CW01523995

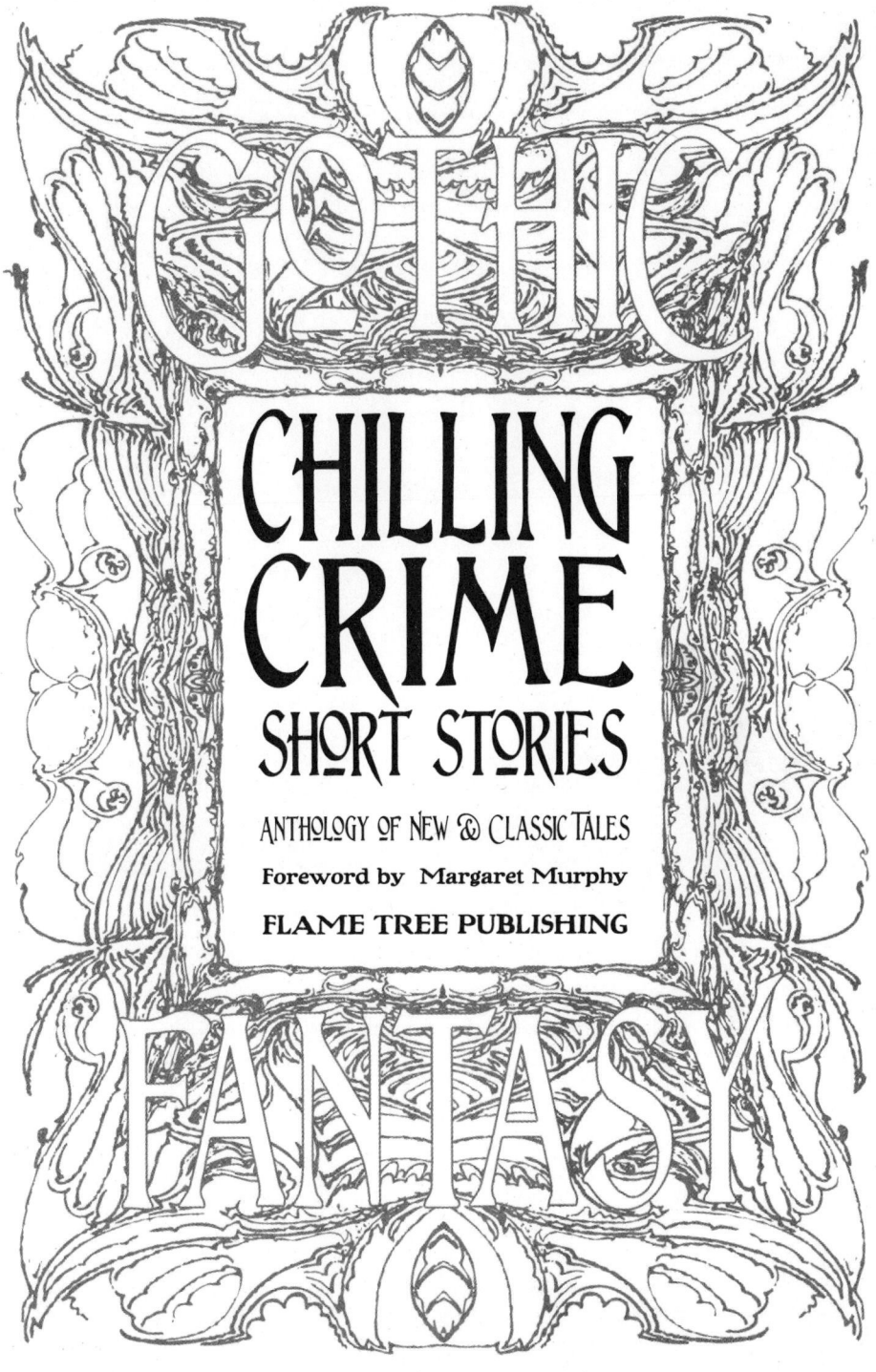

GOTHIC

CHILLING CRIME
SHORT STORIES

ANTHOLOGY OF NEW & CLASSIC TALES

Foreword by Margaret Murphy

FLAME TREE PUBLISHING

FANTASY

This is a FLAME TREE Book

Publisher & Creative Director: Nick Wells
Senior Project Editor: Josie Karani
Editorial Board: Catherine Taylor, Gillian Whitaker and Taylor Bentley

FLAME TREE PUBLISHING
6 Melbray Mews, Fulham,
London SW6 3NS, United Kingdom
www.flametreepublishing.com

First published 2021
Copyright © 2021 Flame Tree Publishing Ltd

21 23 25 24 22
1 3 5 7 9 10 8 6 4 2

ISBN: 978-1-83964-768-0
Special ISBN: 978-1-83964-828-1

The cover image is created by Flame Tree Studio
based on artwork courtesy of Shutterstock.com.

Incidental motif images courtesy of Shutterstock.com:
sacilad and Masterlevsha.

A copy of the CIP data for this book is available from the British Library.

Printed and bound in China

GOTHIC

CHILLING CRIME
SHORT STORIES

ANTHOLOGY OF NEW & CLASSIC TALES

Foreword by Margaret Murphy

FLAME TREE PUBLISHING

FANTASY

Contents

CONTENTS

Foreword: Chilling Crime Short Stories

THE SHORT STORY DAGGER has been a mainstay of the Crime Writers Association's awards for forty years. Surviving even a catastrophic withdrawal of funding from sponsors after the world banking collapse of 2008/9, it remains integral to the awards in 2021 – and with good cause. Modern crime fiction owes its existence to the short story, and while its place in the crime canon has certainly evolved over time, its importance is undiminished, serving today as both a showcase for new talent and a form in which established authors can experiment and take risks.

Reading the new submissions in this collection alongside classic chilling tales dating back two millennia is a rare treat. Contemporary crime can be traced back to the gothic tradition, and there are some fine examples in this collection. The earliest is most likely 'The Three Apples' by Scheherazade – a grisly tale of obsession and murder. The hauntings, nightmarish premonitory dreams and high melodrama typical of early gothic tales persisted through the eighteenth and nineteenth centuries, and Dickens' 'The Old Man's Tale About the Queer Client' and Wilkie Collins' witty and sharply observed 'The Dream Woman', provide excellent examples of these antecedents.

Victorian Gothic stories of all shades had elements of mystery – but supernatural forces, the weird and unexplained often predominated. Then, as Edmond Locard and Alphonse Bertillon's scientific and evidence-based forensic methods gained favour, there was a shift of focus, and from Edgar Allan Poe onwards, the detective-hero's task was to the analyze the subjective narratives of 'supernatural' events and rationalize them in objective, scientific terms. So it is that, although Dupin's first outing in Poe's 'The Murders at the Rue Morgue' has strong gothic motifs, the detective is revealed as a rationalist who develops his theories based on evidence rather than conjecture. Hardly surprising, then, that Arthur Conan Doyle credited Poe with breathing life into the detective story, and many others cite Dupin as the first true fictional detective. Female proponents of the art are too often overlooked or underrated, however; one such being the late-Victorian author, Anna Katharine Green, whose highly entertaining 'The Second Bullet' is represented here. Avidly read and hugely popular in her time, she was named by Agatha Christie as one of her major influences.

Good fiction challenges norms, and both Anna Katharine Green's police detective, Violet Strange, and Baroness Orczy's resourceful Lady Molly of Scotland Yard predate their real-life counterparts by some years. There is much besides to tempt the appetite in these classics of chilling crime, including a story by the prolific feminist writer, L.T. Meade and an extract from Edgar Wallace's 'The Ringer'. If your tastes run to the colloquial, both Irvin Cobb's 'The Belled Buzzard' and Harding Davis' 'Gallegher', vividly evoke time, place and milieu. Indeed, 'Gallegher' compares favourably with the style of master of the vernacular, Damon Runyon.

Glowing like a precious gem at the heart of this collection is F. Scott Fitzgerald's *The Great Gatsby*. While generally regarded as 'literary' fiction, it has everything a crime afficionado could ask for: mystery in the oddly reticent person of Jay Gatsby; scandalous rumours as to how he gained his ostentatious wealth; intrigue from his past relationship with Daisy; violent death and – of course – murder. But it is Fitzgerald's psychological evaluation of the hedonistic years between the two Great Wars which lifts this tale to the truly extraordinary. His acute observation and descriptive powers can load a small, superficially banal encounter with meaning, emotion, sensuality and sexual charge. Although egregiously underrated in his lifetime, it is now considered a strong contender for the Great American Novel.

Despite initial pessimism, booksellers reported increased sales of crime fiction in the first year of the COVID-19 pandemic. It has been speculated that readers were seeking a mental challenge. Perhaps, too, in solving the complex problems authors had set them – effectively finding and neutralising an invisible threat – readers attained at least the illusion of control in a chaotic and frightening world. And with this lovingly compiled and beautifully presented anthology to entice a new generation of readers, crime fiction is clearly alive and well and ready to take on the next millennium.

Margaret Murphy
margaret-murphy.co.uk

Publisher's Note

From ruthless assasins to tormented murderers – this is the darker side of crime. This collection brings together classic stories from well-known and lesser-known writers, including F. Scott Fitzgerald, Irvin S. Cobb and Thomas More. We hope there are a few gems in this collection that you may not have come across before.

We received an incredible number of new submissions for this anthology, and have loved reading so many powerful and gripping stories. The standard of the writing submitted to us has always been impressive and the final selection is always an incredibly hard decision, but ultimately we chose a collection of stories we hope sit alongside each other and with the classic tales, to provide a brilliant *Chilling Crime* book for all to enjoy.

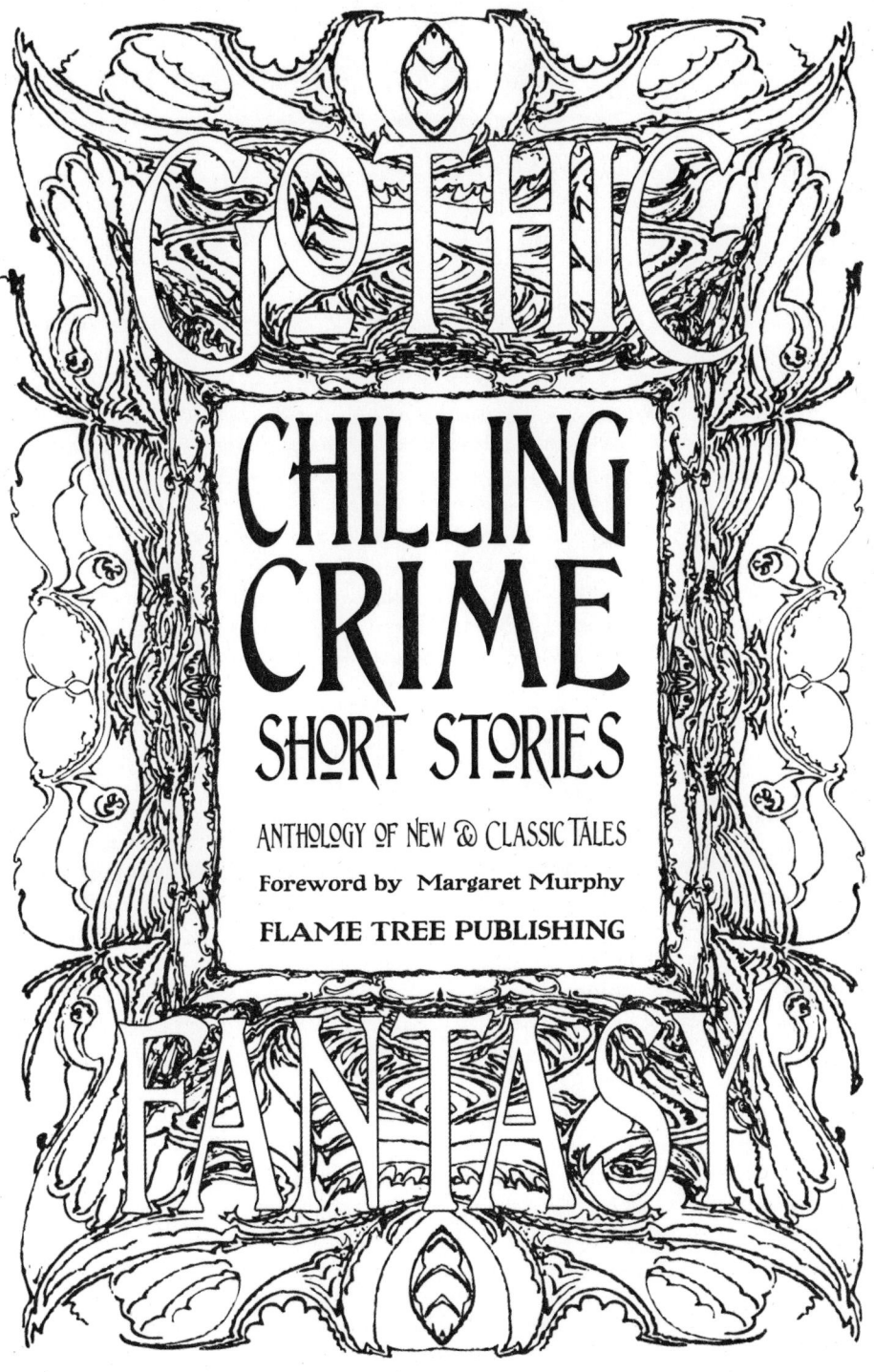

GOTHIC

CHILLING
CRIME
SHORT STORIES

ANTHOLOGY OF NEW & CLASSIC TALES

Foreword by Margaret Murphy

FLAME TREE PUBLISHING

FANTASY

Dinner Date

Jeremy Bates

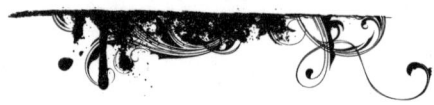

WHAT ARE YOU DOING, *Nia?*

This is crazy! You don't even know him!

You've seen him, what, twice around the building? And now you're going to spend the evening with him? A complete stranger…?

Three times, actually, she corrected herself. She'd seen him three times around the building. So strictly speaking, he wasn't a *complete* stranger. And what's more, he was her neighbor. What's wrong with having dinner with your neighbor? *Absolutely nothing, Nia. That's right, absolutely nothing…if your neighbor is a friendly grandmotherly type who spends her days baking chocolate chip cookies and writing birthday cards to her brood of grandchildren. On the other hand, if your neighbor is of the tall, dark, and handsome variety, as the man in question most certainly is… well, you know where 'dinner' is leading, don't you? And is that what you want? Because if things don't go hunky-dory with Mr. Tall, Dark, and Handsome, if he turns out to have a closetful of bondage paraphernalia, or mirrors on the bedroom ceiling and a video camera on a tripod in the corner, or if he asks you ever so politely if he can take you up the ass while wearing a furry bunny costume…well, what then, Nia…?*

* * *

The first encounter between Titania Christos and her neighbor, Dustin Andrews, occurred the previous Saturday. The movers had finished moving her belongings into her apartment that morning. She had been returning from the delicatessen down the block with her dinner of chopped liver, a made-to-order hot pastrami sandwich, and coleslaw. She'd stepped out of the elevator and saw the man who would later introduce himself as Dustin Andrews at the end of the hallway. Her heart skipped a beat – not because he was a spitting image of a young Gerald Butler, which he was, but because she'd thought he was trying to break into her apartment. In that same cloudy moment, however, she realized he wasn't standing before her door but the one adjacent to it. He glanced at her and tipped a nod. She searched for something to say, yet before anything suitable materialized, he stepped into his apartment and shut the door behind him with an echoing *shu-clack*.

Titania spent an inappropriate amount of time thinking about the man that day and the next before she encountered him again Monday morning. She was leaving the building on her way to work; he was entering with a Starbucks coffee in hand. He held the door open for her and said, "Morning." She said "Morning" back and spent the ten minute walk to her office berating herself for the insipid reply.

They didn't cross paths again until this afternoon. She'd completed a five-mile jog and had taken the stairs up to the third floor, passing the elevator at the very moment it chimed and the doors slid open.

"Oh!" she said, surprised to find her neighbor standing within a few feet from her. She did a mental inventory of her appearance and was grateful she'd put on at least a little makeup earlier.

"Hi," he said, stepping out of the cab to stand next to her – and making her conscious of how sweaty and perhaps smelly she was. "You coming or going?"

"Going…ah, coming…I mean, I'm going to my apartment."

He gestured in a gentlemanly way for her to proceed. She started down the hallway, aware of the fact he was following right behind her, perhaps studying her, judging her, sizing up her butt. She wanted to say something, alleviate the awkwardness of the moment, yet what? She knew nothing about him. She almost chirped over her shoulder that it was forecast to rain later before deciding that would sound inane.

Twenty or so steps later she stopped in front of her door and smiled back at him, as if to say, *Well, this is me! S*he fiddled for her key in the little pocket of her running shorts.

"Huh," he said, passing behind her and stopping in front of the next door.

"Huh?" she said, confused.

"Guess we're neighbors."

"Really?" She feigned surprise. "I didn't know that."

He stuck out his hand. "I'm Dustin. Dustin Andrews."

"I'm Titania."

"Queen of the fairies."

Titania found herself both surprised and impressed that he was familiar with *A Midsummer Night's Dream.* "My mom is a big Shakespeare fan," she explained. "I've never liked my name, but it's better than Ophelia or Desdemona, I suppose."

"Or Goneril," he said, and after a pause they both laughed.

"Most people just call me Nia," she said.

"Nia," he repeated, nodding. "That's nice."

Later, when Titania thought back to this conversation, she would decide it was in this moment, hearing her name spoken from Dustin Andrews' lips, and the simple compliment that followed, when her guard went down, when her natural distrust of strangers, even neighbor-strangers, vanished.

She looked at him now, really *looked* at him, for the first time seeing all the individual parts that made up the face she had been conjuring in her mind for the past week. Full black hair parted on the left, brushed back from his forehead and styled with pomade. Smooth brow and straight eyebrows, shading hazel-green eyes that might have been analyzing her as hers were him. Narrow nose, ending in a bulbous point. Thin lips the same dusty white as his skin.

He was older than her twenty-four years, she decided, but not likely by much.

"I, uh, better get going," she said.

"Sure," Dustin Andrews replied, taking his single key from the back pocket of his blue jeans. It was attached to some sort of brass keychain. He stuck it in his lock. With a quick twist of the handle, he pushed open the door. He took a step forward, hesitated.

"Say," he said, turning toward her. "Would you like to come by for dinner later?"

Titania's pulse spiked. "I…" A litany of excuses scrolled through her mind before she heard herself replying: "What time?"

* * *

7:30 p.m.

Titania stood before Dustin Andrews' door wearing a sleeveless white Calvin Klein dress that was neither slutty nor frumpy, a pair of gold pumps she got on sale at Macy's that were neither too tall nor too modest, and a pearl necklace her mother gave her on her twenty-first birthday that was neither flashy nor cheap. It was, you might say, her Goldilocks outfit, everything just right.

After happily dismissing the naysaying voice in her head that second-guessed her decision to have dinner with a man she knew next to nothing about, Titania knocked on his door.

The quartz ring on her middle finger made partial contact with the wood and added a sharp urgency to the *whud whud whud*. The door opened and Dustin Andrews greeted her with a welcoming smile. He had swapped his jeans and Polo shirt for black corduroys and a matching turtleneck.

"Hi," she said, presenting him with an eight-dollar bottle of white wine. "It's all I had," she added. She didn't drink often. Consequently, she didn't often have alcohol around the house. This bottle, however, had been in the cupboard next to two cereal boxes of Special K and one box of Lucky Charms she would eat like potato chips if she had a late-night sugar craving. She'd bought it to drink her first night in the apartment as a sort of housewarming party for herself. Nevertheless, she'd been so tired from all the unpacking, arranging, rearranging, and cleaning that she'd crashed after dinner and before she had a chance to celebrate.

Dustin Andrews accepted the bottle and read the label. "Can't go wrong with Chardonnay. Thank you, and come in."

He held open the door for her. As she stepped past him, she caught a whiff of a sandalwood aftershave. *No turning back now,* she thought. *One small step for Nia, one giant leap for her sex life!* And this was true. She hadn't had sex for a good spell, and here she was, entering a man's apartment. She knew what this meant. Dustin knew too. Certain things were *expected in* such circumstances. This unspoken agreement frightened her a little, even though it was what she wanted. It was an adult choice she had consciously made, and an adult path she now must follow through to its conclusion.

Titania heard her Greek mother's voice in her head, concerned yet stringent: *Men only want one thing, my sweet. Sex. They don't even care if it's good sex. They just want it with as little emotional commitment as possible.*

Titania wasn't a prude. She'd had her share of relationships in the past. She'd met her first serious boyfriend, Steve Brooks, in her junior year of high school. She went to Louisville High, a Roman Catholic school on Mulholland Drive. Steve went to Taft Charter, a public school a short distance away on Ventura Boulevard. After more than three years together, she took him to her grade-twelve prom, and she'd expected a similar invite to his prom the following week. However, he cancelled at the last minute, telling her he had to leave town for an aunt's funeral. Titania discovered this to be complete and utter bullshit during her first week at college. A girlfriend from Louisville High sent her a photo from the Taft Charter prom – showing Steve Brooks sitting at a big round table with his friends and their dates, a medley of blondes, brunettes, and one Asian. The Asian was seated next to Steve, her arm locked around his, their heads touching.

Her anger red-hot, Titania called Steve, who lived in a different residence hall than she did. He picked up after a few rings, sounding hungover. She let loose on him, calling him all the names under the sun before hanging up, cutting him off mid-excuse.

Over the next four years she dated a handful of other guys, though no one lasted longer than three months. Thanks to Cheatin' Steve Brooks, she'd developed a fear-of-commitment complex. In the back of her mind, where all her doubts and insecurities and paranoias got together for regular cocktails, she had the idea that once she hit that three-month mark, she would be wading into Serious Waters, where Serious Stuff would start to happen, such as leaving a toothbrush at the boyfriend's place, or spending five nights a week in his bed, or God-forbid meeting his parents. All the things she did with Cheatin' Steve and didn't want to do again with anybody else. Because there were only two outcomes when you ventured into Serious Waters: you got married, or you broke up. You had a fifty-fifty chance of one or the other happening. Sure, she could be the one who did the breaking up, but, again, the odds of being the dumper or the dumped were fifty-fifty. And these were not odds she wanted to deal with, her doubts and insecurities and paranoias assured her. She did not want to be hurt again like Cheatin' Steve hurt her. So dating short-term was fine. One-night-flings were fine.

But Serious Stuff?

No thanks.

* * *

Dustin Andrews' apartment was not what Titania had been expecting. Instead of the typical paycheck-to-paycheck young professional fare such as flat-pack ready-to-assemble furniture, clichéd wall art, and maybe a faux-leather sofa or lumpy La-Z-Boy facing a flat-screen TV chosen for size over quality, Dustin's place reflected the tastes of a retiree with a large nest egg. Effeminate oak furniture, a lot of it mid-century; oil on canvas paintings (not prints, mind you) in gilded frames; a giant black steamer trunk adorned with filigreed tin and pressed gold; a child-sized, hand-carved rocking horse sitting by its lonesome in one corner.

"Wow…" Titania said, her eyes picking out ever more bizarre accountments: porcelain figurines, tabletop marble art, a bejeweled Easter egg the size of a football.

"Like the place?" Dustin asked proudly.

"Yes," she lied. "Where'd you get everything?"

"My mom," he said, shrugging. "When my stepdad left her, she needed to downsize. Sold the house and moved into a condo and had to get rid of a lot of her things. Whatever I didn't take she sold at auction." He went to the counter and said, "Red or white? I already have a red open."

"Red then, thank you," she said, still not sure what to make of the furnishings. Regardless of whether they were free or not, did you really want to define your style with your mother's belongings? "So how long have you been here?"

"Five, six years?" He handed her a generously served fishbowl glass and picked up his own. "Cheers!"

"Cheers!" she replied, clinking glasses.

She sipped. The wine was full-bodied with a hint of black cherry. Titania glanced about the apartment and spotted a desk with an angled workspace. "Are you a draftsman?" she asked.

"No, no," he said. He went to the desk and patted the surface affectionately, as if it were the shoulder of a loyal friend. "I'm a graphic novelist."

She was about to ask him if his stuff was published in comic books, but hesitated, not wanting to embarrass him if it wasn't. "Can I see some of your work?" she asked instead.

"You wouldn't like it."

"Sure, I would."

"You're just saying that."

She was, because she had no idea what his work would be like. She moved on. "So what did you study in school to become a graphic novelist?"

"I took some courses in creative writing and illustration. But my degree was in philosophy. Got the top score in my class."

"Did you?" She waited for a self-deprecating remark. None came.

"What did you major in?"

"Marketing."

"How'd you do?"

"Not top of my class."

The remark was a joke, but his response – a silent nod – felt haughty to her.

"So," he said, sipping his wine.

"So," she said, tapping a foot.

"Tell me something about yourself."

"What do you want to know?"

"Entertain me."

"Entertain you?"

CHILLING CRIME SHORT STORIES

"Do you know the Question Game?"

"No, I don't think I do."

"It's simple. I ask you a question. You answer, but you have to finish your answer with a question. Get it? Then I finish my answer with a question. Facilitates conversation."

Titania stared at him.

Slick, Nia. Real slick. You've chosen to have dinner with someone with whom conversation needs to be facilitated.

"So where did you grow up?" he asked her.

"Is this the game?"

"You bet. So where did you grow up?" He placed the back of his hand next to his mouth as if speaking in an aside, then whispered, "See what I just did? Answer-question."

"Okey dokey," she whispered back. She added with exaggerated seriousness, "*I* grew up in *Woodland Hills.* Where did *you* grow up, Dustin?"

"Sherman Oaks," he said. "What's your favorite movie?"

"Let's just say *The Goonies.* What's yours?"

"*Star Wars.* Have you ever been to Europe?"

"No, I haven't. Have you ever been to…oh…New York?"

"Hasn't everyone? Can you ask me different questions than I ask you?"

"Why?"

"You have to answer my question before you ask a new question, remember?"

"*Okay,*" she said with emphasis. "Now: Why?"

"It makes the game more fun! When did you move into this building?"

"Last week. Do you know many other people in it?"

"Not many. Some. Do you like living here so far?"

"It's close to my work. Do you?"

"If you mean, do I like this building, then my answer is yes. Where do you work?"

"In Beverly Hills. Where do *you* work?"

"At home. What do you do?"

"I'm an intern at a talent agency." The question she didn't want to ask earlier, for fear of embarrassing Dustin Andrews, now came easily to her lips: "Are you published?"

He hesitated. "It depends what you mean…" He shrugged, smiled. "This isn't a great game, is it? I know something better."

"Actually, Dustin," she said, "I'm not too hungry tonight. Maybe we could do dinner some other—"

"*No, no, no, no,*" he said adamantly, appearing distressed. "Look…I know this isn't going well, is it? I'm not good at these types of things, dinner dates. They make me nervous. But at least stay for dinner. That's all I'm asking. Promise?"

She opened her mouth, closed it.

"Great!" he said. "Be right back. Gotta go to the loo."

Titania watched Dustin until he disappeared into the bathroom and closed the door behind him. She found it difficult to believe how quickly her opinion of him had flipped. He was like… She didn't even know how to describe him. Like a fifteen-year-old boy manipulating a man's body.

How could she have so misread him?

Because you didn't know one iota about him, Nia, that's how!

I warned you—

"Quit it," she mumbled to herself.

She made a quick calculation in her head. The spaghetti would take fifteen minutes to prepare, ten minutes to eat. It would be rude to call it a night right after the last bite. She would have to stick

⬛ 1 6 ⬛

around for some small talk – hell, maybe another round of the Question Game. So chalk on another five minutes or so. But that would be it. All told, she would be home in roughly half an hour.

Titania chugged what remained of her wine, went to the counter, and refilled her glass, thinking she might as well get a buzz out of this disaster of a date.

While setting the bottle down, she noticed Dustin's key with the brass keychain. It sat on the counter next to a jar of Nescafé instant coffee. She still couldn't make out what the keychain depicted. Curious, she picked up the key between her forefinger and thumb and dangled the brass thingamajig in front of her face as one might a mouse by its tail. She realized she was looking at a pair of testicles.

Brass balls.

"Oh my!" she said. *Dustin Andrews, aren't you something?* She returned the key and keychain to the counter and took another sip of wine. She heard the bathroom door open.

Titania turned – and nearly spit out her wine.

Brass Balls Dustin Andrews was strutting toward her as naked as the day he was born, grinning foolishly, penis swinging.

"Jesus!" she said, averting her eyes.

He stopped a few feet from her. "What?" he said, as if going Full Monty on a date was perfectly acceptable behavior.

"Where are your clothes?"

"I thought this would help break the ice."

She peeked. He stood with his chest puffed heroically, one leg forward, like he was David posing for Michelangelo. He had zero body hair, she noted. His chest, arms, legs – and, yes, even his pubes – were marble-smooth.

The thought of Dustin Andrews shaving, or perhaps waxing, every nook and cranny of his body sickened her stomach.

She turned her back to him.

"You don't know me well, and I don't know you well," he explained. "We got to know each other a little better with the Question Game. But in the bathroom I was thinking there must be a better way to break the ice. And I realized our clothes were the problem. They mask who we really are. So if we get rid of them, we get rid of our pretenses, our defenses, our hypocrisy. Adam and Eve. That's what I'm talking about. Adam and Eve. Vulnerability, transparency, honesty. Are you getting me?"

"Yeah, yeah, I'm getting you," she said, burning with embarrassment. "But – Jesus! Can you please put your clothes back on now?"

"You're not going to take off your clothes?"

"What? No!"

"I don't care if you look at me."

"I'm not looking. In fact, I think I should be leaving—"

"Wait, wait! Don't go! This was stupid. I'm sorry. I'll be right back, and we'll eat."

Titania heard the bathroom door close. She glanced back, saw it was indeed closed, then started for the front door.

She gripped the handle…and hesitated. Because Dustin Andrews was not some random guy she'd met at a bar and came home with. He was her neighbor. If she slipped out without a word, he would be insulted. He might become bitter and angry with her. And she didn't want a bitter and angry neighbor. She would be asking for weeks, months, perhaps years (if she stuck around the building that long), of awkwardness.

She removed her hand from the handle, and instead of leaving, she dug her iPhone from her handbag. She thumbed a Facebook post:

Wow, my neighbor is a freak!! Invited me over for dinner and just came out of the bathroom BUCK NAKED!!

She pressed Share.

As she was about to return her phone to her handbag, she heard a two-tone *dingding!*

Her head snapped toward the kitchen counter.

Where Dustin Andrews' phone was, screen lit up.

Titania's heart locked. Her mind spun.

She went to the counter. The phone's screen had gone dark again. She touched it with a finger. It lit up. An update on the home screen announced:

Titania Christos posted an update.

Titania's hand shot to her mouth.

Why was *Dustin Andrews* her Facebook friend?

How was he her Facebook friend?

Heart pounding, she glanced toward the bathroom door, then back to the phone. Her first instinct was to throw the phone out the window, destroy the evidence. But that wouldn't accomplish what she wanted. The post existed in cyberspace. She had to delete it from her timeline.

She opened the Facebook app on her phone again. The post already had twenty likes and three replies. She deleted it just as the bathroom door opened.

Dustin emerged, fully clothed. Titania slid her phone back into her handbag.

"Need to be somewhere?" he asked.

"Missed call."

"I've decided something great," he declared. "I'm going to show you my stuff."

"Your stuff?"

"My portfolio. Two secs."

He went to his bedroom. Titania thought, *Go, Nia! Leave! Screw his feelings! He's a stalker!*

Yet she didn't move. Because everything was still okay, she told herself. Dustin didn't suspect she knew he was a stalker. And she'd deleted the offensive post. She could still be out of here in thirty minutes with him non-the-wiser about anything.

And what then, Nia? You'll still have a stalker living next door.

Yes, she conceded, but at least it wouldn't be an upset and potentially vengeful stalker.

Dustin Andrews returned from the bedroom with a large artbook. He sat on the sofa and patted the cushion next to him.

After a brief hesitation, Titania crossed the room and sat. Dustin opened the artbook to the first drawing. It was a detailed pencil sketch of a woman. Titania thought it was good, he had talent. But that was all, because as he spoke about the woman, her mind was a world away, wondering, *How was he her Facebook friend? She never friended him. She only met him one week ago. How many people had she friended in those seven days? Two? Her second cousin, April, and a girl named Grace. Titania didn't know Grace, but in the friend request Grace had said she was Joanne Murphy's sister, and Joanne Murphy was a good friend, so Titania accepted…*

She returned her attention to the artbook. Dustin had turned the page, revealing another detailed pencil sketch, this time of a man. He said, "So this is the guy who's stalking her. He's changed everything about himself online, even his gender, to trick her into accepting his friend request."

Titania felt the blood drain from her face.

"I'm thinking of calling the story *Faces*," he continued. "It's a play on the word Facebook. But more, we have all these different faces we present to people online, and nobody really knows who anybody is anymore. Is that deep or what?"

"It's deep," she said. "What happens to her?"

"I haven't really gotten that far yet. Maybe he kills her. Or maybe he just Quaaludes the shit out of her. That's sort of the in-thing right now with Cosby and everything. That's what sells. What do you think?"

"I think – I think we should start making the spaghetti." Standing quickly, Titania headed for the kitchen. Then blurting that she wasn't feeling well, she beelined for the front door.

She wasn't thinking rationally right then. Everything – the room, her thoughts – were a blur, bright and black. She heard Dustin doing something, saying something, maybe coming after her. She heard herself issue a small yelp and realized she was running. She crashed into the door, her hand clawing the handle.

It's going to be locked, he locked it, he's going to grab you by the hair and yank you back and—

*T*he handle turned, the door flung open. She stumbled into the hallway, gasping. In the next instant she was inside her apartment. She shot the deadbolt and shuffled away from the door, never taking her eyes off it.

* * *

Knock-KNOCK.

"Hey, what's wrong?" Dustin called, and she couldn't tell whether he sounded concerned, angry, or what.

"I'm sick!" she managed.

"Let me help you!"

"I'm fine!"

"Let's talk."

"I'm fine!"

"Open the door, Tits!"

Titania blinked. *Tits?* She'd gotten that nickname plenty as a kid, but nobody had called her that since high school.

"Go away!"

"Let me in, Tits!"

"Go away!"

Titania grabbed a chef's knife from the wooden block on the counter and held it before her as she stared, unmoving, at the door.

She half-expected Dustin to kick open the door, come charging in. She heard nothing more. She waited. And waited. A minute passed, then two.

Finally she heard footsteps receding, then the door to Dustin's apartment opening and closing. *Shu-clack.*

* * *

What if he comes back?

What if he's getting a weapon?

She shouldn't have locked herself in her apartment, she decided. She should have run to the stairs, gone outside, found a café or somewhere else with other people around.

Because Brass Balls Dustin Andrews wasn't just a stalker. He was a full-fledged psychopath. He was living out a fantasy from his unpublished comic book. How far would he take the roleplay? Would he kill her if he thought he could get away with it? Quaalude the shit out of her so he could rape her over and over?

Titania needed to get somewhere safe. Now. But…well, what if Dustin hadn't really gone back to his apartment? What if he'd only opened and closed his door to trick her into thinking the coast was clear. What if he was still lurking out there, waiting—

She heard something.

Not from the hallway, but from the wall separating her and Dustin's apartments.

It had been a soft scuffing sound. She'd heard similar noises over the last week, always at night.

She'd believed mice to be the culprits, and she'd made a mental note to speak to the landlord about hiring an exterminator.

She listened – and thought she heard more scuffing, though she couldn't be sure.

Raising the chef's knife, Titania started toward the wall. She spotted a small hole she'd always known to be there. It was about the size of a quarter. There was another one just like it in the bedroom. She'd figured the previous tenants had drilled them to allow the pesky mice into the apartment and waiting mouse traps.

But now she no longer thought that, did she?

Now she thought…what?

That Dustin had made them to spy on her?

No, impossible. She'd peeked into both. They didn't open to his apartment, only the black wall cavity. She bent closer—

Abruptly the hole filled with a swollen white eyeball.

Titania screamed. The eyeball blinked.

Without thinking, she thrust the knife into the wall. It pierced the drywall and sank into something soft yet solid.

A bellow rose from inside the wall. A moment later Dustin Andrews burst through the drywall.

Still screaming, Titania fell onto her behind. Dustin collapsed in front of her. He tore the knife free from his chest and tossed it across the room, a fine red mist following in its wake.

He scrambled toward her on hands and knees. His eyes blazed with rage. His lips were drawn into a rictus of pain.

Titania scooted backward until her back struck the far wall.

"*Going to rip your head off, Tits, you fucking whore,*" he hissed. He snagged one of her ankles with a blood-slimed hand.

Titania brought her right knee to her chest and kicked. The heel of the gold pump she got on sale at Macy's, the one that was neither too tall nor too modest, plugged deeply into Dustin Andrews' left eyeball. His hand released her ankle and he slumped to his side, his head striking the floor with a dull thump.

Titania yanked her heel free from the orifice with a sucking sound, got to her feet, and ran out of her apartment and down the hallway, her screams those of a young woman on the brink of losing her shit.

The Peculiar Affliction of Allison White

Jesse Bethea

WHEN I ARRIVED at the Old Grove Cemetery on Friday, the sun was just over the trees, the leaves were orange and yellow with the first days of Autumn, and the Reverend, the Constable and the Constable's deputies had already lifted the coffin of Sturgis Collins from his grave. In life, he was a man of healthy fortune and typical New England austerity, so the Collins family was able to purchase for their patriarch a lined coffin of polished black cherry with silver handles and fastenings.

Heekins, the young Constable's deputy, pulled his horse to a stop just inside the cemetery's gates so I could depart the buggy, placing my blackthorn on the cold, hard soil and shivering in the morning dew. I turned and reached into the buggy for my medical bag, the contents of which I knew would prove regrettably necessary for this outing. When I retrieved the bag and started into the cemetery grounds, the Reverend Coventry saw my approach and waved, stepping around the lifted coffin with a grave face.

"Doctor!" exclaimed he. "Thank Providence you're here. We only learned the name yesterday."

I joined the Reverend and we commenced to walking side-by-side among the gravestones, back to the site of the exhumation.

"Sturgis Collins?" said I.

"Then you've heard?" said Coventry.

"I was told the name yesterday," said I.

"Was Collins one of your patients?"

"Indeed," said I. "Typhoid fever, the poor man. A full month has passed since his demise."

"Did you notice anything unusual about his affliction?" asked Coventry. "Anything that might relate to the present crisis?"

I chuckled and shook my head, still pumping the blackthorn into the ground to steady every step.

"No, my good man, no," said I. "It was typhoid fever and typhoid fever alone. There was nothing preternatural about Sturgis Collins' life, nor, I expect, his afterlife."

Now it was Reverend Coventry's turn to shake his head at my own naiveté.

"Strange things are afoot, good Doctor," said he. "We must reckon with the spirit realm if we are to survive its conspiracies."

We came to the edge of the coffin, surrounded by the Constable and his deputies, who had managed to extract the box from the ground and lay it next to the hole in the earth where it belonged, yet now they simply milled around it, avoiding the task to come.

"Well, gentlemen," said I. "There is only one thing left to do, don't you suppose?"

The Constable nodded and removed his hat, and his deputies did the same. Then the Constable took it upon himself to unclasp the silver fastenings on Sturgis Collins' coffin and attempt to pry it open. When that proved impossible with bare hands and brute force, one of his deputies approached with a crowbar, shoved it into the coffin's crease and compelled the casket to open.

There lay Sturgis Collins, dressed in his finest shirt, ascot and waistcoat, his silver-topped cane across his heart with both hands upon it. His skin was gray and pallid and heavily sunken against the sharp contours of his bones, but otherwise his corpse was remarkably preserved. The eyes were peacefully shut, but I suppose what caused the chorus of gasps from the deputies around me was the sight of the dead man's mouth, which was wide open in something resembling a mortal shriek.

"My Lord," whispered Reverent Coventry. "His face! That proves it! It's clear as day, he has risen from this grave!"

"Hardly, Reverend, hardly," said I. "It is nothing but common rigor mortis. See here? His ribbon has come undone."

I reached into the coffin and pulled out the black ribbon that was tied around the head and jaw of Sturgis Collins so the family would be spared this same ghastly sight.

"Evidently it came undone sometime after his burial," said I, displaying the black ribbon for the deputies, the Constable and the Reverend. "Thus allowing nature to take its course."

"But Doctor," said Coventry. "You said yourself a full month has passed since he died, yet there is hardly any rot to him at all. How could he be so preserved if not for spectral interference?"

"The answer is simple enough, Reverend," said I. "Sturgis Collins was wealthy, so his coffin is sturdy, well-sealed, protecting his remains from the elements and from predation by worms and maggots. I would venture to guess he should still prove a handsome corpse even six months hence. That is, if you want to dig the old boy up a second time."

I placed the black ribbon back inside the coffin, next to Sturgis' ear, and turned to face Coventry and the rest of them. Their expressions each betrayed a different variety of horror, and the younger of the Constable's deputies kept shifting from foot to foot, due either to nerves or the morning chill or both.

"Shall I do the deed?" I asked of Reverend Coventry. "Or can we finally bury this superstitious nonsense with Sturgis Collins?"

Coventry looked up at me and spoke with a soft, startled cadence.

"We must do what we came to do, Doctor," said Coventry.

"I must remind you, Reverend," said I. "The last two bodies we exhumed showed no signs of anything other than the expected decomposition of human remains."

"And yet, we disposed of them out of an abundance of caution," said Coventry. "As we shall do today, and in the future, so long as Allison White lies abed, tormented by spectral agents. *Something* tortures the girl, Doctor. You have seen it yourself."

"Indeed," I muttered. "Indeed."

So I set my blackthorn and my medical bag on the cold cemetery ground. I unclasped the top of the bag and picked out my favorite bone saw – a sturdy, sharpened instrument. The Constable and the deputies and the Reverend retreated by a few steps as I turned back to the open coffin and quickly set about my work, sawing through what remained of the skin, muscles, tendons and eventually the vertebrae, until Sturgis Collins' head could be separated from his body and placed, facedown, betwixt his legs. Such was the prescribed method, in this state anyway, for the disposal of vampires.

* * *

No force of science or logic, it would seem, can extricate the New Englander from his superstitions. Even now, at the close of this glorious century for reason, this era of Darwin and Pasteur, Edison and Tesla, scientists like myself are forced to contend with the ancient fears of men and the shameful machinations of women.

Our unsavory business of the morning concluded, the Reverend Coventry and I paid a visit to the home of Allison White, the young girl whose peculiar affliction and fantastical accusations compelled these credulous New Englanders to dig up three of their deceased neighbors and examine their corpses for signs of vampirism. She was also, it is my shame to admit, my sister's daughter. We found my niece in the upstairs bedroom of her family's cozy house on Essex Street, in the same bed where she had been confined for nearly a week. There she was looked after, day and night, by my sainted mother, who always doted on pretty little Allison and would never tolerate a negative word against the child.

Though I knew my niece to be a liar, I readily admit young Allison certainly appeared to be at Death's door. She was pale white, blond hair matted to her forehead with sweat, her chest heaving with every labored breath. Beyond outside appearances, however, there was absolutely no medical indication that anything was wrong with the girl, neither on that day nor on any of the prior days when I had occasion to examine her. Her heart rate was normal. A quick observation of her throat and windpipe revealed no physical reason for her labored breathing. All indications were, as they always had been, that the girl was performing an elaborate ruse.

"We wanted to tell you, Allison," said Coventry in his most gentle voice. "The Doctor, the Constable and I visited the grave of Sturgis Collins today, and disposed of his remains in such a way that his spirit can no longer bring harm to you."

"Thank you kindly, Reverend," said Allison in a half-whisper. "Was there anything incorrect about him? Were there any signs?"

"Your uncle says he could see no signs of vampirism with the corpse," said Coventry.

I longed to remind him that I could see no signs of vampirism because there are no signs of things that do not exist, but that was a conversation for another time. The Reverend took the rocking chair by the bed, which had been the post of Allison's loyal grandmother all the nights before.

"Tell me, Allison," said Coventry. "Are you certain now that it was Sturgis Collins who attacked you?"

"I believe so, Reverend," coughed the girl. "But when they come…in the night…it's hard to see their faces…it's just so terrible…so much pain…"

Tears began to form in the corners of her eyes. I retracted my stethoscope and placed my hands in my pockets as I stood over the bedridden child.

"You said quite the same thing about the previous so-called vampires," said I. "Emily Neff and Thomas Summers. Yet we have exhumed their corpses and defiled their remains, and still you experience these nightly torments?"

The Reverend shot me an angry look while the girl squirmed under her quilts.

"I…" she whimpered at the wall behind me. "I cannot explain it."

"Nor can I," I said. "I can only hope now that I have decapitated Sturgis Collins at your behest, you can finally find some peace."

"Doctor," hissed Coventry. "I think it's time we let your niece rest, don't you?"

The Reverend, for good measure, nodded to the door.

"Yes, yes," said I. "We will not be far away, Allison. Send for us if the vampires return."

Coventry stood from his rocking chair and we donned our hats and coats and made for the bedroom door. He left first, and as I was about to follow, I heard a small voice behind me.

"I thank you, Uncle," said Allison. "For all you've done for me. I often think of those summer days when my family visited your cottage. You taught me so much about science."

I glanced back at the girl in the bed. She sighed.

"Knowledge is such a comfort in these terrifying times," she said.

For just a flash of an instant, I saw her "affliction" cured, her complexion rosy, her mind and eyes sharp. I even thought I saw the sparkle of a smile. Was I truly the only one who saw through her lies?

* * *

In the Hermitage Tavern, on the other side of Essex Street from the White household, I again tried to make Reverend Coventry see reason over mugs of beer.

"Emily Neff, Thomas Summers, Sturgis Collins," I repeated. "Not a one of them showed any signs of disturbance upon exhumation."

"Yet the girl says they visit her in the night," said Coventry. "They torture her and steal away her energy, her life force, her very will to live."

"One uniting medical characteristic of lost energy, life force, and will to live is that they are all easy enough to fake," said I. "Allison is lying to us, Reverend, for reasons I cannot say. But I promise you this – her 'affliction' is far from over. She knows she has our attention now, and she intends to keep it. She will tell us the name of another so-called vampire, and I implore you, ignore her lies. Let us not disinter another of our peacefully resting neighbors."

In a moment that, under other circumstances, the good Reverend might have called "divine providence," Heekins, the Constable's deputy, burst into the Hermitage Tavern and rushed to our table.

"Reverend, Doctor," said he. "The girl, Allison, she's been attacked again."

"What?" gasped Coventry. "In broad daylight?"

"It only lasted a few minutes," said Heekins. "I saw it myself, the girl's grandmother called me up to the bedroom. She…she…twisted and wailed…it was like nothing I've ever witnessed…"

"Did she say whose spirit it was that attacked her?" demanded Coventry.

"Yes, sir, yes," said Heekins. "Amid her shrieks, she managed to utter the name of Annabelle Winship."

* * *

I managed to convince Reverend Coventry that there was no need to dig up poor Annabelle Winship that very day. So at sunrise on Saturday, our vampire-hunting party reconvened at Old Grove Cemetery for yet another morning of ghoulish work. The Winships were a poor farming family, living on the outskirts of town and surviving off hard work and not a little charity from Reverend Coventry's parish. The gravestones in their corner of Old Grove were bland and often made from nothing more than fragile shale. When Coventry and I found Annabelle Winship's grave, her casket had already been disinterred. Unlike the previous day's cleansing of Sturgis Collins' remains, Annabelle Winship's family opted to attend the grisly ritual, and I saw the dead woman's father and younger sister standing near the Constable as his deputies pulled her casket from the ground.

"Was she a patient of yours, Doctor?" said Coventry as we approached the grave.

"Yes," I sighed. "Consumption was her killer. Taken much before her time, I'm afraid."

The Winships could scarcely afford such an elaborate coffin as that of Sturgis Collins. Annabelle's casket was cheap, white pine, easily pried open by the Constable, and so we were quickly greeted by the sight of her pretty young corpse, wearing a sky blue dress, her hands still crossed over her stomach. Sitting on the bottom of the casket, I spotted the dried and faded petals of the flowers she held in her hands the day she was buried. Nothing about the corpse seemed out of the ordinary, and even the girl's own black ribbon was still tied around her head, keeping her jaw in place. I hoped that would be enough to show the Reverend, the Constable, and the Winships that there was no reason to go further with this nasty business, but of course I was mistaken.

"It is as I feared," whispered Coventry.

"What are you on about?" said I. "There's not a thing wrong with her."

"That's just it, Doctor! Don't you see?" said Coventry. "You told me yesterday, Sturgis Collins was only preserved because of his coffin. But here Annabelle Winship lies in nothing but a simple pine box, yet just like Sturgis Collins, it's as if she died yesterday!"

I looked again at the corpse before us. Coventry was right; the girl was far better preserved than her interment should have allowed. I tried to think of an explanation to offer when we heard a hoarse shriek from the other side of the casket.

"Her stone!" gasped the girl's father. "Her stone is loose!"

Coventry and I looked and beheld Mr. Winship, easily shoving his daughter's gravestone to and fro. I stuttered, for I was certain a natural explanation would be forthcoming, and yet I could not deny the soil surrounding the stone was severely loosened, allowing the stone to teeter like a child's loose tooth.

"Gentlemen," I said with my arms outstretched. "Gentlemen, please! Let's not panic. We must follow reason and logic."

But as always, I could not be heard over the hysterics of a little girl. Annabelle Winship's little sister stood at the edge of the casket, pointing eagerly at the corpse and shrieking with tears in her eyes.

"Her shoes!" she said. "Daddy, Anna's lost her shoes!"

All of us came around the casket to follow the little girl's pointing finger. Sure enough, the corpse of Annabelle Winship was barefoot, and no shoes could be seen lying anywhere in her coffin.

"She loved those shoes, Daddy!" cried the little girl. "She wanted to be buried in them, she told me herself! The day before she died!"

"It's true, it's true!" said the father. "We made certain she had 'em on when we put her in the ground. Sweet Jesus, my little girl's done walked out of this grave!"

I hung my head. There was simply no reasoning with these people. I knew, of course, there was no vampirism afoot in this cemetery, but yet I had no explanation with which to silence their superstitions. The Winship father and daughter embraced each other and wept over their deceased relation as Reverend Coventry approached me. His eyes were wide and his mouth was agape.

"That settles it, Doctor," said he.

"I've had enough of this business, Reverend," said I.

"You must finish it, Doctor," said he.

"There is nothing to finish!" said I. "This is a farce, I tell you! Allison lies to us!"

"You need more evidence?" said Coventry. "Is what we have seen this morning truly not enough for you?"

In frustration, I threw my medical bag to the ground and withdrew the bone saw, holding its teeth within inches of the Reverend's face.

"If you believe so strongly, you may do it for yourself!" said I. "I tire of decapitating my neighbors on the whims of a child. Perhaps you'd like to take on the Lord's work for today?"

Coventry glanced from the serrated blade of the bone saw to the neck of the young corpse in the casket. He looked as if he would sooner vomit than take the saw's handle.

"Well then," said I. "Let this be the godforsaken end of it!"

With that I stormed over to the coffin and before the Winship father and daughter could stop me, commenced to slicing through Annabelle's neck, her skin, her muscles, her tendons and vertebrae. I cut furiously, and did my best to make it an audible experience for all who surrounded the grave. I wanted them all to know what superstition sounds like.

* * *

Saturday night, I took my supper in the Hermitage Tavern alone, trying to think of what to do next. It happened that the table I'd been given faced the other side of Essex Street, and I could look up to the top of the White household and see the light in Allison's bedroom window. I wondered if my niece was surrounded by doting family members, all while she schemed ways to gain another flash of attention and notoriety. I wondered how she might finally be stopped.

While I ate, one of the Constable's deputies, a different man than Heekins, came to tell me that my niece wanted to see me.

I was shown to Allison's bedroom and found her there alone. She retained her pallid complexion, sleepless red eyes and matted hair, but she was sitting upright with her back against the headboard, hands crossed over the top of her quilt, smiling upon my arrival.

"Hello, Uncle," said she. "I'm real happy you were able to come visit me. I wanted to ask after Annabelle Winship."

"She is still dead," said I.

"Yes," said Allison. "But was there anything incorrect about her corpse?"

"She was missing her shoes," said I.

"Oh," said Allison, looking off into the ether. "How strange."

"Indeed," said I. "The good Reverend interprets it as a sign of vampirism. Tell me, does Annabelle Winship wear shoes when she comes to torment you?"

"Oh…" whimpered Allison. "I'm not sure…it's hard to say…it's all just so…"

"So painful," I grumbled. "Yes, yes, I've heard. Why have you summoned me, Allison?"

"Why, I thought you might look after me, and perhaps give my poor grandmother a rest," said Allison sweetly. "You know, Uncle, I've always wanted to be a doctor like you. I always cherished those family visits to your cottage, watching you work with patients, all the interesting books and instruments and things in your office—"

"Allison," I interrupted. "I should think it would give your grandmother a fine rest indeed if you gave up this foolishness."

"Why, whatever do you mean, Uncle?"

"You know exactly what I mean, girl."

I approached her bed now, and I admit, my aim was menace. I meant to scare the truth out of her, once and for all.

"You may wrap the whole of this town, perhaps the whole of New England round your little finger," I hissed. "But I see through you, Allison. This is all a farce, a fiction! You should be absolutely ashamed of yourself."

Again I saw the wave of perfect health sweep across her face. Her eyes glimmered with malice and the corners of her mouth curled subtly into a smile.

"Yes, it is a shame, isn't it, Uncle?" said she. "When we are finally seen through?"

I prepared a retort, a fierce demand for her to admit her lies before the entire town, but we were disturbed by a commotion from outside the girl's bedroom. The bedroom door flew open and young Heekins appeared, his face ruddy and his chest heaving.

"Doctor!" gasped Heekins. "You must come quickly! There is another one!"

"Another what?" said I.

"Another girl," said he. "Another affliction. Sarah Baldwin was thrown into a rage tonight at her family's table. Attacked, she says, by the vampire of Claudia Linwood."

"Claudia Linwood?" said I, for I recognized the name instantly. She died in my care, of consumption, just like Annabelle Winship.

"Yes, Doctor," said Heekins. "We must go now, the Reverend wants to dispose of the corpse tonight."

"Tonight?" said I. "Why not the morning?"

"The Reverend says time is of the essence," said Heekins. "I believe he means to cleanse the remains himself. Your comments to him at the Winship grave today have put steel in his spine, sir."

Hunched over the bed, I briefly forgot about my niece's presence while I rubbed my chin and tried to decide a course of action.

"No," said I. "We shall do it. Have you any shovels?"

"In the buggy, Doctor."

"Then we must go to Old Grove and spare the good Reverend this ghastly charge."

I left with Heekins, but not before exchanging one, final, angry glance at Allison White.

* * *

At my urging, Heekins drove his horse and buggy hard and fast up the road, bursting through the gates of the Old Grove Cemetery. The sky was clear when we leapt from the buggy with our shovels, but the wind was fierce, tossing and twirling the Autumn leaves about the gravestones. Heekins carried a lantern before his person as he weaved through the stones to the grave of Claudia Linwood. We were once again among the wealthy plots of Old Grove Cemetery, not far from where Sturgis Collins lay at rest with his head between his knees.

"Here it is," announced Heekins, throwing his lantern light on the stone before us so I could clearly see the name of Claudia Linwood. Heekins swung the lantern away and looked at me.

"Are you sure you want to do it now?" said he. "Just the two of us?"

Hesitating, I looked behind us at the gate where we'd left the buggy to see if the Reverend or the Constable had arrived to join us. We were alone.

"Yes," said I. "We should do it ourselves, and be quick about it. Lay down your lantern."

He followed my instruction and gently lowered his lantern to the soil so that its light remained on Claudia Linwood's gravestone. Then, with his back turned to me, I lifted my shovel and swung it against his body.

Young Heekins collapsed against the gravestone, pushing himself over onto his back. In the faint lantern glow I could see him giving me one last, confused, pleading, wide-eyed glance before I lowered the sharp end of my shovel onto his throat. With one quick motion, I pushed the blade through his skin, his trachea, his muscles and tendons until I felt the satisfying snap of the shovel passing through his vertebrae.

So now, driving Heekins' horse and buggy as hard and fast as I can, I make for the Connecticut border. By now, I suspect, the Reverend and the Constable will have found poor, headless Heekins. By now, they have probably opened Claudia Linwood's grave and found it empty. And in a few hours, I expect they shall find her corpse in my cottage wine cellar, where it lay on ice, along with a few others. Presumably, they shall also find Annabelle Winship's shoes down there somewhere, though I never could. I had assumed no one would notice their absence.

I suppose it is my own fault for not keeping a closer eye on my niece whenever her family made visits to my home. I suppose during one such visit, she must have snuck into my office and found the cellar door hidden behind my bookshelf, thus allowing her to discover my crimes. You must understand, of course, that an anatomist is always in need of fresh cadavers upon which to experiment. It was all simply a scientific necessity. I confess, however, that the girl's method of unmasking my deeds was rather clever. She must have believed that she could not accuse me in public, either out of fear of my retribution or simply out of fear that she would not be believed. So she needed the authorities to incidentally discover the empty graves I had left behind, and thus she invented her little vampire crisis. With my mother watching over her day and night, I could hardly make a move to silence her accusations. And when I met each of her challenges, she must have realized that she needed to deprive me of the necessary time to rebury the alleged vampires as she named them. Thus she called me to attend to her tonight, and had her accomplice Sarah Baldwin accuse the final vampire. She left me no time, no choice but to escape.

I should very much like to wring Allison's neck. But instead I drive ever faster for Connecticut. Or perhaps I shall quit New England altogether. I expect this accursed region, where superstition reigns, shall always prove hostile to noble men of science like myself.

The Grim

Allan Burd

JACK STARED at the condo complex on Thomas Street, a five-story building with four upper rows of symmetrical windows and a ground level filled with canopied shops. The building's beige hue washed out under the cloak of the moonless night sky and the reflection of the silent flashing sirens from his police cruiser and the fire engines that beat them to the scene.

"Reeks of garbage and piss out here. When can we enter?" Sal asked him, his eyes scanning the pile of trash bags awaiting morning pickup and the wandering vagrant on the street. Then he checked the Fitbit on his lean wrist and spit. "It's 3 a.m. and I've got a prime piece of pussy waiting for me at home that I'd like to hit again before morning. If you know what I mean?"

Jack glared at him. "I'm forty-five and married half that, so I have no idea what you mean. Not anymore." Jack sized up his young partner. *The bastard.* Even in his jacket, you could tell the fucker was ripped. Like he used to be, he thought, before family life and the job got the better of him. "We'll go in when the professionals tell us it's clear."

A burly fireman exited the building. Jack recognized Kaufman. The seasoned firefighter carried light gear on his back. He had a touch of scruff but otherwise his face was clean, indicating the fire wasn't too bad. Kaufman lit a cigarette, took a long puff then extinguished it under his boot before approaching them.

"Evening, Detective. All clear." Kaufman tilted his head, stretched his neck.

Jack signaled the uniformed men under his command to enter the building while he and Sal hung back. "Wish I could say it was good to see you Kauf, but not like this."

"Never like this," said Kaufman. He glanced at Sal. "New guy. Good. Someone to fill out the paperwork for you."

"You don't look that ruffled," Sal said to Kaufman.

"Fire was out before we even got here. I'd say there's minimal damage, except there's a corpse upstairs whose memory I don't want to diminish."

"Shit," said Sal.

"Aw, fuck." Jack shook his head.

"Young too. Fucking shame. It ain't pretty either. You're not a puker?" Kaufman asked Sal, who shook his head. "I didn't think so. You don't look like a puker. Still, I don't envy you." Kaufman motioned to his crew to load the gear back on the truck so they could pull out.

"Yeah… thanks" Jack patted Kaufman on the back as he left then looked to Sal. "Your dick will have to wait."

A red-vested doorman held the door wide for them as they entered the building.

"How long you been here?" Jack asked him.

"Since ten. Graveyard shift."

"Have you been here the whole time?"

"My bladder's like a camel. Never left my post," the man said proudly.

"Did you see anyone suspicious enter or leave the premises?"

"No, sir," the man replied. "No one out of the ordinary."

"You have video surveillance to back that up?" asked Sal.

"Of course."

"Why don't you get those recordings ready for us before we come back down. The last twenty-four hours should cover it," said Sal.

"Absolutely," said the doorman.

Jack and Sal made their way to the third floor. By the time they got there, the uniformed officers had already prepped the area, cordoning off the apartment with yellow crime tape and interviewing a couple of the neighbors awakened by the commotion.

As Jack reached the door, he immediately placed a handkerchief over his nose to protect his olfactory senses from the pungent smell: a combination of smoke, fried beef, sizzling pork, copper, a hint of charcoal, and excess perfume. "Aw, jeez." He handed an extra cloth to Sal, who turned it down.

"One tour in Iraq got me used to it." Sal lifted the tape so Jack wouldn't have to bend as far to enter the apartment and followed behind him. "Swanky digs. Very spacious. What do you think, two mil?"

"I think it doesn't matter anymore," said Jack.

Jack's experienced eyes scanned the space; polished hardwood floors, eighty-inch TV mounted on a wall, a solid black shelf filled with tchotchkes, a square coffee table with a smattering of woman's magazines, a long leather sofa, a bar with four stools fronting a kitchen. The window at the far end was jammed wide open to vent the room. Kaufman was right. No damage at all, not even from the smoke. Other than the usual mess made by a few in-rushing firefighters, the apartment looked remarkably clean.

Jack followed the source of the offensive odor to the bedroom where a half-charred female lay on a four poster bed covered in scorched white satin sheets. He pocketed his hankie, approached the bedside, and studied the victim. Long curly brunette hair cascaded across her vacant oval face. Along half her body, her melted skin fused with her silk green dress.

"That's how they found her," said a uniformed officer. "They also said every window they opened was locked tight from the inside, so no signs of entry, forced or otherwise."

Jack looked around the neat room. "No signs of a struggle, either. Most of her face escaped the flames. Beautiful girl… figure mid-twenties. Her features are intact enough for facial recognition. We have a name?"

"Tracy McRealy. This is her apartment. Got the info off the driver's license in her purse, along with her cash, credit cards, and some other valuables," replied the officer.

"So, not a robbery." Jack turned to Sal, "You smell that sweetness in the air? That's not perfume. That's cerebrospinal fluid.." Jack slid on a pair of latex gloves. Gently, he turned the victim's head, spying the clump of blood below the sizable gash in the back of her skull. "Aw, jeez. Good news is she didn't burn alive. Bad news is someone caved her head in… judging by the width and depth of the wound with something sharp and heavy like an axe."

"A hatchet," replied Sal.

"That's pretty definitive," said Jack.

"The edge of the blade is sticking out beneath her lower back. Seems to me her killer wanted us to find it. Lift her body a little more and you'll see it," said Sal, snapping his gloves on.

Jack did and Sal called over two crime scene investigators who photographed the evidence then carefully slid the blood-soaked hatchet from beneath her and sealed the weapon in a plastic bag.

Jack looked around again, noting the minimal spatter pattern. "Someone struck her at close range and placed her in this position and it appears she didn't see it coming."

"Lover?" guessed Sal. "Maybe someone who felt burned by her, burned her back. If the doorman's telling the truth, could be someone from a neighboring apartment."

"Maybe they had a fight. After our boys finish canvassing, we'll find out if anyone heard any shouting," said Jack.

"Or maybe it wasn't a lover at all," came a voice from the bedroom entrance. A tall bald man in an overcoat stood in the doorway surveying the crime scene.

"Hey, who let him in here?" Sal asked, tensed to dart forward.

Jack grabbed his arm. "It's okay. He's an old friend."

"He's a crime beat reporter from the *Post*," said Sal.

"The best one," said Jack.

"The best is right. Old is right, too," said the reporter, coming closer.

"Who let you up here?" asked Sal.

"You guys were nice enough to send the doorman away and most of the cops on this beat know me to be a stand-up guy."

"Charlie, meet Sal, my new partner," said Jack. "He's spirited. Like we used to be."

"Speak for yourself." Charlie extended his hand to Sal.

Sal showed him the gloves he was wearing. "Charmed."

"I am charming," said Charlie, lowering his hand. "Damn," he added upon closer inspection of the dead body. He snapped a picture of it with his cell phone.

"Don't do that," said Sal.

"C'mon, Charlie, you know better than that," said Jack.

Charlie quickly pocketed the phone. "I won't use it. But that's only because I know you'll send me a better one." He smiled broadly.

"And I'm going to do that because?" asked Jack.

"Because I'm going to help you figure this one out. Care to take a walk with me, Jack. I might have some insight for you."

Jack viewed the room one more time. Whatever information was to be gleaned could be gleaned without him. "Yeah, sure. Sal, you take it from here."

"I'll handle it," said Sal.

Jack and Charlie exited the apartment, took the elevator down, and stepped outside the building. Jack took a deep breath, inhaling the stale air.

"Does this city look darker to you?" Charlie asked.

Jack shrugged. "It's always darkest before the dawn."

"No, seriously, feels like dark times all around us."

Jack looked up. Maybe it was the sky but even the skyscrapers looked like they had a pall cast over them. "The murder rate's higher. That's for shit sure."

"It's more than that," said Charlie. "These crimes I'm covering… they're crueler, more vicious, more sadistic, more…" Charlie rubbed his bald head, grasping for the right word.

"Inhuman," said Jack, finishing Charlie's thought.

Charlie shivered. "More than that, too… like there's this palpable, malevolent presence suffocating the Big Apple. You notice the waves of icier air, the unexplainable wafts of foul stench."

"It's garbage night," said Jack.

"What about the increase of degenerate scumbags on the streets. They're leaving their crack dens and whorehouses because they feel just as home outside. Heck, even the rats are more comfortable coming out of the sewers, lately. Notice the drop in the homeless, how's there's far less of them. You know why? Because after livin' on these streets for as long as they have, they can sense it, an overwhelming despair, too desperate even for them. New York used to be the city that never sleeps. Now, I think that's only true because people are too afraid to close their eyes."

"That's a little melodramatic but I can't argue. What do you think is going on?"

"I think New York *was* an interesting place to live. Now I think it's a more interesting place to die."

Jack took notice of the glimmer behind Charlie's eyes. "What are you not telling me?"

"This wasn't a crime of passion. This was done as a work of art," said Charlie.

"What the fuck does that mean?"

"Her murder fits the modus operandi of a psychopath I've been tracking who's committed at least a dozen other city crimes and, unfortunately, said psycho has been clever enough to never leave even a whiff of evidence behind."

"I think we'd have noticed a pattern. Plus, I've got a murder weapon with prints on it. None of which fits with what you're telling me. What makes you think this is part of a larger series of crimes and why the hell am I first hearing about this now?"

Charlie shrugged. "Because I wasn't a hundred percent sure until tonight. Now, I've got enough to go to press."

Jack gave him a doubt-filled stare. "You're fishing for a story."

Charlie's shoulders raised. "I'll tell you what. I can wait a few days to present this to my editor. Do your full investigation. Run your prints. When they don't reveal anything, come see me, and I'll tell you what I think is going on. And when you come by, bring my favorite sandwich. You'll owe me at least that." Charlie walked off into the night.

"Shit," said Jack, kicking a cockroach off his shoe and watching it skitter away. "Shit." He looked back up at the condo and reluctantly went back inside.

* * *

Two days later, Jack held something thick wrapped in tinfoil and walked into the crowded offices of *The New York Post* as most everyone else was walking out. He slipped between the bustle and dropped the tinfoil wad on Charlie's desk. Charlie never looked up; just kept typing away furiously on his computer.

"Lean with enough spicy yellow mustard to give you an ulcer. Just the way you like it," said Jack. He produced a can of Dr. Brown's Black Cherry, placed it down next to the sandwich and popped the tab, the fizz of released air finally garnering Charlie's full attention. "I'm ready to listen. Or did you just ask me here to fetch you dinner?"

"Not here," said Charlie. He grabbed a thick file from his middle drawer, piled the food Jack brought on top of it, and tilted his head for Jack to follow him to a nearby conference room. A minute later, he closed the door and locked it.

"Very Deep Throat," said Jack. "Are you going to fill me in?"

"You ain't gonna like it."

"I'm a cop. I don't like most of the things I hear."

"Then I won't sugarcoat it," said Charlie, opening the folder on the table. "There's a serial killer stalking our city, and he, or she, is reenacting… no, recreating old New York City's most infamous crimes."

"You've already lost me," said Jack, his face squinting into a ball.

"Hear me out. The murder on Thomas Street a couple nights ago… that was a recreation of the 1836 murder of Helen Jewett that happened right on that same street." Charlie pulled copies of news articles relating to the Helen Jewett murder out of the file and displayed them on the table for Jack to peruse. "Back in the 1830s, Helen Jewett was an upscale New York City prostitute. A frequent customer of hers killed her with three sharp blows of a hatchet to the back of her skull then set her bed on fire to cover his tracks. Check it out. Same wound. Same burn pattern. Our victim, Tracy, was even wearing a similar green dress to the one that Helen wore when she was killed and she was laid out in the same position. Yeah… the old one's a black and white drawing, but trust me, every reference I found says her dress was green."

"Kaufman told me he thought the perp used a blowtorch," said Jack.

"For a work of art," said Charlie. He placed the drawing of Helen next to the crime photo of Tracy. "Almost identical, right? That's pretty fucked up."

"That's plenty fucked up," said Jack, reviewing the remarkable similarities of the two corpses.

"Tell me, was your victim also a call girl?"

"Yeah," said Jack. "She was an escort with some incredibly wealthy clients. We found their names in her trick book. Sal's been running them down since yesterday morning."

"He's wasting his time. But you already suspect that cause there wasn't a shred of evidence that anyone other than her was even there, was there?"

"The prints we found were unidentifiable," said Jack.

"Thought so." Charlie saw Jack about to speak but held up a finger. "I need you to hold your thoughts a moment. That sandwich is calling to me." He took a long bite, 'mmmm-ing' how good it was. "Damn. You did me right. And here I am ruining your whole day." He spilled more old newspaper articles onto the tabletop and lined them up, matching old articles against current police reports.

Jack took in the enormity of it. "Holy... start at the beginning."

Charlie chugged down some Black Cherry and wiped the excess off his mouth with his sleeve. "My beginning. Remember that case a few months back where a guy committed suicide on the rooftop of Madison Square Garden? He shot himself in the face and based on the closeness of the gunshots, the lack of evidence of anyone else present, and the fact that the victim's fingerprints were found on the weapon as if he was posing for a selfie, no one argued about anything other than how he got up there. But you notice I said gunshots. A few weeks later, when I looked deeper into the case for a personal interest story, I discovered that our suicide victim shot himself three times and at least one of those shots rendered his face almost unrecognizable. How the fuck does someone shoot himself three times?

"So I started to dig. I came across another famous murder that occurred on the rooftop of the Garden. It was a different building in a different place back then, but in 1906, a man named Harry Kendall Thaw shot a guy named Stanford White on the roof of Madison Square Garden because he was screwing around with his wife. *Three times.* According to the records I could find, the bullet wounds were in the same places as our supposed suicide victim. I brought it up to some of your brethren. They gave me a few good chuckles and sent me on my way. But the uncanny coincidence got me thinking, so I got my nose up and started searching for any recent murder scenes that might match with some other notable historical crimes. Guess what? I found a bunch."

Charlie pointed to two matching files, one old and one new. "Earlier this fall, a dismembered pregnant woman with her throat slashed was fished out of the East River. The way she was cut up and dispatched perfectly matched the 1913 killing of Anna Aumuller, a women murdered by her priest slash lover named Hans Schmidt." Charlie tapped two more matching files. "Shortly after that, a torso also floated out of the East River. That body part belonged to a German tourist whose legs were found in the Navy Yard and whose other dismembered body parts turned up in Harlem and parts of the Bronx. That was exactly how a guy named William Guldensuppe was murdered back in 1897, same nationality, same disposal, similar locations. His murder was marked as a probable mob hit due to his alleged money laundering ties to organized crime. I think differently."

Charlie pointed to a picture of a burned-down house. "Five months ago, there was a house fire in Staten Island where they discovered a mother and her baby, not burned, but gruesomely murdered with their skulls bashed in. That was labeled a break-in gone bad with a fire set to burn any evidence. In actuality, I believe it's a re-creation of a Christmas night murder from 1843, similar victim relationship, similar circumstances. And in every case, no leading evidence of any kind. No would-be robbers come arsonists who could fuck up a crime that bad are going to be so careful they don't leave even a shred of evidence behind. But a professional artist painting a scene..."

"You gotta be shittin' me with all this."

"I could see a few happening the same way – bound to be some duplication along the murder train – but this many, with this many similarities. No fucking way. So I made a list of as many infamous old New York City murders as I could find, and I kept my eyes peeled. When Thomas Street came up on my scanner, I got my ass out of bed and over there already knowing what I was going to find."

"Jeez," said Jack with a groan.

"The interesting thing is our killer's far from perfect. He strives for accuracy, but with all the changes to the city that have occurred over time, he can't possibly get everything right. Check this one out," said Charlie, pointing to yet another set of matching crimes. "A fifty-eight-year-old former prostitute was strangled and disemboweled in room 31 of a hotel along the river. You guys arrested her john, a twisted puppy with a rap sheet a block long. I don't think he did it. You ever hear of a case called Jack the Ripper in America? Back in 1891, a fifty-eight-year-old prostitute nicknamed Old Shakespeare was strangled and disemboweled in the same way. Our killer got the room number right but he had to use a different hotel because, similar to the Garden, the old one didn't exist anymore. Our killer's a stickler for details, but when the details aren't available to him, he's forced to improvise. Though, he's getting better.

"Six months back a guy was shot twice in Stanwix Hall. I think that was an attempt to duplicate the botched murder of the infamous Bill the Butcher Poole from the 1850s, you know... the guy they based the movie *Gangs of New York* on. But our guy blew it. Bill the Butcher lived through his wounds whereas the guy who was shot died instantly and our killer didn't shoot him in the same places. I could be wrong here, but I'm theorizing that this was our killer's first attempt. I think he tried to duplicate a very famous murder and learned the hard way that he bit off more than he could chew. So in his quest for historical accuracy, he moved on to easier targets."

"Assuming you're right, we have a sociopath on the loose painting murders in 3D like Picasso."

"Yeah, and lately, he's using a lot of the color red."

Jack sat down and studied everything Charlie had. He reviewed the date order of all the recent killings along with their eerie similarities to the old murders. Everything Charlie said lined up. "This is insane. Do you know the planning it takes to pull off just one of these to this level of detail, let alone this many in this quick a time?"

"Kind of takes evil fucking genius to an all new level," said Charlie.

"Evil, fucking, crazy bastard is more like it. Fuck, I'm going to have to alert the mayor, assemble a task force. And that's assuming they don't push me into retirement early and label me a screw loose because no one is going to want to admit this is going on. You know, when you print this, it's going to cause a panic."

"You mean further panic. People sense something's going on. The city's already on edge."

"This is too fucked up to even think about. I should retire early. You should retire with me. My brother's got a boat up on White Lake. We'll go fishing together."

"No can do. This city's in my blood and, unlike you, I can still do my job when I get fat."

"Now you sound like my missus." Jack patted his pocket after feeling the vibrations from his phone. He swiped the screen and answered, "Yeah. Jack here." His face went pale to the point that even Charlie was startled. "What? No fucking way. I'll be right there." Jack leaned forward, his arms against the table barely holding him up.

"What was that?"

"Sal... Sal's dead. I... I gotta go," stammered Jack, shaking his head.

"How?"

"He didn't say."

"Where?"

"The Empire Hotel," said Jack.

"I'm... I'm going with you," said Charlie.

* * *

Fifteen minutes later, sirens screaming, Jack drove his car between the barricades, and parked in front of the main entrance. Two cops stepped forward to greet him.

"We'll take you to him," said one of the cops.

Charlie quickly moved to join them, but another officer intercepted him. "Please step back, sir. If you aren't a guest at this hotel, you're not allowed inside at this time."

"It's okay, he's with me," said Jack. The officer let him pass and together Jack and Charlie were escorted into the lobby, where patron and staff members stared on in curiosity. "How bad?"

"Fucking bad. As bad as it gets," said the officer. "I know you're a seasoned vet, but still, you're going to want to prepare yourself."

The officer opened a side stairwell leading down to a sub-basement, the smell frighteningly reminiscent of the putrid stench from Thomas Street, only this time made worse by the inclusion of the harsh smell of burnt hair.

"Fuck," muttered Jack, placing a cloth to his nose as his shoes scuffed along the concrete floor. Ahead of him, laying naked and headless, was Sal's body. A cavernous crimson wound across his chest exposed his cracked sternum, broken ribs, meaty muscle, and a bloody mass that used to be his beating heart. Above his open neck, a puddle of coagulated blood pooled into a gel-like consistency. On a nearby worktable rested his smoldering, unrecognizable, blackened head; patches of flesh that clung to a charcoaled skull, hauntingly perfect teeth, and yellow goo stuck inside empty sockets that used to hold his eyes.

Charlie immediately turned and retched.

The cop who brought them down ignored Charlie. "Sal came here by himself, first thing after lunch to track down one of the names in Tracy McRealy's trick book. This hotel was one of the locations listed where she met one of her clients. But nobody comes down here so it took a while for the smell to carry enough where someone noticed. He's been dead at least a few hours. A fireman spotted his head in the open furnace and scooped it out with a shovel. We didn't even realize it was Sal until thirty minutes later when we found his badge lying in the corner."

"Jesus." Jack put his hand over his mouth and stepped back.

The officer pointed to Sal's chest wound. "The damage was done with several blows from a meat cleaver. It's already on its way to the lab for analysis."

Charlie wiped his mouth off and walked over. Sweat dripped from his forehead, his hand trembling. "I know this crime," he said, a tremor in his voice.

"Not here," said Jack. "Outside." Charlie nodded and walked out of the cellar. Jack addressed all the officers present. "I want every molecule of this basement dusted and tested. I want every video feed scoured frame by frame. We use every resource available to us to catch the bastard who did this."

A chorus of *yes sirs* followed behind him as he left the room. He met Charlie on the sidewalk outside. Together they leaned hard against the building. A sliver of moonlight pierced the cloud cover like a dagger.

"Sorry, my friend," said Charlie.

Jack shook his head. "You think this was our killer?"

Charlie took a deep breath. "I know it was. I recently logged a case from 1902 where a guy named Tobin dragged another guy nicknamed Captain Jim into the basement of Hotel Empire and killed him exactly the same way. I'm not sure if this is the same hotel or not, but the name is similar enough where it has to be him."

Something caught Jack's eye, a small white object lying in the gutter. He walked over to it, bent down, and picked up the squished butt of an extinguished cigarette. For a long moment his mind churned. "Two for two," Jack whispered under his breath.

"What is it?" asked Charlie.

Jack scowled at Charlie. "Might be a coincidence. Might be something more. Go back to work, Charlie. Write a story letting the world know the hero Sal was. Not just the great cop this city lost, but the man and war hero he was before he joined us. But don't mention a peep about our serial killer."

"But…"

"No buts. I want this quiet. I don't want this sick bastard to have any idea that we're on to him. And fuck any task force. I'm going to catch this prick in the act myself and bury him somewhere so deep no one will ever find his body." Jack's eyes bore holes into Charlie waiting for a nod of agreement.

"You think you know something?"

Jack didn't answer.

"Come on, Jack. We're partners in this now."

"Just between you and me, okay?" said Jack. Charlie nodded. "Tell me, Charlie, do you know a firefighter by the name of Kaufman?"

* * *

The next day, Charlie wrote a piece that made the city so proud Sal was bound to get a street named after him. And he kept his word… no mention of a serial killer. The day after that, Jack's phone rang.

"I have something on Kaufman," Charlie said over the phone.

"It has to wait. Sal's funeral is in two hours. We're lined up a mile deep."

"It can't. It's time sensitive. I've been watching him. Late last night he left home and checked into the Park Central Hotel. And get this… he paid for the room with cash."

"Did he meet with someone?"

"He did. I think he bought himself a new identity."

"You think he's planning to split?"

"All you cops will be at Sal's funeral. I couldn't think of a better time."

"Shit. You get a room number?"

"Room 349," answered Charlie.

Jack hung up the phone. He tossed his tie on his desk and raced out of the precinct for his squad car. When he arrived at the Park Central Hotel, he took the stairs two at a time, not waiting for the elevator to take him to the right floor. Gun drawn, he strode down the hallway. The door to room 349 was slightly ajar. Jack quietly and cautiously entered the room.

"Close the door," said Charlie, standing behind a cushioned chair in the middle of the room. "Kaufman's not here."

Jack holstered his weapon. "Shit. Where do you think he went?"

Charlie shrugged. "He's probably at work," he said, casually revealing the Smith & Wesson revolver he held in his hand.

"What the fuck?"

Without hesitation Charlie pulled the trigger, placing a bullet in Jack's lower abdomen. Jack yelped and fell against the bed. He reached for his own weapon, but Charlie placed the .38 special against his head.

"Don't you want to hear me out?"

Jack leaned back against the mattress. "What the fuck, Charlie?"

"Do you know who was shot in this room? Arnold Rothstein. November 24, 1928. Mr. Big. The Brain. The Big Bank Roll. This big shot mobster shot through the spleen like a common criminal by a thirty-eight caliber bullet just like the one I placed in you. But Arnold didn't die here. He made his way to the service entrance, stumbled out onto the street, and died the next day in the hospital. I would've preferred that. Heck, I would've preferred not to kill you until much later on, especially in this way because I knew this was a historical crime I could never perfectly duplicate. But I decided to make due."

"I don't get it, Charlie," Jack gasped, his breathing heavy, sweat dripping from his forehead.

"That's because you've never been the imaginative type. I'm an artist, Jack, and what's the point of being an artist if people can't appreciate your work? I showed you my scrapbook and it was pretty great watching you appreciate it. Even better watching you appreciate in person what I did to Sal." Charlie shook his head. "But Kaufman? That was some insulting bullshit."

Jack drooled. "Aw, jeez."

"I love this city, Jack. Everything about it. The architecture, the culture, especially the history. And let's face it… New York's got a very violent history. Manhattan was built with blood, sweat, guts, and tears. What we have now came at a price. I'm just reminding people of that."

"You're out of your mind," said Jack.

"Not really. I like this city better when it's in a dark place. Those old days were the darkest. Killers today don't really put much thought behind it. But the murders they committed in those days… those were the classics."

"That's sick… you're sick. You're gonna get caught. Even if it's not me, someone's going to catch you."

"Maybe. Maybe not. After twenty-five years working in this city, I learned all the ins and outs. You think it was easy getting on the roof of the garden unnoticed. Luckily, I've made friends everywhere… friends with access keys I could duplicate without their knowledge and friends I could use to con my way into places unseen. I'm smart and I'm careful."

"So that's how you got into Thomas Street," said Jack.

Charlie psshawed. "That, no. I was one of Tracy's incredibly wealthy clients. At least I made her think I was wealthy. That piece of art came at a price. But scribbling the Empire Hotel into her little book and waiting to see who came along. That one was free."

"You're a sociopath."

"Always have been. Who else could survive covering the crime beat all these years? But still, I always liked you. Would have been nice to let you walk out that door, too, just to truly emulate the murder of Arnold Rothstein but…"

Charlie raised the pistol and shot Jack in the forehead, killing him instantly, splattering his blood and brains on the bed. Then he wiped the room clean, planted false clues for the police to find that would lead nowhere, and left.

* * *

That afternoon at Sal's funeral, Jack's absence was a noticed concern, but no one was going to stop the proceedings. Charlie sat in a pew next to a pretty blonde from a local news network.

"That was a great piece you wrote yesterday," she whispered to him.

"I appreciate that," said Charlie, admiring her looks, mentally picturing which victim she resembled from New York history.

She stared back at him. "I heard you were there at the crime scene. Do you have any idea who did this?"

"Take a walk with me after this. I might have some insight for you," said Charlie.

She Walks

Laura J. Campbell

CELIA HAD WATCHED PLENTY of those shows on the women's television network where the 'otherwise attractive' frat-boy type slips something in the girl's drink when she isn't watching, and the next thing she knows she's an overnight on-line video sensation. For all the wrong reasons.

So Celia knew better than to leave her drink unattended, even for a moment. But five vodka-and-cranberries into the evening her judgment was impaired. And she only walked a few feet away to pretend to be meeting a friend, in order to avoid eye contact with a man who had whispered "Nice legs" to himself as he looked at her far too long.

After that, she didn't remember much.

* * *

Celia heard her captor walk down the stairs. His cologne had a clean aquatic smell. She could not see him well; he had taken off her prescription glasses. She couldn't say anything due to the gag in her mouth.

"They say if you love something, you should set it free. But I love snakes, and spiders, and tigers," he said. He had a monotone voice.

Celia found herself remembering every forensic and crime show she had seen; she hadn't noticed it before, but now that she thought about it, the villain in those shows always seemed to have a bland voice.

"So, even although I love them, setting them free could be dangerous. I hope that you are a dangerous girl." He walked back upstairs.

He seemed comfortable giving his little soliloquy. As if he was anticipating her questions, expecting her pleading. He seemed well-versed and well-rehearsed.

As if he had done this before.

Celia was alone again. Trying to figure out a way to escape.

And wondering what else is trapped down there with her. There were various tanks and terrariums around the room, she could see (as much as she could without her prescription lenses) into a few of them. She could make out the shapes of some of the caged animals. There were indeed spiders and snakes in them. But no tigers. She wondered if he was trying to get one of those.

There was a window high in the wall, probably at ground level outside. The skies were dark outside; no moonlight entered through the window. She could see a small scattering of snow against the window pane. She was trapped down here in her little black dress and leggings. Fortunately, he kept the basement warm for his critters.

Celia began working at the rope around her wrist. It was tight. Her feet were tied close together but with a little space between them; the cords that bound her were tethered to a nearby pole. There was sufficient length to allow her to crawl or stagger to a little nearby bathroom.

The accommodations suggested he thought there was a degree of permanence to her captivity.

She realized that she was going to need to come up a plan to get out of there. And come up with that plan quickly.

* * *

He came back downstairs with trays and bags. He paused by a glass tank and removed a small clear plastic container from one of the bags. A cricket jumped about inside the container.

"Dinner time," he said. He moved the cover to the glass tank just a little. He dropped the cricket into the terrarium. A spider reached up with hungry arms and caught the doomed insect. In a moment, the spider's venom was injected into the cricket and the cricket went from being alive to being dinner.

"When I have eight legs like you, my precious beast," he said to the spider, "I will be complete. I now own four legs. I am at second base. And my newest pet brings two more…a slide into third."

He came to her and put down a small table. He placed a cheeseburger and a milkshake on the table. She recognized the allusion to major league baseball; she watched baseball with some regularity. The game calmed her mind. She had watched Jeter and Rodriguez when they played for the New York Yankees and watched José Bautista play right-field for the Toronto Blue Jays.

The aim of the game was to hit the ball, run around three bases and end up at home plate. If he was playing baseball, so would she.

She wasn't sure what her captor meant about collecting legs. She really didn't want to know.

"Are you going to be good?" he asked. "No trying to escape?"

She nodded.

He removed the gag. He untied her hands. She couldn't just get up and run. Her feet were still bound. He could easily recapture her if she attempted to escape.

"Eat," he ordered.

"Thank you," she said.

He seemed shocked as the politeness she had extended. "You're welcome," he replied.

He sat back, watching her as she ate. "You are beautiful," he said.

"She walks in beauty, like the night; of cloudless climes and starry skies," Celia said softly. "You like poetry?"

"Byron," he nodded. "A mind at peace with all below."

"Does the spider have a name?" Celia asked, looking at a nearby terrarium. She knew enough from watching those shows on the women's television network that he probably considered her an object; she needed to become a person in his eyes.

"No," he said. "None of you have names."

"What is your name?" she asked.

"Take some advice – don't be too clever. That was the mistake your predecessor made."

"What kind is she, then?"

"A Texas Brown Tarantula."

"I know the species. I had one as a pet when I was a teenager. *Aphonopelma hentzi*. We'll call her Hentzi. And I am Celia." He had drugged her before she had even seen him. It was the first time he had heard her name.

He frowned, taking away the remaining food and quickly whipping the ropes back around her wrists. He stuffed the gag back in her mouth. The fabric grated against her teeth. She was going to brush for hours when she was out of here.

He went upstairs again.

But Celia knew that the damage was already done. He knew her name now.

It was as if she gambled on hitting a low ball and managed to run to first base. She was safe.

For now.

* * *

He brought down soup, a spoon, and a glass of tap water. He took the gag out of her mouth.

She ate in silence.

As he was picking up the utensils, she spoke to him, very calmly. "*She Walks in Beauty* isn't a love poem. The poet is only noting how beautiful the woman is. He never says that he loves her."

"Why even bring that up?" he asked.

"Because you don't want to set the things you *love* free," she said. "But the things you just find beautiful – they are okay, right? You can let the only beautiful go – let them walk in the light?"

He began to mumble the poem to himself. She joined him, the words of the poem spilling simultaneously out of their lips. Whatever code he lived by, she hoped she had tapped into it. He seemed to be a collector. She had to safely opt out of being collected.

"*A mind at peace with all below, a heart whose love is innocent,*" he repeated to himself. "You seem very calm for somebody in your circumstances."

"I just broke up with a man – a narcissistic sociopath," she said. "I guess I'm numb to being a victim. My man - he got mad at me one evening for some insignificant reason that only he knew and he threw my dinner – chicken fried steak with chips – out into the street. You at least let me finish most of the burger you brought me. Heck, you even let me talk with you. I don't seem to have much luck with men."

"Did he hurt you? This ex?" He was filtering her words through some convoluted pinball machine of logic only he could appreciate.

"He hurt me frequently," she replied. "Occasionally physically, but mainly mentally and emotionally. He would convince me that I was the problem. He was normal – the rest of us weren't. '*All you people*' was one of his favorite expressions; he said it when he needed to avoid taking responsibility for the consequences of his own actions. If he hit me, it was my fault that I caused him to hit me. Nice guy, right? But he knew better than me. He knew better than all of us. That was what he told me."

"He told you he was better than you?" That concept had caught the captor's attention.

"All 'us people' are sheep. He didn't need to check the boxes us sheep did. The rules don't apply to him. He would dominate our conversations and chastise me if I tried to interject anything into the conversation – tell me I was rude for interrupting. So, I would bite my tongue while he spoke at me - then he would get mad at me for not saying anything, or not saying it fast enough."

"How long ago did you break up?" The captor seemed to be probing, seeking information without directly asking for it.

Was there an opposite of Stockholm syndrome? Celia wondered. *Something where perhaps the captor began to identify with his captive?* She hoped so.

"We broke up three months ago," Celia replied. She finished the soup, placing the spoon very gracefully into the empty bowl. "It was very good – the soup. Thank you. Split pea is my favorite."

"Why were you at a bar, all dolled up?" he asked. "That seems odd, given your history."

"My friends said it was time – that it would be good for me to ease myself back into being social. Just meet them for a few drinks, get re-acclimated to being around people. People who didn't need to control me. They said that my staying in the house so much was perpetuating his influence over me, keeping me his victim."

Her captor seemed unnerved by the last statement. "*His v*ictim," he muttered unhappily to himself. "*His victim.*" He paused. "I know the type, like your ex," he told her. "My mother was like that. One moment I was her perfect little angel, the next I was a rotten little boy, just as bad as all the other rotten men in her life."

He picked up her bowl, spoon, and glass. "I will leave the gag out, if you promise not to scream."

"I promise that I won't scream," she said. She meant it – there was probably no way anybody would hear her anyway and to have that horrible rag out of her mouth was a delicious freedom. "Can I talk softly to Hentzi?"

He looked towards the tank with the tarantula. "Be my guest," he answered as he walked upstairs. *Guest,* Celia sighed to herself. She had been promoted to *guest*.

"Second base, Hentzi," she said to the spider, after he had gone upstairs. "I have stolen second base." That was the base he said he was at. She wondered what he meant by that.

Four legs. She found herself eyeing a large freezer towards the back of the basement with sudden apprehension.

* * *

He came down with dinner. A chicken fried steak, chips, and a vanilla shake with a glass of water. He put it in front of her. "Eat all of it," he said. It was an order.

She smiled and obeyed. "What's it like out there?" Celia asked. "Is it getting cold?"

"First real snow," he answered. "The skies are very dark. Ominous. They have been dark since I chose you. The skies have never been dark this many days in a row. That concerns me."

He placed a paper flyer in front of her. It had her picture, with a telephone number and plea for information.

"Your friends are looking for you. They were on the local news last night. They confirmed your story. That you were getting over a bad relationship. You seem to be a good girl."

Celia nodded obediently.

"Tell me more, about this ex."

"You don't realize how much damage was done until you look back," she replied, reminiscing on dark times. "Then it hits you. *How isolated you were.* How much you had to adjust your own personality to avoid the volatile temper and navigate the mercurial mood swings. I got used to not saying anything and cleaning up his messes. I was stuck. I couldn't conceive of getting away from him. They call it 'learned helplessness.' An attribute of battered woman's syndrome."

"He still has influence over you," her captor said. "You are still traumatized by him. By *him*."

"He's probably tried to call me about a hundred times. Narcissists don't like to lose any supply." She said. "At least being down here has spared me the temptation to get back together with him."

"Would you be tempted?" he asked.

"Without these few days to realize I could be on my own, maybe," she offered. She was very wary of being too clever. He had hinted that someone before her had tried that. Regardless of the current calm, Celia suspected that her captor was very capable of physical violence. She had indeed gone from the frying pan of her ex into the more dangerous fire of an unknown captor.

"He is a 'person of interest,'" the captor relayed. "The police are asking him questions."

She was quiet for a moment. "He always threatened people – said he could have the people he didn't like done away with. That he knew people who would hurt others for him."

She looked at him, sudden fear in her eyes.

"I am not working for him!" her captor said emphatically.

"He was just always so adamant that he could have me hurt if I crossed him. That he would have a perfect alibi and that I could be hurt…"

"I will not hurt you," her captor said. "I don't even know him. I'm don't do some psychotic little asshole's dirty work for him."

"You brought me the meal he threw away," she said quickly. She had to be very careful of her captor's moods. "Thank you. It means a lot."

"I wish I had known then what I know now," he told her. "I would not have chosen you. You looked like all the other party girls at the club that night. Out there for a cheap fling or to attract a sugar daddy. You had those long legs. You looked like a predator, worthy of being hunted back. You were the wrong one to have chosen. You are not a predator: You are not a black widow."

He noted that she had finished her meal. "Good," he said. "The meal that was thrown away – I replaced that. Never forget. You owe me that memory. You owe me."

He went upstairs. But this time he looked back down before he disappeared. "Good night," he said. In a moment he was gone, closing the door behind him.

Celia nodded to Hentzi. "I was the wrong one to have chosen."

"Third base," she whispered.

The spider pivoted about on its eight legs, as if even she wanted to witness a cricket escape.

* * *

Celia was talking to Hentzi when she heard him coming downstairs again.

"You two getting along?" he asked.

"Famously," she replied.

He put another terrarium beside Hentzi's. "I hate spiders," he told her. "I have about twenty of them down here. She – Hentzi – eats the most."

"Why collect them, then?"

"I collect the dangerous," he reminded her. "Sometimes it is difficult to tell the difference between love and danger."

"I can relate to that," she agreed.

"I suspect that you can," he replied. "I mistook you for something else."

He offered her a can of soda. "Do you like cola?" he asked.

"Yes," she said. She was not going to disagree with him. He seemed to be unsure of what to do with her, and that was a dangerous place to be with any kind of sociopath. He could decide to dispose of his mistake. She sipped from the cola.

"My mother was like your ex," he said. "A woman with a thousand arms and a fist at the end of every one of them. She had severely disturbed relationships. One after another after another. Always wondering why everybody eventually told her to lose their number. To be uncollected. She liked to think of herself as capable of solving everybody else's problems. I learned to duck. I know what it means when you say that you learned to shut up."

He put a newspaper clipping in front of her.

There was a photograph of her ex being interviewed about Celia's disappearance. Celia froze, her face growing pale.

"Interesting," he said. "I walk down and you don't jump. You see his picture and you show fear. *Real fear.* He has a new girlfriend – moving on so quickly is a mark of his personality disorder, from what I have read. She vouches for his whereabouts on the evening you disappeared. That means they will now expand their search."

"I'm a cold case by now," she said, letting sufficient sadness fill her tone. She didn't have to fake the panic that she felt inside, the panic giving credence to the sadness in her voice.

"Somebody will continue searching for you," he noted.

She began to feel very sleepy, very disoriented. In a moment she felt her sense of reality slipping away.

She looked at the can of cola he had handed her. *Really?* She thought to herself. *Again?*

* * *

When Celia regained consciousness, she was lying outside the back door of the club. The one where he had slipped her the flunitrazepam a week or more ago. There was a police officer standing over her.

It was dark; the moon waning gibbous in the sky. It had been a waxing crescent when she was captured. Had her captivity been that long?

"Where am I?" she asked groggily. There was fresh air. She suddenly treasured fresh air.

"You're lucky we found you," the policeman told her. "We were here on a missing person's call and found you lying in the alley. It's below freezing. You don't look dressed for the weather."

There was the sound of sirens; an ambulance backed into the narrow space behind the club. The police officer had wrapped a gray blanket around her. She was still very cold. Little black dresses made for terrible snow gear.

She noted a small glass terrarium next to her. Inside the small box, Hentzi was struggling to stay warm. Celia picked up the box and held it close.

"You were the third woman to go missing from this club. Another woman disappeared last night. They're beginning to call it Club Rohypnol. When you're strong enough, we'd like to ask you some questions."

"Who is the latest missing woman?" Celia asked.

The policeman showed her a photograph. The woman had an unpleasant expression. She looked perpetually angry with the world. She had a skull-and-crossbones tattoo on her upper arm. Her lips were painted blood-red. She looked *dangerous;* she looked like a predator.

The captor would not find empathy with this new victim. He had undoubtedly taken greater care to select her.

The paramedics approached. "You'll have to let go of the terrarium," one of the paramedics told her. 'Viske' was his last name. It was embroidered on his uniform.

Celia held Hentzi close. "We were captives together," she objected.

The paramedics look at one another. "Okay," the other one acquiesced. "The spider can come with you."

"I hate spiders," Viske said.

Hentzi was loaded into the ambulance along with Celia. The policeman jumped into the back with them and the ambulance began to work its way towards the hospital.

Celia looked at the policeman as he took a seat next to her. Viske was pushing fluids into her dehydrated body; Celia was beginning to feel warm again.

"Our priority now is to make sure that you are okay...but anything you can tell us." The policeman was anxious. He was aware that time was the enemy of his investigation.

"He's a man. White male, mid-thirties, nondescript accent. Short brown hair. I didn't have my glasses on, so I didn't get a clear look at him. Just take the boilerplate description of the usual suspect. He knows poetry, so probably at least some college. I think he was abused as a child, at least mentally and emotionally. In the end, I think he saw too much of himself in me to go through with whatever it was that he had planned for me."

The police officer diligently wrote everything down on a field tablet.

"I'm probably lucky to be alive." Celia concluded.

"Anything else? The profilers will want every detail."

"I think he is trying to make himself ... *dangerous,*" Celia said. "Maybe make himself into something to fight his mother's memory with? *The woman of a thousand arms, with a fist at the end of each one.* That's how he described her. He collects spiders – the female of those is always more deadly than the male."

"Kipling," Viske interjected. *"And she knows, because she warns him, and her instincts never fail, that the female of her species is more deadly than the male."*

"How do you even know that?" the cop asked Viske.

"The internet," the paramedic replied. "I listen to podcasts between calls. I got bored with social media – it's all inane memes and girls trying to extort my money by flashing cleavage at me. Me and everybody else with a wallet. So now I listen to poetry."

"Anything else?" The policeman asked. "Anything he said that you think might be important?"

"He said he would be complete when he had eight legs. Eight legs to fight a thousand arms. I think I was the next two of his eight legs. Or I was supposed to be. But it turned out that I wasn't dangerous at all. I was a cricket. I was prey, not predator. So he had no use for me."

"And the place he held you?"

"A basement. With a window. The sunlight and the moonlight were about all I could see."

Celia realized with sadness that she had only paid her captivity forward. That some other woman was now in that same basement, bound with rope and surrounded by the terrariums.

This new captive would not reflect any part of him. The new captive would not know Byron; she would not be pure, dear dwelling-place. The captor would find no home in her, like he had unexpectedly found in Celia.

"Setting me free was the only way he could make me *his* victim," Celia realized aloud. "He knows that I know that he is still out there. That knowledge entraps me. That is enough for him."

She handed the small terrarium holding Hentzi to the police officer. "You should dust this for fingerprints," she suggested. "I think my captor gave the spider to me because he either wants me to remember him, or he doesn't want the spider around to remind him of me."

The police officer accepted the box, as the ambulance pulled up to the sliding glass doors of the emergency department. "I'll get him – or her – back to you. You two are old friends now, right?"

"We're co-survivors," Celia said. "You could maybe keep an eye out for the local pet stores? Perhaps he'll go into one looking for a replacement."

The policemen seemed to brighten up. "That is helpful. A good idea. You are very lucky, you know. To have been released."

"None of the others will be lucky," she said sadly. "Can I suggest something? I think he wants to walk in our beauty, the beauty he never experienced from his mother. Maybe Freud was on to something with all that mother stuff. My choosing to recite Byron's poem *She Walks in Beauty* was dumb luck. I think it went a long way to saving me."

"I don't know the poem," the policeman said. "I don't have time to listen to podcasts." He looked at the paramedic.

"It's a lovely poem," Celia said, as the four wheels of the gurney hit the entrance ramp into the hospital.

"Me? Listen to love poem?" the policeman scoffed.

"No," Celia said in a hushed tone. "The poem is not about love. It's about the one who got away."

A Name for Every Home

Ramsey Campbell

"DON'T YOU KNOW your ABC, Pad? Are they letting people go to university without it now?"

Patrick didn't look up from the map on his phone. A pad was where you lived, he thought, or what a dog did. "Just trying to do my job, Carl."

"Sort your post in alpha order. That's how you'll get round Garden Mile."

"Let Patrick learn for himself." Not quite without a pause their supervisor said "If that's how he works."

"That's not how Frank sorts the Mile, Eunice."

"Frank's off sick," she said.

She gazed at Carl until he returned to filling in a card to tell someone they couldn't have their mail before they paid a customs charge. Even if her rebuke was focused on Carl, Patrick felt less accepted than ever. She couldn't expect him to race through sorting when hardly a house in the suburb was numbered. "I expect he's right," he said and abandoned searching for house names on the map.

Carl watched him set about alphabetising envelopes on the wide desk topped by pigeonholes. "You won't get far if you aren't true to yourself, Pad."

Patrick twisted around, and a muscle throbbed as if someone had punched him in the back. "If you want the real me then for a start that's not my name."

Nearby workmates hooted with amusement. "Don't get in a paddy, Paddy," Carl said.

"That isn't either."

"There'll be time for jokes when everything's delivered," Eunice said.

Patrick tried and failed not to respond. "I didn't hear much of a joke."

"You might like to try a bit harder to get on with your colleagues."

Sensing their contempt, Patrick took a silent breath so fierce it sucked in a smell of envelopes. The huge room put him in mind of a hive – the apian buzz of strip lights, letters fluttering like wings, postal workers bumbling at their honeycombs of pigeonholes – but if this made everybody into drones, didn't that include him? His clammy hands were stained with ink by the time he finished transferring letters and packages to the delivery trolley. "Done," he said, but nobody bothered to respond.

A prematurely autumnal September wind chilled his bare knees as he wheeled the trolley into the shopping precinct, where people were queuing to collect their undelivered mail. The first time he'd worn his postman's uniform he'd felt like an overgrown schoolboy condemned to walk the streets as a punishment for failure. Beyond the precinct – charity shops, off-licences, coin arcades, betting shops – the residential streets began. In ten minutes houses trapped between one another gave way to larger buildings split into apartments, one of which was Patrick's. A carer was coaxing a large slack-faced youth into the house next door, while on the other side two families were sitting on the doorstep and conferring in a language Patrick didn't recognise. They gazed expectantly at him until he realised they saw a postman, not a neighbour. "I'm not your man," he called, "he should be along soon," but all six of them sent him a frown that suggested he was talking nonsense. The Victorian streets led to a wide dual carriageway, across which lay Garden Mile. The suburb appeared to possess its own exclusive stretch of sky, dark with a threat of rain. As Patrick crossed the road, having waited quite some time for a green sketch of a man to scrounge light from the red, a silver Bentley saloon raced in front of him just inches from the trolley. By the time he found breath for an appropriate word the car was swerving through a gap in the central reservation to speed around a bend into Garden Mile.

A car door and a boot slammed somewhere ahead as Patrick wheeled the trolley into the broad road. Every house was resolutely individual and surrounded by a garden several times its area. Each garden boasted at least one vehicle expensive enough to star in a showroom – a Jaguar, a Mercedes, a Rolls Royce – and each gate displayed a name. Patrick was past the first bend by the time he saw a name he recalled from sorting the mail – Dogs Home.

The displaced Swiss chalet didn't look as though it boarded dogs, and no kennels were apparent, but as Patrick dropped a letter in the box attached to the bars of the gate, a Doberman bounded around the house, baring its yellowed teeth. It clawed at the top of the gate as if determined to clamber over, and he'd put the trolley between himself and the animal when a man yelled "Gutter."

Patrick might have felt directed there if the dog hadn't dropped to all fours with a frustrated snarl and trudged back to the house. So that was the dog's name, and the words on the gate could have been a warning. He wheeled the trolley around a bend to the next house he had mail for, an Italianate villa called the Watch. It lived up to its name by taking his photograph with a security camera as he approached the solid seven-foot gate. He pushed a package under the metal flap of the wide slot in the gate, and it was yanked out of his hand. Surprise made him blurt out the last thought he'd had. "I'd have said cheese if I'd known you were after my photograph."

"We don't have smilers in our gallery."

Though the woman's sharp voice invited no response, Patrick retorted "Which one is that?"

"The one we keep rogues in."

"I'm not one of those. I'm your postman."

The metal flap gave him a glimpse of a pair of eyes brimming with moisture and clanked shut at once. "You're not the usual man."

"He's ill. Won't I do?"

"We'll have him back." Her voice was receding, and Patrick heard slippers shuffling along a path. "We trust him," she said.

Patrick wasn't going to let her make him feel like an intruder, never mind a criminal looking for properties to rob or otherwise up to mischief. He trundled the trolley along the middle of the road while he peered at names on gates, and caught sight of a plaque he must be misreading. He had to laugh at his mistake, and then at the mistake the laugh was. When he pushed the trolley up the ramp leading over the pavement to the open gates he saw that the house was indeed called the Pad.

It pointed jazzy angles of white concrete in every direction, no two of them alike. Just the windows were rectangular. One displayed the front room and, beyond sliding doors, a kitchen and an outdoor barbecue. Among the cars parked on the drive he saw a silver Bentley that he recognised from letters on the registration plate – DRG. He was making to move onwards when two rather less than teenage children ran around the house. "Got something for us?" the girl scarcely asked, and the boy supplied a translation or an additional demand. "Got us something?"

They were plainly twins, and they looked oddly familiar – their small skinny angular faces expressive of a dull dogged hunger their owners mightn't even have defined. "Nothing today, I'm afraid," Patrick said.

Their tired eyes narrowed and their thin lips drooped. "It's our birthday," the boy complained, and his sister was anxious to establish "Both of ours."

"Happy birthday, both."

"Kiera," the girl said as if Patrick should have known, and jabbed a finger with a chewed nail at the trolley. "Look for me."

"And Kieron," the boy urged him.

"Trust me, I'd know if there was anything for this house."

"Why would you?" Kiera demanded, and Kieron contributed "You heard, why?"

"You mightn't believe me if I told you." In a bid to end the confrontation Patrick said "Just enjoy your day. I expect that's why you're off school."

"Who's asking that? Who wants to know?"

This came from the man who stalked around the house, a wiry fellow with muscular veinous arms and a larger version of the children's face. Despite its size, the features – meagre eyes and mouth, aggressively pointed nose and chin – looked even more compressed. He halted for a moment, staring at Patrick, and then marched faster at him. "Fucking nora," he said. "Paddy Ransome."

"Mel Cousins. Well, good lord."

Mel stuck out a hand only to take it back. "Weren't you supposed to go to uni?"

"I did." When Mel's red-eyed stare persisted Patrick said "I've been a waiter and worked in a bar, and this is what I'm doing now."

"Fucking nora." Mel jerked his head at the trolley. "Bring it round," he said. "Shouldn't think you're in a panic."

"No rush," Patrick said and followed him around the house.

About a dozen people sat on garden chairs near the paved patio where the barbecue stood. Children were bouncing somewhat desultorily on an inflated castle at the far end of an expansive lawn. "You've done well for yourself," Patrick felt he should remark.

"It's my old man's too."

Patrick thought the women in the audience might appreciate a further comment. "Just yours?"

"We got rid of the wives if they're what you mean. They weren't helping the firm," Mel said and showed Patrick his back. "Dad, here's Paddy Ransome we called Pad at school. He went to uni but this is all it got him."

A stocky man was turning burgers over on the barbecue as though searching under stones for some unwelcome lurker. He raised a puffy instance of the Cousins face to squint at Patrick. "Old friend, are you, Pad?"

Patrick felt it might be unwise to object to the name. "I expect you could say so," he said with equal caution.

"Fancy making yourself a bit of extra? We could use you and your wagon."

"I don't know if I could do that." When not just all the adults but the Cousins twins stared at him, Patrick gave way to saying "What would it involve?"

"Better stuff than I ever sold at school," Mel said. "Give it here, Rod."

A man in a garden chair passed him a device Patrick had assumed was a cigarette substitute. When Mel held it out Patrick said awkwardly "I never liked it much. I'd rather not go back there. My mind's in enough of a state."

"It's the cleanest you can get. It's oil." Since Patrick remained unpersuaded, Mel said "Watch."

He depressed a button on the pipe and applied a lighter, inhaling at such length that Patrick held his breath. As Mel let out a protracted plume of smoke Patrick sucked in a lungful of air, only to find it brought him the smoke. "Whoa," Mel said. "You got some after all."

His delight appeared to spread his features, slowly and relentlessly. His head nodded towards Patrick, bobbing like a balloon on the string of his neck. "I'd rather not have anything to do with it," Patrick heard himself declare too late.

"You just did," an amused spectator told him.

Patrick turned to argue, not least to persuade himself they were wrong, and felt as if he might never stop turning. As he seized the trolley for support Mel's father said "No call for that, Pad. Nobody's going to rob your mail."

"I wasn't. I didn't mean." Patrick left the rest of the sentences behind while he stumbled in search of an empty chair. A herbal odour had lodged in his nostrils and was extending tendrils to net his brain. How could that be? Perhaps if he found words to define the sensation, it would go away – perhaps its effects would. He sank onto a skeletal canvas chair, but he couldn't hide in it when everyone's attention had settled on him like a web. In the hope of subduing his sensations he said "Could I have a drink?"

Mel was refilling the pipe. "Fetch Pad a can, Kieron."

The boy slouched into the kitchen, which was tiled white as a morgue, and hauled open a freezer Patrick could imagine lying in to chill his unhappily clammy self. Of course nobody would shut him in there, but he kept a nervous eye on it until Kieron slammed the lid. When the boy brought him the prize Patrick grabbed the can of lager and rolled it across his forehead, which had grown so tight it was squeezing out trickles of sweat. "Show some fucking manners," Mel's father warned him. "Never mind snatching off the kid."

"Sorry," Patrick blurted, though he wasn't sure to whom. He peeled off the metal tag, remembering barely in time not to lob the grenade, however much he might feel he was acting in a film. He poured a metallic mouthful into himself, belatedly recalling how to swallow. "Needed that," he spluttered before admitting "Thought I did."

Was it quelling the effects of the pipe? When Mel had passed around a sample joint at school there had been nothing to counteract them, and now Patrick couldn't tell how the combination of substances was affecting him. The pipe was advancing towards him along the line of chairs, marking its progress with clouds of smoke he could smell. Mustn't this mean he was breathing them in? He covered his nose and mouth with a moist bloated hand, but his neighbour offered him the pipe. "No, please no," Patrick babbled from behind his hand and made a grab for dignity. "I said not for me, thanks."

Kiera nudged her brother, giggling. "Scared to do a pipe, him."

Patrick lowered his ponderous unwieldy hand so as to deal them a stern look. "I hope you both are. Stay that way."

As the stereoscopic image – one face for each of his eyes – opened its mouths, Mel's father said "Watch out who you think's your friend, son."

"I'd like to think I can tell," Patrick said.

"Not you, you twat. When's he going, Mel?"

The balloon that bobbed at Patrick had regained its dissatisfied look. "Give us what you've got and you can take your can with you," Mel said.

Patrick peered along the line of chairs in search of sympathetic witnesses, but those who weren't indifferent were no better than amused. "Your father said you wouldn't rob me," he pleaded.

Mel's face swelled towards him, and Patrick was afraid it wouldn't stop short of merging with his own head. "What are you calling us, Pad?"

"Nothing if I shouldn't. I didn't think you were that kind of, not that kind of anything, any kind at all."

As Patrick managed to catch up with his own words and restrain them, Mel's father said "Kind of what?"

"No kind. That's what I said, only what do you want to take? I don't mean drugs," Patrick said, outrun by his speech again. "That's nothing to do with me."

"Better believe it. Better remember."

"He's saying we're villains. That right, Pad?"

Patrick would have said anything that might fend off the face, which seemed as huge and hostile as the world. "I was saying you wouldn't steal from me."   "Who'd we rob instead?" The face lurched closer before receding so swiftly that Patrick saw it deflate. "Give us what you've got for us and you can piss off with the rest," the newly shrunken Mel said.

"I told your two, I've got nothing. Perhaps whoever's on the next round will have some."

"What the fuck are you doing here, then?"

"I thought you invited me."

"Guess what I'm telling you now."

For a paralysed moment Patrick assumed he was required to read Mel's thoughts and voice them. As he wobbled to his feet he kept hold of the can of lager, which emitted a screechy creak. "Can I still take this?"

"Take your brew and your walker and best of the lot yourself," Mel's father said. "And get them to send us someone else next time."

He couldn't want that more than Patrick did. Patrick managed to relax his grip on the can as he planted it on one of the lids of the trolley, and felt he ought to say "Thank you for the drink."

"Just keep your garbage to yourself," Mel told him.

"Why do you have to say that? Your father wanted manners. I was trying to be polite."

Mel let his mouth hang open in an idiot's grimace and jerked a thumb at the trolley. "Your garbage there, you stupe."

"I don't think you can call it that just because there wasn't anything for here."

"He's a giggle," Mel's father said without providing any evidence and stared at Patrick. "Mel's saying keep your can out of our road."

"Is it all right if I drop it in somebody else's?"

Presumably Patrick didn't say this, even though he heard himself, since nobody reacted. He was taking care not to dislodge the can while he swivelled the trolley when a woman said "You want to get yourself a car."

"How do you know what I want?" To head off this retort Patrick made haste to ask "Why?"

"Then you wouldn't have to potter about with that contraption. You look like some old feller with a walker."

"At least I won't be killing anyone with it."

This prompted an ominous silence broken only by his irregular rubbery heartbeat – no, the thumps of unshod feet inside the giant blancmange – the castle, rather. "What are you calling us now?" Mel said.

"I was just wondering who nearly ran me over on their way to your house."

"That was you in the road, was it? If we'd wanted you dead you'd be dead."

Patrick saw Kiera and Kieron exchange an eager look, which he was less than anxious to understand. As he turned away he saw the castle set the house prancing. The concrete building calmed down as he hurried past it, and the nearby houses gradually ceased their dance. Perhaps the dark sky was some use if it had restrained them by weighing on them.

Was it safe to walk in the road? Might a car try to run him down? Surely Mel had said not, and Patrick emptied the can of lager down his throat to quell his nervousness. If that made him wander across the roadway, imitating its curves but in reverse, the deliveries ought to keep him on track. He had to veer towards each house to read its name, not the easiest of tasks while the letters jittered like faulty digital displays, if indeed that wasn't what they were. His footsteps and the stormy rumble of the trolley were the only sounds, because everyone in Garden Mile was staying quiet so as to listen to him. They would have heard him announce a name he had mail for – the Spikes, where the package barely fitted through the slot in the gate. Despite the barbs that topped the wall he thought the name might denote needles too, but couldn't be sure if he'd said so aloud. He had a bunch of bills for High Walls, and mustn't think high balls or bills for balls, let alone utter the words, or he might never stop laughing. Wasn't that preferable to feeling afraid? He couldn't afford either while he had a job to finish, and soon he came to Justus with a sheaf of envelopes. "Not justice," he told himself, only to find the comment menacing. The riverine meandering of the road had brought him behind the Pad, and as the antics of the castle threatened to infect the houses he anticipated seeing the Cousins family and all their guests bounce in unison above the wall. He gripped his mouth to trap hilarity, and was glad to find he'd reached another house with mail, the Palms. It greeted him by raising its green hands on their scaly arms above a hedge, and he was about to slip the envelopes through its expressionless mouth on the gate when he recalled sorting just one item for this house. He peered at the second envelope and saw it was addressed to the Pad.

The envelopes must have been stuck together when he'd sorted them. He would surely have noticed if his workmates hadn't distracted him. Best to deliver everything else first, and he drove the trolley through the gathering gloom. Harmoney House, the Manshun, Ray 'n' Beau's End… These and others kept him murmuring observations, and he was sure he'd walked considerably more than a mile by the time he completed the round. As he dropped the empty can in a compartment of the trolley he was overtaken by a notion that he'd misdelivered some item. Surely the recipient could take it to their neighbour.

The engine of his vehicle rattled all the way back to the Pad. If he ever owned a car he suspected that was how it might sound. He should have had it fixed, because the relentless clatter brought Mel around the house as Patrick ventured through the gate. "What are you snooping round here now for?" Mel demanded.

His children were behind him. "It's the old man with his walker," Kieron wanted somebody to know.

"It's a baby with a buggy," Kiera was determined to suggest.

"Shut it, you. What are you after, Pad? Seeing what else we do?"

"I'm just doing my job."

"Not making a bit on the side. Not spying on us for the law." As Patrick made to laugh this off Mel said "Don't waste your time. Some of those are out the back."

Patrick would have been entirely happy not to learn so much. He couldn't judge how closely his answering noise resembled a laugh, and it felt unhelpfully belated. "I'm nothing but a postman," he insisted. "I had mail for you after all."

"You told these you'd got none."

"I'd mixed it up with someone else's." Mel remained suspicious when Patrick retrieved the envelope, which was large and pink. Was he wondering how Patrick could have overlooked such an item? The children ran to seize it, and Patrick was afraid they might rip the contents apart. "Who's going to open it?" he said, holding it above his head. "Better be just one."

"What are you making them jump for? They're not fucking dogs."

"I just thought you mightn't want it destroyed, Mel."

"Never mind thinking what I want. I'll have you destroyed, pal." With no lessening of menace Mel said "Give it here."

Too late Patrick realised he could have ascertained who the mail was for. He'd assumed the birthday card would be addressed to both the children, unless the envelope contained a pair of cards, though was it bulky enough? As he made to examine it, Mel snatched it, and Patrick had to refrain from saying that the elder Cousins would have found that impolite. He was heading for the gate when Mel said "Tell us you're having a laugh."

As Patrick turned, the untimely gloom hindered him like water if not mud. Mel was brandishing the open envelope at him – the empty envelope. "Where's the card?" Patrick protested, he scarcely knew to whom.

"No card in here, Pad. No fucking thing else either."

Patrick stared at the yawning beak, the pink entrance to a woman, the way back into a womb, and fought to concentrate. "Someone must have taken it."

"Who are you calling a thief now?"

"I can't say, can I?" Patrick struggled not to let his gaze stray across Mel and the children in case it looked accusing. Surely it made sense to ask "Who was it for?"

Mel glared at the envelope and then at him. "Looks like you, Pad." Since he didn't move, Patrick had to venture back to him. As Mel turned the envelope towards him he spat on it – no, a large raindrop fell on a line of handwriting. The line was all Patrick had previously seen, and now he saw it was the whole of the address. *To the Pad,* it said. "You're right," Patrick told Mel. "It must be a joke."

"Who's having one of them?"

Patrick watched the letters settle down from writhing and assume a final shape. The scrawl looked childish, which made him think Kiera or Kieron was responsible. Might they have slipped the envelope into the trolley while Mel's father had diverted him away from it? He could equally suspect any of a number of his workmates. "I can't say that either," he said.

"Bet you can't. More like it's an excuse for you to come sneaking back."

"Why would I want to do that?" Patrick saw the answer in Mel's eyes, considerably worse than a warning. If he'd been closer to escaping through the gate he mightn't have lingered to be rational. "Don't be paranoid, Mel," he said.

"What's going to make me that, Pad?"

"What you had before. You won't say you aren't stoned."

"So are we," Kieron said.

"It's our birthday," Kiera said as if this hadn't been made plain.

"I've got to say I am a bit myself." In case it helped, Patrick added "In honour of the occasion."

"Don't try making out you're like us." Some element of the exchange had infuriated Mel. "Pity I didn't run you over," he said, "while I had the chance."

"You can't really mean that. There are children listening." "And don't you fucking tell them what I mean. Here's your message." He thrust the envelope at Patrick and turned to the children. "Watch out for him," he said. "You wouldn't like to be him if he came back."

Patrick dropped the envelope in the compartment that wasn't occupied by the empty can and made with a defiant series of clanks for the gate. From the pavement he saw the children watching him like guards. On his way back to the barbecue Mel shouted "You're not kidding us you didn't write it, Pad."

How could Patrick have been responsible? Where would he have found the envelope or the opportunity to write on it, or a reason? Mel's suggestion had left him feeling that his memory was wrong – that his whole mind was. He needed to show Eunice the item in the hope that somebody owned up. As he headed for the main road he grew anxious to locate a bin where he could bring the clatter of the trolley to an end. The dark sky looked too burdened to keep hold of its rain, but so far not a drop had touched him. Lightning flashed as he passed the Watch – no, the security camera caught him once more. He turned the bend that brought Dogs Home in sight, and Gutter started barking. Patrick wasn't about to be driven off the pavement, and he was marching past the gate when a man called "Hi there, postman. Just wait, will you."

His voice was as clipped as his grey hair and moustache. He was waving an envelope – the first item Patrick had delivered. "This isn't ours," he complained. "It's not remotely like."

The Doberman sprang up as Patrick took the envelope, and the dog's jaws clicked shut only inches from his hand. "Down, you brute," the man said. "It doesn't care for strangers." Patrick had to squint hard at the restless letters to grasp that the house where he should have left it was called Boosome. Even if the name made no sense, how could he have misread it? Mel hadn't affected his mind then, but Patrick felt as if their encounter had undermined time. Though the savage antics of the dog gave him little chance to think, he seemed to recall having seen the name somewhere on his round, surely not just on the envelope. "Sorry to have troubled you," he said.

As the dog bounded at the gate again its owner strode back to the house. For long enough to let the gloom droop lower overhead Patrick tried to think which way to move. He felt as if he was attempting to look down on Garden Mile, still at his desk and searching the map. How distant was the address he had to find? The Doberman was leaping higher, snarling through its teeth, and he had a sense that the entire suburb was growling at him. It wouldn't stop him performing his job. He wasn't going to give anyone an excuse to criticise him, and he tramped back along the road. At the bend he turned to bid some kind of farewell to the dog, which seemed to need no breath to bark. He'd hardly met its eyes when it vaulted over the gate and raced after him.

He wasted seconds in fancying this was his latest hallucination, and then he fled. The Watch greeted his clangourous approach with another flash of lightning, and the pavement around him broke out in a nervous rash. More of the rain streamed down his face, unless that was the juice of his panic. It blurred his vision while he dashed towards the Pad, where he saw faces at an upstairs window. As the dog appeared at the bend in the road Patrick rushed the trolley to the open gates. He hadn't reached them when Kiera and Kieron came out of the house.

They had been at the window, and he thought they'd been watching for him. Kiera was jigging to a repetitive ditty on her phone, and her brother had a gun. Patrick floundered through the gates after the trolley, and the boy pointed the toy at him. "Is that a birthday present?" Patrick said. "It looks real."

"It's our grandad's and you have to piss off."

Kiera continued to jerk like a puppet as if neither she nor the phone felt the rain. "You come in," she warned, "and you'll get what dad said."

Patrick heard claws clacking on the tarmac and a snarl that grew lower but closer. He flung back one of the lids of the trolley to see just his envelope and the Boosome item. "Not them," he pleaded and found the empty can to shy at the dog. It bounced off the animal's head, and the dog gave a yelp before redoubling its snarl and padding towards him. "Let me stay," Patrick begged the children. "I'll make it right with your father."

Through the house he saw Mel and others busy erecting a shelter beyond the crowded kitchen. He took another step, and Kieron raised the pistol. "Not me," Patrick blurted. "The dog."

He stooped to yank the bolt of the left-hand gate out of its socket, and was shutting the gate when he heard his vehicle backfire. It couldn't, since it had no engine, but he'd been distracted by a dull punch on his back. He clung to the gate while he stumbled to face the children. Kiera was continuing to prance, and her brother had him covered. "He's not gone yet," Kiera said.

Patrick tried joining in the dance as he lunged at the other gate. His capering impressed neither of the children, and might even have provoked the blow his chest took. Somebody behind the house – Mel or his father – wondered loudly what had just happened, but nobody came to look. "All right," Patrick said with more dignity than he'd realised he possessed, "I'll take my chances with the dog," and staggered past the gates. Perhaps he hadn't made himself heard, unless it didn't matter, because he received a parting thump on the back of his skull.

It carried him into the road, where he sprawled face down on the tarmac. The sky collapsed on him – the downpour did, at any rate. Perhaps that was why he could barely see the dog until its muzzle met his cheek. He couldn't move enough to flinch, but in any case the dog was only licking rain off him. Was it merely rain that was inundating the road around him? Dance music grew louder as the children came to view him, and he thought lightning had accompanied them until he heard the whir of a shutter on a phone. In the distance a man gave a cry of disgust or frustration about him if not the weather. As Patrick felt himself begin to spread through Garden Mile, he could only wonder if this would help him deliver the last of the mail.

Screams Don't Echo

D.R. Cartwright

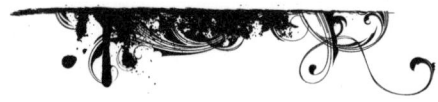

WHAT IS IT ABOUT darkness that scares the soul?

It must be the not knowing, of not seeing what surrounds you, or what to defend yourself against. It plays on your vulnerability, feeds off your weakness. The mind goes into over-drive, filling the blanks where you can't see, but filling them with something much darker than the darkness itself. Terror breeds, muscles tighten, chests become tight. Eyes flicker, left right, heart pounding. Heat. Then the thought: death is imminent.

These are the sensations being felt now. Breath escapes lips in quick bursts, and sweat drips over the body. The surrounding darkness is pitch, impenetrable, and panic is building.

But it isn't just the darkness that's terrifying. There's the inability to move, of being trapped, trapped in a small space. Claustrophobia adds to the panic.

And then there's the noise. It sounds like rain at first, a gentle patter above, followed by loud knocks, thumps and rumbles.

Screams don't echo in the darkness…

* * *

Mrs Heston's strength nearly failed her. She had to cling to her daughter's arm for support as she followed the pallbearers carrying her late husband's coffin to his final resting place. Behind her a trail of people followed, family, friends, acquaintances from town. They had all known Mr Heston, but none were really surprised by the announcement of his passing. He had been sickly for some time, despite only being fifty-six years of age. There were people far older than he, healthier and still working.

Consumption, the doctor had said. A poor unfortunate soul that God had claimed before his time. There was nothing they could do. Mrs Heston had followed the doctor's advice, nursing her husband as best she could, feeding him, giving him warm milk, and even taking daily exercise. Fresh air was supposed to do him good, but as he lay in their bed, drawing his last, ragged breaths, she knew it had all been a waste of time.

The white sickness had always intended to take him, no matter what they did.

The grave had already been dug in preparation for Mr Heston's coffin, a gaping hole amid a sea of gravestones. A pile of loose earth lay heaped next to it, a man leaning on his shovel close by, ready to shift it back into the hole, ready to bury the coffin, to bury her beloved husband. On seeing this, she gave another quiet wail and tightened her grip on her daughter's arm.

No one could see her face. A black veil flowed over her greying hair, hiding her misery. She couldn't afford a black dress for the funeral, and the veil had been a gift from her daughter and son-in-law. This, she knew, would have to suffice. And in this part of town, it was perfectly acceptable. Who could afford new dresses anyway?

The funeral was simple but touching. The priest gave his sermon to silent mourners standing around in the afternoon sun, and the people replied with weeps. After that, the people began to disperse but

Mrs Heston insisted on staying to watch as the earth was replaced, as it left the shovel and fell like rain down on the coffin below, on her Mr Heston.

"Come," her daughter said, her voice soft as she urged her mother away. There was no point watching until the end, but as they walked back to their home, a cloud shrouded Mrs Heston. She wasn't happy to leave her husband there alone, and the feeling continued to eat at her until late in the evening.

"I need to go back to the grave," she said. Her daughter looked up at her, but it was her son-in-law, Christoph, who spoke, standing up from the fireplace, having stoked the fire.

"Whatever for?"

Mrs Heston looked at him with pleading eyes. "I hate to think of him there alone. Anything could happen."

"Mother," he said, for he also called her this since his marriage to her daughter, Anne. "Mr Heston has been laid to rest. His suffering is over. He is at peace now."

"I know this," she replied.

She knew all too well. After all, she had been the one there with him, watching his sufferings. She would miss the man dearly - she loved him well - but he was far better where he was now. And despite her loss, a great weight had been lifted from her shoulders. No longer did she have to suffer, to feel helpless as she watched him slowly be consumed. On the day of his death, he had been a shadow of his former self.

"I fear the resurrection men."

"Resurrection men? Mother, don't talk of such horrors." Anne placed her cup and saucer on the table with unease.

"But all I can think about is your poor father falling prey to their thieving shovels. We should have taken more precautions."

"You knew the cost of a mortsafe, and know full well we couldn't afford one." Christoph said as he sat back on his chair, watching as the small flames took hold in the hearth.

"I just feel there is more we can do. I know we can't afford a mortsafe, but we can guard his grave. Especially tonight while it is still fresh and vulnerable."

Christoph shook his head. "Mother, you're in mourning. You're not talking sense. You need sleep. Rest assured not one grave has been touched here for many months."

Mrs Heston looked from Christoph to Anne. "But the threat is still real. These resurrection men can attack anywhere, any time. I think one of us should go and watch over the grave."

Anne stood from her seat and stepped up to her mother. Reaching down, she took hold of her hand and urged her to her feet. "Mother, you're exhausted. We all are. Come upstairs and get some sleep. It's been a long day and you'll feel better in the morning."

Mrs Heston glanced once more towards Christoph. "Will you make sure father is safe?"

Her son-in-law nodded but she knew full well he wasn't going to leave the house tonight.

* * *

Mrs Heston looks a frail old lady now, he thought as he watched the funeral. Unsurprising under the circumstances. She was a small woman anyway, but today she looked even smaller, hardly able to carry her own weight. So sad about Mr Heston. He had been a decent fellow. But one man's loss was another man's gain, so they say.

He marked the spot in his mind and waited until the cover of darkness, slipping through the back streets with a cart, a wooden shovel, some tools and a tarp rolled up inside. He didn't bring a lantern with him. The moonlight would be bright enough to work by. He hoped his partner, who he was supposed to meet by the gates, wouldn't bring one either. He'd only worked with him on a few occasions and the kid, even though eager, was still a little wet behind the ears. Jittery.

A nice fresh corpse would fetch them around ten guineas if they were lucky.

Did he worry about Mrs Heston ever finding out her husband had been stolen? Of course not. This was business. This was his living. And it was going towards medical science. Surly that was a good thing, right? But still, Mrs Heston was a nice lady, so he made a note that they would leave the grave appearing as untouched as possible. Hopefully she would never find out.

The graveyard loomed in the darkness. He entered the gate and waited just inside. The kid was late, but not by much. His shadow was a little darker than his surroundings as he made his way through the bushes, a shovel of his own in one hand and a bundle of rope slung over the other shoulder.

"Larry," the kid greeted as he approached.

Larry grunted in reply and then turned. They walked up the path, making their way towards the fresh grave. Everything looked different under the cover of night, and he found himself momentarily lost among a sea of gravestones. So much potential money lost out to time here. A corpse had to be fresh, not stinking and rotting like these others would be. They were worthless to him, and worthless to the medical department. Not worth his time.

But one was.

Now, where was it?

"Oh Mr Heston?" he whispered into the night, unsure why. If he received an answer, he'd run a mile and need a new pair of trousers. The kid would be long gone, too. He'd doubt he'd ever see him again.

The mound of disturbed earth shone like a beacon in the moonlight over to their left. It was as if the moon itself was showing them the way. He knew the Hestons had been comfortable financially but the cost of a mortsafe, or any other grave security, was beyond their means, making this an easy job. He indicated to the kid the direction they needed to go in, and then weaved his way through the stones. He parked the cart next to it and stood, looking down at the mound. His mind turned, as it always did at this point. He was never sure why. Doubt? Paying last minute respects? Apologising for the crime and desecration he was about to commit? He stood in silence for a matter of seconds, but to him it felt like minutes. Then he kicked himself back into gear as the kid dropped the rope on the ground and adjusted his grip on his shovel.

"Let's get to it," the kid said. He cut the first strike as Larry grabbed his own shovel from the cart.

"Sorry, Mr Heston, but business is business, as I'm sure you'd appreciate."

Soon the pair were digging, throwing shovels of earth on the side of the grave, making a new mound. Eyes watched them from the shadows, animals going about their own business, scurrying through the bushes and tall grasses. An owl hooted somewhere in the trees, its eyes peeled for its next meal, and a fox called somewhere off in the distance. The night was never truly asleep.

Eventually Larry's shovel met something solid. The sound of it scraping echoed in the darkness and he was glad they were using wooden shovels. They were a lot quieter, something he had learnt through experience. He looked up and his eyes met with the kid's. They were there. They had reached the coffin.

An eagerness waved through them both and they picked up their pace, clearing the mud away from the top of the coffin. They didn't need to uncover the whole thing. They just needed access to the top half. Then the kid would tie his rope around the neck of the late Mr Heston and together they would pull him up. This was a lot easier with fresh corpses. It often turned quite gruesome and messy with older ones. But Mr Heston hadn't even been buried twelve hours. You couldn't get much fresher than him.

Larry was on his knees now, in the grave, brushing the excess mud from the top of the coffin with his hands. The kid watched from above, and the moon illuminated the wood that he needed to break through. He looked up. He didn't need to speak anything for the kid to know what he wanted. He disappeared and came back with the prybar. Reaching down, he handed it to Larry, and then set about readying his rope.

This was the tricky part. Breaking into a coffin without making much noise wasn't the easiest of things to do. And everything sounds louder at night. It carries.

Larry gripped the prybar and set to work. It may have been the trickiest part but he had done this many times before, and he knew how to break into a coffin quickly and efficiently. Tonight was no exception.

He was in.

Mr Heston, God rest his soul, looked peaceful in the dark, resting in his little compartment, despite the sweetly sick smell that arose from him. Mrs Heston had dressed him in his best suit and his hands were closed together across his chest. He looked just as small and frail as his wife did at the funeral, but he never used to look like this. He was once a large, burly man, a worker. This was the result of consumption. It was a wicked sickness, cruel, relentless. It didn't care who it struck down, who it consumed.

But regardless of how much weight the man had lost, he was still the perfect specimen for dissection at the medical school. They just needed to get him out.

"The rope," he called to the kid, looking up. The kid, still standing over the open grave, looked distracted off to the left. "Hey kid!" he called.

Suddenly the kid let out a shrill scream.

Larry jolted, the scream cutting through the night like a knife. He didn't have a chance to ask what was wrong or to shut him up. The kid turned and bolted.

"What the hell?"

Larry stood and looked after him, watching as he disappeared into the shadows. He wanted to call after him but he didn't want to break the silence any more than it had been already. With his prybar still in his hand, ready to use as a weapon if he needed, he climbed from the hole and turned to see what had frightened the kid.

He didn't expect to see the figure in white floating towards him from the shadows.

* * *

The moon was bright in the night sky as the door opened to the house. Christoph and Anne were sleeping soundly in their bed, unaware as Mrs Heston crept past their doorway and headed downstairs, dressed in her white nightdress and a shawl. She knew Christoph wouldn't guard Mr Heston. He was a nice man but his head was for business, not dealing with the horrors of the real world.

This, she had to take care of herself.

Carefully, she closed the front door behind her and set off down the lane towards the graveyard, towards her late Mr Heston.

* * *

The sound! It's deafening now. But knowing what it is doesn't make it any easier. In fact it makes it worse. Knowing what it is a nightmare come true.

It's the sound of earth falling on top of a coffin.

From *above*.

More screams erupt but they fall on deaf ears, if they fall on ears at all. Hands rise, meet an obstruction just inches above. The coffin lid.

Trapped. Confined. Panic.

Fists pound on the coffin top from inside.

The sound is getting duller now. The earth on top of the coffin has settled but more is still being piled on top. It just sounds quieter the deeper it gets.

Deeper.

On top.

How is this happening? What happened that resulted in this? It's all such a blur.

The grave was open. The kid had screamed and bolted. What had happened after that? Think!

Something had struck the side of the head. Stars had flashed brightly before everything fell as dark as it is now. What was it! God damn it, think harder!

A wooden shovel.

Who'd have thought there was strength enough in Mrs Heston to deal such a blow? It had come out of nowhere, breaking the shadows, and there had been no time to react.

Mr Heston lies beside him, slowly rotting, cold and stinking.

Larry continues to scream in the pitch darkness, bile rising in his throat. He calls Mrs Heston's name. He cries that she knows him and please don't do this to him.

Please don't bury him alive!

The darkness plays tricks on the mind, feeding the fear, just as grief plays tricks and make you do crazy things. Mrs Heston was a sweet little lady who had struggled with her sick husband and grieving his loss. No one would ever believe that she was capable of murder, of murdering him, a crime far worse in the eyes of the law than grave robbing.

Sweet, frail, little old Mrs Heston!

And he always knew that if anything happened in the graveyard at night, he would never see that kid again. No one knows he's here.

His screams still don't echo.

The Belled Buzzard

Irvin S. Cobb

THERE WAS A SWAMP known as Little Niggerwool, to distinguish it from Big Niggerwool, which lay across the river. It was traversable only by those who knew it well – an oblong stretch of tawny mud and tawny water, measuring maybe four miles its longest way and two miles roughly at its widest; and it was full of cypress and stunted swamp oak, with edgings of canebrake and rank weeds; and in one place, where a ridge crossed it from side to side, it was snaggled like an old jaw with dead tree trunks, rising close-ranked and thick as teeth. It was untenanted of living things – except, down below, there were snakes and mosquitoes, and a few wading and swimming fowl; and up above, those big woodpeckers that the country people called logcocks – larger than pigeons, with flaming crests and spiky tails – swooping in their long, loping flight from snag to snag, always just out of gunshot of the chance invader, and uttering a strident cry which matched those surroundings so fitly that it might well have been the voice of the swamp itself.

On one side little Niggerwool drained its saffron waters off into a sluggish creek, where summer ducks bred, and on the other it ended abruptly at a natural bank of high ground, along which the county turnpike ran. The swamp came right up to the road and thrust its fringe of reedy, weedy undergrowth forward as though in challenge to the good farm lands that were spread beyond the barrier. At the time I am speaking of it was mid-summer, and from these canes and weeds and waterplants there came a smell so rank as almost to be overpowering. They grew thick as a curtain, making a blank green wall taller than a man's head.

Along the dusty stretch of road fronting the swamp nothing living had stirred for half an hour or more. And so at length the weed-stems rustled and parted, and out from among them a man came forth silently and cautiously. He was an old man – an old man who had once been fat, but with age had grown lean again, so that now his skin was by odds too large for him. It lay on the back of his neck in folds. Under the chin he was pouched like a pelican and about the jowls was wattled like a turkey gobbler.

He came out upon the road slowly and stopped there, switching his legs absently with the stalk of a horseweed. He was in his shirtsleeves – a respectable, snuffy old figure; evidently a man deliberate in words and thoughts and actions. There was something about him suggestive of an old staid sheep that had been engaged in a clandestine transaction and was afraid of being found out.

He had made amply sure no one was in sight before he came out of the swamp, but now, to be doubly certain, he watched the empty road – first up, then down – for a long half minute, and fetched a sighing breath of satisfaction. His eyes fell upon his feet, and, taken with an idea, he stepped back to the edge of the road and with a wisp of crabgrass wiped his shoes clean of the swamp mud, which was of a different color and texture from the soil of the upland. All his life Squire H. B. Gathers had been a careful, canny man, and he had need to be doubly careful on this summer morning. Having disposed of the mud on his feet, he settled his white straw hat down firmly upon his head, and, crossing the road, he climbed a stake-and-rider fence laboriously and went plodding sedately across a weedfield and up a slight slope toward his house, half a mile away, upon the crest of the little hill.

He felt perfectly natural – not like a man who had just taken a fellowman's life – but natural and safe, and well satisfied with himself and with his morning's work. And he was safe; that was the main thing

– absolutely safe. Without hitch or hindrance he had done the thing for which he had been planning and waiting and longing all these months. There had been no slip or mischance; the whole thing had worked out as plainly and simply as two and two make four. No living creature except himself knew of the meeting in the early morning at the head of Little Niggerwool, exactly where the squire had figured they should meet; none knew of the device by which the other man had been lured deeper and deeper in the swamp to the exact spot where the gun was hidden. No one had seen the two of them enter the swamp; no one had seen the squire emerge, three hours later, alone.

The gun, having served its purpose, was hidden again, in a place no mortal eye would ever discover. Face downward, with a hole between his shoulder blades, the dead man was lying where he might lie undiscovered for months or for years, or forever. His pedler's pack was buried in the mud so deep that not even the probing crawfishes could find it. He would never be missed probably. There was but the slightest likelihood that inquiry would ever be made for him – let alone a search. He was a stranger and a foreigner, the dead man was, whose comings and goings made no great stir in the neighborhood, and whose failure to come again would be taken as a matter of course – just one of those shiftless, wandering Dagoes, here today and gone tomorrow. That was one of the best things about it – these Dagoes never had any people in this country to worry about them or look for them when they disappeared. And so it was all over and done with, and nobody the wiser. The squire clapped his hands together briskly with the air of a man dismissing a subject from his mind for good, and mended his gait.

He felt no stabbings of conscience. On the contrary, a glow of gratification filled him. His house was saved from scandal; his present wife would philander no more – before his very eyes – with these young Dagoes, who came from nobody knew where, with packs on their backs and persuasive, wheedling tongues in their heads. At this thought the squire raised his head and considered his homestead. It looked good to him – the small white cottage among the honey locusts, with beehives and flower beds about it; the tidy whitewashed fence; the sound outbuildings at the back, and the well-tilled acres roundabout.

At the fence he halted and turned about, carelessly and casually, and looked back along the way he had come. Everything was as it should be – the weedfield steaming in the heat; the empty road stretching along the crooked ridge like a long gray snake sunning itself; and beyond it, massing up, the dark, cloaking stretch of swamp. Everything was all right, but – The squire's eyes, in their loose sacs of skin, narrowed and squinted. Out of the blue arch away over yonder a small black dot had resolved itself and was swinging to and fro, like a mote. A buzzard – hey? Well, there were always buzzards about on a clear day like this. Buzzards were nothing to worry about – almost any time you could see one buzzard, or a dozen buzzards if you were a mind to look for them.

But this particular buzzard now – wasn't he making for Little Niggerwool? The squire did not like the idea of that. He had not thought of the buzzards until this minute. Sometimes when cattle strayed the owners had been known to follow the buzzards, knowing mighty well that if the buzzards led the way to where the stray was, the stray would be past the small salvage of hide and hoofs – but the owner's doubts would be set at rest for good and all.

There was a grain of disquiet in this. The squire shook his head to drive the thought away – yet it persisted, coming back like a midge dancing before his face. Once at home, however, Squire Gathers deported himself in a perfectly normal manner. With the satisfied proprietorial eye of an elderly husband who has no rivals, he considered his young wife, busied about her household duties. He sat in an easy-chair upon his front gallery and read his yesterday's Courier-Journal which the rural carrier had brought him; but he kept stepping out into the yard to peer up into the sky and all about him. To the second Mrs. Gathers he explained that he was looking for weather signs. A day as hot and still as this one was a regular weather breeder; there ought to be rain before night.

"Maybe so," she said; "but looking's not going to bring rain."

Nevertheless the squire continued to look. There was really nothing to worry about; still at midday he did not eat much dinner, and before his wife was half through with hers he was back on the gallery. His paper was cast aside and he was watching. The original buzzard – or, anyhow, he judged it was the first one he had seen – was swinging back and forth in great pendulum swings, but closer down toward the swamp – closer and closer – until it looked from that distance as though the buzzard flew almost at the level of the tallest snags there. And on beyond this first buzzard, coursing above him, were other buzzards. Were there four of them? No; there were five – five in all.

Such is the way of the buzzard – that shifting black question mark which punctuates a Southern sky. In the woods a shoat or a sheep or a horse lies down to die. At once, coming seemingly out of nowhere, appears a black spot, up five hundred feet or a thousand in the air. In broad loops and swirls this dot swings round and round and round, coming a little closer to earth at every turn and always with one particular spot upon the earth for the axis of its wheel. Out of space also other moving spots emerge and grow larger as they tack and jib and drop nearer, coming in their leisurely buzzard way to the feast. There is no haste – the feast will wait. If it is a dumb creature that has fallen stricken the grim coursers will sooner or later be assembled about it and alongside it, scrouging ever closer and closer to the dying thing, with awkward out-thrustings of their naked necks and great dust-raising flaps of the huge, unkempt wings; lifting their feathered shanks high and stiffly like old crippled grave-diggers in overalls that are too tight – but silent and patient all, offering no attack until the last tremor runs through the stiffening carcass and the eyes glaze over. To humans the buzzard pays a deeper meed of respect – he hangs aloft longer; but in the end he comes. No scavenger shark, no carrion crab, ever chambered more grisly secrets in his digestive processes than this big charnel bird. Such is the way of the buzzard.

* * *

The squire missed his afternoon nap, a thing that had not happened in years. He stayed on the front gallery and kept count. Those moving distant black specks typified uneasiness for the squire – not fear exactly, or panic or anything akin to it, but a nibbling, nagging kind of uneasiness. Time and again he said to himself that he would not think about them any more; but he did – unceasingly.

By supper time there were seven of them.

* * *

He slept light and slept badly. It was not the thought of that dead man lying yonder in Little Niggerwool that made him toss and fume while his wife snored gently alongside him. It was something else altogether. Finally his stirrings roused her and she asked him drowsily what ailed him. Was he sick? Or bothered about anything?

Irritated, he answered her snappishly. Certainly nothing was bothering him, he told her. It was a hot enough night – wasn't it? And when a man got a little along in life he was apt to be a light sleeper – wasn't that so? Well, then? She turned upon her side and slept again with her light, purring snore. The squire lay awake, thinking hard and waiting for day to come.

At the first faint pink-and-gray glow he was up and out upon the gallery. He cut a comic figure standing there in his shirt in the half light, with the dewlap at his throat dangling grotesquely in the neck opening of the unbuttoned garment, and his bare bowed legs showing, splotched and varicose. He kept his eyes fixed on the skyline below, to the south. Buzzards are early risers too. Presently, as the heavens shimmered with the miracle of sunrise, he could make them out – six or seven, or maybe eight.

An hour after breakfast the squire was on his way down through the weedfield to the county road. He went half eagerly, half unwillingly. He wanted to make sure about those buzzards. It might be that they were aiming for the old pasture at the head of the swamp. There were sheep grazing there – and it might be that a sheep had died. Buzzards were notoriously fond of sheep, when dead. Or, if they were pointed for the swamp, he must satisfy himself exactly what part of the swamp it was. He was at the stake-and-rider fence when a mare came jogging down the road, drawing a rig with a man in it. At sight of the squire in the field the man pulled up.

"Hi, squire!" he saluted. "Goin' somewheres?"

"No; jest knockin' about," the squire said: "jest sorter lookin' the place over."

"Hot agin – ain't it?" said the other.

The squire allowed that it was, for a fact, mighty hot. Commonplaces of gossip followed this – county politics and a neighbor's wife sick of breakbone fever down the road a piece. The subject of crops succeeded inevitably. The squire spoke of the need of rain. Instantly he regretted it, for the other man, who was by way of being a weather wiseacre, cocked his head aloft to study the sky for any signs of clouds.

"Wonder whut all them buzzards are doin' yonder, squire," he said, pointing upward with his whipstock.

"Whut buzzards – where?" asked the squire with an elaborate note of carelessness in his voice.

"Right yonder, over Little Niggerwool – see 'em there?"

"Oh, yes," the squire made answer. "Now I see 'em. They ain't doin' nothin', I reckin – jest flyin' round same as they always do in clear weather."

"Must be somethin' dead over there!" speculated the man in the buggy.

"A hawg probably," said the squire promptly – almost too promptly. "There's likely to be hawgs usin' in Niggerwool. Bristow, over on the other side from here – he's got a big drove of hawgs."

"Well, mebbe so," said the man; "but hawgs is a heap more apt to be feedin' on high ground, seems like to me. Well, I'll be gittin' along towards town. G'day, squire." And he slapped the lines down on the mare's flank and jogged off through the dust.

He could not have suspected anything – that man couldn't. As the squire turned away from the road and headed for his house he congratulated himself upon that stroke of his in bringing in Bristow's hogs; and yet there remained this disquieting note in the situation, that buzzards flying, and especially buzzards flying over Little Niggerwool, made people curious – made them ask questions.

He was half-way across the weedfield when, above the hum of insect life, above the inward clamor of his own busy speculations, there came to his ear dimly and distantly a sound that made him halt and cant his head to one side the better to hear it. Somewhere, a good way off, there was a thin, thready, broken strain of metallic clinking and clanking – an eery ghost-chime ringing. It came nearer and became plainer – tonk-tonk-tonk; then the tonks all running together briskly.

A sheep bell or a cowbell – that was it; but why did it seem to come from overhead, from up in the sky, like? And why did it shift so abruptly from one quarter to another – from left to right and back again to left? And how was it that the clapper seemed to strike so fast? Not even the breachiest of breachy young heifers could be expected to tinkle a cowbell with such briskness. The squire's eye searched the earth and the sky, his troubled mind giving to his eye a quick and flashing scrutiny. He had it. It was not a cow at all. It was not anything that went on four legs.

One of the loathly flock had left the others. The orbit of his swing had carried him across the road and over Squire Gathers' land. He was sailing right toward and over the squire now. Craning his flabby neck, the squire could make out the unwholesome contour of the huge bird. He could see the ragged black wings – a buzzard's wings are so often ragged and uneven – and the naked throat; the slim, naked head; the big feet folded up against the dingy belly. And he could see a bell too – an undersized cowbell – that dangled at the creature's breast and jangled incessantly. All his life nearly Squire Gathers had been hearing about the Belled Buzzard. Now with his own eye he was seeing him.

Once, years and years and years ago, some one trapped a buzzard, and before freeing it clamped about its skinny neck a copper band with a cowbell pendent from it. Since then the bird so ornamented has been seen a hundred times – and heard oftener – over an area as wide as half the continent. It has been reported, now in Kentucky, now in Texas, now in North Carolina – now anywhere between the Ohio River and the Gulf. Crossroads correspondents take their pens in hand to write to the country papers that on such and such a date, at such a place, So-and-So saw the Belled Buzzard. Always it is the Belled Buzzard, never a belled buzzard. The Belled Buzzard is an institution.

There must be more than one of them. It seems hard to believe that one bird, even a buzzard in his prime, and protected by law in every Southern state and known to be a bird of great age, could live so long and range so far and wear a clinking cowbell all the time! Probably other jokers have emulated the original joker; probably if the truth were known there have been a dozen such; but the country people will have it that there is only one Belled Buzzard – a bird that bears a charmed life and on his neck a never silent bell.

* * *

Squire Gathers regarded it a most untoward thing that the Belled Buzzard should have come just at this time. The movements of ordinary, unmarked buzzards mainly concerned only those whose stock had strayed; but almost anybody with time to spare might follow this rare and famous visitor, this belled and feathered junkman of the sky. Supposing now that some one followed it today – maybe followed it even to a certain thick clump of cypress in the middle of Little Niggerwool!

But at this particular moment the Belled Buzzard was heading directly away from that quarter. Could it be following him? Of course not! It was just by chance that it flew along the course the squire was taking. But, to make sure, he veered off sharply, away from the footpath into the high weeds so that the startled grasshoppers sprayed up in front of him in fan-like flights.

He was right; it was only a chance. The Belled Buzzard swung off too, but in the opposite direction, with a sharp tonking of its bell, and, flapping hard, was in a minute or two out of hearing and sight, past the trees to the westward.

Again the squire skimped his dinner, and again he spent the long drowsy afternoon upon his front gallery. In all the sky there were now no buzzards visible, belled or unbelled – they had settled to earth somewhere; and this served somewhat to soothe the squire's pestered mind. This does not mean, though, that he was by any means easy in his thoughts. Outwardly he was calm enough, with the ruminative judicial air befitting the oldest justice of the peace in the county; but, within him, a little something gnawed unceasingly at his nerves like one of those small white worms that are to be found in seemingly sound nuts. About once in so long a tiny spasm of the muscles would contract the dewlap under his chin. The squire had never heard of that play, made famous by a famous player, wherein the murdered victim was a pedler too, and a clamoring bell the voice of unappeasable remorse in the murderer's ear. As a strict churchgoer the squire had no use for players or for play actors, and so was spared that added canker to his conscience. It was bad enough as it was.

That night, as on the night before, the old man's sleep was broken and fitful and disturbed by dreaming, in which he heard a metal clapper striking against a brazen surface. This was one dream that came true. Just after daybreak he heaved himself out of bed, with a flop of his broad bare feet upon the floor, and stepped to the window and peered out. Half seen in the pinkish light, the Belled Buzzard flapped directly over his roof and flew due south, right toward the swamp – drawing a direct line through the air between the slayer and the victim – or, anyway, so it seemed to the watcher, grown suddenly tremulous.

* * *

Knee deep in yellow swamp water the squire squatted, with his shotgun cocked and loaded and ready, waiting to kill the bird that now typified for him guilt and danger and an abiding great fear. Gnats plagued him and about him frogs croaked. Almost overhead a log-cock clung lengthwise to a snag, watching him. Snake doctors, limber, long insects with bronze bodies and filmy wings, went back and forth like small living shuttles. Other buzzards passed and repassed, but the squire waited, forgetting the cramps in his elderly limbs and the discomfort of the water in his shoes.

At length he heard the bell. It came nearer and nearer, and the Belled Buzzard swung overhead not sixty feet up, its black bulk a fair target against the blue. He aimed and fired, both barrels bellowing at once and a fog of thick powder smoke enveloping him. Through the smoke he saw the bird careen and its bell jangled furiously; then the buzzard righted itself and was gone, fleeing so fast that the sound of its bell was hushed almost instantly. Two long wing feathers drifted slowly down; torn disks of gunwadding and shredded green scraps of leaves descended about the squire in a little shower.

He cast his empty gun from him so that it fell in the water and disappeared; and he hurried out of the swamp as fast as his shaky legs would take him, splashing himself with mire and water to his eyebrows. Mucked with mud, breathing in great gulps, trembling, a suspicious figure to any eye, he burst through the weed curtain and staggered into the open, his caution all gone and a vast desperation fairly choking him – but the gray road was empty and the field beyond the road was empty; and, except for him, the whole world seemed empty and silent.

As he crossed the field Squire Gathers composed himself. With plucked handfuls of grass he cleansed himself of much of the swamp mire that coated him over; but the little white worm that gnawed at his nerves had become a cold snake that was coiled about his heart, squeezing it tighter and tighter!

This episode of the attempt to kill the Belled Buzzard occurred in the afternoon of the third day. In the forenoon of the fourth, the weather being still hot, with cloudless skies and no air stirring, there was a rattle of warped wheels in the squire's lane and a hail at his yard fence. Coming out upon his gallery from the innermost darkened room of his house, where he had been stretched upon a bed, the squire shaded his eyes from the glare and saw the constable of his own magisterial district sitting in a buggy at the gate waiting.

The old man went down the dirtpath slowly, almost reluctantly, with his head twisted up side wise, listening, watching; but the constable sensed nothing strange about the other's gait and posture; the constable was full of the news he brought. He began to unload the burden of it without preamble.

"Mornin', Squire Gathers. There's been a dead man found in Little Niggerwool – and you're wanted."

He did not notice that the squire was holding on with both hands to the gate; but he did notice that the squire had a sick look out of his eyes and a dead, pasty color in his face; and he noticed – but attached no meaning to it – that when the squire spoke his voice seemed flat and hollow.

"Wanted – fur – whut?" The squire forced the words out of his throat, pumped them out fairly.

"Why, to hold the inquest," explained the constable. "The coroner's sick abed, and he said you bein' the nearest jestice of the peace you should serve."

"Oh," said the squire with more ease. "Well, where is it – the body?"

"They taken it to Bristow's place and put it in his stable for the present. They brought it out over on that side and his place was the nearest. If you'll hop in here with me, squire, I'll ride you right over there now. There's enough men already gathered to make up a jury, I reckin."

"I – I ain't well," demurred the squire. "I've been sleepin' poorly these last few nights. It's the heat," he added quickly.

"Well, suh, you don't look very brash, and that's a fact," said the constable; "but this here job ain't goin' to keep you long. You see it's in such shape – the body is – that there ain't no way of makin' out who the feller was nor whut killed him. There ain't nobody reported missin' in this county as we know of, either; so I jedge a verdict of a unknown person dead from unknown causes would be about the correct thing. And we kin git it all over mighty quick and put him underground right away, suh – if you'll go along now."

"I'll go," agreed the squire, almost quivering in his newborn eagerness. "I'll go right now." He did not wait to get his coat or to notify his wife of the errand that was taking him. In his shirtsleeves he climbed into the buggy, and the constable turned his horse and clucked him into a trot. And now the squire asked the question that knocked at his lips demanding to be asked – the question the answer to which he yearned for and yet dreaded.

"How did they come to find – it?"

"Well, suh, that's a funny thing," said the constable. "Early this mornin' Bristow's oldest boy – that one they call Buddy – he heared a cowbell over in the swamp and so he went to look; Bristow's got cows, as you know, and one or two of 'em is belled. And he kept on followin' after the sound of it till he got way down into the thickest part of them cypress slashes that's near the middle there; and right there he run acrost it – this body.

"But, suh, squire, it wasn't no cow at all. No, suh; it was a buzzard with a cowbell on his neck – that's whut it was. Yes, suh; that there same old Belled Buzzard he's come back agin and is hangin' round. They tell me he ain't been seen round here since the year of the yellow fever – I don't remember myself, but that's whut they tell me. The niggers over on the other side are right smartly worked up over it. They say – the niggers do – that when the Belled Buzzard comes it's a sign of bad luck for somebody, shore!"

The constable drove on, talking on, garrulous as a guinea hen. The squire didn't heed him. Hunched back in the buggy, he harkened only to those busy inner voices filling his mind with thundering portents. Even so, his ear was first to catch above the rattle of the buggy wheels the far-away, faint tonk-tonk! They were about half-way to Bristow's place then. He gave no sign, and it was perhaps half a minute before his companion heard it too.

The constable jerked the horse to a standstill and craned his neck over his shoulder.

"Well, by doctors!" he cried, "if there ain't the old scoundrel now, right here behind us! I kin see him plain as day – he's got an old cowbell hitched to his neck; and he's shy a couple of feathers out of one wing. By doctors, that's somethin' you won't see every day! In all my born days I ain't never seen the beat of that!"

Squire Gathers did not look; he only cowered back farther under the buggy top. In the pleasing excitement of the moment his companion took no heed, though, of anything except the Belled Buzzard.

"Is he followin' us?" asked the squire in a curiously flat, weighted voice.

"Which – him?" answered the constable, still stretching his neck. "No, he's gone now – gone off to the left – jest a-zoomin', like he'd done forgot somethin'."

And Bristow's place was to the left! But there might still be time. To get the inquest over and the body underground – those were the main things. Ordinarily humane in his treatment of stock, Squire Gathers urged the constable to greater speed. The horse was lathered and his sides heaved wearily as they pounded across the bridge over the creek which was the outlet to the swamp and emerged from a patch of woods in sight of Bristow's farm buildings.

The house was set on a little hill among cleared fields and was in other respects much like the squire's own house except that it was smaller and not so well painted. There was a wide yard in front with shade trees and a lye hopper and a well-box, and a paling fence with a stile in it instead of a gate. At the rear, behind a clutter of outbuildings – a barn, a smokehouse and a corncrib – was a little peach orchard, and flanking the house on the right there was a good-sized cowyard, empty of stock at this hour, with feedracks ranged in a row against the fence. A two-year-old negro child, bareheaded and barefooted and wearing but a single garment, was grubbing busily in the dirt under one of these feedracks.

To the front fence a dozen or more riding horses were hitched, flicking their tails at the flies; and on the gallery men in their shirtsleeves were grouped. An old negro woman, with her head tied in a bandanna and a man's old slouch hat perched upon the bandanna, peeped out from behind a corner. There were gaunt hound dogs wandering about, sniffing uneasily.

Before the constable had the horse hitched the squire was out of the buggy and on his way up the footpath, going at a brisker step than the squire usually traveled. The men on the porch hailed him gravely and ceremoniously, as befitting an occasion of solemnity. Afterward some of them recalled the look in his eye; but at the moment they noted it – if they noted it at all – subconsciously.

For all his haste the squire, as was also remembered later, was almost the last to enter the door; and before he did enter he halted and searched the flawless sky as though for signs of rain. Then he hurried on after the others, who clumped single file along a narrow little hall, the bare, uncarpeted floor creaking loudly under their heavy farm shoes, and entered a good-sized room that had in it, among other things, a high-piled feather bed and a cottage organ – Bristow's best room, now to be placed at the disposal of the law's representatives for the inquest. The squire took the largest chair and drew it to the very center of the room, in front of a fireplace, where the grate was banked with withering asparagus ferns. The constable took his place formally at one side of the presiding official. The others sat or stood about where they could find room – all but six of them, whom the squire picked for his coroner's jury, and who backed themselves against the wall.

The squire showed haste. He drove the preliminaries forward with a sort of tremulous insistence. Bristow's wife brought a bucket of fresh drinking water and a gourd, and almost before she was out of the room and the door closed behind her the squire had sworn his jurors and was calling the first witness, who it seemed likely would also be the only witness – Bristow's oldest boy. The boy wriggled in confusion as he sat on a cane-bottomed chair facing the old magistrate. All there, barring one or two, had heard his story a dozen times already, but now it was to be repeated under oath; and so they bent their heads, listening as though it were a brand-new tale. All eyes were on him; none were fastened on the squire as he, too, gravely bent his head, listening – listening.

The witness began – but had no more than started when the squire gave a great, screeching howl and sprang from his chair and staggered backward, his eyes popped and the pouch under his chin quivering as though it had a separate life all its own. Startled, the constable made toward him and they struck together heavily and went down – both on their all fours – right in front of the fireplace.

The constable scrambled free and got upon his feet, in a squat of astonishment, with his head craned; but the squire stayed upon the floor, face downward, his feet flopping among the rustling asparagus greens – a picture of slavering animal fear. And now his gagging screech resolved itself into articulate speech.

"I done it!" they made out his shrieked words. "I done it! I own up – I killed him! He aimed fur to break up my home and I tolled him off into Niggerwool and killed him! There's a hole in his back if you'll look fur it. I done it – oh, I done it – and I'll tell everything jest like it happened if you'll jest keep that thing away from me! Oh, my Lawdy! Don't you hear it? It's a-comin' clos'ter and clos'ter – it's a-comin' after me! Keep it away—" His voice gave out and he buried his head in his hands and rolled upon the gaudy carpet.

And now they all heard what he had heard first – they heard the tonk-tonk-tonk of a cowbell, coming near and nearer toward them along the hallway without. It was as though the sound floated along. There was no creak of footsteps upon the loose, bare boards – and the bell jangled faster than it would dangling from a cow's neck. The sound came right to the door and Squire Gathers wallowed among the chair legs.

The door swung open. In the doorway stood a negro child, barefooted and naked except for a single garment, eyeing them with serious, rolling eyes – and, with all the strength of his two puny arms, proudly but solemnly tolling a small rusty cowbell he had found in the cowyard.

The Dream Woman
A Mystery in Four Narratives
Wilkie Collins

The First Narrative
Introductory Statement of the Facts by Percy Fairbank

Chapter I

"HULLO, there! Hostler! Hullo-o-o!"

"My dear! why don't you look for the bell?"

"I have looked – there is no bell."

"And nobody in the yard. How very extraordinary! Call again, dear."

"Hostler! Hullo, there! Hostler-r-r!"

My second call echoes through empty space, and rouses nobody – produces, in short, no visible result. I am at the end of my resources – I don't know what to say or what to do next. Here I stand in the solitary inn yard of a strange town, with two horses to hold, and a lady to take care of. By way of adding to my responsibilities, it so happens that one of the horses is dead lame, and that the lady is my wife.

Who am I? – you will ask.

There is plenty of time to answer the question. Nothing happens; and nobody appears to receive us. Let me introduce myself and my wife.

I am Percy Fairbank – English gentleman – age (let us say) forty – no profession – moderate politics – middle height – fair complexion – easy character – plenty of money.

My wife is a French lady. She was Mademoiselle Clotilde Delorge – when I was first presented to her at her father's house in France. I fell in love with her – I really don't know why. It might have been because I was perfectly idle, and had nothing else to do at the time. Or it might have been because all my friends said she was the very last woman whom I ought to think of marrying. On the surface, I must own, there is nothing in common between Mrs. Fairbank and me. She is tall; she is dark; she is nervous, excitable, romantic; in all her opinions she proceeds to extremes. What could such a woman see in me? what could I see in her? I know no more than you do. In some mysterious manner we exactly suit each other. We have been man and wife for ten years, and our only regret is, that we have no children. I don't know what you may think; I call that – upon the whole – a happy marriage.

So much for ourselves. The next question is – what has brought us into the inn yard? and why am I obliged to turn groom, and hold the horses?

We live for the most part in France – at the country house in which my wife and I first met. Occasionally, by way of variety, we pay visits to my friends in England. We are paying one of those visits now. Our host is an old college friend of mine, possessed of a fine estate in Somersetshire; and we have arrived at his house – called Farleigh Hall – toward the close of the hunting season.

On the day of which I am now writing – destined to be a memorable day in our calendar – the hounds meet at Farleigh Hall. Mrs. Fairbank and I are mounted on two of the best horses in my friend's stables.

We are quite unworthy of that distinction; for we know nothing and care nothing about hunting. On the other hand, we delight in riding, and we enjoy the breezy Spring morning and the fair and fertile English landscape surrounding us on every side. While the hunt prospers, we follow the hunt. But when a check occurs – when time passes and patience is sorely tried; when the bewildered dogs run hither and thither, and strong language falls from the lips of exasperated sportsmen – we fail to take any further interest in the proceedings. We turn our horses' heads in the direction of a grassy lane, delightfully shaded by trees. We trot merrily along the lane, and find ourselves on an open common. We gallop across the common, and follow the windings of a second lane. We cross a brook, we pass through a village, we emerge into pastoral solitude among the hills. The horses toss their heads, and neigh to each other, and enjoy it as much as we do. The hunt is forgotten. We are as happy as a couple of children; we are actually singing a French song – when in one moment our merriment comes to an end. My wife's horse sets one of his forefeet on a loose stone, and stumbles. His rider's ready hand saves him from falling. But, at the first attempt he makes to go on, the sad truth shows itself – a tendon is strained; the horse is lame.

What is to be done? We are strangers in a lonely part of the country. Look where we may, we see no signs of a human habitation. There is nothing for it but to take the bridle road up the hill, and try what we can discover on the other side. I transfer the saddles, and mount my wife on my own horse. He is not used to carry a lady; he misses the familiar pressure of a man's legs on either side of him; he fidgets, and starts, and kicks up the dust. I follow on foot, at a respectful distance from his heels, leading the lame horse. Is there a more miserable object on the face of creation than a lame horse? I have seen lame men and lame dogs who were cheerful creatures; but I never yet saw a lame horse who didn't look heartbroken over his own misfortune.

For half an hour my wife capers and curvets sideways along the bridle road. I trudge on behind her; and the heartbroken horse halts behind *me*. Hard by the top of the hill, our melancholy procession passes a Somersetshire peasant at work in a field. I summon the man to approach us; and the man looks at me stolidly, from the middle of the field, without stirring a step. I ask at the top of my voice how far it is to Farleigh Hall. The Somersetshire peasant answers at the top of *his* voice:

"Vourteen mile. Gi' oi a drap o' zyder."

I translate (for my wife's benefit) from the Somersetshire language into the English language. We are fourteen miles from Farleigh Hall; and our friend in the field desires to be rewarded, for giving us that information, with a drop of cider. There is the peasant, painted by himself! Quite a bit of character, my dear! Quite a bit of character!

Mrs. Fairbank doesn't view the study of agricultural human nature with my relish. Her fidgety horse will not allow her a moment's repose; she is beginning to lose her temper.

"We can't go fourteen miles in this way," she says. "Where is the nearest inn? Ask that brute in the field!"

I take a shilling from my pocket and hold it up in the sun. The shilling exercises magnetic virtues. The shilling draws the peasant slowly toward me from the middle of the field. I inform him that we want to put up the horses and to hire a carriage to take us back to Farleigh Hall. Where can we do that? The peasant answers (with his eye on the shilling):

"At Oonderbridge, to be zure." (At Underbridge, to be sure.)

"Is it far to Underbridge?"

The peasant repeats, "Var to Oonderbridge?" – and laughs at the question. "Hoo-hoo-hoo!" (Underbridge is evidently close by – if we could only find it.) "Will you show us the way, my man?" "Will you gi' oi a drap of zyder?" I courteously bend my head, and point to the shilling. The agricultural intelligence exerts itself. The peasant joins our melancholy procession. My wife is a fine woman, but he never once looks at my wife – and, more extraordinary still, he never even looks at the horses. His eyes are with his mind – and his mind is on the shilling.

We reach the top of the hill – and, behold on the other side, nestling in a valley, the shrine of our pilgrimage, the town of Underbridge! Here our guide claims his shilling, and leaves us to find out the inn for ourselves. I am constitutionally a polite man. I say "Good morning" at parting. The guide looks at me with the shilling between his teeth to make sure that it is a good one. "Marnin!" he says savagely – and turns his back on us, as if we had offended him. A curious product, this, of the growth of civilization. If I didn't see a church spire at Underbridge, I might suppose that we had lost ourselves on a savage island.

Chapter II

ARRIVING AT THE TOWN, we had no difficulty in finding the inn. The town is composed of one desolate street; and midway in that street stands the inn – an ancient stone building sadly out of repair. The painting on the sign-board is obliterated. The shutters over the long range of front windows are all closed. A cock and his hens are the only living creatures at the door. Plainly, this is one of the old inns of the stage-coach period, ruined by the railway. We pass through the open arched doorway, and find no one to welcome us. We advance into the stable yard behind; I assist my wife to dismount – and there we are in the position already disclosed to view at the opening of this narrative. No bell to ring. No human creature to answer when I call. I stand helpless, with the bridles of the horses in my hand. Mrs. Fairbank saunters gracefully down the length of the yard and does – what all women do, when they find themselves in a strange place. She opens every door as she passes it, and peeps in. On my side, I have just recovered my breath, I am on the point of shouting for the hostler for the third and last time, when I hear Mrs. Fairbank suddenly call to me:

"Percy! come here!"

Her voice is eager and agitated. She has opened a last door at the end of the yard, and has started back from some sight which has suddenly met her view. I hitch the horses' bridles on a rusty nail in the wall near me, and join my wife. She has turned pale, and catches me nervously by the arm.

"Good heavens!" she cries; "look at that!"

I look – and what do I see? I see a dingy little stable, containing two stalls. In one stall a horse is munching his corn. In the other a man is lying asleep on the litter.

A worn, withered, woebegone man in a hostler's dress. His hollow wrinkled cheeks, his scanty grizzled hair, his dry yellow skin, tell their own tale of past sorrow or suffering. There is an ominous frown on his eyebrows – there is a painful nervous contraction on the side of his mouth. I hear him breathing convulsively when I first look in; he shudders and sighs in his sleep. It is not a pleasant sight to see, and I turn round instinctively to the bright sunlight in the yard. My wife turns me back again in the direction of the stable door.

"Wait!" she says. "Wait! he may do it again."

"Do what again?"

"He was talking in his sleep, Percy, when I first looked in. He was dreaming some dreadful dream. Hush! he's beginning again."

I look and listen. The man stirs on his miserable bed. The man speaks in a quick, fierce whisper through his clinched teeth. "Wake up! Wake up, there! Murder!"

There is an interval of silence. He moves one lean arm slowly until it rests over his throat; he shudders, and turns on his straw; he raises his arm from his throat, and feebly stretches it out; his hand clutches at the straw on the side toward which he has turned; he seems to fancy that he is grasping at the edge of something. I see his lips begin to move again; I step softly into the stable; my wife follows me, with her hand fast clasped in mine. We both bend over him. He is talking once more in his sleep – strange talk, mad talk, this time.

"Light gray eyes" (we hear him say), "and a droop in the left eyelid – flaxen hair, with a gold-yellow streak in it – all right, mother! afair, white arms with a down on them – little, lady's hand, with a reddish look round the fingernails – the knife – the cursed knife – first on one side, then on the other – aha, you she-devil! where is the knife?"

He stops and grows restless on a sudden. We see him writhing on the straw. He throws up both his hands and gasps hysterically for breath. His eyes open suddenly. For a moment they look at nothing, with a vacant glitter in them – then they close again in deeper sleep. Is he dreaming still? Yes; but the dream seems to have taken a new course. When he speaks next, the tone is altered; the words are few – sadly and imploringly repeated over and over again. "Say you love me! I am so fond of *you*. Say you love me! say you love me!" He sinks into deeper and deeper sleep, faintly repeating those words. They die away on his lips. He speaks no more.

By this time Mrs. Fairbank has got over her terror; she is devoured by curiosity now. The miserable creature on the straw has appealed to the imaginative side of her character. Her illimitable appetite for romance hungers and thirsts for more. She shakes me impatiently by the arm.

"Do you hear? There is a woman at the bottom of it, Percy! There is love and murder in it, Percy! Where are the people of the inn? Go into the yard, and call to them again."

My wife belongs, on her mother's side, to the South of France. The South of France breeds fine women with hot tempers. I say no more. Married men will understand my position. Single men may need to be told that there are occasions when we must not only love and honor – we must also obey – our wives.

I turn to the door to obey *my* wife, and find myself confronted by a stranger who has stolen on us unawares. The stranger is a tiny, sleepy, rosy old man, with a vacant pudding-face, and a shining bald head. He wears drab breeches and gaiters, and a respectable square-tailed ancient black coat. I feel instinctively that here is the landlord of the inn.

"Good morning, sir," says the rosy old man. "I'm a little hard of hearing. Was it you that was a-calling just now in the yard?"

Before I can answer, my wife interposes. She insists (in a shrill voice, adapted to our host's hardness of hearing) on knowing who that unfortunate person is sleeping on the straw. "Where does he come from? Why does he say such dreadful things in his sleep? Is he married or single? Did he ever fall in love with a murderess? What sort of a looking woman was she? Did she really stab him or not? In short, dear Mr. Landlord, tell us the whole story!"

Dear Mr. Landlord waits drowsily until Mrs. Fairbank has quite done – then delivers himself of his reply as follows:

"His name's Francis Raven. He's an Independent Methodist. He was forty-five year old last birthday. And he's my hostler. That's his story."

My wife's hot southern temper finds its way to her foot, and expresses itself by a stamp on the stable yard.

The landlord turns himself sleepily round, and looks at the horses. "A fine pair of horses, them two in the yard. Do you want to put 'em in my stables?" I reply in the affirmative by a nod. The landlord, bent on making himself agreeable to my wife, addresses her once more. "I'm a-going to wake Francis Raven. He's an Independent Methodist. He was forty-five year old last birthday. And he's my hostler. That's his story."

Having issued this second edition of his interesting narrative, the landlord enters the stable. We follow him to see how he will wake Francis Raven, and what will happen upon that. The stable broom stands in a corner; the landlord takes it – advances toward the sleeping hostler – and coolly stirs the man up with a broom as if he was a wild beast in a cage. Francis Raven starts to his feet with a cry of terror – looks at us wildly, with a horrid glare of suspicion in his eyes – recovers himself the next moment – and suddenly changes into a decent, quiet, respectable serving-man.

"I beg your pardon, ma'am. I beg your pardon, sir."

The tone and manner in which he makes his apologies are both above his apparent station in life. I begin to catch the infection of Mrs. Fairbank's interest in this man. We both follow him out into the yard to see what he will do with the horses. The manner in which he lifts the injured leg of the lame horse tells me at once that he understands his business. Quickly and quietly, he leads the animal into an empty stable; quickly and quietly, he gets a bucket of hot water, and puts the lame horse's leg into it. "The warm water will reduce the swelling, sir. I will bandage the leg afterwards." All that he does is done intelligently; all that he says, he says to the purpose.

Nothing wild, nothing strange about him now. Is this the same man whom we heard talking in his sleep? – the same man who woke with that cry of terror and that horrid suspicion in his eyes? I determine to try him with one or two questions.

Chapter III

"NOT MUCH to do here," I say to the hostler.

"Very little to do, sir," the hostler replies.

"Anybody staying in the house?"

"The house is quite empty, sir."

"I thought you were all dead. I could make nobody hear me."

"The landlord is very deaf, sir, and the waiter is out on an errand."

"Yes; and *you* were fast asleep in the stable. Do you often take a nap in the daytime?"

The worn face of the hostler faintly flushes. His eyes look away from my eyes for the first time. Mrs. Fairbank furtively pinches my arm. Are we on the eve of a discovery at last? I repeat my question. The man has no civil alternative but to give me an answer. The answer is given in these words:

"I was tired out, sir. You wouldn't have found me asleep in the daytime but for that."

"Tired out, eh? You had been hard at work, I suppose?"

"No, sir."

"What was it, then?"

He hesitates again, and answers unwillingly, "I was up all night."

"Up all night? Anything going on in the town?"

"Nothing going on, sir."

"Anybody ill?"

"Nobody ill, sir."

That reply is the last. Try as I may, I can extract nothing more from him. He turns away and busies himself in attending to the horse's leg. I leave the stable to speak to the landlord about the carriage which is to take us back to Farleigh Hall. Mrs. Fairbank remains with the hostler, and favors me with a look at parting. The look says plainly, "*I* mean to find out why he was up all night. Leave him to Me."

The ordering of the carriage is easily accomplished. The inn possesses one horse and one chaise. The landlord has a story to tell of the horse, and a story to tell of the chaise. They resemble the story of Francis Raven – with this exception, that the horse and chaise belong to no religious persuasion. "The horse will be nine year old next birthday. I've had the shay for four-and-twenty year. Mr. Max, of Underbridge, he bred the horse; and Mr. Pooley, of Yeovil, he built the shay. It's my horse and my shay. And that's *their* story!" Having relieved his mind of these details, the landlord proceeds to put the harness on the horse. By way of assisting him, I drag the chaise into the yard. Just as our preparations are completed, Mrs. Fairbank appears. A moment or two later the hostler follows her out. He has bandaged the horse's leg, and is now ready to drive us to Farleigh Hall. I observe signs of agitation in his face and manner, which suggest that my wife has found her way into his confidence. I put the question to her privately in a corner of the yard. "Well? Have you found out why Francis Raven was up all night?"

Mrs. Fairbank has an eye to dramatic effect. Instead of answering plainly, Yes or No, she suspends the interest and excites the audience by putting a question on her side.

"What is the day of the month, dear?"

"The day of the month is the first of March."

"The first of March, Percy, is Francis Raven's birthday."

I try to look as if I was interested – and don't succeed.

"Francis was born," Mrs. Fairbank proceeds gravely, "at two o'clock in the morning."

I begin to wonder whether my wife's intellect is going the way of the landlord's intellect. "Is that all?" I ask.

"It is *not* all," Mrs. Fairbank answers. "Francis Raven sits up on the morning of his birthday because he is afraid to go to bed."

"And why is he afraid to go to bed?"

"Because he is in peril of his life."

"On his birthday?"

"On his birthday. At two o'clock in the morning. As regularly as the birthday comes round."

There she stops. Has she discovered no more than that? No more thus far. I begin to feel really interested by this time. I ask eagerly what it means? Mrs. Fairbank points mysteriously to the chaise – with Francis Raven (hitherto our hostler, now our coachman) waiting for us to get in. The chaise has a seat for two in front, and a seat for one behind. My wife casts a warning look at me, and places herself on the seat in front.

The necessary consequence of this arrangement is that Mrs. Fairbank sits by the side of the driver during a journey of two hours and more. Need I state the result? It would be an insult to your intelligence to state the result. Let me offer you my place in the chaise. And let Francis Raven tell his terrible story in his own words.

The Second Narrative
The Hostler's Story – Told by Himself

Chapter IV

IT IS NOW ten years ago since I got my first warning of the great trouble of my life in the Vision of a Dream.

I shall be better able to tell you about it if you will please suppose yourselves to be drinking tea along with us in our little cottage in Cambridgeshire, ten years since.

The time was the close of day, and there were three of us at the table, namely, my mother, myself, and my mother's sister, Mrs. Chance. These two were Scotchwomen by birth, and both were widows. There was no other resemblance between them that I can call to mind. My mother had lived all her life in England, and had no more of the Scotch brogue on her tongue than I have. My aunt Chance had never been out of Scotland until she came to keep house with my mother after her husband's death. And when *she* opened her lips you heard broad Scotch, I can tell you, if you ever heard it yet!

As it fell out, there was a matter of some consequence in debate among us that evening. It was this: whether I should do well or not to take a long journey on foot the next morning.

Now the next morning happened to be the day before my birthday; and the purpose of the journey was to offer myself for a situation as groom at a great house in the neighboring county to ours. The place was reported as likely to fall vacant in about three weeks' time. I was as well fitted to fill it as any other man. In the prosperous days of our family, my father had been manager of a training stable, and he had kept me employed among the horses from my boyhood upward. Please to excuse my troubling you with these small matters. They all fit into my story farther on, as you will soon find out. My poor mother was dead against my leaving home on the morrow.

"You can never walk all the way there and all the way back again by tomorrow night," she says. "The end of it will be that you will sleep away from home on your birthday. You have never done that yet, Francis, since your father's death, I don't like your doing it now. Wait a day longer, my son – only one day."

For my own part, I was weary of being idle, and I couldn't abide the notion of delay. Even one day might make all the difference. Some other man might take time by the forelock, and get the place.

"Consider how long I have been out of work," I says, "and don't ask me to put off the journey. I won't fail you, mother. I'll get back by tomorrow night, if I have to pay my last sixpence for a lift in a cart."

My mother shook her head. "I don't like it, Francis – I don't like it!" There was no moving her from that view. We argued and argued, until we were both at a deadlock. It ended in our agreeing to refer the difference between us to my mother's sister, Mrs. Chance.

While we were trying hard to convince each other, my aunt Chance sat as dumb as a fish, stirring her tea and thinking her own thoughts. When we made our appeal to her, she seemed as it were to wake up. "Ye baith refer it to my puir judgment?" she says, in her broad Scotch. We both answered Yes. Upon that my aunt Chance first cleared the tea-table, and then pulled out from the pocket of her gown a pack of cards.

Don't run away, if you please, with the notion that this was done lightly, with a view to amuse my mother and me. My aunt Chance seriously believed that she could look into the future by telling fortunes on the cards. She did nothing herself without first consulting the cards. She could give no more serious proof of her interest in my welfare than the proof which she was offering now. I don't say it profanely; I only mention the fact – the cards had, in some incomprehensible way, got themselves jumbled up together with her religious convictions. You meet with people nowadays who believe in spirits working by way of tables and chairs. On the same principle (if there *is* any principle in it) my aunt Chance believed in Providence working by way of the cards.

"Whether *you* are right, Francie, or your mither – whether ye will do weel or ill, the morrow, to go or stay – the cairds will tell it. We are a' in the hands of Proavidence. The cairds will tell it."

Hearing this, my mother turned her head aside, with something of a sour look in her face. Her sister's notions about the cards were little better than flat blasphemy to her mind. But she kept her opinion to herself. My aunt Chance, to own the truth, had inherited, through her late husband, a pension of thirty pounds a year. This was an important contribution to our housekeeping, and we poor relations were bound to treat her with a certain respect. As for myself, if my poor father never did anything else for me before he fell into difficulties, he gave me a good education, and raised me (thank God) above superstitions of all sorts. However, a very little amused me in those days; and I waited to have my fortune told, as patiently as if I believed in it too!

My aunt began her hocus pocus by throwing out all the cards in the pack under seven. She shuffled the rest with her left hand for luck; and then she gave them to me to cut. "Wi' yer left hand, Francie. Mind that! Pet your trust in Proavidence – but dinna forget that your luck's in yer left hand!" A long and roundabout shifting of the cards followed, reducing them in number until there were just fifteen of them left, laid out neatly before my aunt in a half circle. The card which happened to lie outermost, at the right-hand end of the circle, was, according to rule in such cases, the card chosen to represent Me. By way of being appropriate to my situation as a poor groom out of employment, the card was – the King of Diamonds.

"I tak' up the King o' Diamants," says my aunt. "I count seven cairds fra' richt to left; and I humbly ask a blessing on what follows." My aunt shut her eyes as if she was saying grace before meat, and held up to me the seventh card. I called the seventh card – the Queen of Spades. My aunt opened her eyes again in a hurry, and cast a sly look my way. "The Queen o' Spades means a dairk woman. Ye'll be thinking in secret, Francie, of a dairk woman?"

When a man has been out of work for more than three months, his mind isn't troubled much with thinking of women – light or dark. I was thinking of the groom's place at the great house, and I tried to say so. My aunt Chance wouldn't listen. She treated my interpretation with contempt. "Hoot-toot! there's the caird in your hand! If ye're no thinking of her the day, ye'll be thinking of her the morrow. Where's the harm of thinking of a dairk woman! I was ance a dairk woman myself, before my hair was gray. Haud yer peace, Francie, and watch the cairds."

I watched the cards as I was told. There were seven left on the table. My aunt removed two from one end of the row and two from the other, and desired me to call the two outermost of the three cards now left on the table. I called the Ace of Clubs and the Ten of Diamonds. My aunt Chance lifted her eyes to the ceiling with a look of devout gratitude which sorely tried my mother's patience. The Ace of Clubs and the Ten of Diamonds, taken together, signified – first, good news (evidently the news of the groom's place); secondly, a journey that lay before me (pointing plainly to my journey tomorrow!); thirdly and lastly, a sum of money (probably the groom's wages!) waiting to find its way into my pockets. Having told my fortune in these encouraging terms, my aunt declined to carry the experiment any further. "Eh, lad! it's a clean tempting o' Proavidence to ask mair o' the cairds than the cairds have tauld us noo. Gae yer ways tomorrow to the great hoose. A dairk woman will meet ye at the gate; and she'll have a hand in getting ye the groom's place, wi' a' the gratifications and pairquisites appertaining to the same. And, mebbe, when yer poaket's full o' money, ye'll no' be forgetting yer aunt Chance, maintaining her ain unblemished widowhood – wi' Proavidence assisting – on thratty punds a year!"

I promised to remember my aunt Chance (who had the defect, by the way, of being a terribly greedy person after money) on the next happy occasion when my poor empty pockets were to be filled at last. This done, I looked at my mother. She had agreed to take her sister for umpire between us, and her sister had given it in my favor. She raised no more objections. Silently, she got on her feet, and kissed me, and sighed bitterly – and so left the room. My aunt Chance shook her head. "I doubt, Francie, yer puir mither has but a heathen notion of the vairtue of the cairds!"

By daylight the next morning I set forth on my journey. I looked back at the cottage as I opened the garden gate. At one window was my mother, with her handkerchief to her eyes. At the other stood my aunt Chance, holding up the Queen of Spades by way of encouraging me at starting. I waved my hands to both of them in token of farewell, and stepped out briskly into the road. It was then the last day of February. Be pleased to remember, in connection with this, that the first of March was the day, and two o'clock in the morning the hour of my birth.

Chapter V

NOW YOU KNOW how I came to leave home. The next thing to tell is, what happened on the journey.

I reached the great house in reasonably good time considering the distance. At the very first trial of it, the prophecy of the cards turned out to be wrong. The person who met me at the lodge gate was not a dark woman – in fact, not a woman at all – but a boy. He directed me on the way to the servants' offices; and there again the cards were all wrong. I encountered, not one woman, but three – and not one of the three was dark. I have stated that I am not superstitious, and I have told the truth. But I must own that I did feel a certain fluttering at the heart when I made my bow to the steward, and told him what business had brought me to the house. His answer completed the discomfiture of aunt Chance's fortune-telling. My ill-luck still pursued me. That very morning another man had applied for the groom's place, and had got it.

I swallowed my disappointment as well as I could, and thanked the steward, and went to the inn in the village to get the rest and food which I sorely needed by this time.

Before starting on my homeward walk I made some inquiries at the inn, and ascertained that I might save a few miles, on my return, by following a new road. Furnished with full instructions, several times repeated, as to the various turnings I was to take, I set forth, and walked on till the evening with only one stoppage for bread and cheese. Just as it was getting toward dark, the rain came on and the wind began to rise; and I found myself, to make matters worse, in a part of the country with which I was entirely unacquainted, though I guessed myself to be some fifteen miles from home. The first house I found to inquire at, was a lonely roadside inn, standing on the outskirts of a thick wood. Solitary as the place looked, it was welcome to a lost man who was also hungry, thirsty, footsore, and wet. The landlord was civil and respectable-looking; and the price he asked for a bed was reasonable enough. I was grieved to disappoint my mother. But there was no conveyance to be had, and I could go no farther afoot that night. My weariness fairly forced me to stop at the inn.

I may say for myself that I am a temperate man. My supper simply consisted of some rashers of bacon, a slice of home-made bread, and a pint of ale. I did not go to bed immediately after this moderate meal, but sat up with the landlord, talking about my bad prospects and my long run of ill-luck, and diverging from these topics to the subjects of horse-flesh and racing. Nothing was said, either by myself, my host, or the few laborers who strayed into the tap-room, which could, in the slightest degree, excite my mind, or set my fancy – which is only a small fancy at the best of times – playing tricks with my common sense.

At a little after eleven the house was closed. I went round with the landlord, and held the candle while the doors and lower windows were being secured. I noticed with surprise the strength of the bolts, bars, and iron-sheathed shutters.

"You see, we are rather lonely here," said the landlord. "We never have had any attempts to break in yet, but it's always as well to be on the safe side. When nobody is sleeping here, I am the only man in the house. My wife and daughter are timid, and the servant girl takes after her missuses. Another glass of ale, before you turn in? – No! – Well, how such a sober man as you comes to be out of a place is more than I can understand for one. – Here's where you're to sleep. You're the only lodger to-night, and I think you'll say my missus has done her best to make you comfortable. You're quite sure you won't have another glass of ale? – Very well. Good night."

It was half-past eleven by the clock in the passage as we went upstairs to the bedroom. The window looked out on the wood at the back of the house.

I locked my door, set my candle on the chest of drawers, and wearily got me ready for bed. The bleak wind was still blowing, and the solemn, surging moan of it in the wood was very dreary to hear through the night silence. Feeling strangely wakeful, I resolved to keep the candle alight until I began to grow sleepy. The truth is, I was not quite myself. I was depressed in mind by my disappointment of the morning; and I was worn out in body by my long walk. Between the two, I own I couldn't face the prospect of lying awake in the darkness, listening to the dismal moan of the wind in the wood.

Sleep stole on me before I was aware of it; my eyes closed, and I fell off to rest, without having so much as thought of extinguishing the candle.

The next thing that I remember was a faint shivering that ran through me from head to foot, and a dreadful sinking pain at my heart, such as I had never felt before. The shivering only disturbed my slumbers – the pain woke me instantly. In one moment I passed from a state of sleep to a state of wakefulness – my eyes wide open – my mind clear on a sudden as if by a miracle. The candle had burned down nearly to the last morsel of tallow, but the unsnuffed wick had just fallen off, and the light was, for the moment, fair and full.

Between the foot of the bed and the closet door, I saw a person in my room. The person was a woman, standing looking at me, with a knife in her hand. It does no credit to my courage to confess it

– but the truth *is* the truth. I was struck speechless with terror. There I lay with my eyes on the woman; there the woman stood (with the knife in her hand) with *her* eyes on *me*.

She said not a word as we stared each other in the face; but she moved after a little – moved slowly toward the left-hand side of the bed.

The light fell full on her face. A fair, fine woman, with yellowish flaxen hair, and light gray eyes, with a droop in the left eyelid. I noticed these things and fixed them in my mind, before she was quite round at the side of the bed. Without saying a word; without any change in the stony stillness of her face; without any noise following her footfall, she came closer and closer; stopped at the bed-head; and lifted the knife to stab me. I laid my arm over my throat to save it; but, as I saw the blow coming, I threw my hand across the bed to the right side, and jerked my body over that way, just as the knife came down, like lightning, within a hair's breadth of my shoulder.

My eyes fixed on her arm and her hand – she gave me time to look at them as she slowly drew the knife out of the bed. A white, well-shaped arm, with a pretty down lying lightly over the fair skin. A delicate lady's hand, with a pink flush round the finger nails.

She drew the knife out, and passed back again slowly to the foot of the bed; she stopped there for a moment looking at me; then she came on without saying a word; without any change in the stony stillness of her face; without any noise following her footfall – came on to the side of the bed where I now lay.

Getting near me, she lifted the knife again, and I drew myself away to the left side. She struck, as before right into the mattress, with a swift downward action of her arm; and she missed me, as before; by a hair's breadth. This time my eyes wandered from *her* to the knife. It was like the large clasp knives which laboring men use to cut their bread and bacon with. Her delicate little fingers did not hide more than two thirds of the handle; I noticed that it was made of buckhorn, clean and shining as the blade was, and looking like new.

For the second time she drew the knife out of the bed, and suddenly hid it away in the wide sleeve of her gown. That done, she stopped by the bedside watching me. For an instant I saw her standing in that position – then the wick of the spent candle fell over into the socket. The flame dwindled to a little blue point, and the room grew dark.

A moment, or less, if possible, passed so – and then the wick flared up, smokily, for the last time. My eyes were still looking for her over the right-hand side of the bed when the last flash of light came. Look as I might, I could see nothing. The woman with the knife was gone.

I began to get back to myself again. I could feel my heart beating; I could hear the woeful moaning of the wind in the wood; I could leap up in bed, and give the alarm before she escaped from the house. "Murder! Wake up there! Murder!"

Nobody answered to the alarm. I rose and groped my way through the darkness to the door of the room. By that way she must have got in. By that way she must have gone out.

The door of the room was fast locked, exactly as I had left it on going to bed! I looked at the window. Fast locked too!

Hearing a voice outside, I opened the door. There was the landlord, coming toward me along the passage, with his burning candle in one hand, and his gun in the other.

"What is it?" he says, looking at me in no very friendly way.

I could only answer in a whisper, "A woman, with a knife in her hand. In my room. A fair, yellow-haired woman. She jabbed at me with the knife, twice over."

He lifted his candle, and looked at me steadily from head to foot. "She seems to have missed you – twice over."

"I dodged the knife as it came down. It struck the bed each time. Go in, and see."

The landlord took his candle into the bedroom immediately. In less than a minute he came out again into the passage in a violent passion.

"The devil fly away with you and your woman with the knife! There isn't a mark in the bedclothes anywhere. What do you mean by coming into a man's place and frightening his family out of their wits by a dream?"

A dream? The woman who had tried to stab me, not a living human being like myself? I began to shake and shiver. The horrors got hold of me at the bare thought of it.

"I'll leave the house," I said. "Better be out on the road in the rain and dark, than back in that room, after what I've seen in it. Lend me the light to get my clothes by, and tell me what I'm to pay."

The landlord led the way back with his light into the bedroom. "Pay?" says he. "You'll find your score on the slate when you go downstairs. I wouldn't have taken you in for all the money you've got about you, if I had known your dreaming, screeching ways beforehand. Look at the bed – where's the cut of a knife in it? Look at the window – is the lock bursted? Look at the door (which I heard you fasten yourself) – is it broke in? A murdering woman with a knife in my house! You ought to be ashamed of yourself!"

My eyes followed his hand as it pointed first to the bed – then to the window – then to the door. There was no gainsaying it. The bed sheet was as sound as on the day it was made. The window was fast. The door hung on its hinges as steady as ever. I huddled my clothes on without speaking. We went downstairs together. I looked at the clock in the bar-room. The time was twenty minutes past two in the morning. I paid my bill, and the landlord let me out. The rain had ceased; but the night was dark, and the wind was bleaker than ever. Little did the darkness, or the cold, or the doubt about the way home matter to *me*. My mind was away from all these things. My mind was fixed on the vision in the bedroom. What had I seen trying to murder me? The creature of a dream? Or that other creature from the world beyond the grave, whom men call ghost? I could make nothing of it as I walked along in the night; I had made nothing by it by midday – when I stood at last, after many times missing my road, on the doorstep of home.

Chapter VI

MY MOTHER CAME OUT alone to welcome me back. There were no secrets between us two. I told her all that had happened, just as I have told it to you. She kept silence till I had done. And then she put a question to me.

"What time was it, Francis, when you saw the Woman in your Dream?"

I had looked at the clock when I left the inn, and I had noticed that the hands pointed to twenty minutes past two. Allowing for the time consumed in speaking to the landlord, and in getting on my clothes, I answered that I must have first seen the Woman at two o'clock in the morning. In other words, I had not only seen her on my birthday, but at the hour of my birth.

My mother still kept silence. Lost in her own thoughts, she took me by the hand, and led me into the parlor. Her writing-desk was on the table by the fireplace. She opened it, and signed to me to take a chair by her side.

"My son! your memory is a bad one, and mine is fast failing me. Tell me again what the Woman looked like. I want her to be as well known to both of us, years hence, as she is now."

I obeyed; wondering what strange fancy might be working in her mind. I spoke; and she wrote the words as they fell from my lips:

"Light gray eyes, with a droop in the left eyelid. Flaxen hair, with a golden-yellow streak in it. White arms, with a down upon them. Little, lady's hands, with a rosy-red look about the finger nails."

"Did you notice how she was dressed, Francis?"

"No, mother."

"Did you notice the knife?"

"Yes. A large clasp knife, with a buckhorn handle, as good as new."

My mother added the description of the knife. Also the year, month, day of the week, and hour of the day when the Dream-Woman appeared to me at the inn. That done, she locked up the paper in her desk.

"Not a word, Francis, to your aunt. Not a word to any living soul. Keep your Dream a secret between you and me."

The weeks passed, and the months passed. My mother never returned to the subject again. As for me, time, which wears out all things, wore out my remembrance of the Dream. Little by little, the image of the Woman grew dimmer and dimmer. Little by little, she faded out of my mind.

Chapter VII

THE STORY of the warning is now told. Judge for yourself if it was a true warning or a false, when you hear what happened to me on my next birthday.

In the Summer time of the year, the Wheel of Fortune turned the right way for me at last. I was smoking my pipe one day, near an old stone quarry at the entrance to our village, when a carriage accident happened, which gave a new turn, as it were, to my lot in life. It was an accident of the commonest kind – not worth mentioning at any length. A lady driving herself; a runaway horse; a cowardly man-servant in attendance, frightened out of his wits; and the stone quarry too near to be agreeable – that is what I saw, all in a few moments, between two whiffs of my pipe. I stopped the horse at the edge of the quarry, and got myself a little hurt by the shaft of the chaise. But that didn't matter. The lady declared I had saved her life; and her husband, coming with her to our cottage the next day, took me into his service then and there. The lady happened to be of a dark complexion; and it may amuse you to hear that my aunt Chance instantly pitched on that circumstance as a means of saving the credit of the cards. Here was the promise of the Queen of Spades performed to the very letter, by means of "a dark woman," just as my aunt had told me. "In the time to come, Francis, beware o' pettin' yer ain blinded intairpretation on the cairds. Ye're ower ready, I trow, to murmur under dispensation of Proavidence that ye canna fathom – like the Eesraelites of auld. I'll say nae mair to ye. Mebbe when the mony's powering into yer poakets, ye'll no forget yer aunt Chance, left like a sparrow on the housetop, wi' a sma' annuitee o' thratty punds a year."

I remained in my situation (at the West-end of London) until the Spring of the New Year. About that time, my master's health failed. The doctors ordered him away to foreign parts, and the establishment was broken up. But the turn in my luck still held good. When I left my place, I left it – thanks to the generosity of my kind master – with a yearly allowance granted to me, in remembrance of the day when I had saved my mistress's life. For the future, I could go back to service or not, as I pleased; my little income was enough to support my mother and myself.

My master and mistress left England toward the end of February. Certain matters of business to do for them detained me in London until the last day of the month. I was only able to leave for our village by the evening train, to keep my birthday with my mother as usual. It was bedtime when I got to the cottage; and I was sorry to find that she was far from well. To make matters worse, she had finished her bottle of medicine on the previous day, and had omitted to get it replenished, as the doctor had strictly directed. He dispensed his own medicines, and I offered to go and knock him up. She refused to let me do this; and, after giving me my supper, sent me away to my bed.

I fell asleep for a little, and woke again. My mother's bed-chamber was next to mine. I heard my aunt Chance's heavy footsteps going to and fro in the room, and, suspecting something wrong, knocked at the door. My mother's pains had returned upon her; there was a serious necessity for relieving her sufferings as speedily as possible, I put on my clothes, and ran off, with the medicine bottle in my hand, to the other end of the village, where the doctor lived. The church clock chimed the quarter to two on my birthday just as I reached his house. One ring of the night bell brought him to his bedroom window to speak to me. He told me to wait, and he would let me in at the surgery door. I noticed, while I was waiting, that the night was wonderfully fair and warm for the time of year. The old stone quarry where the carriage accident had happened was within view. The moon in the clear heavens lit it up almost as bright as day.

In a minute or two the doctor let me into the surgery. I closed the door, noticing that he had left his room very lightly clad. He kindly pardoned my mother's neglect of his directions, and set to work at once at compounding the medicine. We were both intent on the bottle; he filling it, and I holding the light – when we heard the surgery door suddenly opened from the street.

Chapter VIII

WHO COULD possibly be up and about in our quiet village at the second hour of the morning?

The person who opened the door appeared within range of the light of the candle. To complete our amazement, the person proved to be a woman! She walked up to the counter, and standing side by side with me, lifted her veil. At the moment when she showed her face, I heard the church clock strike two. She was a stranger to me, and a stranger to the doctor. She was also, beyond all comparison, the most beautiful woman I have ever seen in my life.

"I saw the light under the door," she said. "I want some medicine."

She spoke quite composedly, as if there was nothing at all extraordinary in her being out in the village at two in the morning, and following me into the surgery to ask for medicine! The doctor stared at her as if he suspected his own eyes of deceiving him. "Who are you?" he asked. "How do you come to be wandering about at this time in the morning?"

She paid no heed to his questions. She only told him coolly what she wanted. "I have got a bad toothache. I want a bottle of laudanum."

The doctor recovered himself when she asked for the laudanum. He was on his own ground, you know, when it came to a matter of laudanum; and he spoke to her smartly enough this time.

"Oh, you have got the toothache, have you? Let me look at the tooth."

She shook her head, and laid a two-shilling piece on the counter. "I won't trouble you to look at the tooth," she said. "There is the money. Let me have the laudanum, if you please."

The doctor put the two-shilling piece back again in her hand. "I don't sell laudanum to strangers," he answered. "If you are in any distress of body or mind, that is another matter. I shall be glad to help you."

She put the money back in her pocket. "*You* can't help me," she said, as quietly as ever. "Good morning."

With that, she opened the surgery door to go out again into the street. So far, I had not spoken a word on my side. I had stood with the candle in my hand (not knowing I was holding it) – with my eyes fixed on her, with my mind fixed on her like a man bewitched. Her looks betrayed, even more plainly than her words, her resolution, in one way or another, to destroy herself. When she opened the door, in my alarm at what might happen I found the use of my tongue.

"Stop!" I cried out. "Wait for me. I want to speak to you before you go away." She lifted her eyes with a look of careless surprise and a mocking smile on her lips.

"What can *you* have to say to me?" She stopped, and laughed to herself. "Why not?" she said. "I have got nothing to do, and nowhere to go." She turned back a step, and nodded to me. "You're a strange man – I think I'll humor you – I'll wait outside." The door of the surgery closed on her. She was gone.

I am ashamed to own what happened next. The only excuse for me is that I was really and truly a man bewitched. I turned me round to follow her out, without once thinking of my mother. The doctor stopped me.

"Don't forget the medicine," he said. "And if you will take my advice, don't trouble yourself about that woman. Rouse up the constable. It's his business to look after her – not yours."

I held out my hand for the medicine in silence: I was afraid I should fail in respect if I trusted myself to answer him. He must have seen, as I saw, that she wanted the laudanum to poison herself. He had, to my mind, taken a very heartless view of the matter. I just thanked him when he gave me the medicine – and went out.

She was waiting for me as she had promised; walking slowly to and fro – a tall, graceful, solitary figure in the bright moonbeams. They shed over her fair complexion, her bright golden hair, her large gray eyes, just the light that suited them best. She looked hardly mortal when she first turned to speak to me.

"Well?" she said. "And what do you want?"

In spite of my pride, or my shyness, or my better sense – whichever it might me – all my heart went out to her in a moment. I caught hold of her by the hands, and owned what was in my thoughts, as freely as if I had known her for half a lifetime.

"You mean to destroy yourself," I said. "And I mean to prevent you from doing it. If I follow you about all night, I'll prevent you from doing it."

She laughed. "You saw yourself that he wouldn't sell me the laudanum. Do you really care whether I live or die?" She squeezed my hands gently as she put the question: her eyes searched mine with a languid, lingering look in them that ran through me like fire. My voice died away on my lips; I couldn't answer her.

She understood, without my answering. "You have given me a fancy for living, by speaking kindly to me," she said. "Kindness has a wonderful effect on women, and dogs, and other domestic animals. It is only men who are superior to kindness. Make your mind easy – I promise to take as much care of myself as if I was the happiest woman living! Don't let me keep you here, out of your bed. Which way are you going?"

Miserable wretch that I was, I had forgotten my mother – with the medicine in my hand! "I am going home," I said. "Where are you staying? At the inn?"

She laughed her bitter laugh, and pointed to the stone quarry. "There is my inn for to-night," she said. "When I got tired of walking about, I rested there."

We walked on together, on my way home. I took the liberty of asking her if she had any friends.

"I thought I had one friend left," she said, "or you would never have met me in this place. It turns out I was wrong. My friend's door was closed in my face some hours since; my friend's servants threatened me with the police. I had nowhere else to go, after trying my luck in your neighborhood; and nothing left but my two-shilling piece and these rags on my back. What respectable innkeeper would take *me* into his house? I walked about, wondering how I could find my way out of the world without disfiguring myself, and without suffering much pain. You have no river in these parts. I didn't see my way out of the world, till I heard you ringing at the doctor's house. I got a glimpse at the bottles in the surgery, when he let you in, and I thought of the laudanum directly. What were you doing there? Who is that medicine for? Your wife?"

"I am not married!"

She laughed again. "Not married! If I was a little better dressed there might be a chance for ME. Where do you live? Here?"

We had arrived, by this time, at my mother's door. She held out her hand to say good-by. Houseless and homeless as she was, she never asked me to give her a shelter for the night. It was my proposal that she should rest, under my roof, unknown to my mother and my aunt. Our kitchen was built out at the back of the cottage: she might remain there unseen and unheard until the household was astir in the morning. I led her into the kitchen, and set a chair for her by the dying embers of the fire. I dare say I was to blame – shamefully to blame, if you like. I only wonder what *you* would have done in my place.

On your word of honor as a man, would *you* have let that beautiful creature wander back to the shelter of the stone quarry like a stray dog? God help the woman who is foolish enough to trust and love you, if you would have done that!

I left her by the fire, and went to my mother's room.

Chapter IX

IF YOU HAVE EVER felt the heartache, you will know what I suffered in secret when my mother took my hand, and said, "I am sorry, Francis, that your night's rest has been disturbed through *me*." I gave her the medicine; and I waited by her till the pains abated. My aunt Chance went back to her bed; and my mother and I were left alone. I noticed that her writing-desk, moved from its customary place, was on the bed by her side. She saw me looking at it. "This is your birthday, Francis," she said. "Have you anything to tell me?" I had so completely forgotten my Dream, that I had no notion of what was passing in her mind when she said those words. For a moment there was a guilty fear in me that she suspected something. I turned away my face, and said, "No, mother; I have nothing to tell." She signed to me to stoop down over the pillow and kiss her. "God bless you, my love!" she said; "and many happy returns of the day." She patted my hand, and closed her weary eyes, and, little by little, fell off peaceably into sleep.

I stole downstairs again. I think the good influence of my mother must have followed me down. At any rate, this is true: I stopped with my hand on the closed kitchen door, and said to myself: "Suppose I leave the house, and leave the village, without seeing her or speaking to her more?"

Should I really have fled from temptation in this way, if I had been left to myself to decide? Who can tell? As things were, I was not left to decide. While my doubt was in my mind, she heard me, and opened the kitchen door. My eyes and her eyes met. That ended it.

We were together, unsuspected and undisturbed, for the next two hours. Time enough for her to reveal the secret of her wasted life. Time enough for her to take possession of me as her own, to do with me as she liked. It is needless to dwell here on the misfortunes which had brought her low; they are misfortunes too common to interest anybody.

Her name was Alicia Warlock. She had been born and bred a lady. She had lost her station, her character, and her friends. Virtue shuddered at the sight of her; and Vice had got her for the rest of her days. Shocking and common, as I told you. It made no difference to *me*. I have said it already – I say it again – I was a man bewitched. Is there anything so very wonderful in that? Just remember who I was. Among the honest women in my own station in life, where could I have found the like of *her*? Could *they* walk as she walked? and look as she looked? When *they* gave me a kiss, did their lips linger over it as hers did? Had *they* her skin, her laugh, her foot, her hand, her touch? *She* never had a speck of dirt on her: I tell you her flesh was a perfume. When she embraced me, her arms folded round me like the wings of angels; and her smile covered me softly with its light like the sun in heaven. I leave you to laugh at me, or to cry over me, just as your temper may incline. I am not trying to excuse myself – I am trying to explain. You are gentle-folks; what dazzled and maddened *me*, is everyday experience to *you*. Fallen or not, angel or devil, it came to this – she was a lady; and I was a groom.

Before the house was astir, I got her away (by the workmen's train) to a large manufacturing town in our parts.

Here – with my savings in money to help her – she could get her outfit of decent clothes and her lodging among strangers who asked no questions so long as they were paid. Here – now on one pretense and now on another – I could visit her, and we could both plan together what our future lives were to be. I need not tell you that I stood pledged to make her my wife. A man in my station always marries a woman of her sort.

Do you wonder if I was happy at this time? I should have been perfectly happy but for one little drawback. It was this: I was never quite at my ease in the presence of my promised wife.

I don't mean that I was shy with her, or suspicious of her, or ashamed of her. The uneasiness I am speaking of was caused by a faint doubt in my mind whether I had not seen her somewhere, before the morning when we met at the doctor's house. Over and over again, I found myself wondering whether her face did not remind me of some other face – *what* other I never could tell. This strange feeling, this one question that could never be answered, vexed me to a degree that you would hardly credit. It came between us at the strangest times – oftenest, however, at night, when the candles were lit. You have known what it is to try and remember a forgotten name – and to fail, search as you may, to find it in your mind. That was my case. I failed to find my lost face, just as you failed to find your lost name.

In three weeks we had talked matters over, and had arranged how I was to make a clean breast of it at home. By Alicia's advice, I was to describe her as having been one of my fellow servants during the time I was employed under my kind master and mistress in London. There was no fear now of my mother taking any harm from the shock of a great surprise. Her health had improved during the three weeks' interval. On the first evening when she was able to take her old place at tea time, I summoned my courage, and told her I was going to be married. The poor soul flung her arms round my neck, and burst out crying for joy. "Oh, Francis!" she says, "I am so glad you will have somebody to comfort you and care for you when I am gone!" As for my aunt Chance, you can anticipate what *she* did, without being told. Ah, me! If there had really been any prophetic virtue in the cards, what a terrible warning they might have given us that night! It was arranged that I was to bring my promised wife to dinner at the cottage on the next day.

Chapter X

I OWN I WAS proud of Alicia when I led her into our little parlor at the appointed time. She had never, to my mind, looked so beautiful as she looked that day. I never noticed any other woman's dress – I noticed hers as carefully as if I had been a woman myself! She wore a black silk gown, with plain collar and cuffs, and a modest lavender-colored bonnet, with one white rose in it placed at the side. My mother, dressed in her Sunday best, rose up, all in a flutter, to welcome her daughter-in-law that was to be. She walked forward a few steps, half smiling, half in tears – she looked Alicia full in the face – and suddenly stood still. Her cheeks turned white in an instant; her eyes stared in horror; her hands dropped helplessly at her sides. She staggered back, and fell into the arms of my aunt, standing behind her. It was no swoon – she kept her senses. Her eyes turned slowly from Alicia to me. "Francis," she said, "does that woman's face remind you of nothing?"

Before I could answer, she pointed to her writing-desk on the table at the fireside. "Bring it!" she cried, "bring it!".

At the same moment I felt Alicia's hand on my shoulder, and saw Alicia's face red with anger – and no wonder!

"What does this mean?" she asked. "Does your mother want to insult me?".

I said a few words to quiet her; what they were I don't remember – I was so confused and astonished at the time. Before I had done, I heard my mother behind me.

My aunt had fetched her desk. She had opened it; she had taken a paper from it. Step by step, helping herself along by the wall, she came nearer and nearer, with the paper in her hand. She looked at the paper – she looked in Alicia's face – she lifted the long, loose sleeve of her gown, and examined her hand and arm. I saw fear suddenly take the place of anger in Alicia's eyes. She shook herself free of my mother's grasp. "Mad!" she said to herself, "and Francis never told me!" With those words she ran out of the room.

I was hastening out after her, when my mother signed to me to stop. She read the words written on the paper. While they fell slowly, one by one, from her lips, she pointed toward the open door.

"Light gray eyes, with a droop in the left eyelid. Flaxen hair, with a gold-yellow streak in it. White arms, with a down upon them. Little, lady's hand, with a rosy-red look about the finger nails. The Dream Woman, Francis! The Dream Woman!"

Something darkened the parlor window as those words were spoken. I looked sidelong at the shadow. Alicia Warlock had come back! She was peering in at us over the low window blind. There was the fatal face which had first looked at me in the bedroom of the lonely inn. There, resting on the window blind, was the lovely little hand which had held the murderous knife. I *had* seen her before we met in the village. The Dream Woman! The Dream Woman!

Chapter XI

I EXPECT NOBODY to approve of what I have next to tell of myself. In three weeks from the day when my mother had identified her with the Woman of the Dream, I took Alicia Warlock to church, and made her my wife. I was a man bewitched. Again and again I say it – I was a man bewitched!

During the interval before my marriage, our little household at the cottage was broken up. My mother and my aunt quarreled. My mother, believing in the Dream, entreated me to break off my engagement. My aunt, believing in the cards, urged me to marry.

This difference of opinion produced a dispute between them, in the course of which my aunt Chance – quite unconscious of having any superstitious feelings of her own – actually set out the cards which prophesied happiness to me in my married life, and asked my mother how anybody but "a blinded heathen could be fule enough, after seeing those cairds, to believe in a dream!" This was, naturally, too much for my mother's patience; hard words followed on either side; Mrs. Chance returned in dudgeon to her friends in Scotland. She left me a written statement of my future prospects, as revealed by the cards, and with it an address at which a post-office order would reach her. "The day was not that far off," she remarked, "when Francie might remember what he owed to his aunt Chance, maintaining her ain unbleemished widowhood on thratty punds a year."

Having refused to give her sanction to my marriage, my mother also refused to be present at the wedding, or to visit Alicia afterwards. There was no anger at the bottom of this conduct on her part. Believing as she did in this Dream, she was simply in mortal fear of my wife. I understood this, and I made allowances for her. Not a cross word passed between us. My one happy remembrance now – though I did disobey her in the matter of my marriage – is this: I loved and respected my good mother to the last.

As for my wife, she expressed no regret at the estrangement between her mother-in-law and herself. By common consent, we never spoke on that subject. We settled in the manufacturing town which I have already mentioned, and we kept a lodging-house. My kind master, at my request, granted me a lump sum in place of my annuity. This put us into a good house, decently furnished. For a while things went well enough. I may describe myself at this time of my life as a happy man.

My misfortunes began with a return of the complaint with which my mother had already suffered. The doctor confessed, when I asked him the question, that there was danger to be dreaded this time. Naturally, after hearing this, I was a good deal away at the cottage. Naturally also, I left the business of looking after the house, in my absence, to my wife. Little by little, I found her beginning to alter toward me. While my back was turned, she formed acquaintances with people of the doubtful and dissipated sort. One day, I observed something in her manner which forced the suspicion on me that she had been drinking. Before the week was out, my suspicion was a certainty. From keeping company with drunkards, she had grown to be a drunkard herself.

I did all a man could do to reclaim her. Quite useless! She had never really returned the love I felt for her: I had no influence; I could do nothing. My mother, hearing of this last worse trouble, resolved to try what her influence could do. Ill as she was, I found her one day dressed to go out.

"I am not long for this world, Francis," she said. "I shall not feel easy on my deathbed, unless I have done my best to the last to make you happy. I mean to put my own fears and my own feelings out of the question, and go with you to your wife, and try what I can do to reclaim her. Take me home with you, Francis. Let me do all I can to help my son, before it is too late."

How could I disobey her? We took the railway to the town: it was only half an hour's ride. By one o'clock in the afternoon we reached my house. It was our dinner hour, and Alicia was in the kitchen. I was able to take my mother quietly into the parlor and then to prepare my wife for the visit. She had drunk but little at that early hour; and, luckily, the devil in her was tamed for the time.

She followed me into the parlor, and the meeting passed off better than I had ventured to forecast; with this one drawback, that my mother – though she tried hard to control herself – shrank from looking my wife in the face when she spoke to her. It was a relief to me when Alicia began to prepare the table for dinner.

She laid the cloth, brought in the bread tray, and cut some slices for us from the loaf. Then she returned to the kitchen. At that moment, while I was still anxiously watching my mother, I was startled by seeing the same ghastly change pass over her face which had altered it in the morning when Alicia and she first met. Before I could say a word, she started up with a look of horror.

"Take me back! – home, home again, Francis! Come with me, and never go back more!"

I was afraid to ask for an explanation; I could only sign her to be silent, and help her quickly to the door. As we passed the bread tray on the table, she stopped and pointed to it.

"Did you see what your wife cut your bread with?" she asked.

"No, mother; I was not noticing. What was it?"

"Look!"

I did look. A new clasp knife, with a buckhorn handle, lay with the loaf in the bread tray. I stretched out my hand to possess myself of it. At the same moment, there was a noise in the kitchen, and my mother caught me by the arm.

"The knife of the Dream! Francis, I'm faint with fear – take me away before she comes back!"

I couldn't speak to comfort or even to answer her. Superior as I was to superstition, the discovery of the knife staggered me. In silence, I helped my mother out of the house; and took her home.

I held out my hand to say good-by. She tried to stop me.

"Don't go back, Francis! don't go back!".

"I must get the knife, mother. I must go back by the next train." I held to that resolution. By the next train I went back.

Chapter XII

MY WIFE HAD, of course, discovered our secret departure from the house. She had been drinking. She was in a fury of passion. The dinner in the kitchen was flung under the grate; the cloth was off the parlor table. Where was the knife?

I was foolish enough to ask for it. She refused to give it to me. In the course of the dispute between us which followed, I discovered that there was a horrible story attached to the knife. It had been used in a murder – years since – and had been so skillfully hidden that the authorities had been unable to produce it at the trial. By help of some of her disreputable friends, my wife had been able to purchase this relic of a bygone crime. Her perverted nature set some horrid unacknowledged value on the knife. Seeing there was no hope of getting it by fair means, I determined to search for it, later in the day, in secret. The search was unsuccessful. Night came on, and I left the house to walk about the streets. You will understand what a broken man I was by this time, when I tell you I was afraid to sleep in the same room with her!

Three weeks passed. Still she refused to give up the knife; and still that fear of sleeping in the same room with her possessed me. I walked about at night, or dozed in the parlor, or sat watching by my mother's bedside. Before the end of the first week in the new month, the worst misfortune of all befell me – my mother died. It wanted then but a short time to my birthday. She had longed to live till that day. I was present at her death. Her last words in this world were addressed to me. "Don't go back, my son – don't go back!"

I was obliged to go back, if it was only to watch my wife. In the last days of my mother's illness she had spitefully added a sting to my grief by declaring she would assert her right to attend the funeral. In spite of all that I could do or say, she held to her word. On the day appointed for the burial she forced herself, inflamed and shameless with drink, into my presence, and swore she would walk in the funeral procession to my mother's grave.

This last insult – after all I had gone through already – was more than I could endure. It maddened me. Try to make allowances for a man beside himself. I struck her.

The instant the blow was dealt, I repented it. She crouched down, silent, in a corner of the room, and eyed me steadily. It was a look that cooled my hot blood in an instant. There was no time now to think of making atonement. I could only risk the worst, and make sure of her till the funeral was over. I locked her into her bedroom.

When I came back, after laying my mother in the grave, I found her sitting by the bedside, very much altered in look and bearing, with a bundle on her lap. She faced me quietly; she spoke with a curious stillness in her voice – strangely and unnaturally composed in look and manner.

"No man has ever struck me yet," she said. "My husband shall have no second opportunity. Set the door open, and let me go."

She passed me, and left the room. I saw her walk away up the street. Was she gone for good?

All that night I watched and waited. No footstep came near the house. The next night, overcome with fatigue, I lay down on the bed in my clothes, with the door locked, the key on the table, and the candle burning. My slumber was not disturbed. The third night, the fourth, the fifth, the sixth, passed, and nothing happened. I lay down on the seventh night, still suspicious of something happening; still in my clothes; still with the door locked, the key on the table, and the candle burning.

My rest was disturbed. I awoke twice, without any sensation of uneasiness. The third time, that horrid shivering of the night at the lonely inn, that awful sinking pain at the heart, came back again, and roused me in an instant. My eyes turned to the left-hand side of the bed. And there stood, looking at me—

The Dream Woman again? No! My wife. The living woman, with the face of the Dream – in the attitude of the Dream – the fair arm up; the knife clasped in the delicate white hand.

I sprang upon her on the instant; but not quickly enough to stop her from hiding the knife. Without a word from me, without a cry from her, I pinioned her in a chair. With one hand I felt up her sleeve; and there, where the Dream Woman had hidden the knife, my wife had hidden it – the knife with the buckhorn handle, that looked like new.

What I felt when I made that discovery I could not realize at the time, and I can't describe now. I took one steady look at her with the knife in my hand. "You meant to kill me?" I said.

"Yes," she answered; "I meant to kill you." She crossed her arms over her bosom, and stared me coolly in the face. "I shall do it yet," she said. "With that knife."

I don't know what possessed me – I swear to you I am no coward; and yet I acted like a coward. The horrors got hold of me. I couldn't look at her – I couldn't speak to her. I left her (with the knife in my hand), and went out into the night.

There was a bleak wind abroad, and the smell of rain was in the air. The church clocks chimed the quarter as I walked beyond the last house in the town. I asked the first policeman I met what hour that was, of which the quarter past had just struck.

The man looked at his watch, and answered, "Two o'clock." Two in the morning. What day of the month was this day that had just begun? I reckoned it up from the date of my mother's funeral. The horrid parallel between the dream and the reality was complete – it was my birthday!

Had I escaped, the mortal peril which the dream foretold? or had I only received a second warning? As that doubt crossed my mind I stopped on my way out of the town. The air had revived me – I felt in some degree like my own self again. After a little thinking, I began to see plainly the mistake I had made in leaving my wife free to go where she liked and to do as she pleased.

I turned instantly, and made my way back to the house. It was still dark. I had left the candle burning in the bedchamber. When I looked up to the window of the room now, there was no light in it. I advanced to the house door. On going away, I remembered to have closed it; on trying it now, I found it open.

I waited outside, never losing sight of the house till daylight. Then I ventured indoors – listened, and heard nothing – looked into the kitchen, scullery, parlor, and found nothing – went up at last into the bedroom. It was empty.

A picklock lay on the floor, which told me how she had gained entrance in the night. And that was the one trace I could find of the Dream Woman.

Chapter XIII

I WAITED in the house till the town was astir for the day, and then I went to consult a lawyer. In the confused state of my mind at the time, I had one clear notion of what I meant to do: I was determined to sell my house and leave the neighborhood. There were obstacles in the way which I had not counted on. I was told I had creditors to satisfy before I could leave – I, who had given my wife the money to pay my bills regularly every week! Inquiry showed that she had embezzled every farthing of the money I had intrusted to her. I had no choice but to pay over again.

Placed in this awkward position, my first duty was to set things right, with the help of my lawyer. During my forced sojourn in the town I did two foolish things. And, as a consequence that followed, I heard once more, and heard for the last time, of my wife.

In the first place, having got possession of the knife, I was rash enough to keep it in my pocket. In the second place, having something of importance to say to my lawyer, at a late hour of the evening, I went to his house after dark – alone and on foot. I got there safely enough. Returning, I was seized on from behind by two men, dragged down a passage and robbed – not only of the little money I had about me, but also of the knife. It was the lawyer's opinion (as it was mine) that the thieves were among the disreputable acquaintances formed by my wife, and that they had attacked me at her instigation. To confirm this view I received a letter the next day, without date or address, written in Alicia's hand. The first line informed me that the knife was back again in her possession. The second line reminded me of the day when I struck her. The third line warned me that she would wash out the stain of that blow in my blood, and repeated the words, "I shall do it with the knife!"

These things happened a year ago. The law laid hands on the men who had robbed me; but from that time to this, the law has failed completely to find a trace of my wife.

My story is told. When I had paid the creditors and paid the legal expenses, I had barely five pounds left out of the sale of my house; and I had the world to begin over again. Some months since – drifting here and there – I found my way to Underbridge. The landlord of the inn had known something of my father's family in times past. He gave me (all he had to give) my food, and shelter in the yard. Except on market days, there is nothing to do. In the coming winter the inn is to be shut up, and I shall have to shift for myself. My old master would help me if I applied to him – but I don't like to apply: he has done more for me already than I deserve. Besides, in another year who knows but my troubles may all be at an end? Next winter will bring me nigh to my next birthday, and my next birthday may be the day of my death. Yes! it's true I sat up all last night; and I heard two in the morning strike: and nothing happened. Still, allowing for that, the time to come is a time I don't trust. My wife has got the knife – my wife is looking for me. I am above superstition, mind! I don't say I believe in dreams; I only say, Alicia Warlock is looking for me. It is possible I may be wrong. It is possible I may be right. Who can tell?

The Third Narrative
The Story Continued by Percy Fairbank

Chapter XIV

WE TOOK LEAVE of Francis Raven at the door of Farleigh Hall, with the understanding that he might expect to hear from us again.

The same night Mrs. Fairbank and I had a discussion in the sanctuary of our own room. The topic was "The Hostler's Story"; and the question in dispute between us turned on the measure of charitable duty that we owed to the hostler himself.

The view I took of the man's narrative was of the purely matter-of-fact kind. Francis Raven had, in my opinion, brooded over the misty connection between his strange dream and his vile wife, until his mind was in a state of partial delusion on that subject. I was quite willing to help him with a trifle of money, and to recommend him to the kindness of my lawyer, if he was really in any danger and wanted advice. There my idea of my duty toward this afflicted person began and ended.

Confronted with this sensible view of the matter, Mrs. Fairbank's romantic temperament rushed, as usual, into extremes. "I should no more think of losing sight of Francis Raven when his next birthday comes round," says my wife, "than I should think of laying down a good story with the last chapters unread. I am positively determined, Percy, to take him back with us when we return to France, in the capacity of groom. What does one man more or less among the horses matter to people as rich as we are?" In this strain the partner of my joys and sorrows ran on, perfectly impenetrable to everything that I could say on the side of common sense. Need I tell my married brethren how it ended? Of course I allowed my wife to irritate me, and spoke to her sharply.

Of course my wife turned her face away indignantly on the conjugal pillow, and burst into tears. Of course upon that, "Mr." made his excuses, and "Mrs." had her own way.

Before the week was out we rode over to Underbridge, and duly offered to Francis Raven a place in our service as supernumerary groom.

At first the poor fellow seemed hardly able to realize his own extraordinary good fortune. Recovering himself, he expressed his gratitude modestly and becomingly. Mrs. Fairbank's ready sympathies overflowed, as usual, at her lips. She talked to him about our home in France, as if the worn, gray-headed hostler had been a child. "Such a dear old house, Francis; and such pretty gardens! Stables! Stables ten times as big as your stables here – quite a choice of rooms for you. You must learn the name of our house – Maison Rouge. Our nearest town is Metz. We are within a walk of the beautiful River Moselle. And when we want a change we have only to take the railway to the frontier, and find ourselves in Germany."

Listening, so far, with a very bewildered face, Francis started and changed color when my wife reached the end of her last sentence. "Germany?" he repeated.

"Yes. Does Germany remind you of anything?"

The hostler's eyes looked down sadly on the ground. "Germany reminds me of my wife," he replied.

"Indeed! How?"

"She once told me she had lived in Germany – long before I knew her – in the time when she was a young girl."

"Was she living with relations or friends?"

"She was living as governess in a foreign family."

"In what part of Germany?"

"I don't remember, ma'am. I doubt if she told me."

"Did she tell you the name of the family?"

"Yes, ma'am. It was a foreign name, and it has slipped my memory long since. The head of the family was a wine grower in a large way of business – I remember that."

"Did you hear what sort of wine he grew? There are wine growers in our neighborhood. Was it Moselle wine?"

"I couldn't say, ma'am, I doubt if I ever heard."

There the conversation dropped. We engaged to communicate with Francis Raven before we left England, and took our leave. I had made arrangements to pay our round of visits to English friends, and to return to Maison Rouge in the summer. On the eve of departure, certain difficulties in connection with the management of some landed property of mine in Ireland obliged us to alter our plans. Instead of getting back to our house in France in the Summer, we only returned a week or two before Christmas. Francis Raven accompanied us, and was duly established, in the nominal capacity of stable keeper, among the servants at Maison Rouge.

Before long, some of the objections to taking him into our employment, which I had foreseen and had vainly mentioned to my wife, forced themselves on our attention in no very agreeable form. Francis Raven failed (as I had feared he would) to get on smoothly with his fellow-servants They were all French; and not one of them understood English. Francis, on his side, was equally ignorant of French. His reserved manners, his melancholy temperament, his solitary ways – all told against him. Our servants called him "the English Bear." He grew widely known in the neighborhood under his nickname. Quarrels took place, ending once or twice in blows. It became plain, even to Mrs. Fairbank herself, that some wise change must be made. While we were still considering what the change was to be, the unfortunate hostler was thrown on our hands for some time to come by an accident in the stables. Still pursued by his proverbial ill-luck, the poor wretch's leg was broken by a kick from a horse.

He was attended to by our own surgeon, in his comfortable bedroom at the stables. As the date of his birthday drew near, he was still confined to his bed.

Physically speaking, he was doing very well. Morally speaking, the surgeon was not satisfied. Francis Raven was suffering under some mysterious mental disturbance, which interfered seriously with his rest at night. Hearing this, I thought it my duty to tell the medical attendant what was preying on the patient's mind. As a practical man, he shared my opinion that the hostler was in a state of delusion on the subject of his Wife and his Dream. "Curable delusion, in my opinion," the surgeon added, "if the experiment could be fairly tried."

"How can it be tried?" I asked. Instead of replying, the surgeon put a question to me, on his side.

"Do you happen to know," he said, "that this year is Leap Year?"

"Mrs. Fairbank reminded me of it yesterday," I answered. "Otherwise I might *not* have known it."

"Do you think Francis Raven knows that this year is Leap Year?"

(I began to see dimly what my friend was driving at.)

"It depends," I answered, "on whether he has got an English almanac. Suppose he has *not* got the almanac – what then?"

"In that case," pursued the surgeon, "Francis Raven is innocent of all suspicion that there is a twenty-ninth day in February this year. As a necessary consequence – what will he do? He will anticipate the appearance of the Woman with the Knife, at two in the morning of the twenty-ninth of February, instead of the first of March. Let him suffer all his superstitious terrors on the wrong day. Leave him, on the day that is really his birthday, to pass a perfectly quiet night, and to be as sound asleep as other people at two in the morning. And then, when he wakes comfortably in time for his breakfast, shame him out of his delusion by telling him the truth."

I agreed to try the experiment. Leaving the surgeon to caution Mrs. Fairbank on the subject of Leap Year, I went to the stables to see Mr. Raven.

Chapter XV

THE POOR FELLOW was full of forebodings of the fate in store for him on the ominous first of March. He eagerly entreated me to order one of the men servants to sit up with him on the birthday morning. In granting his request, I asked him to tell me on which day of the week his birthday fell. He reckoned the days on his fingers; and proved his innocence of all suspicion that it was Leap Year, by fixing on the twenty-ninth of February, in the full persuasion that it was the first of March. Pledged to try the surgeon's experiment, I left his error uncorrected, of course. In so doing, I took my first step blindfold toward the last act in the drama of the Hostler's Dream.

The next day brought with it a little domestic difficulty, which indirectly and strangely associated itself with the coming end.

My wife received a letter, inviting us to assist in celebrating the "Silver Wedding" of two worthy German neighbors of ours – Mr. and Mrs. Beldheimer. Mr. Beldheimer was a large wine grower on the banks of the Moselle. His house was situated on the frontier line of France and Germany; and the distance from our house was sufficiently considerable to make it necessary for us to sleep under our host's roof. Under these circumstances, if we accepted the invitation, a comparison of dates showed that we should be away from home on the morning of the first of March. Mrs. Fairbank – holding to her absurd resolution to see with her own eyes what might, or might not, happen to Francis Raven on his birthday – flatly declined to leave Maison Rouge. "It's easy to send an excuse," she said, in her off-hand manner.

I failed, for my part, to see any easy way out of the difficulty. The celebration of a "Silver Wedding" in Germany is the celebration of twenty-five years of happy married life; and the host's claim upon the consideration of his friends on such an occasion is something in the nature of a royal "command." After considerable discussion, finding my wife's obstinacy invincible, and feeling that the absence of both of us from the festival would certainly offend our friends, I left Mrs. Fairbank to make her excuses for herself, and directed her to accept the invitation so far as I was concerned. In so doing, I took my second step, blindfold, toward the last act in the drama of the Hostler's Dream.

A week elapsed; the last days of February were at hand. Another domestic difficulty happened; and, again, this event also proved to be strangely associated with the coming end.

My head groom at the stables was one Joseph Rigobert. He was an ill-conditioned fellow, inordinately vain of his personal appearance, and by no means scrupulous in his conduct with women. His one virtue consisted of his fondness for horses, and in the care he took of the animals under his charge. In a word, he was too good a groom to be easily replaced, or he would have quitted my service long since. On the occasion of which I am now writing, he was reported to me by my steward as growing idle and disorderly in his habits. The principal offense alleged against him was, that he had been seen that day in the city of Metz, in the company of a woman (supposed to be an Englishwoman), whom he was entertaining at a tavern, when he ought to have been on his way back to Maison Rouge. The man's defense was that "the lady" (as he called her) was an English stranger, unacquainted with the ways of the place, and that he had only shown her where she could obtain some refreshments at her own request. I administered the necessary reprimand, without troubling myself to inquire further into the matter. In failing to do this, I took my third step, blindfold, toward the last act in the drama of the Hostler's Dream.

On the evening of the twenty-eighth, I informed the servants at the stables that one of them must watch through the night by the Englishman's bedside. Joseph Rigobert immediately volunteered for the duty – as a means, no doubt, of winning his way back to my favor. I accepted his proposal.

That day the surgeon dined with us. Toward midnight he and I left the smoking room, and repaired to Francis Raven's bedside. Rigobert was at his post, with no very agreeable expression on his face. The Frenchman and the Englishman had evidently not got on well together so far. Francis Raven lay helpless on his bed, waiting silently for two in the morning and the Dream Woman.

"I have come, Francis, to bid you good night," I said, cheerfully. "Tomorrow morning I shall look in at breakfast time, before I leave home on a journey."

"Thank you for all your kindness, sir. You will not see me alive tomorrow morning. She will find me this time. Mark my words – she will find me this time."

"My good fellow! she couldn't find you in England. How in the world is she to find you in France?"

"It's borne in on my mind, sir, that she will find me here. At two in the morning on my birthday I shall see her again, and see her for the last time."

"Do you mean that she will kill you?"

"I mean that, sir, she will kill me – with the knife."

"And with Rigobert in the room to protect you?"

"I am a doomed man. Fifty Rigoberts couldn't protect me."

"And you wanted somebody to sit up with you?"

"Mere weakness, sir. I don't like to be left alone on my deathbed."

I looked at the surgeon. If he had encouraged me, I should certainly, out of sheer compassion, have confessed to Francis Raven the trick that we were playing him. The surgeon held to his experiment; the surgeon's face plainly said: "No."

The next day (the twenty-ninth of February) was the day of the "Silver Wedding." The first thing in the morning, I went to Francis Raven's room. Rigobert met me at the door.

"How has he passed the night?" I asked.

"Saying his prayers, and looking for ghosts," Rigobert answered. "A lunatic asylum is the only proper place for him."

I approached the bedside. "Well, Francis, here you are, safe and sound, in spite of what you said to me last night."

His eyes rested on mine with a vacant, wondering look.

"I don't understand it," he said.

"Did you see anything of your wife when the clock struck two?"

"No, sir."

"Did anything happen?"

"Nothing happened, sir."

"Doesn't *this* satisfy you that you were wrong?"

His eyes still kept their vacant, wondering look. He only repeated the words he had spoken already: "I don't understand it."

I made a last attempt to cheer him. "Come, come, Francis! keep a good heart. You will be out of bed in a fortnight."

He shook his head on the pillow. "There's something wrong," he said. "I don't expect you to believe me, sir. I only say there's something wrong – and time will show it."

I left the room. Half an hour later I started for Mr. Beldheimer's house; leaving the arrangements for the morning of the first of March in the hands of the doctor and my wife.

Chapter XVI

THE ONE THING which principally struck me when I joined the guests at the "Silver Wedding" is also the one thing which it is necessary to mention here. On this joyful occasion a noticeable lady present was out of spirits. That lady was no other than the heroine of the festival, the mistress of the house!

In the course of the evening I spoke to Mr. Beldheimer's eldest son on the subject of his mother. As an old friend of the family, I had a claim on his confidence which the young man willingly recognized.

"We have had a very disagreeable matter to deal with," he said; "and my mother has not recovered the painful impression left on her mind. Many years since, when my sisters were children, we had an English governess in the house. She left us, as we then understood, to be married. We heard no more of her until a week or ten days since, when my mother received a letter, in which our ex-governess described herself as being in a condition of great poverty and distress. After much hesitation she had ventured – at the suggestion of a lady who had been kind to her – to write to her former employers, and to appeal to their remembrance of old times. You know my mother: she is not only the most kind-hearted, but the most innocent of women – it is impossible to persuade her of the wickedness that there is in the world. She replied by return of post, inviting the governess to come here and see her, and inclosing the money for her traveling expenses. When my father came home, and heard what had been done, he wrote at once to his agent in London to make inquiries, inclosing the address on the governess' letter. Before he could receive the agent's reply the governess, arrived. She produced the worst possible impression on his mind. The agent's letter, arriving a few days later, confirmed his suspicions. Since we had lost sight of her, the woman had led a most disreputable life. My father spoke to her privately: he offered – on condition of her leaving the house – a sum of money to take her back to England. If she refused, the alternative would be an appeal to the authorities and a public scandal. She accepted the money, and left the house. On her way back to England she appears to have stopped at Metz. You will understand what sort of woman she is when I tell you that she was seen the other day in a tavern, with your handsome groom, Joseph Rigobert."

While my informant was relating these circumstances, my memory was at work. I recalled what Francis Raven had vaguely told us of his wife's experience in former days as governess in a German family. A suspicion of the truth suddenly flashed across my mind. "What was the woman's name?" I asked.

Mr. Beldheimer's son answered: "Alicia Warlock."

I had but one idea when I heard that reply – to get back to my house without a moment's needless delay. It was then ten o'clock at night – the last train to Metz had left long since. I arranged with my young friend – after duly informing him of the circumstances – that I should go by the first train in the morning, instead of staying to breakfast with the other guests who slept in the house.

At intervals during the night I wondered uneasily how things were going on at Maison Rouge. Again and again the same question occurred to me, on my journey home in the early morning – the morning of the first of March. As the event proved, but one person in my house knew what really happened at the stables on Francis Raven's birthday. Let Joseph Rigobert take my place as narrator, and tell the story of the end to You – as he told it, in times past, to his lawyer and to Me.

The Fourth and Last Narrative
Statement of Joseph Rigobert: Addressed to the Advocate who Defended Him at Trial

RESPECTED SIR, – On the twenty-seventh of February I was sent, on business connected with the stables at Maison Rouge, to the city of Metz. On the public promenade I met a magnificent woman. Complexion, blond. Nationality, English. We mutually admired each other; we fell into conversation. (She spoke French perfectly – with the English accent.) I offered refreshment; my proposal was accepted. We had a long and interesting interview – we discovered that we were made for each other. So far, Who is to blame?

Is it my fault that I am a handsome man – universally agreeable as such to the fair sex? Is it a criminal offense to be accessible to the amiable weakness of love? I ask again, Who is to blame? Clearly, nature. Not the beautiful lady – not my humble self.

To resume. The most hard-hearted person living will understand that two beings made for each other could not possibly part without an appointment to meet again.

I made arrangements for the accommodation of the lady in the village near Maison Rouge. She consented to honor me with her company at supper, in my apartment at the stables, on the night of the twenty-ninth. The time fixed on was the time when the other servants were accustomed to retire – eleven o'clock.

Among the grooms attached to the stables was an Englishman, laid up with a broken leg. His name was Francis. His manners were repulsive; he was ignorant of the French language. In the kitchen he went by the nickname of the "English Bear." Strange to say, he was a great favorite with my master and my mistress. They even humored certain superstitious terrors to which this repulsive person was subject – terrors into the nature of which I, as an advanced freethinker, never thought it worth my while to inquire.

On the evening of the twenty-eighth the Englishman, being a prey to the terrors which I have mentioned, requested that one of his fellow servants might sit up with him for that night only. The wish that he expressed was backed by Mr. Fairbank's authority. Having already incurred my master's displeasure – in what way, a proper sense of my own dignity forbids me to relate – I volunteered to watch by the bedside of the English Bear. My object was to satisfy Mr. Fairbank that I bore no malice, on my side, after what had occurred between us. The wretched Englishman passed a night of delirium. Not understanding his barbarous language, I could only gather from his gesture that he was in deadly fear of some fancied apparition at his bedside. From time to time, when this madman disturbed my slumbers, I quieted him by swearing at him. This is the shortest and best way of dealing with persons in his condition.

On the morning of the twenty-ninth, Mr. Fairbank left us on a journey. Later in the day, to my unspeakable disgust, I found that I had not done with the Englishman yet. In Mr. Fairbank's absence, Mrs. Fairbank took an incomprehensible interest in the question of my delirious fellow servant's repose at night. Again, one or the other of us was to watch at his bedside, and report it, if anything happened. Expecting my fair friend to supper, it was necessary to make sure that the other servants at the stables would be safe in their beds that night. Accordingly, I volunteered once more to be the man who kept watch. Mrs. Fairbank complimented me on my humanity. I possess great command over my feelings. I accepted the compliment without a blush.

Twice, after nightfall, my mistress and the doctor (the last staying in the house in Mr. Fairbank's absence) came to make inquiries. Once *before* the arrival of my fair friend – and once *after*. On the second occasion (my apartment being next door to the Englishman's) I was obliged to hide my charming guest in the harness room. She consented, with angelic resignation, to immolate her dignity to the servile necessities of my position. A more amiable woman (so far) I never met with!

After the second visit I was left free. It was then close on midnight. Up to that time there was nothing in the behavior of the mad Englishman to reward Mrs. Fairbank and the doctor for presenting themselves at his bedside. He lay half awake, half asleep, with an odd wondering kind of look in his face. My mistress at parting warned me to be particularly watchful of him toward two in the morning. The doctor (in case anything happened) left me a large hand bell to ring, which could easily be heard at the house.

Restored to the society of my fair friend, I spread the supper table. A pâté, a sausage, and a few bottles of generous Moselle wine, composed our simple meal. When persons adore each other, the intoxicating illusion of Love transforms the simplest meal into a banquet. With immeasurable capacities for enjoyment, we sat down to table. At the very moment when I placed my fascinating companion in a chair, the infamous Englishman in the next room took that occasion, of all others, to become restless and noisy once more. He struck with his stick on the floor; he cried out, in a delirious access of terror, "Rigobert! Rigobert!"

The sound of that lamentable voice, suddenly assailing our ears, terrified my fair friend. She lost all her charming color in an instant. "Good heavens!" she exclaimed. "Who is that in the next room?"

"A mad Englishman."

"An Englishman?"

"Compose yourself, my angel. I will quiet him."

The lamentable voice called out on me again, "Rigobert! Rigobert!"

My fair friend caught me by the arm. "Who is he?" she cried. "What is his name?"

Something in her face struck me as she put that question. A spasm of jealousy shook me to the soul. "You know him?" I said.

"His name!" she vehemently repeated; "his name!"

"Francis," I answered.

"Francis – *what*?"

I shrugged my shoulders. I could neither remember nor pronounce the barbarous English surname. I could only tell her it began with an "R."

She dropped back into the chair. Was she going to faint? No: she recovered, and more than recovered, her lost color. Her eyes flashed superbly. What did it mean? Profoundly as I understand women in general, I was puzzled by *this* woman!

"You know him?" I repeated.

She laughed at me. "What nonsense! How should I know him? Go and quiet the wretch."

My looking-glass was near. One glance at it satisfied me that no woman in her senses could prefer the Englishman to Me. I recovered my self-respect. I hastened to the Englishman's bedside.

The moment I appeared he pointed eagerly toward my room. He overwhelmed me with a torrent of words in his own language. I made out, from his gestures and his looks, that he had, in some incomprehensible manner, discovered the presence of my guest; and, stranger still, that he was scared by the idea of a person in my room. I endeavored to compose him on the system which I have already mentioned – that is to say, I swore at him in *my* language. The result not proving satisfactory, I own I shook my fist in his face, and left the bedchamber.

Returning to my fair friend, I found her walking backward and forward in a state of excitement wonderful to behold. She had not waited for me to fill her glass – she had begun the generous Moselle in my absence. I prevailed on her with difficulty to place herself at the table. Nothing would induce her to eat. "My appetite is gone," she said. "Give me wine."

The generous Moselle deserves its name – delicate on the palate, with prodigious "body." The strength of this fine wine produced no stupefying effect on my remarkable guest. It appeared to strengthen and exhilarate her – nothing more. She always spoke in the same low tone, and always, turn the conversation as I might, brought it back with the same dexterity to the subject of the Englishman in the next room. In any other woman this persistency would have offended me. My lovely guest was irresistible; I answered her questions with the docility of a child. She possessed all the amusing eccentricity of her nation. When I told her of the accident which confined the Englishman to his bed, she sprang to her feet. An extraordinary smile irradiated her countenance. She said, "Show me the horse who broke the Englishman's leg! I must see that horse!" I took her to the stables. She kissed the horse – on my word of honor, she kissed the horse! That struck me. I said. "You *do* know the man; and he has wronged you in some way." No! she would not admit it, even then. "I kiss all beautiful animals," she said. "Haven't I kissed *you?*" With that charming explanation of her conduct, she ran back up the stairs. I only remained behind to lock the stable door again. When I rejoined her, I made a startling discovery. I caught her coming out of the Englishman's room.

"I was just going downstairs again to call you," she said. "The man in there is getting noisy once more."

The mad Englishman's voice assailed our ears once again. "Rigobert! Rigobert!"

He was a frightful object to look at when I saw him this time. His eyes were staring wildly; the perspiration was pouring over his face. In a panic of terror he clasped his hands; he pointed up to heaven. By every sign and gesture that a man can make, he entreated me not to leave him again. I really could not help smiling. The idea of my staying with *him*, and leaving my fair friend by herself in the next room!

I turned to the door. When the mad wretch saw me leaving him he burst out into a screech of despair – so shrill that I feared it might awaken the sleeping servants.

My presence of mind in emergencies is proverbial among those who know me. I tore open the cupboard in which he kept his linen – seized a handful of his handkerchiefs – gagged him with one of them, and secured his hands with the others. There was now no danger of his alarming the servants. After tying the last knot, I looked up.

The door between the Englishman's room and mine was open. My fair friend was standing on the threshold – watching *him* as he lay helpless on the bed; watching *me* as I tied the last knot.

"What are you doing there?" I asked. "Why did you open the door?"

She stepped up to me, and whispered her answer in my ear, with her eyes all the time upon the man on the bed:

"I heard him scream."

"Well?"

"I thought you had killed him."

I drew back from her in horror. The suspicion of me which her words implied was sufficiently detestable in itself. But her manner when she uttered the words was more revolting still. It so powerfully affected me that I started back from that beautiful creature as I might have recoiled from a reptile crawling over my flesh.

Before I had recovered myself sufficiently to reply, my nerves were assailed by another shock. I suddenly heard my mistress's voice calling to me from the stable yard.

There was no time to think – there was only time to act. The one thing needed was to keep Mrs. Fairbank from ascending the stairs, and discovering – not my lady guest only – but the Englishman also, gagged and bound on his bed. I instantly hurried to the yard. As I ran down the stairs I heard the stable clock strike the quarter to two in the morning.

My mistress was eager and agitated. The doctor (in attendance on her) was smiling to himself, like a man amused at his own thoughts.

"Is Francis awake or asleep?" Mrs. Fairbank inquired.

"He has been a little restless, madam. But he is now quiet again. If he is not disturbed" (I added those words to prevent her from ascending the stairs), "he will soon fall off into a quiet sleep."

"Has nothing happened since I was here last?"

"Nothing, madam."

The doctor lifted his eyebrows with a comical look of distress. "Alas, alas, Mrs. Fairbank!" he said. "Nothing has happened! The days of romance are over!"

"It is not two o'clock yet," my mistress answered, a little irritably.

The smell of the stables was strong on the morning air. She put her handkerchief to her nose and led the way out of the yard by the north entrance – the entrance communicating with the gardens and the house. I was ordered to follow her, along with the doctor. Once out of the smell of the stables she began to question me again. She was unwilling to believe that nothing had occurred in her absence. I invented the best answers I could think of on the spur of the moment; and the doctor stood by laughing. So the minutes passed till the clock struck two. Upon that, Mrs. Fairbank announced her intention of personally visiting the Englishman in his room. To my great relief, the doctor interfered to stop her from doing this.

"You have heard that Francis is just falling asleep," he said. "If you enter his room you may disturb him. It is essential to the success of my experiment that he should have a good night's rest, and that he should own it himself, before I tell him the truth. I must request, madam, that you will not disturb the man. Rigobert will ring the alarm bell if anything happens."

My mistress was unwilling to yield. For the next five minutes, at least, there was a warm discussion between the two. In the end Mrs. Fairbank was obliged to give way – for the time. "In half an hour," she said, "Francis will either be sound asleep, or awake again. In half an hour I shall come back." She took the doctor's arm. They returned together to the house.

Left by myself, with half an hour before me, I resolved to take the Englishwoman back to the village – then, returning to the stables, to remove the gag and the bindings from Francis, and to let him screech to his heart's content. What would his alarming the whole establishment matter to *me* after I had got rid of the compromising presence of my guest?

Returning to the yard I heard a sound like the creaking of an open door on its hinges. The gate of the north entrance I had just closed with my own hand. I went round to the west entrance, at the back of the stables. It opened on a field crossed by two footpaths in Mr. Fairbank's grounds. The nearest footpath led to the village. The other led to the highroad and the river.

Arriving at the west entrance I found the door open – swinging to and fro slowly in the fresh morning breeze. I had myself locked and bolted that door after admitting my fair friend at eleven o'clock. A vague dread of something wrong stole its way into my mind. I hurried back to the stables.

I looked into my own room. It was empty. I went to the harness room. Not a sign of the woman was there. I returned to my room, and approached the door of the Englishman's bedchamber. Was it possible that she had remained there during my absence? An unaccountable reluctance to open the door made me hesitate, with my hand on the lock. I listened. There was not a sound inside. I called softly. There was no answer. I drew back a step, still hesitating. I noticed something dark moving slowly in the crevice between the bottom of the door and the boarded floor. Snatching up the candle from the table, I held it low, and looked. The dark, slowly moving object was a stream of blood!

That horrid sight roused me. I opened the door. The Englishman lay on his bed – alone in the room. He was stabbed in two places – in the throat and in the heart. The weapon was left in the second wound. It was a knife of English manufacture, with a handle of buckhorn as good as new.

I instantly gave the alarm. Witnesses can speak to what followed. It is monstrous to suppose that I am guilty of the murder. I admit that I am capable of committing follies: but I shrink from the bare idea of a crime. Besides, I had no motive for killing the man. The woman murdered him in my absence. The woman escaped by the west entrance while I was talking to my mistress. I have no more to say. I swear to you what I have here written is a true statement of all that happened on the morning of the first of March.

Accept, sir, the assurance of my sentiments of profound gratitude and respect.

Joseph Rigobert

Last Lines – Added by Percy Fairbank

TRIED FOR THE MURDER of Francis Raven, Joseph Rigobert was found Not Guilty; the papers of the assassinated man presented ample evidence of the deadly animosity felt toward him by his wife.

The investigations pursued on the morning when the crime was committed showed that the murderess, after leaving the stable, had taken the footpath which led to the river. The river was dragged – without result. It remains doubtful to this day whether she died by drowning or not. The one thing certain is – that Alicia Warlock was never seen again.

So – beginning in mystery, ending in mystery – the Dream Woman passes from your view. Ghost; demon; or living human creature – say for yourselves which she is. Or, knowing what unfathomed wonders are around you, what unfathomed wonders are *in* you, let the wise words of the greatest of all poets be explanation enough:

"We are such stuff As dreams are made of, and our little life Is rounded with, a sleep."

Gallegher

Richard Harding Davis

WE HAD HAD SO MANY office-boys before Gallegher came among us that they had begun to lose the characteristics of individuals, and became merged in a composite photograph of small boys, to whom we applied the generic title of "Here, you"; or "You, boy."

We had had sleepy boys, and lazy boys, and bright, "smart" boys, who became so familiar on so short an acquaintance that we were forced to part with them to save our own self-respect.

They generally graduated into district-messenger boys, and occasionally returned to us in blue coats with nickel-plated buttons, and patronized us.

But Gallegher was something different from anything we had experienced before. Gallegher was short and broad in build, with a solid, muscular broadness, and not a fat and dumpy shortness. He wore perpetually on his face a happy and knowing smile, as if you and the world in general were not impressing him as seriously as you thought you were, and his eyes, which were very black and very bright, snapped intelligently at you like those of a little black-and-tan terrier.

All Gallegher knew had been learnt on the streets; not a very good school in itself, but one that turns out very knowing scholars. And Gallagher had attended both morning and evening sessions. He could not tell you who the Pilgrim Fathers were, nor could he name the thirteen original States, but he knew all the officers of the twenty-second police district by name, and he could distinguish the clang of a fire-engine's gong from that of a patrol-wagon or an ambulance fully two blocks distant. It was Gallegher who rang the alarm when the Woolwich Mills caught fire, while the officer on the beat was asleep, and it was Gallegher who led the "Black Diamonds" against the "Wharf Rats," when they used to stone each other to their hearts' content on the coal-wharves of Richmond.

I am afraid, now that I see these facts written down, that Gallegher was not a reputable character; but he was so very young and so very old for his years that we all liked him very much nevertheless. He lived in the extreme northern part of Philadelphia, where the cotton- and woollen-mills run down to the river, and how he ever got home after leaving the *Press* building at two in the morning, was one of the mysteries of the office. Sometimes he caught a night car, and sometimes he walked all the way, arriving at the little house, where his mother and himself lived alone, at four in the morning. Occasionally he was given a ride on an early milk-cart, or on one of the newspaper delivery wagons, with its high piles of papers still damp and sticky from the press. He knew several drivers of "night hawks" – those cabs that prowl the streets at night looking for belated passengers – and when it was a very cold morning he would not go home at all, but would crawl into one of these cabs and sleep, curled upon the cushions, until daylight.

Besides being quick and cheerful, Gallegher possessed a power of amusing the *Press's* young men to a degree seldom attained by the ordinary mortal. His clog-dancing on the city editor's desk, when that gentleman was upstairs fighting for two more columns of space, was always a source of innocent joy to us, and his imitations of the comedians of the variety halls delighted even the dramatic critic, from whom the comedians themselves failed to force a smile.

But Gallegher's chief characteristic was his love for that element of news generically classed as "crime."

Not that he ever did anything criminal himself. On the contrary, his was rather the work of the criminal specialist, and his morbid interest in the doings of all queer characters, his knowledge of their methods, their present whereabouts, and their past deeds of transgression often rendered him a valuable ally to our police reporter, whose daily feuilletons were the only portion of the paper Gallegher deigned to read.

In Gallegher the detective element was abnormally developed. He had shown this on several occasions, and to excellent purpose.

Once the paper had sent him into a Home for Destitute Orphans which was believed to be grievously mismanaged, and Gallegher, while playing the part of a destitute orphan, kept his eyes open to what was going on around him so faithfully that the story he told of the treatment meted out to the real orphans was sufficient to rescue the unhappy little wretches from the individual who had them in charge, and to have the individual himself sent to jail.

Gallegher's knowledge of the aliases, terms of imprisonment, and various misdoings of the leading criminals in Philadelphia was almost as thorough as that of the chief of police himself, and he could tell to an hour when "Dutchy Mack" was to be let out of prison, and could identify at a glance "Dick Oxford, confidence man," as "Gentleman Dan, petty thief."

There were, at this time, only two pieces of news in any of the papers. The least important of the two was the big fight between the Champion of the United States and the Would-be Champion, arranged to take place near Philadelphia; the second was the Burrbank murder, which was filling space in newspapers all over the world, from New York to Bombay.

Richard F. Burrbank was one of the most prominent of New York's railroad lawyers; he was also, as a matter of course, an owner of much railroad stock, and a very wealthy man. He had been spoken of as a political possibility for many high offices, and, as the counsel for a great railroad, was known even further than the great railroad itself had stretched its system.

At six o'clock one morning he was found by his butler lying at the foot of the hall stairs with two pistol wounds above his heart. He was quite dead. His safe, to which only he and his secretary had the keys, was found open, and $200,000 in bonds, stocks, and money, which had been placed there only the night before, was found missing. The secretary was missing also. His name was Stephen S. Hade, and his name and his description had been telegraphed and cabled to all parts of the world. There was enough circumstantial evidence to show, beyond any question or possibility of mistake, that he was the murderer.

It made an enormous amount of talk, and unhappy individuals were being arrested all over the country, and sent on to New York for identification. Three had been arrested at Liverpool, and one man just as he landed at Sydney, Australia. But so far the murderer had escaped.

We were all talking about it one night, as everybody else was all over the country, in the local room, and the city editor said it was worth a fortune to any one who chanced to run across Hade and succeeded in handing him over to the police. Some of us thought Hade had taken passage from some one of the smaller sea-ports, and others were of the opinion that he had buried himself in some cheap lodging-house in New York, or in one of the smaller towns in New Jersey.

"I shouldn't be surprised to meet him out walking, right here in Philadelphia," said one of the staff. "He'll be disguised, of course, but you could always tell him by the absence of the trigger finger on his right hand. It's missing, you know; shot off when he was a boy."

"You want to look for a man dressed like a tough," said the city editor; "for as this fellow is to all appearances a gentleman, he will try to look as little like a gentleman as possible."

"No, he won't," said Gallegher, with that calm impertinence that made him dear to us. "He'll dress just like a gentleman. Toughs don't wear gloves, and you see he's got to wear 'em. The first thing he thought of after doing for Burrbank was of that gone finger, and how he was to hide it. He stuffed the finger of that glove with cotton so's to make it look like a whole finger, and the first time he takes off that glove they've got him – see, and he knows it. So what youse want to do is to look for a man with gloves on. I've been a-doing it for two weeks now, and I can tell you it's hard work, for everybody wears gloves this kind of weather. But if you look long enough you'll find him. And when you think it's him, go up to him and hold out your hand in a friendly way, like a bunco-steerer, and shake his hand; and if you feel that his forefinger ain't real flesh, but just wadded cotton, then grip to it with your right and grab his throat with your left, and holler for help."

There was an appreciative pause.

"I see, gentlemen," said the city editor, drily, "that Gallegher's reasoning has impressed you; and I also see that before the week is out all of my young men will be under bonds for assaulting innocent pedestrians whose only offence is that they wear gloves in mid-winter."

* * *

It was about a week after this that Detective Hefflefinger, of Inspector Byrnes's staff, came over to Philadelphia after a burglar, of whose whereabouts he had been misinformed by telegraph. He brought the warrant, requisition, and other necessary papers with him, but the burglar had flown. One of our reporters had worked on a New York paper, and knew Hefflefinger, and the detective came to the office to see if he could help him in his so far unsuccessful search.

He gave Gallegher his card, and after Gallegher had read it, and had discovered who the visitor was, he became so demoralized that he was absolutely useless.

"One of Byrnes's men" was a much more awe-inspiring individual to Gallegher than a member of the Cabinet. He accordingly seized his hat and overcoat, and leaving his duties to be looked after by others, hastened out after the object of his admiration, who found his suggestions and knowledge of the city so valuable, and his company so entertaining, that they became very intimate, and spent the rest of the day together.

In the meanwhile the managing editor had instructed his subordinates to inform Gallegher, when he condescended to return, that his services were no longer needed. Gallegher had played truant once too often. Unconscious of this, he remained with his new friend until late the same evening, and started the next afternoon toward the *Press* office.

As I have said, Gallegher lived in the most distant part of the city, not many minutes' walk from the Kensington railroad station, where trains ran into the suburbs and on to New York.

It was in front of this station that a smoothly-shaven, well-dressed man brushed past Gallegher and hurried up the steps to the ticket office.

He held a walking-stick in his right hand, and Gallegher, who now patiently scrutinized the hands of every one who wore gloves, saw that while three fingers of the man's hand were closed around the cane, the fourth stood out in almost a straight line with his palm.

Gallegher stopped with a gasp and with a trembling all over his little body, and his brain asked with a throb if it could be possible. But possibilities and probabilities were to be discovered later. Now was the time for action.

He was after the man in a moment, hanging at his heels and his eyes moist with excitement.

He heard the man ask for a ticket to Torresdale, a little station just outside of Philadelphia, and when he was out of hearing, but not out of sight, purchased one for the same place.

The stranger went into the smoking-car, and seated himself at one end toward the door. Gallegher took his place at the opposite end.

He was trembling all over, and suffered from a slight feeling of nausea. He guessed it came from fright, not of any bodily harm that might come to him, but at the probability of failure in his adventure and of its most momentous possibilities.

The stranger pulled his coat collar up around his ears, hiding the lower portion of his face, but not concealing the resemblance in his troubled eyes and close-shut lips to the likenesses of the murderer Hade.

They reached Torresdale in half an hour, and the stranger, alighting quickly, struck off at a rapid pace down the country road leading to the station.

Gallegher gave him a hundred yards' start, and then followed slowly after. The road ran between fields and past a few frame-houses set far from the road in kitchen gardens.

Once or twice the man looked back over his shoulder, but he saw only a dreary length of road with a small boy splashing through the slush in the midst of it and stopping every now and again to throw snowballs at belated sparrows.

After a ten minutes' walk the stranger turned into a side road which led to only one place, the Eagle Inn, an old roadside hostelry known now as the headquarters for pothunters from the Philadelphia game market and the battle-ground of many a cock-fight.

Gallegher knew the place well. He and his young companions had often stopped there when out chestnutting on holidays in the autumn.

The son of the man who kept it had often accompanied them on their excursions, and though the boys of the city streets considered him a dumb lout, they respected him somewhat owing to his inside knowledge of dog- and cock-fights.

The stranger entered the inn at a side door, and Gallegher, reaching it a few minutes later, let him go for the time being, and set about finding his occasional playmate, young Keppler.

Keppler's offspring was found in the wood-shed.

"'Tain't hard to guess what brings you out here," said the tavern-keeper's son, with a grin; "it's the fight."

"What fight?" asked Gallegher, unguardedly.

"What fight? Why, *the* fight," returned his companion, with the slow contempt of superior knowledge.

"It's to come off here to-night. You knew that as well as me; anyway your sportin' editor knows it. He got the tip last night, but that won't help you any. You needn't think there's any chance of your getting a peep at it. Why, tickets is two hundred and fifty apiece!"

"Whew!" whistled Gallegher, "where's it to be?"

"In the barn," whispered Keppler. "I helped 'em fix the ropes this morning, I did."

"Gosh, but you're in luck," exclaimed Gallegher, with flattering envy. "Couldn't I jest get a peep at it?"

"Maybe," said the gratified Keppler. "There's a winder with a wooden shutter at the back of the barn. You can get in by it, if you have some one to boost you up to the sill."

"Sa-a-y," drawled Gallegher, as if something had but just that moment reminded him. "Who's that gent who come down the road just a bit ahead of me – him with the cape-coat! Has he got anything to do with the fight?"

"Him?" repeated Keppler in tones of sincere disgust. "No-oh, he ain't no sport. He's queer, Dad thinks. He come here one day last week about ten in the morning, said his doctor told him to go out 'en the country for his health. He's stuck up and citified, and wears gloves, and takes his meals private in his room, and all that sort of truck. They was saying in the saloon last night that they thought he was hiding from something, and Dad, just to try him, asks him last night if he was coming to see the fight. He looked sort of scared, and said he didn't want to see no fight. And then Dad says, 'I guess you mean you don't want no fighters to see you.' Dad didn't mean no harm by it, just passed it as a joke; but Mr. Carleton, as he calls himself, got white as a ghost an' says, 'I'll go to the fight willing enough,' and begins to laugh and joke. And this morning he went right into the bar-room, where all the sports were setting, and said he was going in to town to see some friends; and as he starts off he laughs an' says, 'This don't look as if I was afraid of seeing people, does it?' but Dad says it was just bluff that made him do it, and Dad thinks that if he hadn't said what he did, this Mr. Carleton wouldn't have left his room at all."

Gallegher had got all he wanted, and much more than he had hoped for – so much more that his walk back to the station was in the nature of a triumphal march.

He had twenty minutes to wait for the next train, and it seemed an hour. While waiting he sent a telegram to Hefflefinger at his hotel. It read: "Your man is near the Torresdale station, on Pennsylvania Railroad; take cab, and meet me at station. Wait until I come. Gallegher."

With the exception of one at midnight, no other train stopped at Torresdale that evening, hence the direction to take a cab.

The train to the city seemed to Gallegher to drag itself by inches. It stopped and backed at purposeless intervals, waited for an express to precede it, and dallied at stations, and when, at last, it reached the terminus, Gallegher was out before it had stopped and was in the cab and off on his way to the home of the sporting editor.

The sporting editor was at dinner and came out in the hall to see him, with his napkin in his hand. Gallegher explained breathlessly that he had located the murderer for whom the police of two continents were looking, and that he believed, in order to quiet the suspicions of the people with whom he was hiding, that he would be present at the fight that night.

The sporting editor led Gallegher into his library and shut the door. "Now," he said, "go over all that again."

Gallegher went over it again in detail, and added how he had sent for Hefflefinger to make the arrest in order that it might be kept from the knowledge of the local police and from the Philadelphia reporters.

"What I want Hefflefinger to do is to arrest Hade with the warrant he has for the burglar," explained Gallegher; "and to take him on to New York on the owl train that passes Torresdale at one. It don't get to Jersey City until four o'clock, one hour after the morning papers go to press. Of course, we must fix Hefflefinger so's he'll keep quiet and not tell who his prisoner really is."

The sporting editor reached his hand out to pat Gallegher on the head, but changed his mind and shook hands with him instead.

"My boy," he said, "you are an infant phenomenon. If I can pull the rest of this thing off to-night, it will mean the $5,000 reward and fame galore for you and the paper. Now, I'm going to write a note to the managing editor, and you can take it around to him and tell him what you've done and what I am going to do, and he'll take you back on the paper and raise your salary. Perhaps you didn't know you've been discharged?"

"Do you think you ain't a-going to take me with you?" demanded Gallegher.

"Why, certainly not. Why should I? It all lies with the detective and myself now. You've done your share, and done it well. If the man's caught, the reward's yours. But you'd only be in the way now. You'd better go to the office and make your peace with the chief."

"If the paper can get along without me, I can get along without the old paper," said Gallegher, hotly. "And if I ain't a-going with you, you ain't neither, for I know where Hefflefinger is to be, and you don't, and I won't tell you."

"Oh, very well, very well," replied the sporting editor, weakly capitulating. "I'll send the note by a messenger; only mind, if you lose your place, don't blame me."

Gallegher wondered how this man could value a week's salary against the excitement of seeing a noted criminal run down, and of getting the news to the paper, and to that one paper alone.

From that moment the sporting editor sank in Gallegher's estimation.

Mr. Dwyer sat down at his desk and scribbled off the following note:

"I have received reliable information that Hade, the Burrbank murderer, will be present at the fight to-night. We have arranged it so that he will be arrested quietly and in such a manner that the fact may be kept from all other papers. I need not point out to you that this will be the most important piece of news in the country tomorrow.

"Yours, etc.,

"Michael E. Dwyer."

The sporting editor stepped into the waiting cab, while Gallegher whispered the directions to the driver. He was told to go first to a district-messenger office, and from there up to the Ridge Avenue Road, out Broad Street, and on to the old Eagle Inn, near Torresdale.

It was a miserable night. The rain and snow were falling together, and freezing as they fell. The sporting editor got out to send his message to the *Press* office, and then lighting a cigar, and turning up the collar of his great-coat, curled up in the corner of the cab.

"Wake me when we get there, Gallegher," he said. He knew he had a long ride, and much rapid work before him, and he was preparing for the strain.

To Gallegher the idea of going to sleep seemed almost criminal. From the dark corner of the cab his eyes shone with excitement, and with the awful joy of anticipation. He glanced every now and then to where the sporting editor's cigar shone in the darkness, and watched it as it gradually burnt more dimly and went out. The lights in the shop windows threw a broad glare across the ice on the pavements, and the lights from the lamp-posts tossed the distorted shadow of the cab, and the horse, and the motionless driver, sometimes before and sometimes behind them.

After half an hour Gallegher slipped down to the bottom of the cab and dragged out a lap-robe, in which he wrapped himself. It was growing colder, and the damp, keen wind swept in through the cracks until the window-frames and woodwork were cold to the touch.

An hour passed, and the cab was still moving more slowly over the rough surface of partly paved streets, and by single rows of new houses standing at different angles to each other in fields covered with ash-heaps and brick-kilns. Here and there the gaudy lights of a drug-store, and the forerunner of suburban civilization, shone from the end of a new block of houses, and the rubber cape of an occasional policeman showed in the light of the lamp-post that he hugged for comfort.

Then even the houses disappeared, and the cab dragged its way between truck farms, with desolate-looking, glass-covered beds, and pools of water, half-caked with ice, and bare trees, and interminable fences.

Once or twice the cab stopped altogether, and Gallegher could hear the driver swearing to himself, or at the horse, or the roads. At last they drew up before the station at Torresdale. It was quite deserted, and only a single light cut a swath in the darkness and showed a portion of the platform, the ties, and the rails glistening in the rain. They walked twice past the light before a figure stepped out of the shadow and greeted them cautiously.

"I am Mr. Dwyer, of the *Press*," said the sporting editor, briskly. "You've heard of me, perhaps. Well, there shouldn't be any difficulty in our making a deal, should there? This boy here has found Hade, and we have reason to believe he will be among the spectators at the fight to-night. We want you to arrest him quietly, and as secretly as possible. You can do it with your papers and your badge easily enough. We want you to pretend that you believe he is this burglar you came over after. If you will do this, and take him away without any one so much as suspecting who he really is, and on the train that passes here at 1.20 for New York, we will give you $500 out of the $5,000 reward. If, however, one other paper, either in New York or Philadelphia, or anywhere else, knows of the arrest, you won't get a cent. Now, what do you say?"

The detective had a great deal to say. He wasn't at all sure the man Gallegher suspected was Hade; he feared he might get himself into trouble by making a false arrest, and if it should be the man, he was afraid the local police would interfere.

"We've no time to argue or debate this matter," said Dwyer, warmly. "We agree to point Hade out to you in the crowd. After the fight is over you arrest him as we have directed, and you get the money and the credit of the arrest. If you don't like this, I will arrest the man myself, and have him driven to town, with a pistol for a warrant."

Hefflefinger considered in silence and then agreed unconditionally. "As you say, Mr. Dwyer," he returned. "I've heard of you for a thoroughbred sport. I know you'll do what you say you'll do; and as for me I'll do what you say and just as you say, and it's a very pretty piece of work as it stands."

They all stepped back into the cab, and then it was that they were met by a fresh difficulty, how to get the detective into the barn where the fight was to take place, for neither of the two men had $250 to pay for his admittance.

But this was overcome when Gallegher remembered the window of which young Keppler had told him.

In the event of Hade's losing courage and not daring to show himself in the crowd around the ring, it was agreed that Dwyer should come to the barn and warn Hefflefinger; but if he should come, Dwyer was merely to keep near him and to signify by a prearranged gesture which one of the crowd he was.

They drew up before a great black shadow of a house, dark, forbidding, and apparently deserted. But at the sound of the wheels on the gravel the door opened, letting out a stream of warm, cheerful light, and a man's voice said, "Put out those lights. Don't youse know no better than that?" This was Keppler, and he welcomed Mr. Dwyer with effusive courtesy.

The two men showed in the stream of light, and the door closed on them, leaving the house as it was at first, black and silent, save for the dripping of the rain and snow from the eaves.

The detective and Gallegher put out the cab's lamps and led the horse toward a long, low shed in the rear of the yard, which they now noticed was almost filled with teams of many different makes, from the Hobson's choice of a livery stable to the brougham of the man about town.

"No," said Gallegher, as the cabman stopped to hitch the horse beside the others, "we want it nearest that lower gate. When we newspaper men leave this place we'll leave it in a hurry, and the man who is nearest town is likely to get there first. You won't be a-following of no hearse when you make your return trip."

Gallegher tied the horse to the very gate-post itself, leaving the gate open and allowing a clear road and a flying start for the prospective race to Newspaper Row.

The driver disappeared under the shelter of the porch, and Gallegher and the detective moved off cautiously to the rear of the barn. "This must be the window," said Hefflefinger, pointing to a broad wooden shutter some feet from the ground.

"Just you give me a boost once, and I'll get that open in a jiffy," said Gallegher.

The detective placed his hands on his knees, and Gallegher stood upon his shoulders, and with the blade of his knife lifted the wooden button that fastened the window on the inside, and pulled the shutter open.

Then he put one leg inside over the sill, and leaning down helped to draw his fellow-conspirator up to a level with the window. "I feel just like I was burglarizing a house," chuckled Gallegher, as he dropped noiselessly to the floor below and refastened the shutter. The barn was a large one, with a row of stalls on either side in which horses and cows were dozing. There was a haymow over each row of stalls, and at one end of the barn a number of fence-rails had been thrown across from one mow to the other. These rails were covered with hay.

In the middle of the floor was the ring. It was not really a ring, but a square, with wooden posts at its four corners through which ran a heavy rope. The space inclosed by the rope was covered with sawdust.

Gallegher could not resist stepping into the ring, and after stamping the sawdust once or twice, as if to assure himself that he was really there, began dancing around it, and indulging in such a remarkable series of fistic manœuvres with an imaginary adversary that the unimaginative detective precipitately backed into a corner of the barn.

"Now, then," said Gallegher, having apparently vanquished his foe, "you come with me." His companion followed quickly as Gallegher climbed to one of the haymows, and crawling carefully out on the fence-rail, stretched himself at full length, face downward. In this position, by moving the straw a little, he could look down, without being himself seen, upon the heads of whomsoever stood below. "This is better'n a private box, ain't it?" said Gallegher.

The boy from the newspaper office and the detective lay there in silence, biting at straws and tossing anxiously on their comfortable bed.

It seemed fully two hours before they came. Gallegher had listened without breathing, and with every muscle on a strain, at least a dozen times, when some movement in the yard had led him to believe that they were at the door.

And he had numerous doubts and fears. Sometimes it was that the police had learnt of the fight, and had raided Keppler's in his absence, and again it was that the fight had been postponed, or, worst of all, that it would be put off until so late that Mr. Dwyer could not get back in time for the last edition of the paper. Their coming, when at last they came, was heralded by an advance-guard of two sporting men, who stationed themselves at either side of the big door.

"Hurry up, now, gents," one of the men said with a shiver, "don't keep this door open no longer'n is needful."

It was not a very large crowd, but it was wonderfully well selected. It ran, in the majority of its component parts, to heavy white coats with pearl buttons. The white coats were shouldered by long blue coats with astrakhan fur trimmings, the wearers of which preserved a cliqueness not remarkable when one considers that they believed every one else present to be either a crook or a prize-fighter.

There were well-fed, well-groomed clubmen and brokers in the crowd, a politician or two, a popular comedian with his manager, amateur boxers from the athletic clubs, and quiet, close-mouthed sporting men from every city in the country. Their names if printed in the papers would have been as familiar as the types of the papers themselves.

And among these men, whose only thought was of the brutal sport to come, was Hade, with Dwyer standing at ease at his shoulder, – Hade, white, and visibly in deep anxiety, hiding his pale face beneath a cloth travelling-cap, and with his chin muffled in a woollen scarf. He had dared to come because he feared his danger from the already suspicious Keppler was less than if he stayed away. And so he was there, hovering restlessly on the border of the crowd, feeling his danger and sick with fear.

When Hefflefinger first saw him he started up on his hands and elbows and made a movement forward as if he would leap down then and there and carry off his prisoner single-handed.

"Lie down," growled Gallegher; "an officer of any sort wouldn't live three minutes in that crowd."

The detective drew back slowly and buried himself again in the straw, but never once through the long fight which followed did his eyes leave the person of the murderer. The newspaper men took their places in the foremost row close around the ring, and kept looking at their watches and begging the master of ceremonies to "shake it up, do."

There was a great deal of betting, and all of the men handled the great roll of bills they wagered with a flippant recklessness which could only be accounted for in Gallegher's mind by temporary mental derangement. Some one pulled a box out into the ring and the master of ceremonies mounted it, and pointed out in forcible language that as they were almost all already under bonds to keep the peace, it behooved all to curb their excitement and to maintain a severe silence, unless they wanted to bring the police upon them and have themselves "sent down" for a year or two.

Then two very disreputable-looking persons tossed their respective principals' high hats into the ring, and the crowd, recognizing in this relic of the days when brave knights threw down their gauntlets in the lists as only a sign that the fight was about to begin, cheered tumultuously.

This was followed by a sudden surging forward, and a mutter of admiration much more flattering than the cheers had been, when the principals followed their hats, and slipping out of their great-coats, stood forth in all the physical beauty of the perfect brute.

Their pink skin was as soft and healthy-looking as a baby's, and glowed in the lights of the lanterns like tinted ivory, and underneath this silken covering the great biceps and muscles moved in and out and looked like the coils of a snake around the branch of a tree.

Gentleman and blackguard shouldered each other for a nearer view; the coachmen, whose metal buttons were unpleasantly suggestive of police, put their hands, in the excitement of the moment, on the shoulders of their masters; the perspiration stood out in great drops on the foreheads of the backers, and the newspaper men bit somewhat nervously at the ends of their pencils.

And in the stalls the cows munched contentedly at their cuds and gazed with gentle curiosity at their two fellow-brutes, who stood waiting the signal to fall upon, and kill each other if need be, for the delectation of their brothers.

"Take your places," commanded the master of ceremonies.

In the moment in which the two men faced each other the crowd became so still that, save for the beating of the rain upon the shingled roof and the stamping of a horse in one of the stalls, the place was as silent as a church.

"Time!" shouted the master of ceremonies.

The two men sprang into a posture of defence, which was lost as quickly as it was taken, one great arm shot out like a piston-rod; there was the sound of bare fists beating on naked flesh; there was an exultant indrawn gasp of savage pleasure and relief from the crowd, and the great fight had begun.

How the fortunes of war rose and fell, and changed and rechanged that night, is an old story to those who listen to such stories; and those who do not will be glad to be spared the telling of it. It was, they say, one of the bitterest fights between two men that this country has ever known.

But all that is of interest here is that after an hour of this desperate brutal business the champion ceased to be the favorite; the man whom he had taunted and bullied, and for whom the public had but little sympathy, was proving himself a likely winner, and under his cruel blows, as sharp and clean as those from a cutlass, his opponent was rapidly giving way.

The men about the ropes were past all control now; they drowned Keppler's petitions for silence with oaths and in inarticulate shouts of anger, as if the blows had fallen upon them, and in mad rejoicings. They swept from one end of the ring to the other, with every muscle leaping in unison with those of the man they favored, and when a New York correspondent muttered over his shoulder that this would be the biggest sporting surprise since the Heenan-Sayers fight, Mr. Dwyer nodded his head sympathetically in assent.

In the excitement and tumult it is doubtful if any heard the three quickly repeated blows that fell heavily from the outside upon the big doors of the barn. If they did, it was already too late to mend matters, for the door fell, torn from its hinges, and as it fell a captain of police sprang into the light from out of the storm, with his lieutenants and their men crowding close at his shoulder.

In the panic and stampede that followed, several of the men stood as helplessly immovable as though they had seen a ghost; others made a mad rush into the arms of the officers and were beaten back against the ropes of the ring; others dived headlong into the stalls, among the horses and cattle, and still others shoved the rolls of money they held into the hands of the police and begged like children to be allowed to escape.

The instant the door fell and the raid was declared Hefflefinger slipped over the cross rails on which he had been lying, hung for an instant by his hands, and then dropped into the centre of the fighting mob on the floor. He was out of it in an instant with the agility of a pickpocket, was across the room and at Hade's throat like a dog. The murderer, for the moment, was the calmer man of the two.

"Here," he panted, "hands off, now. There's no need for all this violence. There's no great harm in looking at a fight, is there? There's a hundred-dollar bill in my right hand; take it and let me slip out of this. No one is looking. Here."

But the detective only held him the closer.

"I want you for burglary," he whispered under his breath. "You've got to come with me now, and quick. The less fuss you make, the better for both of us. If you don't know who I am, you can feel my badge under my coat there. I've got the authority. It's all regular, and when we're out of this d—d row I'll show you the papers."

He took one hand from Hade's throat and pulled a pair of handcuffs from his pocket.

"It's a mistake. This is an outrage," gasped the murderer, white and trembling, but dreadfully alive and desperate for his liberty. "Let me go, I tell you! Take your hands off of me! Do I look like a burglar, you fool?"

"I know who you look like," whispered the detective, with his face close to the face of his prisoner. "Now, will you go easy as a burglar, or shall I tell these men who you are and what I *do* want you for? Shall I call out your real name or not? Shall I tell them? Quick, speak up; shall I?"

There was something so exultant – something so unnecessarily savage in the officer's face that the man he held saw that the detective knew him for what he really was, and the hands that had held his throat slipped down around his shoulders, or he would have fallen. The man's eyes opened and closed again, and he swayed weakly backward and forward, and choked as if his throat were dry and burning. Even to such a hardened connoisseur in crime as Gallegher, who stood closely by, drinking it in, there was something so abject in the man's terror that he regarded him with what was almost a touch of pity.

"For God's sake," Hade begged, "let me go. Come with me to my room and I'll give you half the money. I'll divide with you fairly. We can both get away. There's a fortune for both of us there. We both can get away. You'll be rich for life. Do you understand – for life!"

But the detective, to his credit, only shut his lips the tighter.

"That's enough," he whispered, in return. "That's more than I expected. You've sentenced yourself already. Come!"

Two officers in uniform barred their exit at the door, but Hefflefinger smiled easily and showed his badge.

"One of Byrnes's men," he said, in explanation; "came over expressly to take this chap. He's a burglar; 'Arlie' Lane, *alias* Carleton. I've shown the papers to the captain. It's all regular. I'm just going to get his traps at the hotel and walk him over to the station. I guess we'll push right on to New York to-night."

The officers nodded and smiled their admiration for the representative of what is, perhaps, the best detective force in the world, and let him pass.

Then Hefflefinger turned and spoke to Gallegher, who still stood as watchful as a dog at his side. "I'm going to his room to get the bonds and stuff," he whispered; "then I'll march him to the station and take that train. I've done my share; don't forget yours!"

"Oh, you'll get your money right enough," said Gallegher. "And, sa-ay," he added, with the appreciative nod of an expert, "do you know, you did it rather well."

Mr. Dwyer had been writing while the raid was settling down, as he had been writing while waiting for the fight to begin. Now he walked over to where the other correspondents stood in angry conclave.

The newspaper men had informed the officers who hemmed them in that they represented the principal papers of the country, and were expostulating vigorously with the captain, who had planned the raid, and who declared they were under arrest.

"Don't be an ass, Scott," said Mr. Dwyer, who was too excited to be polite or politic. "You know our being here isn't a matter of choice. We came here on business, as you did, and you've no right to hold us."

"If we don't get our stuff on the wire at once," protested a New York man, "we'll be too late for tomorrow's paper, and—"

Captain Scott said he did not care a profanely small amount for tomorrow's paper, and that all he knew was that to the station-house the newspaper men would go. There they would have a hearing, and if the magistrate chose to let them off, that was the magistrate's business, but that his duty was to take them into custody.

"But then it will be too late, don't you understand?" shouted Mr. Dwyer. "You've got to let us go *now*, at once."

"I can't do it, Mr. Dwyer," said the captain, "and that's all there is to it. Why, haven't I just sent the president of the Junior Republican Club to the patrol-wagon, the man that put this coat on me, and do you think I can let you fellows go after that? You were all put under bonds to keep the peace not three days ago, and here you're at it – fighting like badgers. It's worth my place to let one of you off."

What Mr. Dwyer said next was so uncomplimentary to the gallant Captain Scott that that overwrought individual seized the sporting editor by the shoulder, and shoved him into the hands of two of his men.

This was more than the distinguished Mr. Dwyer could brook, and he excitedly raised his hand in resistance. But before he had time to do anything foolish his wrist was gripped by one strong, little hand, and he was conscious that another was picking the pocket of his great-coat.

He slapped his hands to his sides, and looking down, saw Gallegher standing close behind him and holding him by the wrist. Mr. Dwyer had forgotten the boy's existence, and would have spoken sharply if something in Gallegher's innocent eyes had not stopped him.

Gallegher's hand was still in that pocket, in which Mr. Dwyer had shoved his note-book filled with what he had written of Gallegher's work and Hade's final capture, and with a running descriptive account of the fight. With his eyes fixed on Mr. Dwyer, Gallegher drew it out, and with a quick movement shoved it inside his waistcoat. Mr. Dwyer gave a nod of comprehension. Then glancing at his two guardsmen, and finding that they were still interested in the wordy battle of the correspondents with their chief, and had seen nothing, he stooped and whispered to Gallegher: "The forms are locked at twenty minutes to three. If you don't get there by that time it will be of no use, but if you're on time you'll beat the town – and the country too."

Gallegher's eyes flashed significantly, and nodding his head to show he understood, started boldly on a run toward the door. But the officers who guarded it brought him to an abrupt halt, and, much to Mr. Dwyer's astonishment, drew from him what was apparently a torrent of tears.

"Let me go to me father. I want me father," the boy shrieked, hysterically. "They've 'rested father. Oh, daddy, daddy. They're a-goin' to take you to prison."

"Who is your father, sonny?" asked one of the guardians of the gate.

"Keppler's me father," sobbed Gallegher. "They're a-goin' to lock him up, and I'll never see him no more."

"Oh, yes, you will," said the officer, good-naturedly; "he's there in that first patrol-wagon. You can run over and say good-night to him, and then you'd better get to bed. This ain't no place for kids of your age."

"Thank you, sir," sniffed Gallegher, tearfully, as the two officers raised their clubs, and let him pass out into the darkness.

The yard outside was in a tumult, horses were stamping, and plunging, and backing the carriages into one another; lights were flashing from every window of what had been apparently an uninhabited house, and the voices of the prisoners were still raised in angry expostulation.

Three police patrol-wagons were moving about the yard, filled with unwilling passengers, who sat or stood, packed together like sheep, and with no protection from the sleet and rain.

Gallegher stole off into a dark corner, and watched the scene until his eyesight became familiar with the position of the land.

Then with his eyes fixed fearfully on the swinging light of a lantern with which an officer was searching among the carriages, he groped his way between horses' hoofs and behind the wheels of carriages to the cab which he had himself placed at the furthermost gate. It was still there, and the horse, as he had left it, with its head turned toward the city. Gallegher opened the big gate noiselessly, and worked nervously at the hitching strap. The knot was covered with a thin coating of ice, and it was several minutes before he could loosen it. But his teeth finally pulled it apart, and with the reins in his hands he sprang upon the wheel. And as he stood so, a shock of fear ran down his back like an electric current, his breath left him, and he stood immovable, gazing with wide eyes into the darkness.

The officer with the lantern had suddenly loomed up from behind a carriage not fifty feet distant, and was standing perfectly still, with his lantern held over his head, peering so directly toward Gallegher that the boy felt that he must see him. Gallegher stood with one foot on the hub of the wheel and with the other on the box waiting to spring. It seemed a minute before either of them moved, and then the officer took a step forward, and demanded sternly, "Who is that? What are you doing there?"

There was no time for parley then. Gallegher felt that he had been taken in the act, and that his only chance lay in open flight. He leaped up on the box, pulling out the whip as he did so, and with a quick sweep lashed the horse across the head and back. The animal sprang forward with a snort, narrowly clearing the gate-post, and plunged off into the darkness.

"Stop!" cried the officer.

So many of Gallegher's acquaintances among the 'longshoremen and mill hands had been challenged in so much the same manner that Gallegher knew what would probably follow if the challenge was disregarded. So he slipped from his seat to the footboard below, and ducked his head.

The three reports of a pistol, which rang out briskly from behind him, proved that his early training had given him a valuable fund of useful miscellaneous knowledge.

"Don't you be scared," he said, reassuringly, to the horse; "he's firing in the air."

The pistol-shots were answered by the impatient clangor of a patrol-wagon's gong, and glancing over his shoulder Gallegher saw its red and green lanterns tossing from side to side and looking in the darkness like the side-lights of a yacht plunging forward in a storm.

"I hadn't bargained to race you against no patrol-wagons," said Gallegher to his animal; "but if they want a race, we'll give them a tough tussle for it, won't we?"

Philadelphia, lying four miles to the south, sent up a faint yellow glow to the sky. It seemed very far away, and Gallegher's braggadocio grew cold within him at the loneliness of his adventure and the thought of the long ride before him.

It was still bitterly cold.

The rain and sleet beat through his clothes, and struck his skin with a sharp chilling touch that set him trembling.

Even the thought of the overweighted patrol-wagon probably sticking in the mud some safe distance in the rear, failed to cheer him, and the excitement that had so far made him callous to the cold died out and left him weaker and nervous.

But his horse was chilled with the long standing, and now leaped eagerly forward, only too willing to warm the half-frozen blood in its veins.

"You're a good beast," said Gallegher, plaintively. "You've got more nerve than me. Don't you go back on me now. Mr. Dwyer says we've got to beat the town." Gallegher had no idea what time it was as he rode through the night, but he knew he would be able to find out from a big clock over a manufactory at a point nearly three-quarters of the distance from Keppler's to the goal.

He was still in the open country and driving recklessly, for he knew the best part of his ride must be made outside the city limits.

He raced between desolate-looking corn-fields with bare stalks and patches of muddy earth rising above the thin covering of snow, truck farms and brick-yards fell behind him on either side. It was very lonely work, and once or twice the dogs ran yelping to the gates and barked after him.

Part of his way lay parallel with the railroad tracks, and he drove for some time beside long lines of freight and coal cars as they stood resting for the night. The fantastic Queen Anne suburban stations were dark and deserted, but in one or two of the block-towers he could see the operators writing at their desks, and the sight in some way comforted him.

Once he thought of stopping to get out the blanket in which he had wrapped himself on the first trip, but he feared to spare the time, and drove on with his teeth chattering and his shoulders shaking with the cold.

He welcomed the first solitary row of darkened houses with a faint cheer of recognition. The scattered lamp-posts lightened his spirits, and even the badly paved streets rang under the beats of his horse's feet like music. Great mills and manufactories, with only a night-watchman's light in the lowest of their many stories, began to take the place of the gloomy farmhouses and gaunt trees that had startled him with their grotesque shapes. He had been driving nearly an hour, he calculated, and in that time the rain had changed to a wet snow, that fell heavily and clung to whatever it touched. He passed block after block of trim workmen's houses, as still and silent as the sleepers within them, and at last he turned the horse's head into Broad Street, the city's great thoroughfare, that stretches from its one end to the other and cuts it evenly in two.

He was driving noiselessly over the snow and slush in the street, with his thoughts bent only on the clock-face he wished so much to see, when a hoarse voice challenged him from the sidewalk. "Hey, you, stop there, hold up!" said the voice.

Gallegher turned his head, and though he saw that the voice came from under a policeman's helmet, his only answer was to hit his horse sharply over the head with his whip and to urge it into a gallop.

This, on his part, was followed by a sharp, shrill whistle from the policeman. Another whistle answered it from a street-corner one block ahead of him. "Whoa," said Gallegher, pulling on the reins. "There's one too many of them," he added, in apologetic explanation. The horse stopped, and stood, breathing heavily, with great clouds of steam rising from its flanks.

"Why in hell didn't you stop when I told you to?" demanded the voice, now close at the cab's side.

"I didn't hear you," returned Gallegher, sweetly. "But I heard you whistle, and I heard your partner whistle, and I thought maybe it was me you wanted to speak to, so I just stopped."

"You heard me well enough. Why aren't your lights lit?" demanded the voice.

"Should I have 'em lit?" asked Gallegher, bending over and regarding them with sudden interest.

"You know you should, and if you don't, you've no right to be driving that cab. I don't believe you're the regular driver, anyway. Where'd you get it?"

"It ain't my cab, of course," said Gallegher, with an easy laugh. "It's Luke McGovern's. He left it outside Cronin's while he went in to get a drink, and he took too much, and me father told me to drive it round to the stable for him. I'm Cronin's son. McGovern ain't in no condition to drive. You can see yourself how he's been misusing the horse. He puts it up at Bachman's livery stable, and I was just going around there now."

Gallegher's knowledge of the local celebrities of the district confused the zealous officer of the peace. He surveyed the boy with a steady stare that would have distressed a less skilful liar, but Gallegher only shrugged his shoulders slightly, as if from the cold, and waited with apparent indifference to what the officer would say next.

In reality his heart was beating heavily against his side, and he felt that if he was kept on a strain much longer he would give way and break down. A second snow-covered form emerged suddenly from the shadow of the houses.

"What is it, Reeder?" it asked.

"Oh, nothing much," replied the first officer. "This kid hadn't any lamps lit, so I called to him to stop and he didn't do it, so I whistled to you. It's all right, though. He's just taking it round to Bachman's. Go ahead," he added, sulkily.

"Get up!" chirped Gallegher. "Good-night," he added, over his shoulder.

Gallegher gave an hysterical little gasp of relief as he trotted away from the two policemen, and poured bitter maledictions on their heads for two meddling fools as he went.

"They might as well kill a man as scare him to death," he said, with an attempt to get back to his customary flippancy. But the effort was somewhat pitiful, and he felt guiltily conscious that a salt, warm tear was creeping slowly down his face, and that a lump that would not keep down was rising in his throat.

"'Tain't no fair thing for the whole police force to keep worrying at a little boy like me," he said, in shame-faced apology. "I'm not doing nothing wrong, and I'm half froze to death, and yet they keep a-nagging at me."

It was so cold that when the boy stamped his feet against the footboard to keep them warm, sharp pains shot up through his body, and when he beat his arms about his shoulders, as he had seen real cabmen do, the blood in his finger-tips tingled so acutely that he cried aloud with the pain.

He had often been up that late before, but he had never felt so sleepy. It was as if some one was pressing a sponge heavy with chloroform near his face, and he could not fight off the drowsiness that lay hold of him.

He saw, dimly hanging above his head, a round disc of light that seemed like a great moon, and which he finally guessed to be the clock-face for which he had been on the lookout. He had passed it before he realized this; but the fact stirred him into wakefulness again, and when his cab's wheels slipped around the City Hall corner, he remembered to look up at the other big clock-face that keeps awake over the railroad station and measures out the night.

He gave a gasp of consternation when he saw that it was half-past two, and that there was but ten minutes left to him. This, and the many electric lights and the sight of the familiar pile of buildings, startled him into a semi-consciousness of where he was and how great was the necessity for haste.

He rose in his seat and called on the horse, and urged it into a reckless gallop over the slippery asphalt. He considered nothing else but speed, and looking neither to the left nor right dashed off down Broad Street into Chestnut, where his course lay straight away to the office, now only seven blocks distant.

Gallegher never knew how it began, but he was suddenly assaulted by shouts on either side, his horse was thrown back on its haunches, and he found two men in cabmen's livery hanging at its head, and patting its sides, and calling it by name. And the other cabmen who have their stand at the corner were swarming about the carriage, all of them talking and swearing at once, and gesticulating wildly with their whips.

They said they knew the cab was McGovern's and they wanted to know where he was, and why he wasn't on it; they wanted to know where Gallegher had stolen it, and why he had been such a fool as to drive it into the arms of its owner's friends; they said that it was about time that a cab-driver could get off his box to take a drink without having his cab run away with, and some of them called loudly for a policeman to take the young thief in charge.

Gallegher felt as if he had been suddenly dragged into consciousness out of a bad dream, and stood for a second like a half-awakened somnambulist.

They had stopped the cab under an electric light, and its glare shone coldly down upon the trampled snow and the faces of the men around him.

Gallegher bent forward, and lashed savagely at the horse with his whip.

"Let me go," he shouted, as he tugged impotently at the reins. "Let me go, I tell you. I haven't stole no cab, and you've got no right to stop me. I only want to take it to the *Press* office," he begged. "They'll send it back to you all right. They'll pay you for the trip. I'm not running away with it. The driver's got the collar – he's 'rested – and I'm only a-going to the *Press* office. Do you hear me?" he cried, his voice rising and breaking in a shriek of passion and disappointment. "I tell you to let go those reins. Let me go, or I'll kill you. Do you hear me? I'll kill you." And leaning forward, the boy struck savagely with his long whip at the faces of the men about the horse's head.

Some one in the crowd reached up and caught him by the ankles, and with a quick jerk pulled him off the box, and threw him on to the street. But he was up on his knees in a moment, and caught at the man's hand.

"Don't let them stop me, mister," he cried, "please let me go. I didn't steal the cab, sir. S'help me, I didn't. I'm telling you the truth. Take me to the *Press* office, and they'll prove it to you. They'll pay you anything you ask 'em. It's only such a little ways now, and I've come so far, sir. Please don't let them stop me," he sobbed, clasping the man about the knees. "For Heaven's sake, mister, let me go!"

* * *

The managing editor of the *Press* took up the india-rubber speaking-tube at his side, and answered, "Not yet" to an inquiry the night editor had already put to him five times within the last twenty minutes.

Then he snapped the metal top of the tube impatiently, and went upstairs. As he passed the door of the local room, he noticed that the reporters had not gone home, but were sitting about on the tables and chairs, waiting. They looked up inquiringly as he passed, and the city editor asked, "Any news yet?" and the managing editor shook his head.

The compositors were standing idle in the composing-room, and their foreman was talking with the night editor.

"Well?" said that gentleman, tentatively.

"Well," returned the managing editor, "I don't think we can wait; do you?"

"It's a half-hour after time now," said the night editor, "and we'll miss the suburban trains if we hold the paper back any longer. We can't afford to wait for a purely hypothetical story. The chances are all against the fight's having taken place or this Hade's having been arrested."

"But if we're beaten on it—" suggested the chief. "But I don't think that is possible. If there were any story to print, Dwyer would have had it here before now."

The managing editor looked steadily down at the floor.

"Very well," he said, slowly, "we won't wait any longer. Go ahead," he added, turning to the foreman with a sigh of reluctance. The foreman whirled himself about, and began to give his orders; but the two editors still looked at each other doubtfully.

As they stood so, there came a sudden shout and the sound of people running to and fro in the reportorial rooms below. There was the tramp of many footsteps on the stairs, and above the confusion they heard the voice of the city editor telling some one to "run to Madden's and get some brandy, quick."

No one in the composing-room said anything; but those compositors who had started to go home began slipping off their overcoats, and every one stood with his eyes fixed on the door.

It was kicked open from the outside, and in the doorway stood a cab-driver and the city editor, supporting between them a pitiful little figure of a boy, wet and miserable, and with the snow melting on his clothes and running in little pools to the floor. "Why, it's Gallegher," said the night editor, in a tone of the keenest disappointment.

Gallegher shook himself free from his supporters, and took an unsteady step forward, his fingers fumbling stiffly with the buttons of his waistcoat.

"Mr. Dwyer, sir," he began faintly, with his eyes fixed fearfully on the managing editor, "he got arrested – and I couldn't get here no sooner, 'cause they kept a-stopping me, and they took me cab from under me – but—" he pulled the note-book from his breast and held it out with its covers damp and limp from the rain, "but we got Hade, and here's Mr. Dwyer's copy."

And then he asked, with a queer note in his voice, partly of dread and partly of hope, " Am I in time, sir?"

The managing editor took the book, and tossed it to the foreman, who ripped out its leaves and dealt them out to his men as rapidly as a gambler deals out cards.

Then the managing editor stooped and picked Gallegher up in his arms, and, sitting down, began to unlace his wet and muddy shoes.

Gallegher made a faint effort to resist this degradation of the managerial dignity; but his protest was a very feeble one, and his head fell back heavily on the managing editor's shoulder.

To Gallegher the incandescent lights began to whirl about in circles, and to burn in different colors; the faces of the reporters kneeling before him and chafing his hands and feet grew dim and unfamiliar, and the roar and rumble of the great presses in the basement sounded far away, like the murmur of the sea.

And then the place and the circumstances of it came back to him again sharply and with sudden vividness.

Gallegher looked up, with a faint smile, into the managing editor's face. "You won't turn me off for running away, will you?" he whispered.

The managing editor did not answer immediately. His head was bent, and he was thinking, for some reason or other, of a little boy of his own, at home in bed. Then he said, quietly, "Not this time, Gallegher."

Gallegher's head sank back comfortably on the older man's shoulder, and he smiled comprehensively at the faces of the young men crowded around him. "You hadn't ought to," he said, with a touch of his old impudence, "'cause – I beat the town."

The Convict's Return

Charles Dickens

WHEN I FIRST settled in this village, which is now just five-and-twenty years ago, the most notorious person among my parishioners was a man of the name of Edmunds, who leased a small farm near this spot. He was a morose, savage-hearted, bad man; idle and dissolute in his habits; cruel and ferocious in his disposition. Beyond the few lazy and reckless vagabonds with whom he sauntered away his time in the fields, or sotted in the ale-house, he had not a single friend or acquaintance; no one cared to speak to the man whom many feared, and every one detested – and Edmunds was shunned by all.

This man had a wife and one son, who, when I first came here, was about twelve years old. Of the acuteness of that woman's sufferings, of the gentle and enduring manner in which she bore them, of the agony of solicitude with which she reared that boy, no one can form an adequate conception. Heaven forgive me the supposition, if it be an uncharitable one, but I do firmly and in my soul believe, that the man systematically tried for many years to break her heart; but she bore it all for her child's sake, and, however strange it may seem to many, for his father's too; for brute as he was, and cruelly as he had treated her, she had loved him once; and the recollection of what he had been to her, awakened feelings of forbearance and meekness under suffering in her bosom, to which all God's creatures, but women, are strangers.

They were poor – they could not be otherwise when the man pursued such courses; but the woman's unceasing and unwearied exertions, early and late, morning, noon, and night, kept them above actual want. These exertions were but ill repaid. People who passed the spot in the evening – sometimes at a late hour of the night – reported that they had heard the moans and sobs of a woman in distress, and the sound of blows; and more than once, when it was past midnight, the boy knocked softly at the door of a neighbour's house, whither he had been sent, to escape the drunken fury of his unnatural father.

During the whole of this time, and when the poor creature often bore about her marks of ill-usage and violence which she could not wholly conceal, she was a constant attendant at our little church. Regularly every Sunday, morning and afternoon, she occupied the same seat with the boy at her side; and though they were both poorly dressed – much more so than many of their neighbours who were in a lower station – they were always neat and clean. Every one had a friendly nod and a kind word for "poor Mrs. Edmunds"; and sometimes, when she stopped to exchange a few words with a neighbour at the conclusion of the service in the little row of elm-trees which leads to the church porch, or lingered behind to gaze with a mother's pride and fondness upon her healthy boy, as he sported before her with some little companions, her careworn face would lighten up with an expression of heartfelt gratitude; and she would look, if not cheerful and happy, at least tranquil and contented.

Five or six years passed away; the boy had become a robust and well-grown youth. The time that had strengthened the child's slight frame and knit his weak limbs into the strength of manhood had bowed his mother's form, and enfeebled her steps; but the arm that should have supported her was no longer locked in hers; the face that should have cheered her, no more looked upon her own. She occupied her old seat, but there was a vacant one beside her. The Bible was kept as carefully as ever, the places were found and folded down as they used to be: but there was no one to read it with her; and the tears fell thick and fast upon the book, and blotted the words from her eyes. Neighbours were as kind as they were wont to be of old, but she shunned their greetings with averted head. There was no lingering among the old elm-trees now – no cheering anticipations of happiness yet in store. The desolate woman drew her bonnet closer over her face, and walked hurriedly away.

Shall I tell you that the young man, who, looking back to the earliest of his childhood's days to which memory and consciousness extended, and carrying his recollection down to that moment, could remember nothing which was not in some way connected with a long series of voluntary privations suffered by his mother for his sake, with ill-usage, and insult, and violence, and all endured for him – shall I tell you, that he, with a reckless disregard for her breaking heart, and a sullen, wilful forgetfulness of all she had done and borne for him, had linked himself with depraved and abandoned men, and was madly pursuing a headlong career, which must bring death to him, and shame to her? Alas for human nature! You have anticipated it long since.

The measure of the unhappy woman's misery and misfortune was about to be completed. Numerous offences had been committed in the neighbourhood; the perpetrators remained undiscovered, and their boldness increased. A robbery of a daring and aggravated nature occasioned a vigilance of pursuit, and a strictness of search, they had not calculated on. Young Edmunds was suspected, with three companions. He was apprehended – committed – tried – condemned – to die.

The wild and piercing shriek from a woman's voice, which resounded through the court when the solemn sentence was pronounced, rings in my ears at this moment. That cry struck a terror to the culprit's heart, which trial, condemnation – the approach of death itself, had failed to awaken. The lips which had been compressed in dogged sullenness throughout, quivered and parted involuntarily; the face turned ashy pale as the cold perspiration broke forth from every pore; the sturdy limbs of the felon trembled, and he staggered in the dock.

In the first transports of her mental anguish, the suffering mother threw herself on her knees at my feet, and fervently sought the Almighty Being who had hitherto supported her in all her troubles to release her from a world of woe and misery, and to spare the life of her only child. A burst of grief, and a violent struggle, such as I hope I may never have to witness again, succeeded. I knew that her heart was breaking from that hour; but I never once heard complaint or murmur escape her lips.

It was a piteous spectacle to see that woman in the prison-yard from day to day, eagerly and fervently attempting, by affection and entreaty, to soften the hard heart of her obdurate son. It was in vain. He remained moody, obstinate, and unmoved. Not even the unlooked-for commutation of his sentence to transportation for fourteen years, softened for an instant the sullen hardihood of his demeanour.

But the spirit of resignation and endurance that had so long upheld her, was unable to contend against bodily weakness and infirmity. She fell sick. She dragged her tottering limbs from the bed to visit her son once more, but her strength failed her, and she sank powerless on the ground.

And now the boasted coldness and indifference of the young man were tested indeed; and the retribution that fell heavily upon him nearly drove him mad. A day passed away and his mother was not there; another flew by, and she came not near him; a third evening arrived, and yet he had not seen her – , and in four-and-twenty hours he was to be separated from her, perhaps for ever. Oh! how the long-forgotten thoughts of former days rushed upon his mind, as he almost ran up and down the narrow yard – as if intelligence would arrive the sooner for his hurrying – and how bitterly a sense of his helplessness and desolation rushed upon him, when he heard the truth! His mother, the only parent he had ever known, lay ill – it might be, dying – within one mile of the ground he stood on; were he free and unfettered, a few minutes would place him by her side. He rushed to the gate, and grasping the iron rails with the energy of desperation, shook it till it rang again, and threw himself against the thick wall as if to force a passage through the stone; but the strong building mocked his feeble efforts, and he beat his hands together and wept like a child.

I bore the mother's forgiveness and blessing to her son in prison; and I carried the solemn assurance of repentance, and his fervent supplication for pardon, to her sick-bed. I heard, with pity and compassion, the repentant man devise a thousand little plans for her comfort and support when he returned; but I knew that many months before he could reach his place of destination, his mother would be no longer of this world.

He was removed by night. A few weeks afterwards the poor woman's soul took its flight, I confidently hope, and solemnly believe, to a place of eternal happiness and rest. I performed the burial service over her remains. She lies in our little churchyard. There is no stone at her grave's head. Her sorrows were known to man; her virtues to God.

It had been arranged previously to the convict's departure, that he should write to his mother as soon as he could obtain permission, and that the letter should be addressed to me. The father had positively refused to see his son from the moment of his apprehension; and it was a matter of indifference to him whether he lived or died. Many years passed over without any intelligence of him; and when more than half his term of transportation had expired, and I had received no letter, I concluded him to be dead, as, indeed, I almost hoped he might be.

Edmunds, however, had been sent a considerable distance up the country on his arrival at the settlement; and to this circumstance, perhaps, may be attributed the fact, that though several letters were despatched, none of them ever reached my hands. He remained in the same place during the whole fourteen years. At the expiration of the term, steadily adhering to his old resolution and the pledge he gave his mother, he made his way back to England amidst innumerable difficulties, and returned, on foot, to his native place.

On a fine Sunday evening, in the month of August, John Edmunds set foot in the village he had left with shame and disgrace seventeen years before. His nearest way lay through the churchyard. The man's heart swelled as he crossed the stile. The tall old elms, through whose branches the declining sun cast here and there a rich ray of light upon the shady part, awakened the associations of his earliest days. He pictured himself as he was then, clinging to his mother's hand, and walking peacefully to church. He remembered how he used to look up into her pale face; and how her eyes would sometimes fill with tears as she gazed upon his features – tears which fell hot upon his forehead as she stooped to kiss him, and made him weep too, although he little knew then what bitter tears hers were. He thought how often he had run merrily down that path with some childish playfellow, looking back, ever and again, to catch his mother's smile, or hear her gentle voice; and then a veil seemed lifted from his memory, and words of kindness unrequited, and warnings despised, and promises broken, thronged upon his recollection till his heart failed him, and he could bear it no longer.

He entered the church. The evening service was concluded and the congregation had dispersed, but it was not yet closed. His steps echoed through the low building with a hollow sound, and he almost feared to be alone, it was so still and quiet. He looked round him. Nothing was changed. The place seemed smaller than it used to be; but there were the old monuments on which he had gazed with childish awe a thousand times; the little pulpit with its faded cushion; the Communion table before which he had so often repeated the Commandments he had reverenced as a child, and forgotten as a man. He approached the old seat; it looked cold and desolate. The cushion had been removed, and the Bible was not there. Perhaps his mother now occupied a poorer seat, or possibly she had grown infirm and could not reach the church alone. He dared not think of what he feared. A cold feeling crept over him, and he trembled violently as he turned away. 'An old man entered the porch just as he reached it. Edmunds started back, for he knew him well; many a time he had watched him digging graves in the churchyard. What would he say to the returned convict?

The old man raised his eyes to the stranger's face, bade him "good-evening," and walked slowly on. He had forgotten him.

He walked down the hill, and through the village. The weather was warm, and the people were sitting at their doors, or strolling in their little gardens as he passed, enjoying the serenity of the evening, and their rest from labour. Many a look was turned towards him, and many a doubtful glance he cast on either side to see whether any knew and shunned him. There were strange faces in almost every house; in some he recognised the burly form of some old schoolfellow – a boy when he last saw him – surrounded by a troop of merry children; in others he saw, seated in an easy-chair at a cottage door, a feeble and infirm old man, whom he only remembered as a hale and hearty labourer; but they had all forgotten him, and he passed on unknown.

The last soft light of the setting sun had fallen on the earth, casting a rich glow on the yellow corn sheaves, and lengthening the shadows of the orchard trees, as he stood before the old house – the home of his infancy – to which his heart had yearned with an intensity of affection not to be described, through long and weary years of captivity and sorrow. The paling was low, though he well remembered the time that it had seemed a high wall to him; and he looked over into the old garden. There were more seeds and gayer flowers than there used to be, but there were the old trees still – the very tree under which he had lain a thousand times when tired of playing in the sun, and felt the soft, mild sleep of happy boyhood steal gently upon him. There were voices within the house. He listened, but they fell strangely upon his ear; he knew them not. They were merry too; and he well knew that his poor old mother could not be cheerful, and he away. The door opened, and a group of little children bounded out, shouting and romping. The father, with a little boy in his arms, appeared at the door, and they crowded round him, clapping their tiny hands, and dragging him out, to join their joyous sports. The convict thought on the many times he had shrunk from his father's sight in that very place. He remembered how often he had buried his trembling head beneath the bedclothes, and heard the harsh word, and the hard stripe, and his mother's wailing; and though the man sobbed aloud with agony of mind as he left the spot, his fist was clenched, and his teeth were set, in a fierce and deadly passion.

And such was the return to which he had looked through the weary perspective of many years, and for which he had undergone so much suffering! No face of welcome, no look of forgiveness, no house to receive, no hand to help him – and this too in the old village. What was his loneliness in the wild, thick woods, where man was never seen, to this!

He felt that in the distant land of his bondage and infamy, he had thought of his native place as it was when he left it; and not as it would be when he returned. The sad reality struck coldly at his heart, and his spirit sank within him. He had not courage to make inquiries, or to present himself to the only person who was likely to receive him with kindness and compassion. He walked slowly on; and shunning the roadside like a guilty man, turned into a meadow he well remembered; and covering his face with his hands, threw himself upon the grass.

He had not observed that a man was lying on the bank beside him; his garments rustled as he turned round to steal a look at the new-comer; and Edmunds raised his head.

The man had moved into a sitting posture. His body was much bent, and his face was wrinkled and yellow. His dress denoted him an inmate of the workhouse: he had the appearance of being very old, but it looked more the effect of dissipation or disease, than the length of years. He was staring hard at the stranger, and though his eyes were lustreless and heavy at first, they appeared to glow with an unnatural and alarmed expression after they had been fixed upon him for a short time, until they seemed to be starting from their sockets. Edmunds gradually raised himself to his knees, and looked more and more earnestly on the old man's face. They gazed upon each other in silence.

The old man was ghastly pale. He shuddered and tottered to his feet. Edmunds sprang to his. He stepped back a pace or two. Edmunds advanced.

"Let me hear you speak," said the convict, in a thick, broken voice.

"Stand off!" cried the old man, with a dreadful oath. The convict drew closer to him.

"Stand off!" shrieked the old man. Furious with terror, he raised his stick, and struck Edmunds a heavy blow across the face.

"Father – devil!" murmured the convict between his set teeth. He rushed wildly forward, and clenched the old man by the throat – but he was his father; and his arm fell powerless by his side.

The old man uttered a loud yell which rang through the lonely fields like the howl of an evil spirit. His face turned black, the gore rushed from his mouth and nose, and dyed the grass a deep, dark red, as he staggered and fell. He had ruptured a blood-vessel, and he was a dead man before his son could raise him.

* * *

In that corner of the churchyard of which I have before spoken, there lies buried a man who was in my employment for three years after this event, and who was truly contrite, penitent, and humbled, if ever man was. No one save myself knew in that man's lifetime who he was, or whence he came – it was John Edmunds, the returned convict.

The Old Man's Tale About the Queer Client

Charles Dickens

IT MATTERS little where, or how, I picked up this brief history. If I were to relate it in the order in which it reached me, I should commence in the middle, and when I had arrived at the conclusion, go back for a beginning. It is enough for me to say that some of its circumstances passed before my own eyes; for the remainder I know them to have happened, and there are some persons yet living, who will remember them but too well.

In the Borough High Street, near St. George's Church, and on the same side of the way, stands, as most people know, the smallest of our debtors' prisons, the Marshalsea. Although in later times it has been a very different place from the sink of filth and dirt it once was, even its improved condition holds out but little temptation to the extravagant, or consolation to the improvident. The condemned felon has as good a yard for air and exercise in Newgate, as the insolvent debtor in the Marshalsea Prison. [Better. But this is past, in a better age, and the prison exists no longer.]

It may be my fancy, or it may be that I cannot separate the place from the old recollections associated with it, but this part of London I cannot bear. The street is broad, the shops are spacious, the noise of passing vehicles, the footsteps of a perpetual stream of people – all the busy sounds of traffic, resound in it from morn to midnight; but the streets around are mean and close; poverty and debauchery lie festering in the crowded alleys; want and misfortune are pent up in the narrow prison; an air of gloom and dreariness seems, in my eyes at least, to hang about the scene, and to impart to it a squalid and sickly hue.

Many eyes, that have long since been closed in the grave, have looked round upon that scene lightly enough, when entering the gate of the old Marshalsea Prison for the first time; for despair seldom comes with the first severe shock of misfortune. A man has confidence in untried friends, he remembers the many offers of service so freely made by his boon companions when he wanted them not; he has hope – the hope of happy inexperience – and however he may bend beneath the first shock, it springs up in his bosom, and flourishes there for a brief space, until it droops beneath the blight of disappointment and neglect. How soon have those same eyes, deeply sunken in the head, glared from faces wasted with famine, and sallow from confinement, in days when it was no figure of speech to say that debtors rotted in prison, with no hope of release, and no prospect of liberty! The atrocity in its full extent no longer exists, but there is enough of it left to give rise to occurrences that make the heart bleed.

Twenty years ago, that pavement was worn with the footsteps of a mother and child, who, day by day, so surely as the morning came, presented themselves at the prison gate; often after a night of restless misery and anxious thoughts, were they there, a full hour too soon, and then the young mother turning meekly away, would lead the child to the old bridge, and raising him in her arms to show him the glistening water, tinted with the light of the morning's sun, and stirring with all the bustling preparations for business and pleasure that the river presented at that early hour, endeavour to interest his thoughts in the objects before him. But she would quickly set him down, and hiding her face in her shawl, give vent to the tears that blinded her; for no expression of interest or amusement lighted up his thin and sickly face. His recollections were few enough, but they were all of one kind – all connected with the poverty and misery of his parents. Hour after hour had he sat on his mother's knee, and with childish sympathy watched the tears that stole down her face, and then crept quietly away into some dark corner, and sobbed himself to sleep. The hard realities of the world, with many of its worst privations – hunger and thirst, and cold and want – had all come home to him, from the first dawnings of reason; and though the form of childhood was there, its light heart, its merry laugh, and sparkling eyes were wanting.

The father and mother looked on upon this, and upon each other, with thoughts of agony they dared not breathe in words. The healthy, strong-made man, who could have borne almost any fatigue of active exertion, was wasting beneath the close confinement and unhealthy atmosphere of a crowded prison. The slight and delicate woman was sinking beneath the combined effects of bodily and mental illness. The child's young heart was breaking.

Winter came, and with it weeks of cold and heavy rain. The poor girl had removed to a wretched apartment close to the spot of her husband's imprisonment; and though the change had been rendered necessary by their increasing poverty, she was happier now, for she was nearer him. For two months, she and her little companion watched the opening of the gate as usual. One day she failed to come, for the first time. Another morning arrived, and she came alone. The child was dead.

They little know, who coldly talk of the poor man's bereavements, as a happy release from pain to the departed, and a merciful relief from expense to the survivor – they little know, I say, what the agony of those bereavements is. A silent look of affection and regard when all other eyes are turned coldly away – the consciousness that we possess the sympathy and affection of one being when all others have deserted us – is a hold, a stay, a comfort, in the deepest affliction, which no wealth could purchase, or power bestow. The child had sat at his parents' feet for hours together, with his little hands patiently folded in each other, and his thin wan face raised towards them. They had seen him pine away, from day to day; and though his brief existence had been a joyless one, and he was now removed to that peace and rest which, child as he was, he had never known in this world, they were his parents, and his loss sank deep into their souls.

It was plain to those who looked upon the mother's altered face, that death must soon close the scene of her adversity and trial. Her husband's fellow-prisoners shrank from obtruding on his grief and misery, and left to himself alone, the small room he had previously occupied in common with two companions. She shared it with him; and lingering on without pain, but without hope, her life ebbed slowly away.

She had fainted one evening in her husband's arms, and he had borne her to the open window, to revive her with the air, when the light of the moon falling full upon her face, showed him a change upon her features, which made him stagger beneath her weight, like a helpless infant.

"Set me down, George," she said faintly. He did so, and seating himself beside her, covered his face with his hands, and burst into tears.

"It is very hard to leave you, George," she said; "but it is God's will, and you must bear it for my sake. Oh! how I thank Him for having taken our boy! He is happy, and in heaven now. What would he have done here, without his mother!"

"You shall not die, Mary, you shall not die;" said the husband, starting up. He paced hurriedly to and fro, striking his head with his clenched fists; then reseating himself beside her, and supporting her in his arms, added more calmly, "Rouse yourself, my dear girl. Pray, pray do. You will revive yet."

"Never again, George; never again," said the dying woman. "Let them lay me by my poor boy now, but promise me, that if ever you leave this dreadful place, and should grow rich, you will have us removed to some quiet country churchyard, a long, long way off – very far from here – where we can rest in peace. Dear George, promise me you will."

"I do, I do," said the man, throwing himself passionately on his knees before her. "Speak to me, Mary, another word; one look – but one!"

He ceased to speak: for the arm that clasped his neck grew stiff and heavy. A deep sigh escaped from the wasted form before him; the lips moved, and a smile played upon the face; but the lips were pallid, and the smile faded into a rigid and ghastly stare. He was alone in the world.

That night, in the silence and desolation of his miserable room, the wretched man knelt down by the dead body of his wife, and called on God to witness a terrible oath, that from that hour, he devoted himself to revenge her death and that of his child; that thenceforth to the last moment of his life, his whole energies should be directed to this one object; that his revenge should be protracted and terrible; that his hatred should be undying and inextinguishable; and should hunt its object through the world.

The deepest despair, and passion scarcely human, had made such fierce ravages on his face and form, in that one night, that his companions in misfortune shrank affrighted from him as he passed by. His eyes were bloodshot and heavy, his face a deadly white, and his body bent as if with age. He had bitten his under lip nearly through in the violence of his mental suffering, and the blood which had flowed from the wound had trickled down his chin, and stained his shirt and neckerchief. No tear, or sound of complaint escaped him; but the unsettled look, and disordered haste with which he paced up and down the yard, denoted the fever which was burning within.

It was necessary that his wife's body should be removed from the prison, without delay. He received the communication with perfect calmness, and acquiesced in its propriety. Nearly all the inmates of the prison had assembled to witness its removal; they fell back on either side when the widower appeared; he walked hurriedly forward, and stationed himself, alone, in a little railed area close to the lodge gate, from whence the crowd, with an instinctive feeling of delicacy, had retired. The rude coffin was borne slowly forward on men's shoulders. A dead silence pervaded the throng, broken only by the audible lamentations of the women, and the shuffling steps of the bearers on the stone pavement. They reached the spot where the bereaved husband stood: and stopped. He laid his hand upon the coffin, and mechanically adjusting the pall with which it was covered, motioned them onward. The turnkeys in the prison lobby took off their hats as it passed through, and in another moment the heavy gate closed behind it. He looked vacantly upon the crowd, and fell heavily to the ground.

Although for many weeks after this, he was watched, night and day, in the wildest ravings of fever, neither the consciousness of his loss, nor the recollection of the vow he had made, ever left him for a moment. Scenes changed before his eyes, place succeeded place, and event followed event, in all the hurry of delirium; but they were all connected in some way with the great object of his mind. He was sailing over a boundless expanse of sea, with a blood-red sky above, and the angry waters, lashed into fury beneath, boiling and eddying up, on every side. There was another vessel before them, toiling and labouring in the howling storm; her canvas fluttering in ribbons from the mast, and her deck thronged with figures who were lashed to the sides, over which huge waves every instant burst, sweeping away some devoted creatures into the foaming sea. Onward they bore, amidst the roaring mass of water, with a speed and force which nothing could resist; and striking the stem of the foremost vessel, crushed her beneath their keel. From the huge whirlpool which the sinking wreck occasioned, arose a shriek so loud and shrill – the death-cry of a hundred drowning creatures, blended into one fierce yell – that it rung far above the war-cry of the elements, and echoed, and re-echoed till it seemed to pierce air, sky, and ocean. But what was that – that old gray head that rose above the water's surface, and with looks of agony, and screams for aid, buffeted with the waves! One look, and he had sprung from the vessel's side, and with vigorous strokes was swimming towards it. He reached it; he was close upon it. They were *his* features. The old man saw him coming, and vainly strove to elude his grasp. But he clasped him tight, and dragged him beneath the water. Down, down with him, fifty fathoms down; his struggles grew fainter and fainter, until they wholly ceased. He was dead; he had killed him, and had kept his oath.

He was traversing the scorching sands of a mighty desert, barefoot and alone. The sand choked and blinded him; its fine thin grains entered the very pores of his skin, and irritated him almost to madness. Gigantic masses of the same material, carried forward by the wind, and shone through by the burning sun, stalked in the distance like pillars of living fire. The bones of men, who had perished in the dreary waste, lay scattered at his feet; a fearful light fell on everything around; so far as the eye could reach, nothing but objects of dread and horror presented themselves. Vainly striving to utter a cry of terror, with his tongue cleaving to his mouth, he rushed madly forward. Armed with supernatural strength, he waded through the sand, until, exhausted with fatigue and thirst, he fell senseless on the earth. What fragrant coolness revived him; what gushing sound was that? Water! It was indeed a well; and the clear fresh stream was running at his feet. He drank deeply of it, and throwing his aching limbs upon the bank, sank into a delicious trance. The sound of approaching footsteps roused him. An old gray-headed man tottered forward to slake his burning thirst. It was *he* again! He wound his arms round the old man's body, and held him back. He struggled, and shrieked for water – for but one drop of water to save his life! But he held the old man firmly, and watched his agonies with greedy eyes; and when his lifeless head fell forward on his bosom, he rolled the corpse from him with his feet.

When the fever left him, and consciousness returned, he awoke to find himself rich and free, to hear that the parent who would have let him die in jail – *would*! who *had* let those who were far dearer to him than his own existence die of want, and sickness of heart that medicine cannot cure – had been found dead in his bed of down. He had had all the heart to leave his son a beggar, but proud even of his health and strength, had put off the act till it was too late, and now might gnash his teeth in the other world, at the thought of the wealth his remissness had left him. He awoke to this, and he awoke to more. To recollect the purpose for which he lived, and to remember that his enemy was his wife's own father – the man who had cast him into prison, and who, when his daughter and her child sued at his feet for mercy, had spurned them from his door. Oh, how he cursed the weakness that prevented him from being up, and active, in his scheme of vengeance!

He caused himself to be carried from the scene of his loss and misery, and conveyed to a quiet residence on the sea-coast; not in the hope of recovering his peace of mind or happiness, for both were fled for ever; but to restore his prostrate energies, and meditate on his darling object. And here, some evil spirit cast in his way the opportunity for his first, most horrible revenge.

It was summer-time; and wrapped in his gloomy thoughts, he would issue from his solitary lodgings early in the evening, and wandering along a narrow path beneath the cliffs, to a wild and lonely spot that had struck his fancy in his ramblings, seat himself on some fallen fragment of the rock, and burying his face in his hands, remain there for hours – sometimes until night had completely closed in, and the long shadows of the frowning cliffs above his head cast a thick, black darkness on every object near him.

He was seated here, one calm evening, in his old position, now and then raising his head to watch the flight of a sea-gull, or carry his eye along the glorious crimson path, which, commencing in the middle of the ocean, seemed to lead to its very verge where the sun was setting, when the profound stillness of the spot was broken by a loud cry for help; he listened, doubtful of his having heard aright, when the cry was repeated with even greater vehemence than before, and, starting to his feet, he hastened in the direction whence it proceeded.

The tale told itself at once: some scattered garments lay on the beach; a human head was just visible above the waves at a little distance from the shore; and an old man, wringing his hands in agony, was running to and fro, shrieking for assistance. The invalid, whose strength was now sufficiently restored, threw off his coat, and rushed towards the sea, with the intention of plunging in, and dragging the drowning man ashore.

"Hasten here, Sir, in God's name; help, help, sir, for the love of Heaven. He is my son, Sir, my only son!" said the old man frantically, as he advanced to meet him. "My only son, Sir, and he is dying before his father's eyes!"

At the first word the old man uttered, the stranger checked himself in his career, and, folding his arms, stood perfectly motionless.

"Great God!" exclaimed the old man, recoiling, "Heyling!"

The stranger smiled, and was silent.

"Heyling!" said the old man wildly; "my boy, Heyling, my dear boy, look, look!" Gasping for breath, the miserable father pointed to the spot where the young man was struggling for life.

"Hark!" said the old man. "He cries once more. He is alive yet. Heyling, save him, save him!"

The stranger smiled again, and remained immovable as a statue.

"I have wronged you," shrieked the old man, falling on his knees, and clasping his hands together. "Be revenged; take my all, my life; cast me into the water at your feet, and, if human nature can repress a struggle, I will die, without stirring hand or foot. Do it, Heyling, do it, but save my boy; he is so young, Heyling, so young to die!"

"Listen," said the stranger, grasping the old man fiercely by the wrist; "I will have life for life, and here is one. *My* child died, before his father's eyes, a far more agonising and painful death than that young slanderer of his sister's worth is meeting while I speak. You laughed – laughed in your daughter's face, where death had already set his hand – at our sufferings, then. What think you of them now! See there, see there!"

As the stranger spoke, he pointed to the sea. A faint cry died away upon its surface; the last powerful struggle of the dying man agitated the rippling waves for a few seconds; and the spot where he had gone down into his early grave, was undistinguishable from the surrounding water.

Three years had elapsed, when a gentleman alighted from a private carriage at the door of a London attorney, then well known as a man of no great nicety in his professional dealings, and requested a private interview on business of importance. Although evidently not past the prime of life, his face was pale, haggard, and dejected; and it did not require the acute perception of the man of business, to discern at a glance, that disease or suffering had done more to work a change in his appearance, than the mere hand of time could have accomplished in twice the period of his whole life.

"I wish you to undertake some legal business for me," said the stranger.

The attorney bowed obsequiously, and glanced at a large packet which the gentleman carried in his hand. His visitor observed the look, and proceeded.

"It is no common business," said he; "nor have these papers reached my hands without long trouble and great expense."

The attorney cast a still more anxious look at the packet; and his visitor, untying the string that bound it, disclosed a quantity of promissory notes, with copies of deeds, and other documents.

"Upon these papers," said the client, "the man whose name they bear, has raised, as you will see, large sums of money, for years past. There was a tacit understanding between him and the men into whose hands they originally went – and from whom I have by degrees purchased the whole, for treble and quadruple their nominal value – that these loans should be from time to time renewed, until a given period had elapsed. Such an understanding is nowhere expressed. He has sustained many losses of late; and these obligations accumulating upon him at once, would crush him to the earth."

"The whole amount is many thousands of pounds," said the attorney, looking over the papers.

"It is," said the client.

"What are we to do?" inquired the man of business.

"Do!" replied the client, with sudden vehemence. "Put every engine of the law in force, every trick that ingenuity can devise and rascality execute; fair means and foul; the open oppression of the law, aided by all the craft of its most ingenious practitioners. I would have him die a harassing and lingering death. Ruin him, seize and sell his lands and goods, drive him from house and home, and drag him forth a beggar in his old age, to die in a common jail."

"But the costs, my dear Sir, the costs of all this," reasoned the attorney, when he had recovered from his momentary surprise. "If the defendant be a man of straw, who is to pay the costs, Sir?"

"Name any sum," said the stranger, his hand trembling so violently with excitement, that he could scarcely hold the pen he seized as he spoke – "any sum, and it is yours. Don't be afraid to name it, man. I shall not think it dear, if you gain my object."

The attorney named a large sum, at hazard, as the advance he should require to secure himself against the possibility of loss; but more with the view of ascertaining how far his client was really disposed to go, than with any idea that he would comply with the demand. The stranger wrote a cheque upon his banker, for the whole amount, and left him.

The draft was duly honoured, and the attorney, finding that his strange client might be safely relied upon, commenced his work in earnest. For more than two years afterwards, Mr. Heyling would sit whole days together, in the office, poring over the papers as they accumulated, and reading again and again, his eyes gleaming with joy, the letters of remonstrance, the prayers for a little delay, the representations of the certain ruin in which the opposite party must be involved, which poured in, as suit after suit, and process after process, was commenced. To all applications for a brief indulgence, there was but one reply – the money must be paid. Land, house, furniture, each in its turn, was taken under some one of the numerous executions which were issued; and the old man himself would have been immured in prison had he not escaped the vigilance of the officers, and fled.

The implacable animosity of Heyling, so far from being satiated by the success of his persecution, increased a hundredfold with the ruin he inflicted. On being informed of the old man's flight, his fury was unbounded. He gnashed his teeth with rage, tore the hair from his head, and assailed with horrid imprecations the men who had been intrusted with the writ. He was only restored to comparative calmness by repeated assurances of the certainty of discovering the fugitive. Agents were sent in quest of him, in all directions; every stratagem that could be invented was resorted to, for the purpose of discovering his place of retreat; but it was all in vain. Half a year had passed over, and he was still undiscovered.

At length late one night, Heyling, of whom nothing had been seen for many weeks before, appeared at his attorney's private residence, and sent up word that a gentleman wished to see him instantly. Before the attorney, who had recognised his voice from above stairs, could order the servant to admit him, he had rushed up the staircase, and entered the drawing-room pale and breathless. Having closed the door, to prevent being overheard, he sank into a chair, and said, in a low voice—

"Hush! I have found him at last."

"No!" said the attorney. "Well done, my dear sir, well done."

"He lies concealed in a wretched lodging in Camden Town," said Heyling. "Perhaps it is as well we *did* lose sight of him, for he has been living alone there, in the most abject misery, all the time, and he is poor – very poor."

"Very good," said the attorney. "You will have the caption made tomorrow, of course?"

"Yes," replied Heyling. "Stay! No! The next day. You are surprised at my wishing to postpone it," he added, with a ghastly smile; "but I had forgotten. The next day is an anniversary in his life: let it be done then."

"Very good," said the attorney. "Will you write down instructions for the officer?"

"No; let him meet me here, at eight in the evening, and I will accompany him myself."

They met on the appointed night, and, hiring a hackney-coach, directed the driver to stop at that corner of the old Pancras Road, at which stands the parish workhouse. By the time they alighted there, it was quite dark; and, proceeding by the dead wall in front of the Veterinary Hospital, they entered a small by-street, which is, or was at that time, called Little College Street, and which, whatever it may be now, was in those days a desolate place enough, surrounded by little else than fields and ditches.

Having drawn the travelling-cap he had on half over his face, and muffled himself in his cloak, Heyling stopped before the meanest-looking house in the street, and knocked gently at the door. It was at once opened by a woman, who dropped a curtsey of recognition, and Heyling, whispering the officer to remain below, crept gently upstairs, and, opening the door of the front room, entered at once.

The object of his search and his unrelenting animosity, now a decrepit old man, was seated at a bare deal table, on which stood a miserable candle. He started on the entrance of the stranger, and rose feebly to his feet.

"What now, what now?" said the old man. "What fresh misery is this? What do you want here?"

"A word with *you*," replied Heyling. As he spoke, he seated himself at the other end of the table, and, throwing off his cloak and cap, disclosed his features.

The old man seemed instantly deprived of speech. He fell backward in his chair, and, clasping his hands together, gazed on the apparition with a mingled look of abhorrence and fear.

"This day six years," said Heyling, "I claimed the life you owed me for my child's. Beside the lifeless form of your daughter, old man, I swore to live a life of revenge. I have never swerved from my purpose for a moment's space; but if I had, one thought of her uncomplaining, suffering look, as she drooped away, or of the starving face of our innocent child, would have nerved me to my task. My first act of requital you well remember: this is my last."

The old man shivered, and his hands dropped powerless by his side.

"I leave England tomorrow," said Heyling, after a moment's pause. "To-night I consign you to the living death to which you devoted her – a hopeless prison—"

He raised his eyes to the old man's countenance, and paused. He lifted the light to his face, set it gently down, and left the apartment.

"You had better see to the old man," he said to the woman, as he opened the door, and motioned the officer to follow him into the street. "I think he is ill." The woman closed the door, ran hastily upstairs, and found him lifeless.

Beneath a plain gravestone, in one of the most peaceful and secluded churchyards in Kent, where wild flowers mingle with the grass, and the soft landscape around forms the fairest spot in the garden of England, lie the bones of the young mother and her gentle child. But the ashes of the father do not mingle with theirs; nor, from that night forward, did the attorney ever gain the remotest clue to the subsequent history of his queer client.

The Great Gatsby

F. Scott Fitzgerald

Chapter I

IN MY YOUNGER and more vulnerable years my father gave me some advice that I've been turning over in my mind ever since.

"Whenever you feel like criticizing anyone," he told me, "just remember that all the people in this world haven't had the advantages that you've had."

He didn't say any more, but we've always been unusually communicative in a reserved way, and I understood that he meant a great deal more than that. In consequence, I'm inclined to reserve all judgements, a habit that has opened up many curious natures to me and also made me the victim of not a few veteran bores. The abnormal mind is quick to detect and attach itself to this quality when it appears in a normal person, and so it came about that in college I was unjustly accused of being a politician, because I was privy to the secret griefs of wild, unknown men. Most of the confidences were unsought – frequently I have feigned sleep, preoccupation, or a hostile levity when I realized by some unmistakable sign that an intimate revelation was quivering on the horizon; for the intimate revelations of young men, or at least the terms in which they express them, are usually plagiaristic and marred by obvious suppressions. Reserving judgements is a matter of infinite hope. I am still a little afraid of missing something if I forget that, as my father snobbishly suggested, and I snobbishly repeat, a sense of the fundamental decencies is parcelled out unequally at birth.

And, after boasting this way of my tolerance, I come to the admission that it has a limit. Conduct may be founded on the hard rock or the wet marshes, but after a certain point I don't care what it's founded on. When I came back from the East last autumn I felt that I wanted the world to be in uniform and at a sort of moral attention forever; I wanted no more riotous excursions with privileged glimpses into the human heart. Only Gatsby, the man who gives his name to this book, was exempt from my reaction – Gatsby, who represented everything for which I have an unaffected scorn. If personality is an unbroken series of successful gestures, then there was something gorgeous about him, some heightened sensitivity to the promises of life, as if he were related to one of those intricate machines that register earthquakes ten thousand miles away. This responsiveness had nothing to do with that flabby impressionability which is dignified under the name of the "creative temperament" – it was an extraordinary gift for hope, a romantic readiness such as I have never found in any other person and which it is not likely I shall ever find again. No – Gatsby turned out all right at the end; it is what preyed on Gatsby, what foul dust floated in the wake of his dreams that temporarily closed out my interest in the abortive sorrows and short-winded elations of men.

* * *

My family have been prominent, well-to-do people in this Middle Western city for three generations. The Carraways are something of a clan, and we have a tradition that we're descended from the Dukes of Buccleuch, but the actual founder of my line was my grandfather's brother, who came here in fifty-one, sent a substitute to the Civil War, and started the wholesale hardware business that my father carries on today.

I never saw this great-uncle, but I'm supposed to look like him – with special reference to the rather hard-boiled painting that hangs in father's office. I graduated from New Haven in 1915, just a quarter of a century after my father, and a little later I participated in that delayed Teutonic migration known as the Great War. I enjoyed the counter-raid so thoroughly that I came back restless. Instead of being the warm centre of the world, the Middle West now seemed like the ragged edge of the universe – so I decided to go East and learn the bond business. Everybody I knew was in the bond business, so I supposed it could support one more single man. All my aunts and uncles talked it over as if they were choosing a prep school for me, and finally said, "Why – ye-es," with very grave, hesitant faces. Father agreed to finance me for a year, and after various delays I came East, permanently, I thought, in the spring of twenty-two.

The practical thing was to find rooms in the city, but it was a warm season, and I had just left a country of wide lawns and friendly trees, so when a young man at the office suggested that we take a house together in a commuting town, it sounded like a great idea. He found the house, a weather-beaten cardboard bungalow at eighty a month, but at the last minute the firm ordered him to Washington, and I went out to the country alone. I had a dog – at least I had him for a few days until he ran away – and an old Dodge and a Finnish woman, who made my bed and cooked breakfast and muttered Finnish wisdom to herself over the electric stove.

It was lonely for a day or so until one morning some man, more recently arrived than I, stopped me on the road.

"How do you get to West Egg village?" he asked helplessly.

I told him. And as I walked on I was lonely no longer. I was a guide, a pathfinder, an original settler. He had casually conferred on me the freedom of the neighbourhood.

And so with the sunshine and the great bursts of leaves growing on the trees, just as things grow in fast movies, I had that familiar conviction that life was beginning over again with the summer.

There was so much to read, for one thing, and so much fine health to be pulled down out of the young breath-giving air. I bought a dozen volumes on banking and credit and investment securities, and they stood on my shelf in red and gold like new money from the mint, promising to unfold the shining secrets that only Midas and Morgan and Maecenas knew. And I had the high intention of reading many other books besides. I was rather literary in college – one year I wrote a series of very solemn and obvious editorials for the Yale News – and now I was going to bring back all such things into my life and become again that most limited of all specialists, the "well-rounded man." This isn't just an epigram – life is much more successfully looked at from a single window, after all.

It was a matter of chance that I should have rented a house in one of the strangest communities in North America. It was on that slender riotous island which extends itself due east of New York – and where there are, among other natural curiosities, two unusual formations of land. Twenty miles from the city a pair of enormous eggs, identical in contour and separated only by a courtesy bay, jut out into the most domesticated body of salt water in the Western hemisphere, the great wet barnyard of Long Island Sound. They are not perfect ovals – like the egg in the Columbus story, they are both crushed flat at the contact end – but their physical resemblance must be a source of perpetual wonder to the gulls that fly overhead. To the wingless a more interesting phenomenon is their dissimilarity in every particular except shape and size.

I lived at West Egg, the – well, the less fashionable of the two, though this is a most superficial tag to express the bizarre and not a little sinister contrast between them. My house was at the very tip of the egg, only fifty yards from the Sound, and squeezed between two huge places that rented for twelve or fifteen thousand a season. The one on my right was a colossal affair by any standard – it was a factual imitation of some Hôtel de Ville in Normandy, with a tower on one side, spanking new under a thin beard of raw ivy, and a marble swimming pool, and more than forty acres of lawn and garden. It was Gatsby's mansion. Or, rather, as I didn't know Mr. Gatsby, it was a mansion inhabited by a gentleman of that name. My own house was an eyesore, but it was a small eyesore, and it had been overlooked, so I had a view of the water, a partial view of my neighbour's lawn, and the consoling proximity of millionaires – all for eighty dollars a month.

Across the courtesy bay the white palaces of fashionable East Egg glittered along the water, and the history of the summer really begins on the evening I drove over there to have dinner with the Tom Buchanans. Daisy was my second cousin once removed, and I'd known Tom in college. And just after the war I spent two days with them in Chicago.

Her husband, among various physical accomplishments, had been one of the most powerful ends that ever played football at New Haven – a national figure in a way, one of those men who reach such an acute limited excellence at twenty-one that everything afterward savours of anticlimax. His family were enormously wealthy – even in college his freedom with money was a matter for reproach – but now he'd left Chicago and come East in a fashion that rather took your breath away: for instance, he'd brought down a string of polo ponies from Lake Forest. It was hard to realize that a man in my own generation was wealthy enough to do that.

Why they came East I don't know. They had spent a year in France for no particular reason, and then drifted here and there unrestfully wherever people played polo and were rich together. This was a permanent move, said Daisy over the telephone, but I didn't believe it – I had no sight into Daisy's heart, but I felt that Tom would drift on forever seeking, a little wistfully, for the dramatic turbulence of some irrecoverable football game.

And so it happened that on a warm windy evening I drove over to East Egg to see two old friends whom I scarcely knew at all. Their house was even more elaborate than I expected, a cheerful red-and-white Georgian Colonial mansion, overlooking the bay. The lawn started at the beach and ran towards the front door for a quarter of a mile, jumping over sundials and brick walks and burning gardens – finally when it reached the house drifting up the side in bright vines as though from the momentum of its run. The front was broken by a line of French windows, glowing now with reflected gold and wide open to the warm windy afternoon, and Tom Buchanan in riding clothes was standing with his legs apart on the front porch.

He had changed since his New Haven years. Now he was a sturdy straw-haired man of thirty, with a rather hard mouth and a supercilious manner. Two shining arrogant eyes had established dominance over his face and gave him the appearance of always leaning aggressively forward. Not even the effeminate swank of his riding clothes could hide the enormous power of that body – he seemed to fill those glistening boots until he strained the top lacing, and you could see a great pack of muscle shifting when his shoulder moved under his thin coat. It was a body capable of enormous leverage – a cruel body.

His speaking voice, a gruff husky tenor, added to the impression of fractiousness he conveyed. There was a touch of paternal contempt in it, even toward people he liked – and there were men at New Haven who had hated his guts.

"Now, don't think my opinion on these matters is final," he seemed to say, "just because I'm stronger and more of a man than you are." We were in the same senior society, and while we were never intimate I always had the impression that he approved of me and wanted me to like him with some harsh, defiant wistfulness of his own.

We talked for a few minutes on the sunny porch.

"I've got a nice place here," he said, his eyes flashing about restlessly.

Turning me around by one arm, he moved a broad flat hand along the front vista, including in its sweep a sunken Italian garden, a half acre of deep, pungent roses, and a snub-nosed motorboat that bumped the tide offshore.

"It belonged to Demaine, the oil man." He turned me around again, politely and abruptly. "We'll go inside."

We walked through a high hallway into a bright rosy-coloured space, fragilely bound into the house by French windows at either end. The windows were ajar and gleaming white against the fresh grass outside that seemed to grow a little way into the house. A breeze blew through the room, blew curtains in at one end and out the other like pale flags, twisting them up toward the frosted wedding-cake of the ceiling, and then rippled over the wine-coloured rug, making a shadow on it as wind does on the sea.

The only completely stationary object in the room was an enormous couch on which two young women were buoyed up as though upon an anchored balloon. They were both in white, and their dresses were rippling and fluttering as if they had just been blown back in after a short flight around the house. I must have stood for a few moments listening to the whip and snap of the curtains and the groan of a picture on the wall. Then there was a boom as Tom Buchanan shut the rear windows and the caught wind died out about the room, and the curtains and the rugs and the two young women ballooned slowly to the floor.

The younger of the two was a stranger to me. She was extended full length at her end of the divan, completely motionless, and with her chin raised a little, as if she were balancing something on it which was quite likely to fall. If she saw me out of the corner of her eyes she gave no hint of it – indeed, I was almost surprised into murmuring an apology for having disturbed her by coming in.

The other girl, Daisy, made an attempt to rise – she leaned slightly forward with a conscientious expression – then she laughed, an absurd, charming little laugh, and I laughed too and came forward into the room.

"I'm p-paralysed with happiness."

She laughed again, as if she said something very witty, and held my hand for a moment, looking up into my face, promising that there was no one in the world she so much wanted to see. That was a way she had. She hinted in a murmur that the surname of the balancing girl was Baker. (I've heard it said that Daisy's murmur was only to make people lean toward her; an irrelevant criticism that made it no less charming.)

At any rate, Miss Baker's lips fluttered, she nodded at me almost imperceptibly, and then quickly tipped her head back again – the object she was balancing had obviously tottered a little and given her something of a fright. Again a sort of apology arose to my lips. Almost any exhibition of complete self-sufficiency draws a stunned tribute from me.

I looked back at my cousin, who began to ask me questions in her low, thrilling voice. It was the kind of voice that the ear follows up and down, as if each speech is an arrangement of notes that will never be played again. Her face was sad and lovely with bright things in it, bright eyes and a bright passionate mouth, but there was an excitement in her voice that men who had cared for her found difficult to forget: a singing compulsion, a whispered "Listen," a promise that she had done gay, exciting things just a while since and that there were gay, exciting things hovering in the next hour.

I told her how I had stopped off in Chicago for a day on my way East, and how a dozen people had sent their love through me.

"Do they miss me?" she cried ecstatically.

"The whole town is desolate. All the cars have the left rear wheel painted black as a mourning wreath, and there's a persistent wail all night along the north shore."

"How gorgeous! Let's go back, Tom. Tomorrow!" Then she added irrelevantly: "You ought to see the baby."

"I'd like to."

"She's asleep. She's three years old. Haven't you ever seen her?"

"Never."

"Well, you ought to see her. She's—"

Tom Buchanan, who had been hovering restlessly about the room, stopped and rested his hand on my shoulder.

"What you doing, Nick?"

"I'm a bond man."

"Who with?"

I told him.

"Never heard of them," he remarked decisively.

This annoyed me.

"You will," I answered shortly. "You will if you stay in the East."

"Oh, I'll stay in the East, don't you worry," he said, glancing at Daisy and then back at me, as if he were alert for something more. "I'd be a God damned fool to live anywhere else."

At this point Miss Baker said: "Absolutely!" with such suddenness that I started – it was the first word she had uttered since I came into the room. Evidently it surprised her as much as it did me, for she yawned and with a series of rapid, deft movements stood up into the room.

"I'm stiff," she complained, "I've been lying on that sofa for as long as I can remember."

"Don't look at me," Daisy retorted, "I've been trying to get you to New York all afternoon."

"No, thanks," said Miss Baker to the four cocktails just in from the pantry. "I'm absolutely in training."

Her host looked at her incredulously.

"You are!" He took down his drink as if it were a drop in the bottom of a glass. "How you ever get anything done is beyond me."

I looked at Miss Baker, wondering what it was she "got done." I enjoyed looking at her. She was a slender, small-breasted girl, with an erect carriage, which she accentuated by throwing her body backward at the shoulders like a young cadet. Her grey sun-strained eyes looked back at me with polite reciprocal curiosity out of a wan, charming, discontented face. It occurred to me now that I had seen her, or a picture of her, somewhere before.

"You live in West Egg," she remarked contemptuously. "I know somebody there."

"I don't know a single—"

"You must know Gatsby."

"Gatsby?" demanded Daisy. "What Gatsby?"

Before I could reply that he was my neighbour dinner was announced; wedging his tense arm imperatively under mine, Tom Buchanan compelled me from the room as though he were moving a checker to another square.

Slenderly, languidly, their hands set lightly on their hips, the two young women preceded us out on to a rosy-coloured porch, open toward the sunset, where four candles flickered on the table in the diminished wind.

"Why *candles*?" objected Daisy, frowning. She snapped them out with her fingers. "In two weeks it'll be the longest day in the year." She looked at us all radiantly. "Do you always watch for the longest day of the year and then miss it? I always watch for the longest day in the year and then miss it."

"We ought to plan something," yawned Miss Baker, sitting down at the table as if she were getting into bed.

"All right," said Daisy. "What'll we plan?" She turned to me helplessly: "What do people plan?"

Before I could answer her eyes fastened with an awed expression on her little finger.

"Look!" she complained; "I hurt it."

We all looked – the knuckle was black and blue.

"You did it, Tom," she said accusingly. "I know you didn't mean to, but you *did* do it. That's what I get for marrying a brute of a man, a great, big, hulking physical specimen of a—"

"I hate that word 'hulking,'" objected Tom crossly, "even in kidding."

"Hulking," insisted Daisy.

Sometimes she and Miss Baker talked at once, unobtrusively and with a bantering inconsequence that was never quite chatter, that was as cool as their white dresses and their impersonal eyes in the absence of all desire. They were here, and they accepted Tom and me, making only a polite pleasant effort to entertain or to be entertained. They knew that presently dinner would be over and a little later the evening too would be over and casually put away. It was sharply different from the West, where an evening was hurried from phase to phase towards its close, in a continually disappointed anticipation or else in sheer nervous dread of the moment itself.

"You make me feel uncivilized, Daisy," I confessed on my second glass of corky but rather impressive claret. "Can't you talk about crops or something?"

I meant nothing in particular by this remark, but it was taken up in an unexpected way.

"Civilization's going to pieces," broke out Tom violently. "I've gotten to be a terrible pessimist about things. Have you read *The Rise of the Coloured Empires* by this man Goddard?"

"Why, no," I answered, rather surprised by his tone.

"Well, it's a fine book, and everybody ought to read it. The idea is if we don't look out the white race will be – will be utterly submerged. It's all scientific stuff; it's been proved."

"Tom's getting very profound," said Daisy, with an expression of unthoughtful sadness. "He reads deep books with long words in them. What was that word we—"

"Well, these books are all scientific," insisted Tom, glancing at her impatiently. "This fellow has worked out the whole thing. It's up to us, who are the dominant race, to watch out or these other races will have control of things."

"We've got to beat them down," whispered Daisy, winking ferociously toward the fervent sun.

"You ought to live in California—" began Miss Baker, but Tom interrupted her by shifting heavily in his chair.

"This idea is that we're Nordics. I am, and you are, and you are, and—" After an infinitesimal hesitation he included Daisy with a slight nod, and she winked at me again. "—And we've produced all the things that go to make civilization – oh, science and art, and all that. Do you see?"

There was something pathetic in his concentration, as if his complacency, more acute than of old, was not enough to him any more. When, almost immediately, the telephone rang inside and the butler left the porch Daisy seized upon the momentary interruption and leaned towards me.

"I'll tell you a family secret," she whispered enthusiastically. "It's about the butler's nose. Do you want to hear about the butler's nose?"

"That's why I came over tonight."

"Well, he wasn't always a butler; he used to be the silver polisher for some people in New York that had a silver service for two hundred people. He had to polish it from morning till night, until finally it began to affect his nose—"

"Things went from bad to worse," suggested Miss Baker.

"Yes. Things went from bad to worse, until finally he had to give up his position."

For a moment the last sunshine fell with romantic affection upon her glowing face; her voice compelled me forward breathlessly as I listened – then the glow faded, each light deserting her with lingering regret, like children leaving a pleasant street at dusk.

The butler came back and murmured something close to Tom's ear, whereupon Tom frowned, pushed back his chair, and without a word went inside. As if his absence quickened something within her, Daisy leaned forward again, her voice glowing and singing.

"I love to see you at my table, Nick. You remind me of a – of a rose, an absolute rose. Doesn't he?" She turned to Miss Baker for confirmation: "An absolute rose?"

This was untrue. I am not even faintly like a rose. She was only extemporizing, but a stirring warmth flowed from her, as if her heart was trying to come out to you concealed in one of those breathless, thrilling words. Then suddenly she threw her napkin on the table and excused herself and went into the house.

Miss Baker and I exchanged a short glance consciously devoid of meaning. I was about to speak when she sat up alertly and said "*Sh!*" in a warning voice. A subdued impassioned murmur was audible in the room beyond, and Miss Baker leaned forward unashamed, trying to hear. The murmur trembled on the verge of coherence, sank down, mounted excitedly, and then ceased altogether.

"This Mr. Gatsby you spoke of is my neighbour—" I began.

"Don't talk. I want to hear what happens."

"Is something happening?" I inquired innocently.

"You mean to say you don't know?" said Miss Baker, honestly surprised. "I thought everybody knew." "I don't."

"Why—" she said hesitantly. "Tom's got some woman in New York."

"Got some woman?" I repeated blankly.

Miss Baker nodded.

"She might have the decency not to telephone him at dinner time. Don't you think?"

Almost before I had grasped her meaning there was the flutter of a dress and the crunch of leather boots, and Tom and Daisy were back at the table.

"It couldn't be helped!" cried Daisy with tense gaiety.

She sat down, glanced searchingly at Miss Baker and then at me, and continued: "I looked outdoors for a minute, and it's very romantic outdoors. There's a bird on the lawn that I think must be a nightingale come over on the Cunard or White Star Line. He's singing away—" Her voice sang: "It's romantic, isn't it, Tom?"

"Very romantic," he said, and then miserably to me: "If it's light enough after dinner, I want to take you down to the stables."

The telephone rang inside, startlingly, and as Daisy shook her head decisively at Tom the subject of the stables, in fact all subjects, vanished into air. Among the broken fragments of the last five minutes at table I remember the candles being lit again, pointlessly, and I was conscious of wanting to look squarely at everyone, and yet to avoid all eyes. I couldn't guess what Daisy and Tom were thinking, but I doubt if even Miss Baker, who seemed to have mastered a certain hardy scepticism, was able utterly to put this fifth guest's shrill metallic urgency out of mind. To a certain temperament the situation might have seemed intriguing – my own instinct was to telephone immediately for the police.

The horses, needless to say, were not mentioned again. Tom and Miss Baker, with several feet of twilight between them, strolled back into the library, as if to a vigil beside a perfectly tangible body, while, trying to look pleasantly interested and a little deaf, I followed Daisy around a chain of connecting verandas to the porch in front. In its deep gloom we sat down side by side on a wicker settee.

Daisy took her face in her hands as if feeling its lovely shape, and her eyes moved gradually out into the velvet dusk. I saw that turbulent emotions possessed her, so I asked what I thought would be some sedative questions about her little girl.

"We don't know each other very well, Nick," she said suddenly. "Even if we are cousins. You didn't come to my wedding."

"I wasn't back from the war."

"That's true." She hesitated. "Well, I've had a very bad time, Nick, and I'm pretty cynical about everything."

Evidently she had reason to be. I waited but she didn't say any more, and after a moment I returned rather feebly to the subject of her daughter.

"I suppose she talks, and – eats, and everything."

"Oh, yes." She looked at me absently. "Listen, Nick; let me tell you what I said when she was born. Would you like to hear?"

"Very much."

"It'll show you how I've gotten to feel about – things. Well, she was less than an hour old and Tom was God knows where. I woke up out of the ether with an utterly abandoned feeling, and asked the nurse right away if it was a boy or a girl. She told me it was a girl, and so I turned my head away and wept. 'All right,' I said, 'I'm glad it's a girl. And I hope she'll be a fool – that's the best thing a girl can be in this world, a beautiful little fool.'

"You see I think everything's terrible anyhow," she went on in a convinced way. "Everybody thinks so – the most advanced people. And I *know*. I've been everywhere and seen everything and done everything." Her eyes flashed around her in a defiant way, rather like Tom's, and she laughed with thrilling scorn. "Sophisticated – God, I'm sophisticated!"

The instant her voice broke off, ceasing to compel my attention, my belief, I felt the basic insincerity of what she had said. It made me uneasy, as though the whole evening had been a trick of some sort to exact a contributory emotion from me. I waited, and sure enough, in a moment she looked at me with an absolute smirk on her lovely face, as if she had asserted her membership in a rather distinguished secret society to which she and Tom belonged.

* * *

Inside, the crimson room bloomed with light. Tom and Miss Baker sat at either end of the long couch and she read aloud to him from the *Saturday Evening Post* – the words, murmurous and uninflected, running together in a soothing tune. The lamplight, bright on his boots and dull on the autumn-leaf yellow of her hair, glinted along the paper as she turned a page with a flutter of slender muscles in her arms.

When we came in she held us silent for a moment with a lifted hand.

"To be continued," she said, tossing the magazine on the table, "in our very next issue."

Her body asserted itself with a restless movement of her knee, and she stood up.

"Ten o'clock," she remarked, apparently finding the time on the ceiling. "Time for this good girl to go to bed."

"Jordan's going to play in the tournament tomorrow," explained Daisy, "over at Westchester."

"Oh – you're *Jor*dan Baker."

I knew now why her face was familiar – its pleasing contemptuous expression had looked out at me from many rotogravure pictures of the sporting life at Asheville and Hot Springs and Palm Beach. I had heard some story of her too, a critical, unpleasant story, but what it was I had forgotten long ago.

"Good night," she said softly. "Wake me at eight, won't you."

"If you'll get up."

"I will. Good night, Mr. Carraway. See you anon."

"Of course you will," confirmed Daisy. "In fact I think I'll arrange a marriage. Come over often, Nick, and I'll sort of – oh – fling you together. You know – lock you up accidentally in linen closets and push you out to sea in a boat, and all that sort of thing—"

"Good night," called Miss Baker from the stairs. "I haven't heard a word."

"She's a nice girl," said Tom after a moment. "They oughtn't to let her run around the country this way."

"Who oughtn't to?" inquired Daisy coldly.

"Her family."

"Her family is one aunt about a thousand years old. Besides, Nick's going to look after her, aren't you, Nick? She's going to spend lots of weekends out here this summer. I think the home influence will be very good for her."

Daisy and Tom looked at each other for a moment in silence.

"Is she from New York?" I asked quickly.

"From Louisville. Our white girlhood was passed together there. Our beautiful white—"

"Did you give Nick a little heart to heart talk on the veranda?" demanded Tom suddenly.

"Did I?" She looked at me. "I can't seem to remember, but I think we talked about the Nordic race. Yes, I'm sure we did. It sort of crept up on us and first thing you know—"

"Don't believe everything you hear, Nick," he advised me.

I said lightly that I had heard nothing at all, and a few minutes later I got up to go home. They came to the door with me and stood side by side in a cheerful square of light. As I started my motor Daisy peremptorily called: "Wait!"

"I forgot to ask you something, and it's important. We heard you were engaged to a girl out West."

"That's right," corroborated Tom kindly. "We heard that you were engaged."

"It's a libel. I'm too poor."

"But we heard it," insisted Daisy, surprising me by opening up again in a flower-like way. "We heard it from three people, so it must be true."

Of course I knew what they were referring to, but I wasn't even vaguely engaged. The fact that gossip had published the banns was one of the reasons I had come East. You can't stop going with an old friend on account of rumours, and on the other hand I had no intention of being rumoured into marriage.

Their interest rather touched me and made them less remotely rich – nevertheless, I was confused and a little disgusted as I drove away. It seemed to me that the thing for Daisy to do was to rush out of the house, child in arms – but apparently there were no such intentions in her head. As for Tom, the fact that he "had some woman in New York" was really less surprising than that he had been depressed by a book. Something was making him nibble at the edge of stale ideas as if his sturdy physical egotism no longer nourished his peremptory heart.

Already it was deep summer on roadhouse roofs and in front of wayside garages, where new red petrol-pumps sat out in pools of light, and when I reached my estate at West Egg I ran the car under its shed and sat for a while on an abandoned grass roller in the yard. The wind had blown off, leaving a loud, bright night, with wings beating in the trees and a persistent organ sound as the full bellows of the earth blew the frogs full of life. The silhouette of a moving cat wavered across the moonlight, and, turning my head to watch it, I saw that I was not alone – fifty feet away a figure had emerged from the shadow of my neighbour's mansion and was standing with his hands in his pockets regarding the silver pepper of the stars. Something in his leisurely movements and the secure position of his feet upon the lawn suggested that it was Mr. Gatsby himself, come out to determine what share was his of our local heavens.

I decided to call to him. Miss Baker had mentioned him at dinner, and that would do for an introduction. But I didn't call to him, for he gave a sudden intimation that he was content to be alone – he stretched out his arms toward the dark water in a curious way, and, far as I was from him, I could have sworn he was trembling. Involuntarily I glanced seaward – and distinguished nothing except a single green light, minute and far away, that might have been the end of a dock. When I looked once more for Gatsby he had vanished, and I was alone again in the unquiet darkness.

Chapter II

ABOUT HALFWAY between West Egg and New York the motor road hastily joins the railroad and runs beside it for a quarter of a mile, so as to shrink away from a certain desolate area of land. This is a valley of ashes – a fantastic farm where ashes grow like wheat into ridges and hills and grotesque gardens; where ashes take the forms of houses and chimneys and rising smoke and, finally, with a transcendent effort, of ash-grey men, who move dimly and already crumbling through the powdery air. Occasionally a line of grey cars crawls along an invisible track, gives out a ghastly creak, and comes to rest, and immediately the ash-grey men swarm up with leaden spades and stir up an impenetrable cloud, which screens their obscure operations from your sight.

But above the grey land and the spasms of bleak dust which drift endlessly over it, you perceive, after a moment, the eyes of Doctor T. J. Eckleburg. The eyes of Doctor T. J. Eckleburg are blue and gigantic – their retinas are one yard high. They look out of no face, but, instead, from a pair of enormous yellow spectacles which pass over a nonexistent nose. Evidently some wild wag of an oculist set them there to fatten his practice in the borough of Queens, and then sank down himself into eternal blindness, or forgot them and moved away. But his eyes, dimmed a little by many paintless days, under sun and rain, brood on over the solemn dumping ground.

The valley of ashes is bounded on one side by a small foul river, and, when the drawbridge is up to let barges through, the passengers on waiting trains can stare at the dismal scene for as long as half an hour. There is always a halt there of at least a minute, and it was because of this that I first met Tom Buchanan's mistress.

The fact that he had one was insisted upon wherever he was known. His acquaintances resented the fact that he turned up in popular cafés with her and, leaving her at a table, sauntered about, chatting with whomsoever he knew. Though I was curious to see her, I had no desire to meet her – but I did. I went up to New York with Tom on the train one afternoon, and when we stopped by the ash-heaps he jumped to his feet and, taking hold of my elbow, literally forced me from the car.

"We're getting off," he insisted. "I want you to meet my girl."

I think he'd tanked up a good deal at luncheon, and his determination to have my company bordered on violence. The supercilious assumption was that on Sunday afternoon I had nothing better to do.

I followed him over a low whitewashed railroad fence, and we walked back a hundred yards along the road under Doctor Eckleburg's persistent stare. The only building in sight was a small block of yellow brick sitting on the edge of the waste land, a sort of compact Main Street ministering to it, and contiguous to absolutely nothing. One of the three shops it contained was for rent and another was an all-night restaurant, approached by a trail of ashes; the third was a garage – *Repairs. George B. Wilson. Cars bought and sold.* – and I followed Tom inside.

The interior was unprosperous and bare; the only car visible was the dust-covered wreck of a Ford which crouched in a dim corner. It had occurred to me that this shadow of a garage must be a blind, and that sumptuous and romantic apartments were concealed overhead, when the proprietor himself appeared in the door of an office, wiping his hands on a piece of waste. He was a blond, spiritless man, anaemic, and faintly handsome. When he saw us a damp gleam of hope sprang into his light blue eyes.

"Hello, Wilson, old man," said Tom, slapping him jovially on the shoulder. "How's business?"

"I can't complain," answered Wilson unconvincingly. "When are you going to sell me that car?"

"Next week; I've got my man working on it now."

"Works pretty slow, don't he?"

"No, he doesn't," said Tom coldly. "And if you feel that way about it, maybe I'd better sell it somewhere else after all."

"I don't mean that," explained Wilson quickly. "I just meant—"

His voice faded off and Tom glanced impatiently around the garage. Then I heard footsteps on a stairs, and in a moment the thickish figure of a woman blocked out the light from the office door.

She was in the middle thirties, and faintly stout, but she carried her flesh sensuously as some women can. Her face, above a spotted dress of dark blue crêpe-de-chine, contained no facet or gleam of beauty, but there was an immediately perceptible vitality about her as if the nerves of her body were continually smouldering. She smiled slowly and, walking through her husband as if he were a ghost, shook hands with Tom, looking him flush in the eye. Then she wet her lips, and without turning around spoke to her husband in a soft, coarse voice:

"Get some chairs, why don't you, so somebody can sit down."

"Oh, sure," agreed Wilson hurriedly, and went toward the little office, mingling immediately with the cement colour of the walls. A white ashen dust veiled his dark suit and his pale hair as it veiled everything in the vicinity – except his wife, who moved close to Tom.

"I want to see you," said Tom intently. "Get on the next train."

"All right."

"I'll meet you by the newsstand on the lower level."

She nodded and moved away from him just as George Wilson emerged with two chairs from his office door.

We waited for her down the road and out of sight. It was a few days before the Fourth of July, and a grey, scrawny Italian child was setting torpedoes in a row along the railroad track.

"Terrible place, isn't it," said Tom, exchanging a frown with Doctor Eckleburg.

"Awful."

"It does her good to get away."

"Doesn't her husband object?"

"Wilson? He thinks she goes to see her sister in New York. He's so dumb he doesn't know he's alive."

So Tom Buchanan and his girl and I went up together to New York – or not quite together, for Mrs. Wilson sat discreetly in another car. Tom deferred that much to the sensibilities of those East Eggers who might be on the train.

She had changed her dress to a brown figured muslin, which stretched tight over her rather wide hips as Tom helped her to the platform in New York. At the newsstand she bought a copy of *Town Tattle* and a moving-picture magazine, and in the station drugstore some cold cream and a small flask of perfume. Upstairs, in the solemn echoing drive she let four taxicabs drive away before she selected a new one, lavender-coloured with grey upholstery, and in this we slid out from the mass of the station into the glowing sunshine. But immediately she turned sharply from the window and, leaning forward, tapped on the front glass.

"I want to get one of those dogs," she said earnestly. "I want to get one for the apartment. They're nice to have – a dog."

We backed up to a grey old man who bore an absurd resemblance to John D. Rockefeller. In a basket swung from his neck cowered a dozen very recent puppies of an indeterminate breed.

"What kind are they?" asked Mrs. Wilson eagerly, as he came to the taxi-window.

"All kinds. What kind do you want, lady?"

"I'd like to get one of those police dogs; I don't suppose you got that kind?"

The man peered doubtfully into the basket, plunged in his hand and drew one up, wriggling, by the back of the neck.

"That's no police dog," said Tom.

"No, it's not exactly a police dog," said the man with disappointment in his voice. "It's more of an Airedale." He passed his hand over the brown washrag of a back. "Look at that coat. Some coat. That's a dog that'll never bother you with catching cold."

"I think it's cute," said Mrs. Wilson enthusiastically. "How much is it?"

"That dog?" He looked at it admiringly. "That dog will cost you ten dollars."

The Airedale – undoubtedly there was an Airedale concerned in it somewhere, though its feet were startlingly white – changed hands and settled down into Mrs. Wilson's lap, where she fondled the weatherproof coat with rapture.

"Is it a boy or a girl?" she asked delicately.

"That dog? That dog's a boy."

"It's a bitch," said Tom decisively. "Here's your money. Go and buy ten more dogs with it."

We drove over to Fifth Avenue, warm and soft, almost pastoral, on the summer Sunday afternoon. I wouldn't have been surprised to see a great flock of white sheep turn the corner.

"Hold on," I said, "I have to leave you here."

"No you don't," interposed Tom quickly. "Myrtle'll be hurt if you don't come up to the apartment. Won't you, Myrtle?"

"Come on," she urged. "I'll telephone my sister Catherine. She's said to be very beautiful by people who ought to know."

"Well, I'd like to, but—"

We went on, cutting back again over the Park toward the West Hundreds. At 158th Street the cab stopped at one slice in a long white cake of apartment-houses. Throwing a regal homecoming glance around the neighbourhood, Mrs. Wilson gathered up her dog and her other purchases, and went haughtily in.

"I'm going to have the McKees come up," she announced as we rose in the elevator. "And, of course, I got to call up my sister, too."

The apartment was on the top floor – a small living-room, a small dining-room, a small bedroom, and a bath. The living-room was crowded to the doors with a set of tapestried furniture entirely too large for it, so that to move about was to stumble continually over scenes of ladies swinging in the gardens of Versailles. The only picture was an over-enlarged photograph, apparently a hen sitting on a blurred rock. Looked at from a distance, however, the hen resolved itself into a bonnet, and the countenance of a stout old lady beamed down into the room. Several old copies of *Town Tattle* lay on the table together with a copy of *Simon Called Peter*, and some of the small scandal magazines of Broadway. Mrs. Wilson was first concerned with the dog. A reluctant elevator boy went for a box full of straw and some milk, to which he added on his own initiative a tin of large, hard dog biscuits – one of which decomposed apathetically in the saucer of milk all afternoon. Meanwhile Tom brought out a bottle of whisky from a locked bureau door.

I have been drunk just twice in my life, and the second time was that afternoon; so everything that happened has a dim, hazy cast over it, although until after eight o'clock the apartment was full of cheerful sun. Sitting on Tom's lap Mrs. Wilson called up several people on the telephone; then there were no cigarettes, and I went out to buy some at the drugstore on the corner. When I came back they had both disappeared, so I sat down discreetly in the living-room and read a chapter of *Simon Called Peter* – either it was terrible stuff or the whisky distorted things, because it didn't make any sense to me.

Just as Tom and Myrtle (after the first drink Mrs. Wilson and I called each other by our first names) reappeared, company commenced to arrive at the apartment door.

The sister, Catherine, was a slender, worldly girl of about thirty, with a solid, sticky bob of red hair, and a complexion powdered milky white. Her eyebrows had been plucked and then drawn on again at a more rakish angle, but the efforts of nature toward the restoration of the old alignment gave a blurred air to her face. When she moved about there was an incessant clicking as innumerable pottery bracelets jingled up and down upon her arms. She came in with such a proprietary haste, and looked around so possessively at the furniture that I wondered if she lived here. But when I asked her she laughed immoderately, repeated my question aloud, and told me she lived with a girl friend at a hotel.

Mr. McKee was a pale, feminine man from the flat below. He had just shaved, for there was a white spot of lather on his cheekbone, and he was most respectful in his greeting to everyone in the room. He informed me that he was in the "artistic game," and I gathered later that he was a photographer and had made the dim enlargement of Mrs. Wilson's mother which hovered like an ectoplasm on the wall. His wife was shrill, languid, handsome, and horrible. She told me with pride that her husband had photographed her a hundred and twenty-seven times since they had been married.

Mrs. Wilson had changed her costume some time before, and was now attired in an elaborate afternoon dress of cream-coloured chiffon, which gave out a continual rustle as she swept about the room. With the influence of the dress her personality had also undergone a change. The intense vitality that had been so remarkable in the garage was converted into impressive hauteur. Her laughter, her gestures, her assertions became more violently affected moment by moment, and as she expanded the room grew smaller around her, until she seemed to be revolving on a noisy, creaking pivot through the smoky air.

"My dear," she told her sister in a high, mincing shout, "most of these fellas will cheat you every time. All they think of is money. I had a woman up here last week to look at my feet, and when she gave me the bill you'd of thought she had my appendicitis out."

"What was the name of the woman?" asked Mrs. McKee.

"Mrs. Eberhardt. She goes around looking at people's feet in their own homes."

"I like your dress," remarked Mrs. McKee, "I think it's adorable."

Mrs. Wilson rejected the compliment by raising her eyebrow in disdain.

"It's just a crazy old thing," she said. "I just slip it on sometimes when I don't care what I look like."

"But it looks wonderful on you, if you know what I mean," pursued Mrs. McKee. "If Chester could only get you in that pose I think he could make something of it."

We all looked in silence at Mrs. Wilson, who removed a strand of hair from over her eyes and looked back at us with a brilliant smile. Mr. McKee regarded her intently with his head on one side, and then moved his hand back and forth slowly in front of his face.

"I should change the light," he said after a moment. "I'd like to bring out the modelling of the features. And I'd try to get hold of all the back hair."

"I wouldn't think of changing the light," cried Mrs. McKee. "I think it's—"

Her husband said "*Sh!*" and we all looked at the subject again, whereupon Tom Buchanan yawned audibly and got to his feet.

"You McKees have something to drink," he said. "Get some more ice and mineral water, Myrtle, before everybody goes to sleep."

"I told that boy about the ice." Myrtle raised her eyebrows in despair at the shiftlessness of the lower orders. "These people! You have to keep after them all the time."

She looked at me and laughed pointlessly. Then she flounced over to the dog, kissed it with ecstasy, and swept into the kitchen, implying that a dozen chefs awaited her orders there.

"I've done some nice things out on Long Island," asserted Mr. McKee.

Tom looked at him blankly.

"Two of them we have framed downstairs."

"Two what?" demanded Tom.

"Two studies. One of them I call *Montauk Point – The Gulls*, and the other I call *Montauk Point – The Sea*."

The sister Catherine sat down beside me on the couch.

"Do you live down on Long Island, too?" she inquired.

"I live at West Egg."

"Really? I was down there at a party about a month ago. At a man named Gatsby's. Do you know him?"

"I live next door to him."

"Well, they say he's a nephew or a cousin of Kaiser Wilhelm's. That's where all his money comes from."

"Really?"

She nodded.

"I'm scared of him. I'd hate to have him get anything on me."

This absorbing information about my neighbour was interrupted by Mrs. McKee's pointing suddenly at Catherine:

"Chester, I think you could do something with *her*," she broke out, but Mr. McKee only nodded in a bored way, and turned his attention to Tom.

"I'd like to do more work on Long Island, if I could get the entry. All I ask is that they should give me a start."

"Ask Myrtle," said Tom, breaking into a short shout of laughter as Mrs. Wilson entered with a tray. "She'll give you a letter of introduction, won't you, Myrtle?"

"Do what?" she asked, startled.

"You'll give McKee a letter of introduction to your husband, so he can do some studies of him." His lips moved silently for a moment as he invented, "'George B. Wilson at the Gasoline Pump,' or something like that."

Catherine leaned close to me and whispered in my ear:

"Neither of them can stand the person they're married to."

"Can't they?"

"Can't *stand* them." She looked at Myrtle and then at Tom. "What I say is, why go on living with them if they can't stand them? If I was them I'd get a divorce and get married to each other right away."

"Doesn't she like Wilson either?"

The answer to this was unexpected. It came from Myrtle, who had overheard the question, and it was violent and obscene.

"You see," cried Catherine triumphantly. She lowered her voice again. "It's really his wife that's keeping them apart. She's a Catholic, and they don't believe in divorce."

Daisy was not a Catholic, and I was a little shocked at the elaborateness of the lie.

"When they do get married," continued Catherine, "they're going West to live for a while until it blows over."

"It'd be more discreet to go to Europe."

"Oh, do you like Europe?" she exclaimed surprisingly. "I just got back from Monte Carlo."

"Really."

"Just last year. I went over there with another girl."

"Stay long?"

"No, we just went to Monte Carlo and back. We went by way of Marseilles. We had over twelve hundred dollars when we started, but we got gyped out of it all in two days in the private rooms. We had an awful time getting back, I can tell you. God, how I hated that town!"

The late afternoon sky bloomed in the window for a moment like the blue honey of the Mediterranean – then the shrill voice of Mrs. McKee called me back into the room.

"I almost made a mistake, too," she declared vigorously. "I almost married a little kike who'd been after me for years. I knew he was below me. Everybody kept saying to me: 'Lucille, that man's way below you!' But if I hadn't met Chester, he'd of got me sure."

"Yes, but listen," said Myrtle Wilson, nodding her head up and down, "at least you didn't marry him."

"I know I didn't."

"Well, I married him," said Myrtle, ambiguously. "And that's the difference between your case and mine."

"Why did you, Myrtle?" demanded Catherine. "Nobody forced you to."

Myrtle considered.

"I married him because I thought he was a gentleman," she said finally. "I thought he knew something about breeding, but he wasn't fit to lick my shoe."

"You were crazy about him for a while," said Catherine.

"Crazy about him!" cried Myrtle incredulously. "Who said I was crazy about him? I never was any more crazy about him than I was about that man there."

She pointed suddenly at me, and everyone looked at me accusingly. I tried to show by my expression that I expected no affection.

"The only *crazy* I was was when I married him. I knew right away I made a mistake. He borrowed somebody's best suit to get married in, and never even told me about it, and the man came after it one day when he was out: 'Oh, is that your suit?' I said. 'This is the first I ever heard about it.' But I gave it to him and then I lay down and cried to beat the band all afternoon."

"She really ought to get away from him," resumed Catherine to me. "They've been living over that garage for eleven years. And Tom's the first sweetie she ever had."

The bottle of whisky – a second one – was now in constant demand by all present, excepting Catherine, who "felt just as good on nothing at all." Tom rang for the janitor and sent him for some celebrated sandwiches, which were a complete supper in themselves. I wanted to get out and walk eastward toward the park through the soft twilight, but each time I tried to go I became entangled in some wild, strident argument which pulled me back, as if with ropes, into my chair. Yet high over the city our line of yellow windows must have contributed their share of human secrecy to the casual watcher in the darkening streets, and I saw him too, looking up and wondering. I was within and without, simultaneously enchanted and repelled by the inexhaustible variety of life.

Myrtle pulled her chair close to mine, and suddenly her warm breath poured over me the story of her first meeting with Tom.

"It was on the two little seats facing each other that are always the last ones left on the train. I was going up to New York to see my sister and spend the night. He had on a dress suit and patent leather shoes, and I couldn't keep my eyes off him, but every time he looked at me I had to pretend to be looking at the advertisement over his head. When we came into the station he was next to me, and his white shirtfront pressed against my arm, and so I told him I'd have to call a policeman, but he knew I lied. I was so excited that when I got into a taxi with him I didn't hardly know I wasn't getting into a subway train. All I kept thinking about, over and over, was 'You can't live forever; you can't live forever.'"

She turned to Mrs. McKee and the room rang full of her artificial laughter.

"My dear," she cried, "I'm going to give you this dress as soon as I'm through with it. I've got to get another one tomorrow. I'm going to make a list of all the things I've got to get. A massage and a wave, and a collar for the dog, and one of those cute little ashtrays where you touch a spring, and a wreath with a black silk bow for mother's grave that'll last all summer. I got to write down a list so I won't forget all the things I got to do."

It was nine o'clock – almost immediately afterward I looked at my watch and found it was ten. Mr. McKee was asleep on a chair with his fists clenched in his lap, like a photograph of a man of action. Taking out my handkerchief I wiped from his cheek the spot of dried lather that had worried me all the afternoon.

The little dog was sitting on the table looking with blind eyes through the smoke, and from time to time groaning faintly. People disappeared, reappeared, made plans to go somewhere, and then lost each other, searched for each other, found each other a few feet away. Some time toward midnight Tom

Buchanan and Mrs. Wilson stood face to face discussing, in impassioned voices, whether Mrs. Wilson had any right to mention Daisy's name.

"Daisy! Daisy! Daisy!" shouted Mrs. Wilson. "I'll say it whenever I want to! Daisy! Dai—"

Making a short deft movement, Tom Buchanan broke her nose with his open hand.

Then there were bloody towels upon the bathroom floor, and women's voices scolding, and high over the confusion a long broken wail of pain. Mr. McKee awoke from his doze and started in a daze toward the door. When he had gone halfway he turned around and stared at the scene – his wife and Catherine scolding and consoling as they stumbled here and there among the crowded furniture with articles of aid, and the despairing figure on the couch, bleeding fluently, and trying to spread a copy of *Town Tattle* over the tapestry scenes of Versailles. Then Mr. McKee turned and continued on out the door. Taking my hat from the chandelier, I followed.

"Come to lunch some day," he suggested, as we groaned down in the elevator.

"Where?"

"Anywhere."

"Keep your hands off the lever," snapped the elevator boy.

"I beg your pardon," said Mr. McKee with dignity, "I didn't know I was touching it."

"All right," I agreed, "I'll be glad to."

… I was standing beside his bed and he was sitting up between the sheets, clad in his underwear, with a great portfolio in his hands.

"Beauty and the Beast… Loneliness… Old Grocery Horse… Brook'n Bridge…"

Then I was lying half asleep in the cold lower level of the Pennsylvania Station, staring at the morning *Tribune*, and waiting for the four o'clock train.

Chapter III

THERE WAS MUSIC from my neighbour's house through the summer nights. In his blue gardens men and girls came and went like moths among the whisperings and the champagne and the stars. At high tide in the afternoon I watched his guests diving from the tower of his raft, or taking the sun on the hot sand of his beach while his two motorboats slit the waters of the Sound, drawing aquaplanes over cataracts of foam. On weekends his Rolls-Royce became an omnibus, bearing parties to and from the city between nine in the morning and long past midnight, while his station wagon scampered like a brisk yellow bug to meet all trains. And on Mondays eight servants, including an extra gardener, toiled all day with mops and scrubbing-brushes and hammers and garden-shears, repairing the ravages of the night before.

Every Friday five crates of oranges and lemons arrived from a fruiterer in New York – every Monday these same oranges and lemons left his back door in a pyramid of pulpless halves. There was a machine in the kitchen which could extract the juice of two hundred oranges in half an hour if a little button was pressed two hundred times by a butler's thumb.

At least once a fortnight a corps of caterers came down with several hundred feet of canvas and enough coloured lights to make a Christmas tree of Gatsby's enormous garden. On buffet tables, garnished with glistening hors-d'oeuvre, spiced baked hams crowded against salads of harlequin designs and pastry pigs and turkeys bewitched to a dark gold. In the main hall a bar with a real brass rail was set up, and stocked with gins and liquors and with cordials so long forgotten that most of his female guests were too young to know one from another.

By seven o'clock the orchestra has arrived, no thin five-piece affair, but a whole pitful of oboes and trombones and saxophones and viols and cornets and piccolos, and low and high drums. The last swimmers have come in from the beach now and are dressing upstairs; the cars from New York are parked five deep in the drive, and already the halls and salons and verandas are gaudy with primary colours, and hair bobbed in strange new ways, and shawls beyond the dreams of Castile. The bar is in full swing, and floating rounds of cocktails permeate the garden outside, until the air is alive with chatter and laughter, and casual innuendo and introductions forgotten on the spot, and enthusiastic meetings between women who never knew each other's names.

The lights grow brighter as the earth lurches away from the sun, and now the orchestra is playing yellow cocktail music, and the opera of voices pitches a key higher. Laughter is easier minute by minute, spilled with prodigality, tipped out at a cheerful word. The groups change more swiftly, swell with new arrivals, dissolve and form in the same breath; already there are wanderers, confident girls who weave here and there among the stouter and more stable, become for a sharp, joyous moment the centre of a group, and then, excited with triumph, glide on through the sea-change of faces and voices and colour under the constantly changing light.

Suddenly one of these gypsies, in trembling opal, seizes a cocktail out of the air, dumps it down for courage and, moving her hands like Frisco, dances out alone on the canvas platform. A momentary hush; the orchestra leader varies his rhythm obligingly for her, and there is a burst of chatter as the erroneous news goes around that she is Gilda Gray's understudy from the Follies. The party has begun.

I believe that on the first night I went to Gatsby's house I was one of the few guests who had actually been invited. People were not invited – they went there. They got into automobiles which bore them out to Long Island, and somehow they ended up at Gatsby's door. Once there they were introduced by somebody who knew Gatsby, and after that they conducted themselves according to the rules of behaviour associated with an amusement park. Sometimes they came and went without having met Gatsby at all, came for the party with a simplicity of heart that was its own ticket of admission.

I had been actually invited. A chauffeur in a uniform of robin's-egg blue crossed my lawn early that Saturday morning with a surprisingly formal note from his employer: the honour would be entirely Gatsby's, it said, if I would attend his "little party" that night. He had seen me several times, and had intended to call on me long before, but a peculiar combination of circumstances had prevented it – signed Jay Gatsby, in a majestic hand.

Dressed up in white flannels I went over to his lawn a little after seven, and wandered around rather ill at ease among swirls and eddies of people I didn't know – though here and there was a face I had noticed on the commuting train. I was immediately struck by the number of young Englishmen dotted about; all well dressed, all looking a little hungry, and all talking in low, earnest voices to solid and prosperous Americans. I was sure that they were selling something: bonds or insurance or automobiles. They were at least agonizingly aware of the easy money in the vicinity and convinced that it was theirs for a few words in the right key.

As soon as I arrived I made an attempt to find my host, but the two or three people of whom I asked his whereabouts stared at me in such an amazed way, and denied so vehemently any knowledge of his movements, that I slunk off in the direction of the cocktail table – the only place in the garden where a single man could linger without looking purposeless and alone.

I was on my way to get roaring drunk from sheer embarrassment when Jordan Baker came out of the house and stood at the head of the marble steps, leaning a little backward and looking with contemptuous interest down into the garden.

Welcome or not, I found it necessary to attach myself to someone before I should begin to address cordial remarks to the passersby.

"Hello!" I roared, advancing toward her. My voice seemed unnaturally loud across the garden.

"I thought you might be here," she responded absently as I came up. "I remembered you lived next door to—"

She held my hand impersonally, as a promise that she'd take care of me in a minute, and gave ear to two girls in twin yellow dresses, who stopped at the foot of the steps.

"Hello!" they cried together. "Sorry you didn't win."

That was for the golf tournament. She had lost in the finals the week before.

"You don't know who we are," said one of the girls in yellow, "but we met you here about a month ago."

"You've dyed your hair since then," remarked Jordan, and I started, but the girls had moved casually on and her remark was addressed to the premature moon, produced like the supper, no doubt, out of a caterer's basket. With Jordan's slender golden arm resting in mine, we descended the steps and sauntered about the garden. A tray of cocktails floated at us through the twilight, and we sat down at a table with the two girls in yellow and three men, each one introduced to us as Mr. Mumble.

"Do you come to these parties often?" inquired Jordan of the girl beside her.

"The last one was the one I met you at," answered the girl, in an alert confident voice. She turned to her companion: "Wasn't it for you, Lucille?"

It was for Lucille, too.

"I like to come," Lucille said. "I never care what I do, so I always have a good time. When I was here last I tore my gown on a chair, and he asked me my name and address – inside of a week I got a package from Croirier's with a new evening gown in it."

"Did you keep it?" asked Jordan.

"Sure I did. I was going to wear it tonight, but it was too big in the bust and had to be altered. It was gas blue with lavender beads. Two hundred and sixty-five dollars."

"There's something funny about a fellow that'll do a thing like that," said the other girl eagerly. "He doesn't want any trouble with *any*body."

"Who doesn't?" I inquired.

"Gatsby. Somebody told me—"

The two girls and Jordan leaned together confidentially.

"Somebody told me they thought he killed a man once."

A thrill passed over all of us. The three Mr. Mumbles bent forward and listened eagerly.

"I don't think it's so much *that*," argued Lucille sceptically; "It's more that he was a German spy during the war."

One of the men nodded in confirmation.

"I heard that from a man who knew all about him, grew up with him in Germany," he assured us positively.

"Oh, no," said the first girl, "it couldn't be that, because he was in the American army during the war." As our credulity switched back to her she leaned forward with enthusiasm. "You look at him sometimes when he thinks nobody's looking at him. I'll bet he killed a man."

She narrowed her eyes and shivered. Lucille shivered. We all turned and looked around for Gatsby. It was testimony to the romantic speculation he inspired that there were whispers about him from those who had found little that it was necessary to whisper about in this world.

The first supper – there would be another one after midnight – was now being served, and Jordan invited me to join her own party, who were spread around a table on the other side of the garden. There were three married couples and Jordan's escort, a persistent undergraduate given to violent innuendo, and obviously under the impression that sooner or later Jordan was going to yield him up her person to a greater or lesser degree. Instead of rambling, this party had preserved a dignified homogeneity, and assumed to itself the function of representing the staid nobility of the countryside – East Egg condescending to West Egg and carefully on guard against its spectroscopic gaiety.

"Let's get out," whispered Jordan, after a somehow wasteful and inappropriate half-hour; "this is much too polite for me."

We got up, and she explained that we were going to find the host: I had never met him, she said, and it was making me uneasy. The undergraduate nodded in a cynical, melancholy way.

The bar, where we glanced first, was crowded, but Gatsby was not there. She couldn't find him from the top of the steps, and he wasn't on the veranda. On a chance we tried an important-looking door, and walked into a high Gothic library, panelled with carved English oak, and probably transported complete from some ruin overseas.

A stout, middle-aged man, with enormous owl-eyed spectacles, was sitting somewhat drunk on the edge of a great table, staring with unsteady concentration at the shelves of books. As we entered he wheeled excitedly around and examined Jordan from head to foot.

"What do you think?" he demanded impetuously.

"About what?"

He waved his hand toward the bookshelves.

"About that. As a matter of fact you needn't bother to ascertain. I ascertained. They're real."

"The books?"

He nodded.

"Absolutely real – have pages and everything. I thought they'd be a nice durable cardboard. Matter of fact, they're absolutely real. Pages and— Here! Lemme show you."

Taking our scepticism for granted, he rushed to the bookcases and returned with Volume One of the *Stoddard Lectures*.

"See!" he cried triumphantly. "It's a bona-fide piece of printed matter. It fooled me. This fella's a regular Belasco. It's a triumph. What thoroughness! What realism! Knew when to stop, too – didn't cut the pages. But what do you want? What do you expect?"

He snatched the book from me and replaced it hastily on its shelf, muttering that if one brick was removed the whole library was liable to collapse.

"Who brought you?" he demanded. "Or did you just come? I was brought. Most people were brought."

Jordan looked at him alertly, cheerfully, without answering.

"I was brought by a woman named Roosevelt," he continued. "Mrs. Claud Roosevelt. Do you know her? I met her somewhere last night. I've been drunk for about a week now, and I thought it might sober me up to sit in a library."

"Has it?"

"A little bit, I think. I can't tell yet. I've only been here an hour. Did I tell you about the books? They're real. They're—"

"You told us."

We shook hands with him gravely and went back outdoors.

There was dancing now on the canvas in the garden; old men pushing young girls backward in eternal graceless circles, superior couples holding each other tortuously, fashionably, and keeping in the corners – and a great number of single girls dancing individually or relieving the orchestra for a moment of the burden of the banjo or the traps. By midnight the hilarity had increased. A celebrated tenor had sung in Italian, and a notorious contralto had sung in jazz, and between the numbers people were doing "stunts" all over the garden, while happy, vacuous bursts of laughter rose toward the summer sky. A pair of stage twins, who turned out to be the girls in yellow, did a baby act in costume, and champagne was served in glasses bigger than finger-bowls. The moon had risen higher, and floating in the Sound was a triangle of silver scales, trembling a little to the stiff, tinny drip of the banjoes on the lawn.

I was still with Jordan Baker. We were sitting at a table with a man of about my age and a rowdy little girl, who gave way upon the slightest provocation to uncontrollable laughter. I was enjoying myself now.

I had taken two finger-bowls of champagne, and the scene had changed before my eyes into something significant, elemental, and profound.

At a lull in the entertainment the man looked at me and smiled.

"Your face is familiar," he said politely. "Weren't you in the First Division during the war?"

"Why yes. I was in the Twenty-eighth Infantry."

"I was in the Sixteenth until June nineteen-eighteen. I knew I'd seen you somewhere before."

We talked for a moment about some wet, grey little villages in France. Evidently he lived in this vicinity, for he told me that he had just bought a hydroplane, and was going to try it out in the morning.

"Want to go with me, old sport? Just near the shore along the Sound."

"What time?"

"Any time that suits you best."

It was on the tip of my tongue to ask his name when Jordan looked around and smiled.

"Having a gay time now?" she inquired.

"Much better." I turned again to my new acquaintance. "This is an unusual party for me. I haven't even seen the host. I live over there—" I waved my hand at the invisible hedge in the distance, "and this man Gatsby sent over his chauffeur with an invitation."

For a moment he looked at me as if he failed to understand.

"I'm Gatsby," he said suddenly.

"What!" I exclaimed. "Oh, I beg your pardon."

"I thought you knew, old sport. I'm afraid I'm not a very good host."

He smiled understandingly – much more than understandingly. It was one of those rare smiles with a quality of eternal reassurance in it, that you may come across four or five times in life. It faced – or seemed to face – the whole eternal world for an instant, and then concentrated on *you* with an irresistible prejudice in your favour. It understood you just so far as you wanted to be understood, believed in you as you would like to believe in yourself, and assured you that it had precisely the impression of you that, at your best, you hoped to convey. Precisely at that point it vanished – and I was looking at an elegant young roughneck, a year or two over thirty, whose elaborate formality of speech just missed being absurd. Some time before he introduced himself I'd got a strong impression that he was picking his words with care.

Almost at the moment when Mr. Gatsby identified himself a butler hurried toward him with the information that Chicago was calling him on the wire. He excused himself with a small bow that included each of us in turn.

"If you want anything just ask for it, old sport," he urged me. "Excuse me. I will rejoin you later."

When he was gone I turned immediately to Jordan – constrained to assure her of my surprise. I had expected that Mr. Gatsby would be a florid and corpulent person in his middle years.

"Who is he?" I demanded. "Do you know?"

"He's just a man named Gatsby."

"Where is he from, I mean? And what does he do?"

"Now *you*'re started on the subject," she answered with a wan smile. "Well, he told me once he was an Oxford man."

A dim background started to take shape behind him, but at her next remark it faded away.

"However, I don't believe it."

"Why not?"

"I don't know," she insisted, "I just don't think he went there."

Something in her tone reminded me of the other girl's "I think he killed a man," and had the effect of stimulating my curiosity. I would have accepted without question the information that Gatsby sprang from the swamps of Louisiana or from the lower East Side of New York. That was comprehensible. But young men didn't – at least in my provincial inexperience I believed they didn't – drift coolly out of nowhere and buy a palace on Long Island Sound.

"Anyhow, he gives large parties," said Jordan, changing the subject with an urban distaste for the concrete. "And I like large parties. They're so intimate. At small parties there isn't any privacy."

There was the boom of a bass drum, and the voice of the orchestra leader rang out suddenly above the echolalia of the garden.

"Ladies and gentlemen," he cried. "At the request of Mr. Gatsby we are going to play for you Mr. Vladmir Tostoff's latest work, which attracted so much attention at Carnegie Hall last May. If you read the papers you know there was a big sensation." He smiled with jovial condescension, and added: "Some sensation!" Whereupon everybody laughed.

"The piece is known," he concluded lustily, "as 'Vladmir Tostoff's Jazz History of the World!'"

The nature of Mr. Tostoff's composition eluded me, because just as it began my eyes fell on Gatsby, standing alone on the marble steps and looking from one group to another with approving eyes. His tanned skin was drawn attractively tight on his face and his short hair looked as though it were trimmed every day. I could see nothing sinister about him. I wondered if the fact that he was not drinking helped to set him off from his guests, for it seemed to me that he grew more correct as the fraternal hilarity increased. When the "Jazz History of the World" was over, girls were putting their heads on men's shoulders in a puppyish, convivial way, girls were swooning backward playfully into men's arms, even into groups, knowing that someone would arrest their falls – but no one swooned backward on Gatsby, and no French bob touched Gatsby's shoulder, and no singing quartets were formed with Gatsby's head for one link.

"I beg your pardon."

Gatsby's butler was suddenly standing beside us.

"Miss Baker?" he inquired. "I beg your pardon, but Mr. Gatsby would like to speak to you alone."

"With me?" she exclaimed in surprise.

"Yes, madame."

She got up slowly, raising her eyebrows at me in astonishment, and followed the butler toward the house. I noticed that she wore her evening-dress, all her dresses, like sports clothes – there was a jauntiness about her movements as if she had first learned to walk upon golf courses on clean, crisp mornings.

I was alone and it was almost two. For some time confused and intriguing sounds had issued from a long, many-windowed room which overhung the terrace. Eluding Jordan's undergraduate, who was now engaged in an obstetrical conversation with two chorus girls, and who implored me to join him, I went inside.

The large room was full of people. One of the girls in yellow was playing the piano, and beside her stood a tall, red-haired young lady from a famous chorus, engaged in song. She had drunk a quantity of champagne, and during the course of her song she had decided, ineptly, that everything was very, very sad – she was not only singing, she was weeping too. Whenever there was a pause in the song she filled it with gasping, broken sobs, and then took up the lyric again in a quavering soprano. The tears coursed down her cheeks – not freely, however, for when they came into contact with her heavily beaded eyelashes they assumed an inky colour, and pursued the rest of their way in slow black rivulets. A humorous suggestion was made that she sing the notes on her face, whereupon she threw up her hands, sank into a chair, and went off into a deep vinous sleep.

"She had a fight with a man who says he's her husband," explained a girl at my elbow.

I looked around. Most of the remaining women were now having fights with men said to be their husbands. Even Jordan's party, the quartet from East Egg, were rent asunder by dissension. One of the men was talking with curious intensity to a young actress, and his wife, after attempting to laugh at the situation in a dignified and indifferent way, broke down entirely and resorted to flank attacks – at intervals she appeared suddenly at his side like an angry diamond, and hissed: "You promised!" into his ear.

The reluctance to go home was not confined to wayward men. The hall was at present occupied by two deplorably sober men and their highly indignant wives. The wives were sympathizing with each other in slightly raised voices.

"Whenever he sees I'm having a good time he wants to go home."

"Never heard anything so selfish in my life."

"We're always the first ones to leave."

"So are we."

"Well, we're almost the last tonight," said one of the men sheepishly. "The orchestra left half an hour ago."

In spite of the wives' agreement that such malevolence was beyond credibility, the dispute ended in a short struggle, and both wives were lifted, kicking, into the night.

As I waited for my hat in the hall the door of the library opened and Jordan Baker and Gatsby came out together. He was saying some last word to her, but the eagerness in his manner tightened abruptly into formality as several people approached him to say goodbye.

Jordan's party were calling impatiently to her from the porch, but she lingered for a moment to shake hands.

"I've just heard the most amazing thing," she whispered. "How long were we in there?"

"Why, about an hour."

"It was… simply amazing," she repeated abstractedly. "But I swore I wouldn't tell it and here I am tantalizing you." She yawned gracefully in my face. "Please come and see me… Phone book… Under the name of Mrs. Sigourney Howard… My aunt…" She was hurrying off as she talked – her brown hand waved a jaunty salute as she melted into her party at the door.

Rather ashamed that on my first appearance I had stayed so late, I joined the last of Gatsby's guests, who were clustered around him. I wanted to explain that I'd hunted for him early in the evening and to apologize for not having known him in the garden.

"Don't mention it," he enjoined me eagerly. "Don't give it another thought, old sport." The familiar expression held no more familiarity than the hand which reassuringly brushed my shoulder. "And don't forget we're going up in the hydroplane tomorrow morning, at nine o'clock."

Then the butler, behind his shoulder:

"Philadelphia wants you on the phone, sir."

"All right, in a minute. Tell them I'll be right there… Good night."

"Good night."

"Good night." He smiled – and suddenly there seemed to be a pleasant significance in having been among the last to go, as if he had desired it all the time. "Good night, old sport… Good night."

But as I walked down the steps I saw that the evening was not quite over. Fifty feet from the door a dozen headlights illuminated a bizarre and tumultuous scene. In the ditch beside the road, right side up, but violently shorn of one wheel, rested a new coupé which had left Gatsby's drive not two minutes before. The sharp jut of a wall accounted for the detachment of the wheel, which was now getting considerable attention from half a dozen curious chauffeurs. However, as they had left their cars blocking the road, a harsh, discordant din from those in the rear had been audible for some time, and added to the already violent confusion of the scene.

A man in a long duster had dismounted from the wreck and now stood in the middle of the road, looking from the car to the tyre and from the tyre to the observers in a pleasant, puzzled way.

"See!" he explained. "It went in the ditch."

The fact was infinitely astonishing to him, and I recognized first the unusual quality of wonder, and then the man – it was the late patron of Gatsby's library.

"How'd it happen?"

He shrugged his shoulders.

"I know nothing whatever about mechanics," he said decisively.

"But how did it happen? Did you run into the wall?"

"Don't ask me," said Owl Eyes, washing his hands of the whole matter. "I know very little about driving – next to nothing. It happened, and that's all I know."

"Well, if you're a poor driver you oughtn't to try driving at night."

"But I wasn't even trying," he explained indignantly, "I wasn't even trying."

An awed hush fell upon the bystanders.

"Do you want to commit suicide?"

"You're lucky it was just a wheel! A bad driver and not even *try*ing!"

"You don't understand," explained the criminal. "I wasn't driving. There's another man in the car."

The shock that followed this declaration found voice in a sustained "Ah-h-h!" as the door of the coupé swung slowly open. The crowd – it was now a crowd – stepped back involuntarily, and when the door had opened wide there was a ghostly pause. Then, very gradually, part by part, a pale, dangling individual stepped out of the wreck, pawing tentatively at the ground with a large uncertain dancing shoe.

Blinded by the glare of the headlights and confused by the incessant groaning of the horns, the apparition stood swaying for a moment before he perceived the man in the duster.

"Wha's matter?" he inquired calmly. "Did we run outa gas?"

"Look!"

Half a dozen fingers pointed at the amputated wheel – he stared at it for a moment, and then looked upward as though he suspected that it had dropped from the sky.

"It came off," someone explained.

He nodded.

"At first I din' notice we'd stopped."

A pause. Then, taking a long breath and straightening his shoulders, he remarked in a determined voice:

"Wonder'ff tell me where there's a gas'line station?"

At least a dozen men, some of them a little better off than he was, explained to him that wheel and car were no longer joined by any physical bond.

"Back out," he suggested after a moment. "Put her in reverse."

"But the *wheel*'s off!"

He hesitated.

"No harm in trying," he said.

The caterwauling horns had reached a crescendo and I turned away and cut across the lawn toward home. I glanced back once. A wafer of a moon was shining over Gatsby's house, making the night fine as before, and surviving the laughter and the sound of his still glowing garden. A sudden emptiness seemed to flow now from the windows and the great doors, endowing with complete isolation the figure of the host, who stood on the porch, his hand up in a formal gesture of farewell.

* * *

Reading over what I have written so far, I see I have given the impression that the events of three nights several weeks apart were all that absorbed me. On the contrary, they were merely casual events in a crowded summer, and, until much later, they absorbed me infinitely less than my personal affairs.

Most of the time I worked. In the early morning the sun threw my shadow westward as I hurried down the white chasms of lower New York to the Probity Trust. I knew the other clerks and young bond-salesmen by their first names, and lunched with them in dark, crowded restaurants on little pig sausages and mashed potatoes and coffee. I even had a short affair with a girl who lived in Jersey City and worked in the accounting department, but her brother began throwing mean looks in my direction, so when she went on her vacation in July I let it blow quietly away.

I took dinner usually at the Yale Club – for some reason it was the gloomiest event of my day – and then I went upstairs to the library and studied investments and securities for a conscientious hour. There were generally a few rioters around, but they never came into the library, so it was a good place to work. After that, if the night was mellow, I strolled down Madison Avenue past the old Murray Hill Hotel, and over 33rd Street to the Pennsylvania Station.

I began to like New York, the racy, adventurous feel of it at night, and the satisfaction that the constant flicker of men and women and machines gives to the restless eye. I liked to walk up Fifth Avenue and pick out romantic women from the crowd and imagine that in a few minutes I was going to enter into their lives, and no one would ever know or disapprove. Sometimes, in my mind, I followed them to their apartments on the corners of hidden streets, and they turned and smiled back at me before they faded through a door into warm darkness. At the enchanted metropolitan twilight I felt a haunting loneliness sometimes, and felt it in others – poor young clerks who loitered in front of windows waiting until it was time for a solitary restaurant dinner – young clerks in the dusk, wasting the most poignant moments of night and life.

Again at eight o'clock, when the dark lanes of the Forties were lined five deep with throbbing taxicabs, bound for the theatre district, I felt a sinking in my heart. Forms leaned together in the taxis as they waited, and voices sang, and there was laughter from unheard jokes, and lighted cigarettes made unintelligible circles inside. Imagining that I, too, was hurrying towards gaiety and sharing their intimate excitement, I wished them well.

For a while I lost sight of Jordan Baker, and then in midsummer I found her again. At first I was flattered to go places with her, because she was a golf champion, and everyone knew her name. Then it was something more. I wasn't actually in love, but I felt a sort of tender curiosity. The bored haughty face that she turned to the world concealed something – most affectations conceal something eventually, even though they don't in the beginning – and one day I found what it was. When we were on a house-party together up in Warwick, she left a borrowed car out in the rain with the top down, and then lied about it – and suddenly I remembered the story about her that had eluded me that night at Daisy's. At her first big golf tournament there was a row that nearly reached the newspapers – a suggestion that she had moved her ball from a bad lie in the semifinal round. The thing approached the proportions of a scandal – then died away. A caddy retracted his statement, and the only other witness admitted that he might have been mistaken. The incident and the name had remained together in my mind.

Jordan Baker instinctively avoided clever, shrewd men, and now I saw that this was because she felt safer on a plane where any divergence from a code would be thought impossible. She was incurably dishonest. She wasn't able to endure being at a disadvantage and, given this unwillingness, I suppose she had begun dealing in subterfuges when she was very young in order to keep that cool, insolent smile turned to the world and yet satisfy the demands of her hard, jaunty body.

It made no difference to me. Dishonesty in a woman is a thing you never blame deeply – I was casually sorry, and then I forgot. It was on that same house-party that we had a curious conversation about driving a car. It started because she passed so close to some workmen that our fender flicked a button on one man's coat.

"You're a rotten driver," I protested. "Either you ought to be more careful, or you oughtn't to drive at all."

"I am careful."

"No, you're not."

"Well, other people are," she said lightly.

"What's that got to do with it?"

"They'll keep out of my way," she insisted. "It takes two to make an accident."

"Suppose you met somebody just as careless as yourself."

"I hope I never will," she answered. "I hate careless people. That's why I like you."

Her grey, sun-strained eyes stared straight ahead, but she had deliberately shifted our relations, and for a moment I thought I loved her. But I am slow-thinking and full of interior rules that act as brakes on my desires, and I knew that first I had to get myself definitely out of that tangle back home. I'd been writing letters once a week and signing them: "Love, Nick," and all I could think of was how, when that certain girl played tennis, a faint moustache of perspiration appeared on her upper lip. Nevertheless there was a vague understanding that had to be tactfully broken off before I was free.

Everyone suspects himself of at least one of the cardinal virtues, and this is mine: I am one of the few honest people that I have ever known.

Chapter IV

ON SUNDAY MORNING while church bells rang in the villages alongshore, the world and its mistress returned to Gatsby's house and twinkled hilariously on his lawn.

"He's a bootlegger," said the young ladies, moving somewhere between his cocktails and his flowers. "One time he killed a man who had found out that he was nephew to Von Hindenburg and second cousin to the devil. Reach me a rose, honey, and pour me a last drop into that there crystal glass."

Once I wrote down on the empty spaces of a timetable the names of those who came to Gatsby's house that summer. It is an old timetable now, disintegrating at its folds, and headed "This schedule in effect July 5th, 1922." But I can still read the grey names, and they will give you a better impression than my generalities of those who accepted Gatsby's hospitality and paid him the subtle tribute of knowing nothing whatever about him.

From East Egg, then, came the Chester Beckers and the Leeches, and a man named Bunsen, whom I knew at Yale, and Doctor Webster Civet, who was drowned last summer up in Maine. And the Hornbeams and the Willie Voltaires, and a whole clan named Blackbuck, who always gathered in a corner and flipped up their noses like goats at whosoever came near. And the Ismays and the Chrysties (or rather Hubert Auerbach and Mr. Chrystie's wife), and Edgar Beaver, whose hair, they say, turned cotton-white one winter afternoon for no good reason at all.

Clarence Endive was from East Egg, as I remember. He came only once, in white knickerbockers, and had a fight with a bum named Etty in the garden. From farther out on the Island came the Cheadles and the O. R. P. Schraeders, and the Stonewall Jackson Abrams of Georgia, and the Fishguards and the Ripley Snells. Snell was there three days before he went to the penitentiary, so drunk out on the gravel drive that Mrs. Ulysses Swett's automobile ran over his right hand. The Dancies came, too, and S. B. Whitebait, who was well over sixty, and Maurice A. Flink, and the Hammerheads, and Beluga the tobacco importer, and Beluga's girls.

From West Egg came the Poles and the Mulreadys and Cecil Roebuck and Cecil Schoen and Gulick the State senator and Newton Orchid, who controlled Films Par Excellence, and Eckhaust and Clyde Cohen and Don S. Schwartz (the son) and Arthur McCarty, all connected with the movies in one way or another. And the Catlips and the Bembergs and G. Earl Muldoon, brother to that Muldoon who afterward strangled his wife. Da Fontano the promoter came there, and Ed Legros and James B. ("Rot-Gut") Ferret and the De Jongs and Ernest Lilly – they came to gamble, and when Ferret wandered into the garden it meant he was cleaned out and Associated Traction would have to fluctuate profitably next day.

A man named Klipspringer was there so often that he became known as "the boarder" – I doubt if he had any other home. Of theatrical people there were Gus Waize and Horace O'Donavan and Lester Myer and George Duckweed and Francis Bull. Also from New York were the Chromes and the Backhyssons and the Dennickers and Russel Betty and the Corrigans and the Kellehers and the Dewars and the Scullys and S. W. Belcher and the Smirkes and the young Quinns, divorced now, and Henry L. Palmetto, who killed himself by jumping in front of a subway train in Times Square.

Benny McClenahan arrived always with four girls. They were never quite the same ones in physical person, but they were so identical one with another that it inevitably seemed they had been there before. I have forgotten their names – Jaqueline, I think, or else Consuela, or Gloria or Judy or June, and their last names were either the melodious names of flowers and months or the sterner ones of the great American capitalists whose cousins, if pressed, they would confess themselves to be.

In addition to all these I can remember that Faustina O'Brien came there at least once and the Baedeker girls and young Brewer, who had his nose shot off in the war, and Mr. Albrucksburger and Miss Haag, his fiancée, and Ardita Fitz-Peters and Mr. P. Jewett, once head of the American Legion, and Miss Claudia Hip, with a man reputed to be her chauffeur, and a prince of something, whom we called Duke, and whose name, if I ever knew it, I have forgotten.

All these people came to Gatsby's house in the summer.

* * *

At nine o'clock, one morning late in July, Gatsby's gorgeous car lurched up the rocky drive to my door and gave out a burst of melody from its three-noted horn.

It was the first time he had called on me, though I had gone to two of his parties, mounted in his hydroplane, and, at his urgent invitation, made frequent use of his beach.

"Good morning, old sport. You're having lunch with me today and I thought we'd ride up together."

He was balancing himself on the dashboard of his car with that resourcefulness of movement that is so peculiarly American – that comes, I suppose, with the absence of lifting work in youth and, even more, with the formless grace of our nervous, sporadic games. This quality was continually breaking through his punctilious manner in the shape of restlessness. He was never quite still; there was always a tapping foot somewhere or the impatient opening and closing of a hand.

He saw me looking with admiration at his car.

"It's pretty, isn't it, old sport?" He jumped off to give me a better view. "Haven't you ever seen it before?"

I'd seen it. Everybody had seen it. It was a rich cream colour, bright with nickel, swollen here and there in its monstrous length with triumphant hatboxes and supper-boxes and toolboxes, and terraced with a labyrinth of windshields that mirrored a dozen suns. Sitting down behind many layers of glass in a sort of green leather conservatory, we started to town.

I had talked with him perhaps half a dozen times in the past month and found, to my disappointment, that he had little to say. So my first impression, that he was a person of some undefined consequence, had gradually faded and he had become simply the proprietor of an elaborate roadhouse next door.

And then came that disconcerting ride. We hadn't reached West Egg village before Gatsby began leaving his elegant sentences unfinished and slapping himself indecisively on the knee of his caramel-coloured suit.

"Look here, old sport," he broke out surprisingly, "what's your opinion of me, anyhow?"

A little overwhelmed, I began the generalized evasions which that question deserves.

"Well, I'm going to tell you something about my life," he interrupted. "I don't want you to get a wrong idea of me from all these stories you hear."

So he was aware of the bizarre accusations that flavoured conversation in his halls.

"I'll tell you God's truth." His right hand suddenly ordered divine retribution to stand by. "I am the son of some wealthy people in the Middle West – all dead now. I was brought up in America but educated at Oxford, because all my ancestors have been educated there for many years. It is a family tradition."

He looked at me sideways – and I knew why Jordan Baker had believed he was lying. He hurried the phrase "educated at Oxford," or swallowed it, or choked on it, as though it had bothered him before. And with this doubt, his whole statement fell to pieces, and I wondered if there wasn't something a little sinister about him, after all.

"What part of the Middle West?" I inquired casually.

"San Francisco."

"I see."

"My family all died and I came into a good deal of money."

His voice was solemn, as if the memory of that sudden extinction of a clan still haunted him. For a moment I suspected that he was pulling my leg, but a glance at him convinced me otherwise.

"After that I lived like a young rajah in all the capitals of Europe – Paris, Venice, Rome – collecting jewels, chiefly rubies, hunting big game, painting a little, things for myself only, and trying to forget something very sad that had happened to me long ago."

With an effort I managed to restrain my incredulous laughter. The very phrases were worn so threadbare that they evoked no image except that of a turbaned "character" leaking sawdust at every pore as he pursued a tiger through the Bois de Boulogne.

"Then came the war, old sport. It was a great relief, and I tried very hard to die, but I seemed to bear an enchanted life. I accepted a commission as first lieutenant when it began. In the Argonne Forest I took the remains of my machine-gun battalion so far forward that there was a half mile gap on either side of us where the infantry couldn't advance. We stayed there two days and two nights, a hundred and thirty men with sixteen Lewis guns, and when the infantry came up at last they found the insignia of three German divisions among the piles of dead. I was promoted to be a major, and every Allied government gave me a decoration – even Montenegro, little Montenegro down on the Adriatic Sea!"

Little Montenegro! He lifted up the words and nodded at them – with his smile. The smile comprehended Montenegro's troubled history and sympathized with the brave struggles of the Montenegrin people. It appreciated fully the chain of national circumstances which had elicited this tribute from Montenegro's warm little heart. My incredulity was submerged in fascination now; it was like skimming hastily through a dozen magazines.

He reached in his pocket, and a piece of metal, slung on a ribbon, fell into my palm.

"That's the one from Montenegro."

To my astonishment, the thing had an authentic look. "Orderi di Danilo," ran the circular legend, "Montenegro, Nicolas Rex."

"Turn it."

"Major Jay Gatsby," I read, "For Valour Extraordinary."

"Here's another thing I always carry. A souvenir of Oxford days. It was taken in Trinity Quad – the man on my left is now the Earl of Doncaster."

It was a photograph of half a dozen young men in blazers loafing in an archway through which were visible a host of spires. There was Gatsby, looking a little, not much, younger – with a cricket bat in his hand.

Then it was all true. I saw the skins of tigers flaming in his palace on the Grand Canal; I saw him opening a chest of rubies to ease, with their crimson-lighted depths, the gnawings of his broken heart.

"I'm going to make a big request of you today," he said, pocketing his souvenirs with satisfaction, "so I thought you ought to know something about me. I didn't want you to think I was just some nobody. You see, I usually find myself among strangers because I drift here and there trying to forget the sad things that happened to me." He hesitated. "You'll hear about it this afternoon."

"At lunch?"

"No, this afternoon. I happened to find out that you're taking Miss Baker to tea."

"Do you mean you're in love with Miss Baker?"

"No, old sport, I'm not. But Miss Baker has kindly consented to speak to you about this matter."

I hadn't the faintest idea what "this matter" was, but I was more annoyed than interested. I hadn't asked Jordan to tea in order to discuss Mr. Jay Gatsby. I was sure the request would be something utterly fantastic, and for a moment I was sorry I'd ever set foot upon his overpopulated lawn.

He wouldn't say another word. His correctness grew on him as we neared the city. We passed Port Roosevelt, where there was a glimpse of red-belted oceangoing ships, and sped along a cobbled slum lined with the dark, undeserted saloons of the faded-gilt nineteen-hundreds. Then the valley of ashes opened out on both sides of us, and I had a glimpse of Mrs. Wilson straining at the garage pump with panting vitality as we went by.

With fenders spread like wings we scattered light through half Astoria – only half, for as we twisted among the pillars of the elevated I heard the familiar "jug-jug-spat!" of a motorcycle, and a frantic policeman rode alongside.

"All right, old sport," called Gatsby. We slowed down. Taking a white card from his wallet, he waved it before the man's eyes.

"Right you are," agreed the policeman, tipping his cap. "Know you next time, Mr. Gatsby. Excuse me!"

"What was that?" I inquired. "The picture of Oxford?"

"I was able to do the commissioner a favour once, and he sends me a Christmas card every year."

Over the great bridge, with the sunlight through the girders making a constant flicker upon the moving cars, with the city rising up across the river in white heaps and sugar lumps all built with a wish out of nonolfactory money. The city seen from the Queensboro Bridge is always the city seen for the first time, in its first wild promise of all the mystery and the beauty in the world.

A dead man passed us in a hearse heaped with blooms, followed by two carriages with drawn blinds, and by more cheerful carriages for friends. The friends looked out at us with the tragic eyes and short upper lips of southeastern Europe, and I was glad that the sight of Gatsby's splendid car was included in their sombre holiday. As we crossed Blackwell's Island a limousine passed us, driven by a white chauffeur, in which sat three modish negroes, two bucks and a girl. I laughed aloud as the yolks of their eyeballs rolled toward us in haughty rivalry.

"Anything can happen now that we've slid over this bridge," I thought; "anything at all…"

Even Gatsby could happen, without any particular wonder.

* * *

Roaring noon. In a well-fanned Forty-second Street cellar I met Gatsby for lunch. Blinking away the brightness of the street outside, my eyes picked him out obscurely in the anteroom, talking to another man.

"Mr. Carraway, this is my friend Mr. Wolfshiem."

A small, flat-nosed Jew raised his large head and regarded me with two fine growths of hair which luxuriated in either nostril. After a moment I discovered his tiny eyes in the half-darkness.

"—so I took one look at him," said Mr. Wolfshiem, shaking my hand earnestly, "and what do you think I did?"

"What?" I inquired politely.

But evidently he was not addressing me, for he dropped my hand and covered Gatsby with his expressive nose.

"I handed the money to Katspaugh and I said: 'All right, Katspaugh, don't pay him a penny till he shuts his mouth.' He shut it then and there."

Gatsby took an arm of each of us and moved forward into the restaurant, whereupon Mr. Wolfshiem swallowed a new sentence he was starting and lapsed into a somnambulatory abstraction.

"Highballs?" asked the head waiter.

"This is a nice restaurant here," said Mr. Wolfshiem, looking at the presbyterian nymphs on the ceiling. "But I like across the street better!"

"Yes, highballs," agreed Gatsby, and then to Mr. Wolfshiem: "It's too hot over there."

"Hot and small – yes," said Mr. Wolfshiem, "but full of memories."

"What place is that?" I asked.

"The old Metropole."

"The old Metropole," brooded Mr. Wolfshiem gloomily. "Filled with faces dead and gone. Filled with friends gone now forever. I can't forget so long as I live the night they shot Rosy Rosenthal there. It was six of us at the table, and Rosy had eat and drunk a lot all evening. When it was almost morning the waiter came up to him with a funny look and says somebody wants to speak to him outside. 'All right,' says Rosy, and begins to get up, and I pulled him down in his chair.

"'Let the bastards come in here if they want you, Rosy, but don't you, so help me, move outside this room.'

"It was four o'clock in the morning then, and if we'd of raised the blinds we'd of seen daylight."

"Did he go?" I asked innocently.

"Sure he went." Mr. Wolfshiem's nose flashed at me indignantly. "He turned around in the door and says: 'Don't let that waiter take away my coffee!' Then he went out on the sidewalk, and they shot him three times in his full belly and drove away."

"Four of them were electrocuted," I said, remembering.

"Five, with Becker." His nostrils turned to me in an interested way. "I understand you're looking for a business gonnegtion."

The juxtaposition of these two remarks was startling. Gatsby answered for me:

"Oh, no," he exclaimed, "this isn't the man."

"No?" Mr. Wolfshiem seemed disappointed.

"This is just a friend. I told you we'd talk about that some other time."

"I beg your pardon," said Mr. Wolfshiem, "I had a wrong man."

A succulent hash arrived, and Mr. Wolfshiem, forgetting the more sentimental atmosphere of the old Metropole, began to eat with ferocious delicacy. His eyes, meanwhile, roved very slowly all around the room – he completed the arc by turning to inspect the people directly behind. I think that, except for my presence, he would have taken one short glance beneath our own table.

"Look here, old sport," said Gatsby, leaning toward me, "I'm afraid I made you a little angry this morning in the car."

There was the smile again, but this time I held out against it.

"I don't like mysteries," I answered, "and I don't understand why you won't come out frankly and tell me what you want. Why has it all got to come through Miss Baker?"

"Oh, it's nothing underhand," he assured me. "Miss Baker's a great sportswoman, you know, and she'd never do anything that wasn't all right."

Suddenly he looked at his watch, jumped up, and hurried from the room, leaving me with Mr. Wolfshiem at the table.

"He has to telephone," said Mr. Wolfshiem, following him with his eyes. "Fine fellow, isn't he? Handsome to look at and a perfect gentleman."

"Yes."

"He's an Oggsford man."

"Oh!"

"He went to Oggsford College in England. You know Oggsford College?"

"I've heard of it."

"It's one of the most famous colleges in the world."

"Have you known Gatsby for a long time?" I inquired.

"Several years," he answered in a gratified way. "I made the pleasure of his acquaintance just after the war. But I knew I had discovered a man of fine breeding after I talked with him an hour. I said to myself: 'There's the kind of man you'd like to take home and introduce to your mother and sister.'" He paused. "I see you're looking at my cuff buttons."

I hadn't been looking at them, but I did now. They were composed of oddly familiar pieces of ivory.

"Finest specimens of human molars," he informed me.

"Well!" I inspected them. "That's a very interesting idea."

"Yeah." He flipped his sleeves up under his coat. "Yeah, Gatsby's very careful about women. He would never so much as look at a friend's wife."

When the subject of this instinctive trust returned to the table and sat down Mr. Wolfshiem drank his coffee with a jerk and got to his feet.

"I have enjoyed my lunch," he said, "and I'm going to run off from you two young men before I outstay my welcome."

"Don't hurry Meyer," said Gatsby, without enthusiasm. Mr. Wolfshiem raised his hand in a sort of benediction.

"You're very polite, but I belong to another generation," he announced solemnly. "You sit here and discuss your sports and your young ladies and your—" He supplied an imaginary noun with another wave of his hand. "As for me, I am fifty years old, and I won't impose myself on you any longer."

As he shook hands and turned away his tragic nose was trembling. I wondered if I had said anything to offend him.

"He becomes very sentimental sometimes," explained Gatsby. "This is one of his sentimental days. He's quite a character around New York – a denizen of Broadway."

"Who is he, anyhow, an actor?"

"No."

"A dentist?"

"Meyer Wolfshiem? No, he's a gambler." Gatsby hesitated, then added, coolly: "He's the man who fixed the World's Series back in 1919."

"Fixed the World's Series?" I repeated.

The idea staggered me. I remembered, of course, that the World's Series had been fixed in 1919, but if I had thought of it at all I would have thought of it as a thing that merely *happened*, the end of some inevitable chain. It never occurred to me that one man could start to play with the faith of fifty million people – with the single-mindedness of a burglar blowing a safe.

"How did he happen to do that?" I asked after a minute.

"He just saw the opportunity."

"Why isn't he in jail?"

"They can't get him, old sport. He's a smart man."

I insisted on paying the check. As the waiter brought my change I caught sight of Tom Buchanan across the crowded room.

"Come along with me for a minute," I said; "I've got to say hello to someone."

When he saw us Tom jumped up and took half a dozen steps in our direction.

"Where've you been?" he demanded eagerly. "Daisy's furious because you haven't called up."

"This is Mr. Gatsby, Mr. Buchanan."

They shook hands briefly, and a strained, unfamiliar look of embarrassment came over Gatsby's face.

"How've you been, anyhow?" demanded Tom of me. "How'd you happen to come up this far to eat?"

"I've been having lunch with Mr. Gatsby."

I turned toward Mr. Gatsby, but he was no longer there.

* * *

One October day in nineteen-seventeen—

(said Jordan Baker that afternoon, sitting up very straight on a straight chair in the tea-garden at the Plaza Hotel)

—I was walking along from one place to another, half on the sidewalks and half on the lawns. I was happier on the lawns because I had on shoes from England with rubber knobs on the soles that bit into the soft ground. I had on a new plaid skirt also that blew a little in the wind, and whenever this happened the red, white, and blue banners in front of all the houses stretched out stiff and said *tut-tut-tut-tut*, in a disapproving way.

The largest of the banners and the largest of the lawns belonged to Daisy Fay's house. She was just eighteen, two years older than me, and by far the most popular of all the young girls in Louisville. She dressed in white, and had a little white roadster, and all day long the telephone rang in her house and excited young officers from Camp Taylor demanded the privilege of monopolizing her that night. "Anyways, for an hour!"

When I came opposite her house that morning her white roadster was beside the kerb, and she was sitting in it with a lieutenant I had never seen before. They were so engrossed in each other that she didn't see me until I was five feet away.

"Hello, Jordan," she called unexpectedly. "Please come here."

I was flattered that she wanted to speak to me, because of all the older girls I admired her most. She asked me if I was going to the Red Cross to make bandages. I was. Well, then, would I tell them that she couldn't come that day? The officer looked at Daisy while she was speaking, in a way that every young girl wants to be looked at sometime, and because it seemed romantic to me I have remembered the incident ever since. His name was Jay Gatsby, and I didn't lay eyes on him again for over four years – even after I'd met him on Long Island I didn't realize it was the same man.

That was nineteen-seventeen. By the next year I had a few beaux myself, and I began to play in tournaments, so I didn't see Daisy very often. She went with a slightly older crowd – when she went with anyone at all. Wild rumours were circulating about her – how her mother had found her packing her bag one winter night to go to New York and say goodbye to a soldier who was going overseas. She was effectually prevented, but she wasn't on speaking terms with her family for several weeks. After that she didn't play around with the soldiers any more, but only with a few flat-footed, shortsighted young men in town, who couldn't get into the army at all.

By the next autumn she was gay again, gay as ever. She had a début after the armistice, and in February she was presumably engaged to a man from New Orleans. In June she married Tom Buchanan of Chicago, with more pomp and circumstance than Louisville ever knew before. He came down with a hundred people in four private cars, and hired a whole floor of the Muhlbach Hotel, and the day before the wedding he gave her a string of pearls valued at three hundred and fifty thousand dollars.

I was a bridesmaid. I came into her room half an hour before the bridal dinner, and found her lying on her bed as lovely as the June night in her flowered dress – and as drunk as a monkey. She had a bottle of Sauterne in one hand and a letter in the other.

"'Gratulate me," she muttered. "Never had a drink before, but oh how I do enjoy it."

"What's the matter, Daisy?"

I was scared, I can tell you; I'd never seen a girl like that before.

"Here, dearies." She groped around in a wastebasket she had with her on the bed and pulled out the string of pearls. "Take 'em downstairs and give 'em back to whoever they belong to. Tell 'em all Daisy's change' her mine. Say: 'Daisy's change' her mine!'"

She began to cry – she cried and cried. I rushed out and found her mother's maid, and we locked the door and got her into a cold bath. She wouldn't let go of the letter. She took it into the tub with her and squeezed it up in a wet ball, and only let me leave it in the soap-dish when she saw that it was coming to pieces like snow.

But she didn't say another word. We gave her spirits of ammonia and put ice on her forehead and hooked her back into her dress, and half an hour later, when we walked out of the room, the pearls were around her neck and the incident was over. Next day at five o'clock she married Tom Buchanan without so much as a shiver, and started off on a three months' trip to the South Seas.

I saw them in Santa Barbara when they came back, and I thought I'd never seen a girl so mad about her husband. If he left the room for a minute she'd look around uneasily, and say: "Where's Tom gone?" and wear the most abstracted expression until she saw him coming in the door. She used to sit on the sand with his head in her lap by the hour, rubbing her fingers over his eyes and looking at him with unfathomable delight. It was touching to see them together – it made you laugh in a hushed, fascinated way. That was in August. A week after I left Santa Barbara Tom ran into a wagon on the Ventura road one night, and ripped a front wheel off his car. The girl who was with him got into the papers, too, because her arm was broken – she was one of the chambermaids in the Santa Barbara Hotel.

The next April Daisy had her little girl, and they went to France for a year. I saw them one spring in Cannes, and later in Deauville, and then they came back to Chicago to settle down. Daisy was popular in Chicago, as you know. They moved with a fast crowd, all of them young and rich and wild, but she came out with an absolutely perfect reputation. Perhaps because she doesn't drink. It's a great advantage not to drink among hard-drinking people. You can hold your tongue and, moreover, you can time any little irregularity of your own so that everybody else is so blind that they don't see or care. Perhaps Daisy never went in for amour at all – and yet there's something in that voice of hers...

Well, about six weeks ago, she heard the name Gatsby for the first time in years. It was when I asked you – do you remember? – if you knew Gatsby in West Egg. After you had gone home she came into my room and woke me up, and said: "What Gatsby?" and when I described him – I was half asleep – she said in the strangest voice that it must be the man she used to know. It wasn't until then that I connected this Gatsby with the officer in her white car.

* * *

When Jordan Baker had finished telling all this we had left the Plaza for half an hour and were driving in a victoria through Central Park. The sun had gone down behind the tall apartments of the movie stars in the West Fifties, and the clear voices of children, already gathered like crickets on the grass, rose through the hot twilight:

> *"I'm the Sheik of Araby.*
> *Your love belongs to me.*
> *At night when you're asleep*
> *Into your tent I'll creep—"*

"It was a strange coincidence," I said.

"But it wasn't a coincidence at all."

"Why not?"

"Gatsby bought that house so that Daisy would be just across the bay."

Then it had not been merely the stars to which he had aspired on that June night. He came alive to me, delivered suddenly from the womb of his purposeless splendour.

"He wants to know," continued Jordan, "if you'll invite Daisy to your house some afternoon and then let him come over."

The modesty of the demand shook me. He had waited five years and bought a mansion where he dispensed starlight to casual moths – so that he could "come over" some afternoon to a stranger's garden.

"Did I have to know all this before he could ask such a little thing?"

"He's afraid, he's waited so long. He thought you might be offended. You see, he's regular tough underneath it all."

Something worried me.

"Why didn't he ask you to arrange a meeting?"

"He wants her to see his house," she explained. "And your house is right next door."

"Oh!"

"I think he half expected her to wander into one of his parties, some night," went on Jordan, "but she never did. Then he began asking people casually if they knew her, and I was the first one he found. It was that night he sent for me at his dance, and you should have heard the elaborate way he worked up to it. Of course, I immediately suggested a luncheon in New York – and I thought he'd go mad:

"'I don't want to do anything out of the way!' he kept saying. 'I want to see her right next door.'

"When I said you were a particular friend of Tom's, he started to abandon the whole idea. He doesn't know very much about Tom, though he says he's read a Chicago paper for years just on the chance of catching a glimpse of Daisy's name."

It was dark now, and as we dipped under a little bridge I put my arm around Jordan's golden shoulder and drew her toward me and asked her to dinner. Suddenly I wasn't thinking of Daisy and Gatsby any more, but of this clean, hard, limited person, who dealt in universal scepticism, and who leaned back jauntily just within the circle of my arm. A phrase began to beat in my ears with a sort of heady excitement: "There are only the pursued, the pursuing, the busy, and the tired."

"And Daisy ought to have something in her life," murmured Jordan to me.

"Does she want to see Gatsby?"

"She's not to know about it. Gatsby doesn't want her to know. You're just supposed to invite her to tea."

We passed a barrier of dark trees, and then the façade of Fifty-Ninth Street, a block of delicate pale light, beamed down into the park. Unlike Gatsby and Tom Buchanan, I had no girl whose disembodied face floated along the dark cornices and blinding signs, and so I drew up the girl beside me, tightening my arms. Her wan, scornful mouth smiled, and so I drew her up again closer, this time to my face.

Chapter V

WHEN I CAME HOME to West Egg that night I was afraid for a moment that my house was on fire. Two o'clock and the whole corner of the peninsula was blazing with light, which fell unreal on the shrubbery and made thin elongating glints upon the roadside wires. Turning a corner, I saw that it was Gatsby's house, lit from tower to cellar.

At first I thought it was another party, a wild rout that had resolved itself into "hide-and-go-seek" or "sardines-in-the-box" with all the house thrown open to the game. But there wasn't a sound. Only wind in the trees, which blew the wires and made the lights go off and on again as if the house had winked into the darkness. As my taxi groaned away I saw Gatsby walking toward me across his lawn.

"Your place looks like the World's Fair," I said.

"Does it?" He turned his eyes toward it absently. "I have been glancing into some of the rooms. Let's go to Coney Island, old sport. In my car."

"It's too late."

"Well, suppose we take a plunge in the swimming pool? I haven't made use of it all summer."

"I've got to go to bed."

"All right."

He waited, looking at me with suppressed eagerness.

"I talked with Miss Baker," I said after a moment. "I'm going to call up Daisy tomorrow and invite her over here to tea."

"Oh, that's all right," he said carelessly. "I don't want to put you to any trouble."

"What day would suit you?"

"What day would suit *you*?" he corrected me quickly. "I don't want to put you to any trouble, you see."

"How about the day after tomorrow?"

He considered for a moment. Then, with reluctance: "I want to get the grass cut," he said.

We both looked down at the grass – there was a sharp line where my ragged lawn ended and the darker, well-kept expanse of his began. I suspected that he meant my grass.

"There's another little thing," he said uncertainly, and hesitated.

"Would you rather put it off for a few days?" I asked.

"Oh, it isn't about that. At least—" He fumbled with a series of beginnings. "Why, I thought – why, look here, old sport, you don't make much money, do you?"

"Not very much."

This seemed to reassure him and he continued more confidently.

"I thought you didn't, if you'll pardon my – you see, I carry on a little business on the side, a sort of side line, you understand. And I thought that if you don't make very much— You're selling bonds, aren't you, old sport?"

"Trying to."

"Well, this would interest you. It wouldn't take up much of your time and you might pick up a nice bit of money. It happens to be a rather confidential sort of thing."

I realize now that under different circumstances that conversation might have been one of the crises of my life. But, because the offer was obviously and tactlessly for a service to be rendered, I had no choice except to cut him off there.

"I've got my hands full," I said. "I'm much obliged but I couldn't take on any more work."

"You wouldn't have to do any business with Wolfshiem." Evidently he thought that I was shying away from the "gonnegtion" mentioned at lunch, but I assured him he was wrong. He waited a moment longer, hoping I'd begin a conversation, but I was too absorbed to be responsive, so he went unwillingly home.

The evening had made me lightheaded and happy; I think I walked into a deep sleep as I entered my front door. So I don't know whether or not Gatsby went to Coney Island, or for how many hours he "glanced into rooms" while his house blazed gaudily on. I called up Daisy from the office next morning, and invited her to come to tea.

"Don't bring Tom," I warned her.

"What?"

"Don't bring Tom."

"Who is 'Tom'?" she asked innocently.

The day agreed upon was pouring rain. At eleven o'clock a man in a raincoat, dragging a lawn-mower, tapped at my front door and said that Mr. Gatsby had sent him over to cut my grass. This reminded me that I had forgotten to tell my Finn to come back, so I drove into West Egg Village to search for her among soggy whitewashed alleys and to buy some cups and lemons and flowers.

The flowers were unnecessary, for at two o'clock a greenhouse arrived from Gatsby's, with innumerable receptacles to contain it. An hour later the front door opened nervously, and Gatsby in a white flannel suit, silver shirt, and gold-coloured tie, hurried in. He was pale, and there were dark signs of sleeplessness beneath his eyes.

"Is everything all right?" he asked immediately.

"The grass looks fine, if that's what you mean."

"What grass?" he inquired blankly. "Oh, the grass in the yard." He looked out the window at it, but, judging from his expression, I don't believe he saw a thing.

"Looks very good," he remarked vaguely. "One of the papers said they thought the rain would stop about four. I think it was *The Journal*. Have you got everything you need in the shape of – of tea?"

I took him into the pantry, where he looked a little reproachfully at the Finn. Together we scrutinized the twelve lemon cakes from the delicatessen shop.

"Will they do?" I asked.

"Of course, of course! They're fine!" and he added hollowly, "… old sport."

The rain cooled about half-past three to a damp mist, through which occasional thin drops swam like dew. Gatsby looked with vacant eyes through a copy of Clay's *Economics*, starting at the Finnish tread that shook the kitchen floor, and peering towards the bleared windows from time to time as if a series of invisible but alarming happenings were taking place outside. Finally he got up and informed me, in an uncertain voice, that he was going home.

"Why's that?"

"Nobody's coming to tea. It's too late!" He looked at his watch as if there was some pressing demand on his time elsewhere. "I can't wait all day."

"Don't be silly; it's just two minutes to four."

He sat down miserably, as if I had pushed him, and simultaneously there was the sound of a motor turning into my lane. We both jumped up, and, a little harrowed myself, I went out into the yard.

Under the dripping bare lilac-trees a large open car was coming up the drive. It stopped. Daisy's face, tipped sideways beneath a three-cornered lavender hat, looked out at me with a bright ecstatic smile.

"Is this absolutely where you live, my dearest one?"

The exhilarating ripple of her voice was a wild tonic in the rain. I had to follow the sound of it for a moment, up and down, with my ear alone, before any words came through. A damp streak of hair lay like a dash of blue paint across her cheek, and her hand was wet with glistening drops as I took it to help her from the car.

"Are you in love with me," she said low in my ear, "or why did I have to come alone?"

"That's the secret of Castle Rackrent. Tell your chauffeur to go far away and spend an hour."

"Come back in an hour, Ferdie." Then in a grave murmur: "His name is Ferdie."

"Does the gasoline affect his nose?"

"I don't think so," she said innocently. "Why?"

We went in. To my overwhelming surprise the living-room was deserted.

"Well, that's funny," I exclaimed.

"What's funny?"

She turned her head as there was a light dignified knocking at the front door. I went out and opened it. Gatsby, pale as death, with his hands plunged like weights in his coat pockets, was standing in a puddle of water glaring tragically into my eyes.

With his hands still in his coat pockets he stalked by me into the hall, turned sharply as if he were on a wire, and disappeared into the living-room. It wasn't a bit funny. Aware of the loud beating of my own heart I pulled the door to against the increasing rain.

For half a minute there wasn't a sound. Then from the living-room I heard a sort of choking murmur and part of a laugh, followed by Daisy's voice on a clear artificial note:

"I certainly am awfully glad to see you again."

A pause; it endured horribly. I had nothing to do in the hall, so I went into the room.

Gatsby, his hands still in his pockets, was reclining against the mantelpiece in a strained counterfeit of perfect ease, even of boredom. His head leaned back so far that it rested against the face of a defunct mantelpiece clock, and from this position his distraught eyes stared down at Daisy, who was sitting, frightened but graceful, on the edge of a stiff chair.

"We've met before," muttered Gatsby. His eyes glanced momentarily at me, and his lips parted with an abortive attempt at a laugh. Luckily the clock took this moment to tilt dangerously at the pressure of his head, whereupon he turned and caught it with trembling fingers, and set it back in place. Then he sat down, rigidly, his elbow on the arm of the sofa and his chin in his hand.

"I'm sorry about the clock," he said.

My own face had now assumed a deep tropical burn. I couldn't muster up a single commonplace out of the thousand in my head.

"It's an old clock," I told them idiotically.

I think we all believed for a moment that it had smashed in pieces on the floor.

"We haven't met for many years," said Daisy, her voice as matter-of-fact as it could ever be.

"Five years next November."

The automatic quality of Gatsby's answer set us all back at least another minute. I had them both on their feet with the desperate suggestion that they help me make tea in the kitchen when the demoniac Finn brought it in on a tray.

Amid the welcome confusion of cups and cakes a certain physical decency established itself. Gatsby got himself into a shadow and, while Daisy and I talked, looked conscientiously from one to the other of us with tense, unhappy eyes. However, as calmness wasn't an end in itself, I made an excuse at the first possible moment, and got to my feet.

"Where are you going?" demanded Gatsby in immediate alarm.

"I'll be back."

"I've got to speak to you about something before you go."

He followed me wildly into the kitchen, closed the door, and whispered: "Oh, God!" in a miserable way.

"What's the matter?"

"This is a terrible mistake," he said, shaking his head from side to side, "a terrible, terrible mistake."

"You're just embarrassed, that's all," and luckily I added: "Daisy's embarrassed too."

"She's embarrassed?" he repeated incredulously.

"Just as much as you are."

"Don't talk so loud."

"You're acting like a little boy," I broke out impatiently. "Not only that, but you're rude. Daisy's sitting in there all alone."

He raised his hand to stop my words, looked at me with unforgettable reproach, and, opening the door cautiously, went back into the other room.

I walked out the back way – just as Gatsby had when he had made his nervous circuit of the house half an hour before – and ran for a huge black knotted tree, whose massed leaves made a fabric against the rain. Once more it was pouring, and my irregular lawn, well-shaved by Gatsby's gardener, abounded in small muddy swamps and prehistoric marshes. There was nothing to look at from under the tree except Gatsby's enormous house, so I stared at it, like Kant at his church steeple, for half an hour. A brewer had built it early in the "period" craze, a decade before, and there was a story that he'd agreed to pay five years' taxes on all the neighbouring cottages if the owners would have their roofs thatched with straw. Perhaps their refusal took the heart out of his plan to Found a Family – he went into an immediate decline. His children sold his house with the black wreath still on the door. Americans, while willing, even eager, to be serfs, have always been obstinate about being peasantry.

After half an hour, the sun shone again, and the grocer's automobile rounded Gatsby's drive with the raw material for his servants' dinner – I felt sure he wouldn't eat a spoonful. A maid began opening the upper windows of his house, appeared momentarily in each, and, leaning from the large central bay, spat meditatively into the garden. It was time I went back. While the rain continued it had seemed like the murmur of their voices, rising and swelling a little now and then with gusts of emotion. But in the new silence I felt that silence had fallen within the house too.

I went in – after making every possible noise in the kitchen, short of pushing over the stove – but I don't believe they heard a sound. They were sitting at either end of the couch, looking at each other as if some question had been asked, or was in the air, and every vestige of embarrassment was gone. Daisy's face was smeared with tears, and when I came in she jumped up and began wiping at it with her handkerchief before a mirror. But there was a change in Gatsby that was simply confounding. He literally glowed; without a word or a gesture of exultation a new well-being radiated from him and filled the little room.

"Oh, hello, old sport," he said, as if he hadn't seen me for years. I thought for a moment he was going to shake hands.

"It's stopped raining."

"Has it?" When he realized what I was talking about, that there were twinkle-bells of sunshine in the room, he smiled like a weather man, like an ecstatic patron of recurrent light, and repeated the news to Daisy. "What do you think of that? It's stopped raining."

"I'm glad, Jay." Her throat, full of aching, grieving beauty, told only of her unexpected joy.

"I want you and Daisy to come over to my house," he said, "I'd like to show her around."

"You're sure you want me to come?"

"Absolutely, old sport."

Daisy went upstairs to wash her face – too late I thought with humiliation of my towels – while Gatsby and I waited on the lawn.

"My house looks well, doesn't it?" he demanded. "See how the whole front of it catches the light."

I agreed that it was splendid.

"Yes." His eyes went over it, every arched door and square tower. "It took me just three years to earn the money that bought it."

"I thought you inherited your money."

"I did, old sport," he said automatically, "but I lost most of it in the big panic – the panic of the war."

I think he hardly knew what he was saying, for when I asked him what business he was in he answered: "That's my affair," before he realized that it wasn't an appropriate reply.

"Oh, I've been in several things," he corrected himself. "I was in the drug business and then I was in the oil business. But I'm not in either one now." He looked at me with more attention. "Do you mean you've been thinking over what I proposed the other night?"

Before I could answer, Daisy came out of the house and two rows of brass buttons on her dress gleamed in the sunlight.

"That huge place *there*?" she cried pointing.

"Do you like it?"

"I love it, but I don't see how you live there all alone."

"I keep it always full of interesting people, night and day. People who do interesting things. Celebrated people."

Instead of taking the shortcut along the Sound we went down to the road and entered by the big postern. With enchanting murmurs Daisy admired this aspect or that of the feudal silhouette against the sky, admired the gardens, the sparkling odour of jonquils and the frothy odour of hawthorn and plum blossoms and the pale gold odour of kiss-me-at-the-gate. It was strange to reach the marble steps and find no stir of bright dresses in and out the door, and hear no sound but bird voices in the trees.

And inside, as we wandered through Marie Antoinette music-rooms and Restoration Salons, I felt that there were guests concealed behind every couch and table, under orders to be breathlessly silent until we had passed through. As Gatsby closed the door of "the Merton College Library" I could have sworn I heard the owl-eyed man break into ghostly laughter.

We went upstairs, through period bedrooms swathed in rose and lavender silk and vivid with new flowers, through dressing-rooms and poolrooms, and bathrooms with sunken baths – intruding into one chamber where a dishevelled man in pyjamas was doing liver exercises on the floor. It was Mr. Klipspringer, the "boarder." I had seen him wandering hungrily about the beach that morning. Finally we came to Gatsby's own apartment, a bedroom and a bath, and an Adam's study, where we sat down and drank a glass of some Chartreuse he took from a cupboard in the wall.

He hadn't once ceased looking at Daisy, and I think he revalued everything in his house according to the measure of response it drew from her well-loved eyes. Sometimes too, he stared around at his possessions in a dazed way, as though in her actual and astounding presence none of it was any longer real. Once he nearly toppled down a flight of stairs.

His bedroom was the simplest room of all – except where the dresser was garnished with a toilet set of pure dull gold. Daisy took the brush with delight, and smoothed her hair, whereupon Gatsby sat down and shaded his eyes and began to laugh.

"It's the funniest thing, old sport," he said hilariously. "I can't— When I try to—"

He had passed visibly through two states and was entering upon a third. After his embarrassment and his unreasoning joy he was consumed with wonder at her presence. He had been full of the idea so long, dreamed it right through to the end, waited with his teeth set, so to speak, at an inconceivable pitch of intensity. Now, in the reaction, he was running down like an over-wound clock.

Recovering himself in a minute he opened for us two hulking patent cabinets which held his massed suits and dressing-gowns and ties, and his shirts, piled like bricks in stacks a dozen high.

"I've got a man in England who buys me clothes. He sends over a selection of things at the beginning of each season, spring and fall."

He took out a pile of shirts and began throwing them, one by one, before us, shirts of sheer linen and thick silk and fine flannel, which lost their folds as they fell and covered the table in many-coloured disarray. While we admired he brought more and the soft rich heap mounted higher – shirts with stripes and scrolls and plaids in coral and apple-green and lavender and faint orange, with monograms of indian blue. Suddenly, with a strained sound, Daisy bent her head into the shirts and began to cry stormily.

"They're such beautiful shirts," she sobbed, her voice muffled in the thick folds. "It makes me sad because I've never seen such – such beautiful shirts before."

* * *

After the house, we were to see the grounds and the swimming pool, and the hydroplane, and the midsummer flowers – but outside Gatsby's window it began to rain again, so we stood in a row looking at the corrugated surface of the Sound.

"If it wasn't for the mist we could see your home across the bay," said Gatsby. "You always have a green light that burns all night at the end of your dock."

Daisy put her arm through his abruptly, but he seemed absorbed in what he had just said. Possibly it had occurred to him that the colossal significance of that light had now vanished forever. Compared to the great distance that had separated him from Daisy it had seemed very near to her, almost touching her. It had seemed as close as a star to the moon. Now it was again a green light on a dock. His count of enchanted objects had diminished by one.

I began to walk about the room, examining various indefinite objects in the half darkness. A large photograph of an elderly man in yachting costume attracted me, hung on the wall over his desk.

"Who's this?"

"That? That's Mr. Dan Cody, old sport."

The name sounded faintly familiar.

"He's dead now. He used to be my best friend years ago."

There was a small picture of Gatsby, also in yachting costume, on the bureau – Gatsby with his head thrown back defiantly – taken apparently when he was about eighteen.

"I adore it," exclaimed Daisy. "The pompadour! You never told me you had a pompadour – or a yacht."

"Look at this," said Gatsby quickly. "Here's a lot of clippings – about you."

They stood side by side examining it. I was going to ask to see the rubies when the phone rang, and Gatsby took up the receiver.

"Yes... Well, I can't talk now... I can't talk now, old sport... I said a *small* town... He must know what a small town is... Well, he's no use to us if Detroit is his idea of a small town..."

He rang off.

"Come here *quick*!" cried Daisy at the window.

The rain was still falling, but the darkness had parted in the west, and there was a pink and golden billow of foamy clouds above the sea.

"Look at that," she whispered, and then after a moment: "I'd like to just get one of those pink clouds and put you in it and push you around."

I tried to go then, but they wouldn't hear of it; perhaps my presence made them feel more satisfactorily alone.

"I know what we'll do," said Gatsby, "we'll have Klipspringer play the piano."

He went out of the room calling "Ewing!" and returned in a few minutes accompanied by an embarrassed, slightly worn young man, with shell-rimmed glasses and scanty blond hair. He was now decently clothed in a "sport shirt," open at the neck, sneakers, and duck trousers of a nebulous hue.

"Did we interrupt your exercise?" inquired Daisy politely.

"I was asleep," cried Mr. Klipspringer, in a spasm of embarrassment. "That is, I'd *been* asleep. Then I got up…"

"Klipspringer plays the piano," said Gatsby, cutting him off. "Don't you, Ewing, old sport?"

"I don't play well. I don't – hardly play at all. I'm all out of prac—"

"We'll go downstairs," interrupted Gatsby. He flipped a switch. The grey windows disappeared as the house glowed full of light.

In the music-room Gatsby turned on a solitary lamp beside the piano. He lit Daisy's cigarette from a trembling match, and sat down with her on a couch far across the room, where there was no light save what the gleaming floor bounced in from the hall.

When Klipspringer had played "The Love Nest" he turned around on the bench and searched unhappily for Gatsby in the gloom.

"I'm all out of practice, you see. I told you I couldn't play. I'm all out of prac—"

"Don't talk so much, old sport," commanded Gatsby.

> *"Play!"*
> *"In the morning,*
> *In the evening,*
> *Ain't we got fun—"*

Outside the wind was loud and there was a faint flow of thunder along the Sound. All the lights were going on in West Egg now; the electric trains, men-carrying, were plunging home through the rain from New York. It was the hour of a profound human change, and excitement was generating on the air.

> *"One thing's sure and nothing's surer*
> *The rich get richer and the poor get – children.*
> *In the meantime,*
> *In between time—"*

As I went over to say goodbye I saw that the expression of bewilderment had come back into Gatsby's face, as though a faint doubt had occurred to him as to the quality of his present happiness. Almost five years! There must have been moments even that afternoon when Daisy tumbled short of his dreams – not through her own fault, but because of the colossal vitality of his illusion. It had gone beyond her, beyond everything. He had thrown himself into it with a creative passion, adding to it all the time, decking it out with every bright feather that drifted his way. No amount of fire or freshness can challenge what a man can store up in his ghostly heart.

As I watched him he adjusted himself a little, visibly. His hand took hold of hers, and as she said something low in his ear he turned toward her with a rush of emotion. I think that voice held him most, with its fluctuating, feverish warmth, because it couldn't be over-dreamed – that voice was a deathless song.

They had forgotten me, but Daisy glanced up and held out her hand; Gatsby didn't know me now at all. I looked once more at them and they looked back at me, remotely, possessed by intense life. Then I went out of the room and down the marble steps into the rain, leaving them there together.

Chapter VI

ABOUT THIS TIME an ambitious young reporter from New York arrived one morning at Gatsby's door and asked him if he had anything to say.

"Anything to say about what?" inquired Gatsby politely.

"Why – any statement to give out."

It transpired after a confused five minutes that the man had heard Gatsby's name around his office in a connection which he either wouldn't reveal or didn't fully understand. This was his day off and with laudable initiative he had hurried out "to see."

It was a random shot, and yet the reporter's instinct was right. Gatsby's notoriety, spread about by the hundreds who had accepted his hospitality and so become authorities upon his past, had increased all summer until he fell just short of being news. Contemporary legends such as the "underground pipeline to Canada" attached themselves to him, and there was one persistent story that he didn't live in a house at all, but in a boat that looked like a house and was moved secretly up and down the Long Island shore. Just why these inventions were a source of satisfaction to James Gatz of North Dakota, isn't easy to say.

James Gatz – that was really, or at least legally, his name. He had changed it at the age of seventeen and at the specific moment that witnessed the beginning of his career – when he saw Dan Cody's yacht drop anchor over the most insidious flat on Lake Superior. It was James Gatz who had been loafing along the beach that afternoon in a torn green jersey and a pair of canvas pants, but it was already Jay Gatsby who borrowed a rowboat, pulled out to the *Tuolomee*, and informed Cody that a wind might catch him and break him up in half an hour.

I suppose he'd had the name ready for a long time, even then. His parents were shiftless and unsuccessful farm people – his imagination had never really accepted them as his parents at all. The truth was that Jay Gatsby of West Egg, Long Island, sprang from his Platonic conception of himself. He was a son of God – a phrase which, if it means anything, means just that – and he must be about His Father's business, the service of a vast, vulgar, and meretricious beauty. So he invented just the sort of Jay Gatsby that a seventeen-year-old boy would be likely to invent, and to this conception he was faithful to the end.

For over a year he had been beating his way along the south shore of Lake Superior as a clam-digger and a salmon-fisher or in any other capacity that brought him food and bed. His brown, hardening body lived naturally through the half-fierce, half-lazy work of the bracing days. He knew women early, and since they spoiled him he became contemptuous of them, of young virgins because they were ignorant, of the others because they were hysterical about things which in his overwhelming self-absorption he took for granted.

But his heart was in a constant, turbulent riot. The most grotesque and fantastic conceits haunted him in his bed at night. A universe of ineffable gaudiness spun itself out in his brain while the clock ticked on the washstand and the moon soaked with wet light his tangled clothes upon the floor. Each night he added to the pattern of his fancies until drowsiness closed down upon some vivid scene with an oblivious embrace. For a while these reveries provided an outlet for his imagination; they were a satisfactory hint of the unreality of reality, a promise that the rock of the world was founded securely on a fairy's wing.

An instinct toward his future glory had led him, some months before, to the small Lutheran College of St. Olaf's in southern Minnesota. He stayed there two weeks, dismayed at its ferocious indifference to the drums of his destiny, to destiny itself, and despising the janitor's work with which he was to pay his way through. Then he drifted back to Lake Superior, and he was still searching for something to do on the day that Dan Cody's yacht dropped anchor in the shallows alongshore.

Cody was fifty years old then, a product of the Nevada silver fields, of the Yukon, of every rush for metal since seventy-five. The transactions in Montana copper that made him many times a millionaire found him physically robust but on the verge of soft-mindedness, and, suspecting this, an infinite number of women tried to separate him from his money. The none too savoury ramifications by which Ella Kaye, the newspaper woman, played Madame de Maintenon to his weakness and sent him to sea in a yacht, were common property of the turgid journalism in 1902. He had been coasting along all too hospitable shores for five years when he turned up as James Gatz's destiny in Little Girl Bay.

To young Gatz, resting on his oars and looking up at the railed deck, that yacht represented all the beauty and glamour in the world. I suppose he smiled at Cody – he had probably discovered that people liked him when he smiled. At any rate Cody asked him a few questions (one of them elicited the brand new name) and found that he was quick and extravagantly ambitious. A few days later he took him to Duluth and bought him a blue coat, six pairs of white duck trousers, and a yachting cap. And when the *Tuolomee* left for the West Indies and the Barbary Coast, Gatsby left too.

He was employed in a vague personal capacity – while he remained with Cody he was in turn steward, mate, skipper, secretary, and even jailor, for Dan Cody sober knew what lavish doings Dan Cody drunk might soon be about, and he provided for such contingencies by reposing more and more trust in Gatsby. The arrangement lasted five years, during which the boat went three times around the Continent. It might have lasted indefinitely except for the fact that Ella Kaye came on board one night in Boston and a week later Dan Cody inhospitably died.

I remember the portrait of him up in Gatsby's bedroom, a grey, florid man with a hard, empty face – the pioneer debauchee, who during one phase of American life brought back to the Eastern seaboard the savage violence of the frontier brothel and saloon. It was indirectly due to Cody that Gatsby drank so little. Sometimes in the course of gay parties women used to rub champagne into his hair; for himself he formed the habit of letting liquor alone.

And it was from Cody that he inherited money – a legacy of twenty-five thousand dollars. He didn't get it. He never understood the legal device that was used against him, but what remained of the millions went intact to Ella Kaye. He was left with his singularly appropriate education; the vague contour of Jay Gatsby had filled out to the substantiality of a man.

* * *

He told me all this very much later, but I've put it down here with the idea of exploding those first wild rumours about his antecedents, which weren't even faintly true. Moreover he told it to me at a time of confusion, when I had reached the point of believing everything and nothing about him. So I take advantage of this short halt, while Gatsby, so to speak, caught his breath, to clear this set of misconceptions away.

It was a halt, too, in my association with his affairs. For several weeks I didn't see him or hear his voice on the phone – mostly I was in New York, trotting around with Jordan and trying to ingratiate myself with her senile aunt – but finally I went over to his house one Sunday afternoon. I hadn't been there two minutes when somebody brought Tom Buchanan in for a drink. I was startled, naturally, but the really surprising thing was that it hadn't happened before.

They were a party of three on horseback – Tom and a man named Sloane and a pretty woman in a brown riding-habit, who had been there previously.

"I'm delighted to see you," said Gatsby, standing on his porch. "I'm delighted that you dropped in."

As though they cared!

"Sit right down. Have a cigarette or a cigar." He walked around the room quickly, ringing bells. "I'll have something to drink for you in just a minute."

He was profoundly affected by the fact that Tom was there. But he would be uneasy anyhow until he had given them something, realizing in a vague way that that was all they came for. Mr. Sloane wanted nothing. A lemonade? No, thanks. A little champagne? Nothing at all, thanks… I'm sorry—

"Did you have a nice ride?"

"Very good roads around here."

"I suppose the automobiles—"

"Yeah."

Moved by an irresistible impulse, Gatsby turned to Tom, who had accepted the introduction as a stranger.

"I believe we've met somewhere before, Mr. Buchanan."

"Oh, yes," said Tom, gruffly polite, but obviously not remembering. "So we did. I remember very well."

"About two weeks ago."

"That's right. You were with Nick here."

"I know your wife," continued Gatsby, almost aggressively.

"That so?"

Tom turned to me.

"You live near here, Nick?"

"Next door."

"That so?"

Mr. Sloane didn't enter into the conversation, but lounged back haughtily in his chair; the woman said nothing either – until unexpectedly, after two highballs, she became cordial.

"We'll all come over to your next party, Mr. Gatsby," she suggested. "What do you say?"

"Certainly; I'd be delighted to have you."

"Be ver' nice," said Mr. Sloane, without gratitude. "Well – think ought to be starting home."

"Please don't hurry," Gatsby urged them. He had control of himself now, and he wanted to see more of Tom. "Why don't you – why don't you stay for supper? I wouldn't be surprised if some other people dropped in from New York."

"You come to supper with *me*," said the lady enthusiastically. "Both of you."

This included me. Mr. Sloane got to his feet.

"Come along," he said – but to her only.

"I mean it," she insisted. "I'd love to have you. Lots of room."

Gatsby looked at me questioningly. He wanted to go and he didn't see that Mr. Sloane had determined he shouldn't.

"I'm afraid I won't be able to," I said.

"Well, you come," she urged, concentrating on Gatsby.

Mr. Sloane murmured something close to her ear.

"We won't be late if we start now," she insisted aloud.

"I haven't got a horse," said Gatsby. "I used to ride in the army, but I've never bought a horse. I'll have to follow you in my car. Excuse me for just a minute."

The rest of us walked out on the porch, where Sloane and the lady began an impassioned conversation aside.

"My God, I believe the man's coming," said Tom. "Doesn't he know she doesn't want him?"

"She says she does want him."

"She has a big dinner party and he won't know a soul there." He frowned. "I wonder where in the devil he met Daisy. By God, I may be old-fashioned in my ideas, but women run around too much these days to suit me. They meet all kinds of crazy fish."

Suddenly Mr. Sloane and the lady walked down the steps and mounted their horses.

"Come on," said Mr. Sloane to Tom, "we're late. We've got to go." And then to me: "Tell him we couldn't wait, will you?"

Tom and I shook hands, the rest of us exchanged a cool nod, and they trotted quickly down the drive, disappearing under the August foliage just as Gatsby, with hat and light overcoat in hand, came out the front door.

Tom was evidently perturbed at Daisy's running around alone, for on the following Saturday night he came with her to Gatsby's party. Perhaps his presence gave the evening its peculiar quality of oppressiveness – it stands out in my memory from Gatsby's other parties that summer. There were the same people, or at least the same sort of people, the same profusion of champagne, the same many-coloured, many-keyed commotion, but I felt an unpleasantness in the air, a pervading harshness that hadn't been there before. Or perhaps I had merely grown used to it, grown to accept West Egg as a world complete in itself, with its own standards and its own great figures, second to nothing because it had no consciousness of being so, and now I was looking at it again, through Daisy's eyes. It is invariably saddening to look through new eyes at things upon which you have expended your own powers of adjustment.

They arrived at twilight, and, as we strolled out among the sparkling hundreds, Daisy's voice was playing murmurous tricks in her throat.

"These things excite me *so*," she whispered. "If you want to kiss me any time during the evening, Nick, just let me know and I'll be glad to arrange it for you. Just mention my name. Or present a green card. I'm giving out green—"

"Look around," suggested Gatsby.

"I'm looking around. I'm having a marvellous—"

"You must see the faces of many people you've heard about."

Tom's arrogant eyes roamed the crowd.

"We don't go around very much," he said; "in fact, I was just thinking I don't know a soul here."

"Perhaps you know that lady." Gatsby indicated a gorgeous, scarcely human orchid of a woman who sat in state under a white-plum tree. Tom and Daisy stared, with that peculiarly unreal feeling that accompanies the recognition of a hitherto ghostly celebrity of the movies.

"She's lovely," said Daisy.

"The man bending over her is her director."

He took them ceremoniously from group to group:

"Mrs. Buchanan… and Mr. Buchanan—" After an instant's hesitation he added: "the polo player."

"Oh no," objected Tom quickly, "not me."

But evidently the sound of it pleased Gatsby for Tom remained "the polo player" for the rest of the evening.

"I've never met so many celebrities," Daisy exclaimed. "I liked that man – what was his name? – with the sort of blue nose."

Gatsby identified him, adding that he was a small producer.

"Well, I liked him anyhow."

"I'd a little rather not be the polo player," said Tom pleasantly, "I'd rather look at all these famous people in – in oblivion."

Daisy and Gatsby danced. I remember being surprised by his graceful, conservative foxtrot – I had never seen him dance before. Then they sauntered over to my house and sat on the steps for half an hour, while at her request I remained watchfully in the garden. "In case there's a fire or a flood," she explained, "or any act of God."

Tom appeared from his oblivion as we were sitting down to supper together. "Do you mind if I eat with some people over here?" he said. "A fellow's getting off some funny stuff."

"Go ahead," answered Daisy genially, "and if you want to take down any addresses here's my little gold pencil.".... She looked around after a moment and told me the girl was "common but pretty," and I knew that except for the half-hour she'd been alone with Gatsby she wasn't having a good time.

We were at a particularly tipsy table. That was my fault – Gatsby had been called to the phone, and I'd enjoyed these same people only two weeks before. But what had amused me then turned septic on the air now.

"How do you feel, Miss Baedeker?"

The girl addressed was trying, unsuccessfully, to slump against my shoulder. At this inquiry she sat up and opened her eyes.

"Wha'?"

A massive and lethargic woman, who had been urging Daisy to play golf with her at the local club tomorrow, spoke in Miss Baedeker's defence:

"Oh, she's all right now. When she's had five or six cocktails she always starts screaming like that. I tell her she ought to leave it alone."

"I do leave it alone," affirmed the accused hollowly.

"We heard you yelling, so I said to Doc Civet here: 'There's somebody that needs your help, Doc.'"

"She's much obliged, I'm sure," said another friend, without gratitude, "but you got her dress all wet when you stuck her head in the pool."

"Anything I hate is to get my head stuck in a pool," mumbled Miss Baedeker. "They almost drowned me once over in New Jersey."

"Then you ought to leave it alone," countered Doctor Civet.

"Speak for yourself!" cried Miss Baedeker violently. "Your hand shakes. I wouldn't let you operate on me!"

It was like that. Almost the last thing I remember was standing with Daisy and watching the moving-picture director and his Star. They were still under the white-plum tree and their faces were touching except for a pale, thin ray of moonlight between. It occurred to me that he had been very slowly bending toward her all evening to attain this proximity, and even while I watched I saw him stoop one ultimate degree and kiss at her cheek.

"I like her," said Daisy, "I think she's lovely."

But the rest offended her – and inarguably because it wasn't a gesture but an emotion. She was appalled by West Egg, this unprecedented "place" that Broadway had begotten upon a Long Island fishing village – appalled by its raw vigour that chafed under the old euphemisms and by the too obtrusive fate that herded its inhabitants along a shortcut from nothing to nothing. She saw something awful in the very simplicity she failed to understand.

I sat on the front steps with them while they waited for their car. It was dark here in front; only the bright door sent ten square feet of light volleying out into the soft black morning. Sometimes a shadow moved against a dressing-room blind above, gave way to another shadow, an indefinite procession of shadows, who rouged and powdered in an invisible glass.

"Who is this Gatsby anyhow?" demanded Tom suddenly. "Some big bootlegger?"

"Where'd you hear that?" I inquired.

"I didn't hear it. I imagined it. A lot of these newly rich people are just big bootleggers, you know."

"Not Gatsby," I said shortly.

He was silent for a moment. The pebbles of the drive crunched under his feet.

"Well, he certainly must have strained himself to get this menagerie together."

A breeze stirred the grey haze of Daisy's fur collar.

"At least they are more interesting than the people we know," she said with an effort.

"You didn't look so interested."

"Well, I was."

Tom laughed and turned to me.

"Did you notice Daisy's face when that girl asked her to put her under a cold shower?"

Daisy began to sing with the music in a husky, rhythmic whisper, bringing out a meaning in each word that it had never had before and would never have again. When the melody rose her voice broke up sweetly, following it, in a way contralto voices have, and each change tipped out a little of her warm human magic upon the air.

"Lots of people come who haven't been invited," she said suddenly. "That girl hadn't been invited. They simply force their way in and he's too polite to object."

"I'd like to know who he is and what he does," insisted Tom. "And I think I'll make a point of finding out."

"I can tell you right now," she answered. "He owned some drugstores, a lot of drugstores. He built them up himself."

The dilatory limousine came rolling up the drive.

"Good night, Nick," said Daisy.

Her glance left me and sought the lighted top of the steps, where "Three O'Clock in the Morning," a neat, sad little waltz of that year, was drifting out the open door. After all, in the very casualness of Gatsby's party there were romantic possibilities totally absent from her world. What was it up there in the song that seemed to be calling her back inside? What would happen now in the dim, incalculable hours? Perhaps some unbelievable guest would arrive, a person infinitely rare and to be marvelled at, some authentically radiant young girl who with one fresh glance at Gatsby, one moment of magical encounter, would blot out those five years of unwavering devotion.

I stayed late that night. Gatsby asked me to wait until he was free, and I lingered in the garden until the inevitable swimming party had run up, chilled and exalted, from the black beach, until the lights were extinguished in the guestrooms overhead. When he came down the steps at last the tanned skin was drawn unusually tight on his face, and his eyes were bright and tired.

"She didn't like it," he said immediately.

"Of course she did."

"She didn't like it," he insisted. "She didn't have a good time."

He was silent, and I guessed at his unutterable depression.

"I feel far away from her," he said. "It's hard to make her understand."

"You mean about the dance?"

"The dance?" He dismissed all the dances he had given with a snap of his fingers. "Old sport, the dance is unimportant."

He wanted nothing less of Daisy than that she should go to Tom and say: "I never loved you." After she had obliterated four years with that sentence they could decide upon the more practical measures to be taken. One of them was that, after she was free, they were to go back to Louisville and be married from her house – just as if it were five years ago.

"And she doesn't understand," he said. "She used to be able to understand. We'd sit for hours—"

He broke off and began to walk up and down a desolate path of fruit rinds and discarded favours and crushed flowers.

"I wouldn't ask too much of her," I ventured. "You can't repeat the past."

"Can't repeat the past?" he cried incredulously. "Why of course you can!"

He looked around him wildly, as if the past were lurking here in the shadow of his house, just out of reach of his hand.

"I'm going to fix everything just the way it was before," he said, nodding determinedly. "She'll see."

He talked a lot about the past, and I gathered that he wanted to recover something, some idea of himself perhaps, that had gone into loving Daisy. His life had been confused and disordered since then, but if he could once return to a certain starting place and go over it all slowly, he could find out what that thing was…

… One autumn night, five years before, they had been walking down the street when the leaves were falling, and they came to a place where there were no trees and the sidewalk was white with moonlight. They stopped here and turned toward each other. Now it was a cool night with that mysterious excitement in it which comes at the two changes of the year. The quiet lights in the houses were humming out into the darkness and there was a stir and bustle among the stars. Out of the corner of his eye Gatsby saw that the blocks of the sidewalks really formed a ladder and mounted to a secret place above the trees – he could climb to it, if he climbed alone, and once there he could suck on the pap of life, gulp down the incomparable milk of wonder.

His heart beat faster as Daisy's white face came up to his own. He knew that when he kissed this girl, and forever wed his unutterable visions to her perishable breath, his mind would never romp again like the mind of God. So he waited, listening for a moment longer to the tuning-fork that had been struck upon a star. Then he kissed her. At his lips' touch she blossomed for him like a flower and the incarnation was complete.

Through all he said, even through his appalling sentimentality, I was reminded of something – an elusive rhythm, a fragment of lost words, that I had heard somewhere a long time ago. For a moment a phrase tried to take shape in my mouth and my lips parted like a dumb man's, as though there was more struggling upon them than a wisp of startled air. But they made no sound, and what I had almost remembered was uncommunicable forever.

Chapter VII

IT WAS WHEN CURIOSITY about Gatsby was at its highest that the lights in his house failed to go on one Saturday night – and, as obscurely as it had begun, his career as Trimalchio was over. Only gradually did I become aware that the automobiles which turned expectantly into his drive stayed for just a minute and then drove sulkily away. Wondering if he were sick I went over to find out – an unfamiliar butler with a villainous face squinted at me suspiciously from the door.

"Is Mr. Gatsby sick?"

"Nope." After a pause he added "sir" in a dilatory, grudging way.

"I hadn't seen him around, and I was rather worried. Tell him Mr. Carraway came over."

"Who?" he demanded rudely.

"Carraway."

"Carraway. All right, I'll tell him."

Abruptly he slammed the door.

My Finn informed me that Gatsby had dismissed every servant in his house a week ago and replaced them with half a dozen others, who never went into West Egg village to be bribed by the tradesmen, but ordered moderate supplies over the telephone. The grocery boy reported that the kitchen looked like a pigsty, and the general opinion in the village was that the new people weren't servants at all.

Next day Gatsby called me on the phone.

"Going away?" I inquired.

"No, old sport."

"I hear you fired all your servants."

"I wanted somebody who wouldn't gossip. Daisy comes over quite often – in the afternoons."

So the whole caravansary had fallen in like a card house at the disapproval in her eyes.

"They're some people Wolfshiem wanted to do something for. They're all brothers and sisters. They used to run a small hotel."

"I see."

He was calling up at Daisy's request – would I come to lunch at her house tomorrow? Miss Baker would be there. Half an hour later Daisy herself telephoned and seemed relieved to find that I was coming. Something was up. And yet I couldn't believe that they would choose this occasion for a scene – especially for the rather harrowing scene that Gatsby had outlined in the garden.

The next day was broiling, almost the last, certainly the warmest, of the summer. As my train emerged from the tunnel into sunlight, only the hot whistles of the National Biscuit Company broke the simmering hush at noon. The straw seats of the car hovered on the edge of combustion; the woman next to me perspired delicately for a while into her white shirtwaist, and then, as her newspaper dampened under her fingers, lapsed despairingly into deep heat with a desolate cry. Her pocketbook slapped to the floor.

"Oh, my!" she gasped.

I picked it up with a weary bend and handed it back to her, holding it at arm's length and by the extreme tip of the corners to indicate that I had no designs upon it – but everyone near by, including the woman, suspected me just the same.

"Hot!" said the conductor to familiar faces. "Some weather!... Hot!... Hot!... Hot!... Is it hot enough for you? Is it hot? Is it...?"

My commutation ticket came back to me with a dark stain from his hand. That anyone should care in this heat whose flushed lips he kissed, whose head made damp the pyjama pocket over his heart!

... Through the hall of the Buchanans' house blew a faint wind, carrying the sound of the telephone bell out to Gatsby and me as we waited at the door.

"The master's body?" roared the butler into the mouthpiece. "I'm sorry, madame, but we can't furnish it – it's far too hot to touch this noon!"

What he really said was: "Yes... Yes... I'll see."

He set down the receiver and came toward us, glistening slightly, to take our stiff straw hats.

"Madame expects you in the salon!" he cried, needlessly indicating the direction. In this heat every extra gesture was an affront to the common store of life.

The room, shadowed well with awnings, was dark and cool. Daisy and Jordan lay upon an enormous couch, like silver idols weighing down their own white dresses against the singing breeze of the fans.

"We can't move," they said together.

Jordan's fingers, powdered white over their tan, rested for a moment in mine.

"And Mr. Thomas Buchanan, the athlete?" I inquired.

Simultaneously I heard his voice, gruff, muffled, husky, at the hall telephone.

Gatsby stood in the centre of the crimson carpet and gazed around with fascinated eyes. Daisy watched him and laughed, her sweet, exciting laugh; a tiny gust of powder rose from her bosom into the air.

"The rumour is," whispered Jordan, "that that's Tom's girl on the telephone."

We were silent. The voice in the hall rose high with annoyance: "Very well, then, I won't sell you the car at all... I'm under no obligations to you at all... and as for your bothering me about it at lunch time, I won't stand that at all!"

"Holding down the receiver," said Daisy cynically.

"No, he's not," I assured her. "It's a bona-fide deal. I happen to know about it."

Tom flung open the door, blocked out its space for a moment with his thick body, and hurried into the room.

"Mr. Gatsby!" He put out his broad, flat hand with well-concealed dislike. "I'm glad to see you, sir... Nick..."

"Make us a cold drink," cried Daisy.

As he left the room again she got up and went over to Gatsby and pulled his face down, kissing him on the mouth.

"You know I love you," she murmured.

"You forget there's a lady present," said Jordan.

Daisy looked around doubtfully.

"You kiss Nick too."

"What a low, vulgar girl!"

"I don't care!" cried Daisy, and began to clog on the brick fireplace. Then she remembered the heat and sat down guiltily on the couch just as a freshly laundered nurse leading a little girl came into the room.

"Bles-sed pre-cious," she crooned, holding out her arms. "Come to your own mother that loves you."

The child, relinquished by the nurse, rushed across the room and rooted shyly into her mother's dress.

"The bles-sed pre-cious! Did mother get powder on your old yellowy hair? Stand up now, and say – How-de-do."

Gatsby and I in turn leaned down and took the small reluctant hand. Afterward he kept looking at the child with surprise. I don't think he had ever really believed in its existence before.

"I got dressed before luncheon," said the child, turning eagerly to Daisy.

"That's because your mother wanted to show you off." Her face bent into the single wrinkle of the small white neck. "You dream, you. You absolute little dream."

"Yes," admitted the child calmly. "Aunt Jordan's got on a white dress too."

"How do you like mother's friends?" Daisy turned her around so that she faced Gatsby. "Do you think they're pretty?"

"Where's Daddy?"

"She doesn't look like her father," explained Daisy. "She looks like me. She's got my hair and shape of the face."

Daisy sat back upon the couch. The nurse took a step forward and held out her hand.

"Come, Pammy."

"Goodbye, sweetheart!"

With a reluctant backward glance the well-disciplined child held to her nurse's hand and was pulled out the door, just as Tom came back, preceding four gin rickeys that clicked full of ice.

Gatsby took up his drink.

"They certainly look cool," he said, with visible tension.

We drank in long, greedy swallows.

"I read somewhere that the sun's getting hotter every year," said Tom genially. "It seems that pretty soon the earth's going to fall into the sun – or wait a minute – it's just the opposite – the sun's getting colder every year.

"Come outside," he suggested to Gatsby, "I'd like you to have a look at the place."

I went with them out to the veranda. On the green Sound, stagnant in the heat, one small sail crawled slowly toward the fresher sea. Gatsby's eyes followed it momentarily; he raised his hand and pointed across the bay.

"I'm right across from you."

"So you are."

Our eyes lifted over the rose-beds and the hot lawn and the weedy refuse of the dog-days alongshore. Slowly the white wings of the boat moved against the blue cool limit of the sky. Ahead lay the scalloped ocean and the abounding blessed isles.

"There's sport for you," said Tom, nodding. "I'd like to be out there with him for about an hour."

We had luncheon in the dining-room, darkened too against the heat, and drank down nervous gaiety with the cold ale.

"What'll we do with ourselves this afternoon?" cried Daisy, "and the day after that, and the next thirty years?"

"Don't be morbid," Jordan said. "Life starts all over again when it gets crisp in the fall."

"But it's so hot," insisted Daisy, on the verge of tears, "and everything's so confused. Let's all go to town!"

Her voice struggled on through the heat, beating against it, moulding its senselessness into forms.

"I've heard of making a garage out of a stable," Tom was saying to Gatsby, "but I'm the first man who ever made a stable out of a garage."

"Who wants to go to town?" demanded Daisy insistently. Gatsby's eyes floated toward her. "Ah," she cried, "you look so cool."

Their eyes met, and they stared together at each other, alone in space. With an effort she glanced down at the table.

"You always look so cool," she repeated.

She had told him that she loved him, and Tom Buchanan saw. He was astounded. His mouth opened a little, and he looked at Gatsby, and then back at Daisy as if he had just recognized her as someone he knew a long time ago.

"You resemble the advertisement of the man," she went on innocently. "You know the advertisement of the man—"

"All right," broke in Tom quickly, "I'm perfectly willing to go to town. Come on – we're all going to town."

He got up, his eyes still flashing between Gatsby and his wife. No one moved.

"Come on!" His temper cracked a little. "What's the matter, anyhow? If we're going to town, let's start."

His hand, trembling with his effort at self-control, bore to his lips the last of his glass of ale. Daisy's voice got us to our feet and out on to the blazing gravel drive.

"Are we just going to go?" she objected. "Like this? Aren't we going to let anyone smoke a cigarette first?"

"Everybody smoked all through lunch."

"Oh, let's have fun," she begged him. "It's too hot to fuss."

He didn't answer.

"Have it your own way," she said. "Come on, Jordan."

They went upstairs to get ready while we three men stood there shuffling the hot pebbles with our feet. A silver curve of the moon hovered already in the western sky. Gatsby started to speak, changed his mind, but not before Tom wheeled and faced him expectantly.

"Have you got your stables here?" asked Gatsby with an effort.

"About a quarter of a mile down the road."

"Oh."

A pause.

"I don't see the idea of going to town," broke out Tom savagely. "Women get these notions in their heads—"

"Shall we take anything to drink?" called Daisy from an upper window.

"I'll get some whisky," answered Tom. He went inside.

Gatsby turned to me rigidly:

"I can't say anything in his house, old sport."

"She's got an indiscreet voice," I remarked. "It's full of—" I hesitated.

"Her voice is full of money," he said suddenly.

That was it. I'd never understood before. It was full of money – that was the inexhaustible charm that rose and fell in it, the jingle of it, the cymbals' song of it… High in a white palace the king's daughter, the golden girl…

Tom came out of the house wrapping a quart bottle in a towel, followed by Daisy and Jordan wearing small tight hats of metallic cloth and carrying light capes over their arms.

"Shall we all go in my car?" suggested Gatsby. He felt the hot, green leather of the seat. "I ought to have left it in the shade."

"Is it standard shift?" demanded Tom.

"Yes."

"Well, you take my coupé and let me drive your car to town."

The suggestion was distasteful to Gatsby.

"I don't think there's much gas," he objected.

"Plenty of gas," said Tom boisterously. He looked at the gauge. "And if it runs out I can stop at a drugstore. You can buy anything at a drugstore nowadays."

A pause followed this apparently pointless remark. Daisy looked at Tom frowning, and an indefinable expression, at once definitely unfamiliar and vaguely recognizable, as if I had only heard it described in words, passed over Gatsby's face.

"Come on, Daisy" said Tom, pressing her with his hand toward Gatsby's car. "I'll take you in this circus wagon."

He opened the door, but she moved out from the circle of his arm.

"You take Nick and Jordan. We'll follow you in the coupé."

She walked close to Gatsby, touching his coat with her hand. Jordan and Tom and I got into the front seat of Gatsby's car, Tom pushed the unfamiliar gears tentatively, and we shot off into the oppressive heat, leaving them out of sight behind.

"Did you see that?" demanded Tom.

"See what?"

He looked at me keenly, realizing that Jordan and I must have known all along.

"You think I'm pretty dumb, don't you?" he suggested. "Perhaps I am, but I have a – almost a second sight, sometimes, that tells me what to do. Maybe you don't believe that, but science—"

He paused. The immediate contingency overtook him, pulled him back from the edge of theoretical abyss.

"I've made a small investigation of this fellow," he continued. "I could have gone deeper if I'd known—"

"Do you mean you've been to a medium?" inquired Jordan humorously.

"What?" Confused, he stared at us as we laughed. "A medium?"

"About Gatsby."

"About Gatsby! No, I haven't. I said I'd been making a small investigation of his past."

"And you found he was an Oxford man," said Jordan helpfully.

"An Oxford man!" He was incredulous. "Like hell he is! He wears a pink suit."

"Nevertheless he's an Oxford man."

"Oxford, New Mexico," snorted Tom contemptuously, "or something like that."

"Listen, Tom. If you're such a snob, why did you invite him to lunch?" demanded Jordan crossly.

"Daisy invited him; she knew him before we were married – God knows where!"

We were all irritable now with the fading ale, and aware of it we drove for a while in silence. Then as Doctor T. J. Eckleburg's faded eyes came into sight down the road, I remembered Gatsby's caution about gasoline.

"We've got enough to get us to town," said Tom.

"But there's a garage right here," objected Jordan. "I don't want to get stalled in this baking heat."

Tom threw on both brakes impatiently, and we slid to an abrupt dusty stop under Wilson's sign. After a moment the proprietor emerged from the interior of his establishment and gazed hollow-eyed at the car.

"Let's have some gas!" cried Tom roughly. "What do you think we stopped for – to admire the view?"

"I'm sick," said Wilson without moving. "Been sick all day."

"What's the matter?"

"I'm all run down."

"Well, shall I help myself?" Tom demanded. "You sounded well enough on the phone."

With an effort Wilson left the shade and support of the doorway and, breathing hard, unscrewed the cap of the tank. In the sunlight his face was green.

"I didn't mean to interrupt your lunch," he said. "But I need money pretty bad, and I was wondering what you were going to do with your old car."

"How do you like this one?" inquired Tom. "I bought it last week."

"It's a nice yellow one," said Wilson, as he strained at the handle.

"Like to buy it?"

"Big chance," Wilson smiled faintly. "No, but I could make some money on the other."

"What do you want money for, all of a sudden?"

"I've been here too long. I want to get away. My wife and I want to go West."

"Your wife does," exclaimed Tom, startled.

"She's been talking about it for ten years." He rested for a moment against the pump, shading his eyes. "And now she's going whether she wants to or not. I'm going to get her away."

The coupé flashed by us with a flurry of dust and the flash of a waving hand.

"What do I owe you?" demanded Tom harshly.

"I just got wised up to something funny the last two days," remarked Wilson. "That's why I want to get away. That's why I been bothering you about the car."

"What do I owe you?"

"Dollar twenty."

The relentless beating heat was beginning to confuse me and I had a bad moment there before I realized that so far his suspicions hadn't alighted on Tom. He had discovered that Myrtle had some sort of life apart from him in another world, and the shock had made him physically sick. I stared at him and then at Tom, who had made a parallel discovery less than an hour before – and it occurred to me that there was no difference between men, in intelligence or race, so profound as the difference between the sick and the well. Wilson was so sick that he looked guilty, unforgivably guilty – as if he had just got some poor girl with child.

"I'll let you have that car," said Tom. "I'll send it over tomorrow afternoon."

That locality was always vaguely disquieting, even in the broad glare of afternoon, and now I turned my head as though I had been warned of something behind. Over the ash-heaps the giant eyes of Doctor T. J. Eckleburg kept their vigil, but I perceived, after a moment, that other eyes were regarding us with peculiar intensity from less than twenty feet away.

In one of the windows over the garage the curtains had been moved aside a little, and Myrtle Wilson was peering down at the car. So engrossed was she that she had no consciousness of being observed, and one emotion after another crept into her face like objects into a slowly developing picture. Her expression was curiously familiar – it was an expression I had often seen on women's faces, but on Myrtle Wilson's face it seemed purposeless and inexplicable until I realized that her eyes, wide with jealous terror, were fixed not on Tom, but on Jordan Baker, whom she took to be his wife.

* * *

There is no confusion like the confusion of a simple mind, and as we drove away Tom was feeling the hot whips of panic. His wife and his mistress, until an hour ago secure and inviolate, were slipping precipitately from his control. Instinct made him step on the accelerator with the double purpose of overtaking Daisy and leaving Wilson behind, and we sped along toward Astoria at fifty miles an hour, until, among the spidery girders of the elevated, we came in sight of the easygoing blue coupé.

"Those big movies around Fiftieth Street are cool," suggested Jordan. "I love New York on summer afternoons when everyone's away. There's something very sensuous about it – overripe, as if all sorts of funny fruits were going to fall into your hands."

The word "sensuous" had the effect of further disquieting Tom, but before he could invent a protest the coupé came to a stop, and Daisy signalled us to draw up alongside.

"Where are we going?" she cried.

"How about the movies?"

"It's so hot," she complained. "You go. We'll ride around and meet you after." With an effort her wit rose faintly. "We'll meet you on some corner. I'll be the man smoking two cigarettes."

"We can't argue about it here," Tom said impatiently, as a truck gave out a cursing whistle behind us. "You follow me to the south side of Central Park, in front of the Plaza."

Several times he turned his head and looked back for their car, and if the traffic delayed them he slowed up until they came into sight. I think he was afraid they would dart down a side-street and out of his life forever.

But they didn't. And we all took the less explicable step of engaging the parlour of a suite in the Plaza Hotel.

The prolonged and tumultuous argument that ended by herding us into that room eludes me, though I have a sharp physical memory that, in the course of it, my underwear kept climbing like a damp snake around my legs and intermittent beads of sweat raced cool across my back. The notion originated with Daisy's suggestion that we hire five bathrooms and take cold baths, and then assumed more tangible form as "a place to have a mint julep." Each of us said over and over that it was a "crazy idea" – we all talked at once to a baffled clerk and thought, or pretended to think, that we were being very funny…

The room was large and stifling, and, though it was already four o'clock, opening the windows admitted only a gust of hot shrubbery from the Park. Daisy went to the mirror and stood with her back to us, fixing her hair.

"It's a swell suite," whispered Jordan respectfully, and everyone laughed.

"Open another window," commanded Daisy, without turning around.

"There aren't any more."

"Well, we'd better telephone for an axe—"

"The thing to do is to forget about the heat," said Tom impatiently. "You make it ten times worse by crabbing about it."

He unrolled the bottle of whisky from the towel and put it on the table.

"Why not let her alone, old sport?" remarked Gatsby. "You're the one that wanted to come to town."

There was a moment of silence. The telephone book slipped from its nail and splashed to the floor, whereupon Jordan whispered, "Excuse me" – but this time no one laughed.

"I'll pick it up," I offered.

"I've got it." Gatsby examined the parted string, muttered "Hum!" in an interested way, and tossed the book on a chair.

"That's a great expression of yours, isn't it?" said Tom sharply.

"What is?"

"All this 'old sport' business. Where'd you pick that up?"

"Now see here, Tom," said Daisy, turning around from the mirror, "if you're going to make personal remarks I won't stay here a minute. Call up and order some ice for the mint julep."

As Tom took up the receiver the compressed heat exploded into sound and we were listening to the portentous chords of Mendelssohn's Wedding March from the ballroom below.

"Imagine marrying anybody in this heat!" cried Jordan dismally.

"Still – I was married in the middle of June," Daisy remembered. "Louisville in June! Somebody fainted. Who was it fainted, Tom?"

"Biloxi," he answered shortly.

"A man named Biloxi. 'Blocks' Biloxi, and he made boxes – that's a fact – and he was from Biloxi, Tennessee."

"They carried him into my house," appended Jordan, "because we lived just two doors from the church. And he stayed three weeks, until Daddy told him he had to get out. The day after he left Daddy died." After a moment she added. "There wasn't any connection."

"I used to know a Bill Biloxi from Memphis," I remarked.

"That was his cousin. I knew his whole family history before he left. He gave me an aluminium putter that I use today."

The music had died down as the ceremony began and now a long cheer floated in at the window, followed by intermittent cries of "Yea – ea – ea!" and finally by a burst of jazz as the dancing began.

"We're getting old," said Daisy. "If we were young we'd rise and dance."

"Remember Biloxi," Jordan warned her. "Where'd you know him, Tom?"

"Biloxi?" He concentrated with an effort. "I didn't know him. He was a friend of Daisy's."

"He was not," she denied. "I'd never seen him before. He came down in the private car."

"Well, he said he knew you. He said he was raised in Louisville. Asa Bird brought him around at the last minute and asked if we had room for him."

Jordan smiled.

"He was probably bumming his way home. He told me he was president of your class at Yale."

Tom and I looked at each other blankly.

"Biloxi?"

"First place, we didn't have any president—"

Gatsby's foot beat a short, restless tattoo and Tom eyed him suddenly.

"By the way, Mr. Gatsby, I understand you're an Oxford man."

"Not exactly."

"Oh, yes, I understand you went to Oxford."

"Yes – I went there."

A pause. Then Tom's voice, incredulous and insulting:

"You must have gone there about the time Biloxi went to New Haven."

Another pause. A waiter knocked and came in with crushed mint and ice but the silence was unbroken by his "thank you" and the soft closing of the door. This tremendous detail was to be cleared up at last.

"I told you I went there," said Gatsby.

"I heard you, but I'd like to know when."

"It was in nineteen-nineteen, I only stayed five months. That's why I can't really call myself an Oxford man."

Tom glanced around to see if we mirrored his unbelief. But we were all looking at Gatsby.

"It was an opportunity they gave to some of the officers after the armistice," he continued. "We could go to any of the universities in England or France."

I wanted to get up and slap him on the back. I had one of those renewals of complete faith in him that I'd experienced before.

Daisy rose, smiling faintly, and went to the table.

"Open the whisky, Tom," she ordered, "and I'll make you a mint julep. Then you won't seem so stupid to yourself... Look at the mint!"

"Wait a minute," snapped Tom, "I want to ask Mr. Gatsby one more question."

"Go on," Gatsby said politely.

"What kind of a row are you trying to cause in my house anyhow?"

They were out in the open at last and Gatsby was content.

"He isn't causing a row," Daisy looked desperately from one to the other. "You're causing a row. Please have a little self-control."

"Self-control!" repeated Tom incredulously. "I suppose the latest thing is to sit back and let Mr. Nobody from Nowhere make love to your wife. Well, if that's the idea you can count me out... Nowadays people begin by sneering at family life and family institutions, and next they'll throw everything overboard and have intermarriage between black and white."

Flushed with his impassioned gibberish, he saw himself standing alone on the last barrier of civilization.

"We're all white here," murmured Jordan.

"I know I'm not very popular. I don't give big parties. I suppose you've got to make your house into a pigsty in order to have any friends – in the modern world."

Angry as I was, as we all were, I was tempted to laugh whenever he opened his mouth. The transition from libertine to prig was so complete.

"I've got something to tell *you*, old sport—" began Gatsby. But Daisy guessed at his intention.

"Please don't!" she interrupted helplessly. "Please let's all go home. Why don't we all go home?"

"That's a good idea," I got up. "Come on, Tom. Nobody wants a drink."

"I want to know what Mr. Gatsby has to tell me."

"Your wife doesn't love you," said Gatsby. "She's never loved you. She loves me."

"You must be crazy!" exclaimed Tom automatically.

Gatsby sprang to his feet, vivid with excitement.

"She never loved you, do you hear?" he cried. "She only married you because I was poor and she was tired of waiting for me. It was a terrible mistake, but in her heart she never loved anyone except me!"

At this point Jordan and I tried to go, but Tom and Gatsby insisted with competitive firmness that we remain – as though neither of them had anything to conceal and it would be a privilege to partake vicariously of their emotions.

"Sit down, Daisy," Tom's voice groped unsuccessfully for the paternal note. "What's been going on? I want to hear all about it."

"I told you what's been going on," said Gatsby. "Going on for five years – and you didn't know."

Tom turned to Daisy sharply.

"You've been seeing this fellow for five years?"

"Not seeing," said Gatsby. "No, we couldn't meet. But both of us loved each other all that time, old sport, and you didn't know. I used to laugh sometimes" – but there was no laughter in his eyes – "to think that you didn't know."

"Oh – that's all." Tom tapped his thick fingers together like a clergyman and leaned back in his chair. "You're crazy!" he exploded. "I can't speak about what happened five years ago, because I didn't know Daisy then – and I'll be damned if I see how you got within a mile of her unless you brought the groceries to the back door. But all the rest of that's a God damned lie. Daisy loved me when she married me and she loves me now."

"No," said Gatsby, shaking his head.

"She does, though. The trouble is that sometimes she gets foolish ideas in her head and doesn't know what she's doing." He nodded sagely. "And what's more, I love Daisy too. Once in a while I go off on a spree and make a fool of myself, but I always come back, and in my heart I love her all the time."

"You're revolting," said Daisy. She turned to me, and her voice, dropping an octave lower, filled the room with thrilling scorn: "Do you know why we left Chicago? I'm surprised that they didn't treat you to the story of that little spree."

Gatsby walked over and stood beside her.

"Daisy, that's all over now," he said earnestly. "It doesn't matter any more. Just tell him the truth – that you never loved him – and it's all wiped out forever."

She looked at him blindly. "Why – how could I love him – possibly?"

"You never loved him."

She hesitated. Her eyes fell on Jordan and me with a sort of appeal, as though she realized at last what she was doing – and as though she had never, all along, intended doing anything at all. But it was done now. It was too late.

"I never loved him," she said, with perceptible reluctance.

"Not at Kapiolani?" demanded Tom suddenly.

"No."

From the ballroom beneath, muffled and suffocating chords were drifting up on hot waves of air.

"Not that day I carried you down from the Punch Bowl to keep your shoes dry?" There was a husky tenderness in his tone… "Daisy?"

"Please don't." Her voice was cold, but the rancour was gone from it. She looked at Gatsby. "There, Jay," she said – but her hand as she tried to light a cigarette was trembling. Suddenly she threw the cigarette and the burning match on the carpet.

"Oh, you want too much!" she cried to Gatsby. "I love you now – isn't that enough? I can't help what's past." She began to sob helplessly. "I did love him once – but I loved you too."

Gatsby's eyes opened and closed.

"You loved me *too*?" he repeated.

"Even that's a lie," said Tom savagely. "She didn't know you were alive. Why – there's things between Daisy and me that you'll never know, things that neither of us can ever forget."

The words seemed to bite physically into Gatsby.

"I want to speak to Daisy alone," he insisted. "She's all excited now—"

"Even alone I can't say I never loved Tom," she admitted in a pitiful voice. "It wouldn't be true."

"Of course it wouldn't," agreed Tom.

She turned to her husband.

"As if it mattered to you," she said.

"Of course it matters. I'm going to take better care of you from now on."

"You don't understand," said Gatsby, with a touch of panic. "You're not going to take care of her any more."

"I'm not?" Tom opened his eyes wide and laughed. He could afford to control himself now. "Why's that?"

"Daisy's leaving you."

"Nonsense."

"I am, though," she said with a visible effort.

"She's not leaving me!" Tom's words suddenly leaned down over Gatsby. "Certainly not for a common swindler who'd have to steal the ring he put on her finger."

"I won't stand this!" cried Daisy. "Oh, please let's get out."

"Who are you, anyhow?" broke out Tom. "You're one of that bunch that hangs around with Meyer Wolfshiem – that much I happen to know. I've made a little investigation into your affairs – and I'll carry it further tomorrow."

"You can suit yourself about that, old sport," said Gatsby steadily.

"I found out what your 'drugstores' were." He turned to us and spoke rapidly. "He and this Wolfshiem bought up a lot of side-street drugstores here and in Chicago and sold grain alcohol over the counter. That's one of his little stunts. I picked him for a bootlegger the first time I saw him, and I wasn't far wrong."

"What about it?" said Gatsby politely. "I guess your friend Walter Chase wasn't too proud to come in on it."

"And you left him in the lurch, didn't you? You let him go to jail for a month over in New Jersey. God! You ought to hear Walter on the subject of *you*."

"He came to us dead broke. He was very glad to pick up some money, old sport."

"Don't you call me 'old sport'!" cried Tom. Gatsby said nothing. "Walter could have you up on the betting laws too, but Wolfshiem scared him into shutting his mouth."

That unfamiliar yet recognizable look was back again in Gatsby's face.

"That drugstore business was just small change," continued Tom slowly, "but you've got something on now that Walter's afraid to tell me about."

I glanced at Daisy, who was staring terrified between Gatsby and her husband, and at Jordan, who had begun to balance an invisible but absorbing object on the tip of her chin. Then I turned back to Gatsby – and was startled at his expression. He looked – and this is said in all contempt for the babbled slander of his garden – as if he had "killed a man." For a moment the set of his face could be described in just that fantastic way.

It passed, and he began to talk excitedly to Daisy, denying everything, defending his name against accusations that had not been made. But with every word she was drawing further and further into herself, so he gave that up, and only the dead dream fought on as the afternoon slipped away, trying to touch what was no longer tangible, struggling unhappily, undespairingly, toward that lost voice across the room.

The voice begged again to go.

"*Please*, Tom! I can't stand this any more."

Her frightened eyes told that whatever intentions, whatever courage she had had, were definitely gone.

"You two start on home, Daisy," said Tom. "In Mr. Gatsby's car."

She looked at Tom, alarmed now, but he insisted with magnanimous scorn.

"Go on. He won't annoy you. I think he realizes that his presumptuous little flirtation is over."

They were gone, without a word, snapped out, made accidental, isolated, like ghosts, even from our pity.

After a moment Tom got up and began wrapping the unopened bottle of whisky in the towel.

"Want any of this stuff? Jordan?… Nick?"

I didn't answer.

"Nick?" He asked again.

"What?"

"Want any?"

"No… I just remembered that today's my birthday."

I was thirty. Before me stretched the portentous, menacing road of a new decade.

It was seven o'clock when we got into the coupé with him and started for Long Island. Tom talked incessantly, exulting and laughing, but his voice was as remote from Jordan and me as the foreign clamour on the sidewalk or the tumult of the elevated overhead. Human sympathy has its limits, and we were content to let all their tragic arguments fade with the city lights behind. Thirty – the promise of a decade of loneliness, a thinning list of single men to know, a thinning briefcase of enthusiasm, thinning hair. But there was Jordan beside me, who, unlike Daisy, was too wise ever to carry well-forgotten dreams from age to age. As we passed over the dark bridge her wan face fell lazily against my coat's shoulder and the formidable stroke of thirty died away with the reassuring pressure of her hand.

So we drove on toward death through the cooling twilight.

* * *

The young Greek, Michaelis, who ran the coffee joint beside the ash-heaps was the principal witness at the inquest. He had slept through the heat until after five, when he strolled over to the garage, and found George Wilson sick in his office – really sick, pale as his own pale hair and shaking all over. Michaelis advised him to go to bed, but Wilson refused, saying that he'd miss a lot of business if he did. While his neighbour was trying to persuade him a violent racket broke out overhead.

"I've got my wife locked up there," explained Wilson calmly. "She's going to stay there till the day after tomorrow, and then we're going to move away."

Michaelis was astonished; they had been neighbours for four years, and Wilson had never seemed faintly capable of such a statement. Generally he was one of these worn-out men: when he wasn't working, he sat on a chair in the doorway and stared at the people and the cars that passed along the road. When anyone spoke to him he invariably laughed in an agreeable, colourless way. He was his wife's man and not his own.

So naturally Michaelis tried to find out what had happened, but Wilson wouldn't say a word – instead he began to throw curious, suspicious glances at his visitor and ask him what he'd been doing at certain times on certain days. Just as the latter was getting uneasy, some workmen came past the door bound for his restaurant, and Michaelis took the opportunity to get away, intending to come back later. But he didn't. He supposed he forgot to, that's all. When he came outside again, a little after seven, he was reminded of the conversation because he heard Mrs. Wilson's voice, loud and scolding, downstairs in the garage.

"Beat me!" he heard her cry. "Throw me down and beat me, you dirty little coward!"

A moment later she rushed out into the dusk, waving her hands and shouting – before he could move from his door the business was over.

The "death car" as the newspapers called it, didn't stop; it came out of the gathering darkness, wavered tragically for a moment, and then disappeared around the next bend. Mavro Michaelis wasn't even sure of its colour – he told the first policeman that it was light green. The other car, the one going toward New York, came to rest a hundred yards beyond, and its driver hurried back to where Myrtle Wilson, her life violently extinguished, knelt in the road and mingled her thick dark blood with the dust.

Michaelis and this man reached her first, but when they had torn open her shirtwaist, still damp with perspiration, they saw that her left breast was swinging loose like a flap, and there was no need to listen for the heart beneath. The mouth was wide open and ripped a little at the corners, as though she had choked a little in giving up the tremendous vitality she had stored so long.

* * *

We saw the three or four automobiles and the crowd when we were still some distance away.

"Wreck!" said Tom. "That's good. Wilson'll have a little business at last."

He slowed down, but still without any intention of stopping, until, as we came nearer, the hushed, intent faces of the people at the garage door made him automatically put on the brakes.

"We'll take a look," he said doubtfully, "just a look."

I became aware now of a hollow, wailing sound which issued incessantly from the garage, a sound which as we got out of the coupé and walked toward the door resolved itself into the words "Oh, my God!" uttered over and over in a gasping moan.

"There's some bad trouble here," said Tom excitedly.

He reached up on tiptoes and peered over a circle of heads into the garage, which was lit only by a yellow light in a swinging metal basket overhead. Then he made a harsh sound in his throat, and with a violent thrusting movement of his powerful arms pushed his way through.

The circle closed up again with a running murmur of expostulation; it was a minute before I could see anything at all. Then new arrivals deranged the line, and Jordan and I were pushed suddenly inside.

Myrtle Wilson's body, wrapped in a blanket, and then in another blanket, as though she suffered from a chill in the hot night, lay on a worktable by the wall, and Tom, with his back to us, was bending over it, motionless. Next to him stood a motorcycle policeman taking down names with much sweat and correction in a little book. At first I couldn't find the source of the high, groaning words that echoed clamorously through the bare garage – then I saw Wilson standing on the raised threshold of his office, swaying back and forth and holding to the doorposts with both hands. Some man was talking to him in a low voice and attempting, from time to time, to lay a hand on his shoulder, but Wilson neither heard nor saw. His eyes would drop slowly from the swinging light to the laden table by the wall, and then jerk back to the light again, and he gave out incessantly his high, horrible call:

"Oh, my Ga-od! Oh, my Ga-od! Oh, Ga-od! Oh, my Ga-od!"

Presently Tom lifted his head with a jerk and, after staring around the garage with glazed eyes, addressed a mumbled incoherent remark to the policeman.

"M-a-v—" the policeman was saying, "—o—"

"No, r—" corrected the man, "M-a-v-r-o—"

"Listen to me!" muttered Tom fiercely.

"r—" said the policeman, "o—"

"g—"

"g—" He looked up as Tom's broad hand fell sharply on his shoulder. "What you want, fella?"

"What happened? – that's what I want to know."

"Auto hit her. Ins'antly killed."

"Instantly killed," repeated Tom, staring.

"She ran out ina road. Son-of-a-bitch didn't even stopus car."

"There was two cars," said Michaelis, "one comin', one goin', see?"

"Going where?" asked the policeman keenly.

"One goin' each way. Well, she" – his hand rose toward the blankets but stopped halfway and fell to his side – "she ran out there an' the one comin' from N'York knock right into her, goin' thirty or forty miles an hour."

"What's the name of this place here?" demanded the officer.

"Hasn't got any name."

A pale well-dressed negro stepped near.

"It was a yellow car," he said, "big yellow car. New."

"See the accident?" asked the policeman.

"No, but the car passed me down the road, going faster'n forty. Going fifty, sixty."

"Come here and let's have your name. Look out now. I want to get his name."

Some words of this conversation must have reached Wilson, swaying in the office door, for suddenly a new theme found voice among his grasping cries:

"You don't have to tell me what kind of car it was! I know what kind of car it was!"

Watching Tom, I saw the wad of muscle back of his shoulder tighten under his coat. He walked quickly over to Wilson and, standing in front of him, seized him firmly by the upper arms.

"You've got to pull yourself together," he said with soothing gruffness.

Wilson's eyes fell upon Tom; he started up on his tiptoes and then would have collapsed to his knees had not Tom held him upright.

"Listen," said Tom, shaking him a little. "I just got here a minute ago, from New York. I was bringing you that coupé we've been talking about. That yellow car I was driving this afternoon wasn't mine – do you hear? I haven't seen it all afternoon."

Only the negro and I were near enough to hear what he said, but the policeman caught something in the tone and looked over with truculent eyes.

"What's all that?" he demanded.

"I'm a friend of his." Tom turned his head but kept his hands firm on Wilson's body. "He says he knows the car that did it... It was a yellow car."

Some dim impulse moved the policeman to look suspiciously at Tom.

"And what colour's your car?"

"It's a blue car, a coupé."

"We've come straight from New York," I said.

Someone who had been driving a little behind us confirmed this, and the policeman turned away.

"Now, if you'll let me have that name again correct—"

Picking up Wilson like a doll, Tom carried him into the office, set him down in a chair, and came back.

"If somebody'll come here and sit with him," he snapped authoritatively. He watched while the two men standing closest glanced at each other and went unwillingly into the room. Then Tom shut the door on them and came down the single step, his eyes avoiding the table. As he passed close to me he whispered: "Let's get out."

Self-consciously, with his authoritative arms breaking the way, we pushed through the still gathering crowd, passing a hurried doctor, case in hand, who had been sent for in wild hope half an hour ago.

Tom drove slowly until we were beyond the bend – then his foot came down hard, and the coupé raced along through the night. In a little while I heard a low husky sob, and saw that the tears were overflowing down his face.

"The God damned coward!" he whimpered. "He didn't even stop his car."

* * *

The Buchanans' house floated suddenly toward us through the dark rustling trees. Tom stopped beside the porch and looked up at the second floor, where two windows bloomed with light among the vines.

"Daisy's home," he said. As we got out of the car he glanced at me and frowned slightly.

"I ought to have dropped you in West Egg, Nick. There's nothing we can do tonight."

A change had come over him, and he spoke gravely, and with decision. As we walked across the moonlight gravel to the porch he disposed of the situation in a few brisk phrases.

"I'll telephone for a taxi to take you home, and while you're waiting you and Jordan better go in the kitchen and have them get you some supper – if you want any." He opened the door. "Come in."

"No, thanks. But I'd be glad if you'd order me the taxi. I'll wait outside."

Jordan put her hand on my arm.

"Won't you come in, Nick?"

"No, thanks."

I was feeling a little sick and I wanted to be alone. But Jordan lingered for a moment more.

"It's only half-past nine," she said.

I'd be damned if I'd go in; I'd had enough of all of them for one day, and suddenly that included Jordan too. She must have seen something of this in my expression, for she turned abruptly away and ran up the porch steps into the house. I sat down for a few minutes with my head in my hands, until I heard the phone taken up inside and the butler's voice calling a taxi. Then I walked slowly down the drive away from the house, intending to wait by the gate.

I hadn't gone twenty yards when I heard my name and Gatsby stepped from between two bushes into the path. I must have felt pretty weird by that time, because I could think of nothing except the luminosity of his pink suit under the moon.

"What are you doing?" I inquired.

"Just standing here, old sport."

Somehow, that seemed a despicable occupation. For all I knew he was going to rob the house in a moment; I wouldn't have been surprised to see sinister faces, the faces of "Wolfshiem's people," behind him in the dark shrubbery.

"Did you see any trouble on the road?" he asked after a minute.

"Yes."

He hesitated.

"Was she killed?"

"Yes."

"I thought so; I told Daisy I thought so. It's better that the shock should all come at once. She stood it pretty well."

He spoke as if Daisy's reaction was the only thing that mattered.

"I got to West Egg by a side road," he went on, "and left the car in my garage. I don't think anybody saw us, but of course I can't be sure."

I disliked him so much by this time that I didn't find it necessary to tell him he was wrong.

"Who was the woman?" he inquired.

"Her name was Wilson. Her husband owns the garage. How the devil did it happen?"

"Well, I tried to swing the wheel—" He broke off, and suddenly I guessed at the truth.

"Was Daisy driving?"

"Yes," he said after a moment, "but of course I'll say I was. You see, when we left New York she was very nervous and she thought it would steady her to drive – and this woman rushed out at us just as we were passing a car coming the other way. It all happened in a minute, but it seemed to me that she wanted to speak to us, thought we were somebody she knew. Well, first Daisy turned away from the woman toward the other car, and then she lost her nerve and turned back. The second my hand reached the wheel I felt the shock – it must have killed her instantly."

"It ripped her open—"

"Don't tell me, old sport." He winced. "Anyhow – Daisy stepped on it. I tried to make her stop, but she couldn't, so I pulled on the emergency brake. Then she fell over into my lap and I drove on.

"She'll be all right tomorrow," he said presently. "I'm just going to wait here and see if he tries to bother her about that unpleasantness this afternoon. She's locked herself into her room, and if he tries any brutality she's going to turn the light out and on again."

"He won't touch her," I said. "He's not thinking about her."

"I don't trust him, old sport."

"How long are you going to wait?"

"All night, if necessary. Anyhow, till they all go to bed."

A new point of view occurred to me. Suppose Tom found out that Daisy had been driving. He might think he saw a connection in it – he might think anything. I looked at the house; there were two or three bright windows downstairs and the pink glow from Daisy's room on the ground floor.

"You wait here," I said. "I'll see if there's any sign of a commotion."

I walked back along the border of the lawn, traversed the gravel softly, and tiptoed up the veranda steps. The drawing-room curtains were open, and I saw that the room was empty. Crossing the porch where we had dined that June night three months before, I came to a small rectangle of light which I guessed was the pantry window. The blind was drawn, but I found a rift at the sill.

Daisy and Tom were sitting opposite each other at the kitchen table, with a plate of cold fried chicken between them, and two bottles of ale. He was talking intently across the table at her, and in his earnestness his hand had fallen upon and covered her own. Once in a while she looked up at him and nodded in agreement.

They weren't happy, and neither of them had touched the chicken or the ale – and yet they weren't unhappy either. There was an unmistakable air of natural intimacy about the picture, and anybody would have said that they were conspiring together.

As I tiptoed from the porch I heard my taxi feeling its way along the dark road toward the house. Gatsby was waiting where I had left him in the drive.

"Is it all quiet up there?" he asked anxiously.

"Yes, it's all quiet." I hesitated. "You'd better come home and get some sleep."

He shook his head.

"I want to wait here till Daisy goes to bed. Good night, old sport."

He put his hands in his coat pockets and turned back eagerly to his scrutiny of the house, as though my presence marred the sacredness of the vigil. So I walked away and left him standing there in the moonlight – watching over nothing.

Chapter VIII

I COULDN'T SLEEP ALL NIGHT; a foghorn was groaning incessantly on the Sound, and I tossed half-sick between grotesque reality and savage, frightening dreams. Toward dawn I heard a taxi go up Gatsby's drive, and immediately I jumped out of bed and began to dress – I felt that I had something to tell him, something to warn him about, and morning would be too late.

Crossing his lawn, I saw that his front door was still open and he was leaning against a table in the hall, heavy with dejection or sleep.

"Nothing happened," he said wanly. "I waited, and about four o'clock she came to the window and stood there for a minute and then turned out the light."

His house had never seemed so enormous to me as it did that night when we hunted through the great rooms for cigarettes. We pushed aside curtains that were like pavilions, and felt over innumerable feet of dark wall for electric light switches – once I tumbled with a sort of splash upon the keys of a ghostly piano. There was an inexplicable amount of dust everywhere, and the rooms were musty, as though they hadn't been aired for many days. I found the humidor on an unfamiliar table, with two stale, dry cigarettes inside. Throwing open the French windows of the drawing-room, we sat smoking out into the darkness.

"You ought to go away," I said. "It's pretty certain they'll trace your car."

"Go away *now*, old sport?"

"Go to Atlantic City for a week, or up to Montreal."

He wouldn't consider it. He couldn't possibly leave Daisy until he knew what she was going to do. He was clutching at some last hope and I couldn't bear to shake him free.

It was this night that he told me the strange story of his youth with Dan Cody – told it to me because "Jay Gatsby" had broken up like glass against Tom's hard malice, and the long secret extravaganza was played out. I think that he would have acknowledged anything now, without reserve, but he wanted to talk about Daisy.

She was the first "nice" girl he had ever known. In various unrevealed capacities he had come in contact with such people, but always with indiscernible barbed wire between. He found her excitingly desirable. He went to her house, at first with other officers from Camp Taylor, then alone. It amazed him – he had never been in such a beautiful house before. But what gave it an air of breathless intensity, was that Daisy lived there – it was as casual a thing to her as his tent out at camp was to him. There was a ripe mystery about it, a hint of bedrooms upstairs more beautiful and cool than other bedrooms, of gay and radiant activities taking place through its corridors, and of romances that were not musty and laid away already in lavender but fresh and breathing and redolent of this year's shining motorcars and of dances whose flowers were scarcely withered. It excited him, too, that many men had already loved Daisy – it increased her value in his eyes. He felt their presence all about the house, pervading the air with the shades and echoes of still vibrant emotions.

But he knew that he was in Daisy's house by a colossal accident. However glorious might be his future as Jay Gatsby, he was at present a penniless young man without a past, and at any moment the invisible cloak of his uniform might slip from his shoulders. So he made the most of his time. He took what he could get, ravenously and unscrupulously – eventually he took Daisy one still October night, took her because he had no real right to touch her hand.

He might have despised himself, for he had certainly taken her under false pretences. I don't mean that he had traded on his phantom millions, but he had deliberately given Daisy a sense of security; he let her believe that he was a person from much the same strata as herself – that he was fully able to take care of her. As a matter of fact, he had no such facilities – he had no comfortable family standing behind him, and he was liable at the whim of an impersonal government to be blown anywhere about the world.

But he didn't despise himself and it didn't turn out as he had imagined. He had intended, probably, to take what he could and go – but now he found that he had committed himself to the following of a grail. He knew that Daisy was extraordinary, but he didn't realize just how extraordinary a "nice" girl could be. She vanished into her rich house, into her rich, full life, leaving Gatsby – nothing. He felt married to her, that was all.

When they met again, two days later, it was Gatsby who was breathless, who was, somehow, betrayed. Her porch was bright with the bought luxury of star-shine; the wicker of the settee squeaked fashionably as she turned toward him and he kissed her curious and lovely mouth. She had caught a cold, and it made her voice huskier and more charming than ever, and Gatsby was overwhelmingly aware of the youth and mystery that wealth imprisons and preserves, of the freshness of many clothes, and of Daisy, gleaming like silver, safe and proud above the hot struggles of the poor.

* * *

"I can't describe to you how surprised I was to find out I loved her, old sport. I even hoped for a while that she'd throw me over, but she didn't, because she was in love with me too. She thought I knew a lot because I knew different things from her… Well, there I was, way off my ambitions, getting deeper in love every minute, and all of a sudden I didn't care. What was the use of doing great things if I could have a better time telling her what I was going to do?"

On the last afternoon before he went abroad, he sat with Daisy in his arms for a long, silent time. It was a cold fall day, with fire in the room and her cheeks flushed. Now and then she moved and he changed his arm a little, and once he kissed her dark shining hair. The afternoon had made them tranquil for a while, as if to give them a deep memory for the long parting the next day promised. They had never been closer in their month of love, nor communicated more profoundly one with another, than when she brushed silent lips against his coat's shoulder or when he touched the end of her fingers, gently, as though she were asleep.

* * *

He did extraordinarily well in the war. He was a captain before he went to the front, and following the Argonne battles he got his majority and the command of the divisional machine-guns. After the armistice he tried frantically to get home, but some complication or misunderstanding sent him to Oxford instead. He was worried now – there was a quality of nervous despair in Daisy's letters. She didn't see why he couldn't come. She was feeling the pressure of the world outside, and she wanted to see him and feel his presence beside her and be reassured that she was doing the right thing after all.

For Daisy was young and her artificial world was redolent of orchids and pleasant, cheerful snobbery and orchestras which set the rhythm of the year, summing up the sadness and suggestiveness of life in new tunes. All night the saxophones wailed the hopeless comment of the "Beale Street Blues" while a hundred pairs of golden and silver slippers shuffled the shining dust. At the grey tea hour there were always rooms that throbbed incessantly with this low, sweet fever, while fresh faces drifted here and there like rose petals blown by the sad horns around the floor.

Through this twilight universe Daisy began to move again with the season; suddenly she was again keeping half a dozen dates a day with half a dozen men, and drowsing asleep at dawn with the beads and chiffon of an evening-dress tangled among dying orchids on the floor beside her bed. And all the time something within her was crying for a decision. She wanted her life shaped now, immediately – and the decision must be made by some force – of love, of money, of unquestionable practicality – that was close at hand.

That force took shape in the middle of spring with the arrival of Tom Buchanan. There was a wholesome bulkiness about his person and his position, and Daisy was flattered. Doubtless there was a certain struggle and a certain relief. The letter reached Gatsby while he was still at Oxford.

* * *

It was dawn now on Long Island and we went about opening the rest of the windows downstairs, filling the house with grey-turning, gold-turning light. The shadow of a tree fell abruptly across the dew and ghostly birds began to sing among the blue leaves. There was a slow, pleasant movement in the air, scarcely a wind, promising a cool, lovely day.

"I don't think she ever loved him." Gatsby turned around from a window and looked at me challengingly. "You must remember, old sport, she was very excited this afternoon. He told her those things in a way that frightened her – that made it look as if I was some kind of cheap sharper. And the result was she hardly knew what she was saying."

He sat down gloomily.

"Of course she might have loved him just for a minute, when they were first married – and loved me more even then, do you see?"

Suddenly he came out with a curious remark.

"In any case," he said, "it was just personal."

What could you make of that, except to suspect some intensity in his conception of the affair that couldn't be measured?

He came back from France when Tom and Daisy were still on their wedding trip, and made a miserable but irresistible journey to Louisville on the last of his army pay. He stayed there a week, walking the streets where their footsteps had clicked together through the November night and revisiting the out-of-the-way places to which they had driven in her white car. Just as Daisy's house had always seemed to him more mysterious and gay than other houses, so his idea of the city itself, even though she was gone from it, was pervaded with a melancholy beauty.

He left feeling that if he had searched harder, he might have found her – that he was leaving her behind. The day-coach – he was penniless now – was hot. He went out to the open vestibule and sat down on a folding-chair, and the station slid away and the backs of unfamiliar buildings moved by. Then out into the spring fields, where a yellow trolley raced them for a minute with people in it who might once have seen the pale magic of her face along the casual street.

The track curved and now it was going away from the sun, which, as it sank lower, seemed to spread itself in benediction over the vanishing city where she had drawn her breath. He stretched out his hand desperately as if to snatch only a wisp of air, to save a fragment of the spot that she had made lovely for him. But it was all going by too fast now for his blurred eyes and he knew that he had lost that part of it, the freshest and the best, forever.

It was nine o'clock when we finished breakfast and went out on the porch. The night had made a sharp difference in the weather and there was an autumn flavour in the air. The gardener, the last one of Gatsby's former servants, came to the foot of the steps.

"I'm going to drain the pool today, Mr. Gatsby. Leaves'll start falling pretty soon, and then there's always trouble with the pipes."

"Don't do it today," Gatsby answered. He turned to me apologetically. "You know, old sport, I've never used that pool all summer?"

I looked at my watch and stood up.

"Twelve minutes to my train."

I didn't want to go to the city. I wasn't worth a decent stroke of work, but it was more than that – I didn't want to leave Gatsby. I missed that train, and then another, before I could get myself away.

"I'll call you up," I said finally.

"Do, old sport."

"I'll call you about noon."

We walked slowly down the steps.

"I suppose Daisy'll call too." He looked at me anxiously, as if he hoped I'd corroborate this.

"I suppose so."

"Well, goodbye."

We shook hands and I started away. Just before I reached the hedge I remembered something and turned around.

"They're a rotten crowd," I shouted across the lawn. "You're worth the whole damn bunch put together."

I've always been glad I said that. It was the only compliment I ever gave him, because I disapproved of him from beginning to end. First he nodded politely, and then his face broke into that radiant and understanding smile, as if we'd been in ecstatic cahoots on that fact all the time. His gorgeous pink rag of a suit made a bright spot of colour against the white steps, and I thought of the night when I first came to his ancestral home, three months before. The lawn and drive had been crowded with the faces of those who guessed at his corruption – and he had stood on those steps, concealing his incorruptible dream, as he waved them goodbye.

I thanked him for his hospitality. We were always thanking him for that – I and the others.

"Goodbye," I called. "I enjoyed breakfast, Gatsby."

* * *

Up in the city, I tried for a while to list the quotations on an interminable amount of stock, then I fell asleep in my swivel-chair. Just before noon the phone woke me, and I started up with sweat breaking out on my forehead. It was Jordan Baker; she often called me up at this hour because the uncertainty of her own movements between hotels and clubs and private houses made her hard to find in any other way. Usually her voice came over the wire as something fresh and cool, as if a divot from a green golf-links had come sailing in at the office window, but this morning it seemed harsh and dry.

"I've left Daisy's house," she said. "I'm at Hempstead, and I'm going down to Southampton this afternoon."

Probably it had been tactful to leave Daisy's house, but the act annoyed me, and her next remark made me rigid.

"You weren't so nice to me last night."

"How could it have mattered then?"

Silence for a moment. Then:

"However – I want to see you."

"I want to see you, too."

"Suppose I don't go to Southampton, and come into town this afternoon?"

"No – I don't think this afternoon."

"Very well."

"It's impossible this afternoon. Various—"

We talked like that for a while, and then abruptly we weren't talking any longer. I don't know which of us hung up with a sharp click, but I know I didn't care. I couldn't have talked to her across a tea-table that day if I never talked to her again in this world.

I called Gatsby's house a few minutes later, but the line was busy. I tried four times; finally an exasperated central told me the wire was being kept open for long distance from Detroit. Taking out my timetable, I drew a small circle around the three-fifty train. Then I leaned back in my chair and tried to think. It was just noon.

* * *

When I passed the ash-heaps on the train that morning I had crossed deliberately to the other side of the car. I supposed there'd be a curious crowd around there all day with little boys searching for dark spots in the dust, and some garrulous man telling over and over what had happened, until it became less and less real even to him and he could tell it no longer, and Myrtle Wilson's tragic achievement was forgotten. Now I want to go back a little and tell what happened at the garage after we left there the night before.

They had difficulty in locating the sister, Catherine. She must have broken her rule against drinking that night, for when she arrived she was stupid with liquor and unable to understand that the ambulance had already gone to Flushing. When they convinced her of this, she immediately fainted, as if that was the intolerable part of the affair. Someone, kind or curious, took her in his car and drove her in the wake of her sister's body.

Until long after midnight a changing crowd lapped up against the front of the garage, while George Wilson rocked himself back and forth on the couch inside. For a while the door of the office was open, and everyone who came into the garage glanced irresistibly through it. Finally someone said it was a shame, and closed the door. Michaelis and several other men were with him; first, four or five men, later two or three men. Still later Michaelis had to ask the last stranger to wait there fifteen minutes longer, while he went back to his own place and made a pot of coffee. After that, he stayed there alone with Wilson until dawn.

About three o'clock the quality of Wilson's incoherent muttering changed – he grew quieter and began to talk about the yellow car. He announced that he had a way of finding out whom the yellow car belonged to, and then he blurted out that a couple of months ago his wife had come from the city with her face bruised and her nose swollen.

But when he heard himself say this, he flinched and began to cry "Oh, my God!" again in his groaning voice. Michaelis made a clumsy attempt to distract him.

"How long have you been married, George? Come on there, try and sit still a minute, and answer my question. How long have you been married?"

"Twelve years."

"Ever had any children? Come on, George, sit still – I asked you a question. Did you ever have any children?"

The hard brown beetles kept thudding against the dull light, and whenever Michaelis heard a car go tearing along the road outside it sounded to him like the car that hadn't stopped a few hours before. He didn't like to go into the garage, because the work bench was stained where the body had been lying, so he moved uncomfortably around the office – he knew every object in it before morning – and from time to time sat down beside Wilson trying to keep him more quiet.

"Have you got a church you go to sometimes, George? Maybe even if you haven't been there for a long time? Maybe I could call up the church and get a priest to come over and he could talk to you, see?"

"Don't belong to any."

"You ought to have a church, George, for times like this. You must have gone to church once. Didn't you get married in a church? Listen, George, listen to me. Didn't you get married in a church?"

"That was a long time ago."

The effort of answering broke the rhythm of his rocking – for a moment he was silent. Then the same half-knowing, half-bewildered look came back into his faded eyes.

"Look in the drawer there," he said, pointing at the desk.

"Which drawer?"

"That drawer – that one."

Michaelis opened the drawer nearest his hand. There was nothing in it but a small, expensive dog-leash, made of leather and braided silver. It was apparently new.

"This?" he inquired, holding it up.

Wilson stared and nodded.

"I found it yesterday afternoon. She tried to tell me about it, but I knew it was something funny."

"You mean your wife bought it?"

"She had it wrapped in tissue paper on her bureau."

Michaelis didn't see anything odd in that, and he gave Wilson a dozen reasons why his wife might have bought the dog-leash. But conceivably Wilson had heard some of these same explanations before, from Myrtle, because he began saying "Oh, my God!" again in a whisper – his comforter left several explanations in the air.

"Then he killed her," said Wilson. His mouth dropped open suddenly.

"Who did?"

"I have a way of finding out."

"You're morbid, George," said his friend. "This has been a strain to you and you don't know what you're saying. You'd better try and sit quiet till morning."

"He murdered her."

"It was an accident, George."

Wilson shook his head. His eyes narrowed and his mouth widened slightly with the ghost of a superior "Hm!"

"I know," he said definitely. "I'm one of these trusting fellas and I don't think any harm to *no*body, but when I get to know a thing I know it. It was the man in that car. She ran out to speak to him and he wouldn't stop."

Michaelis had seen this too, but it hadn't occurred to him that there was any special significance in it. He believed that Mrs. Wilson had been running away from her husband, rather than trying to stop any particular car.

"How could she of been like that?"

"She's a deep one," said Wilson, as if that answered the question. "Ah-h-h—"

He began to rock again, and Michaelis stood twisting the leash in his hand.

"Maybe you got some friend that I could telephone for, George?"

This was a forlorn hope – he was almost sure that Wilson had no friend: there was not enough of him for his wife. He was glad a little later when he noticed a change in the room, a blue quickening by the window, and realized that dawn wasn't far off. About five o'clock it was blue enough outside to snap off the light.

Wilson's glazed eyes turned out to the ash-heaps, where small grey clouds took on fantastic shapes and scurried here and there in the faint dawn wind.

"I spoke to her," he muttered, after a long silence. "I told her she might fool me but she couldn't fool God. I took her to the window" – with an effort he got up and walked to the rear window and leaned with his face pressed against it—"and I said 'God knows what you've been doing, everything you've been doing. You may fool me, but you can't fool God!'"

Standing behind him, Michaelis saw with a shock that he was looking at the eyes of Doctor T. J. Eckleburg, which had just emerged, pale and enormous, from the dissolving night.

"God sees everything," repeated Wilson.

"That's an advertisement," Michaelis assured him. Something made him turn away from the window and look back into the room. But Wilson stood there a long time, his face close to the window pane, nodding into the twilight.

* * *

By six o'clock Michaelis was worn out, and grateful for the sound of a car stopping outside. It was one of the watchers of the night before who had promised to come back, so he cooked breakfast for three, which he and the other man ate together. Wilson was quieter now, and Michaelis went home to sleep; when he awoke four hours later and hurried back to the garage, Wilson was gone.

His movements – he was on foot all the time – were afterward traced to Port Roosevelt and then to Gad's Hill, where he bought a sandwich that he didn't eat, and a cup of coffee. He must have been tired and walking slowly, for he didn't reach Gad's Hill until noon. Thus far there was no difficulty in accounting for his time – there were boys who had seen a man "acting sort of crazy," and motorists at whom he stared oddly from the side of the road. Then for three hours he disappeared from view. The police, on the strength of what he said to Michaelis, that he "had a way of finding out," supposed that he spent that time going from garage to garage thereabout, inquiring for a yellow car. On the other hand, no garage man who had seen him ever came forward, and perhaps he had an easier, surer way of finding out what he wanted to know. By half-past two he was in West Egg, where he asked someone the way to Gatsby's house. So by that time he knew Gatsby's name.

* * *

At two o'clock Gatsby put on his bathing-suit and left word with the butler that if anyone phoned word was to be brought to him at the pool. He stopped at the garage for a pneumatic mattress that had amused his guests during the summer, and the chauffeur helped him to pump it up. Then he gave instructions that the open car wasn't to be taken out under any circumstances – and this was strange, because the front right fender needed repair.

Gatsby shouldered the mattress and started for the pool. Once he stopped and shifted it a little, and the chauffeur asked him if he needed help, but he shook his head and in a moment disappeared among the yellowing trees.

No telephone message arrived, but the butler went without his sleep and waited for it until four o'clock – until long after there was anyone to give it to if it came. I have an idea that Gatsby himself didn't believe it would come, and perhaps he no longer cared. If that was true he must have felt that he had lost the old warm world, paid a high price for living too long with a single dream. He must have looked up at an unfamiliar sky through frightening leaves and shivered as he found what a grotesque thing a rose is and how raw the sunlight was upon the scarcely created grass. A new world, material without being real, where poor ghosts, breathing dreams like air, drifted fortuitously about... like that ashen, fantastic figure gliding toward him through the amorphous trees.

The chauffeur – he was one of Wolfshiem's protégés – heard the shots – afterwards he could only say that he hadn't thought anything much about them. I drove from the station directly to Gatsby's house and my rushing anxiously up the front steps was the first thing that alarmed anyone. But they knew then, I firmly believe. With scarcely a word said, four of us, the chauffeur, butler, gardener, and I hurried down to the pool.

There was a faint, barely perceptible movement of the water as the fresh flow from one end urged its way toward the drain at the other. With little ripples that were hardly the shadows of waves, the laden mattress moved irregularly down the pool. A small gust of wind that scarcely corrugated the surface was enough to disturb its accidental course with its accidental burden. The touch of a cluster of leaves revolved it slowly, tracing, like the leg of transit, a thin red circle in the water.

It was after we started with Gatsby toward the house that the gardener saw Wilson's body a little way off in the grass, and the holocaust was complete.

Chapter IX

AFTER TWO YEARS I remember the rest of that day, and that night and the next day, only as an endless drill of police and photographers and newspaper men in and out of Gatsby's front door. A rope stretched across the main gate and a policeman by it kept out the curious, but little boys soon discovered that they could enter through my yard, and there were always a few of them clustered open-mouthed about the pool. Someone with a positive manner, perhaps a detective, used the expression "madman" as he bent over Wilson's body that afternoon, and the adventitious authority of his voice set the key for the newspaper reports next morning.

Most of those reports were a nightmare – grotesque, circumstantial, eager, and untrue. When Michaelis's testimony at the inquest brought to light Wilson's suspicions of his wife I thought the whole tale would shortly be served up in racy pasquinade – but Catherine, who might have said anything, didn't say a word. She showed a surprising amount of character about it too – looked at the coroner with determined eyes under that corrected brow of hers, and swore that her sister had never seen Gatsby, that her sister was completely happy with her husband, that her sister had been into no mischief whatever. She convinced herself of it, and cried into her handkerchief, as if the very suggestion was more than she could endure. So Wilson was reduced to a man "deranged by grief" in order that the case might remain in its simplest form. And it rested there.

But all this part of it seemed remote and unessential. I found myself on Gatsby's side, and alone. From the moment I telephoned news of the catastrophe to West Egg village, every surmise about him, and every practical question, was referred to me. At first I was surprised and confused; then, as he lay in his house and didn't move or breathe or speak, hour upon hour, it grew upon me that I was responsible, because no one else was interested – interested, I mean, with that intense personal interest to which everyone has some vague right at the end.

I called up Daisy half an hour after we found him, called her instinctively and without hesitation. But she and Tom had gone away early that afternoon, and taken baggage with them.

"Left no address?"

"No."

"Say when they'd be back?"

"No."

"Any idea where they are? How I could reach them?"

"I don't know. Can't say."

I wanted to get somebody for him. I wanted to go into the room where he lay and reassure him: "I'll get somebody for you, Gatsby. Don't worry. Just trust me and I'll get somebody for you—"

Meyer Wolfshiem's name wasn't in the phone book. The butler gave me his office address on Broadway, and I called Information, but by the time I had the number it was long after five, and no one answered the phone.

"Will you ring again?"

"I've rung three times."

"It's very important."

"Sorry. I'm afraid no one's there."

I went back to the drawing-room and thought for an instant that they were chance visitors, all these official people who suddenly filled it. But, though they drew back the sheet and looked at Gatsby with shocked eyes, his protest continued in my brain:

"Look here, old sport, you've got to get somebody for me. You've got to try hard. I can't go through this alone."

Someone started to ask me questions, but I broke away and going upstairs looked hastily through the unlocked parts of his desk – he'd never told me definitely that his parents were dead. But there was nothing – only the picture of Dan Cody, a token of forgotten violence, staring down from the wall.

Next morning I sent the butler to New York with a letter to Wolfshiem, which asked for information and urged him to come out on the next train. That request seemed superfluous when I wrote it. I was sure he'd start when he saw the newspapers, just as I was sure there'd be a wire from Daisy before noon – but neither a wire nor Mr. Wolfshiem arrived; no one arrived except more police and photographers and newspaper men. When the butler brought back Wolfshiem's answer I began to have a feeling of defiance, of scornful solidarity between Gatsby and me against them all.

Dear Mr. Carraway. This has been one of the most terrible shocks of my life to me I hardly can believe it that it is true at all. Such a mad act as that man did should make us all think. I cannot come down now as I am tied up in some very important business and cannot get mixed up in this thing now. If there is anything I can do a little later let me know in a letter by Edgar. I hardly know where I am when I hear about a thing like this and am completely knocked down and out.

    Yours truly
    Meyer Wolfshiem

and then hasty addenda beneath:

Let me know about the funeral etc do not know his family at all.

When the phone rang that afternoon and Long Distance said Chicago was calling I thought this would be Daisy at last. But the connection came through as a man's voice, very thin and far away.

"This is Slagle speaking…"

"Yes?" The name was unfamiliar.

"Hell of a note, isn't it? Get my wire?"

"There haven't been any wires."

"Young Parke's in trouble," he said rapidly. "They picked him up when he handed the bonds over the counter. They got a circular from New York giving 'em the numbers just five minutes before. What d'you know about that, hey? You never can tell in these hick towns—"

"Hello!" I interrupted breathlessly. "Look here – this isn't Mr. Gatsby. Mr. Gatsby's dead."

There was a long silence on the other end of the wire, followed by an exclamation… then a quick squawk as the connection was broken.

* * *

I think it was on the third day that a telegram signed Henry C. Gatz arrived from a town in Minnesota. It said only that the sender was leaving immediately and to postpone the funeral until he came.

It was Gatsby's father, a solemn old man, very helpless and dismayed, bundled up in a long cheap ulster against the warm September day. His eyes leaked continuously with excitement, and when I took the bag and umbrella from his hands he began to pull so incessantly at his sparse grey beard that I had difficulty in getting off his coat. He was on the point of collapse, so I took him into the music-room and made him sit down while I sent for something to eat. But he wouldn't eat, and the glass of milk spilled from his trembling hand.

"I saw it in the Chicago newspaper," he said. "It was all in the Chicago newspaper. I started right away."

"I didn't know how to reach you."

His eyes, seeing nothing, moved ceaselessly about the room.

"It was a madman," he said. "He must have been mad."

"Wouldn't you like some coffee?" I urged him.

"I don't want anything. I'm all right now, Mr.—"

"Carraway."

"Well, I'm all right now. Where have they got Jimmy?"

I took him into the drawing-room, where his son lay, and left him there. Some little boys had come up on the steps and were looking into the hall; when I told them who had arrived, they went reluctantly away.

After a little while Mr. Gatz opened the door and came out, his mouth ajar, his face flushed slightly, his eyes leaking isolated and unpunctual tears. He had reached an age where death no longer has the quality of ghastly surprise, and when he looked around him now for the first time and saw the height and splendour of the hall and the great rooms opening out from it into other rooms, his grief began to be mixed with an awed pride. I helped him to a bedroom upstairs; while he took off his coat and vest I told him that all arrangements had been deferred until he came.

"I didn't know what you'd want, Mr. Gatsby—"

"Gatz is my name."

"—Mr. Gatz. I thought you might want to take the body West."

He shook his head.

"Jimmy always liked it better down East. He rose up to his position in the East. Were you a friend of my boy's, Mr.—?"

"We were close friends."

"He had a big future before him, you know. He was only a young man, but he had a lot of brain power here."

He touched his head impressively, and I nodded.

"If he'd of lived, he'd of been a great man. A man like James J. Hill. He'd of helped build up the country."

"That's true," I said, uncomfortably.

He fumbled at the embroidered coverlet, trying to take it from the bed, and lay down stiffly – was instantly asleep.

That night an obviously frightened person called up, and demanded to know who I was before he would give his name.

"This is Mr. Carraway," I said.

"Oh!" He sounded relieved. "This is Klipspringer."

I was relieved too, for that seemed to promise another friend at Gatsby's grave. I didn't want it to be in the papers and draw a sightseeing crowd, so I'd been calling up a few people myself. They were hard to find.

"The funeral's tomorrow," I said. "Three o'clock, here at the house. I wish you'd tell anybody who'd be interested."

"Oh, I will," he broke out hastily. "Of course I'm not likely to see anybody, but if I do."

His tone made me suspicious.

"Of course you'll be there yourself."

"Well, I'll certainly try. What I called up about is—"

"Wait a minute," I interrupted. "How about saying you'll come?"

"Well, the fact is – the truth of the matter is that I'm staying with some people up here in Greenwich, and they rather expect me to be with them tomorrow. In fact, there's a sort of picnic or something. Of course I'll do my best to get away."

I ejaculated an unrestrained "Huh!" and he must have heard me, for he went on nervously:

"What I called up about was a pair of shoes I left there. I wonder if it'd be too much trouble to have the butler send them on. You see, they're tennis shoes, and I'm sort of helpless without them. My address is care of B. F.—"

I didn't hear the rest of the name, because I hung up the receiver.

After that I felt a certain shame for Gatsby – one gentleman to whom I telephoned implied that he had got what he deserved. However, that was my fault, for he was one of those who used to sneer most bitterly at Gatsby on the courage of Gatsby's liquor, and I should have known better than to call him.

The morning of the funeral I went up to New York to see Meyer Wolfshiem; I couldn't seem to reach him any other way. The door that I pushed open, on the advice of an elevator boy, was marked "The Swastika Holding Company," and at first there didn't seem to be anyone inside. But when I'd shouted "hello" several times in vain, an argument broke out behind a partition, and presently a lovely Jewess appeared at an interior door and scrutinized me with black hostile eyes.

"Nobody's in," she said. "Mr. Wolfshiem's gone to Chicago."

The first part of this was obviously untrue, for someone had begun to whistle "The Rosary," tunelessly, inside.

"Please say that Mr. Carraway wants to see him."

"I can't get him back from Chicago, can I?"

At this moment a voice, unmistakably Wolfshiem's, called "Stella!" from the other side of the door.

"Leave your name on the desk," she said quickly. "I'll give it to him when he gets back."

"But I know he's there."

She took a step toward me and began to slide her hands indignantly up and down her hips.

"You young men think you can force your way in here any time," she scolded. "We're getting sickantired of it. When I say he's in Chicago, he's in Chicago."

I mentioned Gatsby.

"Oh-h!" She looked at me over again. "Will you just – What was your name?"

She vanished. In a moment Meyer Wolfshiem stood solemnly in the doorway, holding out both hands. He drew me into his office, remarking in a reverent voice that it was a sad time for all of us, and offered me a cigar.

"My memory goes back to when first I met him," he said. "A young major just out of the army and covered over with medals he got in the war. He was so hard up he had to keep on wearing his uniform because he couldn't buy some regular clothes. First time I saw him was when he came into Winebrenner's poolroom at Forty-third Street and asked for a job. He hadn't eat anything for a couple of days. 'Come on have some lunch with me,' I said. He ate more than four dollars' worth of food in half an hour."

"Did you start him in business?" I inquired.

"Start him! I made him."

"Oh."

"I raised him up out of nothing, right out of the gutter. I saw right away he was a fine-appearing, gentlemanly young man, and when he told me he was at Oggsford I knew I could use him good. I got him to join the American Legion and he used to stand high there. Right off he did some work for a client of mine up to Albany. We were so thick like that in everything" – he held up two bulbous fingers – "always together."

I wondered if this partnership had included the World's Series transaction in 1919.

"Now he's dead," I said after a moment. "You were his closest friend, so I know you'll want to come to his funeral this afternoon."

"I'd like to come."

"Well, come then."

The hair in his nostrils quivered slightly, and as he shook his head his eyes filled with tears.

"I can't do it – I can't get mixed up in it," he said.

"There's nothing to get mixed up in. It's all over now."

"When a man gets killed I never like to get mixed up in it in any way. I keep out. When I was a young man it was different – if a friend of mine died, no matter how, I stuck with them to the end. You may think that's sentimental, but I mean it – to the bitter end."

I saw that for some reason of his own he was determined not to come, so I stood up.

"Are you a college man?" he inquired suddenly.

For a moment I thought he was going to suggest a "gonnegtion," but he only nodded and shook my hand.

"Let us learn to show our friendship for a man when he is alive and not after he is dead," he suggested. "After that my own rule is to let everything alone."

When I left his office the sky had turned dark and I got back to West Egg in a drizzle. After changing my clothes I went next door and found Mr. Gatz walking up and down excitedly in the hall. His pride in his son and in his son's possessions was continually increasing and now he had something to show me.

"Jimmy sent me this picture." He took out his wallet with trembling fingers. "Look there."

It was a photograph of the house, cracked in the corners and dirty with many hands. He pointed out every detail to me eagerly. "Look there!" and then sought admiration from my eyes. He had shown it so often that I think it was more real to him now than the house itself.

"Jimmy sent it to me. I think it's a very pretty picture. It shows up well."

"Very well. Had you seen him lately?"

"He come out to see me two years ago and bought me the house I live in now. Of course we was broke up when he run off from home, but I see now there was a reason for it. He knew he had a big future in front of him. And ever since he made a success he was very generous with me."

He seemed reluctant to put away the picture, held it for another minute, lingeringly, before my eyes. Then he returned the wallet and pulled from his pocket a ragged old copy of a book called *Hopalong Cassidy*.

"Look here, this is a book he had when he was a boy. It just shows you."

He opened it at the back cover and turned it around for me to see. On the last flyleaf was printed the word schedule, and the date September 12, 1906. And underneath:

Rise from bed	6:00 a.m.
Dumbell exercise and wall-scaling	6:15–6:30
Study electricity, etc.	7:15–8:15
Work	8:30–4:30 p.m.
Baseball and sports	4:30–5:00
Practise elocution, poise and how to attain it	5:00–6:00
Study needed inventions	7:00–9:00

General Resolves

- No wasting time at Shafters or [a name, indecipherable]
- No more smokeing or chewing.
- Bath every other day
- Read one improving book or magazine per week
- Save $5.00 [crossed out] $3.00 per week
- Be better to parents

"I came across this book by accident," said the old man. "It just shows you, don't it?"

"It just shows you."

"Jimmy was bound to get ahead. He always had some resolves like this or something. Do you notice what he's got about improving his mind? He was always great for that. He told me I et like a hog once, and I beat him for it."

He was reluctant to close the book, reading each item aloud and then looking eagerly at me. I think he rather expected me to copy down the list for my own use.

A little before three the Lutheran minister arrived from Flushing, and I began to look involuntarily out the windows for other cars. So did Gatsby's father. And as the time passed and the servants came in and stood waiting in the hall, his eyes began to blink anxiously, and he spoke of the rain in a worried, uncertain way. The minister glanced several times at his watch, so I took him aside and asked him to wait for half an hour. But it wasn't any use. Nobody came.

* * *

About five o'clock our procession of three cars reached the cemetery and stopped in a thick drizzle beside the gate – first a motor hearse, horribly black and wet, then Mr. Gatz and the minister and me in the limousine, and a little later four or five servants and the postman from West Egg, in Gatsby's station wagon, all wet to the skin. As we started through the gate into the cemetery I heard a car stop and then the sound of someone splashing after us over the soggy ground. I looked around. It was the man with owl-eyed glasses whom I had found marvelling over Gatsby's books in the library one night three months before.

I'd never seen him since then. I don't know how he knew about the funeral, or even his name. The rain poured down his thick glasses, and he took them off and wiped them to see the protecting canvas unrolled from Gatsby's grave.

I tried to think about Gatsby then for a moment, but he was already too far away, and I could only remember, without resentment, that Daisy hadn't sent a message or a flower. Dimly I heard someone murmur "Blessed are the dead that the rain falls on," and then the owl-eyed man said "Amen to that," in a brave voice.

We straggled down quickly through the rain to the cars. Owl-eyes spoke to me by the gate.

"I couldn't get to the house," he remarked.

"Neither could anybody else."

"Go on!" He started. "Why, my God! they used to go there by the hundreds."

He took off his glasses and wiped them again, outside and in.

"The poor son-of-a-bitch," he said.

* * *

One of my most vivid memories is of coming back West from prep school and later from college at Christmas time. Those who went farther than Chicago would gather in the old dim Union Station at six o'clock of a December evening, with a few Chicago friends, already caught up into their own holiday gaieties, to bid them a hasty goodbye. I remember the fur coats of the girls returning from Miss This-or-That's and the chatter of frozen breath and the hands waving overhead as we caught sight of old acquaintances, and the matchings of invitations: "Are you going to the Ordways'? the Herseys'? the Schultzes'?" and the long green tickets clasped tight in our gloved hands. And last the murky yellow cars of the Chicago, Milwaukee and St. Paul railroad looking cheerful as Christmas itself on the tracks beside the gate.

When we pulled out into the winter night and the real snow, our snow, began to stretch out beside us and twinkle against the windows, and the dim lights of small Wisconsin stations moved by, a sharp wild brace came suddenly into the air. We drew in deep breaths of it as we walked back from dinner through the cold vestibules, unutterably aware of our identity with this country for one strange hour, before we melted indistinguishably into it again.

That's my Middle West – not the wheat or the prairies or the lost Swede towns, but the thrilling returning trains of my youth, and the street lamps and sleigh bells in the frosty dark and the shadows of holly wreaths thrown by lighted windows on the snow. I am part of that, a little solemn with the feel of those long winters, a little complacent from growing up in the Carraway house in a city where dwellings are still called through decades by a family's name. I see now that this has been a story of the West, after all – Tom and Gatsby, Daisy and Jordan and I, were all Westerners, and perhaps we possessed some deficiency in common which made us subtly unadaptable to Eastern life.

Even when the East excited me most, even when I was most keenly aware of its superiority to the bored, sprawling, swollen towns beyond the Ohio, with their interminable inquisitions which spared only the children and the very old – even then it had always for me a quality of distortion. West Egg, especially, still figures in my more fantastic dreams. I see it as a night scene by El Greco: a hundred houses, at once conventional and grotesque, crouching under a sullen, overhanging sky and a lustreless moon. In the foreground four solemn men in dress suits are walking along the sidewalk with a stretcher on which lies a drunken woman in a white evening dress. Her hand, which dangles over the side, sparkles cold with jewels. Gravely the men turn in at a house – the wrong house. But no one knows the woman's name, and no one cares.

After Gatsby's death the East was haunted for me like that, distorted beyond my eyes' power of correction. So when the blue smoke of brittle leaves was in the air and the wind blew the wet laundry stiff on the line I decided to come back home.

There was one thing to be done before I left, an awkward, unpleasant thing that perhaps had better have been let alone. But I wanted to leave things in order and not just trust that obliging and indifferent sea to sweep my refuse away. I saw Jordan Baker and talked over and around what had happened to us together, and what had happened afterward to me, and she lay perfectly still, listening, in a big chair.

She was dressed to play golf, and I remember thinking she looked like a good illustration, her chin raised a little jauntily, her hair the colour of an autumn leaf, her face the same brown tint as the fingerless glove on her knee. When I had finished she told me without comment that she was engaged to another man. I doubted that, though there were several she could have married at a nod of her head, but I pretended to be surprised. For just a minute I wondered if I wasn't making a mistake, then I thought it all over again quickly and got up to say goodbye.

"Nevertheless you did throw me over," said Jordan suddenly. "You threw me over on the telephone. I don't give a damn about you now, but it was a new experience for me, and I felt a little dizzy for a while."

We shook hands.

"Oh, and do you remember" – she added – "a conversation we had once about driving a car?"

"Why – not exactly."

"You said a bad driver was only safe until she met another bad driver? Well, I met another bad driver, didn't I? I mean it was careless of me to make such a wrong guess. I thought you were rather an honest, straightforward person. I thought it was your secret pride."

"I'm thirty," I said. "I'm five years too old to lie to myself and call it honour."

She didn't answer. Angry, and half in love with her, and tremendously sorry, I turned away.

* * *

One afternoon late in October I saw Tom Buchanan. He was walking ahead of me along Fifth Avenue in his alert, aggressive way, his hands out a little from his body as if to fight off interference, his head moving sharply here and there, adapting itself to his restless eyes. Just as I slowed up to avoid overtaking him he stopped and began frowning into the windows of a jewellery store. Suddenly he saw me and walked back, holding out his hand.

"What's the matter, Nick? Do you object to shaking hands with me?"

"Yes. You know what I think of you."

"You're crazy, Nick," he said quickly. "Crazy as hell. I don't know what's the matter with you."

"Tom," I inquired, "what did you say to Wilson that afternoon?"

He stared at me without a word, and I knew I had guessed right about those missing hours. I started to turn away, but he took a step after me and grabbed my arm.

"I told him the truth," he said. "He came to the door while we were getting ready to leave, and when I sent down word that we weren't in he tried to force his way upstairs. He was crazy enough to kill me if I hadn't told him who owned the car. His hand was on a revolver in his pocket every minute he was in the house—" He broke off defiantly. "What if I did tell him? That fellow had it coming to him. He threw dust into your eyes just like he did in Daisy's, but he was a tough one. He ran over Myrtle like you'd run over a dog and never even stopped his car."

There was nothing I could say, except the one unutterable fact that it wasn't true.

"And if you think I didn't have my share of suffering – look here, when I went to give up that flat and saw that damn box of dog biscuits sitting there on the sideboard, I sat down and cried like a baby. By God it was awful—"

I couldn't forgive him or like him, but I saw that what he had done was, to him, entirely justified. It was all very careless and confused. They were careless people, Tom and Daisy – they smashed up things and creatures and then retreated back into their money or their vast carelessness, or whatever it was that kept them together, and let other people clean up the mess they had made…

I shook hands with him; it seemed silly not to, for I felt suddenly as though I were talking to a child. Then he went into the jewellery store to buy a pearl necklace – or perhaps only a pair of cuff buttons – rid of my provincial squeamishness forever.

* * *

Gatsby's house was still empty when I left – the grass on his lawn had grown as long as mine. One of the taxi drivers in the village never took a fare past the entrance gate without stopping for a minute and pointing inside; perhaps it was he who drove Daisy and Gatsby over to East Egg the night of the accident, and perhaps he had made a story about it all his own. I didn't want to hear it and I avoided him when I got off the train.

I spent my Saturday nights in New York because those gleaming, dazzling parties of his were with me so vividly that I could still hear the music and the laughter, faint and incessant, from his garden, and the cars going up and down his drive. One night I did hear a material car there, and saw its lights stop at his front steps. But I didn't investigate. Probably it was some final guest who had been away at the ends of the earth and didn't know that the party was over.

On the last night, with my trunk packed and my car sold to the grocer, I went over and looked at that huge incoherent failure of a house once more. On the white steps an obscene word, scrawled by some boy with a piece of brick, stood out clearly in the moonlight, and I erased it, drawing my shoe raspingly along the stone. Then I wandered down to the beach and sprawled out on the sand.

Most of the big shore places were closed now and there were hardly any lights except the shadowy, moving glow of a ferryboat across the Sound. And as the moon rose higher the inessential houses began to melt away until gradually I became aware of the old island here that flowered once for Dutch sailors' eyes – a fresh, green breast of the new world. Its vanished trees, the trees that had made way for Gatsby's house, had once pandered in whispers to the last and greatest of all human dreams; for a transitory enchanted moment man must have held his breath in the presence of this continent, compelled into an aesthetic contemplation he neither understood nor desired, face to face for the last time in history with something commensurate to his capacity for wonder.

And as I sat there brooding on the old, unknown world, I thought of Gatsby's wonder when he first picked out the green light at the end of Daisy's dock. He had come a long way to this blue lawn, and his dream must have seemed so close that he could hardly fail to grasp it. He did not know that it was already behind him, somewhere back in that vast obscurity beyond the city, where the dark fields of the republic rolled on under the night.

Gatsby believed in the green light, the orgastic future that year by year recedes before us. It eluded us then, but that's no matter – tomorrow we will run faster, stretch out our arms further… And one fine morning—

So we beat on, boats against the current, borne back ceaselessly into the past.

T.H.O.R.N.
The Human Organ Repossession Network

Robert Ford

"**COUPLE OF GUYS** came lookin' for you while you were gone."

Mike glanced at his foreman without replying, and then walked to the rear of the flatbed truck. His guts had been twisted since before his alarm clock went off, and he was certain whatever Hanlon was going to tell him wasn't going to improve things. Mike took his hat off and wiped his forehead with the sleeve of his flannel shirt. "What'd they want?"

Hanlon drank from his ever-present steel travel mug of black coffee and shrugged. "Didn't say, but they seemed pretty damned keen on talking with you. Slick-suited pricks, too. Full of themselves." He looked at the crew of men, took a step closer to Mike, and lowered his voice. "You ain't in trouble with… you owe somebody you shouldn't?"

"No, no. Of course not." Mike put his hat back on and pulled a pair of gloves from the right rear pocket of his jeans. "Medical bills, yeah, but we're getting by."

"Sammy still doin' okay? He need clothes or anything?"

A lump threatened to form in Mike's throat, but he coughed and shook his head. "He still misses his mother, but he brings her up less and less. But yeah, man, he's good. Won a ribbon last week for best animal drawing."

Hanlon grinned. "That's good, Mike. That's real good. Having a kid is stressful enough, but I know Sammy's gotta be—"

"He's my son." Mike felt himself bristle a little inside, even though he should be used to it by now.

Most people don't understand what the reality is of having an autistic child. His mother certainly hadn't.

She didn't much care to find out, either.

Hanlon smiled a genuine smile and took another drink from his mug. "Well, as long as you're not gettin' bills with big red letters…"

"Nothing like that." Mike's guts turned into a barrel of eels. His lunch threatened to come back up, but he forced a smile.

Hanlon's gaze lingered on Mike's face a moment, and then he nodded. "Alright, then. Get to it." Mud squelched beneath the man's work boots as he walked back toward the crew.

He was gruff and rude and raw at times, but Hanlon was a good foreman. He was fair and to the point when he wanted something, and beyond that, he was a decent man. Mike had heard about Hanlon loaning some of the crew money to keep the electric on, or buy baby formula when wallets were tight.

But he can't loan the kind of money I owe, can he? And hell, what would be the use, even if he did? I couldn't pay him back any better than—

"It's an hour 'til quittin' time, Mike! You gonna unload the damned sheetrock or you gonna stand there and play with yourself?"

He turned toward the voice of one of the crewmen, a young, likeable kid, full of piss and vinegar. Mike gave him the finger and watched as the kid laughed and headed back inside the framed home. After unbuckling the shipping straps, Mike unloaded the truck. He tried to focus on the labor, but the red envelopes he'd been throwing away for the past several months kept coming to the forefront of his mind.

* * *

"If this isn't the definition of F.U.B.A.R., then I don't know what the hell is." Detective Jacobs daubed a small smear of Vicks VapoRub beneath his nose, and turned to an officer on scene. "Open a window. There's *ripe,* and then there's this."

Detective Noble took the jar when Jacobs offered it, applied his own smudge of mentholated ointment in the same spot, and then tucked the container in his suit pocket. "What the hell happened? Poor bastard looks like he was hit by a train."

The corpse on the living room floor was almost split in half at the waist, the body held together by the spinal cord alone. A massive puddle of dried blood surrounded him on the carpet. The body was bloated, mottled a terrible greenish hue, and the eye sockets and open mouth were still filled with a writhing assembly of maggots.

A man with CORONER stamped in bright yellow on his black windbreaker stood up from his crouched position by the dead man. "He's missing his hips."

Noble stared at him. "Excuse me?"

The coroner removed one latex glove, and then the next. "The top of both femurs, and partial sections on both sides of his hips have been cut out. And not cleanly." He tossed the gloves to a spot on the carpet, joining a small pile of others used at the scene.

Jacobs winced and looked away from the body. "Post or pre-mortem?"

The coroner gave a slight shrug. "I'll know for sure after the autopsy, but from the blood loss alone, I'd say the poor son of a bitch was alive when it happened."

* * *

"No sidecar for me today, Denise."

The bartender raised an eyebrow, a slight smirk on her face as she set a mug of Budweiser in front of him. "On a diet this week?"

Mike snickered. "My wallet is."

"Ain't it the truth for everyone." She took a towel from her shoulder and leaned closer. "Hear about Lombardo?"

Mike took a drink from the cold draft. "Haven't seen him in a while."

"Neither has anyone else. Been almost a month." Denise wiped some drops of water from the bar. "Smitty said he saw the Coroner's wagon outside Lombardo's place earlier."

"Oh hell. Outside of the hip replacement, he seemed a healthy enough guy. Son of a bitch could outwork me or any of the crew I'm with."

"Ticker gave out maybe? Hell, we're all living on borrowed time anyway." Denise shrugged and wandered off to the other side of the bar.

Mike stared into the yellow depths of his frosted mug.

Living on borrowed time. Isn't it the damned truth?

The thought made an ache pulse inside him, and the long-healed scar on his abdomen began to itch. Mike ignored it, pulled a five-dollar bill from his pocket and laid it on the top of the bar. He lifted his mug and drained it. The urge to have another, along with a shot of Jack Daniels, rose up inside him and wanted to take over. But it was time to pick up Sammy from the sitters, and besides, every dollar counted right now. Even a single cold draft in this dive bar made him feel guilty as sin.

* * *

The men got into the patrol car without a word. Jacobs slid into the passenger seat and chewed on his bottom lip.

Detective Jacobs started the car and drove in silence until he caught a glance of Jacobs shaking his head, as if he was arguing with his thoughts.

"What's eating you? You look like you're waiting for results on a STD test." Noble picked up a napkin from the center console and wiped the menthol away from his upper lip. It had come in handy to cover the smell – as the old man's body had been rotting for at least a week.

Crossing his arms, Jacobs turned toward him. "You really okay with this?"

Detective Noble lowered the driver's side window slightly. He reached into his suit jacket and pulled a pack of Winstons, shook one free with a practiced hand, and then lit the cigarette as he drove. "We've been busting our asses for how long? I'm looking at twenty years next month, and you're not far behind me."

"What's your point?"

"All I'm saying is… look, I've got a daughter in college, my son starts next year. I've got alimony, a hell of a nice boat I never get to use and—"

"I get it, man, but holy hell. They took his goddamn *hip replacements*." Jacobs uncrossed his arms, put his palms on his knees and let out a long exhale.

Noble took a drag from his cigarette and exhaled the smoke from his nostrils. "It's business. Gotta be close to forty-grand to—"

"Business?" Jacobs scoffed and reached into an inner suit pocket. He pulled out several red envelopes and shook them in his hand. "This is way more than—"

"*Jesus Christ, Jacobs!*" Noble screamed out loud, swerved the patrol car to the shoulder of the road and came to a stop. He glared at the other man, and then lowered his voice, speaking in an even tone, but one with a razor-honed edge. "You asked if I'm okay with all of this, and the honest answer is I don't know. I don't know, okay?"

Noble took an angry puff off his Winston and flicked the butt through the open window. "But I know I want life to be *nice and comfortable.* I don't want a freakin' mansions or a Corvette or a Rolex. I want *nice and comfortable,* that's all. So, if *this* shit is what I need to do to get it, then it is what the hell it is."

* * *

Mike was headed toward his truck when he heard footsteps on gravel behind him. It was an okay neighborhood, where everybody kept to their own business, but times were hard all over. He paused and turned to see two men approaching him. Both were dressed in business suits that were definitely not off-the-rack, and both walked toward him with purpose. The one on the left was a little taller than Mike, sporting a trimmed mustache and goatee, and had a pate as bald and gleaming as the hull of a rocket ship.

The man on the right was built like a silverback gorilla, and wore a similar expression.

"Mr. Tandy." The bald man walked closer, though he made no move to put his hand out to shake.

Mike thought of the tools in the bed of his truck, wondered if he could reach his hammer if he needed it. "Who's asking?"

The bald man smiled, glanced at the suited giant beside him, and then turned back to Mike. "We represent Harrington Medical Corporation. We've repeatedly tried to—"

"Hospital bills?" Mike crossed his arms and stared. *"That's* what this is about?" He shook his head and spat on the ground. "I know I'm behind, okay? I know. It's been…"

Mike glanced at the front door of the bar. "It's been a rough year. I got laid off, and then I needed a kidney transplant, and…"

As Mike let his words fade, the bald man nodded and then withdrew a small notebook from his inner suit pocket. He flipped several sheets and studied the page. "While you were laid off, your wife left you with an autistic son of four."

Mike swallowed hard. A wet knot of rope swelled in his stomach. "Who the hell—"

"She's living in southern Maryland, not too far from a beach actually, place called the Briarwood Estates trailer park." He closed the notebook and put it in his pocket." Lot number forty-three."

"How do *you* know where she is?" Mike glared at the man. *"I* don't even know where the hell she ran off—"

"Mr. Tandy…" The bald man inhaled sharply, irritated, and then released his breath slowly. "There are *lots* of things we know. Knowledge, as they say, is power. But none of those things matter presently. What *does* matter is you've ignored your financial obligations, as well as your…" He waved his hand toward Mike's abdomen. "Your responsibilities as ward of the kidney you received. You're simply not taking care of it."

Mike shifted his eyes back and forth over the two men, and then settled back on the bald man. "Not taking care of it? What the—"

"The amount of alcohol you've consumed over the past four months is one indication. Not taking the necessary medications you are—"

"How in the blue hell am I supposed to afford the prescriptions?" Mike took a step back toward his pick-up.

The bald man shook his head in an exaggerated action of disappointment. "Mr. Tandy, you are neither paying the money you owe for the transplant, nor are you taking care of the investment."

"Can't get blood from a rock, alright? I'll start paying a little at a time, pick up a second job or—"

"No, no, no." Now it was the bald man's turn to cross his arms. He shook his head and stared down at the gravel lot. "We've sent many notices in hopes of coming to a solution, however you've chosen to ignore them, as well as our *phone calls,* and *voicemails,* and *emails.* No, Mr. Tandy…" He uncrossed his arms and put his hands on his hips. "The time for talking is over."

"What're you gonna do, take it back?" Mike snickered as he studied the man, noting his attempt at alpha-male body language.

The two men glanced at each other, and then they turned back to Mike. The bald man nodded. "Yes."

There was a beat of silence, and then Mike laughed, the sound loud and crisp in the half-empty parking lot. "You can't just take back my freakin' kidney."

The big man shifted slightly, and Mike saw something he hadn't noticed earlier – the man gripped the handle of a small Igloo cooler in his right hand.

"Why not?" The tone in the bald man's voice was very matter of fact, without a hint of amusement.

Mike swallowed hard and the twisted feeling in his stomach turned cold. There was no way he was going to be able to reach the hammer in his toolbox, and from the size of the man holding the cooler, Mike knew he was outmatched. That left one option. He broke into a sprint across the parking lot, heading for the chain link fence protecting the warehouse next door.

He jumped as high as he could and gripped the mesh, climbed until he reached the top of the fence, and swung himself over. Heavy footsteps crunched on gravel behind him as Mike landed on the other side, steadied his footing, and ran.

The warehouse yard was lined with rows of fifteen-foot high stacks of cinderblocks. Some of them were ready to be shipped, with thick metal straps over their bulk, others were partially complete, like the remains of a lost temple. Mike ran past two of the large stacks, turned left, then right, and stopped.

His heart hammered in his chest, and Mike felt a twinge of pain zig-zag through his abdomen. Sweat dripped down his spine, and he heard footsteps – cautious and methodical.

Mike rose to his feet, readying himself to break into a run at the first glimpse of movement. He heard a soft *huffing* noise behind him and slowly turned in the direction of the sound.

The Rottweiler was as thick as a barrel of Kentucky bourbon, its collar a rusted length of chain secured with a padlock. A low rumble escaped from its chest, and the dog bared its teeth with a moist licking sound.

Mike kept his gaze on the dog, but reached blindly to find handholds on the stack of cinderblocks. The Rottweiler took one step forward, flicking its tongue over its lips and snout. Even in the light of dusk, its teeth were bright white and full of violence. A line of silver drool stretched from the side of its mouth and swung like a pendulum.

Gripping onto the cinderblock, Mike snapped his head around and jumped as high as he could, found another handhold and scrambled with his feet to climb. A thick snarl burst from the dog as it charged.

The toe of his left work boot found a hold in the blocks, and Mike felt the dog lunge at him, its mouth grazing the heel of his right foot. He reached the top of the stack, pulled himself over and lay there, as the dog barked and jumped against the stack of concrete.

Mike heard the big man's footsteps, right on the other side of the stack.

Goddamn.

He rolled onto his stomach and pushed himself up to a crouch. He looked around, saw the other stacks of cinderblocks and bricks around him. There was a narrow opening to the right side of the building, and Mike knew it had to lead to the street in front of the warehouse.

He took a deep breath, stood up and ran, jumped to another stack, and raced ahead. Behind him, the Rottweiler's barks changed, and there was another sound, a sharp crackling noise, and the dog yelped.

End of the line, pal.

Mike jumped onto the last column of cinderblocks, and when he ran to the edge, he crouched, sat down, and slid off as quickly as he could. His knees took the landing better than he thought, and Mike broke into a sprint until his lungs burned, heading toward the side of the building.

He ran through the narrow space until he reached the fence and climbed, throwing one leg over the top and letting momentum take care of the rest. Behind him, Mike saw the big man's silhouette, barreling toward him like a freight train.

To his right was the parking lot for the bar, and there was no way the bald man wasn't still there. Mike ran to his left, down the sidewalk and past a dry cleaner and a tobacco shop. He cut right, into a small alleyway, and saw the rusted frame of a fire escape bolted to the side of the building. Mike climbed the ladder to the first landing and grabbed the chain looped around the railing. He pulled, raising the ladder of the escape until it latched in place.

Continuing up the clanking stairs, Mike reached the tar and gravel rooftop of the building. He spun around, dropped flat on his stomach, and peered over the edge of the building.

Below, he saw the big man on the sidewalk, pausing at the alleyway. Mike pulled away and rolled onto his back. He stayed there, letting his pulse and breathing return to normal, and watched the indigo sky darken to a deep midnight blue.

* * *

"This shit's gonna come to a head, you know that, right?"

Noble glanced at Jacobs. "What, me and you?"

"Them and us." Jacobs rolled his window down and spat. "When this started, it was… It was for bigger reasons then."

"Bigger makes it okay with you?"

Jacobs put his hands out. "I didn't say that. It's…" He sighed heavily and shook his head. "Where's the line, huh?"

Noble glared at him. "I'm not sure there is a line in this."

"There has to be. There has to be a line you… we, don't cross."

"So, what's yours, then, Jacobs? What's the line you don't cross?" He reached for his pack of Winstons and shook a fresh one loose. "We're deliberately hiding evidence, taking bribes, aiding and abetting, accessory to murder…" He pinched the filter between his teeth and then lit the cigarette. "Want me to go on? So, now that you've developed a conscience or some bullshit, what's your line?"

Jacobs remained quiet, staring ahead as they drove. "I don't know," he whispered.

"You don't know?"

"I don't know, alright? I don't know what my line is, but this is some shit… it's a big pile of shit."

Noble took an irritated drag from his cigarette. "We've been stepping in it up to our knees, haven't we, Jacobs? We're in it, now. Nothing to do but keep walking until the stink wears off."

A low buzzing came from Noble's suit and he clenched his cigarette in his teeth, pulled his cellphone free, and answered the call. "Yeah."

Jacobs leaned against the headrest of his seat as Noble listened for a moment.

"The rate you guys are going, we'll be working double overtime as it is, and do you think it's possible to be less sloppy next time? That old guy looked like—

"Yeah, I know." Noble held the phone away from his ear, staring at it with an expression of rage, before he put it back in place. "What the hell did you say?"

Jacobs straightened in his seat, watching his partner.

"That's her college, yeah, but…" The look of anger on Noble's face shifted to something else. "He turned seventeen, yeah. Leave my kids out of this and… hello? Hello?"

Noble clenched the phone in his hand and then threw it in the center console.

"Feeling nice and comfortable now?" Jacobs asked as he stared at the man.

* * *

I've got about five hundred in the checking account. Maybe another two hundred in savings bonds for Sammy.

Mike had been going through his inventory as he sped toward the sitters to pick up Sammy. Nothing in the apartment mattered, not *anymore*.

It's time to cut and run.

Sammy had been going to the same sitter since his mom had walked out. Jess was barely sixteen, but a good kid. She had the caring, mothering personality of a much older woman, and Sammy adored her. Most days, Mike wasn't sure what he would do without Jess, thankful he could rely on her for a few more years before she left for college.

When she answered the door, her expression shifted almost immediately from surprise to worry. "Mr. Tandry? What's… why are you here?"

"I'm here to get Sammy, what do you—"

"The school called and told me you were gonna pick him up." Now the worry changed to fear on her face.

Ice trailed along Mike's spine. The world appeared through a funhouse mirror, twisting, turning. His chest tightened. "They told you…"

"Is everything—"

"It's good, Jess. Everything's good." Mike ran toward his pickup and spun his tires as he left the driveway and roared toward his house.

Seeing the shining black Denali parked on the street beside his driveway didn't come as a surprise to Mike. It gave him a sick feeling to see the lights inside his house were turned on. He took a heavy breath, reached into his toolbox, and grabbed his Estwing framing hammer. He hefted the tool, feeling the heavy twenty-eight-ounce weight in his grip.

The front door was unlocked, and Mike eased it open and stepped into the front hallway. On his right was the small dining room, brightly lit, but vacant. Mike paused, tightened his grip on the hammer, and took a step forward to look at the living room on his left.

The big man from earlier stood against the far wall, his arms crossed in front of him. On the couch, with Sammy in his lap, the bald man sat and stared at Mike as he came into view. The Igloo cooler rested on the coffee table in front of him. His gaze flicked to the hammer in Mike's hand, and then he shook his head slightly.

"Mr. Tandy, drop the hammer, come in, and sit down." He leaned forward, hugging an arm around Sammy, who was focused on a handheld video game.

Rage coursed through Mike's veins and he clenched his jaw. King Kong took a step away from the wall, his expression daring Mike to do something, *anything,* to justify violence.

Mike let the hammer fall to the floor, walked into the living room, and sat on the edge of the reclining chair.

"I hate this, I really do." The bald man straightened up, reached for the headphones around Sammy's neck, and fitted them snugly against the boy's ears. "But since you—"

"If you don't release my son—"

"Shut up." The bald man spoke with an abrupt authority, sniffled, and then cleared his throat. "First, you're in no position to threaten anything. Second, you need to understand we're protecting our investment, Mr. Tandy. Someone else *died* in order for you to receive that kidney. Doesn't that mean anything to you?"

Mike felt his hands ball into fists, but he remained quiet.

The bald man inhaled and exhaled slowly, through his nose. "We've given more than ample opportunity to rectify the situation." He turned and gave a nod to the big man, and then it was nothing but a tornado of motion and pain.

* * *

Mike blinked his eyes and looked at his vibrating phone on the carpet in front of him. His living room floor looked skewed and out of focus, and he had to concentrate to reach forward and answer the call from Jess. Shadows danced in front of his eyes, but he caught a glimpse of her face as the video chat started.

"Mr. Tandry? Are you okay? I tried calling so many—"

"Jess," Mike's voice was a whisper against sandpaper. "Call the—"

There were noises behind him, the rattle of the front door.

Christ, they're still here.

Mike pressed the button to mute Jess on the other end of the call. He put a finger over his lips to *Shhhh* her, tucked his phone beneath the edge of the reclining chair, and put his head down against the carpet.

His body felt detached and cold. His mouth was bone dry. He stared at Jess and listened as the front door swung open. There was a silent pause, and then footsteps entered his house. Jess stepped away from her camera and then came back on screen, holding up a sheet of paper with large handwritten letters on it:

IS THAT THE COPS??

Mike stared at her and blinked twice slowly.

She leaned down, and a moment later, held up another sign:

ARE YOU IN DANGER?

Mike blinked once, and for the first time, saw complete and utter fear on her face. She nodded and stepped away from her camera again.

"In here."

The man's voice was gruff, and Mike lay still as he heard the man release a heavy exhale. Jess came back on screen, and then she stood and held out another paper:

MY MOM CALLED THE COPS

"Oh Jesus... Fucking hell."

Another man's voice.

And neither of them belong to the bald man, Mike thought.

"This doesn't change anything. We do what—"

"This is over, man. It *has* to be over." The sound of scuffing feet in the foyer.

"Bullshit. They *know* things, Jacobs. They know things about my kids. You think they don't know anything about you, too?"

Mike watched as Jess listened to the conversation. He felt a surge of nausea and bit down on his lower lip.

"I don't give a damn if they do or not. I'm out."

"But not the way you think."

The sound of a gunshot thundered inside the house, and Mike heard the sound of a body falling to the wooden floor.

On the phone screen, Mike saw Jess in a silent scream.

The man's voice, full of gravel, whispered. "What a goddamn mess."

Footsteps came into the living room to stop beside Mike and the man's knees popped as he lowered to a crouch. On the screen of Mike's phone, he watched the smaller square of video from his side of the call.

The man's face came into frame, and then his expression changed as he saw the phone beneath the chair. The man stared at it a moment and then reached over Mike's body and grabbed the phone.

"Son of a bitch!" The man hissed into the room.

He threw the phone, and Mike heard it thud against the wall and fall to the floor.

Mike lay still, scared to even breathe, and he waited as the man stood in the living room. A moment longer, and footsteps retreated to the hall, and then Mike heard the front door open and close. A sea of razors flowed inside of Mike's body, and he turned his head to look around the living room.

Mike's attention rose to his son's body, saw the boy's shirt pushed up to his armpits, baring his ribs. An incision curved along the side of his stomach, dashed with a train track of staples.

Sammy's limp arm lay stretched off the edge of the sofa, but what drew Mike's attention was the sheet of paper on the floor between them:

LATE FEES

Mike began to scream.

The Second Bullet

Anna Katharine Green

"YOU MUST SEE HER."

"No. No."

"She's a most unhappy woman. Husband and child both taken from her in a moment; and now, all means of living as well, unless some happy thought of yours – some inspiration of your genius – shows us a way of re-establishing her claims to the policy voided by this cry of suicide."

But the small wise head of Violet Strange continued its slow shake of decided refusal.

"I'm sorry," she protested, "but it's quite out of my province. I'm too young to meddle with so serious a matter."

"Not when you can save a bereaved woman the only possible compensation left her by untoward fate?"

"Let the police try their hand at that."

"They have had no success with the case."

"Or you?"

"Nor I either."

"And you expect—"

"Yes, Miss Strange. I expect you to find the missing bullet which will settle the fact that murder and not suicide ended George Hammond's life. If you cannot, then a long litigation awaits this poor widow, ending, as such litigation usually does, in favour of the stronger party. There's the alternative. If you once saw her—"

"But that's what I'm not willing to do. If I once saw her I should yield to her importunities and attempt the seemingly impossible. My instincts bid me say no. Give me something easier."

"Easier things are not so remunerative. There's money in this affair, if the insurance company is forced to pay up. I can offer you—"

"What?"

There was eagerness in the tone despite her effort at nonchalance. The other smiled imperceptibly, and briefly named the sum.

It was larger than she had expected. This her visitor saw by the way her eyelids fell and the peculiar stillness which, for an instant, held her vivacity in check.

"And you think I can earn that?"

Her eyes were fixed on his in an eagerness as honest as it was unrestrained.

He could hardly conceal his amazement, her desire was so evident and the cause of it so difficult to understand. He knew she wanted money – that was her avowed reason for entering into this uncongenial work. But to want it so much! He glanced at her person; it was simply clad but very expensively – how expensively it was his business to know. Then he took in the room in which they sat. Simplicity again, but the simplicity of high art – the drawing-room of one rich enough to indulge in the final luxury of a highly cultivated taste, viz.: unostentatious elegance and the subjection of each carefully chosen ornament to the general effect.

What did this favoured child of fortune lack that she could be reached by such a plea, when her whole being revolted from the nature of the task he offered her? It was a question not new to him; but one he had never heard answered and was not likely to hear answered now. But the fact remained that the consent he had thought dependent upon sympathetic interest could be reached much more readily by the promise of large emolument, – and he owned to a feeling of secret disappointment even while he recognized the value of the discovery.

But his satisfaction in the latter, if satisfaction it were, was of very short duration. Almost immediately he observed a change in her. The sparkle which had shone in the eye whose depths he had never been able to penetrate, had dissipated itself in something like a tear and she spoke up in that vigorous tone no one but himself had ever heard, as she said:

"No. The sum is a good one and I could use it; but I will not waste my energy on a case I do not believe in. The man shot himself. He was a speculator, and probably had good reason for his act. Even his wife acknowledges that he has lately had more losses than gains."

"See her. She has something to tell you which never got into the papers."

"You say that? You know that?"

"On my honour, Miss Strange."

Violet pondered; then suddenly succumbed.

"Let her come, then. Prompt to the hour. I will receive her at three. Later I have a tea and two party calls to make."

Her visitor rose to leave. He had been able to subdue all evidence of his extreme gratification, and now took on a formal air. In dismissing a guest, Miss Strange was invariably the society belle and that only. This he had come to recognize.

The case (well known at the time) was, in the fewest possible words, as follows:

On a sultry night in September, a young couple living in one of the large apartment houses in the extreme upper portion of Manhattan were so annoyed by the incessant crying of a child in the adjoining suite, that they got up, he to smoke, and she to sit in the window for a possible breath of cool air. They were congratulating themselves upon the wisdom they had shown in thus giving up all thought of sleep – for the child's crying had not ceased – when (it may have been two o'clock and it may have been a little later) there came from somewhere near, the sharp and somewhat peculiar detonation of a pistol-shot.

He thought it came from above; she, from the rear, and they were staring at each other in the helpless wonder of the moment, when they were struck by the silence. The baby had ceased to cry. All was as still in the adjoining apartment as in their own – too still – much too still. Their mutual stare turned to one of horror. "It came from there!" whispered the wife. "Some accident has occurred to Mr. or Mrs. Hammond – we ought to go—"

Her words – very tremulous ones – were broken by a shout from below. They were standing in their window and had evidently been seen by a passing policeman. "Anything wrong up there?" they heard him cry. Mr. Saunders immediately looked out. "Nothing wrong here," he called down. (They were but two stories from the pavement.) "But I'm not so sure about the rear apartment. We thought we heard a shot. Hadn't you better come up, officer? My wife is nervous about it. I'll meet you at the stair-head and show you the way."

The officer nodded and stepped in. The young couple hastily donned some wraps, and, by the time he appeared on their floor, they were ready to accompany him.

Meanwhile, no disturbance was apparent anywhere else in the house, until the policeman rang the bell of the Hammond apartment. Then, voices began to be heard, and doors to open above and below, but not the one before which the policeman stood.

Another ring, and this time an insistent one; – and still no response. The officer's hand was rising for the third time when there came a sound of fluttering from behind the panels against which he had laid his ear, and finally a choked voice uttering unintelligible words. Then a hand began to struggle with the lock, and the door, slowly opening, disclosed a woman clad in a hastily donned wrapper and giving every evidence of extreme fright.

"Oh!" she exclaimed, seeing only the compassionate faces of her neighbours. "You heard it, too! a pistol-shot from there – there – my husband's room. I have not dared to go – I – I – O, have mercy and see if anything is wrong! It is so still – so still, and only a moment ago the baby was crying. Mrs. Saunders, Mrs. Saunders, why is it so still?"

She had fallen into her neighbour's arms. The hand with which she had pointed out a certain door had sunk to her side and she appeared to be on the verge of collapse.

The officer eyed her sternly, while noting her appearance, which was that of a woman hastily risen from bed.

"Where were you?" he asked. "Not with your husband and child, or you would know what had happened there."

"I was sleeping down the hall," she managed to gasp out. "I'm not well – I – Oh, why do you all stand still and do nothing? My baby's in there. Go! go!" and, with sudden energy, she sprang upright, her eyes wide open and burning, her small well featured face white as the linen she sought to hide.

The officer demurred no longer. In another instant he was trying the door at which she was again pointing.

It was locked.

Glancing back at the woman, now cowering almost to the floor, he pounded at the door and asked the man inside to open.

No answer came back.

With a sharp turn he glanced again at the wife.

"You say that your husband is in this room?"

She nodded, gasping faintly, "And the child!"

He turned back, listened, then beckoned to Mr. Saunders. "We shall have to break our way in," said he. "Put your shoulder well to the door. Now!"

The hinges of the door creaked; the lock gave way (this special officer weighed two hundred and seventy-five, as he found out, next day), and a prolonged and sweeping crash told the rest.

Mrs. Hammond gave a low cry; and, straining forward from where she crouched in terror on the floor, searched the faces of the two men for some hint of what they saw in the dimly-lighted space beyond. Something dreadful, something which made Mr. Saunders come rushing back with a shout:

"Take her away! Take her to our apartment, Jennie. She must not see—"

Not see! He realized the futility of his words as his gaze fell on the young woman who had risen up at his approach and now stood gazing at him without speech, without movement, but with a glare of terror in her eyes, which gave him his first realization of human misery.

His own glance fell before it. If he had followed his instinct he would have fled the house rather than answer the question of her look and the attitude of her whole frozen body.

Perhaps in mercy to his speechless terror, perhaps in mercy to herself, she was the one who at last found the word which voiced their mutual anguish.

"Dead?"

No answer. None was needed.

"And my baby?"

O, that cry! It curdled the hearts of all who heard it. It shook the souls of men and women both inside and outside the apartment; then all was forgotten in the wild rush she made. The wife and mother had flung herself upon the scene, and, side by side with the not unmoved policeman, stood looking down upon the desolation made in one fatal instant in her home and heart.

They lay there together, both past help, both quite dead. The child had simply been strangled by the weight of his father's arm which lay directly across the upturned little throat. But the father was a victim of the shot they had heard. There was blood on his breast, and a pistol in his hand.

Suicide! The horrible truth was patent. No wonder they wanted to hold the young widow back. Her neighbour, Mrs. Saunders, crept in on tiptoe and put her arms about the swaying, fainting woman; but there was nothing to say – absolutely nothing.

At least, they thought not. But when they saw her throw herself down, not by her husband, but by the child, and drag it out from under that strangling arm and hug and kiss it and call out wildly for a doctor, the officer endeavoured to interfere and yet could not find the heart to do so, though he knew the child was dead and should not, according to all the rules of the coroner's office, be moved before that official arrived. Yet because no mother could be convinced of a fact like this, he let her sit with it on the floor and try all her little arts to revive it, while he gave orders to the janitor and waited himself for the arrival of doctor and coroner.

She was still sitting there in wide-eyed misery, alternately fondling the little body and drawing back to consult its small set features for some sign of life, when the doctor came, and, after one look at the child, drew it softly from her arms and laid it quietly in the crib from which its father had evidently lifted it but a short time before. Then he turned back to her, and found her on her feet, upheld by her two friends. She had understood his action, and without a groan had accepted her fate. Indeed, she seemed incapable of any further speech or action. She was staring down at her husband's body, which she, for the first time, seemed fully to see. Was her look one of grief or of resentment for the part he had played so unintentionally in her child's death? It was hard to tell; and when, with slowly rising finger, she pointed to the pistol so tightly clutched in the other outstretched hand, no one there – and by this time the room was full – could foretell what her words would be when her tongue regained its usage and she could speak.

What she did say was this:

"Is there a bullet gone? Did he fire off that pistol?" A question so manifestly one of delirium that no one answered it, which seemed to surprise her, though she said nothing till her glance had passed all around the walls of the room to where a window stood open to the night, – its lower sash being entirely raised. "There! look there!" she cried, with a commanding accent, and, throwing up her hands, sank a dead weight into the arms of those supporting her.

No one understood; but naturally more than one rushed to the window. An open space was before them. Here lay the fields not yet parcelled out into lots and built upon; but it was not upon these they looked, but upon the strong trellis which they found there, which, if it supported no vine, formed a veritable ladder between this window and the ground.

Could she have meant to call attention to this fact; and were her words expressive of another idea than the obvious one of suicide?

If so, to what lengths a woman's imagination can go! Or so their combined looks seemed to proclaim, when to their utter astonishment they saw the officer, who had presented a calm appearance up till now, shift his position and with a surprised grunt direct their eyes to a portion of the wall just visible beyond the half-drawn curtains of the bed. The mirror hanging there showed a star-shaped breakage, such as follows the sharp impact of a bullet or a fiercely projected stone.

"He fired two shots. One went wild; the other straight home."

It was the officer delivering his opinion.

Mr. Saunders, returning from the distant room where he had assisted in carrying Mrs. Hammond, cast a look at the shattered glass, and remarked forcibly:

"I heard but one; and I was sitting up, disturbed by that poor infant. Jennie, did you hear more than one shot?" he asked, turning toward his wife.

"No," she answered, but not with the readiness he had evidently expected. "I heard only one, but that was not quite usual in its tone. I'm used to guns," she explained, turning to the officer. "My father was an army man, and he taught me very early to load and fire a pistol. There was a prolonged sound to this shot; something like an echo of itself, following close upon the first ping. Didn't you notice that, Warren?"

"I remember something of the kind," her husband allowed.

"He shot twice and quickly," interposed the policeman, sententiously. "We shall find a spent bullet back of that mirror."

But when, upon the arrival of the coroner, an investigation was made of the mirror and the wall behind, no bullet was found either there or any where else in the room, save in the dead man's breast. Nor had more than one been shot from his pistol, as five full chambers testified. The case which seemed so simple had its mysteries, but the assertion made by Mrs. Saunders no longer carried weight, nor was the evidence offered by the broken mirror considered as indubitably establishing the fact that a second shot had been fired in the room.

Yet it was equally evident that the charge which had entered the dead speculator's breast had not been delivered at the close range of the pistol found clutched in his hand. There were no powder-marks to be discerned on his pajama-jacket, or on the flesh beneath. Thus anomaly confronted anomaly, leaving open but one other theory: that the bullet found in Mr. Hammond's breast came from the window and the one he shot went out of it. But this would necessitate his having shot his pistol from a point far removed from where he was found; and his wound was such as made it difficult to believe that he would stagger far, if at all, after its infliction.

Yet, because the coroner was both conscientious and alert, he caused a most rigorous search to be made of the ground overlooked by the above mentioned window; a search in which the police joined, but which was without any result save that of rousing the attention of people in the neighbourhood and leading to a story being circulated of a man seen some time the night before crossing the fields in a great hurry. But as no further particulars were forthcoming, and not even a description of the man to be had, no emphasis would have been laid upon this story had it not transpired that the moment a report of it had come to Mrs. Hammond's ears (why is there always some one to carry these reports?) she roused from the torpor into which she had fallen, and in wild fashion exclaimed:

"I knew it! I expected it! He was shot through the window and by that wretch. He never shot himself." Violent declarations which trailed off into the one continuous wail, "O, my baby! my poor baby!"

Such words, even though the fruit of delirium, merited some sort of attention, or so this good coroner thought, and as soon as opportunity offered and she was sufficiently sane and quiet to respond to his questions, he asked her whom she had meant by that wretch, and what reason she had, or thought she had, of attributing her husband's death to any other agency than his own disgust with life.

And then it was that his sympathies, although greatly roused in her favour began to wane. She met the question with a cold stare followed by a few ambiguous words out of which he could make nothing. Had she said wretch? She did not remember. They must not be influenced by anything she might have uttered in her first grief. She was well-nigh insane at the time. But of one thing they might be sure: her husband had not shot himself; he was too much afraid of death for such an act. Besides, he was too happy. Whatever folks might say he was too fond of his family to wish to leave it.

Nor did the coroner or any other official succeed in eliciting anything further from her. Even when she was asked, with cruel insistence, how she explained the fact that the baby was found lying on the floor instead of in its crib, her only answer was: "His father was trying to soothe it. The child was crying dreadfully, as you have heard from those who were kept awake by him that night, and my husband was carrying him about when the shot came which caused George to fall and overlay the baby in his struggles."

"Carrying a baby about with a loaded pistol in his hand?" came back in stern retort.

She had no answer for this. She admitted when informed that the bullet extracted from her husband's body had been found to correspond exactly with those remaining in the five chambers of the pistol taken from his hand, that he was not only the owner of this pistol but was in the habit of sleeping with it under his pillow; but, beyond that, nothing; and this reticence, as well as her manner which was cold and repellent, told against her.

A verdict of suicide was rendered by the coroner's jury, and the life-insurance company, in which Mr. Hammond had but lately insured himself for a large sum, taking advantage of the suicide clause embodied in the policy, announced its determination of not paying the same.

Such was the situation, as known to Violet Strange and the general public, on the day she was asked to see Mrs. Hammond and learn what might alter her opinion as to the justice of this verdict and the stand taken by the Shuler Life Insurance Company.

The clock on the mantel in Miss Strange's rose-coloured boudoir had struck three, and Violet was gazing in some impatience at the door, when there came a gentle knock upon it, and the maid (one of the elderly, not youthful, kind) ushered in her expected visitor.

"You are Mrs. Hammond?" she asked, in natural awe of the too black figure outlined so sharply against the deep pink of the sea-shell room.

The answer was a slow lifting of the veil which shadowed the features she knew only from the cuts she had seen in newspapers.

"You are – Miss Strange?" stammered her visitor; "the young lady who—"

"I am," chimed in a voice as ringing as it was sweet. "I am the person you have come here to see. And this is my home. But that does not make me less interested in the unhappy, or less desirous of serving them. Certainly you have met with the two greatest losses which can come to a woman – I know your story well enough to say that – ; but what have you to tell me in proof that you should not lose your anticipated income as well? Something vital, I hope, else I cannot help you; something which you should have told the coroner's jury – and did not."

The flush which was the sole answer these words called forth did not take from the refinement of the young widow's expression, but rather added to it; Violet watched it in its ebb and flow and, seriously affected by it (why, she did not know, for Mrs. Hammond had made no other appeal either by look or gesture), pushed forward a chair and begged her visitor to be seated.

"We can converse in perfect safety here," she said. "When you feel quite equal to it, let me hear what you have to communicate. It will never go any further. I could not do the work I do if I felt it necessary to have a confidant."

"But you are so young and so – so—"

"So inexperienced you would say and so evidently a member of what New Yorkers call 'society.' Do not let that trouble you. My inexperience is not likely to last long and my social pleasures are more apt to add to my efficiency than to detract from it."

With this Violet's face broke into a smile. It was not the brilliant one so often seen upon her lips, but there was something in its quality which carried encouragement to the widow and led her to say with obvious eagerness:

"You know the facts?"

"I have read all the papers."

"I was not believed on the stand."

"It was your manner—"

"I could not help my manner. I was keeping something back, and, being unused to deceit, I could not act quite naturally."

"Why did you keep something back? When you saw the unfavourable impression made by your reticence, why did you not speak up and frankly tell your story?"

"Because I was ashamed. Because I thought it would hurt me more to speak than to keep silent. I do not think so now; but I did then – and so made my great mistake. You must remember not only the awful shock of my double loss, but the sense of guilt accompanying it; for my husband and I had quarreled that night, quarreled bitterly – that was why I had run away into another room and not because I was feeling ill and impatient of the baby's fretful cries."

"So people have thought." In saying this, Miss Strange was perhaps cruelly emphatic. "You wish to explain that quarrel? You think it will be doing any good to your cause to go into that matter with me now?"

"I cannot say; but I must first clear my conscience and then try to convince you that quarrel or no quarrel, he never took his own life. He was not that kind. He had an abnormal fear of death. I do not like to say it but he was a physical coward. I have seen him turn pale at the least hint of danger. He could no more have turned that muzzle upon his own breast than he could have turned it upon his baby. Some other hand shot him, Miss Strange. Remember the open window, the shattered mirror; and I think I know that hand."

Her head had fallen forward on her breast. The emotion she showed was not so eloquent of grief as of deep personal shame.

"You think you know the man?" In saying this, Violet's voice sunk to a whisper. It was an accusation of murder she had just heard.

"To my great distress, yes. When Mr. Hammond and I were married," the widow now proceeded in a more determined tone, "there was another man – a very violent one – who vowed even at the church door that George and I should never live out two full years together. We have not. Our second anniversary would have been in November."

"But—"

"Let me say this: the quarrel of which I speak was not serious enough to occasion any such act of despair on his part. A man would be mad to end his life on account of so slight a disagreement. It was not even on account of the person of whom I've just spoken, though that person had been mentioned between us earlier in the evening, Mr. Hammond having come across him face to face that very afternoon in the subway. Up to this time neither of us had seen or heard of him since our wedding-day."

"And you think this person whom you barely mentioned, so mindful of his old grudge that he sought out your domicile, and, with the intention of murder, climbed the trellis leading to your room and turned his pistol upon the shadowy figure which was all he could see in the semi-obscurity of a much lowered gas-jet?"

"A man in the dark does not need a bright light to see his enemy when he is intent upon revenge." Miss Strange altered her tone.

"And your husband? You must acknowledge that he shot off his pistol whether the other did or not."

"It was in self-defence. He would shoot to save his own life – or the baby's."

"Then he must have heard or seen—"

"A man at the window."

"And would have shot there?"

"Or tried to."

"Tried to?"

"Yes; the other shot first – oh, I've thought it all out – causing my husband's bullet to go wild. It was his which broke the mirror."

Violet's eyes, bright as stars, suddenly narrowed.

"And what happened then?" she asked. "Why cannot they find the bullet?"

"Because it went out of the window; – glanced off and went out of the window."

Mrs. Hammond's tone was triumphant; her look spirited and intense.

Violet eyed her compassionately.

"Would a bullet glancing off from a mirror, however hung, be apt to reach a window so far on the opposite side?"

"I don't know; I only know that it did," was the contradictory, almost absurd, reply.

"What was the cause of the quarrel you speak of between your husband and yourself? You see, I must know the exact truth and all the truth to be of any assistance to you."

"It was – it was about the care I gave, or didn't give, the baby. I feel awfully to have to say it, but George did not think I did my full duty by the child. He said there was no need of its crying so; that if I gave it the proper attention it would not keep the neighbours and himself awake half the night. And I – I got angry and insisted that I did the best I could; that the child was naturally fretful and that if he wasn't satisfied with my way of looking after it, he might try his. All of which was very wrong and unreasonable on my part, as witness the awful punishment which followed."

"And what made you get up and leave him?"

"The growl he gave me in reply. When I heard that, I bounded out of bed and said I was going to the spare room to sleep; and if the baby cried he might just try what he could do himself to stop it."

"And he answered?"

"This, just this – I shall never forget his words as long as I live – 'If you go, you need not expect me to let you in again no matter what happens.'"

"He said that?"

"And locked the door after me. You see I could not tell all that."

"It might have been better if you had. It was such a natural quarrel and so unprovocative of actual tragedy."

Mrs. Hammond was silent. It was not difficult to see that she had no very keen regrets for her husband personally. But then he was not a very estimable man nor in any respect her equal.

"You were not happy with him," Violet ventured to remark.

"I was not a fully contented woman. But for all that he had no cause to complain of me except for the reason I have mentioned. I was not a very intelligent mother. But if the baby were living now – O, if he were living now – with what devotion I should care for him."

She was on her feet, her arms were raised, her face impassioned with feeling. Violet, gazing at her, heaved a little sigh. It was perhaps in keeping with the situation, perhaps extraneous to it, but whatever its source, it marked a change in her manner. With no further check upon her sympathy, she said very softly:

"It is well with the child."

The mother stiffened, swayed, and then burst into wild weeping.

"But not with me," she cried, "not with me. I am desolate and bereft. I have not even a home in which to hide my grief and no prospect of one."

"But," interposed Violet, "surely your husband left you something? You cannot be quite penniless?"

"My husband left nothing," was the answer, uttered without bitterness, but with all the hardness of fact. "He had debts. I shall pay those debts. When these and other necessary expenses are liquidated, there will be but little left. He made no secret of the fact that he lived close up to his means. That is why he was induced to take on a life insurance. Not a friend of his but knows his improvidence. I – I have not even jewels. I have only my determination and an absolute conviction as to the real nature of my husband's death."

"What is the name of the man you secretly believe to have shot your husband from the trellis?"

Mrs. Hammond told her.

It was a new one to Violet. She said so and then asked:

"What else can you tell me about him?"

"Nothing, but that he is a very dark man and has a club-foot."

"Oh, what a mistake you've made."

"Mistake? Yes, I acknowledge that."

"I mean in not giving this last bit of information at once to the police. A man can be identified by such a defect. Even his footsteps can be traced. He might have been found that very day. Now, what have we to go upon?"

"You are right, but not expecting to have any difficulty about the insurance money I thought it would be generous in me to keep still. Besides, this is only surmise on my part. I feel certain that my husband was shot by another hand than his own, but I know of no way of proving it. Do you?"

Then Violet talked seriously with her, explaining how their only hope lay in the discovery of a second bullet in the room which had already been ransacked for this very purpose and without the shadow of a result.

A tea, a musicale, and an evening dance kept Violet Strange in a whirl for the remainder of the day. No brighter eye nor more contagious wit lent brilliance to these occasions, but with the passing of the midnight hour no one who had seen her in the blaze of electric lights would have recognized this favoured child of fortune in the earnest figure sitting in the obscurity of an up-town apartment, studying the walls, the ceilings, and the floors by the dim light of a lowered gas-jet. Violet Strange in society was a very different person from Violet Strange under the tension of her secret and peculiar work.

She had told them at home that she was going to spend the night with a friend; but only her old coachman knew who that friend was. Therefore a very natural sense of guilt mingled with her emotions at finding herself alone on a scene whose gruesome mystery she could solve only by identifying herself with the place and the man who had perished there.

Dismissing from her mind all thought of self, she strove to think as he thought, and act as he acted on the night when he found himself (a man of but little courage) left in this room with an ailing child.

At odds with himself, his wife, and possibly with the child screaming away in its crib, what would he be apt to do in his present emergency? Nothing at first, but as the screaming continued he would remember the old tales of fathers walking the floor at night with crying babies, and hasten to follow suit. Violet, in her anxiety to reach his inmost thought, crossed to where the crib had stood, and, taking that as a start, began pacing the room in search of the spot from which a bullet, if shot, would glance aside from the mirror in the direction of the window. (Not that she was ready to accept this theory of Mrs. Hammond, but that she did not wish to entirely dismiss it without putting it to the test.)

She found it in an unexpected quarter of the room and much nearer the bed-head than where his body was found. This, which might seem to confuse matters, served, on the contrary to remove from the case one of its most serious difficulties. Standing here, he was within reach of the pillow under which his pistol lay hidden, and if startled, as his wife believed him to have been by a noise at the other end of the room, had but to crouch and reach behind him in order to find himself armed and ready for a possible intruder.

Imitating his action in this as in other things, she had herself crouched low at the bedside and was on the point of withdrawing her hand from under the pillow, when a new surprise checked her movement and held her fixed in her position, with eyes staring straight at the adjoining wall. She had seen there what he must have seen in making this same turn – the dark bars of the opposite window-frame outlined in the mirror – and understood at once what had happened. In the nervousness and terror of the moment, George Hammond had mistaken this reflection of the window for the window itself, and shot impulsively at the man he undoubtedly saw covering him from the trellis without. But while this explained the shattering of the mirror, how about the other and still more vital question, of where the bullet went afterward? Was the angle at which it had been fired acute enough to send it out of a window diagonally opposed? No; even if the pistol had been held closer to the man firing it than she had reason to believe, the angle still would be oblique enough to carry it on to the further wall.

But no sign of any such impact had been discovered on this wall. Consequently, the force of the bullet had been expended before reaching it, and when it fell—

Here, her glance, slowly traveling along the floor, impetuously paused. It had reached the spot where the two bodies had been found, and unconsciously her eyes rested there, conjuring up the picture of the bleeding father and the strangled child. How piteous and how dreadful it all was. If she could only understand— Suddenly she rose straight up, staring and immovable in the dim light. Had the idea – the explanation – the only possible explanation covering the whole phenomena come to her at last?

It would seem so, for as she so stood, a look of conviction settled over her features, and with this look, evidences of a horror which for all her fast accumulating knowledge of life and its possibilities made her appear very small and very helpless.

A half-hour later, when Mrs. Hammond, in her anxiety at hearing nothing more from Miss Strange, opened the door of her room, it was to find, lying on the edge of the sill, the little detective's card with these words hastily written across it:

I do not feel as well as I could wish, and so have telephoned to my own coachman to come and take me home. I will either see or write you within a few days. But do not allow yourself to hope. I pray you do not allow yourself the least hope; the outcome is still very problematical.

When Violet's employer entered his office the next morning it was to find a veiled figure awaiting him which he at once recognized as that of his little deputy. She was slow in lifting her veil and when it finally came free he felt a momentary doubt as to his wisdom in giving her just such a matter as this to investigate. He was quite sure of his mistake when he saw her face, it was so drawn and pitiful.

"You have failed," said he.

"Of that you must judge," she answered; and drawing near she whispered in his ear.

"No!" he cried in his amazement.

"Think," she murmured, "think. Only so can all the facts be accounted for."

"I will look into it; I will certainly look into it," was his earnest reply. "If you are right— But never mind that. Go home and take a horseback ride in the Park. When I have news in regard to this I will let you know. Till then forget it all. Hear me, I charge you to forget everything but your balls and your parties."

And Violet obeyed him.

Some few days after this, the following statement appeared in all the papers:

"Owing to some remarkable work done by the firm of — & —, the well-known private detective agency, the claim made by Mrs. George Hammond against the Shuler Life Insurance Company is likely to be allowed without further litigation. As our readers will remember, the contestant has insisted from the first that the bullet causing her husband's death came from another pistol than the one found clutched in his own hand. But while reasons were not lacking to substantiate this assertion, the failure to discover more than the disputed track of a second bullet led to a verdict of suicide, and a refusal of the company to pay.

"But now that bullet has been found. And where? In the most startling place in the world, viz.: in the larynx of the child found lying dead upon the floor beside his father, strangled as was supposed by the weight of that father's arm. The theory is, and there seems to be none other, that the father, hearing a suspicious noise at the window, set down the child he was endeavouring to soothe and made for the bed and his own pistol, and, mistaking a reflection of the assassin for the assassin himself, sent his shot sidewise at a mirror just as the other let go the trigger which drove a similar bullet into his breast. The course of the one was straight and fatal and that of the other deflected. Striking the mirror at an oblique angle, the bullet fell to the floor where it was picked up by the crawling child, and, as was most natural, thrust at once into his mouth. Perhaps it felt hot to the little tongue; perhaps the child was simply frightened by some convulsive movement of the father who evidently spent his last moment in an endeavour to reach the child, but, whatever the cause, in the quick gasp it gave, the bullet was drawn into the larynx, strangling him.

"That the father's arm, in his last struggle, should have fallen directly across the little throat is one of those anomalies which confounds reason and misleads justice by stopping investigation at the very point where truth lies and mystery disappears.

"Mrs. Hammond is to be congratulated that there are detectives who do not give too much credence to outward appearances."

We expect soon to hear of the capture of the man who sped home the death-dealing bullet.

A Tragedy of Error

Henry James

Chapter I

A LOW English phaeton was drawn up before the door of the post office of a French seaport town. In it was seated a lady, with her veil down and her parasol held closely over her face. My story begins with a gentleman coming out of the office and handing her a letter.

He stood beside the carriage a moment before getting in. She gave him her parasol to hold, and then lifted her veil, showing a very pretty face. This couple seemed to be full of interest for the passers by, most of whom stared hard and exchanged significant glances. Such persons as were looking on at the moment saw the lady turn very pale as her eyes fell on the direction of the letter. Her companion saw it too, and instantly stepping into the place beside her, took up the reins, and drove rapidly along the main street of the town, past the harbor, to an open road skirting the sea. Here he slackened pace. The lady was leaning back, with her veil down again, and the letter lying open in her lap. Her attitude was almost that of unconsciousness, and he could see that her eyes were closed. Having satisfied himself of this, he hastily possessed himself of the letter, and read as follows:

> Southampton, July 16th, 18—.
>
> *My Dear Hortense: You will see by my postmark that I am a thousand leagues nearer home than when I last wrote, but I have hardly time to explain the change. M. P— has given me a most unlooked-for congé. After so many months of separation, we shall be able to spend a few weeks together. God be praised! We got in here from New York this morning, and I have had the good luck to find a vessel, the Armorique, which sails straight for H—. The mail leaves directly, but we shall probably be detained a few hours by the tide; so this will reach you a day before I arrive: the master calculates we shall get in early Thursday morning. Ah, Hortense! how the time drags! Three whole days. If I did not write from New York, it is because I was unwilling to torment you with an expectancy which, as it is, I venture to hope, you will find long enough. Farewell. To a warmer greeting! Your devoted C. B.*

When the gentleman replaced the paper on his companion's lap, his face was almost as pale as hers. For a moment he gazed fixedly and vacantly before him, and a half-suppressed curse escaped his lips. Then his eyes reverted to his neighbor. After some hesitation, during which he allowed the reins to hang so loose that the horse lapsed into a walk, he touched her gently on the shoulder.

"Well, Hortense," said be, in a very pleasant tone, "what's the matter; have you fallen asleep?"

Hortense slowly opened her eyes, and, seeing that they had left the town behind them, raised her veil. Her features were stiffened with horror.

"Read that," said she, holding out the open letter.

The gentleman took it, and pretended to read it again.

"Ah! M. Bernier returns. Delightful!" he exclaimed.

"How, delightful?" asked Hortense; "we mustn't jest at so serious a crisis, my friend."

"True," said the other, "it will be a solemn meeting. Two years of absence is a great deal."

"O Heaven! I shall never dare to face him," cried Hortense, bursting into tears.

Covering her face with one hand, she put out the other toward that of her friend. But he was plunged in so deep a reverie, that he did not perceive the movement. Suddenly he came to, aroused by her sobs.

"Come, come," said he, in the tone of one who wishes to coax another into mistrust of a danger before which he does not himself feel so secure but that the sight of a companion's indifference will give him relief. "What if he does come? He need learn nothing. He will stay but a short time, and sail away again as unsuspecting as he came."

"Learn nothing! You surprise me. Every tongue that greets him, if only to say *bon jour*, will wag to the tune of a certain person's misconduct."

"Bah! People don't think about us quite as much as you fancy. You and I, *n'est-ce-pas?* we have little time to concern ourselves about our neighbors' failings. Very well, other people are in the same box, better or worse. When a ship goes to pieces on those rocks out at sea, the poor devils who are pushing their way to land on a floating spar, don't bestow many glances on those who are battling with the waves beside them. Their eyes are fastened to the shore, and all their care is for their own safety. In life we are all afloat on a tumultuous sea; we are all struggling toward some *terra firma* of wealth or love or leisure. The roaring of the waves we kick up about us and the spray we dash into our eyes deafen and blind us to the sayings and doings of our fellows. Provided we climb high and dry, what do we care for them?"

"Ay, but if we don't? When we've lost hope ourselves, we want to make others sink. We hang weights about their necks, and dive down into the dirtiest pools for stones to cast at them. My friend, you don't feel the shots which are not aimed at you. It isn't of you the town talks, but of me: a poor woman throws herself off the pier yonder, and drowns before a kind hand has time to restrain her, and her corpse floats over the water for all the world to look at. When her husband comes up to see what the crowd means, is there any lack of kind friends to give him the good news of his wife's death?"

"As long as a woman is light enough to float, Hortense, she is not counted drowned. It's only when she sinks out of sight that they give her up."

Hortense was silent a moment, looking at the sea with swollen eyes.

"Louis," she said at last, "we were speaking metaphorically: I have half a mind to drown myself literally."

"Nonsense!" replied Louis; "an accused pleads 'not guilty,' and hangs himself in prison. What do the papers say? People talk, do they? Can't you talk as well as they? A woman is in the wrong from the moment she holds her tongue and refuses battle. And that you do too often. That pocket handkerchief is always more or less of a flag of truce."

"I'm sure I don't know," said Hortense indifferently; "perhaps it is."

There are moments of grief in which certain aspects of the subject of our distress seems as irrelevant as matters entirely foreign to it. Her eyes were still fastened on the sea. There was another silence. "O my poor Charles!" she murmured, at length, "to what a hearth do you return!"

"Hortense," said the gentleman, as if he had not heard her, although, to a third person, it would have appeared that it was because he had done so that he spoke: "I do not need to tell you that it will never happen to me to betray our secret. But I will answer for it that so long as M. Bernier is at home no mortal shall breathe a syllable of it."

"What of that?" sighed Hortense. "He will not be with me ten minutes without guessing it."

"Oh, as for that," said her companion, dryly, "that's your own affair."

"Monsieur de Meyrau!" cried the lady.

"It seems to me," continued the other, "that in making such a guarantee, I have done my part of the business."

"Your part of the business!" sobbed Hortense.

M. de Meyrau made no reply, but with a great cut of the whip sent the horse bounding along the road. Nothing more was said. Hortense lay back in the carriage with her face buried in her handkerchief, moaning. Her companion sat upright, with contracted brows and firmly set teeth, looking straight before him, and by an occasional heavy lash keeping the horse at a furious pace. A wayfarer might have taken him for a ravisher escaping with a victim worn out with resistance. Travellers to whom they were known would perhaps have seen a deep meaning in this accidental analogy. So, by a *détour*, they returned to the town.

When Hortense reached home, she went straight up to a little boudoir on the second floor, and shut herself in. This room was at the back of the house, and her maid, who was at that moment walking in the long garden which stretched down to the water, where there was a landing place for small boats, saw her draw in the window blind and darken the room, still in her bonnet and cloak. She remained alone for a couple of hours. At five o'clock, some time after the hour at which she was usually summoned to dress her mistress for the evening, the maid knocked at Hortense's door, and offered her services. Madame called out, from within, that she had a *migraine*, and would not be dressed.

"Can I get anything for madame?" asked Josephine; "a *tisane*, a warm drink, something?"

"Nothing, nothing."

"Will madame dine?"

"No."

"Madame had better not go wholly without eating."

"Bring me a bottle of wine – of brandy."

Josephine obeyed. When she returned, Hortense was standing in the doorway, and as one of the shutters had meanwhile been thrown open, the woman could see that, although her mistress's hat had been tossed upon the sofa, her cloak had not been removed, and that her face was very pale. Josephine felt that she might not offer sympathy nor ask questions.

"Will madame have nothing more?" she ventured to say, as she handed her the tray.

Madame shook her head, and closed and locked the door.

Josephine stood a moment vexed, irresolute, listening. She heard no sound. At last she deliberately stooped down and applied her eye to the keyhole.

This is what she saw:

Her mistress had gone to the open window, and stood with her back to the door, looking out at the sea. She held the bottle by the neck in one hand, which hung listlessly by her side; the other was resting on a glass half filled with water, standing, together with an open letter, on a table beside her. She kept this position until Josephine began to grow tired of waiting. But just as she was about to arise in despair of gratifying her curiosity, madame raised the bottle and glass, and filled the latter full. Josephine looked more eagerly. Hortense held it a moment against the light, and then drained it down.

Josephine could not restrain an involuntary whistle. But her surprise became amazement when she saw her mistress prepare to take a second glass. Hortense put it down, however, before its contents were half gone, as if struck by a sudden thought, and hurried across the room. She stooped down before a cabinet, and took out a small opera glass. With this she returned to the window, put it to her eyes, and again spent some moments in looking seaward. The purpose of this proceeding Josephine could not make out. The only result visible to her was that her mistress suddenly dropped the lorgnette on the table, and sank down on an armchair, covering her face with her hands.

Josephine could contain her wonderment no longer. She hurried down to the kitchen.

"Valentine," said she to the cook, "what on earth can be the matter with Madame? She will have no dinner, she is drinking brandy by the glassful, a moment ago she was looking out to sea with a lorgnette, and now she is crying dreadfully with an open letter in her lap."

The cook looked up from her potato-peeling with a significant wink.

"What can it be," said she, "but that monsieur returns?"

Chapter II

AT SIX O'CLOCK, Josephine and Valentine were still sitting together, discussing the probable causes and consequences of the event hinted at by the latter. Suddenly Madame Bernier's bell rang. Josephine was only too glad to answer it. She met her mistress descending the stairs, combed, cloaked, and veiled, with no traces of agitation, but a very pale face.

"I am going out," said Madame Bernier; "if M. le Vicomte comes, tell him I am at my mother-in-law's, and wish him to wait till I return."

Josephine opened the door, and let her mistress pass; then stood watching her as she crossed the court.

"Her mother-in-law's," muttered the maid; "she has the face!"

When Hortense reached the street, she took her way, not through the town, to the ancient quarter where that ancient lady, her husband's mother, lived, but in a very different direction. She followed the course of the quay, beside the harbor, till she entered a crowded region, chiefly the residence of fishermen and boatmen. Here she raised her veil. Dusk was beginning to fall. She walked as if desirous to attract as little observation as possible, and yet to examine narrowly the population in the midst of which she found herself. Her dress was so plain that there was nothing in her appearance to solicit attention; yet, if for any reason a passer by had happened to notice her, he could not have helped being struck by the contained intensity with which she scrutinized every figure she met. Her manner was that of a person seeking to recognize a long-lost friend, or perhaps, rather, a long-lost enemy, in a crowd. At last she stopped before a flight of steps, at the foot of which was a landing place for half a dozen little boats, employed to carry passengers between the two sides of the port, at times when the drawbridge above was closed for the passage of vessels. While she stood she was witness of the following scene:

A man, in a red woollen fisherman's cap, was sitting on the top of the steps, smoking the short stump of a pipe, with his face to the water. Happening to turn about, his eye fell on a little child, hurrying along the quay toward a dingy tenement close at hand, with a jug in its arms.

"Hullo, youngster!" cried the man; "what have you got there? Come here."

The little child looked back, but, instead of obeying, only quickened its walk.

"The devil take you, come here!" repeated the man, angrily, "or I'll wring your beggarly neck. You won't obey your own uncle, eh?"

The child stopped, and ruefully made its way to its relative, looking around several times toward the house, as if to appeal to some counter authority.

"Come, make haste!" pursued the man, "or I shall go and fetch you. Move!"

The child advanced to within half a dozen paces of the steps, and then stood still, eyeing the man cautiously, and hugging the jug tight.

"Come on, you little beggar, come up close."

The youngster kept a stolid silence, however, and did not budge. Suddenly its self-styled uncle leaned forward, swept out his arm, clutched hold of its little sunburnt wrist, and dragged it toward him.

"Why didn't you come when you were called?" he asked, running his disengaged hand into the infant's frowsy mop of hair, and shaking its head until it staggered. "Why didn't you come, you unmannerly little brute, eh? – eh? – eh?" accompanying every interrogation with a renewed shake.

The child made no answer. It simply and vainly endeavored to twist its neck around under the man's gripe, and transmit some call for succor to the house.

"Come, keep your head straight. Look at me, and answer me. What's in that jug? Don't lie."

"Milk."

"Who for?"

"Granny."

"Granny be hanged."

The man disengaged his hands, lifted the jug from the child's feeble grasp, tilted it toward the light, surveyed its contents, put it to his lips, and exhausted them. The child, although liberated, did not retreat. It stood watching its uncle drink until he lowered the jug. Then, as he met its eyes, it said:

"It was for the baby."

For a moment the man was irresolute. But the child seemed to have a foresight of the parental resentment, for it had hardly spoken when it darted backward and scampered off, just in time to elude a blow from the jug, which the man sent clattering at its heels. When it was out of sight, he faced about to the water again, and replaced the pipe between his teeth with a heavy scowl and a murmur that sounded to Madame Bernier very like: "I wish the baby'd choke."

Hortense was a mute spectator of this little drama. When it was over, she turned around, and retraced her steps twenty yards with her hand to her head. Then she walked straight back, and addressed the man.

"My good man," she said, in a very pleasant voice, "are you the master of one of these boats?"

He looked up at her. In a moment the pipe was out of his mouth, and a broad grin in its place. He rose, with his hand to his cap.

"I am, madame, at your service."

"Will you take me to the other side?"

"You don't need a boat; the bridge is closed," said one of his comrades at the foot of the steps, looking that way.

"I know it," said Madame Bernier; "but I wish to go to the cemetery, and a boat will save me half a mile walking."

"The cemetery is shut at this hour."

"*Allons*, leave madame alone," said the man first spoken to. "This way, my lady."

Hortense seated herself in the stern of the boat. The man took the sculls.

"Straight across?" he asked.

Hortense looked around her. "It's a line evening," said she; "suppose you row me out to the lighthouse, and leave me at the point nearest the cemetery on our way back."

"Very well," rejoined the boatman; "fifteen sous," and began to pull lustily.

"*Allez*, I'll pay you well," said Madame.

"Fifteen sous is the fare," insisted the man.

"Give me a pleasant row, and I'll give you a hundred," said Hortense.

Her companion said nothing. He evidently wished to appear not to have heard her remark. Silence was probably the most dignified manner of receiving a promise too munificent to be anything but a jest.

For some time this silence was maintained, broken only by the trickling of the oars and the sounds from the neighboring shores and vessels. Madame Bernier was plunged in a sidelong scrutiny of her ferryman's countenance. He was a man of about thirty-five. His face was dogged, brutal, and sullen. These indications were perhaps exaggerated by the dull monotony of his exercise. The eyes lacked a certain rascally gleam which had appeared in them when he was so *empressé* with the offer of his services. The face was better then – that is, if vice is better than ignorance. We say a countenance is 'lit up' by a smile; and indeed that momentary flicker does the office of a candle in a dark room. It sheds a ray upon the dim upholstery of our souls. The visages of poor men, generally, know few alternations. There is a large class of human beings whom fortune restricts to a single change of expression, or, perhaps, rather to a single expression. Ah me! the faces which wear either nakedness or rags; whose repose is stagnation, whose activity vice; ingorant at their worst, infamous at their best!

"Don't pull too hard," said Hortense at last. "Hadn't you better take breath a moment?"

"Madame is very good," said the man, leaning upon his oars. "But if you had taken me by the hour," he added, with a return of the vicious grin, "you wouldn't catch me loitering."

"I suppose you work very hard," said Madame Bernier.

The man gave a little toss of his head, as if to intimate the inadequacy of any supposition to grasp the extent of his labors.

"I've been up since four o'clock this morning, wheeling bales and boxes on the quay, and plying my little boat. Sweating without five minutes' intermission. *C'est comme ça.* Sometimes I tell my mate I think I'll take a plunge in the basin to dry myself. Ha! ha! ha!"

"And of course you gain little," said Madame Bernier.

"Worse than nothing. Just what will keep me fat enough for starvation to feed on."

"How? you go without your necessary food?"

"Necessary is a very elastic word, madame. You can narrow it down, so that in the degree above nothing it means luxury. My necessary food is sometimes thin air. If I don't deprive myself of that, it's because I can't."

"Is it possible to be so unfortunate?"

"Shall I tell you what I have eaten today?"

"Do," said Madame Bernier.

"A piece of black bread and a salt herring are all that have passed my lips for twelve hours."

"Why don't you get some better work?"

"If I should die to-night," pursued the boatman, heedless of the question, in the manner of a man whose impetus on the track of self-pity drives him past the signal flags of relief, "what would there be left to bury me? These clothes I have on might buy me a long box. For the cost of this shabby old suit, that hasn't lasted me a twelvemonth, I could get one that I wouldn't wear out in a thousand years. *La bonne idée!*"

"Why don't you get some work that pays better?" repeated Hortense.

The man dipped his oars again.

"Work that pays better? I must work for work. I must earn that too. Work is wages. I count the promise of the next week's employment the best part of my Saturday night's pocketings. Fifty casks rolled from the ship to the storehouse mean two things: thirty sous and fifty more to roll the next day. Just so a crushed hand, or a dislocated shoulder, mean twenty francs to the apothecary and *bon jour* to my business."

"Are you married?" asked Hortense.

"No, I thank you. I'm not cursed with that blessing. But I've an old mother, a sister, and three nephews, who look to me for support. The old woman's too old to work; the lass is too lazy, and the little ones are too young. But they're none of them too old or young to be hungry, *allez*. I'll be hanged if I'm not a father to them all."

There was a pause. The man had resumed rowing. Madame Bernier sat motionless, still examining her neighbor's physiognomy. The sinking sun, striking full upon his face, covered it with an almost lurid glare. Her own features being darkened against the western sky, the direction of them was quite indistinguishable to her companion.

"Why don't you leave the place?" she said at last.

"Leave it! how?" he replied, looking up with the rough avidity with which people of his class receive proposals touching their interests, extending to the most philanthropic suggestions that mistrustful eagerness with which experience has taught them to defend their own side of a bargain – the only form of proposal that she has made them acquainted with.

"Go somewhere else," said Hortense.

"Where, for instance!"

"To some new country – America."

The man burst into a loud laugh. Madame Bernier's face bore more evidence of interest in the play of his features than of that discomfiture which generally accompanies the consciousness of ridicule.

"There's a lady's scheme for you! If you'll write for furnished apartments, *là-bas*, I don't desire anything better. But no leaps in the dark for me. America and Algeria are very fine words to cram into an empty stomach when you're lounging in the sun, out of work, just as you stuff tobacco into your pipe and let the smoke curl around your head. But they fade away before a cutlet and a bottle of wine. When the earth grows so smooth and the air so pure that you can see the American coast from the pier yonder, then I'll make up my bundle. Not before."

"You're afraid, then, to risk anything?"

"I'm afraid of nothing, *moi*. But I am not a fool either. I don't want to kick away my *sabots* till I am certain of a pair of shoes. I can go barefoot here. I don't want to find water where I counted on land. As for America, I've been there already."

"Ah! you've been there?"

"I've been to Brazil and Mexico and California and the West Indies."

"Ah!"

"I've been to Asia, too."

"Ah!"

"*Pardio*, to China and India. Oh, I've seen the world! I've been three times around the Cape."

"You've been a seaman then?"

"Yes, ma'am; fourteen years."

"On what ship?"

"Bless your heart, on fifty ships."

"French?"

"French and English and Spanish; mostly Spanish."

"Ah?"

"Yes, and the more fool I was."

"How so?"

"Oh, it was a dog's life. I'd drown any dog that would play half the mean tricks I used to see."

"And you never had a hand in any yourself?"

"*Pardon*, I gave what I got. I was as good a Spaniard and as great a devil as any. I carried my knife with the best of them, and drew it as quickly, and plunged it as deep. I've got scars, if you weren't a lady. But I'd warrant to find you their mates on a dozen Spanish hides!"

He seemed to pull with renewed vigor at the recollection. There was a short silence.

"Do you suppose," said Madame Bernier, in a few moments – "do you remember – that is, can you form any idea whether you ever killed a man?"

There was a momentary slackening of the boatman's oars. He gave a sharp glance at his passenger's countenance, which was still so shaded by her position, however, as to be indistinguishable. The tone of her interrogation had betrayed a simple, idle curiosity. He hesitated a moment, and then gave one of those conscious, cautious, dubious smiles, which may cover either a criminal assumption of more than the truth or a guilty repudiation of it.

"*Min Dieu!*" said he, with a great shrug, "there's a question! ..... I never killed one without a reason."

"Of course not," said Hortense.

"Though a reason in South America, *ma foi!*" added the boatman, "wouldn't be a reason here."

"I suppose not. What would be a reason there?"

"Well, if I killed a man in Valparaiso – I don't say I did, mind – it's because my knife went in farther than I intended."

"But why did you use it at all?"

"I didn't. If I had, it would have been because he drew his against me."

"And why should he have done so?"

"*Ventrebleu!* for as many reasons as there are craft in the harbor."

"For example?"

"Well, that I should have got a place in a ship's company that he was trying for."

"Such things as that? is it possible?"

"Oh, for smaller things. That a lass should have given me a dozen oranges she had promised him."

"How odd!" said Madame Bernier, with a shrill kind of laugh. "A man who owed you a grudge of this kind would just come up and stab you, I suppose, and think nothing of it?"

"Precisely. Drive a knife up to the hilt into your back, with an oath, and slice open a melon with it, with, a song, five minutes afterward."

"And when a person is afraid, or ashamed, or in some way unable to take revenge himself, does he – or it may be a woman – does she, get some one else to do it for her?"

"*Parbleu!* Poor devils on the lookout for such work are as plentiful all along the South American coast as *commissionaires* on the street corners here." The ferryman was evidently surprised at the fascination possessed by this infamous topic for so lady-like a person; but having, as you see, a very ready tongue, is is probable that his delight in being able to give her information and hear himself talk were still greater. "And then down there," he went on, "they never forget a grudge. If a fellow doesn't serve you one day, he'll do it another. A Spaniard's hatred is like lost sleep – you can put it off for a time, but it will gripe you in the end. The rascals always keep their promises to themselves. .... An enemy on shipboard is jolly fun. It's like bulls tethered in the same field. You can't stand still half a minute except against a wall. Even when he makes friends with you, his favors never taste right. Messing with him is like drinking out of a pewter mug. And so it is everywhere. Let your shadow once flit across a Spaniard's path, and he'll always see it there. If you've never lived in any but these damned clockworky European towns, you can't imagine the state of things in a South American seaport – one half the population waiting round the corner for the other half. But I don't see that it's so much better here, where every man's a spy on every other. There you meet an assassin at every turn, here a *sergent de ville*. .... At all events, the life *là bas* used to remind me, more than anything else, of sailing in a shallow channel, where you don't know what infernal rock you may ground on. Every man has a standing account with his neighbor, just as madame has at her *fournisseur's*; and, *ma foi*, those are the only accounts they settle. The master of the *Santiago* may pay me one of these days for the pretty names I heaved after him when we parted company, but he'll never pay me my wages."

A short pause followed this exposition of the virtues of the Spaniard.

"You yourself never put a man out of the world, then?" resumed Hortense.

"Oh, *que si!* .... Are you horrified?"

"Not at all. I know that the thing is often justifiable."

The man was silent a moment, perhaps with surprise, for the next thing he said was:

"Madame is Spanish?"

"In that, perhaps, I am," replied Hortense.

Again her companion was silent. The pause was prolonged. Madame Bernier broke it by a question which showed that she had been following the same train of thought.

"What is sufficient ground in this country for killing a man?"

The boatman sent a loud laugh over the water. Hortense drew her cloak closer about her.

"I'm afraid there is none."

"Isn't there a right of self-defence?"

"To be sure there is – it's one I ought to know something about. But it's one that *ces messieurs* at the Palais make short work with."

"In South America and those countries, when a man makes life insupportable to you, what do you do?"

"*Mon Dieu!* I suppose you kill him."

"And in France?"

"I suppose you kill yourself. Ha! ha! ha!"

By this time they had reached the end of the great breakwater, terminating in a lighthouse, the limit, on one side, of the inner harbor. The sun had set.

"Here we are at the lighthouse," said the man; "it's growing dark. Shall we turn?"

Hortense rose in her place a few moments, and stood looking out to sea. "Yes," she said at last, "you may go back – slowly." When the boat had headed round she resumed her old position, and put one of her hands over the side, drawing it through the water as they moved, and gazing into the long ripples.

At last she looked up at her companion. Now that her face caught some of the lingering light of the west, he could see that it was deathly pale.

"You find it hard to get along in the world," said she: "I shall be very glad to help you."

The man started, and stared a moment. Was it because this remark jarred upon the expression which he was able faintly to discern in her eyes? The next, he put his hand to his cap.

"Madame is very kind. What will you do?"

Madame Bernier returned his gaze.

"I will trust you."

"Ah!"

"And reward you."

"Ah? Madame has a piece of work for me?"

"A piece of work," Hortense nodded.

The man said nothing, waiting apparently for an explanation. His face wore the look of lowering irritation which low natures feel at being puzzled.

"Are you a bold man?"

Light seemed to come in this question. The quick expansion of his features answered it. You cannot touch upon certain subjects with an inferior but by the sacrifice of the barrier which separates you from him. There are thoughts and feelings and glimpses and foreshadowings of thoughts which level all inequalities of station.

"I'm bold enough," said the boatman, "for anything *you* want me to do."

"Are you bold enough to commit a crime?"

"Not for nothing."

"If I ask you to endanger your peace of mind, to risk your personal safety for me, it is certainly not as a favor. I will give you ten times the weight in gold of every grain by which your conscience grows heavier in my service."

The man gave her a long, hard look through the dim light.

"I know what you want me to do," he said at last.

"Very well," said Hortense; "will you do it?"

He continued to gaze. She met his eyes like a woman who has nothing more to conceal.

"State your case."

"Do you know a vessel named the *Armorique*, a steamer?"

"Yes; it runs from Southampton."

"It will arrive tomorrow morning early. Will it be able to cross the bar?"

"No; not till noon."

"I thought so. I expect a person by it – a man."

Madame Bender appeared unable to continue, as if her voice had given way.

"Well, well?" said her companion.

"He's the person" – she stopped again.

"The person who—?"

"The person whom I wish to get rid of."

For some moments nothing was said. The boatman was the first to speak again.

"Have you formed a plan?"

Hortense nodded.

"Let's hear it."

"The person in question," said Madame Bernier, "will be impatient to land before noon. The house to which he returns will be in view of the vessel if, as you say, she lies at anchor. If he can get a boat, he will be sure to come ashore. *Eh bien!* – but you understand me."

"Aha! you mean my boat – *this* boat?"

"O God!"

Madame Bernier sprang up in her seat, threw out her arms, and sank down again, burying her face in her knees. Her companion hastily shipped his oars, and laid his hands on her shoulders.

"*Allons donc*, in the devil's name, don't break down," said he; "we'll come to an understanding."

Kneeling in the bottom of the boat, and supporting her by his grasp, he succeeded in making her raise herself, though her head still drooped.

"You want me to finish him in the boat?"

No answer.

"Is he an old man?"

Hortense shook her head faintly.

"My age?"

She nodded.

"*Sapristi!* it isn't so easy."

"He can't swim," said Hortense, without looking up; "he – he is lame."

"*Nom de Dieu!*" The boatman dropped his hands. Hortense looked up quickly. Do you read the pantomime?

"Never mind," added the man at last, "it will serve as a sign."

"*Mais oui.* And besides that, he will ask to be taken to the Maison Bernier, the house with its back to the water, on the extension of the great quay. *Tenez*, you can almost see it from here."

"I know the place," said the boatman, and was silent, as if asking and answering himself a question.

Hortense was about to interrupt the train of thought which she apprehended he was following, when he forestalled her.

"How am I to be sure of my affair?" asked he.

"Of your reward? I've thought of that. This watch is a pledge of what I shall be able and glad to give you afterward. There are two thousand francs' worth of pearls in the case."

"*Il faut fiver la somme*," said the man, leaving the watch untouched.

"That lies with you."

"Good. You know that I have the right to ask a high price."

"Certainly. Name it."

"It's only on the supposition of a large sum that I will so much as consider your proposal. *Songez donc*, that it's a MURDER you ask of me."

"The price – the price?"

"*Tenez*," continued the man, "poached game is always high. The pearls in that watch are costly because it's worth a man's life to get at them. You want me to be your pearl diver. Be it so. You must guarantee me a safe descent, – it's a descent, you know – ha! – you must furnish me the armor of safety; a little gap to breathe through while I'm at my work – the thought of a capful of Napoleons!"

"My good man, I don't wish to talk to you or to listen to your sallies. I wish simply to know your price. I'm not bargaining for a pair of chickens. Propose a sum."

The boatman had by this time resumed his seat and his oars. He stretched out for a long, slow pull, which brought him closely face to face with his temptress. This position, his body bent forward, his eyes fixed on Madame Bernier's face, he kept for some seconds. It was perhaps fortunate for Hortense's purpose at that moment – it had often aided her purposes before – that she was a pretty woman.[1] A plain face might have emphasized the utterly repulsive nature of the negotiation. Suddenly, with a quick, convulsive movement, the man completed the stroke.

"*Pas si bête!* propose one yourself."

"Very well," said Hortense, "if you wish it. *Voyons:* I'll give you what I can. I have fifteen thousand francs' worth of jewels. I'll give you them, or, if they will get you into trouble, their value. At home, in a box I have a thousand francs in gold. You shall have those. I'll pay your passage and outfit to America. I have friends in New York. I'll write to them to get you work."

"And you'll give your washing to my mother and sister, *hein?* Ha! ha! Jewels, fifteen thousand francs; one thousand more makes sixteen; passage to America – first class – five hundred francs; outfit – what does Madame understand by that?"

"Everything needful for your success *là bas.*"

"A written denial that I am an assassin? *Ma foi*, it were better not to remove the impression. It's served me a good turn, on this side of the water at least. Call it twenty-five thousand francs."

"Very well; but not a sous more."

"Shall I trust you?"

"Am I not trusting you? It is well for you that I do not allow myself to think of the venture I am making."

"Perhaps we're even there. We neither of us can afford to make account of certain possibilities. Still, I'll trust you, too. .... *Tiens!*" added the boatman, "here we are near the quay." Then with a mock-solemn touch of his cap, "Will Madame still visit the cemetery?"

"Come, quick, let me land," said Madame Bernier, impatiently.

"We *have* been among the dead, after a fashion," persisted the boatman, as he gave her his hand.

Chapter III

IT WAS MORE than eight o'clock when Madame Bernier reached her own house.

"Has M. de Meyrau been here?" she asked of Josephine.

"Yes, ma'am; and on learning that Madame was out, he left a note, *chez monsieur.*"

Hortense found a sealed letter on the table in her husband's old study. It ran as follows:

> "*I was desolated at finding you out. I had a word to tell you. I have accepted an invitation to sup and pass the night at C—, thinking it would look well. For the same reason I have resolved to take the bull by the horns, and go aboard the steamer on my return, to welcome M. Bernier home – the privilege of an old friend. I am told the Armorique will anchor off the bar by daybreak. What do you think? But it's too late to let me know. Applaud my savoir faire – you will, at all events, in the end. You will see how it will smoothe matters.*"

"Baffled! baffled!" hissed Madame, when she had read the note; "God deliver me from my friends!" She paced up and down the room several times, and at last began to mutter to herself, as people often do in moments of strong emotion: "Bah! but he'll never get up by daybreak. He'll oversleep himself, especially after to-night's supper. The other will be before him. .... Oh, my poor head, you've suffered too much to fail in the end!"

Josephine reappeared to offer to remove her mistress's things. The latter, in her desire to reassure herself, asked the first question that occurred to her. "Was M. le Vicomte alone?"

"No, madame; another gentleman was with him – M. de Saulges, I think. They came in a hack, with two portmanteaus."

Though I have judged best, hitherto, often from an exaggerated fear of trenching on the ground of fiction, to tell you what this poor lady did and said, rather than what she thought, I may disclose what passed in her mind now:

"Is he a coward? is he going to leave me? or is he simply going to pass these last hours in play and drink? He might have stayed with me. Ah! my friend, you do little for me, who do so much for you; who commit murder, and – Heaven help me! – suicide for you! .... But I suppose he knows best. At all events, he will make a night of it."

When the cook came in late that evening, Josephine, who had sat up for her, said: "You've no idea how Madame is looking. She's ten years older since this morning. Holy mother! what a day this has been for her!"

"Wait till tomorrow," said the oracular Valentine.

Later, when the women went up to bed in the attic, they saw a light under Hortense's door, and during the night Josephine, whose chamber was above Madame's, and who couldn't sleep (for sympathy, let us say), heard movements beneath her, which told that her mistress was even more wakeful than she.

Chapter IV

THERE WAS considerable bustle around the *Armorique* as she anchored outside the harbor of H—, in the early dawn of the following day. A gentleman, with an overcoat, walking stick, and small valise, came alongside in a little fishing boat, and got leave to go aboard.

"Is M. Bernier here?" he asked of one of the officers, the first man he met.

"I fancy he's gone ashore, sir. There was a boatman inquiring for him a few minutes ago, and I think he carried him off."

M. de Meyrau reflected a moment. Then he crossed over to the other side of the vessel, looking landward. Leaning over the bulwarks he saw an empty boat moored to the ladder which ran up the vessel's side.

"That's a town boat, isn't it?" he said to one of the hands standing by.

"Yes, sir."

"Where's the master?"

"I suppose he'll be here in a moment. I saw him speaking to one of the officers just now."

De Meyrau descended the ladder, and seated himself at the stern of the boat. As the sailor he had just addressed was handing down his bag, a face with a red cap looked over the bulwarks.

"Hullo, my man!" cried De Meyrau, "is this your boat?"

"Yes, sir, at your service," answered the red cap, coming to the top of the ladder, and looking hard at the gentleman's stick and portmanteau.

"Can you take me to town, to Madame Bernier's, at the end of the new quay?"

"Certainly, sir," said the boatman, scuttling down the ladder, "you're just the gentleman I want."

* * *

An hour later Hortense Bernier came out of the house, and began to walk slowly through the garden toward the terrace which overlooked the water. The servants, when they came down at an early hour, had found her up and dressed, or rather, apparently, not undressed, for she wore the same clothes as the evening before.

"*Tiens!*" exclaimed Josephine, after seeing her, "Madame gained ten years yesterday; she has gained ten more during the night."

When Madame Bernier reached the middle of the garden she halted, and stood for a moment motionless, listening. The next, she uttered a great cry. For she saw a figure emerge from below the terrace, and come limping toward her with outstretched arms.

Footnotes for 'A Tragedy of Error'

1. I am told that there was no resisting her smile; and that she had at her command, in moments of grief, a certain look of despair which filled even the roughest hearts with sympathy, and won over the kindest to the cruel cause.

"Trigger"

Tyler Jones

I FALLED ASLEEP to Pa and Booker shouting, and I woke up to the high whine of Pa's electric saw. Somewhere in there I heard the scream of a cougar echo 'cross the field. Probably took one a Jacoby's sheep again. I get outta bed and go downstairs. The table where we never eat is still covered in cards and poker chips and empty beer cans.

That saw sound is coming from the garage. High whine as it cuts through something. Low whine as it comes out the end.

Pa, Booker, and two other guys from the mill come over on Mondays after work to shoot the shit and play cards. Loser has to buy beer for the next week. But the way the chips is scattered, I can't tell who won. One chair is knocked down and some of the chips is on the ground.

I go outside in bare feet, rubbing my eyes with one hand and my crotch with the other. Cold fall night with crickets singing in the fields. Big ole' moon hangin' there like a diseased eye. Nothing but field as far as I can see. Our nearest neighbor is Jacoby's farm, and his house is just one light way out there in the dark.

The saw stops and starts and stops again.

I make it to the side door, wait until the saw stop, and knock. I know better than to walk in on Pa doing anything. Especially with a 'lectric saw. He's liable to cut a finger off, and he'd take off his belt and whip me good, even while blood still all spurting out the end of his stump.

It ain't unlikely. After all, that's what happened to Booker. He lost half his ring finger at the mill. Got a buncha time off work and some money 'cause of it and he was always goin' on about his good fortune.

The saw drops to the dirt floor of the garage and boots crunch over to the door. It opens a bit and Pa's eye stares out the crack.

"What're you doing up, Travis?" His breath fresh Camels and Pabst.

"Did you hear the cougar?" I ask him.

Pa lowers his head, then opens the door wider and steps outside. He takes the pack of cigarettes out the pocket of his flannel shirt. Slips one out and lights it. His face glows all red in the cherry and it makes him look like something outta one of them scary movies we ain't allowed to watch but sometimes do when he's at work.

"Listen," he says, "I need you to do something for me."

The gravel is sharp ice under my bare feet. I shove my hands into my pajama pockets and clench my teeth. I don't want him to see me shiver. Pa's car is still parked in front of the house. Old brown Chevy with black primer covering the spots where the paint's peeled. He calls it "the Turd."

"How'd Booker get home?" I ask him.

Pa takes a drag. His eyes squint in the smoke that goes up into his face.

"He walked," Pa says, his voice like he's sick.

There's a smell comin' off him, reminds me like when we butchered the hog. The smell of insides and blood. The cherry glows again and I see dark little stains all over his shirt. One of his only good shirts. All the others have small burn holes, just like the couch.

Pa blows out smoke, squints at me. "Trigger got killed tonight. The cougar got 'im."

"Shit," I say.

Pa's two fingers with the cigarette slash down and point at my face. The cherry glows hot at my nose.

"Language, boy," he says.

"Sorry, Pa."

The fingers lift and he takes another drag. "Jonah's gonna be hurt something awful. He loved that dog. I don't want him to know yet. He's still worked up about your ma."

I nod and a piece of gravel digs into the bottom of my foot, but it feels kinda good the way pain sometimes does.

"I need you to bury 'im out in the field. Didn't want your brother to see 'im so I cut 'im up, put 'im in trash bags and put those in some old duffels."

"Like the deer," I say.

Pa nods and breathes smoke out his nose like a dragon.

"You gotta bury it out there too," he says.

I can't hold it anymore and I shiver. Pa doesn't even notice.

"Bags'll be in here. Make your brother help. Tell 'im the cougar got Trigger."

"Yes, Pa," I say.

He drops the cigarette and it hits the ground like a tiny Fourth of July. A spark lands on my foot and it burns like the cold gravel.

Pa turns and starts to open the garage door. I let out a breath I didn't know I was holdin', and he stops and looks back at me. I swallow but it's one of those bad ones that makes your chest hurt.

"Why was you up?" he asks.

Pa don't like it when I shrug, says it's a dumb thing to do when God gave us words, but I shrug and I'm glad he ignores it.

"Thinkin', I guess," I tell him.

Pa's hand is still on the garage door. "Your ma?"

It's been since school started up that she's been gone, and Pa didn't make Jonah and me go back, but since we ain't in school we have to do lots of chores. He ain't said nothin' 'bout ma since he told us she run off, and I sort of believed he didn't feel nothin' over it 'cept maybe anger.

But his face now, it's what I see in Jonah sometimes when he's all worked up about ma leaving us. Usually when I look at Jonah I see ma all in his eyes and the way his smile is crooked, and that hurts.

Pa looks down at my bare feet. "Try not to think 'bout her," he says. "'Cause she sure as hell ain't thinkin' 'bout us."

He sighs and the breath comes out like smoke, hangs there a little while. He comes closer and puts a hand on my shoulder. I feel the hard calluses even through my shirt.

"I gotta finish cleanin' up and get to work. Make sure your brother eats breakfast. He's lookin' weak, you know?" He jerks his head at the garage. "Job better be done when I get back. Don't wanna hear no excuses."

When he opens the garage door that butchered hog smell comes out again. Pa turns around, tries to smile but his face just looks like it does when he's lost at poker.

"We'll have chili for dinner, tonight, okay?" he says, then he goes into the garage and shuts the door. I stand there in the cold, watch the smoke of my breath go up into the air like a ghost leavin' my body.

* * *

I know Jonah's up 'cause I hear his piss hittin' water, and then he's walkin' like an elephant down the stairs. Each step bangs like a hand inside my head and it makes me want to make him wear pillows on his feet.

When he comes into the kitchen he's rubbin' his eyes and his belly at the same time, and Pa is right. He looks all skinny and stringy.

"Mornin'," he says.

I slide him a bowl and spoon and fill the bowl with plain Cheerios.

"Pa says you need to eat," I tell him.

Jonah yawns and reaches for the sugar bowl, starts scoopin' one spoon after the other until there's a hill of the stuff.

He's got ma's hair. It's thick and the color of the dust at the bottom of the Cheerio bag. He's got her green eyes too, and maybe that's why Pa is so hard on him. The bruise on Jonah's cheek is faded to the color of a smashed blueberry but he never cried so hard as when Pa whooped him for mouthin' off.

"Can I watch a cartoon?" He asks.

"Not today, we got work to do," I tell him.

Jonah sighs, takes a bite, and milk dribbles down his chin.

* * *

Outside the garage, Jonah folds in half and barfs up breakfast when I tell him 'bout Trigger. He cries so hard he starts wheezin' when he breathes and I have to go get his medicine. He sucks on the inhaler which calms him down a bit, but his chin won't stop movin' and some part of me wants to hold it shut.

Jonah got Ma's weak stomach too. When she and Pa used to fight she'd wrap her arms 'round her belly like her guts were gonna fall out. And she'd fold up just like Jonah is, and the sounds she'd make were like Jacoby's sheep giving birth.

At least she could cover her bruises with makeup. She didn't ever go nowhere anyway.

Jonah's sobbin'. Steam comes off his barf and I tell him I'm sorry, but he needs to calm down.

"He didn't never do nothin' to nobody," Jonah says.

I tell him he needs to brush his teeth. The smell of the barf makes me think of what it tastes like and it make me want to barf.

I tell him the cougar's like a monster in one of them books Ma used to read to him. It's just out there hungry and waitin', and sometimes it comes to take things. I tell him that's what life is, this monster with teeth rippin' stuff away from us.

He stops blubberin' just enough to look at me with big wet eyes.

"Did the monster take Ma?" He says.

I tell him, no. But sometimes people get so beat up by the world they start rippin' stuff apart themselves just 'cause they know the monster's gonna do it anyway. Someday.

Jonah turns to go back inside. He whispers, "Goddamn it," but I don't hit him like Pa would. There's a lot I don't know, but I know he ain't just cryin' for Trigger.

* * *

When Jonah comes back out of the house he's got Pa's huntin' rifle over his shoulder. The stock hangs down to behind his knee.

"What the hell you doing with that?" I ask him.

Jonah's not cryin' anymore but his eyes is all red, and he's got this look like when I pretended to flush his comic books down the toilet. I shouldn't of done it because those mean more to him than anything. Ma got 'em at a garage sale and he's read 'em so many times the covers are all falling off the staples.

"In case we see the monster," he says.

Pa would be so mad if he saw Jonah with that gun, but Pa ain't here and if it makes Jonah feel better, I figure I won't say nothin' 'bout it.

When I open the side door of the garage the smell's not as bad as it was, but there's still the stink of something dead in the air. The blood smell's mostly gone, but now the burnt meat stink of when the saw cut through Trigger is stronger. I yank the chain and the light comes on and the bulb swings back and forth over two duffels sittin' on the floor. Jonah won't notice, but the table saw is cleaner than it has been since Ma left, and the dirt on the floor is raked.

Jonah steps in behind me, wrinkles his nose. "Why's there two bags?"

"Trigger was a big dog," I tell him. I grab the straps of one and start to lift, but it's heavier than I thought it'd be. I test the other one and it's a bit lighter so I tell Jonah to take that one, and to use both hands.

There's stuff movin' around in the bag. It shifts like carryin' a cooler full of beer after all the ice has melted. Heavy things movin' inside liquid.

Jonah can't quite carry his bag, he's more draggin' it than anything. The gun slaps against the back of his legs and one of his shoelaces is untied. I hold up my hand for him to stop, then kneel down and tie it for him.

He smells like B.O., which is the first time I ever noticed it on him. He's still young and sometimes he smells a bit ripe, but this is different. I bet he's getting pubes too. So maybe Pa is wrong, maybe Jonah isn't weak. Maybe he's just growin'.

We go out behind the house, me carryin' the heavier bag, and Jonah pullin' his through the grass like it's a shitty sled. His face all serious and tight lipped like that, he looks older too. Pa always said brushin' up against Death ages the ones still livin'. Guess he was right.

My arms are burnin' so I drop the duffel and take a breather in the middle of the field. Jonah stops too, puts his hands on his knees and breathes heavy like a smoker.

The old dead tree is still a ways off, and that's where the field dips down into a valley, and then the forest begins after that. When you're down in that valley, no can see you. That's where we buried the deer Pa hit with his truck. He said it was an elk but we never saw no antlers, so maybe he got that part wrong. I think he'd been out drinkin' with Booker that night because it was so late he had to wake me up and it was morning by the time he finished tellin' me what happened.

I shake my arms out and lift the duffel back up. Jonah starts draggin' his again, pullin' a trail of flat grass behind him. When we get to the tree I stop again. It stings in my chest to breathe and I wish I thought to bring some water. Or shovels for that matter.

Jonah reaches me and drops to the ground. The shirt under his armpits is all wet and I ain't never seen that before either. Not on him. He looks down the hill to the valley floor. I see it too. The mound where the deer is buried. Young grass grows over the top of it.

The ground is rocky down there. I 'member sparks flying when the shovel blade hit them, and Jonah and I takin' turns but me gettin' pissed 'cause he's not as strong as me and the job'd take longer, so I did most the diggin'.

I look back across the field to the house, and there's somethin' dark and low to the ground runnin' at us.

My balls tighten up and I say, "Jonah, gun."

He looks up like he been caught with his pants down and looks where I'm lookin'. He struggles to get the rifle off his shoulder, and still this thing is runnin' at us full speed, but the closer it gets it don't look like no cougar.

This thing barks twice and I know the sound 'cause I been hearin' it for years, and it's gotta be a ghost, or me wishing things was different than they are.

Jonah's got the gun held out, fightin' to the hold the barrel steady. It swings past me and my stomach falls lower 'cause if he twitches at the wrong moment he's gonna hit me.

The thing is close enough now to hear panting and Jonah is sayin' my name over and over, and then the thing is right on me and Trigger jumps up, puts his muddy paws all over my chest.

I get all dizzy because I ain't sure if time stopped or the world started spinnin' backwards, but sure as hell this dog is real. It barks again and I get down on my knees, rubbing his neck and head. He's covered in mud and some of his fur is all matted down with dark red stuff, dry and crusty.

Jonah drops the rifle on the ground, somethin' Pa would've given him a black eye for, and comes over. "Is it him?" he asks.

Trigger didn't never have no collar, but the tip of his tail is gone from when Pa backed over it in the truck, and his one ear is almost the color of a blonde lady's hair. This dog has both them things.

I nod at Jonah and he smiles so big and laughs. Trigger runs to him next, rubbing the mud and blood all over Jonah's clothes. Licking his face, nubby tail waggin' like he ain't never been so happy in his life.

But then the tail stops waggin' and Trigger puts his nose up in the air. Jonah keep rubbin' but the dog don't notice. Trigger puts his face to ground, waves it back and forth, leaves Jonah and walks like he's on the trail of somethin'.

He goes over to the duffel and makes a whinin' sound like he does when he's gotta go outside to pee. Trigger paws at the bag and nips at the corner.

"Trigger, knock it off," I tell him.

But then I get that feelin' again. My balls shrink and I feel like I'm gonna have diarrhea.

Trigger bites at the bag then jumps back, moves forward and bites at it again. Shakes his head with the bag between his teeth until the fabric rips a little and some dark liquid comes dribblin' out.

Jonah grabs Trigger by the scruff and pulls him back, then lifts up the bag and drops it just as quick and backs away, shaking his head and saying no no no. He trips over a root of the dead tree and goes down on his ass. All the color leaves his face until it looks like the skin of that dead hog. All grey and lifeless and bled out.

He points at the bag and says somethin' but I don't hear it. I lift the bag up too and somethin' is pokin' out the through the hole. I know what it is but my brain is slow to believe it, because I know what's in the bag. Pa told me. But this thing hangin' out is not what Pa said.

It's a hand. Pale skin like when you've been in the bath too long, no hair. Stained in that same black red stuff that leaked out on the grass. I lift the bag up more and the stuff inside moves around. The butchered hog smell comes rushin' out and hits my throat. The rip gets wider and this dead person's hand flops out more, all five fingers. One finger shorter'n the others. There's a rippin' sound and the tear gets bigger and there's the trash bag in the duffel, torn open too, and staring up at me from inside is an open eyeball. I can't tell if it's on a face or just floatin' there in all the blood.

I let go the bag and it drops and makes a waterbed sound and a bunch a dark liquid comes splashin' out onto my jeans.

"Jesus, Travis," Jonah says. "What the hell is that?"

His mouth hangs open and his chin is shakin' and there's a big wet spot on the crotch of his jeans.

"It's Booker," I tell him, and I almost can't breathe when I say it, because of what it means.

"You sure?" Jonah says.

I hold up my hand and tap the ring finger. Jonah knows what I mean.

Jonah starts cryin' and I wish he'd stop. I can't think any thoughts.

Pa lied, and that's a cold knife slippin' between my ribs. My throat's closin' up and I'm seein' black. Oh Jesus, I just wanna lay down and be nowhere.

Jonah's just wailin' now, rockin' back and forth with his arms 'round his knees and he don't look so old anymore. He looks just like he did when he was small enough to fit inside the dresser drawer where he'd hide and fall asleep and make everyone lookin' for him sick with worry.

The sun's behind some clouds and I stare at it until my eyes go white and I see lights floatin'. When things clear I turn back to the house and there's someone coming 'cross the field. A big woman with curly hair piled on top her head. She looks kinda familiar but she's just a shape right now.

I go over and slap Jonah on the face. "Stop your blubberin' and get down there." Pointin' to the valley and the grass covered mound where we buried the deer. "Take the duffel."

Jonah looks up, sees the woman comin' closer. He grabs the duffel and drags it down the hillside, and all the sloshin' makes more blood come spillin' out. A long pink tube squeezes out past the eye and the hand, trails behind the bag like a tail. Trigger takes off running after Jonah.

The woman's voice calls out, "Howdy. What are you boys doing out here?"

I look back and Jonah is almost at the bottom of the hill. He doesn't notice that Booker's hand has come all the way out of the bag and sits there in the blood trail like a dead fish. The pink tube has come out too. My whole stomach clenches up like a fist and acid burns my throat. Good thing I didn't eat breakfast, or it'd be all over my shoes.

"Just buryin' our dog," I yell back to the woman.

She's closer now. Close enough to see she's wearin' an Eddie's Diner waitress uniform and the name "Lena" is stitched on the breast pocket.

Her perfume smells like a grandma but she don't look quite that old. Her eyeslids is blue and the makeup on her cheeks cracks when she smiles. There's some wetness just under her nose. Her face is wide and the uniform fits pretty snug, shows the rolls of her arms, her belly.

She says. "Shouldn't you be in school?"

I glance back and see Jonah doing his best to drag the duffel behind the grass mound, but if the woman looks down there, it ain't gonna matter. A snail trail of blood with a dead man's hand and a piece of his guts. Trigger's runnin' in circles 'round that hand.

"No, ma'am," I say. "Me and my brother is sick. Dog died last night and Pa told us to bury him."

The woman is close enough for me to hear the creak of her leather shoes. She stops and stares at me and her eyes are kind, but there's some worry in there too. She's got a handkerchief all bunched up in one hand and a purse hangin' from the other.

"Travis, isn't it?" she says. "Do you remember me?"

"No, ma'am," I say.

The woman wipes at her nose, says, "I'm not surprised, we haven't seen each other in a while, and I'm a little bigger than I used to be. I'm Lena Crenshaw, Booker's wife."

I feel like there's another person inside me, living in my stomach, and he's tryin' to push everything up out my throat.

She says, "Booker didn't come home last night and I'm getting kinda nervous. You haven't seen him have you?"

I shake my head but I can't speak, and I don't trust my legs no more. They're going all jelly. I suddenly have to pee real bad, and I got that bad taste in my throat like I wanna barf.

Lena takes a few steps to me. "Is your daddy home?"

I swallow and say, "No, ma'am. He's at work."

Lena opens her mouth but she doesn't say nothin'. She looks at me like Ma used to when I'd got scraped up or fallen down.

"Oh sweetie," she says, and reaches out a hand like she wants to touch my face. "You're all covered in blood. What happened?"

I look behind me real quick, but I don't see Jonah. He must have run into the woods. I don't blame him. I see Trigger and I can't get any air. He's sniffin' at Booker's hand and it takes all I got to not yell at him.

Lena comes so close her perfume's all I smell. My eyes is burnin' somethin' awful when she puts a hand on my arm.

"Come on," she says," let's go inside and get you cleaned up. I'll make you some food. You're all skin and bones. Your daddy ain't cookin' much these days, is he?"

Her foot moves into the blood on the grass. She feels it, looks down and sees the dark red liquid on her shoe.

"Travis, sweetie, what's all the blood from? Are you hurt?"

"I told you," I say, and hold one arm over my belly. I can't help it. "Our dog died."

Lena looks over my shoulder. "Where were you gonna bury him?"

Oh Jesus, my stomach. It hurts so much I hunch over. Tears are comin', I feel 'em.

Then Trigger barks and Lena's eyes go big. She walks past me to the edge of the hill. She's quiet as long as it takes me to stand up straight, then she's screaming and it's so loud and full of hurt that her voice breaks into big wheezy sobs like she can't breathe. I go to the edge all hunched over and look down and see the dog has Booker's hand hangin' out of his mouth and he's pawin' at the piece of guts like it's a red snake. Lena's whisperin' "Sweet Jesus, dear sweet God in heaven." She spins around and her face is pain and fear and anger and I see her eyes real clear and they look the same color as the gravel, and my stomach clenches again so tight I swear it's twisting itself into a knot, and Lena's shakin' her head and breathin' heavy like a dog that's chased somethin' and I smell her sweat now and her perfume makes my head hurt like allergies and she's sayin' somethin' about callin' the cops and she doesn't know what's going on but she's gonna find out and take us away from Pa and oh sweet Jesus what have you done, and I sink to the dirt and dry heave just like Jonah does, and then Lena puts a hand to her forehead and her skin is turnin' red, and she calls me a monster and she screams again and there's a thunder crack but it don't come from the sky, it comes from the hill, and a hole bursts open in Lena's chest and I feel a warm mist fall on my face, and her mouth opens and her eyes get big and she stumbles forward a step or two, and she goes down to her knees, looking at me at the whole time, and I see her lips movin' and I want to know what she's sayin' but I also don't because it's probably bad, and blood comes up over her lips and down her chin, and then she falls forward straight onto her face and her nose makes a snappin' sound, and from behind her comes Jonah holdin' the rifle, a little smoke still comin' from the barrel.

Jonah don't look like no killer. His lips and nose are movin' like he's tryin' not to cry. I get up and go over to him and he hands me the gun like it's somethin' horrible he don't want to hold no more.

Lena's hands are grabbin' grass and her thick legs are twitchin', tryin' to push herself forward. She scrapes her belly along the grass. Bubblin' sounds come from her mouth and she's moanin', but it's weak. She's draggin' a big trail of bright blood now and the moanin' drives me crazy, like a squeaky wheel on a shoppin' cart.

Jonah pushes into my leg, both his hands held together up by his heart, like prayin'. He sniffs against my jeans and says, "Can you make her stop? That sound is hurtin' in my head."

And Lena moans and gurgle breathes as she drags herself further into the field. I leave Jonah and walk over to her. I could take the blame when it all comes out, but that don't help Jonah none. He knows what he did and he can't carry that all by hisself. Lena coughs and sprays blood on the grass and her moanin' has a wheeze in it, like a balloon leakin' air.

I raise up the rifle, look back at Jonah and tell him to cover his ears and close his eyes. He does as I say then I aim the gun and pull the trigger.

* * *

Jonah and I sit at the top of the hill. He chews his nails until they bleed and there's red smeared around his mouth. Trigger dropped the hand a while ago and now he's pawin' at the grass mound and whinin'.

"Are we thinkin' the same thing?" Jonah says.

"I figure we probably are," I tell him.

Jonah's chin is shakin' and his eyes are full of water.

"Can you say it?" he asks. "Please, I don't want to."

I breathe out as far as I can. "We're thinkin', if it wasn't Trigger in them duffels, that means Pa lied, and now we're wonderin' if it was really a deer in them duffels we buried down there." Noddin' at the green mound.

Jonah sniffs and nods.

"Stay here," I tell him.

* * *

He's sittin' in the same place, chewin' the nails on his other hand when I come back with the shovels. I hand him one and we go down the hill to the grass covered mound where we buried the deer. We don't say nothin'. We just stab the blades into the ground and dig.

Justice

Theresa Konwinski

A FULL MOON provided abundant light as George Miller tamped down the last few shovels full of dirt on top of a makeshift grave, approximately five and one-half feet in length by four feet wide. He stopped to wipe sweat from his brow. It was hot for October. Most days were cool and crisp, and the trees were in the process of emptying themselves into yards, blowing up into small, annoying piles close to the back door of his house. He constantly tracked them into the kitchen, where Alma griped about it every day. *That* and his snoring…she never tired of bitching about either one. He knew it wouldn't be long before the first hard frost, and he had kept this fact in the back of his mind as he planned Alma's murder. Better to get everything done and over with before he was unable to break through frozen ground.

Sunday, October 2, 2016 – that day was the final straw. They went to church that morning. Alma's loud, off-key singing irritated him first.

Why do people who sing the worst sing the loudest? George was sullen. Even God himself couldn't be happy about Alma's caterwauling. He had to stuff his hands in his pocket that day just to keep himself from putting them around her flabby, loose-skinned throat. To make matters worse, after church she spent forty minutes gabbing to other old crones about making quilts, getting ready for some kind of ladies' group to knit baby booties, and jawing about a meeting to plan Christmas festivities for the church. He was hungry and wanted some lunch. He finally had to grab her arm and lead her away from the group or she would have stayed there half the afternoon.

"George Miller, what do you mean pulling on my arm like that?" Alma angrily started as soon as they were safely in the car and the doors closed. "We were trying to get ourselves organized for…."

"I don't give a good goddamn about what you were getting organized for," he seethed. "I'm hungry. You need to pay a little attention to your obligations towards your husband instead of everything *but*. Quilts! Baby booties! That's a young woman's activity." He was in no mood for her goody-two-shoes routine.

Alma sat quietly for a few minutes, then started again, a voice of quiet judgment. "You are a selfish man, George Miller. You are selfish and hateful. If it weren't for the children…."

"Why let the children stop you? They couldn't care less about us. If you want out, get out, only don't think you'll take one penny with you. You'll get nothing but the clothes on your back."

"Oh, don't you worry. I wouldn't want anything. I would want *nothing* that would remind me of the last fifty-three miserable years I've had under your roof." Alma turned to face out the passenger side window. "Of course, there's always the land," she said in a menacing tone. "I'm sure a lawyer would help me get what's rightfully mine after all my contributions to this joke of a marriage."

That was the exact moment George Miller made his decision. She had to go. There hadn't been a day of their marriage he hadn't regretted. Alma was never beautiful, never possessed a pleasing personality. The only things she had ever been any good for were hard work and sex, which she was free about even before they got married. Now, she didn't participate in either. Over their years together they built a thriving farm and raised three successful children, but the kids hardly ever came around, and the farming business was slowly winding down as he moved closer to retirement. The kids didn't want the farm – they were city-dwellers. It was just George and Alma and echoes in an empty house where the two of them kept to themselves in separate rooms.

The moon was a silver sliver the night he hatched his plan. For over a week, he watched the moon pass through its phases while a strategy took form and cemented itself in his brain. The moon was just right on October 12 – bright enough for final resolution. Alma was in her bedroom, watching television, leafing through a *People* magazine, and pulling Russell Stover chocolates out of the box which seemed to be next to her bed in perpetuity. She stuffed them into her mouth, and the sight of her with chocolate slobber at the corners of her mouth was so abhorrent that he could barely maintain control as he peeked through the door of her bedroom, open just a crack. He knocked lightly.

"Alma, may I come in?" he said sweetly but cautiously, hoping not to tip his hand.

"What is it?" she answered, abrupt and cold.

He entered the room and sat down on the bed next to her, pulling the magazine gently out of her hand, placing it on the nightstand beside her bed. She looked at him warily.

"Remember the way we used to be? Remember the old days? Why isn't it like that anymore?" He spoke in a soothing voice, sweet talking her the way he had done when they were teenagers in the back of his Studebaker.

"Whatever has gotten into you?" she harrumphed, brushing aside the hand he had placed on her thigh. "Have you been hitting the bottle? Go on back to your own room. You can't do anything with that shriveled, wilted up little corn cob of yours, anyway. Don't think I can't read your mind after all these years."

He leaned over in a pretense of kissing her. She resisted and tried to push him away.

"Come on, Alma. Don't you see how I feel?"

"How you *feel?* You haven't loved me in fifty years, that is, if you *ever* did. Leave me alone," she screeched.

He kneeled at the side of the bed, feigning affection, trying to coax her. "Come on, darlin' – let me put my arms around you," he said, as he slid his left arm around her shoulders. He felt her shudder. "Let me just touch you for old time's sake," he purred, stroking her cheek, allowing his right hand to slide down slowly to rest on her shoulder.

"Get away from me," she hissed as he slid his hand around, covering her throat in what first seemed a tender gesture. Then George began to push with his left hand from the back of Alma's neck.

"Let go of me! You're *choking* me!" she sputtered. Her eyes widened as she recognized the menacing, self-satisfied smile creeping over his face. His hands grew tighter around her neck. She struggled against the vice-like grip, no longer able to speak. Her face darkened, her eyeballs bulged, and George knew he was almost loose from this anchor, once and for all. She thrashed, floundering her arms and legs as he squeezed every ounce of life out of his toad of a wife. He wanted to laugh, feeling free and powerful, and when Alma finally stopped struggling, he knew it was all over.

He stopped to catch his breath. *She was stronger than I thought she'd be.* He walked out to the kitchen and got a drink of water from the tap. It tasted like blood in his mouth, full of iron. He spat it into the sink and got a beer instead, gulping it down like a college kid at a frat party, returning to Alma's bedroom to survey the scene.

She was somewhat upright in bed. Her lips were parted, her face dark purple, and her eyes were open, staring him down – a lifeless indictment.

"You fat, purple, old hag," he grunted to the accusing eyes, diverting his own gaze.

He took her comforter off, laying it on the floor. He jerked her body towards the edge of the bed. It landed with a heavy thud onto the comforter, which he wrapped up as best he could around her corpulent torso. Then he grabbed the foot end and began dragging her through the house, not caring that her head bounced over thresholds or off the legs of furniture. Amazed at his own strength, he thought about the perfection of his plan as he dragged her out to the hay wagon waiting near the back door. It had all worked out so well....

One of their sows, Bessie, had come down with dysentery, and though there was treatment that could be administered, but he would tell people that to reduce stress on his herd, he shot Bessie before any of the other hogs could come down with it.

That night, he would bury not one, but *two* sows.

Lifting Alma onto the hay wagon was no easy feat, and the comforter kept coming unwrapped. He finally gave up on the cover, linked his arms under her armpits and pulled her up into the wagon. Once there, he concealed Alma and the sow with the comforter. He whistled to himself as he started up the John Deere and drove toward the grave site he had created near the woods at the back of his wheat field. The winter wheat was planted. In time, it would provide adequate cover for the grave, where the bodies could decompose together and fertilize his ground.

And now, with the bright, full moon shining over him, the two of them were buried, Alma on the bottom, pink rose comforter separating her and the dysenteric pig. Surveying his work, he heard a long, low howl, and a shiver went up his spine. Coyotes had been spotted recently around these parts. He would have to be on the lookout so that they didn't try to dig up the grave.

Excited with his new freedom, he slept fitfully that night. At 6 a.m., he decided to just get up and put on a pot of coffee. He didn't have anything to worry about. He had spent a week planning this act and knew how to answer the inevitable questions that would be asked.

Alma? She just up and left without an explanation. No, she took nothing. No, she left no clues as to where she was going. No, she didn't have any family except for the kids.

And as for the kids, he didn't expect them to call – not even at the holidays. He knew they recognized the cold charade of a relationship he and Alma had maintained. They were unlikely to ever want to be part of that again. Not one of the three of them had been close for years. If they did happen to call, he would report that Mother took off. She didn't leave a note. She hadn't been seen or heard from since October.

He puttered around the house for a while, read the daily news, and when it was finally daylight, he went out to the pigpen to check the rest of his livestock. He was just finishing slopping the hogs when he heard tires on the gravel of his driveway. He exited the barn to see Jim Yoder getting out of his truck.

Jim waved in greeting. "Good morning, George. How ya doin' today?"

"Good, good. You?" George answered. He wanted to shout that today was like Christmas for him.

"Oh, I'm good, but I wanted to come check on you. I wasn't sure you knew about the coyotes that've been hanging around lately. I heard a gunshot over here yesterday and wanted to see if you had maybe run across one of them," Jim stated. "They got a couple of my chickens a week ago. I don't know much about whether they would go after hogs."

"I haven't seen any, but I *did* hear one of them howling last night. As for the gunshot you heard, I had to kill Bessie. She had dysentery and I figured it was time to thin the herd anyway, so old Bessie is a goner," George answered him.

"Gees, George. Isn't there a treatment for that?" Jim was astonished at the killing of a prized sow. "That was a lot of feed and care down the drain."

"Yes, but you know, it spreads fast and I didn't want to mess around, take a chance on any of the other hogs getting it. She was old." George hoped Jim would buy it.

"Well, you know best about hogs. They're definitely not my area of expertise," Jim answered. "Listen, if you see the coyotes, let me know. Maybe you and I can do some hunting."

"Sure thing, Jim, sure thing. Yeah, we've gotta protect our livestock, don't we?" George responded.

"That's the truth. I tell ya, I can't get over you shootin' Bessie. That must've been rough, as long as you've had *that* old sow." Jim shook his head in disbelief.

"Yeah, it was hard all right, but it was the best thing to do." George had to look away for fear his face might give away something he didn't want Jim to see.

"All right, George. I'll check in with you in a day or two, but just call if you see those coyotes and I'll come over." Jim turned and walked back to his truck, pulling slowly out of the driveway.

For a few days, George just enjoyed having the house to himself. He ate what and when he wanted. He slept in every morning. In the evening, he built a fire in the fireplace and enjoyed a glass of whiskey in front of it, listening to the pop and crackle, watching the red and orange flames snaking up, then receding, swirling at times into tongues, licking at the glass doors that kept embers from bursting out onto the wood floor. *I wonder if that's what hell looks like,* he thought. *If it is, hell shouldn't be so bad as Preacher Martin lets on.* He laughed out loud, a hollow sound in the empty house.

Then one evening, he was restless. He decided to go for a walk out to survey the grave. *Pay my respects,* he snorted. He grabbed a flashlight, knowing the daylight would soon be gone. He started out through the wheat field, dim yellow light guiding his footing. When he got to the gravesite, he was stupefied…the grave was as loose and wet-looking as the night he tamped it down. He put his toe in the soil…it was like mud. And it was putrid. He had never smelled a more horrible smell in all his days. He pulled his shirt collar up over his nose to help block the horrific odor, but it was little help. *We need a good, hard freeze soon,* he thought as he turned to go back to the house.

The next day, he spied two coyotes at the very back of the wheat field. They were pawing at the grave. He went right to his gun cabinet, retrieved his twelve-gauge, and walked out the back door. He focused his site on one of the coyotes and fired. The two coyotes bolted off in the same direction – back into the woods. George knew he had to take care of those animals. It wouldn't be good for them to dig up anything he might have trouble explaining.

Over coffee, he ruminated about the best thing to do. That afternoon, he called Jim Yoder.

"Jim, this is George Miller. I saw those coyotes again this morning. They were out back where I buried Bessie. If we don't shoot them before long, you're likely to find sow guts in your yard."

"Geeminy, George. Didn't you put her in any kind of box or bag or anything?" Jim asked.

"Nah, I was in a hurry and I didn't have anything big enough. I just dumped her in the ground," George said.

"Did you bury her deep? They wouldn't be able to dig her up if she's deep," Jim posed.

"Well, I'm just one man. I couldn't dig a hole *that d*eep, I suppose. I got it as deep as I could." The hole had to be deep enough for two, but George couldn't tell Jim that.

"Give me half an hour. I'll be over, and we can take a walk back there – see what we can find," Jim said.

George hung up. Jim could unknowingly help George protect his secret and keep Bessie and Alma where they belonged. He thought about the look on Alma's face as he tossed her in the shallow hole he had dug. Those bugged-out eyes remained wide open, condemning him. He would never forget that face. Moreover, he would never regret being the cause of it.

Jim Yoder's Chevy truck pulled into the driveway, and George walked out to greet him. Jim was already stepping out onto the running board, pulling his gun case from the front seat where it had been beside him for the short trip to the Miller farm.

"Thanks for coming over, Jim. Let's get right to it. I know where to start looking for those dogs. I shot at them once this morning, and they took off west into the woods." George was matter of fact, ready to get down to business.

"Do you think I could get Alma to make me a cup of coffee first? I sure need one. It's getting cold out here," Jim said.

George jumped a little at the sound of Alma's name coming out of another human's mouth. "Oh, she's not home right now. She went into town." He saw Jim observing Alma's car and his own truck still in the driveway. "Sally Ann came home and picked her mother up to go shopping for the day," he quickly added.

"I'd love to see Sally Ann. Did she bring the kids with her?" Jim asked.

"No." Wanting to refocus, George asked, "Have you lost any more chickens?"

"Yeah, just a couple, but every chicken counts, so I reckon we ought to just get to it, shouldn't we?" Jim replied.

"I'll grab my 12-gauge and meet you by the back door." George walked into the house, grabbed his gun and donned his hunting jacket. Camouflage would be needed to sneak up on the coyotes. Jim could get one, and he could get one.

The two men started through the winter wheat, which was in its vegetative phase. They were quiet in their steps, looking around the landscape for any signs of recent coyote activity. As they came upon the gravesite, Jim began to gag and sputter. He stepped his boot into the top of the muddy grave. His boot was sucked down into the muck, and he had a difficult time pulling it back out.

"George, don't you smell that? Good God, man. Is that Bessie? And look at this ground! It's like black quicksand." Jim retched, as if he were going to vomit. He tried pulling a red handkerchief up over his nose, but the gagging continued.

"Yeah, I suppose that's her. Can't do anything about it. Here." George reached into his pocket and pulled out a box of cough drops. "Try one of these. Maybe that will help block the smell of old Bessie." *And old Alma,* he thought.

Jim took the lozenge, but he soon knew it wouldn't help. Nothing in the world could block *that* smell...the smell of rotting flesh.

"I can't take it, George. I've got to head back. I'll be puking my guts up if I don't." The only response from George was a look of disgust.

"I'm sorry, George. I just can't take that smell." Jim retched once more, then jogged to his truck.

Dusk replaced daylight as Jim pulled out of George Miller's driveway, throwing stones in his hurry to get away. George paid no attention, intent on the object of his search.

He saw two coyotes stick their noses out of the woods. Stealthy, cautious, they made their way towards George. They didn't seem to pick up his scent, maybe because of the noxious odor Bessie and Alma infected the soil with.

He needed to kill both creatures. It wouldn't do any good to kill only one, and if he fired too soon, the second coyote would run. George ducked behind a large tree near the edge of the woods. He waited, patient, until he felt a chill up his spine and hair standing up on the back of his neck. He whirled around to see a third coyote behind him, teeth bared. He stumbled back out from behind the tree and into the wheat field, realizing he was triangulated by the three coyotes. Hoping to scare them off, he now fired at one of them but missed. Adjusting his stance to re-aim, his boot sunk into the mucky, muddy grave he had made. He tried to pull his boot up but couldn't move it an inch. The gunk was like soft concrete in his boot, pulling him deeper into the rotten, fetid glop. Panicked, he dropped his gun, and it discharged. His heartbeat pounded in his temples. His eyes darted from one coyote to the next as he tried to extricate himself from the mud. It was oozing farther up his leg, and to balance himself, he pulled his other foot closer. The result was devastating – he was in putrefied mud up to his waist. He reached for his gun – maybe he could utilize it as leverage to pull himself up. But it was no use. Desperate flailing pulled him deeper and deeper into the black decay. Jim Yoder was right...it was quicksand, and at the bottom was rotten old Alma, waiting for him, sucking him down with her. When he was up to his neck, he tried to scream, but his mouth was quickly filled with rancid mud and decomposing flesh. He couldn't even gag, the pressure of the oozing mud preventing all his muscles from normal function. His ears and eyes were just above the mud and wide open when he saw three sets of yellow eyes walking towards him. The coyotes stared as he sank, then threw back their heads and howled justice into the night sky.

Shadows

Alexes Lester

I STILL REMEMBER the things he brought me, afterwards. A bent copper bracelet. A tiny purse with some coins still in it. A dirty straw bonnet. Frail, miserable things that had once been loved, had once held importance, yet in his hands were shameful reminders of poverty and death. Worthless offerings, yet he placed them on my lap with care, blood still under his fingernails.

"This reminded me of you," he would say, and smile that infectious smile. The one that had once won me over, the one that had made me think the word "No" would never be part of my vocabulary again. There were, once, no negatives with him. Nothing to naysay, nothing to dispute.

With that smile he would give me the dead woman's trinkets, and then he would lean in.

"A large lass, this one," he would whisper. Or "More buxom than you would expect from looking at her." Their bodies always seemed to fascinate him. He liked to take his time describing them to me. "She had paper white skin," or, with the last one, "A bonny lass she was, good and tall." But no matter what he would say, his left hand on the back of my chair, his right holding my chin, turning my face up to meet his, he would always end the moment the same way.

"She was on the street, waiting," he would say, the smile falling into a frown. "She wasn't waiting for someone. She was waiting for anyone. Anyone."

At that, he would lean in and press his forehead to mine. "And the smell of her. She smelled. Of gin. Just like you."

* * *

As my collection of stolen trinkets grew, my chances of escape dwindled. Such a well known man, in his work. Such a good, Christian man. An example of grace and honor in difficult, cruel times. Who would ever question his word? Who would ever think to look him in the eye?

"Lord, lord!" they would call, when they saw him on the street. "Lord, lord!" It was biblical, their obeisance. Their unthinking trust. "Lord," they would say, doffing their hats, "when do you think he will be caught?"

My husband, so splendid in his self-possession, his exquisite poise, always smiled and demurred, referring them to the police with some faint praise for the poor fools leading the investigation, but then he would add that he was sure the end was coming ever closer.

"It will be over soon," he would say to them over his shoulder as he helped me up into the waiting carriage. "I am sure of it." The ride, after denying the throng any scrap of information, any faint hope, was always quiet, his face turned to the window, his hand possessively on my thigh.

* * *

"For your sake, I loved her," he would say, later, in bed. "For your sake, she was my love, but just then. Not for always." He would reach for me, and I would never resist. I slid limply into his arms as he pulled me across the sheets, gave no sign that I understood, or at least objected. How could I object? My body, as the law said, was his to do with as he pleased, and he pleased to do so much that was evil. Objection was not wise.

"They are always my love for your sake, darling, so don't be jealous," he would whisper into my throat, and then he would kiss me.

* * *

The worst for me, though certainly not for his "love" of that night, was the half kidney. Handed to me with that same beautiful smile, just after he had taken me by the hand and led me into the kitchen.

This, followed by the request for me to prepare the kidney in a pan so that he could eat it, almost broke my mind. My spirit. Fear stopped me from screaming but I did moan, and sagged to the floor. Soft, paper-wrapped package in my hands, I bent over my folded knees and pressed my forehead to the tiles, rocking like a mother with her child. Never before had one of his gifts been anything but a trinket. Never before had it bled in my hands.

He surprised me by lifting me gently to my feet and then removing the pins from my hair, his hands shaking as though with eagerness to see my curls unbound.

"Cook for me, love," he said, stroking my head like he might a hound. "Cook for me." And then "She smelled of gin. Just like you. I wonder if we will taste it."

* * *

The knife was never far away. A token from his slumming, from time spent with his "loves", he would keep it in his pocket. When irritated by some parliamentary debate that had kept him away from me overlong, he would absentmindedly display it, flicking in and out as he recited the failings of the other lords. In and out, over and over. Like a metronome ticking away the seconds before his anger would take him to the streets once again. Anger at lords more powerful than himself. Anger at the commoners he called "The great unwashed." Anger at his own lengthening years.

And anger at me. Anger at me, at my one betrayal, for which I would not repent.

Who could give him a child? Who could allow such a man to hold their newborn? Not I. Not willingly. When I knew without doubt that I was expecting again, I did not hesitate. As I had once before, I sought release from my state, but unlike the last time, he moved to stop me before I could succeed. This time, the second time, was different. There were no beatings, there was no rough, bone-bending assault on my person, for this time he got there first. No clever little potion for me. No well planned miscarriage, under the guidance of a merciful doctor. A mixture of pennyroyal oil, tansy and opium could not save me, for I was not allowed out of the house to find it, nor was anyone permitted to visit without his lordship's permission. The servants even brought him my mail, so that he might read it, searching for any defiance of his will. To my horror, his child remained inside of me. Unabated, the shadow within my womb grew and grew, my collection from the dead growing apace. What satisfaction he could not cut into his "loves" he forced into me, and there was no stopping it. Not a second time.

* * *

My heart goes out to the police, still, to this day, though they disappointed me terribly. They never really stood a chance. His lordship, ever the sadist, sent them frequent dinner invitations, so that he might hear news of their progress and, more importantly, enjoy their frustration. Sir Charles Warren was the most regular guest, and from the beginning the most certain of success, which pleased my husband no end. As a solider Sir Warren felt little trepidation when facing violence, and he was certain from the first that there would be no more than two murders. On those nights in the early fall, his uniformed presence lent me much needed hope, but by the end of the investigation, when the weather had changed and news of the fifth and most violent death had reached around the world, he was reduced, nothing more than a wounded, broken man, defeat written plainly on his face.

"We cannot seem to make any headway with this Whitechapel problem," he admitted one night. The newspapers had been vicious to him, suggesting he was a buffoon or corrupt, and it was plain to see he keenly felt the need to retrieve his honor from the muck. "We simply cannot get a grip on the fiend."

And if you did, I wondered as I stared at my untouched plate, what excuse would you make for him, this lord beside you? What embarrassed justification for lack of action against him? Would you blame another, or simply tell no one? Would you retreat in fear? Or would you make the effort to take Jack down, only to be sent away to an endless war for the empire's glory, never to return home again? If you did tell, would anyone believe? Would anyone listen? Would anything be done?

My husband had nodded at Sir Warren's comment and made sympathetic noises, but offered no real comfort to the poor man.

Later, in bed, I was pushed face-first into the sheets and strangled from behind until I began to see spots before my eyes. My husband was so excited I began to wonder if I would be found in the street, intestines hanging out of my body, face disfigured until I was unrecognizable.

"The baby," I gasped, clawing at the pillows. "Please, the baby!"

The response was immediate. He withdrew his hands, turned me around, apologized, and lifted me to lean against his chest, his excitement lessened a little. When he caught his breath, he bent down and began to speak into my ear.

"My love," he whispered, "you are an excellent hostess. So lovely. So quiet. Absolutely serene. You made me proud."

Unable to stop myself, I wept as he kissed my shoulders.

* * *

It did not begin with murder, or with street crime of other kinds. He was neither prone to intemperance, nor wild behavior in public. He was not indiscrete, unaware of his responsibility to his name, or self destructive. It did not begin out there, with anyone else. It began inside with us, those that belonged to him.

The beatings he laid upon the stable boy were kept quiet with money, as was the shameful abuse of the maid. Both were given references and a tidy sum to send them on their way, just weeks before we were joined in marriage. Had I known, I would have begged my father to let me out of the arrangement, but I had not, and so did not. Who could claim to be prepared for such a monster? What virgin could know of such a beast? For me it began with his hands on my flesh and his teeth against my throat. On our wedding night, once he had undressed me, he took my trachea between his jaws and held me there, pinned under his body, gasping for breath. When I struggled, he pinched the flesh of my breasts between his thumb and forefinger, until I squealed from the pain of it.

When I spoke of it later, my mother believed it was a simple lack of understanding of a wife's duties, and my father said nothing at all. Nothing at all when I spoke of the legal impossibility of leaving the lord my husband. Nothing until the bruises rode my neck up onto my face. Nothing until my corset held my broken ribs rigidly in place. But by then, when they began to understand and found their voice, it was too late.

By then, all I had for help was a wicked little potion.

* * *

When I gave birth, he came to me in our bloody marriage bed and smiled, that same heart stopping smile. The one that had, not so long ago, made me feel safe.

"I love you," he whispered to me, over our child's head. "I love you both."

Then, with his liar's lips, he bent to kiss me and our daughter, before reaching into my nightgown to squeeze my breast with his murderer's fingers.

"It will stop, now," he said quietly. "It will stop."

This he promised as he moved his hand to rest on my deflated belly.

A promise I fear he has not kept. Though her cradle is always close by my bed, it is not always under my eye. When I sleep, which I do as infrequently as possible, I fear looking down to see her upon waking. There is no worry of blood or bruises. Because of her status, there is no fear of a ruined body.

It is just that my baby girl, with her paper white skin and cubby hands, with her curling blond hair and rosy cheeks, always has something new beside her on the bedclothes. A barrette. A cheap, lacy garter. A single, broken earring.

Gifts from her father. Her father, the lord who is untouchable. The lord who is the ripper.

We are so alike, those of us he called his "loves", despite all outward appearances. I too am alone. I too cannot escape my situation. I too feel nothing but the need for rescue, or, failing that, at least a moment's respite.

Here in the shadows, I wait. Waiting, as always, with a glass of gin in my hand.

Waiting, not for someone, but for anyone.

Anyone.

The Present

Robert Lopresti

MAGGIE FROWNED at the woman pushing the stroller. A girl really, not more than twenty, with high heels, tight jeans, and a tiny cell phone pressed to her ear. She was talking loudly, so as to be heard over the sound of her baby crying.

Maggie shook her head. *When he's grown up and gone you'll never, ever remember one of those phone calls, but you'll remember every chance you missed to talk to him.*

No point in saying that to the girl, Maggie knew. In the past she had tried once or twice to correct some awful bit of parenting she'd seen. That used to drive Frank crazy. Obsessive, he called it. *Do you think you're everybody's mother?*

No, she always replied. Just Kevin's mother, and he's plenty.

The young woman pushed the stroller into one of the mall's many clothing stores, still talking.

Maggie sighed and returned to the task as hand. The dentist she worked for was out with the flu and the unexpected day off gave her the perfect chance to shop for Kevin's birthday, coming up in October.

She strolled past the toy store and the computer software shop. Her first choice for gifts for her son was Newton's Kingdom, the mall's emporium of volcano wall charts, dolphin videos, fossils, geodes, and other treasures of the natural world. It had been Kevin's favorite shop since the first time she took him to the mall. She remembered the wide-eyed toddler staring in delight at toys powered by magnets and gravity.

"Can I help you?" The salesman was perhaps thirty-five, a few years older than Maggie, and he had the earnest look of a science nerd. It made her smile.

"I'm looking for a birthday present for a bright eight-year-old boy," she said. "I was thinking of a chemistry set."

The salesman politely disagreed. The really good sets were aimed at a slightly older child. But he had another idea.

"How does he feel about astronomy?"

"He could name all the planets by the time he was four. What have you got in mind?"

"Take a look at this." He pointed to a beautiful copper-colored telescope, a yard long. "It's copied from a classic model, but it's absolutely modern. He can see the planets through it, even the rings of Saturn."

"It's perfect," said Maggie. "How much?"

* * *

A lot, as it turned out, but she was sure Kevin would love it. The box, containing scope and tripod, was long, bulky, and heavy. The salesman stuffed one end into a sky-blue bag with the Newton's Kingdom logo.

Maggie found that the only way to carry the present was as if it were a flagpole, hugging it to her chest, and letting it soar above her head. It felt silly but that was fine. She'd show her marching style to Kevin and they'd have a good laugh about it.

The long walk across the mall made her arms tired. She decided to stop for lunch at the food court before trekking out to her car.

On the way she passed a couple with a toddler. The little boy was in a harness and his father was holding the other end of the leash.

Maggie had mixed feelings about that arrangement. It seemed degrading treating the child like an animal. But it let the boy wander a little in a crowded place and still be safe. She certainly understood the parents' desire to keep him close.

This was the sort of thing that used to drive her husband nuts. "You're fixated," Frank said, before *he* fixated on his secretary and ran off.

The hell with him. She and Kevin didn't need him. They would be better off without him.

In the food court she put the telescope down beside a table and placed her coat over it. Then she bought a spinach salad and a strawberry smoothie.

A family was seated two tables away and she had a good view of them. The father was a tall, thin man and his daughter was a cute little girl of about six. The little angel was in a bad mood, possibly because her father had bought her a healthy lunch instead of the junk food that was available at most booths around the food court.

Maggie liked the way the father responded to the little girl's sulk. She couldn't hear his exact words but they were clearly along the lines of *eat what's in front of you and stop complaining*. So many parents these days treated their child as an adult to negotiate with, but the tall man seemed both gentle and firm.

When the little girl still refused to eat, her father tried a different tack. He got up and went to one of the hamburger places. Giving in? No. He came back with crayons and a place mat and centered them in front of the little girl. *If you aren't going to eat, then keep yourself busy while I do.*

*N*ot bad, Maggie thought, but the place mat was a mistake. It was coloring-book style and the little girl no doubt thought she was too old for such things. By the time Kevin was four he used to get furious if he was "treated like a baby," and this girl was no different. She pushed the crayons away. Her father calmly picked one of them up and put it into her right hand. He said something to her.

The girl rolled her eyes. *Little drama queen,* Maggie thought, amused The kid transferred the crayon to her left hand, flipped the paper over elaborately and began to draw on the blank side.

She enjoyed this clever defiance. *I'm too big to color in the lines. I'll do my own drawing.* And now the girl was working away. It looked like an animal, something running—

Maggie stopped, smoothie halfway to her mouth.

What kind of father doesn't know that his six-year-old daughter is left-handed?

Surely no one in this day and age would try to change their child's dominant hand? And from the way the girl was drawing, she was a definite southpaw.

Maggie studied the two faces. Was there any hint of a family resemblance? She couldn't see any, except that their hair was the same shade of black. Come to think of it, the girl was awfully pale for such dark hair. And it had been cut recently and not too well.

For that matter, shouldn't the girl be in school?

Maggie swallowed hard. Could this be an abducted child?

She had read a lot about child abductions – more of the supposed obsessiveness that so bugged Frank. One writer estimated that in at least half the cases an adult had seen some part of the event and missed its significance. There were long-term abductions where a child lived with the criminal for months or even years before being recognized and rescued.

Maggie stared at the girl and the tall man – she could no longer think of him as the father. Her heart was pounding. What should she do?

There were no security guards in sight. She could open her cell phone and step out of the food court. Or go to one of the vendors. The main entrance of the mall was to the right, just beyond the court. If the tall man suspected anything – if he weren't really the girl's father – he could grab her and be gone in a minute. The girl stood up and said something to the man, who nodded and rose as well.

The girl walked out of the food court and to the left, to the ladies' room. The tall man stood outside in the hallway. Protecting her, or making sure she couldn't run away?

You'll never, ever get a better chance, Maggie thought. She stood up and then considered the telescope. Bring it or not? Deciding it would be suspicious to do otherwise, she picked it up.

Maggie entered the ladies' room without a glance at the tall man. The little girl stood by the sinks staring at herself in the mirror. *At her new hair color?*

Maggie put down her burden with an exaggerated sigh. "Heavy. How are you, dear?"

Wide eyes looked back at her in the mirror. "Okay."

Maggie turned on a faucet and began to scrub her hands. "It looked like you and your father were having a little quarrel. Didn't you like the food?"

"Wasn't hungry." She turned toward the stalls. "Gotta use the bathroom."

"Listen— Oh, my name is Maggie. What's yours?"

The little girl looked back over her shoulder. "Dorrie."

"Is he your father, Dorrie?"

The child's eyes went wide. Maggie thought she was going to let out a scream of pure terror. "I didn't say anything! Tell him I didn't say anything!"

Maggie dropped to her knees. She put her hands on the little girl's shoulders. "It's all right, Dorrie. It's all right. Tell me what happened."

Tears were coming now. "He said— he said he'll kill my family if I tell anyone. Tell him I didn't say anything!"

Maggie hugged her. "It's all right, Dorrie. Nobody's going to get hurt. We're going to take you back to your family." Her heart was beating so fast that she wasn't sure she could stand up. She took a deep breath, smiled, and rose.

"Here's what we're going to do. You get in that last stall, that's right. Now lock it. Good girl.

"Listen to me, Dorrie. I'm going to call the police for help. Don't open that door for me, or that man, or anyone except a police officer in uniform. If anyone else tries to get in, you *scream.* Do you understand?"

"I want my mommy and daddy!"

Maggie thought her heart would break. "We'll get you there, honey. Just keep that door shut."

She opened her cell phone. No signal. *Dammit.*

Maggie closed her eyes and took a deep breath. *Think. You may never, ever do anything this important again.*

All right. She had her plan. She hefted the telescope and walked out.

In the mall corridor she made a point of looking past the tall man – the *rat* – as if she weren't sure who she was looking for. Then she focussed on him and walked up with a smile.

"Excuse me. Are you the father of the little girl in the ladies' room?"

He looked surprised, and nervous. "Why do you ask?"

Maggie lowered Kevin's birthday present to the floor. "She said her father was waiting outside for her."

"Oh. Yes, I'm her dad. What's wrong?"

"Nothing serious. She had a little accident." Maggie shrugged. "Nervous tummy? My sister is in there helping her clean up."

He started toward the door. Maggie put a hand on his arm gently, resisting the temptation to latch on like a bear-trap. "Please don't. She's embarassed emough."

"Oh." He stopped, but stood staring at the door, undecided.

"You know what would be a big help? There's a clothing store around the corner, by the jeweler's. If you could buy a package of girl's underwear..."

"Sure. I'll be right back. Thanks."

Maggie smiled and nodded as he left. Then she flipped her cell phone open. A signal!

"911. What's your emergency?"

"This is Maggie Wells. I'm at the Mayhill Mall, near the food court. A child's been kidnapped. You need to—"

Running footsteps. The phony father hadn't stayed fooled for long. He was rushing back down the hall, straight toward the ladies' room.

"Stop!" yelled Maggie, dropping her phone. But he was coming faster, not even looking at her.

Maggie bent down and grabbed the bottom end of the telescope. She heaved the box with all her might, straight at the kidnapper.

It bounced off his chest. He stumbled over it and crashed to the floor, face first.

"Hey!" somebody yelled.

The tall man rose fast. Maggie jumped onto his back, but he threw her off easily.

A fat man in a sports coat pressed between them. "Stop it, you two." Others were gathering now; a gray-haired woman, two teenagers in basketball jackets.

"That bitch is crazy," said the tall man. "She attacked me."

"He's a kidnapper!" said Maggie. "There's a little girl in the ladies' room who says he took her."

"You're nuts," he said.

The fat man looked around at the small group that had gathered. "You! Call 911. And you – find a security guard."

"I want to make sure my daughter's all right," said the tall man and headed towards the ladies' room. "God knows what this lunatic did to her."

"You stay here," said the gray-haired woman. "I'll check on her."

"Good, good." The tall man wiped his hand across his mouth. His eyes darted nervously. "Where are those cops?"

He walked into the main corridor, as if he were looking for the security guards. Maggie watched him pace back and forth twice. As he turned the third time he began to run, heading for the main door.

"Stop him!" yelled Maggie and the fat man together. The two basketball players were already moving and didn't slow down until all three men bounced off one of the mall's doors and landed in a heap on the floor.

* * *

The girl's name was Dorrie Sommers. She had been abducted out of her backyard a few days before in a small town three states away. The kidnapper's driver's license said his name was Nick O'Ryan, but the cops assumed that was a lie.

The police told Maggie all this while men in suits argued about Kevin's birthday present. The telescope had been banged up in the fall. The manager of the science store and the assistant head of the mall were fighting over the honor of paying for a replacement.

They finally agreed that Newton's Kingdom would immediately provide a new telescope and the mall would gather an assortment of birthday gifts for Kevin from its other fine stores.

"I'll bring him in as soon as I can," Maggie promised. "He loves the mall."

Just when she thought they would let her go home a TV reporter arrived and wanted an interview. Maggie thought she'd skip it, but then decided it might do some good. The reporter – a youngster with a huge pile of blond hair – was a good audience, growing wide-eyed as she heard Maggie's story. She promised the interview would be on the news that night.

Finally, with a new telescope wrapped in the finest recycleable gift paper, courtesy of Newton's Kingdom, she was allowed to leave. Maggie was bone-tired and barely remembered the drive home. *Adrenalin overloads really wear you out,* she remembered.

In the apartment she carried the telescope into Kevin's room. The walls were covered with dinosaurs and jet planes, with a few mementos of his cowboy phase visible as well.

Maggie opened the closet door and tucked the telescope in beside the other gifts. There was the globe she had purchased for Christmas. The rock polishing set for his seventh birthday. And so on back to the set of plastic sharks she had bought when he was five.

Each was neatly wrapped, ready to be opened and played with.

Maggie closed the closet door. She looked around the room.

"I told the TV reporter about you, Kevin," she said. "I gave her your photo. Who knows? Maybe someone will remember something. Maybe tomorrow will be the day you come home."

She straightened the calendar that hung on the wall. It was wild animals this year. "But I know one thing. Someday I *will* find you. And whenever that happens, we will open every one of those presents together and you'll know that, no matter what your dad said, and no matter what the police said, I never, ever doubted it for one second."

And then she turned out the light and closed the door. Because she never, ever cried in that room.

The Horrible

Guy de Maupassant

THE SHADOWS OF A BALMY night were slowly falling. The women remained in the drawing-room of the villa. The men, seated, or astride of garden chairs, were smoking outside the door of the house, around a table laden with cups and liqueur glasses.

Their lighted cigars shone like eyes in the darkness, which was gradually becoming more dense. They had been talking about a frightful accident which had occurred the night before – two men and three women drowned in the river before the eyes of the guests.

General de G— remarked:

"Yes, these things are affecting, but they are not horrible.

"Horrible, that well-known word, means much more than terrible. A frightful accident like this affects, upsets, terrifies; it does not horrify. In order that we should experience horror, something more is needed than emotion, something more than the spectacle of a dreadful death; there must be a shuddering sense of mystery, or a sensation of abnormal terror, more than natural. A man who dies, even under the most tragic circumstances, does not excite horror; a field of battle is not horrible; blood is not horrible; the vilest crimes are rarely horrible.

"Here are two personal examples which have shown me what is the meaning of horror.

"It was during the war of 1870. We were retreating toward Pont-Audemer, after having passed through Rouen. The army, consisting of about twenty thousand men, twenty thousand routed men, disbanded, demoralized, exhausted, were going to disband at Havre.

"The earth was covered with snow. The night was falling. They had not eaten anything since the day before. They were fleeing rapidly, the Prussians not being far off.

"All the Norman country, sombre, dotted with the shadows of the trees surrounding the farms, stretched out beneath a black, heavy, threatening sky.

"Nothing else could be heard in the wan twilight but the confused sound, undefined though rapid, of a marching throng, an endless tramping, mingled with the vague clink of tin bowls or swords. The men, bent, round-shouldered, dirty, in many cases even in rags, dragged themselves along, hurried through the snow, with a long, broken-backed stride.

"The skin of their hands froze to the butt ends of their muskets, for it was freezing hard that night. I frequently saw a little soldier take off his shoes in order to walk barefoot, as his shoes hurt his weary feet; and at every step he left a track of blood. Then, after some time, he would sit down in a field for a few minutes' rest, and he never got up again. Every man who sat down was a dead man.

"Should we have left behind us those poor, exhausted soldiers, who fondly counted on being able to start afresh as soon as they had somewhat refreshed their stiffened legs? But scarcely had they ceased to move, and to make their almost frozen blood circulate in their veins, than an unconquerable torpor congealed them, nailed them to the ground, closed their eyes, and paralyzed in one second this overworked human mechanism. And they gradually sank down, their foreheads on their knees, without, however, falling over, for their loins and their limbs became as hard and immovable as wood, impossible to bend or to stand upright.

"And the rest of us, more robust, kept straggling on, chilled to the marrow, advancing by a kind of inertia through the night, through the snow, through that cold and deadly country, crushed by pain, by defeat, by despair, above all overcome by the abominable sensation of abandonment, of the end, of death, of nothingness.

"I saw two gendarmes holding by the arm a curious-looking little man, old, beardless, of truly surprising aspect.

"They were looking for an officer, believing that they had caught a spy. The word 'spy' at once spread through the midst of the stragglers, and they gathered in a group round the prisoner. A voice exclaimed: 'He must be shot!' And all these soldiers who were falling from utter prostration, only holding themselves on their feet by leaning on their guns, felt all of a sudden that thrill of furious and bestial anger which urges on a mob to massacre.

"I wanted to speak. I was at that time in command of a battalion; but they no longer recognized the authority of their commanding officers; they would even have shot me.

"One of the gendarmes said: 'He has been following us for the three last days. He has been asking information from every one about the artillery.'"

I took it on myself to question this person.

"What are you doing? What do you want? Why are you accompanying the army?"

"He stammered out some words in some unintelligible dialect. He was, indeed, a strange being, with narrow shoulders, a sly look, and such an agitated air in my presence that I really no longer doubted that he was a spy. He seemed very aged and feeble. He kept looking at me from under his eyes with a humble, stupid, crafty air.

"The men all round us exclaimed.

"'To the wall! To the wall!'

"I said to the gendarmes:

"'Will you be responsible for the prisoner?'

"I had not ceased speaking when a terrible shove threw me on my back, and in a second I saw the man seized by the furious soldiers, thrown down, struck, dragged along the side of the road, and flung against a tree. He fell in the snow, nearly dead already.

"And immediately they shot him. The soldiers fired at him, reloaded their guns, fired again with the desperate energy of brutes. They fought with each other to have a shot at him, filed off in front of the corpse, and kept on firing at him, as people at a funeral keep sprinkling holy water in front of a coffin.

"But suddenly a cry arose of 'The Prussians! the Prussians!'

"And all along the horizon I heard the great noise of this panic-stricken army in full flight.

"A panic, the result of these shots fired at this vagabond, had filled his very executioners with terror; and, without realizing that they were themselves the originators of the scare, they fled and disappeared in the darkness.

"I remained alone with the corpse, except for the two gendarmes whose duty compelled them to stay with me.

"They lifted up the riddled mass of bruised and bleeding flesh.

"'He must be searched,' I said. And I handed them a box of taper matches which I had in my pocket. One of the soldiers had another box. I was standing between the two.

"The gendarme who was examining the body announced:

"'Clothed in a blue blouse, a white shirt, trousers, and a pair of shoes.'

"The first match went out; we lighted a second. The man continued, as he turned out his pockets:

"'A horn-handled pocketknife, check handkerchief, a snuffbox, a bit of pack thread, a piece of bread.'

"The second match went out; we lighted a third. The gendarme, after having felt the corpse for a long time, said:

"'That is all.'

"I said:

"'Strip him. We shall perhaps find something next his skin."

"And in order that the two soldiers might help each other in this task, I stood between them to hold the lighted match. By the rapid and speedily extinguished flame of the match, I saw them take off the garments one by one, and expose to view that bleeding bundle of flesh, still warm, though lifeless.

"And suddenly one of them exclaimed:

"'Good God, general, it is a woman!'

"I cannot describe to you the strange and poignant sensation of pain that moved my heart. I could not believe it, and I knelt down in the snow before this shapeless pulp of flesh to see for myself: it was a woman.

"The two gendarmes, speechless and stunned, waited for me to give my opinion on the matter. But I did not know what to think, what theory to adopt.

"Then the brigadier slowly drawled out:

"'Perhaps she came to look for a son of hers in the artillery, whom she had not heard from.'

"And the other chimed in:

"'Perhaps, indeed, that is so.'

"And I, who had seen some very terrible things in my time, began to cry. And I felt, in the presence of this corpse, on that icy cold night, in the midst of that gloomy plain; at the sight of this mystery, at the sight of this murdered stranger, the meaning of that word 'horror.'

"I had the same sensation last year, while interrogating one of the survivors of the Flatters Mission, an Algerian sharpshooter.

"You know the details of that atrocious drama. It is possible, however, that you are unacquainted with one of them.

"The colonel travelled through the desert into the Soudan, and passed through the immense territory of the Touaregs, who, in that great ocean of sand which stretches from the Atlantic to Egypt and from the Soudan to Algeria, are a kind of pirates, resembling those who ravaged the seas in former days.

"The guides who accompanied the column belonged to the tribe of the Chambaa, of Ouargla.

"Now, one day we encamped in the middle of the desert, and the Arabs declared that, as the spring was still some distance away, they would go with all their camels to look for water.

"One man alone warned the colonel that he had been betrayed. Flatters did not believe this, and accompanied the convoy with the engineers, the doctors, and nearly all his officers.

"They were massacred round the spring, and all the camels were captured.

"The captain of the Arab Intelligence Department at Ouargla, who had remained in the camp, took command of the survivors, spahis and sharpshooters, and they began to retreat, leaving behind them the baggage and provisions, for want of camels to carry them.

"Then they started on their journey through this solitude without shade and boundless, beneath the devouring sun, which burned them from morning till night.

"One tribe came to tender its submission and brought dates as a tribute. The dates were poisoned. Nearly all the Frenchmen died, and, among them, the last officer.

"There now only remained a few spahis with their quartermaster, Pobeguin, and some native sharpshooters of the Chambaa tribe. They had still two camels left. They disappeared one night, along with two, Arabs.

"Then the survivors understood that they would be obliged to eat each other, and as soon as they discovered the flight of the two men with the two camels, those who remained separated, and proceeded to march, one by one, through the soft sand, under the glare of a scorching sun, at a distance of more than a gunshot from each other.

"So they went on all day, and when they reached a spring each of them came to drink at it in turn, as soon as each solitary marcher had moved forward the number of yards arranged upon. And thus they continued marching the whole day, raising everywhere they passed, in that level, burnt up expanse, those little columns of dust which, from a distance, indicate those who are trudging through the desert.

"But one morning one of the travellers suddenly turned round and approached the man behind him. And they all stopped to look.

"The man toward whom the famished soldier drew near did not flee, but lay flat on the ground, and took aim at the one who was coming toward him. When he believed he was within gunshot, he fired. The other was not hit, and he continued then to advance, and levelling his gun, in turn, he killed his comrade.

"Then from all directions the others rushed to seek their share. And he who had killed the fallen man, cutting the corpse into pieces, distributed it.

"And they once more placed themselves at fixed distances, these irreconcilable allies, preparing for the next murder which would bring them together.

"For two days they lived on this human flesh which they divided between them. Then, becoming famished again, he who had killed the first man began killing afresh. And again, like a butcher, he cut up the corpse and offered it to his comrades, keeping only his own portion of it.

"And so this retreat of cannibals continued.

"The last Frenchman, Pobeguin, was massacred at the side of a well, the very night before the supplies arrived.

"Do you understand now what I mean by the horrible?"

This was the story told us a few nights ago by General de G—.

Invisible Death

Tom Mead

SNOW IS FALLING outside, and I am thinking about the Samodiva. It seems strange now, but there was once a time when I had never even heard the word. Since then, the Samodiva has infected the course of my life in many ways.

The story was told to me in 1935. War was still a few years off but England was in the grip of a fierce winter. My fiancée Ruby Soames (as she was then) had invited me out to stay with her family over the Christmas period. It was a comparatively small house, but set in a wide expanse of snow-dappled land. As we drove up the gravel drive, I saw Ruby's mother and father waiting for us, framed in the glowing doorway like a couple of phantoms.

Ruby's mother was a quiet and insipid woman. She was stout and dignified, with a sweet little voice. She always wore black, and today favoured us with a funereal dress that reached her ankles and culminated at her neck in a rippling ruff. With her white skin and sunken eyes, she looked like nothing so much as one of those Victorian *memento mori* photographs. Mrs Soames gave us a faint smile as Ruby and I climbed from the car, our breath snatched from us by a biting wind.

Ruby's father was more garrulous in his greeting. He stepped forward and gripped my hand in a tight shake: "How are you, my boy?"

"Well, thank you Major."

He wore a fabulous silk smoking jacket embroidered with an oriental dragon. His breath smelt of hot brandy. They each hugged Ruby tight then ushered us into the house, where the rooms were well-lit and fires blazed in comfort and warmth. We settled in the parlour and enjoyed a brandy as we told them tales of London and made plans for our festive visit.

We had not been there long when the front door was flung open and a young man tumbled into the house. This was Bill, Ruby's cousin. He beamed when he saw us and snatched us both to him in a great enveloping hug.

Though he was handsome and clean-shaven, with black brylcreemed hair, Bill was bundled up in a furry overcoat at least two sizes too large, and resembled some Appalachian bear trapper.

He joined us in a brandy and told us of his latest exploits. Bill fancied himself an adventurer and had just got back from the Australian outback. This, Ruby told me, was the influence of his uncle.

While these days Major Soames's life was largely sedentary, I knew that he had been quite the daredevil in his time. Recently, the memoirs of his time in Europe during the Balkans Campaign had been published. I made sure to compliment him on the volume's success as we ambled through to the dining room.

"Tip of the iceberg, you know," said the major, "there are things I saw that are so horrible and fantastic they could never see print."

We sat down to dine and as the soup dishes were placed in front of us by two housemaids, Major Soames began to tell us the story of the Samodiva. He looked from Bill to Ruby to myself, but never once did he lock eyes with his wife as he spoke.

"We were stationed in Albania in the winter of 1915. Like yourself, Michael, I am a medical man, and I was operating a field hospital out of an abandoned church. You've never fought in a war, Michael, nor you, Bill, and I pray that you never do. But it can do funny things to a soldier's mind. The Slavs have their own ghoulish folklore just like any other region, but it began to exert an insidious effect on the soldiers. It seemed to infect them like a sickness.

"We had established a sort of 'common room' at the rear of the church, in the vestry, and there the healing soldiers would congregate. I would go in there to talk with them sometimes, and to drink with them.

"One of the soldiers I encountered was a chap called Anderson. He was missing his right hand. We'd bandaged him up and doped him, but for a while I was afraid infection had set in. He was starting to get delirious. It was touch and go. By November of 1916 we'd been there for close to a year. It felt like the end of the world. Anderson's recovery was long and there was no chance of us getting out anytime soon.

"There was a civilian settlement nearby. Anderson used to socialise with them. They took him in as one of their own. And once, we were drinking together in the vestry and he started to tell me a story about the Samodiva.

"I'd never heard the word, but Anderson was full of it.

"'They told me about it in the village,' he said. 'At first I didn't believe them. I thought it was just silly talk. But last night I saw it.'

"'Take it easy, Anderson,' I said. 'You've had too much to drink.'

"'It came to the church gates. It wanted to follow me in but it couldn't. You see,' he leaned toward me, 'it can't walk on consecrated ground.'

"Well, as you can imagine I didn't think too much of it. But the next time I spoke to him, he said 'It came a little closer last night.' There was terror in his eyes.

"'It can't get in, Anderson,' I said, trying to placate him. 'The consecrated ground, remember?'

"'I was wrong,' he whispered. 'I must have been wrong.'

"But that night, something happened. I saw the creature for myself.

"It was a white shape, much like our most trite conception of a ghost. Anderson stood in the doorway of the church, watching it move toward him. Its feet did not touch the ground. I opened my mouth to speak, but I was struck dumb. I saw its bright white face. It extended its white-robed arms and enveloped him in a dark embrace.

"Within seconds, I snapped from my reverie and dashed over to Anderson. He dropped to the ground like a stone. The Samodiva loomed over him. It was tall and white and inhuman. And this is the sight that will haunt me forever. It still crops up in my darkest dreams. You see: *it looked at me.*"

You could have heard a pin drop in that room. The very lights dimmed around us.

"That's enough," said Mrs Soames.

The major seemed to snap awake. "Of course. Apologies, all. Hardly fit subject matter for the dinner table."

"But what happened to Anderson?" asked Bill.

"He, ah, he died. I am sorry I mentioned it. I seem to have soured the mood."

A silence.

"Well," Ruby chipped in, "you must have mentioned it for a reason."

Another lengthy pause. Then, Major Soames said something that has stuck with me ever since. "It's just that lately I have started to feel that same dread as I felt the night Anderson died. As if the Samodiva might have remembered my face. As if it might be coming for me."

* * *

Morning came – a Sunday – and I confess I had not much slept. The house creaked and moaned in the rattling wind and my lonely little room on the top floor looked out on a vast empty expanse of snow-caked earth. The light was insufficient to read, and besides I did not think my concentration was up to it. So I lay there, my eyes wide, staring at the blank ceiling and picturing Major Soames face to face with the Samodiva.

I almost missed breakfast; the family were avid churchgoers and were preparing for the morning's service. All, that is, except Major Soames. He ate little and gazed vacantly at nothing. I was unsurprised when Ruby quietly informed me that he would not be joining us today.

When I spoke to him he responded with the conventional bluster, but in the cold light of day it seemed somehow hollow. "Case of nerves, that's all," he said. "I just need to take a few hours and catch my breath."

"My husband is going to spend the morning at his painting," said Mrs Soames. "He gets the melancholy sometimes. All he needs is a little quiet contemplation."

Mrs Soames wore her usual black. That morning I mentioned it to Ruby: "Why does your mother dress like that all the time?"

Ruby gave a sad little smile, but did not answer.

Cousin Bill too was oddly subdued, but his appetite was hearty and he was the first among us to don his coat and linger at the front door waiting for the off. While the rest of us scrambled into our winter-wear, Major Soames approached his daughter and gave her a damp little peck on the cheek. Then he shook Bill's hand firmly and gave his wife a kiss, at which she almost seemed to shy away. Finally he gave me a warm handshake and when I looked into his eyes I could not escape the feeling that this was a gesture of farewell.

While Bill warmed up the car to take us into the village, Mrs Soames perched on a little stool in the hallway with all the dignity of a crown princess. She wore a curious pair of spectacles, faintly tinted, so her intractable gaze was masked from view.

Major Soames began to mount the stairs and Ruby, unexpectedly, followed him. Half-way up, she turned to me: "Come on!"

I followed. We trailed behind her father as he unlocked the door of the little upstairs room which served as his studio. Then she sprang.

"Daddy!" she called.

He jumped and turned to face us. "What is it, Ruby? I thought you were leaving."

"We just wanted to give you something. A little gift we picked up in London. I was saving it for later, but since you're down in the dumps you might as well have it now."

It was a little trinket we snagged in a pawn shop in Bond Street, but Ruby had fallen in love with it. The old man's face lit up as she produced from her handbag the small velvet box. He plucked it open and studied the object inside.

"And this is from both of you?" he said. We nodded. "It's absolutely marvellous," he went on, placing the object on the flat of his palm. It was an old fob watch, an antique, that Ruby was convinced her father would adore.

"Come in, come in," he said, ushering us into the dank little wood-panelled room. His easel was already set up, with a half-finished still life in place. Various paint pots and jars brimmed with multi-coloured fluids and a row of brushes were lined on a trestle table like a surgeon's instruments. Over in the far corner, covered by a beige tarpaulin, his other paintings lay propped against the wall. The major placed the watch on the large oak sideboard beside a bronze candlestick and began to struggle into his paint-spattered dungarees.

"Thank you both. I know I'm just a superstitious old fool."

"Our pleasure, sir," I said.

"Now get along, both of you, or you'll have my wife to answer to."

We made to go, but before we reached the top of the stairs Ruby turned back and gave her father a hug. She whispered something to him I could not hear. He retreated with that same smile on his face.

Mrs Soames was still waiting in the hall. "Car trouble," she said.

I went out to assist and found Bill in the driveway with the bonnet up and his head buried in the engine.

"Nothing to fret about," he informed me in his gung-ho fashion, "just a loose gasket."

Bill dashed back into the house like an eager schoolboy. I watched him bound past his mother and up the stairs – two at a time – to hammer on the door of his uncle's studio. From my vantage point I could not see the door but I heard it creak open.

"Yes?" said the old man's voice.

"We need the wrench, Major, do you have it in there?"

"One moment." The sound of footsteps from the studio. Then the old man's voice again: "Here, take it."

The door slammed and the lock clicked before Bill could even thank his uncle. Bill returned looking faintly nonplussed. "The old man uses it to adjust the easel," he explained.

Within five minutes the engine was chugging and the four of us were climbing into the car. As we drove away from the house, there was no doubt in my mind that Major Soames was safe and secure in his studio.

* * *

The events of our return from church at half-past twelve now unfold in front of me on an endless loop, like some infinite cinema reel, or spinning zoetrope. The sun was low and orange in the sky. It already seemed like twilight. After a number of hours in an ice-caked church, we rushed into the house to get warm. Ruby and her mother immediately headed for the blazing fireplace in the lounge, while Bill poured out four glasses of brandy.

"Go and see if father's all right will you?" Ruby instructed me.

I took my time going up the stairs. When I rapped on the door I was unsurprised that the old man did not answer straight away. Probably hard at work, or lost in some artistic reverie. But then I knocked again. No answer this time either.

I tried the door handle but it held firm. I dropped to one knee and screwed up my eye at the keyhole, but could see nothing. The key, I concluded, must be in the lock on the other side.

Just as I was getting ready to barge the door open with my shoulder, Bill came up the stairs behind me. "What is it?"

"I can't get any answer out of the old man," I said softly.

Then Ruby joined us, her arms wrapped round her shoulders and a shiver in her voice: "What's going on up here?"

"The old man's locked himself in and fallen asleep or something."

Ruby tried the handle for herself and found the door stuck firm. "Daddy," she called through the wood. No answer.

It took the three of us a good fifteen minutes to break open the door. When we gained entry to the room, what we saw inside is now burned into my memory. That hideous tableau of death. The floor, drenched in blood. The old man himself, seated in a small wooden chair by the window, cold and dead. His half-lidded eyes were fixed on something beyond the glass. On his face was an expression of icy dread.

The events of the crime itself have been recorded and studied in minute detail by criminologists and theorists over the years, but it is perhaps worth outlining them again purely for myself. Major Soames had been dead perhaps half an hour when we found him, though the medical examiner estimated from the amount of blood that he had been stabbed in the stomach perhaps an hour before that. Since we had been out of the house for over three hours, this left the family in the clear.

The room was locked on the inside; the major's were the only fingerprints on the key. The window too was bolted from within. There was no visible weapon, no secret door by which an assailant could have gained entrance. Major Soames had been stabbed in a hermetically sealed room.

We were all questioned and re-questioned. Ruby was hysterical, her mother stoic. Only Bill surprised us in his response: I caught him in the kitchen an hour after the discovery dabbing at his eyes with a tea-towel. He had been crying genuine tears for his dead uncle.

And what of the room itself? Its contents were catalogued and re-catalogued, but no weapon was ever found. The easel, and its never-to-be completed still life of a fruit bowl, had been carelessly knocked over, as though in a struggle. The bowl itself, piled with green apples, stood on a high wooden stool near the window. The trestle table of paint pots and brushes of varying length had also been knocked over. Several jars had been smashed. Interestingly, the beige tarpaulin had been wrenched from the completed paintings in the corner and now lay in a ball in the middle of the floor. Beneath it, investigators found a blackened patch on the bare boards, as though they had been scorched somehow. The walls were bare and white and cold winter sun sent chilly rays through the glass.

I sit now in my own study, watching the snow fall beyond the window. Much has changed in the twenty intervening years. Ruby is now my wife, and sleeps upstairs. She is older; plumper; her hair is greying. Mrs Soames died perhaps a year after her husband. It was pneumonia rather than a broken heart that saw her off.

And today – this morning – I received through the post an answer to the riddle. I now know that when Major Soames told us his story the night before he died, and predicted that his own personal Samodiva would soon catch up with him, he was speaking the truth. I do not know what to do. There is no one to whom I can confide my fears, so I am setting them down in ink. The pieces have always been there, just waiting for me to slot them together. And today it came to me.

* * *

It wasn't until some years after the major's death that I got my first inkling.

In 1942, Cousin Bill was killed. I've mentioned his lust for adventure, so it was no surprise when he expressed a desire to join the RAF. He was to be a pilot.

It was such a stupid and senseless death. Bill lost in a ball of flame. It felt like the end of everything; I do not know quite how Ruby survived the loss.

When the war was over, we travelled for a while. Through battle-scarred Europe to Africa, where I worked as a surgeon. When we got back to England in 1949, we found a country much changed. It was an end of innocence. But somewhere in the back of my mind, lingering like an errant shadow which should not move but does, I had never quite got rid of the Samodiva.

At a surgeon's conference in the spring of 1950, I bumped into a former associate of mine called Barney. Barney had risen to a high-up clerical post in the British Medical Association, and was privy to all the latest gossip.

Taking me by the elbow, he drew me aside. "Have you heard about Hutchings?"

"What about him?" I said, startled, sloshing my cuff with champagne from a brimming glass.

"Arraigned two days ago."

"No! What charge?"

"Bribery. Apparently he was taking kickbacks in order to falsify medical records."

I took a swig of champagne.

"The reason I'm telling you this," Barney went on, "is that I wouldn't want Ruby to find out."

"Find out what?"

"Find out, old chum, that if not for Hutchings then her cousin Bill might still be alive today."

"How so?"

"Bill evidently paid Hutchings to fudge his medical records, so they'd have him in the Air Force. Everybody knows you can't have a colour-blind pilot!"

* * *

I thought back to that weekend – to the furtive glances amongst the family. To the story the major had told. I remember the chilly dread in his eyes when he said he felt the Samodiva was coming for him at last. I remember the way he looked at Ruby and myself on the morning of his death, when he said that final goodbye.

And of course, poor colour-blind Bill, who darted up the stairs to retrieve a wrench. Bill only described in the vaguest terms what he saw in that room: his uncle, he said, was a little curt and strode directly to the wrench in the corner. He seized it and handed it to Bill.

"It was almost as if," I remember Bill saying, "he couldn't wait for me to leave."

That caused considerable intrigue among the investigators. Was the major waiting for someone? No one was ever identified, and of course the snow around the house betrayed no unidentified footprints.

I thought back to that dinner party of the previous evening, and the behaviour of each guest. Ruby was as lively as ever – perhaps more boisterous than usual. The major was in campfire storytelling mode – all sepulchral tones and arched eyebrows. Bill was the adventurer – just a boy at heart really. Mrs Soames was deathly quiet. But the major never quite met her eye.

Perhaps it is easy to construe significance from the most benign circumstances, but I can look back now and see a silent conversation taking place between man and wife at that dinner table. A conversation that was dark and deep, like some burbling underground river. What could be read from that connubial silence? He did not look at his wife as he spoke because his eyes were fixed on Ruby.

* * *

Recently, I attended a lecture at the British Library. The speech was dull enough, but as I was leaving I happened to pass the section labelled 'occult.' I had never noticed this before, and took a few minutes to wander among the stacks.

I was looking for nothing in particular, but when I spotted one title it felt as if providence had led me to it. *Slavic Folklore: A Compendium of Demons and Ghosts.* I picked up the book from the shelf and flipped to the index. There, sure enough, was the word I had been half looking for all along: "Samodiva." The entry was brief, but it was enough to set my imagination in motion.

The Samodiva, it read, *is a fabled fairy or wood-nymph of Indo-European origin. It commonly takes a female, humanoid form, with an affinity for fire.*

The last three words were the key. I replaced the book on the shelf. I was thinking of the blackened boards on the floor of the murder room. And the way Major Soames spoke on the morning of his death, as though he knew something was coming for him.

But I could not leave it there. I needed to know more. Subsequently, I tracked down a more comprehensive overview – a tome bound in yak-skin – from an occult book shop in Camden. This book was titled *Gremlins of Carpathia a*nd it had this to say of the Samodiva:

The Samodiva is less a fleshly creature, and more a manifestation from within. An extrapolation of man's weaknesses and his desires, visited upon him and transmuted into horror.

Of course I said nothing of my endeavours to Ruby. But ideas were forming, and when she was out of the house one day I made certain arrangements, the object of which will soon become clear.

Today – that is, November 30th 1955 – a parcel arrived. It contained a pair of spectacles, slightly tinted, much like the ones Ruby's mother wore that fateful day. I was careful to examine them when Ruby was elsewhere, I do not know what I would have done if she found out.

Slipping the spectacles on, I found myself disorientated. The room around me took on the hue of overexposed photographic negatives. Colours blared like sirens.

Colour-blindness is a hereditary complaint. It is passed down through the genes. Thus, both Mrs Soames and her nephew were apparently afflicted. To my knowledge, Ruby is not. But these spectacles – with corrective lenses – gave me an idea of the effect of the condition upon everyday perceptions. They also gave me the only viable solution to the major's death.

It was a conclusion no one had seriously considered at the time: that when Bill visited the studio to retrieve the wrench, the fatal wound had already been struck. That it was struck in my presence, by the woman who is now my wife.

With a hatpin or some such unobtrusive implement she clutched her father in an embrace and punctured it deep into his guts. *Before my eyes.* The narrowness of the blade belied the depth of the wound. The shock meant he did not necessarily feel the instant pain. But he knew he had been struck.

When Bill visited the room, it is likely the major's wound had only just begun to bleed. But why, if this was the case, did Cousin Bill not react? When I found out Bill was colour blind, that provided me with my answer. To his eye the crimson blood would be indistinguishable from the green paint with which the major's apron was already smeared. And so perhaps he noticed a certain abruptness in the major's demeanour, or the odd twinge in his movements. But he could not have known that he was speaking with a walking dead man.

With the door safely locked behind him, Major Soames had quite a task on his hands. Acutely trained in survival techniques, his first instinct would be to staunch the flow of blood. This is how the blackened patch on the floor came into being – he removed the tarpaulin from the completed canvases and, from the underside of one such canvas, wrenched away the copper wire designed to append the picture to the wall. This, he looped and heated over the candle before – I can only imagine the agony – holding it close to the wound in an attempt to cauterise it. This may have been sufficient to close up the wound temporarily, and staunch the heavy flow of blood.

But then things went wrong. He must have grown woozy, and spilt the contents of a jar with a careless arm. The content was turpentine. This, with the flame of the candle, explains the blackened patch in the centre of the floor. In his panic, the major seized the tarpaulin and used it to suffocate the flames. But this action was enough to wrench open the wound. A wound that had been sealed shut, then wrenched open again: that is the explanation for the time discrepancy of the coroner's report. How the amount of blood the major lost could indicate that he had been stabbed two hours *later.*

The fire completely burned away the fragments of jar and the loop of copper wire, so no trace of them was ever found. All that remained of the fire itself was the black patch on the floor and the lingering smell of chemical fumes in the air. Major Soames collapsed soon after that, the blood loss was too great for him. The blood pooled on the floor, spreading out to cover the black patch left by the fire. But he struggled to the chair, his imminent mortality dawning on him. He sat and looked out at the snow. And that was where he died.

A patricide is a terrible crime to consider. But I am afraid the motive is more troubling still. I remember the major, so certain that the Samodiva was coming for him. But my failing then was that I did not fully understand the *nature* of the Samodiva. It is an embodiment of man's wickedest desires, come back to torment him, and to seek vengeance. I think back to that ill-fated dinner party, and the story the old man told us. He could not meet his wife's eyes – because his gaze was fixed on his daughter.

So you have heard my story. And my theory, such as it is. I will go upstairs now, to Ruby. I shall lean over and kiss her sleeping face, before stretching out fully-clothed on the bed. I think I shall lie there, silent and still as the dead, staring up at the blank white ceiling, waiting for morning.

To Prove an Alibi

L.T. Meade and Robert Eustace

I FIRST MET Arthur Cressley in the late spring of 1892. I had been spending the winter in Egypt, and was returning to Liverpool. One calm evening, about eleven o'clock, while we were still in the Mediterranean, I went on deck to smoke a final cigar before turning in. After pacing up and down for a time I leant over the taff-rail and began idly watching the tiny wavelets with their crests of white fire as they rippled away from the vessel's side. Presently I became aware of some one standing near me, and, turning, saw that it was one of my fellow-passengers, a young man whose name I knew but whose acquaintance I had not yet made. He was entered in the passenger list as Arthur Cressley, belonged to an old family in Derbyshire, and was returning home from Western Australia, where he had made a lot of money. I offered him a light, and after a few preliminary remarks we drifted into a desultory conversation. He told me that he had been in Australia for fifteen years, and having done well was now returning to settle in his native land.

"Then you do not intend going out again?" I asked.

"No," he replied; "I would not go through the last fifteen years for double the money I have made."

"I suppose you will make London your headquarters?"

"Not altogether; but I shall have to spend a good deal of time there. My wish is for a quiet country life, and I intend to take over the old family property. We have a place called Cressley Hall, in Derbyshire, which has belonged to us for centuries. It would be a sort of white elephant, for it has fallen into pitiable decay; but, luckily, I am now in a position to restore it and set it going again in renewed prosperity."

"You are a fortunate man," I answered.

"Perhaps I am," he replied. "Yes, as far as this world's goods go I suppose I am lucky, considering that I arrived in Australia fifteen years ago with practically no money in my pocket. I shall be glad to be home again for many reasons, chiefly because I can save the old property from being sold."

"It is always a pity when a fine old family seat has to go to the hammer for want of funds," I remarked.

"That is true, and Cressley Hall is a superb old place. There is only one drawback to it; but I don't believe there is anything in that," added Cressley in a musing tone.

Knowing him so little I did not feel justified in asking for an explanation. I waited, therefore, without speaking. He soon proceeded:

"I suppose I am rather foolish about it," he continued; "but if I am superstitious, I have abundant reason. For more than a century and a half there has been a strange fatality about any Cressley occupying the Hall. This fatality was first exhibited in 1700, when Barrington Cressley, one of the most abandoned libertines of that time, led his infamous orgies there – of these even history takes note. There are endless legends as to their nature, one of which is that he had personal dealings with the devil in the large turret room, the principal bedroom at the Hall, and was found dead there on the following morning. Certainly since that date a curious doom has hung over the family, and this doom shows itself in a strange way, only attacking those victims who are so unfortunate as to sleep in the turret room. Gilbert Cressley, the young Court favourite of George the Third, was found mysteriously murdered there, and my own great-grandfather paid the penalty by losing his reason within those gloomy walls."

"If the room has such an evil reputation, I wonder that it is occupied," I replied.

"It happens to be far and away the best bedroom in the house, and people always laugh at that sort of thing until they are brought face to face with it. The owner of the property is not only born there, as a rule, but also breathes his last in the old four-poster, the most extraordinary, wonderful old bedstead you ever laid eyes on. Of course I do not believe in any malevolent influences from the unseen world, but the record of disastrous coincidences in that one room is, to say the least of it, curious. Not that this sort of thing will deter me from going into possession, and I intend to put a lot of money into Cressley Hall."

"Has no one been occupying it lately?" I asked.

"Not recently. An old housekeeper has had charge of the place for the last few years. The agent had orders to sell the Hall long ago, but though it has been in the market for a long time I do not believe there was a single offer. Just before I left Australia I wired to Murdock, my agent, that I intended taking over the place, and authorised its withdrawal from the market."

"Have you no relations?" I inquired.

"None at all. Since I have been away my only brother died. It is curious to call it going home when one has no relatives and only friends who have probably forgotten one."

I could not help feeling sorry for Cressley as he described the lonely outlook. Of course, with heaps of money and an old family place he would soon make new friends; but he looked the sort of chap who might be imposed upon, and although he was as nice a fellow as I had ever met, I could not help coming to the conclusion that he was not specially strong, either mentally or physically. He was essentially good-looking, however, and had the indescribable bearing of a man of old family. I wondered how he had managed to make his money. What he told me about his old Hall also excited my interest, and as we talked I managed to allude to my own peculiar hobby, and the delight I took in such old legends.

As the voyage flew by our acquaintance grew apace, ripening into a warm friendship. Cressley told me much of his past life, and finally confided to me one of his real objects in returning to England.

While prospecting up country he had come across some rich veins of gold, and now his intention was to bring out a large syndicate in order to acquire the whole property, which, he anticipated, was worth at least a million. He spoke confidently of this great scheme, but always wound up by informing me that the money which he hoped to make was only of interest to him for the purpose of re-establishing Cressley Hall in its ancient splendour.

As we talked I noticed once or twice that a man stood near us who seemed to take an interest in our conversation. He was a thickly set individual with a florid complexion and a broad German cast of face. He was an inveterate smoker, and when he stood near us with a pipe in his mouth the expression of his face was almost a blank; but watching him closely I saw a look in his eyes which betokened the shrewd man of business, and I could scarcely tell why, but I felt uncomfortable in his presence. This man, Wickham by name, managed to pick up an acquaintance with Cressley, and soon they spent a good deal of time together. They made a contrast as they paced up and down on deck, or played cards in the evening; the Englishman being slight and almost fragile in build, the German of the bulldog order, with a manner at once curt and overbearing. I took a dislike to Wickham, and wondered what Cressley could see in him.

"Who is the fellow?" I asked on one occasion, linking my hand in Cressley's arm and drawing him aside as I spoke.

"Do you mean Wickham?" he answered. "I am sure I cannot tell you. I never met the chap before this voyage. He came on board at King George's Sound, where I also embarked; but he never spoke to me until we were in the Mediterranean. On the whole, Bell, I am inclined to like him; he seems to be downright and honest. He knows a great deal about the bush, too, as he has spent several years there."

"And he gives you the benefit of his information?" I asked.

"I don't suppose he knows more than I do, and it is doubtful whether he has had so rough a time."

"Then in that case he picks your brains."

"What do you mean?"

The young fellow looked at me with those clear grey eyes which were his most attractive feature.

"Nothing," I answered, "nothing; only if you will be guided by a man nearly double your age, I would take care to tell Wickham as little as possible. Have you ever observed that he happens to be about when you and I are engaged in serious conversation?"

"I can't say that I have."

"Well, keep your eyes open and you'll see what I mean. Be as friendly as you like, but don't give him your confidence – that is all."

"You are rather late in advising me on that score," said Cressley, with a somewhat nervous laugh. "Wickham knows all about the old Hall by this time."

"And your superstitious fears with regard to the turret room?" I queried.

"Well, I have hinted at them. You will be surprised, but he is full of sympathy."

"Tell him no more," I said in conclusion.

Cressley made a sort of half-promise, but looked as if he rather resented my interference.

A day or two later we reached Liverpool; I was engaged long ago to stay with some friends in the suburbs, and Cressley took up his abode at the Prince's Hotel. His property was some sixty miles away, and when we parted he insisted on my agreeing to come down and see his place as soon as he had put things a little straight.

I readily promised to do so, provided we could arrange a visit before my return to London.

Nearly a week went by and I saw nothing of Cressley; then, on a certain morning, he called to see me.

"How are you getting on?" I asked.

"Capitally," he replied. "I have been down to the Hall several times with my agent, Murdock, and though the place is in the most shocking condition I shall soon put things in order. But what I have come specially to ask you now is whether you can get away today and come with me to the Hall for a couple of nights. I had arranged with the agent to go down this afternoon in his company, but he has been suddenly taken ill – he is rather bad, I believe – and cannot possibly come with me. He has ordered the housekeeper to get a couple of rooms ready, and though I am afraid it will be rather roughing it, I shall be awfully glad if you can come."

I had arranged to meet a man in London on special business that very evening, and could not put him off; but my irresistible desire to see the old place from the description I had heard of it decided me to make an effort to fall in as well as I could with Cressley's plans.

"I wish I could go with you today," I said; "but that, as it happens, is out of the question. I must run up to town on some pressing business; but if you will allow me I can easily come back again tomorrow. Can you not put off your visit until tomorrow evening?"

"No, I am afraid I cannot do that. I have to meet several of the tenants, and have made all arrangements to go by the five o'clock train this afternoon."

He looked depressed at my refusal, and after a moment said thoughtfully:

"I wish you could have come with me today. When Murdock could not come I thought of you at once – it would have made all the difference."

"I am sorry," I replied; "but I can promise faithfully to be with you tomorrow. I shall enjoy seeing your wonderful old Hall beyond anything; and as to roughing it, I am used to that. You will not mind spending one night there by yourself?"

He looked at me as if he were about to speak, but no words came from his lips.

"What is the matter?" I said, giving him an earnest glance. "By the way, are you going to sleep in the turret room?"

"I am afraid there is no help for it; the housekeeper is certain to get it ready for me. The owner of the property always sleeps there, and it would look like a confession of weakness to ask to be put into another bedroom."

"Nevertheless, if you are nervous, I should not mind that," I said.

"Oh, I don't know that I am absolutely nervous, Bell, but all the same I have a superstition. At the present moment I have the queerest sensation; I feel as if I ought not to pay this visit to the Hall."

"If you intend to live there by-and-by, you must get over this sort of thing," I remarked.

"Oh yes, I must, and I would not yield to it on any account whatever. I am sorry I even mentioned it to you. It is good of you to promise to come tomorrow, and I shall look forward to seeing you. By what train will you come?"

We looked up the local time-table, and I decided on a train which would leave Liverpool about five o'clock.

"The very one that I shall go down by today," said Cressley; "that's capital, I'll meet you with a conveyance of some sort and drive you over. The house is a good two hours' drive from the station, and you cannot get a trap there for love or money."

"By the way," I said, "is there much the matter with your agent?"

"I cannot tell you; he seems bad enough. I went up to his house this morning and saw the wife. It appears that he was suddenly taken ill with a sort of asthmatic attack to which he is subject. While I was talking to Mrs. Murdock, a messenger came down to say that her husband specially wished to see me, so we both went to his room, but he had dozed off into a queer restless sleep before we arrived. The wife said he must not be awakened on any account, but I caught a glimpse of him and he certainly looked bad, and was moaning as if in a good deal of pain. She gave me the keys of a bureau in his room, and I took out some estimates, and left a note for him telling him to come on as soon as he was well enough."

"And your visit to his room never roused him?" I said.

"No, although Mrs. Murdock and I made a pretty good bit of noise moving about and opening and shutting drawers. His moans were quite heartrending – he was evidently in considerable pain; and I was glad to get away, as that sort of thing always upsets me."

"Who is this Murdock?" I asked.

"Oh, the man who has looked after the place for years. I was referred to him by my solicitors. He seems a most capable person, and I hope to goodness he won't be ill long. If he is I shall find myself in rather a fix."

I made no reply to this, and soon afterwards Cressley shook hands with me and departed on his way. I went to my room, packed my belongings, and took the next train to town. The business which I had to get through occupied the whole of that evening and also some hours of the following day. I found I was not able to start for Liverpool before the 12.10 train at Euston, and should not therefore arrive at Lime Street before five o'clock – too late to catch the train for Brent, the nearest station to Cressley's place. Another train left Central Station for Brent, however, at seven o'clock, and I determined to wire to Cressley to tell him to meet me by the latter train. This was the last train in the day, but there was no fear of my missing it.

I arrived at Lime Street almost to the moment and drove straight to the Prince's Hotel, where I had left my bag the day before. Here a telegram awaited me; it was from Cressley, and ran as follows:

"Hope this will reach you time; if so, call at Murdock's house, No. 12, Melville Gardens. If possible see him and get the documents referred to in Schedule A – he will know what you mean. Most important.

"Cressley"

I glanced at the clock in the hall; it was now a quarter past five – my train would leave at seven. I had plenty of time to get something to eat and then go to Murdock's.

Having despatched my telegram to Cressley, telling him to look out for me by the train which arrived at Brent at nine o'clock, I ordered a meal, ate it, and then hailing a cab, gave the driver the number of Murdock's house. Melville Gardens was situated somewhat in the suburbs, and it was twenty minutes' drive from my hotel. When we drew up at Murdock's door I told the cabman to wait, and, getting out, rang the bell. The servant who answered my summons told me that the agent was still very ill and could not be seen by any one. I then inquired for the wife. I was informed that she was out, but would be back soon. I looked at my watch. It was just six o'clock. I determined to wait to see Mrs. Murdock if possible.

Having paid and dismissed my cab, I was shown into a small, untidily kept parlour, where I was left to my own meditations. The weather was hot and the room close. I paced up and down restlessly. The minutes flew by and Mrs. Murdock did not put in an appearance. I looked at my watch, which now pointed to twenty minutes past six. It would take me, in an ordinary cab, nearly twenty minutes to reach the station. In order to make all safe I ought to leave Murdock's house in ten minutes from now at the latest.

I went and stood by the window watching anxiously for Mrs. Murdock to put in an appearance. Melville Gardens was a somewhat lonely place, and few people passed the house, which was old and shabby; it had evidently not been done up for years. I was just turning round in order to ring the bell to leave a message with the servant, when the room door was opened and, to my astonishment, in walked Wickham, the man I had last seen on board the *Euphrates*. He came up to me at once and held out his hand.

"No doubt you are surprised at seeing me here, Mr. Bell," he exclaimed.

"I certainly was for a moment," I answered; but then I added, "The world is a small place, and one soon gets accustomed to acquaintances cropping up in all sorts of unlikely quarters."

"Why unlikely?" said Wickham. "Why should I not know Murdock, who happens to be a very special and very old friend of mine? I might as well ask you why you are interested in him."

"Because I happen to be a friend of Arthur Cressley's," I answered, "and have come here on his business."

"And so am I also a friend of Cressley's. He has asked me to go and see him at Cressley Hall some day, and I hope to avail myself of his invitation. The servant told me that you were waiting for Mrs. Murdock – can I give her any message from you?"

"I want to see Murdock himself," I said, after a pause. "Do you think that it is possible for me to have an interview with him?"

"I left him just now and he was asleep," said Wickham. "He is still very ill, and I think the doctor is a little anxious about him. It would not do to disturb him on any account. Of course, if he happens to awake he might be able to tell you what you want to know. By the way, has it anything to do with Cressley Hall?"

"Yes; I have just had a telegram from Cressley, and the message is somewhat important. You are quite sure that Murdock is asleep?"

"He was when I left the room, but I will go up again and see. Are you going to London to-night, Mr. Bell?"

"No; I am going down to Cressley Hall, and must catch the seven o'clock train. I have not a moment to wait." As I spoke I took out my watch.

"It only wants five-and-twenty minutes to seven," I said, "and I never care to run a train to the last moment. There is no help for it, I suppose I must go without seeing Murdock. Cressley will in all probability send down a message tomorrow for the papers he requires."

"Just stay a moment," said Wickham, putting on an anxious expression; "it is a great pity that you should not see Cressley's agent if it is as vital as all that. Ah! and here comes Mrs. Murdock; wait one moment, I'll go and speak to her."

He went out of the room, and I heard him say something in a low voice in the passage – a woman's voice replied, and the next instant Mrs. Murdock stood before me. She was a tall woman with a sallow face and sandy hair; she had a blank sort of stare about her, and scarcely any expression. Now she fixed her dull, light-blue eyes on my face and held out her hand.

"You are Mr. Bell?" she said. "I have heard of you, of course, from Mr. Cressley. So you are going to spend to-night with him at Cressley Hall. I am glad, for it is a lonely place – the most lonely place I know."

"Pardon me," I interrupted, "I cannot stay to talk to you now or I shall miss my train. Can I see your husband or can I not?"

She glanced at Wickham, then she said with hesitation, –

"If he is asleep it would not do to disturb him, but there is a chance of his being awake now. I don't quite understand about the papers, I wish I did. It would be best for you to see him certainly; follow me upstairs."

"And I tell you what," called Wickham after us, "I'll go and engage a cab, so that you shall lose as short a time as possible, Mr. Bell."

I thanked him and followed the wife upstairs. The stairs were narrow and steep, and we soon reached the small landing at the top. Four bedrooms opened into it. Mrs. Murdock turned the handle of the one which exactly faced the stairs, and we both entered. Here the blinds were down, and the chamber was considerably darkened. The room was a small one, and the greater part of the space was occupied by an old-fashioned Albert bedstead with the curtains pulled forward. Within I could just see the shadowy outline of a figure, and I distinctly heard the feeble groans of the sick man.

"Ah! what a pity, my husband is still asleep," said Mrs. Murdock, as she turned softly round to me and put her finger to her lips. "It would injure him very much to awaken him," she said. "You can go and look at him if you like; you will see how very ill he is. I wonder if I could help you with regard to the papers you want, Mr. Bell?"

"I want the documents referred to in Schedule A," I answered.

"Schedule A?" she repeated, speaking under her breath. "I remember that name. Surely all the papers relating to it are in this drawer. I think I can get them for you."

She crossed the room as she spoke, and standing with her back to the bedstead, took a bunch of keys from a table which stood near and fitted one into the lock of a high bureau made of mahogany. She pulled open a drawer and began to examine its contents.

While she was so occupied I approached the bed, and bending slightly forward, took a good stare at the sick man. I had never seen Murdock before. There was little doubt that he was ill – he looked very ill, indeed. His face was long and cadaverous, the cheek bones were high, and the cheeks below were much sunken in; the lips, which were clean-shaven, were slightly drawn apart, and some broken irregular teeth were visible. The eyebrows were scanty, and the hair was much worn away from the high and hollow forehead. The man looked sick unto death. I had seldom seen any one with an expression like his – the closed eyes were much sunken, and the moaning which came from the livid lips was horrible to listen to.

After giving Murdock a long and earnest stare, I stepped back from the bed, and was just about to speak to Mrs. Murdock, who was rustling papers in the drawer, when the most strong and irresistible curiosity assailed me. I could not account for it, but I felt bound to yield to its suggestions. I turned again and bent close over the sick man. Surely there was something monotonous about that deep-drawn breath; those moans, too, came at wonderfully regular intervals. Scarcely knowing why I did it, I stretched out my hand and laid it on the forehead. Good God! what was the matter? I felt myself turning cold; the perspiration stood out on my own brow. I had not touched a living forehead at all. Flesh was flesh, it was impossible to mistake the feel, but there was no flesh here. The figure in the bed was neither a living nor a dead man, it was a wax representation of one; but why did it moan, and how was it possible for it not to breathe?

Making the greatest effort of my life, I repressed an exclamation, and when Mrs. Murdock approached me with the necessary papers in her hand, took them from her in my usual manner.

"These all relate to Schedule A," she said. "I hope I am not doing wrong in giving them to you without my husband's leave. He looks very ill, does he not?"

"He looks as bad as he can look," I answered. I moved towards the door. Something in my tone must have alarmed her, for a curious expression of fear dilated the pupils of her light blue eyes. She followed me downstairs. A hansom was waiting for me. I nodded to Wickham, did not even wait to shake hands with Mrs. Murdock, and sprang into the cab.

"Central Station!" I shouted to the man; and then as he whipped up his horse and flew down the street, "A sovereign if you get there before seven o'clock."

We were soon dashing quickly along the streets. I did not know Liverpool well, and consequently could not exactly tell where the man was going. When I got into the hansom it wanted twelve minutes to seven o'clock; these minutes were quickly flying, and still no station.

"Are you sure you are going right?" I shouted through the hole in the roof.

"You'll be there in a minute, sir," he answered. "It's Lime Street Station you want, isn't it?"

"No; Central Station," I answered. "I told you Central Station; drive there at once like the very devil. I must catch that train, for it is the last one to-night."

"All right, sir; I can do it," he cried, whipping up his horse again.

Once more I pulled out my watch; the hands pointed to three minutes to seven.

At ten minutes past we were driving into the station. I flung the man half a sovereign, and darted into the booking-office.

"To Brent, sir? The last train has just gone," said the clerk, with an impassive stare at me through the little window.

I flung my bag down in disgust and swore a great oath. But for that idiot of a driver I should have just caught the train. All of a sudden a horrible thought flashed through my brain. Had the cabman been bribed by Wickham? No directions could have been plainer than mine. I had told the man to drive to Central Station. Central Station did not sound the least like Lime Street Station. How was it possible for him to make so grave a mistake?

The more I considered the matter the more certain I was that a black plot was brewing, and that Wickham was in the thick of it. My brain began to whirl with excitement. What was the matter? Why was a lay figure in Murdock's bed? Why had I been taken upstairs to see it? Without any doubt both Mrs. Murdock and Wickham wished me to see what was such an admirable imitation of a sick man – an imitation so good, with those ghastly moans coming from the lips, that it would have taken in the sharpest detective in Scotland Yard. I myself was deceived until I touched the forehead. This state of things had not been brought to pass without a reason. What was the reason? Could it be possible that Murdock was wanted elsewhere, and it was thought well that I should see him in order to prove an alibi, should he be suspected of a ghastly crime? My God! what could this mean? From the first I had mistrusted Wickham. What was he doing in Murdock's house? For what purpose had he bribed the driver of the cab in order to make me lose my train?

The more I thought, the more certain I was that Cressley was in grave danger; and I now determined, cost what it might, to get to him that night.

I left the station, took a cab, and drove back to my hotel. I asked to see the manager. A tall, dark man in a frock-coat emerged from a door at the back of the office and inquired what he could do for me. I begged permission to speak to him alone, and we passed into his private room.

"I am in an extraordinary position," I began. "Circumstances of a private nature make it absolutely necessary that I should go to a place called Cressley Hall, about fourteen miles from Brent. Brent is sixty miles down the line, and the last train has gone. I could take a 'special,' but there might be an interminable delay at Brent, and I prefer to drive straight to Cressley Hall across country. Can you assist me by directing me to some good jobmaster from whom I can hire a carriage and horses?"

The man looked at me with raised eyebrows. He evidently thought I was mad.

"I mean what I say," I added, "and am prepared to back my words with a substantial sum. Can you help me?"

"I dare say you might get a carriage and horses to do it," he replied; "but it is a very long way, and over a hilly country. No two horses could go such a distance without rest. You would have to change from time to time as you went. I will send across to the hotel stables for my man, and you can see him about it."

He rang the bell and gave his orders. In a few moments the jobmaster came in. I hurriedly explained to him what I wanted. At first he said it was impossible, that his best horses were out, and that those he had in his stables could not possibly attempt such a journey; but when I brought out my cheque-book and offered to advance any sum in reason, he hesitated.

"Of course there is one way in which it might be managed, sir. I would take you myself as far as Ovenden, which is five-and-twenty miles from here. There, I know, we could get a pair of fresh horses from the Swan; and if we wired at once from here, horses might be ready at Carlton, which is another twenty miles on the road. But, at our best, sir, it will be between two and three in the morning before we get to Brent."

"I am sorry to hear you say so," I answered; "but it is better to arrive then than to wait until tomorrow. Please send the necessary telegram off without a moment's delay, and get the carriage ready."

"Put the horses in at once, John," said the manager. "You had better take the light wagonette. You ought to get there between one and two in the morning with that."

Then he added, as the man left the room, –

"I suppose, sir, your business is very urgent?"

"It is," I replied shortly.

He looked as if he would like to question me further, but refrained.

A few moments later I had taken my seat beside the driver, and we were speeding at a good round pace through the streets of Liverpool. We passed quickly through the suburbs, and out into the open country. The evening was a lovely one, and the country looked its best. It was difficult to believe, as I drove through the peaceful landscape, that in all probability a dark deed was in contemplation, and that the young man to whom I had taken a most sincere liking was in danger of his life.

As I drove silently by my companion's side I reviewed the whole situation. The more I thought of it the less I liked it. On board the *Euphrates* Wickham had been abnormally interested in Cressley. Cressley had himself confided to him his superstitious dread with regard to the turret room. Cressley had come home with a fortune; and if he floated his syndicate he would be a millionaire. Wickham scarcely looked like a rich man. Then why should he know Murdock, and why should a lay figure be put in Murdock's bed? Why, also, through a most unnatural accident, should I have lost my train?

The more I thought, the graver and graver became my fears. Gradually darkness settled over the land, and then a rising moon flooded the country in its weird light. I had been on many a wild expedition before, but in some ways never a wilder than this. Its very uncertainty, wrapped as it was in unformed suspicions, gave it an air of inexpressible mystery.

On and on we went, reaching Ovenden between nine and ten at night. Here horses were ready for us, and we again started on our way. When we got to Carlton, however, there came a hitch in my well-formed arrangements. We drew up at the little inn, to find the place in total darkness, and all the inhabitants evidently in bed and asleep. With some difficulty we roused the landlord, and asked why the horses which had been telegraphed for had not been got ready.

"We did not get them when the second telegram arrived," was the reply.

"The second telegram!" I cried, my heart beating fast. "What do you mean?"

"There were two, sir, both coming from the same stables. The first was written desiring us to have the horses ready at any cost. The second contradicted the first, and said that the gentleman had changed his mind, and was not going. On receipt of that, sir, I shut up the house as usual, and we all went to bed. I am very sorry if there has been any mistake."

"There has, and a terrible one," I could not help muttering under my breath. My fears were getting graver than ever. Who had sent the second telegram? Was it possible that I had been followed by Wickham, who took these means of circumventing me?

"We must get horses, and at once," I said. "Never mind about the second telegram; it was a mistake."

Peach, the jobmaster, muttered an oath.

"I can't understand what is up," he said. He looked mystified and not too well pleased. Then he added, –

"These horses can't go another step, sir."

"They must if we can get no others," I said. I went up to him, and began to whisper in his ear.

"This is a matter of life and death, my good friend. Only the direst necessity takes me on this journey. The second telegram without doubt was sent by a man whom I am trying to circumvent. I know what I am saying. We must get horses, or these must go on. We have not an instant to lose. There is a conspiracy afoot to do serious injury to the owner of Cressley Hall."

"What! the young gentleman who has just come from Australia? You don't mean to say he is in danger?" said Peach.

"He is in the gravest danger. I don't mind who knows. I have reason for my fears."

While I was speaking the landlord drew near. He overheard some of my last words. The landlord and Peach now exchanged glances. After a moment the landlord spoke, –

"A neighbour of ours, sir, has got two good horses," he said. "He is the doctor in this village. I believe he'll lend them if the case is as urgent as you say."

"Go and ask him," I cried. "You shall have ten pounds if we are on the road in five minutes from the present moment."

At this hint the landlord flew. He came back in an incredibly short space of time, accompanied by the doctor's coachman leading the horses. They were quickly harnessed to the wagonette, and once more we started on our way.

"Now drive as you never drove before in the whole course of your life," I said to Peach. "Money is no object. We have still fifteen miles to go, and over a rough country. You can claim any reward in reason if you get to Cressley Hall within an hour."

"It cannot be done, sir," he replied; but then he glanced at me, and some of the determination in my face was reflected in his. He whipped up the horses. They were thoroughbred animals, and worked well under pressure.

We reached the gates of Cressley Hall between two and three in the morning. Here I thought it best to draw up, and told my coachman that I should not need his services any longer.

"If you are afraid of mischief, sir, would it not be best for me to lie about here?" he asked. "I'd rather be in the neighbourhood in case you want me. I am interested in this here job, sir."

"You may well be, my man. God grant it is not a black business. Well, walk the horses up and down, if you like. If you see nothing of me within the next couple of hours, judge that matters are all right, and return with the horses to Carlton."

This being arranged, I turned from Peach and entered the lodge gates. Just inside was a low cottage surrounded by trees. I paused for a moment to consider what I had better do. My difficulty now was how to obtain admittance to the Hall, for of course it would be shut up and all its inhabitants asleep at this hour. Suddenly an idea struck me. I determined to knock up the lodge-keeper, and to enlist her assistance. I went across to the door, and presently succeeded in rousing the inmates. A woman of about fifty appeared. I explained to her my position, and begged of her to give me her help. She hesitated at first in unutterable astonishment; but then, seeing something in my face which convinced her, I suppose, of the truth of my story, for it was necessary to alarm her in order to induce her to do anything, she said she would do what I wished.

"I know the room where Mitchell, the old housekeeper, sleeps," she said, "and we can easily wake him by throwing stones up at his window. If you'll just wait a minute I'll put a shawl over my head and go with you."

She ran into an inner room and quickly re-appeared. Together we made our way along the drive which, far as I could see, ran through a park studded with old timber. We went round the house to the back entrance, and the woman, after a delay of two or three moments, during which I was on thorns, managed to wake up Mitchell the housekeeper. He came to his window, threw it open, and poked out his head.

"What can be wrong?" he said.

"It is Mr. Bell, James," was the reply, "the gentleman who has been expected at the Hall all the evening; he has come now, and wants you to admit him."

The old man said that he would come downstairs. He did so, and opening a door, stood in front of it, barring my entrance.

"Are you really the gentleman Mr. Cressley has been expecting?" he said.

"I am," I replied; "I missed my train, and was obliged to drive out. There is urgent need why I should see your master immediately; where is he?"

"I hope in bed, sir, and asleep; it is nearly three o'clock in the morning."

"Never mind the hour," I said; "I must see Mr. Cressley immediately. Can you take me to his room?"

"If I am sure that you are Mr. John Bell," said the old man, glancing at me with not unnatural suspicion.

"Rest assured on that point. Here, this is my card, and here is a telegram which I received today from your master."

"But master sent no telegram today."

"You must be mistaken, this is from him."

"I don't understand it, sir, but you look honest, and I suppose I must trust you."

"You will do well to do so," I said.

He moved back and I entered the house. He took me down a passage, and then into a lofty chamber, which probably was the old banqueting-hall. As well as I could see by the light of the candle, it was floored, and panelled with black oak. Round the walls stood figures of knights in armour, with flags and banners hanging from the panels above. I followed the old man up a broad staircase and along endless corridors to a more distant part of the building. We turned now abruptly to our right, and soon began to ascend some turret stairs.

"In which room is your master?" I asked.

"This is his room, sir," said the man. He stood still and pointed to a door.

"Stay where you are; I may want you," I said.

I seized his candle, and holding it above my head, opened the door. The room was a large one, and when I entered was in total darkness. I fancied I heard a rustling in the distance, but could see no one. Then, as my eyes got accustomed to the faint light caused by the candle, I observed at the further end of the chamber a large four-poster bedstead. I immediately noticed something very curious about it. I turned round to the old housekeeper.

"Did you really say that Mr. Cressley was sleeping in this room?" I asked.

"Yes, sir; he must be in bed some hours ago. I left him in the library hunting up old papers, and he told me he was tired and was going to rest early."

"He is not in the bed," I said.

"Not in the bed, sir! Good God!" a note of horror came into the man's voice. "What in the name of fortune is the matter with the bed?"

As the man spoke I rushed forward. Was it really a bed at all? If it was, I had never seen a stranger one. Upon it, covering it from head to foot, was a thick mattress, from the sides of which tassels were hanging. There was no human being lying on the mattress, nor was it made up with sheets and blankets like an ordinary bed. I glanced above me. The posts at the four corners of the bedstead stood like masts. I saw at once what had happened. The canopy had descended upon the bed. Was Cressley beneath? With a shout I desired the old man to come forward, and between us we seized the mattress, and exerting all our force, tried to drag it from the bed. In a moment I saw it was fixed by cords that held it tightly in its place. Whipping out my knife, I severed these, and then hurled the heavy weight from the bed. Beneath lay Cressley, still as death. I put my hand on his heart and uttered a thankful exclamation. It was still beating. I was in time; I had saved him. After all, nothing else mattered during that supreme moment of thankfulness. A few seconds longer beneath that smothering mass and he would have been dead. By what a strange sequence of events had I come to his side just in the nick of time!

"We must take him from this room before he recovers consciousness," I said to the old man, who was surprised and horror-stricken.

"But, sir, in the name of Heaven, what has happened?"

"Let us examine the bed, and I will tell you," I said. I held up the candle as I spoke. A glance at the posts was all-sufficient to show me how the deed had been done. The canopy above, on which the heavy mattress had been placed, was held in position by strong cords which ran through pulleys at the top of the posts. These were thick and heavy enough to withstand the strain. When the cords were released, the canopy, with its heavy weight, must quickly descend upon the unfortunate sleeper, who would be smothered beneath it in a few seconds. Who had planned and executed this murderous device?

There was not a soul to be seen.

"We will take Mr. Cressley into another room and then come back," I said to the housekeeper. "Is there one where we can place him?"

"Yes, sir," was the instant reply; "there's a room on the next floor which was got ready for you."

"Capital," I answered; "we will convey him there at once."

We did so, and after using some restoratives, he came to himself. When he saw me he gazed at me with an expression of horror on his face.

"Am I alive, or is it a dream?" he said.

"You are alive, but you have had a narrow escape of your life," I answered. I then told him how I had found him.

He sat up as I began to speak, and as I continued my narrative his eyes dilated with an expression of terror which I have seldom seen equalled.

"You do not know what I have lived through," he said at last. "I only wonder I retain my reason. Oh, that awful room! no wonder men died and went mad there!"

"Well, speak, Cressley; I am all attention," I said; "you will be the better when you have unburdened yourself."

"I can tell you what happened in a few words," he answered. "You know I mentioned the horrid sort of presentiment I had about coming here at all. That first night I could not make up my mind to sleep in the house, so I went to the little inn at Brent. I received your telegram yesterday, and went to meet you by the last train. When you did not come, I had a tussle with myself; but I could think of no decent excuse for deserting the old place, and so came back. My intention was to sit up the greater part of the night arranging papers in the library. The days are long now, and I thought I might go to bed when morning broke. I was irresistibly sleepy, however, and went up to my room soon after one o'clock. I was determined to think of nothing unpleasant, and got quickly into bed, taking the precaution first to lock the door. I placed the key under my pillow, and, being very tired, soon fell into a heavy sleep. I awoke suddenly, after what seemed but a few minutes, to find the room dark, for the moon must just have set. I was very sleepy, and I wondered vaguely why I had awakened; and then suddenly, without warning, and without cause, a monstrous, unreasonable fear seized me. An indefinable intuition told me that I was not alone – that some horrible presence was near. I do not think the certainty of immediate death could have inspired me with a greater dread than that which suddenly came upon me. I dared not stir hand nor foot. My powers of reason and resistance were paralysed. At last, by an immense effort, I nerved myself to see the worst. Slowly, very slowly, I turned my head and opened my eyes. Against the tapestry at the further corner of the room, in the dark shadow, stood a figure. It stood out quite boldly, emanating from itself a curious light. I had no time to think of phosphorus. It never occurred to me that any trick was being played upon me. I felt certain that I was looking at my ancestor, Barrington Cressley, who had come back to torture me in order to make me give up possession. The figure was that of a man six feet high, and broad in proportion. The face was bent forward and turned toward me, but in the uncertain light I could neither see the features nor the expression. The figure stood as still as a statue, and was evidently watching me. At the end of a moment, which seemed to me an eternity, it began to move, and, with a slow and silent step, approached me. I lay perfectly still, every muscle braced, and watched the figure between half-closed eyelids. It was now within a foot or two of me, and I could distinctly see the face. What was my horror to observe that it wore the features of my agent Murdock.

"'Murdock!' I cried, the word coming in a strangled sound from my throat. The next instant he had sprung upon me. I heard a noise of something rattling above, and saw a huge shadow descending upon me. I did not know what it was, and I felt certain that I was being murdered. The next moment all was lost in unconsciousness. Bell, how queer you look! Was it – was it Murdock? But it could not have been; he was very ill in bed at Liverpool. What in the name of goodness was the awful horror through which I had lived?"

"I can assure you on one point," I answered; "it was no ghost. And as to Murdock, it is more than likely that you did see him."

I then told the poor fellow what I had discovered with regard to the agent, and also my firm conviction that Wickham was at the bottom of it.

Cressley's astonishment was beyond bounds, and I saw at first that he scarcely believed me; but when I said that it was my intention to search the house, he accompanied me.

We both, followed by Mitchell, returned to the ill-fated room; but, though we examined the tapestry and panelling, we could not find the secret means by which the villain had obtained access to the chamber.

"The carriage which brought me here is still waiting just outside the lodge gates," I said. "What do you say to leaving this place at once, and returning, at least, as far as Carlton? We might spend the remainder of the night there, and take the very first train to Liverpool."

"Anything to get away," said Cressley. "I do not feel that I can ever come back to Cressley Hall again."

"You feel that now, but by-and-by your sensations will be different," I answered. As I spoke I called Mitchell to me. I desired him to go at once to the lodge gates and ask the driver of the wagonette to come down to the Hall.

This was done, and half an hour afterwards Cressley and I were on our way back to Carlton. Early the next morning we went to Liverpool. There we visited the police, and I asked to have a warrant taken out for the apprehension of Murdock.

The superintendent, on hearing my tale, suggested that we should go at once to Murdock's house in Melville Gardens. We did so, but it was empty, Murdock, his wife, and Wickham having thought it best to decamp. The superintendent insisted, however, on having the house searched, and in a dark closet at the top we came upon a most extraordinary contrivance. This was no less than an exact representation of the agent's head and neck in wax. In it was a wonderfully skilful imitation of a human larynx, which, by a cunning mechanism of clockwork, could be made exactly to simulate the breathing and low moaning of a human being. This the man had, of course, utilized with the connivance of his wife and Wickham in order to prove an alibi, and the deception was so complete that only my own irresistible curiosity could have enabled me to discover the secret. That night the police were fortunate enough to capture both Murdock and Wickham in a Liverpool slum. Seeing that all was up, the villains made complete confession, and the whole of the black plot was revealed. It appeared that two adventurers, the worst form of scoundrels, knew of Cressley's great discovery in Western Australia, and had made up their minds to forestall him in his claim. One of these men had come some months ago to England, and while in Liverpool had made the acquaintance of Murdock. The other man, Wickham, accompanied Cressley on the voyage in order to keep him in view, and worm as many secrets as possible from him. When Cressley spoke of his superstition with regard to the turret room, it immediately occurred to Wickham to utilize the room for his destruction. Murdock proved a ready tool in the hands of the rogues. They offered him an enormous bribe. And then the three between them evolved the intricate and subtle details of the crime. It was arranged that Murdock was to commit the ghastly deed, and for this purpose he was sent down quietly to Brent disguised as a journeyman the day before Cressley went to the Hall. The men had thought that Cressley would prove an easy prey, but they distrusted me from the first. Their relief was great when they discovered that I could not accompany Cressley to the Hall. And had he spent the first night there, the murder would have been committed; but his nervous terrors inducing him to spend the night at Brent foiled this attempt. Seeing that I was returning to Liverpool, the men now thought that they would use me for their own devices, and made up their minds to decoy me into Murdock's bedroom in order that I might see the wax figure, their object, of course, being that I should be forced to prove an alibi in case Murdock was suspected of the crime. The telegram which reached me at Prince's Hotel on my return from London was sent by one of the ruffians, who was lying in ambush at Brent. When I left Murdock's house, the wife informed Wickham that she thought from my manner I suspected something. He had already taken steps to induce the cab-driver to take me in a wrong direction, in order that I should miss my train, and it was not until he visited the stables outside the Prince's Hotel that he found that I intended to go by road. He then played his last card, when he telegraphed to the inn at Carlton to stop the horses. By Murdock's means Wickham and his confederate had the run of the rooms at the Hall ever since the arrival of Wickham from Australia, and they had rigged up the top of the old bedstead in the way I have described. There was, needless to say, a secret passage at the back of the tapestry, which was so cunningly hidden in the panelling as to baffle all ordinary means of discovery.

Monsters

Marshall J. Moore

"PLEASE DON'T KILL ME," the dead man begged.

As last words went, they were uninspired. Nor was I moved by the tears running down his cheeks, or the dribble of snot clinging to one nostril.

"I'm not going to, Mr. Durant," I said, though the barrel of my silenced pistol remained trained on his temples.

His lower lip trembled. "You're not?"

"No," I said. I pulled a second pistol from my belt, a revolver. Durant's eyes widened. "You're going to kill yourself."

Durant licked his lips, eyes darting from the gun to me. "Is this – this is some sort of trick—"

"It's not," I said. "Put the gun in your mouth, then pull the trigger."

Even to my own ears, my voice sounded flat and clipped. I was in no mood to play games with this groveling wretch.

A laugh escaped his mouth, high and hysterical. "Why the hell would I do that?"

"Because of your daughter."

What little color remained in Durant's face drained away completely.

"Susie is eight years old," I said. "Her favorite school subject is math. She wants to be an astronaut. She sleeps in the second-story bedroom of your townhouse—"

"That's enough!" Spittle sprayed from his lips, his eyes wide and white behind his glasses. "You sick bastard—"

"You will put this gun in your mouth," I repeated, raising my voice over his objections. A rare flash of anger boiled in my stomach. I disliked being interrupted. "You will pull the trigger. You were dead the moment I entered this room, Mr. Durant. It is your choice whether Susie shares your fate or not."

He took the proffered weapon in a shaking hand. He looked down at it, then back up at me. I saw the fear in his eyes, the moment of decision.

Durant raised the revolver –not to his mouth, but at me. The fear in his eyes turned to triumph.

I sidestepped faster than he could track me. The barrel of my silencer pressed against Durant's temple at the exact moment his finger closed on his trigger.

A dull *click* filled the silence, louder than any gunfire.

"Please don't try that again," I said, my voice perfectly level as I pressed the silencer hard against his skull.

Durant licked his lips. "You gave me an unloaded gun?"

"I've been doing this a long time," I said. "There's only one round in the chamber of that revolver. Now, unless you want to ensure little Susie never grows up to become an astronaut, put the gun back in your mouth and pull the trigger as many times as it takes."

The revolver shook violently as Durant raised it to his lips, planting the lightest kiss on the barrel. He looked back up at me, no doubt searching me for some trace of mercy. Others had done the same in his position. If any such feeling existed in me, none of them had found it yet.

"You're a monster," he whispered. As though his condemnation would matter to me.

"The gun, Mr. Durant. Don't make me repeat myself again."

Durant's lips wet the revolver's barrel. His finger tightened around the trigger.

He was wrong about me, I thought as the gunshot roared. A monster would take pleasure in what he had just done.

I felt nothing at all.

* * *

"It's done," I told my broker.

We sat at the bar of an upscale hotel, all dim light and jazz music. The bartender hovered near enough that we could call for her, but far enough that there was no chance of us being overheard. Wealth buys many things, privacy among them.

Anatoly nodded without looking at me. "Any complications?"

"None." Durant's pathetic attempt at self-defense hardly counted.

"Verification?"

I slid an unmarked manila envelope across the bar to him. He opened it, studied the photographs inside. Not for very long. His stomach was weaker than mine.

"I see you convinced Durant to do it himself," he said, placing the envelope in a briefcase leaning against his barstool. He pulled an identical envelope from it and slid it across the bar to me.

"Just a matter of knowing how to apply pressure," I said. I opened the envelope and counted out the bills inside. The agreed upon amount, minus Anatoly's cut.

He wrinkled his nose, unable to hide his distaste. "I don't want to know."

"No," I agreed. "You don't."

Anatoly raised his glass to his lips, swirling the amber liquid within. His pale eyes, watery at the best of times, blinked furiously at the whiskey fumes.

"Do you like what you do?" he asked abruptly.

I looked over at him. He was hunched over the bar, staring fixedly at his Scotch.

"I don't understand the question," I said.

"You know." His watery eyes darted around, making sure the bartender wasn't nearby. "Killing people for money."

"I'm good at it."

"That's not—" Anatoly shook his head, lowered his lips to the glass. "Never mind."

I shrugged. I had no moral compunctions regarding my work. If Anatoly did, that was his problem, not mine.

"Found you another job." Anatoly reached into his briefcase and pulled out yet another envelope, slid it across the bar to me.

"That was fast." I took the envelope but didn't open it. "You verified the client?"

Anatoly nodded. "They're legit."

That was enough to satisfy me. Anatoly dealt with the clients; I handled the targets. Neither of us asked about the other's side of the business. Safer that way.

I pulled the files from the folder. A glossy photo topped the stack, from which a man with blindingly white teeth grinned up at me. Square-jawed and broad-shouldered, with a mop of wavy hair and light blue eyes. He wore a white coat, a stethoscope around his neck.

"A doctor?" I looked back up at Anatoly.

"Dr. Joseph Augustin," he nodded. "Head physician of the geriatric ICU in a Chicago hospital. Pay's seven figures."

He cocked his head, waiting for me to ask the obvious question: why anyone would want to pay upwards of a million dollars to kill a doctor?

I refused to take the bait. If the reason for the hit on Dr. Augustin was relevant, it'd come out during the course of the job. "How do they want it done?"

"No collateral damage or unnecessary casualties. I assured the client you could handle it cleanly and quietly. They want results within a week."

"They'll have them." I stood. "I'll arrange a drop point when it's done."

Anatoly raised his glass in salute. "Good hunting."

* * *

The flight from Paris to Chicago was nine hours –more than long enough to familiarize myself with the contents of Dr. Augustin's dossier.

On first gloss, nothing about him warranted hiring a professional killer to end his life. Hospital newsletters and social media posts indicated he was well-liked by both patients and coworkers, and he had positive relationships with his family. He paid his student loans and mortgage on time but was otherwise debt-free.

"Squeaky clean," I muttered, sipping my water bottle as the plane rumbled around me. I returned to the first page and read again, this time searching for irregularities.

This time a few things stood out. At age twelve, Joseph Augustin had brought home a bad case of the measles, infecting his entire family. He had recovered, but the grandfather who lived with them hadn't.

When Augustin was fifteen, he and a friend had gone swimming in a lake. The friend had drowned, despite what a yellowed local paper described as Augustin's "heroic efforts to resuscitate him." In college he and a girlfriend had gotten into a car wreck. Again Augustin survived, but the girlfriend died in the ambulance, still holding his hand. And his father had passed just after Joseph had graduated medical school, a victim of a sudden and massive heart attack.

More deaths followed. I paged through newspaper clippings and obituaries of friends, relatives, neighbors. Though the losses in Augustin's personal life had abated in recent years, the hospital records of the ICU where he worked painted a bleak picture. Intensive care units in general had a high mortality rate, but the one Augustin oversaw was practically an abattoir. Patients in his care died with grim regularity.

I perused medical files of the deceased over my inflight meal. Of the dozen coroner's reports, all had died of complications after surgery, downward turns in already-precarious illnesses, and other natural causes.

I closed the dossier and stared out at the black Atlantic passing below. Death followed Joseph Augustin wherever he went, through all stages of his life. Some, like those of his grandfather and many of his patients, were apparently natural. Others, like his childhood friend and college girlfriend, seemed like tragic accidents. But I wasn't fooled.

I recognized the work of a fellow killer when I saw it.

* * *

I landed just after midnight and took a cab straight from O'Hare to Augustin's hospital. As I stepped from the car into the muggy Chicago night, I began to understand why the staggering death toll of his ICU had gone unnoticed. The hospital's lack of funding was written across its exterior: half-crumbling brick adorned with spray painted gang tags, broken windows covered over with cardboard and plastic wrap, and a chain-link fence topped with razor wire. Small wonder an institution with visible financial troubles had more to worry about than a high patient mortality rate.

The EMTs lounging against the wall on their smoke break had shadowed eyes and grim-set mouths that spoke to long shifts full of ugly sights. We exchanged vague nods as I passed them unremarked. I was dressed in maroon nurse's scrubs and had a forged lanyard hanging around my neck, both provided by Anatoly's unnamed client upon my arrival in Chicago via an airport lockbox. The security guard barely glanced at my credentials before waving me through.

Gooseflesh prickled on my arms as I walked the corridors. The scent of antiseptics stung my nostrils. Most people disliked hospitals, discomfited by the reminder of their own mortality. But I appreciated the spartan layout of the long hallways, the way the harsh fluorescent lights painted everything in stark relief. I imagine my mind was built along a similar blueprint.

According to the schedule in his dossier, Dr. Augustin was currently on hour forty of a sixty-hour shift. I had a three-minute window where he was alone in the ICU while the attending nurses changed shifts. Tight, but I had worked under worse constraints.

The ICU was at the end of a long third floor hallway lined with storage closets. I jimmied the lock on one and slipped inside. Thirty seconds later I stepped back into the hallway, a hypodermic needle filled with ninety milligrams of morphine tucked into the pocket of my scrubs.

"What do you think you're doing?"

A tall woman was walking down the hall towards me. Her features were Mediterranean, with sharp cheekbones and a slender neck, her hair pulled back in a ponytail. She wore a white coat over her scrubs, with *Dr. Alexandria Brandt* sewn onto it in blue thread.

"Those supply closets are off-limits for nonpharmaceutical staff," she said, coming to a halt a few paces away. "Your scrubs are the wrong color for pharma, Nurse...?"

"Hunt," I said. I shifted my weight from foot to foot, playing the part of the cringing nurse. "Dr. Mehtani sent me to find him some prescription painkillers..."

Dr. Brandt snorted. "The only painkiller in that closet is morphine, Hunt. You get lost or what?"

"Sorry," I said. "I just transferred here from County General. Still learning my way around."

Brandt furrowed her brow and peered over my shoulder. "How'd you get into that closet, anyway? It should be locked."

"It wasn't," I said, slipping a hand into the pocket containing the morphine-filled needle. Two steps and I could plunge it into her neck, injecting her with the lethal dose I had prepared for Augustin. Then I could drag her into the supply closet, refill the needle, and finish Augustin in the same way.

"Dammit," Brandt ground her teeth, ran a hand through her hair. "Augustin must have left it unlocked. I'm going to kill him."

Not if I do first, I thought. "Augustin's the one Dr. Mehtani wanted me to get the prescription pills for. Said he'd requested them for one of the ICU patients." I looked at the double doors at the end of the hallway. "That *is* the ICU, right?"

"Right." Brandt pursed her lips, looking frankly at me. "Tell you what, Hunt. I'll go find you your pills, and you go in there and let Augustin know that I'll be along shortly to tell him how he badly he fucked up. Alright?"

"Sure," I said. "Thank you."

"Don't mention it." Brandt turned and walked down the hall. I watched her go, waiting until she had descended the stairs before I turned back to the ICU.

By the time she came back, Augustin would already be dead.

* * *

The ICU smelled like death.

It was a smell I was intimately familiar with: stale and dry, yet somehow cloying. It hung in the mouth more than the nose, as though it were trying to force its way down my throat.

I adjusted my grip on the needle in my pocket and moved down the rows of hospital beds. Most were empty, but a few were occupied by elderly patients, frail and wrinkled in their hospital gowns. Some had cannula sticking from their nostrils, while others slept with ventilators covering their entire faces. The machines hooked to them beeped intermittently.

A wild impulse to unplug those machines seized me as I walked the aisles of the dying. These people were already corpses. Their minds hadn't accepted that truth yet, but their bodies had. Their time was over, and lingering would only prolong their suffering.

At least the death I gave was clean.

"Can I help you?"

Joseph Augustin stood before me in the flesh, standing over a patient's bedside. There were deep bags under his eyes, but he looked alert and wary as he regarded me.

"Dr. Augustin?" I gave him a nervous smile. "I'm your new attending. Dan Hunt."

I held out a hand for him to shake, the other gripping the needle in my pocket. One quick jab and my job was done.

Augustin frowned down at my hand, then back up at me. He was a handsome man in his late thirties, but up close I could see the hollow look in his eyes, the gauntness of his cheeks.

"Joseph Augustin," he said at last. He reached for my hand. My fingers tightened on the needle.

A beeping split the air, high and frantic. Augustin whirled towards one of the occupied beds. The elderly woman in it twitched feebly, as though in the grips of a nightmare. The heartrate monitor above her leapt erratically from wild spikes to deep valleys.

"Get the defibrillator!" Augustin shouted, rushing towards the dying woman's bed. "Hurry!"

He was already out of reach. Grinding my teeth in frustration, I looked around, found the defibrillator affixed to the wall. I hurried towards it, an idea forming in my head. The device delivered a powerful electric shock, enough to restart a stopped heart –or to still a beating one.

I pulled the defibrillator from the wall and raced across the room to where Augustin bent over the elderly woman, rhythmically pumping at her chest with his closed fists. I was once again struck by the gauntness of his features.

I drew nearer, arming the defibrillator. One swift shock would incapacitate Augustin. And if that didn't kill him, there was still the morphine in my pocket.

Augustin bent over the elderly woman and pressed his mouth to hers. I reached him, raised the defibrillator paddles.

Something moved beneath the skin of his face.

It was subtle, just a slight bulge against the flesh of his hollow cheeks. I stood in paralyzed fascination as it traveled along his jaw and down his throat, like an insect that had burrowed under his skin.

The dying woman whimpered, but Augustin's lips didn't leave hers. He made a sick gulping sound, and another bulge appeared on his face.

He's drinking her. The thought came to me, absurd and impossible. Yet there was no denying what I was seeing.

The heartrate monitor wailed a high, keening note as its green line flattened.

Augustin jerked away from the dead woman, his lips wet with something clear and viscous. His eyes shone red, like some nocturnal animal caught in the headlights.

"Shit," he said. His voice was throaty and raw. "You weren't supposed to see that."

Instinct overcame my shock. I thrust the defibrillator paddles against his chest.

"Clear," I said.

The shock threw Augustin across the room, into the far wall. I heard the sound of bones snapping as he landed in a heap on the floor. The heart monitor still sang its dirge as I stalked towards him, needle in hand.

My suspicion had been right. Augustin *had* been killing off his patients, and likely the people who had died around him prior to that. Not only that, but he had been...feeding off them, somehow.

Time to worry about that later. I had a job to complete.

Augustin rose suddenly, a hideous cracking filling the air as his broken bones knit themselves back together. His red eyes fixed on me, glimmering balefully. He snarled, revealing a mouth full of snaggle teeth like something that had evolved in the most lightless reaches of the deep ocean.

I reached for the morphine needle in my pocket, but Augustin leapt for me, blindingly fast. A high ringing filled my ears as my head cracked against the tile floor. The needle went rolling from my hand.

My lungs screamed in protest as Augustin pressed his knees against my chest, one hand on my throat.

"I should have known," he said through his nightmare teeth, his voice a throaty rasp. "Someone was going to catch on eventually. Who sent you?"

I said nothing.

"Talk!" Augustin snarled. He slammed his fist into my brow, and my vision blurred. My free hand clawed blindly across the floor. Where was the needle?

"I'm going to ask you again." Augustin clamped both hands around my neck and squeezed. "Who. Sent. You?"

"I don't know," I wheezed. I shook my head wildly, hoping the motion would distract from my searching hand. "I don't know, I swear."

"Too bad for you," Augustin growled, tightening around my throat. The heartrate monitor continued to wail. Augustin glanced up at the line of hospital beds, at the woman he had killed.

"You don't know what it's like," he said, his ragged voice a whisper. "The hunger. I try to ignore it, to resist, but it always wins. I lost control, just now. Couldn't help myself from taking all that poor woman had left."

My fingertips brushed something plastic. The needle, just out of reach.

Augustin's hands tightened around my throat, so hard that my vision went wholly black. When it returned his red eyes were inches from mine.

"But you?" he said, snaggleteeth splitting in a horrific parody of a grin. "I'm going to enjoy draining you."

A creak split the air. Augustin's head whipped to the side.

"Joe," Dr. Brandt said, shutting the door behind her. "Do you have any idea where I just caught one of your nurses—"

She trailed off at the sight of Augustin crouched over me, his face something out of a nightmare. Her hand flew to her mouth.

"Alex," Augustin rasped. "I—"

His grip around my neck loosened just enough for me to reach the needle.

I stabbed it into his throat, directly into his carotid artery. Augustin's head jerked back towards me, red eyes widening.

Then he pitched to the side like a felled tree, crashing against the tile floor.

"Hunt?" Footsteps rang against the tiles as Brandt hurried over to me. She reached down a hand and pulled me roughly to my feet. "God, are you okay?"

I nodded feebly. My bruised throat screamed in protest as I gasped down a deep lungful of air.

"Yeah," I croaked. "I'm fine. I—"

Brandt's hand darted out, jabbing my neck. A stinging sensation pierced the bruises already forming around my throat.

"That's good," Brandt said, pulling her hand away. A clear droplet of glistening liquid hung from the tip of the needle in her hand. Her expression was no longer terrified, but bemused. "We wanted you alive."

"Alive?" I repeated thickly. My vision was going blurry again, the world swimming out of focus. I reached for Brandt, stumbled to the floor.

"Alive," Brandt repeated, a blurred shadow above me. "But first we needed to see that you were worth the effort. An audition…"

I didn't hear the rest. I was already deep inside the sweet poppy-dreams.

* * *

The interrogation room was identical to those others I'd found myself in over the course of my career: bare cinderblock walls lit by a flickering fluorescent overhead lamp. My hands were cuffed to the metal table, leaving me to stare at my reflection in the two-way mirror.

I'd looked better. A purple bruise bloomed over my left temple, and my throat looked green where Augustin had choked me. I ran my tongue over my chapped lips, but my mouth was so dry it made no difference.

The door screeched open on rusting hinges. Dr. Alexandria Brandt entered, though not as I'd last seen her. She had exchanged the scrubs for a suit, and her hair was a neat bun instead of a ponytail. Her heels clacked across the concrete floor.

She sat in the chair opposite me and set a file folder on the table between us.

"Ms. Brandt," I said, my chapped lips splitting in a thin smile. "You're looking well."

She studied me for a moment before replying, her dark eyes searching. "Can't say the same for you."

"I'm guessing Brandt isn't your real name."

"No more than Hunt is yours." She pursed her lips, paging through the folder. I caught brief glimpses of typewritten pages, thick black redactions scored through them like tiger stripes. Black and white photographs with the grainy, unfocused resolution of security footage. Color photos of blood and bodies, some of which I recognized.

"Jakarta, Mexico City, San Francisco, Paris," Brandt said. "All within the last two months. You're quite the globetrotter."

"Lots of people travel for work."

"Not all of them leave a trail of bodies behind them when they do." She checked her files again. "By our estimation you're responsible for some thirty-two killings over the last five years alone. Corporate bigwigs, oil tycoons, crime bosses. Even the odd politician here and there."

I glanced over Brandt's shoulder at my reflection. "Who's on the other side of the mirror? FBI, CIA? Interpol?"

"None of those." She leaned forward, elbows resting on the table. "As you've no doubt noticed, Mr. Augustin was not…typical of your victims."

The sound of Augustin's bones rippling and twisting beneath his skin came to me, stark in its clarity. I licked my chapped lips.

"No," I said. "He wasn't."

"Most of our targets aren't."

My gaze flicked to the mirror, back to her. "Not a fed. Not Interpol. Who are you really, Miss Brandt?"

"Call me Roth." She steepled her fingers. "I work with a black ops agency that specializes in extrahuman entities."

"Extrahuman?"

"You and I were in the same room," Brandt –no, Roth—said. "Do you think Joseph Augustin was a member of *homo sapiens?*"

"I suppose not," I said, remembering the gleam of those snaggle teeth, the red glint of Augustin's eyes. "He died like one, though."

"Indeed he did," Roth nodded. "Which is why you're here, Mr. Hunt."

"Handcuffed to a chair," I said, jangling my manacles. "Poor thanks for a job well done."

"Consider it a precaution," Roth said. "You have a reputation for not leaving witnesses."

That was true. "Am I under arrest?"

"That depends on you." She leaned forward. "There's no shortage of things out there in the dark corners of the world. Creatures like the one that called itself Joseph Augustin, lurking in the shadows to prey on humanity. My agency's role is to keep those creatures on the margins. Shine a light into the dark so that they scatter like cockroaches, and stomp out any that don't crawl into their holes quickly enough."

"Let me guess," I said, my tone as dry as my chapped lips. "You want me to do the stomping."

The corner of Roth's mouth quirked upwards. "Precisely."

"And if I say no?"

Roth threw a meaningful glance over her shoulder. "I can get Interpol on the other side of that mirror in half an hour."

I matched Roth's false smile with one of my own. "You're putting me on a leash."

"A long one," she said, folding her arms. "We've been watching you for some time, Mr. Hunt. We know you work best operating under your own constraints –and we *are* admirers of your work, believe it or not."

She pulled a file from the folder, slid it across the table.

"That's your annual stipend," she said, tapping a six-digit figure near the top. "Enough to cover your travel, lodging, equipment, and other expenses. You'll go where we tell you to, kill who and what we tell you to. Hardly a difference from how you live now, really."

The gulf between working as an independent operator and doing so collared by an unknown government agency was vast, but this wasn't the time to split hairs. Roth had backed me into a corner with an efficiency I couldn't help admiring.

"Say I accept," I said, studying the document before me. "What's to keep me from running the moment I'm out of this room? Or on a job?"

"Practically?" Roth shrugged. "Nothing. But we found you once, Mr. Hunt. We can do it again. And if we do…"

She selected a photograph from the folder and slid it to me. Older than the others, the colors faded. Four bodies, two of them smaller than the others. Much smaller.

"We're in the business of hunting monsters." Her voice was tight as a coiled spring.

I didn't need to look at that photograph. The sight had been etched into my memory well before I had awoken in this room. An early job, back when I was young and arrogant. That overconfidence in my capability had botched the job, made things messy.

There should only have been one body in that photo.

I looked down at my manacled hands. Augustin's blood was a brown crust beneath my fingernails.

If what Roth said was true, there were other creatures out there. Parasites like Augustin that preyed on those too weak to fight back. I was no great judge of morality, but if any creatures truly deserved death, these did. Perhaps it was only fitting that Roth had selected someone just as removed from common humanity to hunt her monsters.

I looked up to see her watching me. Silent. Waiting.

Keeping someone with my skillset was a double-edged sword for her and her unnamed agency. Right now Roth regarded me with naked suspicion. But the longer I worked for her, the more that initial misapprehension would fade. If I followed her orders to the letter –went where I was told to go, killed who I was told to kill – she might even come to regard me with some measure of trust.

It was human nature. Familiarity breeds comfort. Eventually, she would let her guard down.

And that was the moment I would plant a knife in her back.

"Alright," I said, holding out my bloodstained hand for her to shake. "I'll be your monster."

Princes in the Tower
An Extract
Thomas More

[Publisher's Note: This extract from The History of King Richard III *tells the tale of the two young sons of King Edward IV who were kept in the Tower of London, supposedly in preparation for Edward V's forthcoming coronation. They were never seen again.]*

WHEN HE HADDE BEGONNE his reygne the – daye of June, after this mockishe eleccion, than was he crowned the – day of the same moneth. And that solemnitie was furnished for the most part with the selfe same prouision that was appointed for the coronacion of his nephew.

Now fell ther mischieues thick. And as the thinge euill gotten is neuer well kept, through all the time of his reygne, neuer ceased there cruel death and slaughter, till his owne destruccion ended it. But as he finished his time with the beste death, and the most righteous, that is to wyt his own; so began he with the most piteous and wicked, I meane the lamentable murther of his innocent nephewes, the young king and his tender brother. Whose death and final infortune hathe natheles so far comen in question, that some remain yet in doubt, whither they wer in his dayes destroyde or no. Not for that onely that Perken Werbecke, by many folkes malice, and more folkes foly, so long space abusyng the worlde, was, as wel with princes as the porer people, reputed and taken for the yonger of those two, but for that also that all thynges wer in late daies so couertly demeaned one thing pretended and an other ment, that there was nothyng so plaine and openly proued, but that yet for the comen custome of close and couert dealing, men had it euer inwardely suspect, as many well counterfaited jewels make the true mistrusted. Howbeit concerning the opinion, with the occasions mouing either partie, we shal haue place more at large to entreate, yf we hereafter happen to write the time of the late noble prince of famous memory king Henry the seuenth, or parcase that history of Perkin in any compendious processe by it selfe. But in the meane time for this present matter, I shall rehearse you the dolorous end of those babes, not after euery way that I haue heard, but after that way that I haue so hard by suche men and by such meanes, as me thinketh it wer hard but it should be true. King Richarde after his coronacion, takyng his way to Gloucester to visit, in his newe honor, the towne of which he bare the name of his old, deuised as he roode to fulfil that thing which he before had intended. And forasmuch as his minde gaue him that, his nephewes liuing, men woulde not recken that hee could haue right to the realm, he thought therfore without delay to rid them, as though the killing of his kinsmen could amend his cause, and make him a kindly king. Whereuppon he sent one John Grene, whom he specially trusted, vnto sir Robert Brakenbery constable of the Tower, with a letter and credence also, that the same sir Robert shoulde in any wise put the two children to death. This John Grene did his errande vnto Brakenbery kneling before our Lady in the Tower, who plainely answered that he would neuer putte them to death to dye therfore, with which answer Jhon Grene returning recounted the same to Kynge Richarde at Warwick yet in his way.

Wherwith he toke such displeasure and thought, that the same night, he said vnto a secrete page of his: Ah whome shall a man trust? those that I haue broughte vp my selfe, those that I had went would most surely serue me, euen those fayle me, and at my commaundemente wyll do nothyng for me. Sir, quod his page, there lyeth one on your paylet without, that I dare well say, to do your grace pleasure, the thyng were right harde that he wold refuse, meaning this by sir James Tyrell, which was a man of right goodlye parsonage, and for natures gyftes, worthy to haue serued a muche better prince, if he had well serued God, and by grace obtayned as muche trouthe and good wil as he had strength and wilte. The man had an high heart, and sore longed vpwarde, not rising yet so fast as he had hoped, being hindered and kept vnder by the meanes of sir Richarde Ratclifc and sir William Catesby, which longing for no moo parteners of the princes fauour, and namely not for hym, whose pride thei wist would beare no pere, kept him by secrete driftes oute of all secrete trust. Whiche thyng this page wel had marked and knowen. Wherefore thys occasion offered, of very speciall frendship he toke his time to put him forward, and by such wise doe him good, that al the enemies he had except the deuil, could neuer haue done him so muche hurte. For vpon this pages wordes king Richard arose. (For this communicacion had he sitting at the draught, a conuenient carpet for such a counsaile) and came out in to the pallet chamber, on which he found in bed sir James and sir Thomas Tyrels, of parson like and brethren of blood, but nothing of kin in condicions. Then said the king merely to them: What, sirs, be ye in bed so soone? And calling vp syr James, brake to him secretely his mind in this mischieuous matter. In whiche he founde him nothing strange. Wherfore on the morow he sente him to Brakenbury with a letter, by which he was commaunded to deliuer sir James all the kayes of the Tower for one nyght, to the ende he might there accomplish the kinges pleasure, in such thing as he had geuen him commaundement. After which letter deliuered and the kayes receiued, sir James appointed the night nexte ensuing to destroy them, deuysing before and preparing the meanes. The prince, as soone as the protector left that name and toke himself as king, had it shewed vnto him, that he should not reigne, but his vncle should haue the crowne. At which worde the prince sore abashed, began to sigh and said: Alas I woulde my vncle woulde lette me haue my lyfe yet, though I lese my kingdome. Then he that tolde him the tale, vsed him with good wordes, and put him in the best comfort he could. But forthwith was the prince and his brother bothe shet vp, and all other remoued from them, onely one called black Wil or William Slaughter except, set to serue them and see them sure. After whiche time the prince neuer tyed his pointes, nor ought rought of hymselfe, but with that young babe hys brother, lingered in thought and heauines til this tratorous death delivered them of that wretchednes. F'or sir James Tirel deuised that thei shold be murthered in their beddes. To the execucion wherof, he appointed Miles Forest, one of the foure that kept them, a felowe fleshed in murther before time. To him he joyned one John Dighton, bis own horsekeper, a big brode square strong knaue. Then al the other beeing remoued from them, thys Miles Forest and John Dighton, about midnight (the sely children lying in their beddes) came into the chamber, and sodainly lapped them vp among the clothes, so bewrapped them and entangled them, keping down by force the fetherbed and pillowes hard vnto their mouthes, that within a while smored and stifled, theyr breath failing, thei gaue vp to God their innocent soules into the joyes of heauen, leauing to the tormentors their bodyes dead in the bed. Whiche after that the wretches parceiued, first by the strugling with the paines of death, and after long lying styll, to be throughly dead; they laide their bodies naked out vppon the bed, and fetched sir James to see them. Which vpon the sight of them, caused those murtherers to burye them at the stayre foote, metely depe in the grounde vnder a great heape of stones. Than rode sir James in great hast to king Richarde, and shewed him al the maner of the murther, who gaue bym gret thanks and, as som say, there made him knight.

Rockin' Around the Murder Tree

Jane Nightshade

AND NOW *on this crisp and crunchy Christmas Eve in the fast-disappearing year of 1958, let's ease into the hottest new Christmas song of the season,* Rockin' Around the Christmas Tree, *by the little lady with the great big voice, lovely Miss Brenda Lee. This is Howlin' Howie Holtzman for K-K-R-S Merrivale, the station that puts the C-H-R-I-S in Christmas!*

Sally turned the radio dial up and smiled happily: the new song by Brenda Lee was one of her favorites. It was just past six and Ben would be home soon; she hummed along while pinning pineapple rings with dried cloves to a hunk of pressed ham. Into the oven soon, and then she'd turn the Jell-O out of the mold onto a bed of cottage cheese and crimson radishes carved into rosettes; it was Ben's favorite treat, lime Jell-O with fruit cocktail inside. The mold was a special aluminum one that Sally had bought just before quitting her job at the five-and-dime, shaped like a Christmas tree. She'd bought a jar of maraschino cherries and planned to put one on top of each quivery, Jell-O'd tree branch, to look like ornaments.

"Red, green, and white – cheerful Christmas colors!" she thought as she fussed with the Jell-O. That, with the ham and the mashed potatoes with tomato gravy and the Parkerhouse rolls would make quite a perfect Christmas Eve dinner for the two of them. Simple but hearty.

They didn't have much, Sally and Ben. Nineteen and twenty-one years old respectively, married for just one year and one month. Ben worked the forklift at a paint plant in the big city, and Sally had worked at the only five-and-dime in Merrivale until six weeks before; the store manager wouldn't let her stay on when they found out she was expecting Ben Junior – or maybe a little Sally-ette! – she wasn't picky, but she knew that Ben had his heart set on a boy. They had to live now on just Ben's wages, but so far, so good. Ben was doing well at the plant and had his eye on advancing to forklift supervisor soon. Sally saved as much as she could and the rent on their apartment was cheap. Someday they would have a little house of their own, filled with children. Sally, who was raised by her grandparents after her mother died and her father ran off, drinking to forget his grief, wanted at least four.

After dinner they'd have their special treat, ginger sponge cake washed down with Borden's eggnog, and then they'd walk around the neighborhood arm-in-arm, looking at all the Christmas lights. Sally loved the Christmas lights in Merrivale.

This is Howlin' Howie again with Santa Baby *from that p-u-r-r-i-n-g Hollywood kittenish sensation, Miss Eartha Kitt, and then we'll have a special recorded holiday message from President Eisenhower – Wait! here's a live bulletin just in from the Merrivale police...*

Sally didn't get to hear the beginning of the special police bulletin; the door buzzer sounded, and she turned reluctantly away from the kitchen and puttered to the front door, looking through the peephole. It was Lewis, the grown son of Mrs. Popkin from 2G down the hall, who still lived with his mother despite, at twenty-two, being a whole year older than Ben; Sally was sure he'd never even had a girlfriend before. He could barely look her in the eye whenever they met; according to Mrs. Popkin, he spent most of his free time in his room, putting together Bakelite plastic models of dinosaurs and movie monsters. Their apartment always smelled of model glue and enamel paint, whenever Sally would go over to watch her favorite daytime shows, *Queen for a Day* or *The Secret Storm*.

She and Ben did not have a television; they made do with the radio and Sally's neat little aqua-colored suitcase record player, which Grammy Ammy had bought her in high school. Ben said they'd get a TV sometime soon, but in the meantime, Mrs. Popkin was plenty generous with hers. Anyways, Ben didn't like Sally watching the serial television dramas that people were just starting to call by the derisive term, "soap operas," so Sally was deliberately vague when he asked about her visits with Mrs. Popkin. "Women *like that!*" Ben would shake his head whenever he heard a woman talking about soap operas, frowning and disapproving. "The trashy ideas they get from those shows!"

Sally opened her front door. Lewis had started working as a delivery boy for McKenna's Scotch Country Market six months before. He was dressed neatly in his delivery uniform: white cotton twill overalls under a zip-up dark blue nylon jacket, finished at the top with a jaunty navy-blue bow tie. On his awkwardly red-haired head, there perched a dark blue, billed cap with *McKenna's* spelled out across the front in white embroidery. Sally had heard that he'd been let go from his old job in the big city because of some vague "trouble" or other; Mrs. Popkin said his boss was cruel and unfair because Lewis was "shy" and "delicate."

"Good evening, Lewis! Merry Christmas!"

Lewis gulped jerkily. "U-m-m-m, M-M-Merry Christmas to you too, Sall— uh—*Miz*— uh—*Kelly.* I've got your Borden's eggnog and the fruitcake for your Grammy Ammy and a little something extra too! McKenna's is giving a special gift out to all of its steady customers for the holiday season." He handed her a small grocery sack and a gaily wrapped package, about the size of a shoebox, with a big, satiny, red bow on top.

"Oh, swell," said Sally. "What is it?" Lewis got an odd, furtive smirk on his face – or at least that was how Sally saw it – and then sputtered, "It's a secret. You're not supposed to open it until tomorrow."

"Oh," said Sally. "I won't! I promise...Well, I've got to get back to the kitchen and get my ham out of the oven and finish the mashed potatoes. And this eggnog needs to go in the icebox. Nice talking to you, Lewis."

"Mashed potatoes? With tomato gravy? They're...they're my favorites." He stood expectantly in the doorway, as if he thought she would invite him to stay for dinner at any minute. "Lewis, your mother needs you home tonight, of all nights! You need to get home as soon as you finish your deliveries, or it will ruin her Christmas Eve," said Sally, kindly but firmly.

Lewis shrugged, ungainly as always, with his slightly crooked shoulders. It always seemed to Sally as if something would come flying off whenever Lewis moved too quickly. "See ya around, Miz Kelly. Okey-dokey. I'm goin' home."

"See you around. Merry Christmas."

She closed the door after him quickly, glad he was gone. He always made her feel ever-so-slightly uncomfortable. "He gives me the heebie-jeebies," she'd told Ben once. "He's put together like a Tinkertoy; his clothes never fit right even when Mrs. Popkin has them altered at Swanson's department store." "He's harmless," Ben had said at the time, shaking his head disapprovingly. "An overgrown boy, because she treats him like a baby, and bosses him around so much. Women *like that*—"

Sally shoved the gift-wrapped package from McKenna's under the little tabletop tree on the coffee table in the living room, barely glancing at it. It was six-thirty now; she had hardly enough time to finish dinner and make herself presentable before Ben was expected at seven. He was working late for the double overtime; he deserved to see her look nice. It wouldn't do for her to greet him at the door dressed the way she currently looked, in a pair of red pedal pushers, which she'd let out at the waist to accommodate her slightly expanding middle, and a baggy sweatshirt with her high school letters printed on the front. She would change after getting dinner settled, just before Ben got home.

She planned to wear her red-and-green plaid dress with the full, New Look skirt, and the black velvet collar and cuffs, her good black pumps, and her tiny seed-pearl necklace that Ben had given her on their wedding day. And, of course, she'd have to pull out her hair-curlers and comb her curls out, and put a slick of Tangee on her lips. She didn't need much make-up, and Ben didn't like it anyway, but he didn't mind a thin coat of Tangee and a little light dust of rouge.

Surprisingly, Howlin' Howie was still reading his police bulletin over the radio as Sally trotted quickly back into the kitchen. She didn't pay much attention to the radio as she checked on the ham, but then she stiffened up sharply when she heard the words, "gift giver." Quickly she turned the dial up again.

...the package was found at 5:45 p.m. on top of a freestanding mailbox on Carpenter Blvd. Passers- by describe a tall, thin boy or man who looked to be wearing some sort of light-colored work uniform or overalls, with a dark jacket over it, and a dark cap with embroidered script on the front. Detectives aren't willing to say at this juncture whether or not it was left by The Gift Giver but it follows his established pattern. Merrivale residents are cautioned to stay calm, but keep an eye out for any suspicious, unattended packages in public places, especially if they are wrapped in the distinctive, green-red-and-white striped wrapping paper with gold glitter sprinkled on it, which The Gift Giver always prefers to use...

The Gift Giver! Sally shuddered. *The Gift Giver was in Merrivale!* She could hardly believe it.

Two years ago, at Christmastime, the packages had started to appear in public places in the big city, perched on park benches or freestanding mailboxes or fence pillars, always wrapped in the same paper – and always containing the freshly detached body part of a young woman – an arm, a foot, a head. The mutilated, headless torsos of two young women had eventually been discovered in a remote gorge off the highway, but police had not been able to catch the murderer, whom the newspapers had sensationally dubbed The Gift Giver.

Now he was back, and he was in Merrivale! It was almost too much to comprehend, Sally thought, shuddering. She hoped fervently that Ben would get home soon. "I'm glad I stayed in today," she told herself. "That poor young woman. And that poor person, whoever found it and opened it!"

The bulletin ended with more police talk, and then Howlin' Howie switched over to a Burma-Shave jingle. *In this vale of toil and sin, your head grows bald but not your chin...*

The jaunty jingle clashed horribly with the gruesome news. Sally ran to the sink and instinctively, started to wash her hands. For what reason, she could not say, but somehow, washing her hands always made her feel safer and able to deal with trouble. Maybe it was because Grammy Ammy had always told her that "cleanliness is next to Godliness, dear."

She turned on the tap and then caught a glimpse of her right hand and started suddenly – why, how strange! *The skin on her hand was sprinkled with sticky glitter.* Gold glitter. The other one too. What on earth? There was nothing in the apartment that would brush off gold glitter... except...*except*...the package that Lewis had given her! Intent as she was on getting dinner finished, she'd hardly glanced at it; she couldn't even say what the wrapping paper looked like without going back into the living room and peering under the tabletop tree.

"Don't open until tomorrow!" Lewis had said with an odd smirk – and now the smirk and the words seemed sinister, malevolent, frightening. Sally steadied herself against the kitchen table, for she suddenly realized something important. *Lewis!* Lewis wore a dark jacket over light-colored overalls! Lewis wore a dark, billed cap with embroidery across the front! And Lewis had worked in the big city two years ago, just when the horrible deeds of The Gift Giver had first surfaced, and had been let go because of some kind of "trouble".

"It can't be," thought Sally, looking wildly around her neat, snug little kitchen. The room looked the same as always, everything in its place but for the various mixing bowls soaking in the sink; yet it was different now, somehow, some way. The Mamie Pink curtains at the window, and the matching Mamie Pink gingham oilcloth covering the kitchen table – they looked disturbing now, the cheerful color mocking her sudden sense of fear. The three chalkware fruit plaques on the wall – apple, peach, and banana – each with grinning anthropomorphic faces, which Ben had won for her at the County Fair last summer, seemed leering and grotesque.

"It can't be," she thought, fighting the odd, thudding terror that was rising in her throat. If it's true, then – then – *The Gift Giver lived right in her building, right on her floor, just down the hall in Mrs. Popkin's apartment at 2G!* She, Sally Kelly, humble housewife and expectant mother from Apartment 2A, personally *k*new The Gift Giver! Oh poor, poor Mrs. Popkin, if she only knew! But – but – Sally didn't *know,* for sure. She had to know – *for sure.*

There was one way of finding out, she realized: The package under the tree in the living room! If the wrapping paper on the package that Lewis had given her matched the description that the police bulletin had given out, then she would know. If not, all her worrying and upset would be for nothing, and she and Ben would have a chuckle about it over dinner.

She forced herself into the living room and crept up to the coffee table where the tree sat, gaily trimmed and festive. She'd taken a long-handled wooden spoon from the kitchen drawer, and she used it to lift up a bottom branch of the tree to get a closer look – *I'm not going to touch it, ever!* – she vowed silently. There it was, the shoe-box-sized package with the big, red, satiny bow, a bow which looked bloody and obscene, now that she suspected what it was hiding. She pushed the red satin loops aside with the spoon handle and peered in closer at the package.

Red-green-and-white-striped wrapping paper. Sally gasped. With glittery, gold sprinkles over the stripes. You could fit a woman's arm in it easily, she thought unwillingly, if you had cut the arm off just below the elbow. She felt horribly sick. "I am either going to throw up or I'm going to faint!"

She did neither. Instead, she sat heavily on the couch and thought. "I should call the police and tell them my suspicions. Yes, call the police, let *them* open the package!" The radio bulletin had urged the public to report all suspicious packages. But then, a nagging doubt began to claw in her mind. What if she were wrong about Lewis? Mrs. Popkin would never forgive her and that would be the end of the long, pleasant afternoons drinking tea and watching *The Secret Storm* on the Popkin television – not to mention the many times Lewis would fetch groceries for her from McKenna's without charging the delivery fee. And of course, she would look ridiculous in front of the police if she were wrong. "Hysterical pregnant woman fantasizing about crazy things and wasting the police's time!" It might even make the papers and she'd never be able to hold her head up again while shopping at McKenna's or the five-and-dime.

No…it wouldn't do. She had to make sure before calling the police. She had to…*open*…it. There were no two ways of getting around it. Sally clutched the wooden spoon and poked forcefully at the package…and she heard a definite, dull thud, as if something long and tube-like were bumping against the sides of the package. Her heart sank into her throat. "*Definitely* something long and tube-like," she told herself. She had to open it; there were no two ways about. Steeling herself, she crouched down to the coffee table and leaned in for a sniff, then pulled back sharply. There was a faint but definite… *meaty*…aroma coming from the package. *Meaty* was the only way to describe it.

"I have to do it, I have to make myself open it…for Ben…for the baby," she thought frantically. Maybe Lewis would go after her next, or even the baby, after it was born. Anybody as disturbed as The Gift Giver wouldn't think twice about hurting a baby. She put the spoon down and forced herself to take the package, shuddering and heart-pounding all the way…she sat on the couch, the horrible thing resting heavily on her lap…what would it be like, she thought? Would it be bloody and goey? Or purple-black and fetid, strips of skin and green nails peeling off the fingers, exposing white bone underneath. She shuddered again and turned away, nauseous. . .but the wave of nausea passed, and she started to work on a corner of the wrapping paper.

B-z-z-z-z – t*he doorbell buzzer! It was the door buzzer!! Sally's heart leapt and pounded in her breast, as she sat still on the couch and pondered whether to answer it or not.

"Miz Kelly? Sally?"

My God! Lewis! It was *Lewis!!* Sally put her hand to her mouth and bit the back of it to keep from screaming.

"I know you are in there? Miz Kelly," he shouted through the door after buzzing again and again. "I've got something for you from my mother."

"Leave it on the doorstep there, Lewis," she finally croaked out loudly, in a strangled voice.

"I can't, I told Mother I'd hand it to you personally. It's a Christmas gift." Right, thought Sally grimly, maybe it's a *foot* this time.

He wasn't going away, Sally realized. Sinking to the floor, she crawled, trembling to the front door on her hands and knees; feeling safer and stronger somehow close to the floor, like Antaeus, the Greek mythical character who gained his strength from the earth, that she'd read about in high school. With a huge effort, she drew herself up and looked through the peephole. Lewis was red-faced and sweating, his mouth set in an uncharacteristically angry gash.

"Mother *told* me," he growled petulantly, through the door. "She *told* me."

Sally's voice was raw and strangled from yelling through the door; in a hoarse but more normal tone of voice, she spoke: "It's okay, Lewis, you needn't shout anymore. I can't open the door; I'm not decent. I just got out of the bathtub and I'm in my housecoat (she was sure that Grammy Ammy would forgive her this lie)," she explained. "So, I can't open the door."

What if he didn't want to leave, thought Sally frantically? What if he stayed at the door until Ben came home and attacked Ben? But surely, Ben would have no problem taking care of himself.

Sally screwed up all her courage and said, with a firmness and resolve she didn't really feel: "Tell your mother I will come by after dinner and pick it up, when I'm *decent* – I've got something for her also." Another lie which she was sure that Grammy Ammy wouldn't mind.

"All right," Lewis said finally, still growling. "But if you don't come by, I'll come back. Mother *told me.*"

She watched him clump away through the peephole, holding her breath, her pulse pounding. As usual, he moved awkwardly and reminded her of a Tinkertoy structure. A very *dangerous* and *disturbed* Tinkertoy structure.

"There it is! I've got to make myself open *that thing*…there isn't time. If it's true I *must* call the police immediately! Maybe he means to do in Mrs. Popkin herself, *his own mother,* you never know." She crawled back on all fours to the couch and grabbed the package. This time, she tore through the glittery paper, determinedly and aggressively. She took a deep breath and opened the lid of the box, stifling again the urge to scream; the meaty smell got much stronger, until…*My God, what on earth?"*

Nestled in the box, within a bed of crunchy, white tissue paper, was a long, dried salami sausage. Attached to the salami was a small, printed card that read in gold script: *"Merry Christmas and Happy New Year to one of our best customers from McKenna's Scotch Country Market."*

There was no sound anywhere in the whole apartment for a long, still moment – even the muffled buzz of sound from Howlin' Howie in the kitchen seemed to have gone silent, and then—

Sally began to laugh. She laughed and laughed out loud, until tears streamed down her face in great big rivulets, laughing and crying at the same time. "It's a salami," she cried through her tears. "It has a *definite* meaty smell."

Then she laughed and laughed again, more of a scream than a laugh, for at least five minutes… on and on. "I'm going to wet my pants at this rate," she thought, when she finally stopped laughing.

Then she caught sight of the electric starburst clock on the wall behind the couch. Ten minutes past seven! The minute hand relentlessly approached the Westinghouse brand name spelled out under the thirty-minute mark.

"The ham!" she cried. "The Jell-O! The tomato gravy! And look at me – I'm a mess! I'm still wearing my pedal pushers!" Ben would be home soon, and he disliked seeing women in any kind of slacks or pants. "Women *like that!*" he would glower whenever he saw a woman in pants out in public.

"No, it's too late," she thought, as she heard Ben's key in the door. He was whistling a cheerful tune, the way he always did when he got home; this time, Sally realized, it was *Rockin' Around the Christmas Tree*, strangely enough.

"I'll just have to be *a woman like that* for one night only! The important thing is, I'm alive, I'm alive! The Gift Giver doesn't live down the hall and I'm not a cold, dead torso thrown in a ditch somewhere, with my arms and feet chopped off and wrapped up in red-and-green-and white wrapping paper with gold glitter sprinkled on it." She shot up quickly and ran to meet Ben at the doorway.

"Oh Ben!" she cried joyously, through her still-wet eyes, throwing her arms around her tall, solid, protective husband. "I'm alive! I'm not chopped up! I'm alive!"

"You're wearing pants," Ben said stiffly, pushing her gently but firmly away. Your hair is in curlers… *women like that.*"

There's something *wrong*, thought Sally, backing away slowly. "Where's Ben? That's not *my* Ben! *My Ben* has kind eyes and a sweet smile. *My Ben* would never push me away like that—"

She looked at him, her face flushed, her hands dangling awkwardly by her sides…yes, it *was* Ben, different somehow, but standing there in his familiar light-gray overalls, with his dark, olive drab Eisenhower jacket buttoned over it, and his matching cap with "Starling Bros. Paint and Trim" embroidered on the front in yellow.

"Ben?" she asked, uncertainly. "Ben?"

Slowly, Ben stretched his hands out in front of his waist, and stared down at them with an odd stare, as if he were seeing them for the first time. Sally looked down at his outstretched hands as well. Ben? she thought, backing further away from the man in the doorway, the man with the suddenly odd, staring eyes – and the outstretched hands, covered in gold glitter.

Move-in Weekend

Christi Nogle

MOMMY DIED IN '60, and life has been happy for me and Daddy ever since. Can it have been nearly ten years?

Hired women stayed with me whenever Daddy went away on business. He wasn't ever home all that much, but he was always back for Christmas bearing gifts from around the world, and anyway absence makes the heart grow fonder – or stops love from spoiling for a little while longer, at least.

He hasn't been out of the country in the past two years. He's not handsome anymore either, poor Daddy. I've been thinking more often lately, what's going to happen to him?

There are still so many arrangements he needs to make before I'm settled at college. He has to check on my tuition and help me shop, he needs to help me unpack and make sure the movers didn't break any of my things, and of course he needs to drive me and Princess to the apartment tomorrow. He has to worry about the cost of the apartment, too, but he knows I couldn't bear to live in a dormitory without Princess close by.

On the way there, I think I'll change my mind about having a car. I'll start to wonder whether it would be such a bad idea after all. Parking will be an expense, but on the other hand I'll be able to shop – I won't have to call him for every little thing – and I can take Princess to the beach.

Daddy worries about her. As soon as he came home tonight, he wondered what will little Precious do all day while I'm in classes, all night when I'm on dates?

"Oh, do you really think I'll be asked on any dates, Daddy?"

He only looks away. He always used to praise my face, but now that I'm grown, it's too much for him. Like looking at the sun, it hurts him. He says, "Maybe Princess ought to stay at home after all. I'll be lonely enough without you."

Daddy worries too much. Some people like to worry, like to suffer.

"Oh, but I'll be too lonely without *you*," I say. I pout. Princess wriggles at my feet, and I take her up in my arms, stroke the fawn-colored fluff on her foxy little head. I could crush her in my hands right here and now. I'd like to.

I'd like to see it all settle on Daddy, finally. I'd like to make a proper scene.

Stop, I tell myself. Put that out of mind. I never get to have that kind of gratification. Funny, other people get to gratify themselves over and over, every day and sometimes all day. They gorge themselves with whatever they want, whether it's warm kisses or food, cigarettes, sex. Liquor.

Speaking of. He's looking at the bar-cart again.

"I'm so sorry I forgot to ask, Daddy," I say, Would you like a drink?" I don't wait for an answer. I settle Princess on her pillow and rush to fix his drink.

I'm Mommy in these moments – well dressed and shapely, graceful and gracious, a perfect hostess. I take my time putting ice in the glass, measure out everything just as slowly and carefully as if it were a science experiment. My face is beautiful in concentration, and at this distance safe for Daddy to watch.

Mommy died in '60, but her image lives on in me. That's all right. Her image was all she had, anyway.

It's certainly all she cared about. I was rotten through and through, but after all, I had all those strawberry-gold curls. I wore those ridiculous dresses with the fluffy crinolines and sat on a blanket in the grass so she could watch me from the window.

I haven't thought of that in years. The neighbor at that awful apartment building, what was his name? Sam? He used to come out and bother me while I played. Why'd she let him do that?

Daddy smokes and sips his drink. He doesn't try to talk, so I turn on his television. I take Princess to my room so she can watch me get ready for one last night with the girls.

I sit down at the vanity, but there's nothing that needs doing. My bob is perfect, my green turtleneck snug enough to flatter but still sophisticated.

There's a '66 Mustang in a used car lot that we'll pass on the way to college. Convertible, burgundy. I feel like it's going to set me off well. I sit at the vanity watching my face as I see the car. Surprise, delight, a quiet, "Oh Daddy, did you *see* that?" It'll be on his side. He'll look at me, and I'll be looking back at it. We'll be passing it, but we will make a U-turn.

* * *

Some people like to suffer. Mommy always did.

Mary and Joan, my best friends, they like to suffer. We're going to a movie tonight, but before that we sit drinking milkshakes. We all look so very pretty at the high bistro table, and all of us notice the other patrons approving of us.

Joan drones on and on about her sister's wedding. She's so jealous of that sister I'm amazed she can still breathe. Mary drones and drones about her mother's ill health. I think how uncalled-for all of this is. We're supposed to be celebrating something – the end of childhood, I suppose – and I only said I'd come because I thought it would be a good time.

While I smile and nod, I think of breaking the rim of my milkshake glass on the table and screwing the shattered glass into Mary's face. The wet vanilla dregs dripping pink with her blood.

Why don't we ever talk about my mommy, Mary? Would you like to do that?

I see the actions over and over while Mary speaks: the pills in Mommy's hand and the quick dash of the thick glass against the Formica table, the pressing and screwing motion. I feel it in my hands. I feel it in my back. I taste Mommy's lime and grenadine in my throat.

Fantasies like this are the closest I get to suffering. Something has to relieve them. I have to have gratification, and then I'll be happy again.

I fix things when they're wrong instead of bawling about them. That's the difference between me and other people.

"We're about to be late," says Joan with a gesture toward her wristwatch.

We hurriedly pay and cross the street, get our tickets to *Beyond the Valley of the D*olls at our filthy little hometown theater. We go in late, giggling apologies to the people we step over. Everyone admires us as we go, thinking it strange that girls like us are not in the city on dates tonight. The truth is we all had to turn down dates so we could have this last time together.

I notice, as we are finding our seats, how Joan touches Mary's arm and her back. Neither of them ever touch me like that, and as the stupid movie plays, that's all I can think about. I only seem to be laughing along with the silly movie. Really, I'm watching a private movie of my own, a much sharper and funnier one.

Mary goes to the ladies' room an hour into the show. I follow her – in my movie I see her blood dripping down the side of a broken porcelain sink and pooling onto the tile – but no, I do not follow her. She gets back in her seat, finishes her popcorn. Joan gives her a ride home.

She'd have given me a ride, too, but the night's so nice I want to walk. I take time putting on my gloves as we say good night so that Joan and Mary won't have to be awkward, deciding whether or not to give me a goodbye hug. I stop across the street for a bottle of Coke and take a turn into an alley, and a few moments later I'm strolling down the street towards home.

Mary gets home in one piece.

That's how much I restrain myself, every hour of every day.

* * *

My new apartment's front windows look out onto the courtyard, very pretty with its bougainvillea on the balconies, its Mexican tile and its little kidney-shaped pool, but the kitchen window looks out on the side street where my new baby is parked. I walk over to the sink to look down at it every five minutes, and Daddy is proud again each time I do.

I open the lightest box, and inside is the pink hatbox. Daddy says, "I don't know why you'd bring that."

"It was Bea's, don't you remember?" Dear Aunt Bea, Mommy's older sister and only friend. We all used to go ice skating together – only that one time, yes, that one time Mommy was sick and stayed home. I laugh a little remembering it. After her accident, I got Bea's hatbox with her best hat in it. I still remember the accident and later, Mommy in a fever destroying that beautiful hat.

I still remember the surprise in Bea's face just before her accident – or during the accident, maybe I should say.

I'm holding up the hatbox, and Daddy's looking at my face in a strange way.

"Oh, what's the matter?" I say.

He shakes his head, opens another box.

My china kitten is packed in with the towels. He hands the kitten up to me, and I hold it close.

That was the very first time I gratified myself. I can barely remember it, though. Mommy told the story to me when I was older, and I had forgotten most of it by then. It was a neighbor woman who liked me – spinster women and widows were always wanting to make a pet out of me. She told me I could have this kitten if ever she died, and then she died.

I couldn't have been more than three or four. I was stupid, as all kids are. Zero control. I'd just gratify myself in the most direct way possible and then get all hurt if anyone noticed.

I laugh, thinking of all of these old stories, and I set the shiny white kitten on my pretty white mantel.

I turn back to get more things out of the packing box, and Daddy's crouched there pulling out towels, stacking things. My music box sits on the hardwood by his feet.

I take the music box to the highboy in my bedroom and stand there looking over Mommy's jewelry and all of my other best things. A little mother-of-pearl lighter I got from a little boy, a teacher's coral-pink lipstick. All of that was before we moved.

I can't remember the teacher or the little boy's names, but suddenly I laugh because I remember the upstairs neighbor's name: not Sam but Simon. That smelly little old man would come down and bother me when I played, but without warning him in any way, one morning I tiptoed up to the landing and found his door unlocked.

How stupid he looked sleeping his drunk-sleep, mouth wide open like that. Wide open just like a jar so you could pour things right in.

I'm cracking up thinking of it. He came pounding down the stairs later making a great big fuss – everyone in the apartments staring and shrieking from their windows – and poor old stupid Simon sprawled and crawled across the yard. He was vomiting blood in between the screaming, everyone screaming with him like they felt it too.

Simon says scream your absolute head off!

That's when I knew for sure that I was different. I could well imagine what it might feel like for my guts to get all poisoned and turn liquid, but there was no connection between that and what it would feel like for Simon's guts to burn away. He was a whole different person from them, and nobody liked him anyway. What were they so upset about? Why were they acting like they were liquefying and dying in the grass?

"Oh Daddy, you're positively green," I say. He's staring at me from the bedroom doorway, swaying, more of an old man than I've ever realized.

"Sit down. Let me fix you a drink."

Thee bottles are in a brown paper bag on the kitchen counter, the glasses already arranged on the shelves. I measure everything out carefully just as if it were a science experiment. Well, maybe it is.

* * *

Daddy's gotten home in one piece. He just called.

I did think about popping something into his drink, and then when we went out to dinner, I thought about pushing him into the street. He slept on my new sofa last night, and I thought about covering his face with a pillow. I thought of an accident in the shower, an accident with the kitchen counter, a problem with his brakes. I thought of the kidney-shaped pool.

If I only had a dime for every moment I've devoted over the years to thinking of the sharp edges of ceramic objects! That pool is going to feature in some fantasies to come, I'm sure.

I twist myself in knots thinking it really would be better for Daddy to just die, but then if I want to take the risk, I want it to be really gratifying. If it's just a matter of killing somebody, well, I'm in the city now. I guess I can kill whomever I want.

No, when it's him, I want it to be special. I want him to know what's happening.

He made a last comment about Precious Princess just before shuffling out to his car. Shouldn't she really go home with him, where there's a yard and squirrels to chase and him at home so much? Wouldn't I be happier knowing she was safe?

Princess is eight years old now, the longest-lived pet I've ever had. The others were all so accident-prone.

We stood in the courtyard when he said all of that, and I was looking up at a marmalade cat deciding whether to jump from one balcony to the other. *Don't worry, Daddy,* I wanted to say. *Maybe I'll feel like killing Princess sometime, but I won't do it. I'll go and wring that little kitty's neck instead. It will be all right.*

I wonder how soon he'll call to tell me about what he read in the paper. He'll read it, surely, as soon as he gets a drink and gets settled: A middle-aged woman was murdered in the alley behind the movie theater night before last, the very night that Mary and Joan and I had our last ladies' date. The night I walked home. I was that close to danger.

He'll worry about me, especially tomorrow when he hears some of the more gruesome details of the case (the lady's face), things that weren't yet described in the paper but that people will be talking about in town.

He'll call again tomorrow when he hears more about it, but he'll call me tonight, I'm sure. I listen for the phone while I get Princess's dinner. Should I go out tonight? There's really nothing here, but I don't feel like walking to a restaurant. I certainly don't feel like driving.

That was a stupid idea, the car. I'm never going to drive it. I was thinking I ought to have a car in case Daddy died, but it seems like Daddy's going to be around for a while now.

I find I'm afraid. I hate this feeling.

I keep thinking of the Coke bottle, how it screwed into the lady's face, how it ought to have been Mary's face instead.

Precious stares up at me. "That would have been a thousand times more gratifying, wouldn't it?" I say. She takes two slow steps back when I reach for her.

I can't go out. I need to be here for Daddy's call, and so I lie back on the sofa looking through the pile of textbooks we bought yesterday and decide I'm not going to like college all that much. The new college clothes are nice, anyway. They're hanging already, but I rearrange them. I eat from a tube of saltines.

Nine o'clock, and it dawns on me. Daddy's not calling. He's finished the paper, and yet he is not calling to tell me about it, and that can mean only one thing.

He knows. Just like Mommy knew.

Princess licks the back of my hand now. She smells my anger, doesn't she?

I get up to set my hair. I haven't worn curls for a while, but I think how they'll look with a scarf and sunglasses when I'm driving around town tomorrow. I'm going to be driving a lot after all, and so I need just the right look for it.

Daddy knows, and he wanted free of me, didn't he? He thinks he's safe now that I'm on my own. He's worried about himself all this time, all these years, and now he thinks he's safe.

But I never killed Mommy! She drove herself crazy thinking I would, but I never touched a hair on my sweetest, prettiest Mommy's tender little head. She did it all by herself.

I sit at my new vanity in new satin pajamas, curlers in my hair. Suddenly the lights go out. Out the window, lights are off across the way. On a nearby roof, the black silhouette of a cat stands tall against gray city sky.

Suffering. That's what I've been doing tonight – and for how long?

Dry lightning cracks in the distance, heat lightning. Princess is smart. She's made herself scarce.

I rise to the highboy and pull on my driving gloves. There's something I need to do tonight.

The Ninescore Mystery

Baroness Emma Orczy

Chapter I

WELL, YOU KNOW, some say she is the daughter of a duke, others that she was born in the gutter, and that the handle has been soldered on to her name in order to give her style and influence.

I could say a lot, of course, but "my lips are sealed," as the poets say. All through her successful career at the Yard she honoured me with her friendship and confidence, but when she took me in partnership, as it were, she made me promise that I would never breathe a word of her private life, and this I swore on my Bible oath – "wish I may die," and all the rest of it.

Yes, we always called her "my lady," from the moment that she was put at the head of our section; and the chief called her "Lady Molly" in our presence. We of the Female Department are dreadfully snubbed by the men, though don't tell me that women have not ten times as much intuition as the blundering and sterner sex; my firm belief is that we shouldn't have half so many undetected crimes if some of the so-called mysteries were put to the test of feminine investigation.

Do you suppose for a moment, for instance, that the truth about that extraordinary case at Ninescore would ever have come to light if the men alone had had the handling of it? Would any man have taken so bold a risk as Lady Molly did when – But I am anticipating.

Let me go back to that memorable morning when she came into my room in a wild state of agitation.

"The chief says I may go down to Ninescore if I like, Mary," she said in a voice all a-quiver with excitement.

"You!" I ejaculated. "What for?"

"What for – what for?" she repeated eagerly. "Mary, don't you understand? It is the chance I have been waiting for – the chance of a lifetime? They are all desperate about the case up at the Yard; the public is furious, and columns of sarcastic letters appear in the daily press. None of our men know what to do; they are at their wits' end, and so this morning I went to the chief—"

"Yes?" I queried eagerly, for she had suddenly ceased speaking.

"Well, never mind now how I did it – I will tell you all about it on the way, for we have just got time to catch the 11 a.m. down to Canterbury. The chief says I may go, and that I may take whom I like with me. He suggested one of the men, but somehow I feel that this is woman's work, and I'd rather have you, Mary, than anyone. We will go over the preliminaries of the case together in the train, as I don't suppose that you have got them at your fingers' ends yet, and you have only just got time to put a few things together and meet me at Charing Cross booking-office in time for that 11.0 sharp."

She was off before I could ask her any more questions, and anyhow I was too flabbergasted to say much. A murder case in the hands of the Female Department! Such a thing had been unheard of until now. But I was all excitement, too, and you may be sure I was at the station in good time.

Fortunately Lady Molly and I had a carriage to ourselves. It was a non-stop run to Canterbury, so we had plenty of time before us, and I was longing to know all about this case, you bet, since I was to have the honour of helping Lady Molly in it.

The murder of Mary Nicholls had actually been committed at Ash Court, a fine old mansion which stands in the village of Ninescore. The Court is surrounded by magnificently timbered grounds, the most fascinating portion of which is an island in the midst of a small pond, which is spanned by a tiny rustic bridge. The island is called "The Wilderness," and is at the furthermost end of the grounds, out of sight and earshot of the mansion itself. It was in this charming spot, on the edge of the pond, that the body of a girl was found on the 5th of February last.

I will spare you the horrible details of this gruesome discovery. Suffice it to say for the present that the unfortunate woman was lying on her face, with the lower portion of her body on the small grass-covered embankment, and her head, arms, and shoulders sunk in the slime of the stagnant water just below.

It was Timothy Coleman, one of the under-gardeners at Ash Court, who first made this appalling discovery. He had crossed the rustic bridge and traversed the little island in its entirety, when he noticed something blue lying half in and half out of the water beyond. Timothy is a stolid, unemotional kind of yokel, and, once having ascertained that the object was a woman's body in a blue dress with white facings, he quietly stooped and tried to lift it out of the mud.

But here even his stolidity gave way at the terrible sight which was revealed before him. That the woman – whoever she might be – had been brutally murdered was obvious, her dress in front being stained with blood; but what was so awful that it even turned old Timothy sick with horror, was that, owing to the head, arms and shoulders having apparently been in the slime for some time, they were in an advanced state of decomposition.

Well, whatever was necessary was immediately done, of course. Coleman went to get assistance from the lodge, and soon the police were on the scene and had removed the unfortunate victim's remains to the small local police-station.

Ninescore is a sleepy, out-of-the-way village, situated some seven miles from Canterbury and four from Sandwich. Soon everyone in the place had heard that a terrible murder had been committed in the village, and all the details were already freely discussed at the Green Man.

To begin with, everyone said that though the body itself might be practically unrecognisable, the bright blue serge dress with the white facings was unmistakable, as were the pearl and ruby ring and the red leather purse found by Inspector Meisures close to the murdered woman's hand.

Within two hours of Timothy Coleman's gruesome find the identity of the unfortunate victim was firmly established as that of Mary Nicholls, who lived with her sister Susan at 2, Elm Cottages, in Ninescore Lane, almost opposite Ash Court. It was also known that when the police called at that address they found the place locked and apparently uninhabited.

Mrs. Hooker, who lived at No. 1 next door, explained to Inspector Meisures that Susan and Mary Nicholls had left home about a fortnight ago, and that she had not seen them since.

"It'll be a fortnight tomorrow," she said. "I was just inside my own front door a-calling to the cat to come in. It was past seven o'clock, and as dark a night as ever you did see. You could hardly see your 'and afore your eyes, and there was a nasty damp drizzle comin' from everywhere. Susan and Mary come out of their cottage; I couldn't rightly see Susan, but I 'eard Mary's voice quite distinck. She says: 'We'll have to 'urry,' says she. I, thinkin' they might be goin' to do some shoppin' in the village, calls out to them that I'd just 'eard the church clock strike seven, and that bein' Thursday, and early closin', they'd find all the shops shut at Ninescore. But they took no notice, and walked off towards the village, and that's the last I ever seed o' them two."

Further questioning among the village folk brought forth many curious details. It seems that Mary Nicholls was a very flighty young woman, about whom there had already been quite a good deal of scandal, whilst Susan, on the other hand – who was very sober and steady in her conduct

– had chafed considerably under her younger sister's questionable reputation, and, according to Mrs. Hooker, many were the bitter quarrels which occurred between the two girls. These quarrels, it seems, had been especially violent within the last year whenever Mr. Lionel Lydgate called at the cottage. He was a London gentleman, it appears – a young man about town, it afterwards transpired – but he frequently stayed at Canterbury, where he had some friends, and on those occasions he would come over to Ninescore in his smart dogcart and take Mary out for drives.

Mr. Lydgate is brother to Lord Edbrooke, the multi-millionaire, who was the recipient of birthday honours last year. His lordship resides at Edbrooke Castle, but he and his brother Lionel had rented Ash Court once or twice, as both were keen golfers and Sandwich Links are very close by. Lord Edbrooke, I may add, is a married man. Mr. Lionel Lydgate, on the other hand, is just engaged to Miss Marbury, daughter of one of the canons of Canterbury.

No wonder, therefore, that Susan Nicholls strongly objected to her sister's name being still coupled with that of a young man far above her in station, who, moreover, was about to marry a young lady in his own rank of life.

But Mary seemed not to care. She was a young woman who only liked fun and pleasure, and she shrugged her shoulders at public opinion, even though there were ugly rumours anent the parentage of a little baby girl whom she herself had placed under the care of Mrs. Williams, a widow who lived in a somewhat isolated cottage on the Canterbury road. Mary had told Mrs. Williams that the father of the child, who was her own brother, had died very suddenly, leaving the little one on her and Susan's hands; and, as they couldn't look after it properly, they wished Mrs. Williams to have charge of it. To this the latter readily agreed.

The sum for the keep of the infant was decided upon, and thereafter Mary Nicholls had come every week to see the little girl, and always brought the money with her.

Inspector Meisures called on Mrs. Williams, and certainly the worthy widow had a very startling sequel to relate to the above story.

"A fortnight tomorrow," explained Mrs. Williams to the inspector, "a little after seven o'clock, Mary Nicholls come runnin' into my cottage. It was an awful night, pitch dark and a nasty drizzle. Mary says to me she's in a great hurry; she is goin' up to London by a train from Canterbury and wants to say good-bye to the child. She seemed terribly excited, and her clothes were very wet. I brings baby to her, and she kisses it rather wild-like and says to me: 'You'll take great care of her, Mrs. Williams,' she says; 'I may be gone some time.' Then she puts baby down and gives me £2, the child's keep for eight weeks."

After which, it appears, Mary once more said "good-bye" and ran out of the cottage, Mrs. Williams going as far as the front door with her. The night was very dark, and she couldn't see if Mary was alone or not, until presently she heard her voice saying tearfully: "I had to kiss baby—" then the voice died out in the distance "on the way to Canterbury," Mrs. Williams said most emphatically.

So far, you see, Inspector Meisures was able to fix the departure of the two sisters Nicholls from Ninescore on the night of January 23rd. Obviously they left their cottage about seven, went to Mrs. Williams, where Susan remained outside while Mary went in to say good-bye to the child.

After that all traces of them seem to have vanished. Whether they did go to Canterbury, and caught the last up train, at what station they alighted, or when poor Mary came back, could not at present be discovered.

According to the medical officer, the unfortunate girl must have been dead twelve or thirteen days at the very least, as, though the stagnant water may have accelerated decomposition, the head could not have got into such an advanced state much under a fortnight.

At Canterbury station neither the booking-clerk nor the porters could throw any light upon the subject. Canterbury West is a busy station, and scores of passengers buy tickets and go through the barriers every day. It was impossible, therefore, to give any positive information about two young women who may or may not have travelled by the last up train on Saturday, January 23rd – that is, a fortnight before.

One thing only was certain – whether Susan went to Canterbury and travelled by that up train or not, alone or with her sister – Mary had undoubtedly come back to Ninescore either the same night or the following day, since Timothy Coleman found her half-decomposed remains in the grounds of Ash Court a fortnight later.

Had she come back to meet her lover, or what? And where was Susan now?

From the first, therefore, you see, there was a great element of mystery about the whole case, and it was only natural that the local police should feel that, unless something more definite came out at the inquest, they would like to have the assistance of some of the fellows at the Yard.

So the preliminary notes were sent up to London, and some of them drifted into our hands. Lady Molly was deeply interested in it from the first, and my firm belief is that she simply worried the chief into allowing her to go down to Ninescore and see what she could do.

Chapter II

AT FIRST it was understood that Lady Molly should only go down to Canterbury after the inquest, if the local police still felt that they were in want of assistance from London. But nothing was further from my lady's intentions than to wait until then.

"I was not going to miss the first act of a romantic drama," she said to me just as our train steamed into Canterbury station. "Pick up your bag, Mary. We're going to tramp it to Ninescore – two lady artists on a sketching tour, remember – and we'll find lodgings in the village, I dare say."

We had some lunch in Canterbury, and then we started to walk the six and a half miles to Ninescore, carrying our bags. We put up at one of the cottages, where the legend "Apartments for single respectable lady or gentleman" had hospitably invited us to enter, and at eight o'clock the next morning we found our way to the local police-station, where the inquest was to take place. Such a funny little place, you know – just a cottage converted for official use – and the small room packed to its utmost holding capacity. The entire able-bodied population of the neighbourhood had, I verily believe, congregated in these ten cubic yards of stuffy atmosphere.

Inspector Meisures, apprised by the chief of our arrival, had reserved two good places for us well in sight of witnesses, coroner and jury. The room was insupportably close, but I assure you that neither Lady Molly nor I thought much about our comfort then. We were terribly interested.

From the outset the case seemed, as it were, to wrap itself more and more in its mantle of impenetrable mystery. There was precious little in the way of clues, only that awful intuition, that dark unspoken suspicion with regard to one particular man's guilt, which one could feel hovering in the minds of all those present.

Neither the police nor Timothy Coleman had anything to add to what was already known. The ring and purse were produced, also the dress worn by the murdered woman. All were sworn to by several witnesses as having been the property of Mary Nicholls.

Timothy, on being closely questioned, said that, in his opinion, the girl's body had been pushed into the mud, as the head was absolutely embedded in it, and he didn't see how she could have fallen like that.

Medical evidence was repeated; it was as uncertain – as vague – as before. Owing to the state of the head and neck it was impossible to ascertain by what means the death blow had been dealt. The doctor repeated his statement that the unfortunate girl must have been dead quite a fortnight. The body was discovered on February 5th – a fortnight before that would have been on or about January 23rd.

The caretaker who lived at the lodge at Ash Court could also throw but little light on the mysterious event. Neither he nor any member of his family had seen or heard anything to arouse their suspicions. Against that he explained that "The Wilderness," where the murder was committed, is situated some 200 yards from the lodge, with the mansion and flower garden lying between. Replying to a question put to him by a juryman, he said that that portion of the grounds is only divided off from Ninescore Lane by a low, brick wall, which has a door in it, opening into the lane almost opposite Elm Cottages. He added that the mansion had been empty for over a year, and that he succeeded the last man, who died, about twelve months ago. Mr. Lydgate had not been down for golf since witness had been in charge.

It would be useless to recapitulate all that the various witnesses had already told the police, and were now prepared to swear to. The private life of the two sisters Nicholls was gone into at full length, as much, at least, as was publicly known. But you know what village folk are; except when there is a bit of scandal and gossip, they know precious little of one another's inner lives.

The two girls appeared to be very comfortably off. Mary was always smartly dressed; and the baby girl, whom she had placed in Mrs. Williams's charge, had plenty of good and expensive clothes, whilst her keep, 5s. a week, was paid with unfailing regularity. What seemed certain, however, was that they did not get on well together, that Susan violently objected to Mary's association with Mr. Lydgate, and that recently she had spoken to the vicar asking him to try to persuade her sister to go away from Ninescore altogether, so as to break entirely with the past. The Reverend Octavius Ludlow, Vicar of Ninescore, seems thereupon to have had a little talk with Mary on the subject, suggesting that she should accept a good situation in London.

"But," continued the reverend gentleman, "I didn't make much impression on her. All she replied to me was that she certainly need never go into service, as she had a good income of her own, and could obtain £5,000 or more quite easily at any time if she chose."

"Did you mention Mr. Lydgate's name to her at all?" asked the coroner.

"Yes, I did," said the vicar, after a slight hesitation.

"Well, what was her attitude then?"

"I am afraid she laughed," replied the Reverend Octavius, primly, "and said very picturesquely, if somewhat ungrammatically, that 'some folks didn't know what they was talkin' about.'"

All very indefinite, you see. Nothing to get hold of, no motive suggested – beyond a very vague suspicion, perhaps, of blackmail – to account for a brutal crime. I must not, however, forget to tell you the two other facts which came to light in the course of this extraordinary inquest. Though, at the time, these facts seemed of wonderful moment for the elucidation of the mystery, they only helped ultimately to plunge the whole case into darkness still more impenetrable than before.

I am alluding, firstly, to the deposition of James Franklin, a carter in the employ of one of the local farmers. He stated that about half-past six on that same Saturday night, January 23rd, he was walking along Ninescore Lane leading his horse and cart, as the night was indeed pitch dark. Just as he came somewhere near Elm Cottages he heard a man's voice saying in a kind of hoarse whisper:

"Open the door, can't you? It's as dark as blazes!"

Then a pause, after which the same voice added:

"Mary, where the dickens are you?" Whereupon a girl's voice replied: "All right, I'm coming."

James Franklin heard nothing more after that, nor did he see anyone in the gloom.

With the stolidity peculiar to the Kentish peasantry, he thought no more of this until the day when he heard that Mary Nicholls had been murdered; then he voluntarily came forward and told his story to the police. Now, when he was closely questioned, he was quite unable to say whether these voices proceeded from that side of the lane where stand Elm Cottages or from the other side, which is edged by the low, brick wall.

Finally, Inspector Meisures, who really showed an extraordinary sense of what was dramatic, here produced a document which he had reserved for the last. This was a piece of paper which he had found in the red leather purse already mentioned, and which at first had not been thought very important, as the writing was identified by several people as that of the deceased, and consisted merely of a series of dates and hours scribbled in pencil on a scrap of notepaper. But suddenly these dates had assumed a weird and terrible significance: two of them, at least – December 26th and January 1st followed by "10 a.m." – were days on which Mr. Lydgate came over to Ninescore and took Mary for drives. One or two witnesses swore to this positively. Both dates had been local meets of the harriers, to which other folk from the village had gone, and Mary had openly said afterwards how much she had enjoyed these.

The other dates (there were six altogether) were more or less vague. One Mrs. Hooker remembered as being coincident with a day Mary Nicholls had spent away from home; but the last date, scribbled in the same handwriting, was January 23rd, and below it the hour – 6 p.m.

The coroner now adjourned the inquest. An explanation from Mr. Lionel Lydgate had become imperative.

Chapter III

PUBLIC EXCITEMENT had by now reached a very high pitch; it was no longer a case of mere local interest. The country inns all round the immediate neighbourhood were packed with visitors from London, artists, journalists, dramatists, and actor-managers, whilst the hotels and fly-proprietors of Canterbury were doing a roaring trade.

Certain facts and one vivid picture stood out clearly before the thoughtful mind in the midst of a chaos of conflicting and irrelevant evidence: the picture was that of the two women tramping in the wet and pitch dark night towards Canterbury. Beyond that everything was a blur.

When did Mary Nicholls come back to Ninescore, and why?

To keep an appointment made with Lionel Lydgate, it was openly whispered; but that appointment – if the rough notes were interpreted rightly – was for the very day on which she and her sister went away from home. A man's voice called to her at half-past six certainly, and she replied to it. Franklin, the carter, heard her; but half an hour afterwards Mrs. Hooker heard her voice when she left home with her sister, and she visited Mrs. Williams after that.

The only theory compatible with all this was, of course, that Mary merely accompanied Susan part of the way to Canterbury, then went back to meet her lover, who enticed her into the deserted grounds of Ash Court, and there murdered her.

The motive was not far to seek. Mr. Lionel Lydgate, about to marry, wished to silence for ever a voice that threatened to be unpleasantly persistent in its demands for money and in its threats of scandal.

But there was one great argument against that theory – the disappearance of Susan Nicholls. She had been extensively advertised for. The murder of her sister was published broadcast in every newspaper in the United Kingdom – she could not be ignorant of it. And, above all, she hated Mr. Lydgate. Why did she not come and add the weight of her testimony against him if, indeed, he was guilty?

And if Mr. Lydgate was innocent, then where was the criminal? And why had Susan Nicholls disappeared?

Why? Why? Why?

Well, the next day would show. Mr. Lionel Lydgate had been cited by the police to give evidence at the adjourned inquest.

Good-looking, very athletic, and obviously frightfully upset and nervous, he entered the little courtroom, accompanied by his solicitor, just before the coroner and jury took their seats.

He looked keenly at Lady Molly as he sat down, and from the expression on his face I guessed that he was much puzzled to know who she was.

He was the first witness called. Manfully and clearly he gave a concise account of his association with the deceased.

"She was pretty and amusing," he said. "I liked to take her out when I was in the neighborhood; it was no trouble to me. There was no harm in her, whatever the village gossips might say. I know she had been in trouble, as they say, but that had nothing to do with me. It wasn't for me to be hard on a girl, and I fancy that she has been very badly treated by some scoundrel."

Here he was hard pressed by the coroner, who wished him to explain what he meant. But Mr. Lydgate turned obstinate, and to every leading question he replied stolidly and very emphatically:

"I don't know who it was. It had nothing to do with me, but I was sorry for the girl because of everyone turning against her, including her sister, and I tried to give her a little pleasure when I could."

That was all right. Very sympathetically told. The public quite liked this pleasing specimen of English cricket-, golf- and football-loving manhood. Subsequently Mr. Lydgate admitted meeting Mary on December 26th and January 1st, but he swore most emphatically that that was the last he ever saw of her.

"But the 23rd of January," here insinuated the coroner; "you made an appointment with the deceased then?"

"Certainly not," he replied.

"But you met her on that day?"

"Most emphatically no," he replied quietly. "I went down to Edbrooke Castle, my brother's place in Lincolnshire, on the 20th of last month, and only got back to town about three days ago."

"You swear to that, Mr. Lydgate?" asked the coroner.

"I do, indeed, and there are a score of witnesses to bear me out. The family, the house-party, the servants."

He tried to dominate his own excitement. I suppose, poor man, he had only just realised that certain horrible suspicions had been resting upon him. His solicitor pacified him, and presently he sat down, whilst I must say that everyone there present was relieved at the thought that the handsome young athlete was not a murderer, after all. To look at him it certainly seemed preposterous.

But then, of course, there was the deadlock, and as there were no more witnesses to be heard, no new facts to elucidate, the jury returned the usual verdict against some person or persons unknown; and we, the keenly interested spectators, were left to face the problem – Who murdered Mary Nicholls, and where was her sister Susan?

Chapter IV

AFTER THE VERDICT we found our way back to our lodgings. Lady Molly tramped along silently, with that deep furrow between her brows which I knew meant that she was deep in thought.

"Now we'll have some tea," I said, with a sigh of relief, as soon as we entered the cottage door.

"No, you won't," replied my lady, dryly. "I am going to write out a telegram, and we'll go straight on to Canterbury and send it from there."

"To Canterbury!" I gasped. "Two hours' walk at least, for I don't suppose we can get a trap, and it is past three o'clock. Why not send your telegram from Ninescore?"

"Mary, you are stupid," was all the reply I got.

She wrote out two telegrams – one of which was at least three dozen words long – and, once more calling to me to come along, we set out for Canterbury.

I was tea-less, cross, and puzzled. Lady Molly was alert, cheerful, and irritatingly active.

We reached the first telegraph office a little before five. My lady sent the telegram without condescending to tell me anything of its destination or contents; then she took me to the Castle Hotel and graciously offered me tea.

"May I be allowed to inquire whether you propose tramping back to Ninescore to-night?" I asked with a slight touch of sarcasm, as I really felt put out.

"No, Mary," she replied, quietly munching a bit of Sally Lunn; "I have engaged a couple of rooms at this hotel and wired the chief that any message will find us here tomorrow morning."

After that there was nothing for it but quietude, patience, and finally supper and bed.

The next morning my lady walked into my room before I had finished dressing. She had a newspaper in her hand, and threw it down on the bed as she said calmly:

"It was in the evening paper all right last night. I think we shall be in time."

No use asking her what "it" meant. It was easier to pick up the paper, which I did. It was a late edition of one of the leading London evening shockers, and at once the front page, with its startling headline, attracted my attention:

THE NINESCORE MYSTERY
MARY NICHOLL'S BABY DYING

Then, below that, a short paragraph: –

> *"We regret to learn that the little baby daughter of the unfortunate girl who was murdered recently at Ash Court, Ninescore, Kent, under such terrible and mysterious circumstances, is very seriously ill at the cottage of Mrs. Williams, in whose charge she is. The local doctor who visited her today declares that she cannot last more than a few hours. At the time of going to press the nature of the child's complaint was not known to our special representative at Ninescore."*

"What does this mean?" I gasped.

But before she could reply there was a knock at the door.

"A telegram for Miss Granard," said the voice of the hall-porter.

"Quick, Mary," said Lady Molly, eagerly. "I told the chief and also Meisures to wire here and to you."

The telegram turned out to have come from Ninescore, and was signed "Meisures." Lady Molly read it aloud:

"Mary Nicholls arrived here this morning. Detained her at station. Come at once."

"Mary Nicholls! I don't understand," was all I could contrive to say.

But she only replied:

"I knew it! I knew it! Oh, Mary, what a wonderful thing is human nature, and how I thank Heaven that gave me a knowledge of it!"

She made me get dressed all in a hurry, and then we swallowed some breakfast hastily whilst a fly was being got for us. I had, perforce, to satisfy my curiosity from my own inner consciousness. Lady Molly was too absorbed to take any notice of me. Evidently the chief knew what she had done and approved of it: the telegram from Meisures pointed to that.

My lady had suddenly become a personality. Dressed very quietly, and in a smart close-fitting hat, she looked years older than her age, owing also to the seriousness of her mien.

The fly took us to Ninescore fairly quickly. At the little police-station we found Meisures awaiting us. He had Elliot and Pegram from the Yard with him. They had obviously got their orders, for all three of them were mighty deferential.

"The woman is Mary Nicholls, right enough," said Meisures, as Lady Molly brushed quickly past him, "the woman who was supposed to have been murdered. It's that silly bogus paragraph about the infant brought her out of her hiding-place. I wonder how it got in," he added blandly; "the child is well enough."

"I wonder," said Lady Molly, whilst a smile – the first I had seen that morning – lit up her pretty face.

"I suppose the other sister will turn up too, presently," rejoined Elliot. "Pretty lot of trouble we shall have now. If Mary Nicholls is alive and kickin', who was murdered at Ash Court, say I?"

"I wonder," said Lady Molly, with the same charming smile.

Then she went in to see Mary Nicholls.

The Reverend Octavius Ludlow was sitting beside the girl, who seemed in great distress, for she was crying bitterly.

Lady Molly asked Elliott and the others to remain in the passage whilst she herself went into the room, I following behind her.

When the door was shut, she went up to Mary Nicholls, and assuming a hard and severe manner, she said:

"Well, you have at last made up your mind, have you, Nicholls? I suppose you know that we have applied for a warrant for your arrest?"

The woman gave a shriek which unmistakably was one of fear.

"My arrest?" she gasped. "What for?"

"The murder of your sister Susan."

"'Twasn't me!" she said quickly.

"Then Susan *is* dead?" retorted Lady Molly, quietly.

Mary saw that she had betrayed herself. She gave Lady Molly a look of agonised horror, then turned as white as a sheet and would have fallen had not the Reverend Octavius Ludlow gently led her to a chair.

"It wasn't me," she repeated, with a heart-broken sob.

"That will be for you to prove," said Lady Molly dryly. "The child cannot now, of course remain with Mrs. Williams; she will be removed to the workhouse, and—"

"No, that shan't be," said the mother excitedly. "She shan't be, I tell you. The workhouse, indeed," she added in a paroxysm of hysterical tears, "and her father a lord!"

The reverend gentleman and I gasped in astonishment; but Lady Molly had worked up to this climax so ingeniously that it was obvious she had guessed it all along, and had merely led Mary Nicholls on in order to get this admission from her.

How well she had known human nature in pitting the child against the sweetheart! Mary Nicholls was ready enough to hide herself, to part from her child even for a while, in order to save the man she had once loved from the consequences of his crime; but when she heard that her child was dying, she no longer could bear to leave it among strangers, and when Lady Molly taunted her with the workhouse, she exclaimed in her maternal pride:

"The workhouse! And her father a lord!"

Driven into a corner, she confessed the whole truth.

Lord Edbrooke, then Mr. Lydgate, was the father of her child. Knowing this, her sister Susan had, for over a year now, systematically blackmailed the unfortunate man – not altogether, it seems, without Mary's connivance. In January last she got him to come down to Ninescore under the distinct promise that Mary would meet him and hand over to him the letters she had received from him, as well as the ring he had given her, in exchange for the sum of £5,000.

The meeting-place was arranged, but at the last moment Mary was afraid to go in the dark. Susan, nothing daunted, but anxious about her own reputation in case she should be seen talking to a man so late at night, put on Mary's dress, took the ring and the letters, also her sister's purse, and went to meet Lord Edbrooke.

What happened at that interview no one will ever know. It ended with the murder of the blackmailer. I suppose the fact that Susan had, in measure, begun by impersonating her sister, gave the murderer the first thought of confusing the identity of his victim by the horrible device of burying the body in the slimy mud. Anyway, he almost did succeed in hoodwinking the police, and would have done so entirely but for Lady Molly's strange intuition in the matter.

After his crime he ran instinctively to Mary's cottage. He had to make a clean breast of it to her, as, without her help, he was a doomed man.

So he persuaded her to go away from home and to leave no clue or trace of herself or her sister in Ninescore. With the help of money which he would give her, she could begin life anew somewhere else, and no doubt he deluded the unfortunate girl with promises that her child would be restored to her very soon.

Thus he enticed Mary Nicholls away, who would have been the great and all-important witness against him the moment his crime was discovered. A girl of Mary's type and class instinctively obeys the man she has once loved, the man who is the father of her child. She consented to disappear and to allow all the world to believe that she had been murdered by some unknown miscreant.

Then the murderer quietly returned to his luxurious home at Edbrooke Castle, unsuspected. No one had thought of mentioning his name in connection with that of Mary Nicholls. In the days when he used to come down to Ash Court he was Mr. Lydgate, and, when he became a peer, sleepy, out-of-the-way Ninescore ceased to think of him.

Perhaps Mr. Lionel Lydgate knew all about his brother's association with the village girl. From his attitude at the inquest I should say he did, but of course he would not betray his own brother unless forced to do so.

Now, of course, the whole aspect of the case was changed: the veil of mystery had been torn asunder owing to the insight, the marvelous intuition, of a woman who, in my opinion, is the most wonderful psychologist of her time.

You know the sequel. Our fellows at the Yard, aided by the local police, took their lead from Lady Molly, and began their investigations of Lord Edbrooke's movements on or about the 23rd of January.

Even their preliminary inquiries revealed the fact that his lordship had left Edbrooke Castle on the 21st. He went up to town, saying to his wife and household that he was called away on business, and not even taking his valet with him. He put up at the Langham Hotel.

But here police investigations came to an abrupt ending. Lord Edbrooke evidently got wind of them. Anyway, the day after Lady Molly so cleverly enticed Mary Nicholls out of her hiding-place, and surprised her into an admission of the truth, the unfortunate man threw himself in front of the express train at Grantham railway station, and was instantly killed. Human justice cannot reach him now!

But don't tell me that a man would have thought of that bogus paragraph, or of the taunt which stung the motherly pride of the village girl to the quick, and thus wrung from her an admission which no amount of male ingenuity would ever have obtained.

The Walker

Michael Penncavage

A HARD WIND blew against the car and globs of rain slammed the windshield as Norman and Betty drove down the gloomy, pothole-strewn road. It was only three in the afternoon but the grey brown sky made it look like the sun was going to set at any moment.

"This weather," Betty said as she anxiously clutched the arm rest. "It's just horrible."

Norman grunted in reply as he squinted through the streaked window.

"You didn't get the wiper blades replaced like I told you, did you?"

"I forgot."

Betty looked annoyed. "You got the oil changed last week. That place could have changed the wipers as well."

Norman dismissed the comment. "Do you know how much the car shop charges for something like that? Money doesn't grow on trees, Betty. I can do it myself."

"With your arthritis? I'd be surprised if you were able to get the wipers out of the package let alone fasten them onto the windshield."

"I'm not *that* feeble, Betty."

"How long has it been since we both retired? Ten years?"

Norman applied some cleaner on the windshield. It did little good. "Eleven. I would have thought *you* would've remembered something like that."

"Ten years. Eleven years. Either way, it's been a long time."

Norman turned up the heat. "That's what happens when you retire. You forget things. Your mind goes soft. Your body falls apart."

"You're being a little hard on yourself, don't you think? I don't think we fell off the wagon *that* much. We still stay active."

"Really? Like when?"

"Well, we have church on Sunday. Every other Wednesday I get together with the girls for bridge. You have your model trains…"

Norman sighed as navigated around a large puddle. "You're making me depressed."

Betty leaned up slightly in her seat. Two hundred feet ahead a figure was trudging along the side of the road. "I wonder what that person is doing all the way out here."

They slowly approached. It was a man. He was wrapped in a dirty green windbreaker. Or what seemed like a windbreaker. It wasn't doing a good job keeping him dry.

"Should we ask if he needs any help?" asked Betty.

"We didn't pass any broken-down vehicles. He's probably just passing through the area." Norman looked more carefully at the man. They were about fifty feet away. "He looks like a vagrant."

"Vagrants are only up north," corrected Betty. "Down here we have *misplaced souls.*"

They drove slowly past the man. His arms were close to his chest and his head was bowed down. He was lost in his own thoughts and paid no attention to them or the car.

Norman caught a good look at the man. "He looks like a mess, Betty. Like he hasn't seen a shower in the past month."

Betty shook her head. "Pull over."

Norman looked at her surprised. "Are you crazy? *We're retired.*"

"Pull over," she commanded.

Harold slowly drifted into the shoulder of the road. The man was about a hundred feet back. He glanced up for a moment but then returned his head down to the ground and made no attempt to hasten his pace to the car. "Maybe he doesn't want any help."

"In this rain?"

He looked over at his wife. "I just want to go on record and say that this is a bad idea."

Betty looked over her shoulder. "And why is that?"

"We don't know who he is, where he's been, or where he's going."

"Fine," she looked over to him. "We've got about ten seconds before he reaches the car. Your choice. You can roll down the window or simply drive off."

"And you won't badger me later about my decision?"

"Not a word."

Harold drummed his hands on the steering wheel and looked down at the shifter. It was now or never.

Decisions. Decisions.

"Fine," he placed the car into Park and unlocked the doors. Betty smiled brightly at him.

"It's the right choice," she said calmly.

The window rolled down with a squeak. The man was almost to the car. "Good afternoon," she called. "You need any help?"

The man looked up at them as he walked by the passenger side. "That's all right, ma'am. I'm fine."

Betty glanced over to Norman and mouthed the word manners at him. "Are you sure? I don't mean to pry but you seem pretty miserable out here in the rain."

The man stopped and turned to them. "You're very kind to offer, but I'm fine."

"We seem to be heading the same direction as you. Why don't you jump in the backseat? We'll take you are far as we are going on this road. Maybe the rain will have stopped by then."

The man stared at her for a moment and then looked back down at the ground, uncertain.

"I'm afraid I'm not going to be able to take no for an answer."

The man looked back at her for a long moment and smiled. "Thank you, ma'am."

He got into the backseat of the Oldsmobile. Norman and Betty introduced themselves.

"I'm Wade," he replied. "I appreciate your help."

Norman looked at him in the rear-view mirror. The man's eyes were bloodshot and his skin as pale as photocopy paper. He looked like he was in his late forties. "You're not going to carjack us are you, Wade?"

"No, sir," he replied. "And no offense, if I were, I wouldn't go after a late model Oldsmobile."

They shared a chuckle and Norman eased the car back onto the highway. "Where are you heading to, Wade?"

"West," he replied.

"That's not a destination," he corrected.

Wade rubbed his hands together. "It's the best I can do."

"What town do you live in?"

"I used to live in Henderson."

"Henderson," replied Betty. "I think I know Henderson. That's quite a distance from here."

"I don't live there anymore," he said with a strong senses of sadness in his voice. "Not for a long time."

"So what were you doing all the way out here?" asked Norman. "Not much out here on these roads."

"Just doing some walking. And thinking."

"We didn't see any cars off to the side of the road."

"No. I don't own one. At least not anymore."

"Are you saying that you walked all the way from Henderson to here?"

Wade remained silent as he looked out of the car window. Rivulets of water streamed down the glass.

"We can drop you off at a payphone if you need to make a call. Norman and I haven't gotten around to purchasing one of those cellphones yet."

Wade shook his head. "No thanks."

"No one that you need to speak to? Friends? Family? No one to let them know you're doing all right?" asked Betty.

Norman shot her a glance. She didn't return his gaze.

"No. No one."

Betty turned in her seat so that she could see Wade better. "Would you like to stop at our house to have something to eat?"

"That's very nice of you but I wouldn't want to impose."

"Nonsense. It's no trouble at all." She turned to her husband. "Isn't that right?"

Norman didn't reply as he kept his eyes on the road.

Wade noticed his stoic look. "You can take me as far as you are going on this road and that will be good enough."

"Young man, it's simply rude to turn down an offer of dinner," said Betty in a joking voice.

Wade smirked. "I didn't mean to insult."

There was silence for a moment before Norman sighed heavily. "If we take you to our house you promise not to murder us, right? You're not some sort of serial killer, are you?"

"Norman!" exclaimed Betty, appalled.

For an instant a smirk formed on the corner of Wade's mouth. "No. I'm no serial killer."

Norman turned up the heater a little more. "Thank goodness for that."

* * *

They continued on for another half hour. The rain gave up but the sky remained overcast. A solitary rusted and neglected mailbox was off to the side. Tall weeds grew around it.

They turned onto a small, unmarked road. It was bumpy and uneven and took them deep into the woods.

The road ended to reveal a mansion-sized house. Years of neglect and weathering had taken its toll on the structure. Huge vines of ivy blanketed one side. The wood siding, once a pristine white, was now a dirty grey.

Norman turned the car off. "You're going to have to excuse the condition. These old hands aren't what they used to be."

Wade looked up at the house. "It's very nice. Very grand. You must have had a large family."

Norman and Betty looked at each other. Sadness was in their eyes.

"I'm sorry. I didn't mean to pry."

Norman patted his hand on Wade's shoulder. "Not to worry, my boy. That's all in the past."

They walked up the porch stairs. They creaked so loudly that the wood sounded like it was going to snap from their weight.

Wade looked down at the planks. "You should be careful. The wood has rotted through. You wouldn't want to hurt yourself."

"You sound just like Betty. I bought replacements. Just been meaning to get up the energy to replace them."

Wade coughed slightly. "I'll tell you what. I'll trade you the meal for fixing the stairs."

Norman rubbed his chin. "That's a deal. The wood and tools are in the barn out back of the house." He looked at his watch and then at Betty. "How long do you need to get things ready?"

"Oh…about an hour. Maybe a little more." she replied.

Wade looked over the staircase again. "That's good. I can have this fixed by then."

Gripping the railing, Norman continued up the stairs. "We'll give you a shout when we're ready."

* * *

The wood had deteriorated so badly that Wade was able to remove the rot almost by hand. Fortunately, the support beams were still in good condition or else Wade would have underestimated the scope of the project. Using the hammer's claw he scraped away the bits of pine, clusters of decomposing leaves, and rusted nails from earlier attempts to patch the steps.

Wade was just about to lay the first new piece of timber when an object caught his eye. It was set away back under the porch. It had been there for a while as years of rain had softened the ground around it, causing it to sink partially into the dirt. Wade reached out and was just able to grab it. He pried it loose and removed it. It was a shoe. A woman's heeled shoe. He looked at it again, running his thumb across the side of the shoe. Beneath the mud and grime, red shined through. The name of the manufacturer was stamped on the interior. *Bartigales.*

Wade had shopped there many times.

* * *

Betty stamped her foot as hard as she could. A pleased look washed over her face. "It's as solid as a rock. Better than when we moved in."

"I'm glad you like it," replied Wade as he gathered up the bits of wood that he had not used.

"I can't thank you enough. It's going to be so nice to leave the house for my morning walks without having to worry about breaking my leg on these stairs." She wiped her hands on the underside of her sunflower and daffodil apron. "I'm sure you've worked up an appetite. Let's get you washed up. Dinner is almost on the table."

Wade followed her inside to the kitchen. The interior of the house was grand but it showed just as much neglect as the porch. The wallpaper was faded and curling. The ceiling had large areas where the paint had cracked and chipped off.

"I don't mean to sound like a broken recorder but you're going to have to forgive the appearance. It's hard to keep up with the chores these days."

The warm water from the kitchen sink felt good on his hands as it washed away the cold and the aches and the pain. Wade sighed in relief. How long had it been since he had come in from the outside? Days? Weeks? He had lost track.

Wade followed them into the dining room. It was immense and the table sat a dozen comfortably. Norman motioned for him to sit at the head of the table. The chair was large and regal, with a high back, sturdy legs, and made of mahogany. It slid loudly against the wood floor as he pulled it out from the table.

Betty placed a glass of water down in front of him. "The roast needs about fifteen more minutes. Can I get you anything to eat in the meantime?"

"No, thank you." Wade looked around the room. Dated portraits hung around the room. "Are those pictures of your family?"

Betty nodded as she looked cheerily around. "Yes. Going back to the mid 1800s when our ancestors emigrated from Europe. There's five generations on the walls. Norman's family came over at the end of the century."

Norman looked over at Wade. "So how about yourself? Any family?"

"I was married. Once. A long time ago."

"What happened?" asked Norman.

Betty looked over at him with disdain. "Please excuse my husband's bad manners. We don't mean to pry."

Wade looked down at his water glass. "That's all right. My wife…she disappeared."

Betty's eyebrows rose. "Disappeared? What do you mean?"

A distant look appeared in Wade's eyes. "It was a long time ago. She was driving from Davenport. She left her sister Kate's house early Friday morning. It was a long drive but she always liked to do it in one day. She normally would arrive home by midnight." He paused for a moment, lost in thought. "But she never arrived."

"Oh, dear," replied Betty. "I am so sorry to hear that. What was her name?"

"Nora."

"The police were never able to come up with any leads?"

"They conducted a manhunt, but since the distance was over six hundred miles they had no idea where to start looking. They called it off after three months of searching. Soon after I was accused of being involved in her disappearance."

Betty was slicing pieces of bread and stopped instantly after hearing this. Wade saw the fear in her eyes and quickly continued. "But I was exonerated shortly thereafter. We had taken out life insurance policies on each other just before she went missing. The police got suspicious."

"That's understandable," said Norman as he passed the wicker bread basket to Wade. "Betty and I have a policy on each other as well. These days you can never be too careful."

Wade took a piece and reached for the butter. "We were planning on having children and thought that if something happened to one of us the other would be financially secure."

"Were you able to collect on the policy?"

"Norman Hawthorn!" exclaimed Betty. "Your manners have gone completely out the window!" She placed her napkin on the table and stood up. "I'm going to check on dinner. It should be ready. I hope that in the few minutes I'm gone you won't insult our guest any more."

Norman looked down at the floor like a puppy that that had been scolded. Betty left the room.

"I hope you didn't take any offense in my questions there, son."

Wade smirked. "No offense taken."

"Good," he winked at him and then lowered his voice. "So, were you able to collect?"

"Yes."

"And they weren't able to ever find out what happened to your wife?"

"No. After two years the police moved the murder to their cold case files. I realized it was up to me to try and find her killer."

"Did you have any luck?" asked Norman. "Any leads?"

"One of the private investigators I hired found a witness who claimed to have seen Nora at a rest stop."

"That sounds encouraging."

Wade shook his head. "Nothing came from it. The gas station's security cameras didn't have any footage of her. The surrounding area was searched but nothing was found." Wade rubbed his brow. "It was another in a long string of dead ends."

Norman sat back in his chair. "So what were you doing out there on such a dreary day?"

Wade rubbed his hands. "Just thinking. I like to go for long walks and think."

"Well, you certainly did a lot of that," he joked. "All of that walking. You must be in fine shape. It takes a Herculean effort for me to just get to the end of the driveway."

"What did you do before you retired?"

"Betty and myself...well, we lived an active lifestyle."

"Doing what?"

Norman stared at Wade for a moment. "It's a little hard to explain. It's probably easier to just show you."

A faint *creak* in the wood flooring behind Wade made him turn around. Betty was standing beside the chair. For an old person she was quiet. Her arm swung out at him. She didn't move quickly, but it was unexpected. The blackjack in her hand smacked Wade across the side of his head.

A black tide washed over Wade, pulling him under.

* * *

Dancing globes of white and green paraded across Wade's vision as he cracked open his eyes. He was still in the dining-room chair, though he was slumped backwards. His head was wet and it stuck to the wood. He glanced at his watch to see how much time had passed when he realized his wrists were handcuffed to the chair. He jerked his hand up but the wood was thick and solid and it held firm. He tried to break free again but all he managed to do was cause the steel handcuffs to dig into his skin.

"That's Kentucky mahogany, son." Betty sat at the other end of the table slowly turning the pages of a large, weathered photo album. "I've lost count of how many people that chair has held down over the years." She picked up a small key from the table and dropped it into her apron pocket. "You're not going anywhere."

A trickle of blood was trailing down over Wade's right eye. He blinked rapidly in an effort to clear his vision. "What... what are you doing?"

The door to the kitchen opened and Norman came hobbling into the room. His limp was more pronounced that before. Betty took notice of his pain. "Are you all right?"

He grunted. "Damn sciatica. Flared up again as I was running the sharpener." He dropped a hand axe onto the table and sat down wearily in the chair. "But I was still able to get it pretty sharp."

"You take your pain reliever? You know that you'll never get to sleep tonight unless you take it a few hours in advance."

Norman shook his head. "Couldn't find it."

Betty sighed. "It's in the medicine cabinet. Middle shelf. Left hand side."

"I looked there. Didn't see it."

Wade forcefully tugged his hand again, this time making the handcuffs cut into his skin and start to bleed.

Betty shook her head and flipped to the next page of the photo album. "Your last name wouldn't happen to be Billings, would it?"

Wade's eyes widened and she continued. "It was just a guess. You didn't have any identification on you. But you had mentioned your wife's first name and when she went missing. I was able to put two and two together."

Norman smiled at his wife. "She was always the brains of the bunch."

Betty looked directly at Wade. She smiled at him and cleared her throat, "Would you like to know how she died?"

She spun the photo album around. Wade let out a gasp. The photo in the upper left corner was blurry from the lack of light where it had been taken but there was no mistaking it.

It was Nora.

She was staring at the camera. Her eyes were wide and red. Duct tape covered her mouth.

"This was taken a day after we got her. My notes say that it took her three days to die." Betty shook her head in dismay. "I'm just glad that I wrote everything down. To be honest, I don't really remember too much about her. That was an *active* summer for Norman and me. It all seemed to go by with such a blur."

Norman nodded. "That witness that your investigator dug up. They were right."

"What?"

"The rest stop. That's where we got her. She had walked in off the road and was leaving the restroom, probably to make her phone call. Didn't take much to get her in the trunk of our car. As a matter of fact, it would have been the very same car that you drove in. Isn't that right, Betty?"

She smiled proudly. "Yes, Norman. Your memory hasn't gone on you just yet."

Wade gripped the chair arms and tried to leap forward. The heavy chair moved only a few inches.

Norman picked up the axe from the table and pointed it at him. "That will be quite enough of that. I just polished the floorboards. I don't need you scraping and scuffing them all up."

Wade bowed his head and shifted himself slightly upwards in the chair. "What did you do with the body?"

Betty looked at him surprised. "Aren't you curious why we did it? Virtually all of the people who were in that chair wanted to know."

Wade shook his head. "After Nora went missing I read all sorts of books on serial killers. Most important thing I learned was that there was never any real motive behind the murders. Just insanity."

"Is that it?" said Norman. "You think Betty and I are crazies?"

Wade shrugged. "I don't know what to think. Nor do I care. All that matters is I was able to find you." He spat out a wad of blood and phlegm onto the floor. "After all of these years I've *finally* been able to find you. I've *finally* been able to learn the truth."

"What's that supposed to mean?" asked Betty.

"After the case went into the cold case files I grew desperate. I knew she had been abducted. In my gut I just *knew* it. So I decided to find her myself. I knew that if anyone was going to unlock the mystery to what happened to her it was going to be me."

Norman began spinning the axe blade on the table. "So you took to walking the roads? Son, that sounds like some bad country music song."

Wade cleared his throat. "I've took to the roads in hopes that maybe, *just maybe* the person who abducted Nora would try to do the same to me."

Norman stared at him curiously but Wade's expression did not change. "You're serious?" He looked over at Betty. "How long ago did we come across that girl?"

Betty reviewed her notes. "Fifteen years this June."

"Fifteen years?" Norman repeated, sounding surprised. "You've been searching for us for fifteen years?"

"I needed to find out the truth. It didn't matter how many years it took. I knew once I found you, I would find her."

"Damn. Now that's tenacity." Norman picked up the axe. "You know what the funny thing is? Betty and I...we're retired. We haven't killed in over ten years."

"Eleven," corrected Betty.

Norman grinned. "Like I said before. She's the brains of the bunch. But seeing you walking alongside the road...well, you were like a fawn who decided to wander into the backyard of a hunter."

Wade picked up his right leg and rested his shoe on the chair so that it was near his handcuffed hand. The position contorted him somewhat. Norman frowned at the blatant gesture. "You mind taking your foot off my furniture?"

Wade ignored him. "I have two questions I want to ask."

Norman ran his finger over the axe. "Go right ahead. Least we can do before we get to work."

"My wife. Did she suffer?"

Norman glanced over to Betty who spoke. "Yes. I'm afraid she did. Greatly."

Wade stared at her with emotionless eyes for a moment before he continued. "Where is the body buried?"

"The woods behind the barn. There's a clearing about a half mile in. That's where we put them *all*."

"What about her car?"

Betty shook her head. "Her car? That's a silly thing to ask. And that's three questions. You were only allowed two." She turned to Norman. "What do you think? Should we extend our generosity to…"

An explosion echoed across the room. The back of Betty's head exploded, projecting bits of bone and gobs of blood against the wall behind her. She collapsed face first against the dining-room table and then slowly slid off onto the floor.

Norman spun around. A gun was in Wade's handcuffed hand, pointing in Norman's general direction. "Did you think that after all of these years looking for you that I wouldn't be prepared for when I actually *found* you?"

Norman slowly extended his hand towards the axe. "Betty searched you."

"Ankle holster. Sloppy work on your part."

Norman grabbed the hand axe but it was as far as he got. A bullet tore into his shoulder. The weapon fell to the floor with a dull thud.

Wade fired again. A second bullet tore into Norman's other shoulder.

"Wait!" he gasped as he sunk deep into the chair. "You need me!"

"For what?" asked Wade.

"The…the keys. How do you expect to unlock the handcuff? You're going to need my help finding them."

"They're in your wife's pocket."

Norman stared at him, surprised. "She's on the other side of the room. How are you going to get over to her in that chair?"

"I managed to find you." Wade leveled the gun at Norman's brow. "I think I'll be able to figure out that."

* * *

An hour later Wade emerged from the house. He rubbed his bandaged wrists gingerly. He walked past the barn. It was getting late in the day. The clouds had finally given way to some blue skies. The sun was beginning its slow descent down over the horizon. As he walked a dark plume of smoke curled and lifted up from the house behind him. By the time Wade entered the woods the entire house was engulfed in flames.

Norman was right. The clearing was easy to locate. It was the size of a baseball diamond. The ground was patchy and uneven. None of the dirt had been disturbed in a while. Wade walked out to the middle of the field and knelt down. The tall blades of grass swayed in the breeze and brushed gently against his arms and legs. He laid down on the ground. It was surprisingly comfortable. Wade closed his eyes.

And for the first time in a long time he slept.

The Murders in the Rue Morgue

Edgar Allan Poe

What song the Syrens sang, or what name Achilles assumed when he hid himself among women, although puzzling questions, are not beyond all conjecture. – Sir Thomas Browne.

THE MENTAL FEATURES discoursed of as the analytical, are, in themselves, but little susceptible of analysis. We appreciate them only in their effects. We know of them, among other things, that they are always to their possessor, when inordinately possessed, a source of the liveliest enjoyment. As the strong man exults in his physical ability, delighting in such exercises as call his muscles into action, so glories the analyst in that moral activity which *disentangles*. He derives pleasure from even the most trivial occupations bringing his talent into play. He is fond of enigmas, of conundrums, of hieroglyphics; exhibiting in his solutions of each a degree of *acumen* which appears to the ordinary apprehension praeternatural. His results, brought about by the very soul and essence of method, have, in truth, the whole air of intuition.

The faculty of re-solution is possibly much invigorated by mathematical study, and especially by that highest branch of it which, unjustly, and merely on account of its retrograde operations, has been called, as if *par excellence*, analysis. Yet to calculate is not in itself to analyse. A chess-player, for example, does the one without effort at the other. It follows that the game of chess, in its effects upon mental character, is greatly misunderstood. I am not now writing a treatise, but simply prefacing a somewhat peculiar narrative by observations very much at random; I will, therefore, take occasion to assert that the higher powers of the reflective intellect are more decidedly and more usefully tasked by the unostentatious game of draughts than by all the elaborate frivolity of chess. In this latter, where the pieces have different and *bizarre* motions, with various and variable values, what is only complex is mistaken (a not unusual error) for what is profound. The *attention* is here called powerfully into play. If it flag for an instant, an oversight is committed resulting in injury or defeat. The possible moves being not only manifold but involute, the chances of such oversights are multiplied; and in nine cases out of ten it is the more concentrative rather than the more acute player who conquers. In draughts, on the contrary, where the moves are *unique* and have but little variation, the probabilities of inadvertence are diminished, and the mere attention being left comparatively unemployed, what advantages are obtained by either party are obtained by superior *acumen*. To be less abstract—Let us suppose a game of draughts where the pieces are reduced to four kings, and where, of course, no oversight is to be expected. It is obvious that here the victory can be decided (the players being at all equal) only by some *recherché* movement, the result of some strong exertion of the intellect. Deprived of ordinary resources, the analyst throws himself into the spirit of his opponent, identifies himself therewith, and not unfrequently sees thus, at a glance, the sole methods (sometime indeed absurdly simple ones) by which he may seduce into error or hurry into miscalculation.

Whist has long been noted for its influence upon what is termed the calculating power; and men of the highest order of intellect have been known to take an apparently unaccountable delight in it, while eschewing chess as frivolous. Beyond doubt there is nothing of a similar nature so greatly tasking the faculty of analysis. The best chess-player in Christendom *may* be little more than the best player of chess; but proficiency in whist implies capacity for success in all those more important undertakings where mind struggles with mind. When I say proficiency, I mean that perfection in the game which includes a comprehension of *all* the sources whence legitimate advantage may be derived. These are not only manifold but multiform, and lie frequently among recesses of thought altogether inaccessible to the ordinary understanding. To observe attentively is to remember distinctly; and, so far, the concentrative chess-player will do very well at whist; while the rules of Hoyle (themselves based upon the mere mechanism of the game) are sufficiently and generally comprehensible. Thus to have a retentive memory, and to proceed by "the book," are points commonly regarded as the sum total of good playing. But it is in matters beyond the limits of mere rule that the skill of the analyst is evinced. He makes, in silence, a host of observations and inferences. So, perhaps, do his companions; and the difference in the extent of the information obtained, lies not so much in the validity of the inference as in the quality of the observation. The necessary knowledge is that of *what* to observe. Our player confines himself not at all; nor, because the game is the object, does he reject deductions from things external to the game. He examines the countenance of his partner, comparing it carefully with that of each of his opponents. He considers the mode of assorting the cards in each hand; often counting trump by trump, and honor by honor, through the glances bestowed by their holders upon each. He notes every variation of face as the play progresses, gathering a fund of thought from the differences in the expression of certainty, of surprise, of triumph, or of chagrin. From the manner of gathering up a trick he judges whether the person taking it can make another in the suit. He recognises what is played through feint, by the air with which it is thrown upon the table. A casual or inadvertent word; the accidental dropping or turning of a card, with the accompanying anxiety or carelessness in regard to its concealment; the counting of the tricks, with the order of their arrangement; embarrassment, hesitation, eagerness or trepidation – all afford, to his apparently intuitive perception, indications of the true state of affairs. The first two or three rounds having been played, he is in full possession of the contents of each hand, and thenceforward puts down his cards with as absolute a precision of purpose as if the rest of the party had turned outward the faces of their own.

The analytical power should not be confounded with ample ingenuity; for while the analyst is necessarily ingenious, the ingenious man is often remarkably incapable of analysis. The constructive or combining power, by which ingenuity is usually manifested, and to which the phrenologists (I believe erroneously) have assigned a separate organ, supposing it a primitive faculty, has been so frequently seen in those whose intellect bordered otherwise upon idiocy, as to have attracted general observation among writers on morals. Between ingenuity and the analytic ability there exists a difference far greater, indeed, than that between the fancy and the imagination, but of a character very strictly analogous. It will be found, in fact, that the ingenious are always fanciful, and the *truly* imaginative never otherwise than analytic.

The narrative which follows will appear to the reader somewhat in the light of a commentary upon the propositions just advanced.

Residing in Paris during the spring and part of the summer of 18—, I there became acquainted with a Monsieur C. Auguste Dupin. This young gentleman was of an excellent – indeed of an illustrious family, but, by a variety of untoward events, had been reduced to such poverty that the energy of his character succumbed beneath it, and he ceased to bestir himself in the world, or to care for the retrieval of his fortunes. By courtesy of his creditors, there still remained in his possession a small remnant of his patrimony; and, upon the income arising from this, he managed, by means of a rigorous economy, to procure the necessaries of life, without troubling himself about its superfluities. Books, indeed, were his sole luxuries, and in Paris these are easily obtained.

Our first meeting was at an obscure library in the Rue Montmartre, where the accident of our both being in search of the same very rare and very remarkable volume, brought us into closer communion. We saw each other again and again. I was deeply interested in the little family history which he detailed to me with all that candor which a Frenchman indulges whenever mere self is his theme. I was astonished, too, at the vast extent of his reading; and, above all, I felt my soul enkindled within me by the wild fervor, and the vivid freshness of his imagination. Seeking in Paris the objects I then sought, I felt that the society of such a man would be to me a treasure beyond price; and this feeling I frankly confided to him. It was at length arranged that we should live together during my stay in the city; and as my worldly circumstances were somewhat less embarrassed than his own, I was permitted to be at the expense of renting, and furnishing in a style which suited the rather fantastic gloom of our common temper, a time-eaten and grotesque mansion, long deserted through superstitions into which we did not inquire, and tottering to its fall in a retired and desolate portion of the Faubourg St. Germain.

Had the routine of our life at this place been known to the world, we should have been regarded as madmen – although, perhaps, as madmen of a harmless nature. Our seclusion was perfect. We admitted no visitors. Indeed the locality of our retirement had been carefully kept a secret from my own former associates; and it had been many years since Dupin had ceased to know or be known in Paris. We existed within ourselves alone.

It was a freak of fancy in my friend (for what else shall I call it?) to be enamored of the Night for her own sake; and into this *bizarrerie*, as into all his others, I quietly fell; giving myself up to his wild whims with a perfect *abandon*. The sable divinity would not herself dwell with us always; but we could counterfeit her presence. At the first dawn of the morning we closed all the messy shutters of our old building; lighting a couple of tapers which, strongly perfumed, threw out only the ghastliest and feeblest of rays. By the aid of these we then busied our souls in dreams – reading, writing, or conversing, until warned by the clock of the advent of the true Darkness. Then we sallied forth into the streets arm in arm, continuing the topics of the day, or roaming far and wide until a late hour, seeking, amid the wild lights and shadows of the populous city, that infinity of mental excitement which quiet observation can afford.

At such times I could not help remarking and admiring (although from his rich ideality I had been prepared to expect it) a peculiar analytic ability in Dupin. He seemed, too, to take an eager delight in its exercise – if not exactly in its display – and did not hesitate to confess the pleasure thus derived. He boasted to me, with a low chuckling laugh, that most men, in respect to himself, wore windows in their bosoms, and was wont to follow up such assertions by direct and very startling proofs of his intimate knowledge of my own. His manner at these moments was frigid and abstract; his eyes were vacant in expression; while his voice, usually a rich tenor, rose into a treble which would have sounded petulantly but for the deliberateness and entire distinctness of the enunciation. Observing him in these moods, I often dwelt meditatively upon the old philosophy of the Bi-Part Soul, and amused myself with the fancy of a double Dupin – the creative and the resolvent.

Let it not be supposed, from what I have just said, that I am detailing any mystery, or penning any romance. What I have described in the Frenchman, was merely the result of an excited, or perhaps of a diseased intelligence. But of the character of his remarks at the periods in question an example will best convey the idea.

We were strolling one night down a long dirty street in the vicinity of the Palais Royal. Being both, apparently, occupied with thought, neither of us had spoken a syllable for fifteen minutes at least. All at once Dupin broke forth with these words:

"He is a very little fellow, that's true, and would do better for the *Théâtre des Variétés*."

"There can be no doubt of that," I replied unwittingly, and not at first observing (so much had I been absorbed in reflection) the extraordinary manner in which the speaker had chimed in with my meditations. In an instant afterward I recollected myself, and my astonishment was profound.

"Dupin," said I, gravely, "this is beyond my comprehension. I do not hesitate to say that I am amazed, and can scarcely credit my senses. How was it possible you should know I was thinking of —?" Here I paused, to ascertain beyond a doubt whether he really knew of whom I thought.

"—of Chantilly," said he, "why do you pause? You were remarking to yourself that his diminutive figure unfitted him for tragedy."

This was precisely what had formed the subject of my reflections. Chantilly was a *quondam* cobbler of the Rue St. Denis, who, becoming stage-mad, had attempted the *rôle* of Xerxes, in Crébillon's tragedy so called, and been notoriously Pasquinaded for his pains.

"Tell me, for Heaven's sake," I exclaimed, "the method – if method there is – by which you have been enabled to fathom my soul in this matter." In fact I was even more startled than I would have been willing to express.

"It was the fruiterer," replied my friend, "who brought you to the conclusion that the mender of soles was not of sufficient height for Xerxes *et id genus omne*."

"The fruiterer! – you astonish me – I know no fruiterer whomsoever."

"The man who ran up against you as we entered the street – it may have been fifteen minutes ago."

I now remembered that, in fact, a fruiterer, carrying upon his head a large basket of apples, had nearly thrown me down, by accident, as we passed from the Rue C — into the thoroughfare where we stood; but what this had to do with Chantilly I could not possibly understand.

There was not a particle of *charlatanerie* about Dupin. "I will explain," he said, "and that you may comprehend all clearly, we will first retrace the course of your meditations, from the moment in which I spoke to you until that of the *rencontre* with the fruiterer in question. The larger links of the chain run thus – Chantilly, Orion, Dr. Nichols, Epicurus, Stereotomy, the street stones, the fruiterer."

There are few persons who have not, at some period of their lives, amused themselves in retracing the steps by which particular conclusions of their own minds have been attained. The occupation is often full of interest and he who attempts it for the first time is astonished by the apparently illimitable distance and incoherence between the starting-point and the goal. What, then, must have been my amazement when I heard the Frenchman speak what he had just spoken, and when I could not help acknowledging that he had spoken the truth. He continued:

"We had been talking of horses, if I remember aright, just before leaving the Rue C —. This was the last subject we discussed. As we crossed into this street, a fruiterer, with a large basket upon his head, brushing quickly past us, thrust you upon a pile of paving stones collected at a spot where the causeway is undergoing repair. You stepped upon one of the loose fragments, slipped, slightly strained your ankle, appeared vexed or sulky, muttered a few words, turned to look at the pile, and then proceeded in silence. I was not particularly attentive to what you did; but observation has become with me, of late, a species of necessity.

"You kept your eyes upon the ground – glancing, with a petulant expression, at the holes and ruts in the pavement, (so that I saw you were still thinking of the stones,) until we reached the little alley called Lamartine, which has been paved, by way of experiment, with the overlapping and riveted blocks. Here your countenance brightened up, and, perceiving your lips move, I could not doubt that you murmured the word 'stereotomy,' a term very affectedly applied to this species of pavement. I knew that you could not say to yourself 'stereotomy' without being brought to think of atomies, and thus of the theories of Epicurus; and since, when we discussed this subject not very long ago, I mentioned to you how singularly, yet with how little notice, the vague guesses of that noble Greek had met with confirmation in the late nebular cosmogony, I felt that you could not avoid casting your eyes upward to the great *nebula* in Orion, and I certainly expected that you would do so. You did look up; and I was now assured that I had correctly followed your steps. But in that bitter *tirade* upon Chantilly, which appeared in yesterday's 'Musée,' the satirist, making some disgraceful allusions to the cobbler's change of name upon assuming the buskin, quoted a Latin line about which we have often conversed. I mean the line

Perdidit antiquum litera sonum.

"I had told you that this was in reference to Orion, formerly written Urion; and, from certain pungencies connected with this explanation, I was aware that you could not have forgotten it. It was clear, therefore, that you would not fail to combine the two ideas of Orion and Chantilly. That you did combine them I saw by the character of the smile which passed over your lips. You thought of the poor cobbler's immolation. So far, you had been stooping in your gait; but now I saw you draw yourself up to your full height. I was then sure that you reflected upon the diminutive figure of Chantilly. At this point I interrupted your meditations to remark that as, in fact, he was a very little fellow – that Chantilly – he would do better at the *Théatre des Variétés.*"

Not long after this, we were looking over an evening edition of the "Gazette des Tribunaux," when the following paragraphs arrested our attention.

"*EXTRAORDINARY MURDERS. – This morning, about three o'clock, the inhabitants of the Quartier St. Roch were aroused from sleep by a succession of terrific shrieks, issuing, apparently, from the fourth story of a house in the Rue Morgue, known to be in the sole occupancy of one Madame L'Espanaye, and her daughter Mademoiselle Camille L'Espanaye. After some delay, occasioned by a fruitless attempt to procure admission in the usual manner, the gateway was broken in with a crowbar, and eight or ten of the neighbors entered accompanied by two gendarmes. By this time the cries had ceased; but, as the party rushed up the first flight of stairs, two or more rough voices in angry contention were distinguished and seemed to proceed from the upper part of the house. As the second landing was reached, these sounds, also, had ceased and everything remained perfectly quiet. The party spread themselves and hurried from room to room. Upon arriving at a large back chamber in the fourth story, (the door of which, being found locked, with the key inside, was forced open,) a spectacle presented itself which struck every one present not less with horror than with astonishment.*

"*The apartment was in the wildest disorder – the furniture broken and thrown about in all directions. There was only one bedstead; and from this the bed had been removed, and thrown into the middle of the floor. On a chair lay a razor, besmeared with blood. On the hearth were two or three long and thick tresses of grey human hair, also dabbled in blood, and seeming to have been pulled out by the roots. Upon the floor were found four Napoleons, an ear-ring of topaz, three large silver spoons, three smaller of métal d'Alger and two bags, containing nearly four thousand francs in gold. The drawers of a bureau, which stood in one corner were open, and had been, apparently, rifled, although many articles still remained in them. A small iron safe was discovered under the bed (not under the bedstead). It was open, with the key still in the door. It had no contents beyond a few old letters, and other papers of little consequence.*

"*Of Madame L'Espanaye no traces were here seen; but an unusual quantity of soot being observed in the fire-place, a search was made in the chimney, and (horrible to relate!) the corpse of the daughter, head downward, was dragged therefrom; it having been thus forced up the narrow aperture for a considerable distance. The body was quite warm. Upon examining it, many excoriations were perceived, no doubt occasioned by the violence with which it had been thrust up and disengaged. Upon the face were many severe scratches, and, upon the throat, dark bruises, and deep indentations of finger nails, as if the deceased had been throttled to death.*

"After a thorough investigation of every portion of the house, without farther discovery, the party made its way into a small paved yard in the rear of the building, where lay the corpse of the old lady, with her throat so entirely cut that, upon an attempt to raise her, the head fell off. The body, as well as the head, was fearfully mutilated – the former so much so as scarcely to retain any semblance of humanity.

"To this horrible mystery there is not as yet, we believe, the slightest clew."

The next day's paper had these additional particulars.

"The Tragedy in the Rue Morgue. Many individuals have been examined in relation to this most extraordinary and frightful affair. [The word 'affaire' has not yet, in France, that levity of import which it conveys with us,] "but nothing whatever has transpired to throw light upon it. We give below all the material testimony elicited.

"Pauline Dubourg, laundress, deposes that she has known both the deceased for three years, having washed for them during that period. The old lady and her daughter seemed on good terms – very affectionate towards each other. They were excellent pay. Could not speak in regard to their mode or means of living. Believed that Madame L. told fortunes for a living. Was reputed to have money put by. Never met any persons in the house when she called for the clothes or took them home. Was sure that they had no servant in employ. There appeared to be no furniture in any part of the building except in the fourth story.

"Pierre Moreau, tobacconist, deposes that he has been in the habit of selling small quantities of tobacco and snuff to Madame L'Espanaye for nearly four years. Was born in the neighborhood, and has always resided there. The deceased and her daughter had occupied the house in which the corpses were found, for more than six years. It was formerly occupied by a jeweller, who under-let the upper rooms to various persons. The house was the property of Madame L. She became dissatisfied with the abuse of the premises by her tenant, and moved into them herself, refusing to let any portion. The old lady was childish. Witness had seen the daughter some five or six times during the six years. The two lived an exceedingly retired life – were reputed to have money. Had heard it said among the neighbors that Madame L. told fortunes – did not believe it. Had never seen any person enter the door except the old lady and her daughter, a porter once or twice, and a physician some eight or ten times.

"Many other persons, neighbors, gave evidence to the same effect. No one was spoken of as frequenting the house. It was not known whether there were any living connexions of Madame L. and her daughter. The shutters of the front windows were seldom opened. Those in the rear were always closed, with the exception of the large back room, fourth story. The house was a good house – not very old.

"Isidore Muset, gendarme, deposes that he was called to the house about three o'clock in the morning, and found some twenty or thirty persons at the gateway, endeavoring to gain admittance. Forced it open, at length, with a bayonet – not with a crowbar. Had but little difficulty in getting it open, on account of its being a double or folding gate, and bolted neither at bottom not top. The shrieks were continued until the gate was forced

– and then suddenly ceased. They seemed to be screams of some person (or persons) in great agony – were loud and drawn out, not short and quick. Witness led the way up stairs. Upon reaching the first landing, heard two voices in loud and angry contention – the one a gruff voice, the other much shriller – a very strange voice. Could distinguish some words of the former, which was that of a Frenchman. Was positive that it was not a woman's voice. Could distinguish the words 'sacré' and 'diable.' The shrill voice was that of a foreigner. Could not be sure whether it was the voice of a man or of a woman. Could not make out what was said, but believed the language to be Spanish. The state of the room and of the bodies was described by this witness as we described them yesterday.

"Henri Duval, a neighbor, and by trade a silver-smith, deposes that he was one of the party who first entered the house. Corroborates the testimony of Muset in general. As soon as they forced an entrance, they reclosed the door, to keep out the crowd, which collected very fast, notwithstanding the lateness of the hour. The shrill voice, this witness thinks, was that of an Italian. Was certain it was not French. Could not be sure that it was a man's voice. It might have been a woman's. Was not acquainted with the Italian language. Could not distinguish the words, but was convinced by the intonation that the speaker was an Italian. Knew Madame L. and her daughter. Had conversed with both frequently. Was sure that the shrill voice was not that of either of the deceased.

"—Odenheimer, restaurateur. This witness volunteered his testimony. Not speaking French, was examined through an interpreter. Is a native of Amsterdam. Was passing the house at the time of the shrieks. They lasted for several minutes – probably ten. They were long and loud – very awful and distressing. Was one of those who entered the building. Corroborated the previous evidence in every respect but one. Was sure that the shrill voice was that of a man – of a Frenchman. Could not distinguish the words uttered. They were loud and quick – unequal – spoken apparently in fear as well as in anger. The voice was harsh – not so much shrill as harsh. Could not call it a shrill voice. The gruff voice said repeatedly 'sacré' 'diable,' and once 'mon Dieu.'

"Jules Mignaud, banker, of the firm of Mignaud et Fils, Rue Deloraine. Is the elder Mignaud. Madame L'Espanaye had some property. Had opened an account with his banking house in the spring of the year – (eight years previously). Made frequent deposits in small sums. Had checked for nothing until the third day before her death, when she took out in person the sum of 4000 francs. This sum was paid in gold, and a clerk went home with the money.

"Adolphe Le Bon, clerk to Mignaud et Fils, deposes that on the day in question, about noon, he accompanied Madame L'Espanaye to her residence with the 4000 francs, put up in two bags. Upon the door being opened, Mademoiselle L. appeared and took from his hands one of the bags, while the old lady relieved him of the other. He then bowed and departed. Did not see any person in the street at the time. It is a bye-street – very lonely.

"William Bird, tailor deposes that he was one of the party who entered the house. Is an Englishman. Has lived in Paris two years. Was one of the first to ascend the stairs. Heard the voices in contention. The gruff voice was that of a Frenchman. Could make out several words, but cannot now remember all. Heard distinctly 'sacré' and 'mon Dieu.' There was a sound at the moment as if of several persons struggling – a scraping and scuffling sound. The shrill voice was very loud – louder than the gruff one. Is sure that it was not the voice of an Englishman. Appeared to be that of a German. Might have been a woman's voice. Does not understand German.

"*Four of the above-named witnesses, being recalled, deposed that the door of the chamber in which was found the body of Mademoiselle L. was locked on the inside when the party reached it. Every thing was perfectly silent – no groans or noises of any kind. Upon forcing the door no person was seen. The windows, both of the back and front room, were down and firmly fastened from within. A door between the two rooms was closed, but not locked. The door leading from the front room into the passage was locked, with the key on the inside. A small room in the front of the house, on the fourth story, at the head of the passage was open, the door being ajar. This room was crowded with old beds, boxes, and so forth. These were carefully removed and searched. There was not an inch of any portion of the house which was not carefully searched. Sweeps were sent up and down the chimneys. The house was a four story one, with garrets (mansardes.) A trap-door on the roof was nailed down very securely – did not appear to have been opened for years. The time elapsing between the hearing of the voices in contention and the breaking open of the room door, was variously stated by the witnesses. Some made it as short as three minutes – some as long as five. The door was opened with difficulty.*

"*Alfonzo Garcio, undertaker, deposes that he resides in the Rue Morgue. Is a native of Spain. Was one of the party who entered the house. Did not proceed up stairs. Is nervous, and was apprehensive of the consequences of agitation. Heard the voices in contention. The gruff voice was that of a Frenchman. Could not distinguish what was said. The shrill voice was that of an Englishman – is sure of this. Does not understand the English language, but judges by the intonation.*

"*Alberto Montani, confectioner, deposes that he was among the first to ascend the stairs. Heard the voices in question. The gruff voice was that of a Frenchman. Distinguished several words. The speaker appeared to be expostulating. Could not make out the words of the shrill voice. Spoke quick and unevenly. Thinks it the voice of a Russian. Corroborates the general testimony. Is an Italian. Never conversed with a native of Russia.*

"*Several witnesses, recalled, here testified that the chimneys of all the rooms on the fourth story were too narrow to admit the passage of a human being. By 'sweeps' were meant cylindrical sweeping brushes, such as are employed by those who clean chimneys. These brushes were passed up and down every flue in the house. There is no back passage by which any one could have descended while the party proceeded up stairs. The body of Mademoiselle L'Espanaye was so firmly wedged in the chimney that it could not be got down until four or five of the party united their strength.*

"*Paul Dumas, physician, deposes that he was called to view the bodies about day-break. They were both then lying on the sacking of the bedstead in the chamber where Mademoiselle L. was found. The corpse of the young lady was much bruised and excoriated. The fact that it had been thrust up the chimney would sufficiently account for these appearances. The throat was greatly chafed. There were several deep scratches just below the chin, together with a series of livid spots which were evidently the impression of fingers. The face was fearfully discolored, and the eye-balls protruded. The tongue had been partially bitten through. A large bruise was discovered upon the pit of the stomach, produced, apparently, by the pressure of a knee. In the opinion of M. Dumas, Mademoiselle L'Espanaye had been throttled to death by some person or persons unknown. The corpse of the mother was horribly mutilated. All the bones of the right leg and arm were more or less shattered. The left tibia much splintered, as well as all the ribs of the left side. Whole body dreadfully bruised and discolored. It was not possible to say how the injuries had been inflicted. A heavy club of wood, or a broad bar of iron – a chair – any large, heavy, and obtuse weapon would have produced such results, if wielded by the hands of a very powerful man. No woman could have inflicted the blows with any weapon. The head of the deceased, when seen by witness, was entirely separated from the body, and was also greatly shattered. The throat had evidently been cut with some very sharp instrument – probably with a razor.*

"Alexandre Etienne, surgeon, was called with M. Dumas to view the bodies. Corroborated the testimony, and the opinions of M. Dumas.

"Nothing farther of importance was elicited, although several other persons were examined. A murder so mysterious, and so perplexing in all its particulars, was never before committed in Paris – if indeed a murder has been committed at all. The police are entirely at fault – an unusual occurrence in affairs of this nature. There is not, however, the shadow of a clew apparent."

The evening edition of the paper stated that the greatest excitement still continued in the Quartier St. Roch – that the premises in question had been carefully re-searched, and fresh examinations of witnesses instituted, but all to no purpose. A postscript, however, mentioned that Adolphe Le Bon had been arrested and imprisoned – although nothing appeared to criminate him, beyond the facts already detailed.

Dupin seemed singularly interested in the progress of this affair – at least so I judged from his manner, for he made no comments. It was only after the announcement that Le Bon had been imprisoned, that he asked me my opinion respecting the murders.

I could merely agree with all Paris in considering them an insoluble mystery. I saw no means by which it would be possible to trace the murderer.

"We must not judge of the means," said Dupin, "by this shell of an examination. The Parisian police, so much extolled for *acumen*, are cunning, but no more. There is no method in their proceedings, beyond the method of the moment. They make a vast parade of measures; but, not unfrequently, these are so ill adapted to the objects proposed, as to put us in mind of Monsieur Jourdain's calling for his *robe-de-chambre – pour mieux entendre la musique.* The results attained by them are not unfrequently surprising, but, for the most part, are brought about by simple diligence and activity. When these qualities are unavailing, their schemes fail. Vidocq, for example, was a good guesser and a persevering man. But, without educated thought, he erred continually by the very intensity of his investigations. He impaired his vision by holding the object too close. He might see, perhaps, one or two points with unusual clearness, but in so doing he, necessarily, lost sight of the matter as a whole. Thus there is such a thing as being too profound. Truth is not always in a well. In fact, as regards the more important knowledge, I do believe that she is invariably superficial. The depth lies in the valleys where we seek her, and not upon the mountain-tops where she is found. The modes and sources of this kind of error are well typified in the contemplation of the heavenly bodies. To look at a star by glances – to view it in a side-long way, by turning toward it the exterior portions of the *retina* (more susceptible of feeble impressions of light than the interior), is to behold the star distinctly – is to have the best appreciation of its lustre – a lustre which grows dim just in proportion as we turn our vision *fully* upon it. A greater number of rays actually fall upon the eye in the latter case, but, in the former, there is the more refined capacity for comprehension. By undue profundity we perplex and enfeeble thought; and it is possible to make even Venus herself vanish from the firmament by a scrutiny too sustained, too concentrated, or too direct.

"As for these murders, let us enter into some examinations for ourselves, before we make up an opinion respecting them. An inquiry will afford us amusement," [I thought this an odd term, so applied, but said nothing] "and, besides, Le Bon once rendered me a service for which I am not ungrateful. We will go and see the premises with our own eyes. I know G —, the Prefect of Police, and shall have no difficulty in obtaining the necessary permission."

The permission was obtained, and we proceeded at once to the Rue Morgue. This is one of those miserable thoroughfares which intervene between the Rue Richelieu and the Rue St. Roch. It was late in the afternoon when we reached it; as this quarter is at a great distance from that in which we resided. The house was readily found; for there were still many persons gazing up at the closed shutters, with an objectless curiosity, from the opposite side of the way. It was an ordinary Parisian house, with a gateway, on one side of which was a glazed watch-box, with a sliding panel in the window, indicating a *loge de concierge*. Before going in we walked up the street, turned down an alley, and then, again turning, passed in the rear of the building – Dupin, meanwhile examining the whole neighborhood, as well as the house, with a minuteness of attention for which I could see no possible object.

Retracing our steps, we came again to the front of the dwelling, rang, and, having shown our credentials, were admitted by the agents in charge. We went up stairs – into the chamber where the body of Mademoiselle L'Espanaye had been found, and where both the deceased still lay. The disorders of the room had, as usual, been suffered to exist. I saw nothing beyond what had been stated in the "Gazette des Tribunaux." Dupin scrutinized every thing – not excepting the bodies of the victims. We then went into the other rooms, and into the yard; a *gendarme* accompanying us throughout. The examination occupied us until dark, when we took our departure. On our way home my companion stepped in for a moment at the office of one of the daily papers.

I have said that the whims of my friend were manifold, and that *Je les ménagais*: – for this phrase there is no English equivalent. It was his humor, now, to decline all conversation on the subject of the murder, until about noon the next day. He then asked me, suddenly, if I had observed any thing *peculiar* at the scene of the atrocity.

There was something in his manner of emphasizing the word "peculiar," which caused me to shudder, without knowing why.

"No, nothing *peculiar*," I said; "nothing more, at least, than we both saw stated in the paper."

"The 'Gazette,'" he replied, "has not entered, I fear, into the unusual horror of the thing. But dismiss the idle opinions of this print. It appears to me that this mystery is considered insoluble, for the very reason which should cause it to be regarded as easy of solution – I mean for the *outré* character of its features. The police are confounded by the seeming absence of motive – not for the murder itself – but for the atrocity of the murder. They are puzzled, too, by the seeming impossibility of reconciling the voices heard in contention, with the facts that no one was discovered up stairs but the assassinated Mademoiselle L'Espanaye, and that there were no means of egress without the notice of the party ascending. The wild disorder of the room; the corpse thrust, with the head downward, up the chimney; the frightful mutilation of the body of the old lady; these considerations, with those just mentioned, and others which I need not mention, have sufficed to paralyze the powers, by putting completely at fault the boasted *acumen*, of the government agents. They have fallen into the gross but common error of confounding the unusual with the abstruse. But it is by these deviations from the plane of the ordinary, that reason feels its way, if at all, in its search for the true. In investigations such as we are now pursuing, it should not be so much asked 'what has occurred,' as 'what has occurred that has never occurred before.' In fact, the facility with which I shall arrive, or have arrived, at the solution of this mystery, is in the direct ratio of its apparent insolubility in the eyes of the police."

I stared at the speaker in mute astonishment.

"I am now awaiting," continued he, looking toward the door of our apartment – "I am now awaiting a person who, although perhaps not the perpetrator of these butcheries, must have been in some measure implicated in their perpetration. Of the worst portion of the crimes committed, it is probable that he is innocent. I hope that I am right in this supposition; for upon it I build my expectation of reading the entire riddle. I look for the man here – in this room – every moment. It is true that he may not arrive; but the probability is that he will. Should he come, it will be necessary to detain him. Here are pistols; and we both know how to use them when occasion demands their use."

I took the pistols, scarcely knowing what I did, or believing what I heard, while Dupin went on, very much as if in a soliloquy. I have already spoken of his abstract manner at such times. His discourse was addressed to myself; but his voice, although by no means loud, had that intonation which is commonly employed in speaking to some one at a great distance. His eyes, vacant in expression, regarded only the wall.

"That the voices heard in contention," he said, "by the party upon the stairs, were not the voices of the women themselves, was fully proved by the evidence. This relieves us of all doubt upon the question whether the old lady could have first destroyed the daughter and afterward have committed suicide. I speak of this point chiefly for the sake of method; for the strength of Madame L'Espanaye would have been utterly unequal to the task of thrusting her daughter's corpse up the chimney as it was found; and the nature of the wounds upon her own person entirely preclude the idea of self-destruction. Murder, then, has been committed by some third party; and the voices of this third party were those heard in contention. Let me now advert – not to the whole testimony respecting these voices – but to what was *peculiar* in that testimony. Did you observe any thing peculiar about it?"

I remarked that, while all the witnesses agreed in supposing the gruff voice to be that of a Frenchman, there was much disagreement in regard to the shrill, or, as one individual termed it, the harsh voice.

"That was the evidence itself," said Dupin, "but it was not the peculiarity of the evidence. You have observed nothing distinctive. Yet there *was* something to be observed. The witnesses, as you remark, agreed about the gruff voice; they were here unanimous. But in regard to the shrill voice, the peculiarity is – not that they disagreed – but that, while an Italian, an Englishman, a Spaniard, a Hollander, and a Frenchman attempted to describe it, each one spoke of it as that *of a foreigner*. Each is sure that it was not the voice of one of his own countrymen. Each likens it – not to the voice of an individual of any nation with whose language he is conversant – but the converse. The Frenchman supposes it the voice of a Spaniard, and 'might have distinguished some words *had he been acquainted with the Spanish.*' The Dutchman maintains it to have been that of a Frenchman; but we find it stated that '*not understanding French this witness was examined through an interpreter.*' The Englishman thinks it the voice of a German, and '*does not understand German.*' The Spaniard 'is sure' that it was that of an Englishman, but 'judges by the intonation' altogether, '*as he has no knowledge of the English.*' The Italian believes it the voice of a Russian, but '*has never conversed with a native of Russia.*' A second Frenchman differs, moreover, with the first, and is positive that the voice was that of an Italian; but, *not being cognizant of that tongue*, is, like the Spaniard, 'convinced by the intonation.' Now, how strangely unusual must that voice have really been, about which such testimony as this *could* have been elicited! – in whose *tones*, even, denizens of the five great divisions of Europe could recognise nothing familiar! You will say that it might have been the voice of an Asiatic – of an African. Neither Asiatics nor Africans abound in Paris; but, without denying the inference, I will now merely call your attention to three points. The voice is termed by one witness 'harsh rather than shrill.' It is represented by two others to have been 'quick and *unequal.*' No words – no sounds resembling words – were by any witness mentioned as distinguishable.

"I know not," continued Dupin, "what impression I may have made, so far, upon your own understanding; but I do not hesitate to say that legitimate deductions even from this portion of the testimony – the portion respecting the gruff and shrill voices – are in themselves sufficient to engender a suspicion which should give direction to all farther progress in the investigation of the mystery. I said 'legitimate deductions;' but my meaning is not thus fully expressed. I designed to imply that the deductions are the *sole* proper ones, and that the suspicion arises *inevitably* from them as the single result. What the suspicion is, however, I will not say just yet. I merely wish you to bear in mind that, with myself, it was sufficiently forcible to give a definite form – a certain tendency – to my inquiries in the chamber.

"Let us now transport ourselves, in fancy, to this chamber. What shall we first seek here? The means of egress employed by the murderers. It is not too much to say that neither of us believe in prÃ¦ternatural events. Madame and Mademoiselle L'Espanaye were not destroyed by spirits. The doers of the deed were material, and escaped materially. Then how? Fortunately, there is but one mode of reasoning upon the point, and that mode *must* lead us to a definite decision. – Let us examine, each by each, the possible means of egress. It is clear that the assassins were in the room where Mademoiselle L'Espanaye was found, or at least in the room adjoining, when the party ascended the stairs. It is then only from these two apartments that we have to seek issues. The police have laid bare the floors, the ceilings, and the masonry of the walls, in every direction. No *secret* issues could have escaped their vigilance. But, not trusting to *their* eyes, I examined with my own. There were, then, no secret issues. Both doors leading from the rooms into the passage were securely locked, with the keys inside. Let us turn to the chimneys. These, although of ordinary width for some eight or ten feet above the hearths, will not admit, throughout their extent, the body of a large cat. The impossibility of egress, by means already stated, being thus absolute, we are reduced to the windows. Through those of the front room no one could have escaped without notice from the crowd in the street. The murderers *must* have passed, then, through those of the back room. Now, brought to this conclusion in so unequivocal a manner as we are, it is not our part, as reasoners, to reject it on account of apparent impossibilities. It is only left for us to prove that these apparent 'impossibilities' are, in reality, not such.

"There are two windows in the chamber. One of them is unobstructed by furniture, and is wholly visible. The lower portion of the other is hidden from view by the head of the unwieldy bedstead which is thrust close up against it. The former was found securely fastened from within. It resisted the utmost force of those who endeavored to raise it. A large gimlet-hole had been pierced in its frame to the left, and a very stout nail was found fitted therein, nearly to the head. Upon examining the other window, a similar nail was seen similarly fitted in it; and a vigorous attempt to raise this sash, failed also. The police were now entirely satisfied that egress had not been in these directions. And, *therefore*, it was thought a matter of supererogation to withdraw the nails and open the windows.

"My own examination was somewhat more particular, and was so for the reason I have just given – because here it was, I knew, that all apparent impossibilities *must* be proved to be not such in reality.

"I proceeded to think thus – *a posteriori*. The murderers did escape from one of these windows. This being so, they could not have refastened the sashes from the inside, as they were found fastened; – the consideration which put a stop, through its obviousness, to the scrutiny of the police in this quarter. Yet the sashes *were* fastened. They *must*, then, have the power of fastening themselves. There was no escape from this conclusion. I stepped to the unobstructed casement, withdrew the nail with some difficulty and attempted to raise the sash. It resisted all my efforts, as I had anticipated. A concealed spring must, I now know, exist; and this corroboration of my idea convinced me that my premises at least, were correct, however mysterious still appeared the circumstances attending the nails. A careful search soon brought to light the hidden spring. I pressed it, and, satisfied with the discovery, forbore to upraise the sash.

"I now replaced the nail and regarded it attentively. A person passing out through this window might have reclosed it, and the spring would have caught – but the nail could not have been replaced. The conclusion was plain, and again narrowed in the field of my investigations. The assassins *must* have escaped through the other window. Supposing, then, the springs upon each sash to be the same, as was probable, there *must* be found a difference between the nails, or at least between the modes of their fixture. Getting upon the sacking of the bedstead, I looked over the head-board minutely at the second casement. Passing my hand down behind the board, I readily discovered and pressed the spring, which was, as I had supposed, identical in character with its neighbor. I now looked at the nail. It was as stout as the other, and apparently fitted in the same manner – driven in nearly up to the head.

"You will say that I was puzzled; but, if you think so, you must have misunderstood the nature of the inductions. To use a sporting phrase, I had not been once 'at fault.' The scent had never for an instant been lost. There was no flaw in any link of the chain. I had traced the secret to its ultimate result, – and that result was *the nail*. It had, I say, in every respect, the appearance of its fellow in the other window; but this fact was an absolute nullity (conclusive us it might seem to be) when compared with the consideration that here, at this point, terminated the clew. 'There *must* be something wrong,' I said, 'about the nail.' I touched it; and the head, with about a quarter of an inch of the shank, came off in my fingers. The rest of the shank was in the gimlet-hole where it had been broken off. The fracture was an old one (for its edges were incrusted with rust), and had apparently been accomplished by the blow of a hammer, which had partially imbedded, in the top of the bottom sash, the head portion of the nail. I now carefully replaced this head portion in the indentation whence I had taken it, and the resemblance to a perfect nail was complete – the fissure was invisible. Pressing the spring, I gently raised the sash for a few inches; the head went up with it, remaining firm in its bed. I closed the window, and the semblance of the whole nail was again perfect.

"The riddle, so far, was now unriddled. The assassin had escaped through the window which looked upon the bed. Dropping of its own accord upon his exit (or perhaps purposely closed), it had become fastened by the spring; and it was the retention of this spring which had been mistaken by the police for that of the nail, – farther inquiry being thus considered unnecessary.

"The next question is that of the mode of descent. Upon this point I had been satisfied in my walk with you around the building. About five feet and a half from the casement in question there runs a lightning-rod. From this rod it would have been impossible for any one to reach the window itself, to say nothing of entering it. I observed, however, that the shutters of the fourth story were of the peculiar kind called by Parisian carpenters *ferrades* – a kind rarely employed at the present day, but frequently seen upon very old mansions at Lyons and Bordeaux. They are in the form of an ordinary door, (a single, not a folding door) except that the lower half is latticed or worked in open trellis – thus affording an excellent hold for the hands. In the present instance these shutters are fully three feet and a half broad. When we saw them from the rear of the house, they were both about half open – that is to say, they stood off at right angles from the wall. It is probable that the police, as well as myself, examined the back of the tenement; but, if so, in looking at these *ferrades* in the line of their breadth (as they must have done), they did not perceive this great breadth itself, or, at all events, failed to take it into due consideration. In fact, having once satisfied themselves that no egress could have been made in this quarter, they would naturally bestow here a very cursory examination. It was clear to me, however, that the shutter belonging to the window at the head of the bed, would, if swung fully back to the wall, reach to within two feet of the lightning-rod. It was also evident that, by exertion of a very unusual degree of activity and courage, an entrance into the window, from the rod, might have been thus effected. – By reaching to the distance of two feet and a half (we now suppose the shutter open to its whole extent) a robber might have taken a firm grasp upon the trellis-work. Letting go, then, his hold upon the rod, placing his feet securely against the wall, and springing boldly from it, he might have swung the shutter so as to close it, and, if we imagine the window open at the time, might even have swung himself into the room.

"I wish you to bear especially in mind that I have spoken of a *very* unusual degree of activity as requisite to success in so hazardous and so difficult a feat. It is my design to show you, first, that the thing might possibly have been accomplished: – but, secondly and *chiefly*, I wish to impress upon your understanding the *very extraordinary* – the almost prÃ¦ternatural character of that agility which could have accomplished it.

"You will say, no doubt, using the language of the law, that 'to make out my case,' I should rather undervalue, than insist upon a full estimation of the activity required in this matter. This may be the practice in law, but it is not the usage of reason. My ultimate object is only the truth. My immediate purpose is to lead you to place in juxtaposition, that *very unusual* activity of which I have just spoken with that *very peculiar* shrill (or harsh) and *unequal* voice, about whose nationality no two persons could be found to agree, and in whose utterance no syllabification could be detected."

At these words a vague and half-formed conception of the meaning of Dupin flitted over my mind. I seemed to be upon the verge of comprehension without power to comprehend – men, at times, find themselves upon the brink of remembrance without being able, in the end, to remember. My friend went on with his discourse.

"You will see," he said, "that I have shifted the question from the mode of egress to that of ingress. It was my design to convey the idea that both were effected in the same manner, at the same point. Let us now revert to the interior of the room. Let us survey the appearances here. The drawers of the bureau, it is said, had been rifled, although many articles of apparel still remained within them. The conclusion here is absurd. It is a mere guess – a very silly one – and no more. How are we to know that the articles found in the drawers were not all these drawers had originally contained? Madame L'Espanaye and her daughter lived an exceedingly retired life – saw no company – seldom went out – had little use for numerous changes of habiliment. Those found were at least of as good quality as any likely to be possessed by these ladies. If a thief had taken any, why did he not take the best – why did he not take all? In a word, why did he abandon four thousand francs in gold to encumber himself with a bundle of linen? The gold *was* abandoned. Nearly the whole sum mentioned by Monsieur Mignaud, the banker, was discovered, in bags, upon the floor. I wish you, therefore, to discard from your thoughts the blundering idea of *motive*, engendered in the brains of the police by that portion of the evidence which speaks of money delivered at the door of the house. Coincidences ten times as remarkable as this (the delivery of the money, and murder committed within three days upon the party receiving it), happen to all of us every hour of our lives, without attracting even momentary notice. Coincidences, in general, are great stumbling-blocks in the way of that class of thinkers who have been educated to know nothing of the theory of probabilities – that theory to which the most glorious objects of human research are indebted for the most glorious of illustration. In the present instance, had the gold been gone, the fact of its delivery three days before would have formed something more than a coincidence. It would have been corroborative of this idea of motive. But, under the real circumstances of the case, if we are to suppose gold the motive of this outrage, we must also imagine the perpetrator so vacillating an idiot as to have abandoned his gold and his motive together.

"Keeping now steadily in mind the points to which I have drawn your attention – that peculiar voice, that unusual agility, and that startling absence of motive in a murder so singularly atrocious as this – let us glance at the butchery itself. Here is a woman strangled to death by manual strength, and thrust up a chimney, head downward. Ordinary assassins employ no such modes of murder as this. Least of all, do they thus dispose of the murdered. In the manner of thrusting the corpse up the chimney, you will admit that there was something *excessively outré* – something altogether irreconcilable with our common notions of human action, even when we suppose the actors the most depraved of men. Think, too, how great must have been that strength which could have thrust the body *up* such an aperture so forcibly that the united vigor of several persons was found barely sufficient to drag it *down!*

"Turn, now, to other indications of the employment of a vigor most marvellous. On the hearth were thick tresses – very thick tresses – of grey human hair. These had been torn out by the roots. You are aware of the great force necessary in tearing thus from the head even twenty or thirty hairs together. You saw the locks in question as well as myself. Their roots (a hideous sight!) were clotted with fragments of the flesh of the scalp – sure token of the prodigious power which had been exerted in uprooting perhaps half a million of hairs at a time. The throat of the old lady was not merely cut, but the head absolutely severed from the body: the instrument was a mere razor. I wish you also to look at the *brutal* ferocity of these deeds. Of the bruises upon the body of Madame L'Espanaye I do not speak. Monsieur Dumas, and his worthy coadjutor Monsieur Etienne, have pronounced that they were inflicted by some obtuse instrument; and so far these gentlemen are very correct. The obtuse instrument was clearly the stone pavement in the yard, upon which the victim had fallen from the window which looked in upon the bed. This idea, however simple it may now seem, escaped the police for the same reason that the breadth of the shutters escaped them – because, by the affair of the nails, their perceptions had been hermetically sealed against the possibility of the windows having ever been opened at all.

"If now, in addition to all these things, you have properly reflected upon the odd disorder of the chamber, we have gone so far as to combine the ideas of an agility astounding, a strength superhuman, a ferocity brutal, a butchery without motive, a *grotesquerie* in horror absolutely alien from humanity, and a voice foreign in tone to the ears of men of many nations, and devoid of all distinct or intelligible syllabification. What result, then, has ensued? What impression have I made upon your fancy?"

I felt a creeping of the flesh as Dupin asked me the question. "A madman," I said, "has done this deed – some raving maniac, escaped from a neighboring *Maison de Santé*."

"In some respects," he replied, "your idea is not irrelevant. But the voices of madmen, even in their wildest paroxysms, are never found to tally with that peculiar voice heard upon the stairs. Madmen are of some nation, and their language, however incoherent in its words, has always the coherence of syllabification. Besides, the hair of a madman is not such as I now hold in my hand. I disentangled this little tuft from the rigidly clutched fingers of Madame L'Espanaye. Tell me what you can make of it."

"Dupin!" I said, completely unnerved; "this hair is most unusual – this is no *human* hair."

"I have not asserted that it is," said he; "but, before we decide this point, I wish you to glance at the little sketch I have here traced upon this paper. It is a *fac-simile* drawing of what has been described in one portion of the testimony as 'dark bruises, and deep indentations of finger nails,' upon the throat of Mademoiselle L'Espanaye, and in another, (by Messrs. Dumas and Etienne,) as a 'series of livid spots, evidently the impression of fingers.'

"You will perceive," continued my friend, spreading out the paper upon the table before us, "that this drawing gives the idea of a firm and fixed hold. There is no *slipping* apparent. Each finger has retained – possibly until the death of the victim – the fearful grasp by which it originally imbedded itself. Attempt, now, to place all your fingers, at the same time, in the respective impressions as you see them."

I made the attempt in vain.

"We are possibly not giving this matter a fair trial," he said. "The paper is spread out upon a plane surface; but the human throat is cylindrical. Here is a billet of wood, the circumference of which is about that of the throat. Wrap the drawing around it, and try the experiment again."

I did so; but the difficulty was even more obvious than before. "This," I said, "is the mark of no human hand."

"Read now," replied Dupin, "this passage from Cuvier."

It was a minute anatomical and generally descriptive account of the large fulvous Ourang-Outang of the East Indian Islands. The gigantic stature, the prodigious strength and activity, the wild ferocity, and the imitative propensities of these mammalia are sufficiently well known to all. I understood the full horrors of the murder at once.

"The description of the digits," said I, as I made an end of reading, "is in exact accordance with this drawing. I see that no animal but an Ourang-Outang, of the species here mentioned, could have impressed the indentations as you have traced them. This tuft of tawny hair, too, is identical in character with that of the beast of Cuvier. But I cannot possibly comprehend the particulars of this frightful mystery. Besides, there were *two* voices heard in contention, and one of them was unquestionably the voice of a Frenchman."

"True; and you will remember an expression attributed almost unanimously, by the evidence, to this voice, – the expression, '*mon Dieu!*' This, under the circumstances, has been justly characterized by one of the witnesses (Montani, the confectioner,) as an expression of remonstrance or expostulation. Upon these two words, therefore, I have mainly built my hopes of a full solution of the riddle. A Frenchman was cognizant of the murder. It is possible – indeed it is far more than probable – that he was innocent of all participation in the bloody transactions which took place. The Ourang-Outang may have escaped from him. He may have traced it to the chamber; but, under the agitating circumstances which ensued, he could never have re-captured it. It is still at large. I will not pursue these guesses – for I have no right to call them more – since the shades of reflection upon which they are based are scarcely of sufficient depth to be appreciable by my own intellect, and since I could not pretend to make them intelligible to the understanding of another. We will call them guesses then, and speak of them as such. If the Frenchman in question is indeed, as I suppose, innocent of this atrocity, this advertisement which I left last night, upon our return home, at the office of 'Le Monde,' (a paper devoted to the shipping interest, and much sought by sailors,) will bring him to our residence."

He handed me a paper, and I read thus:

CAUGHT – *In the Bois de Boulogne, early in the morning of the — inst., (the morning of the murder,) a very large, tawny Ourang-Outang of the Bornese species. The owner, (who is ascertained to be a sailor, belonging to a Maltese vessel,) may have the animal again, upon identifying it satisfactorily, and paying a few charges arising from its capture and keeping. Call at No. —, Rue —, Faubourg St. Germain— au troisième.*

"How was it possible," I asked, "that you should know the man to be a sailor, and belonging to a Maltese vessel?"

"I do *not* know it," said Dupin. "I am not *sure* of it. Here, however, is a small piece of ribbon, which from its form, and from its greasy appearance, has evidently been used in tying the hair in one of those long *queues* of which sailors are so fond. Moreover, this knot is one which few besides sailors can tie, and is peculiar to the Maltese. I picked the ribbon up at the foot of the lightning-rod. It could not have belonged to either of the deceased. Now if, after all, I am wrong in my induction from this ribbon, that the Frenchman was a sailor belonging to a Maltese vessel, still I can have done no harm in saying what I did in the advertisement. If I am in error, he will merely suppose that I have been misled by some circumstance into which he will not take the trouble to inquire. But if I am right, a great point is gained. Cognizant although innocent of the murder, the Frenchman will naturally hesitate about replying to the advertisement – about demanding the Ourang-Outang. He will reason thus: – 'I am innocent; I am poor; my Ourang-Outang is of great value – to one in my circumstances a fortune of itself – why should I lose it through idle apprehensions of danger? Here it is, within my grasp. It was found in the Bois de Boulogne – at a vast distance from the scene of that butchery. How can it ever be suspected that a brute beast should have done the deed? The police are at fault – they have failed to procure the slightest clew. Should they even trace the animal, it would be impossible to prove me cognizant of the murder, or to implicate me in guilt on account of that cognizance. Above all, *I am known*. The advertiser designates me as the possessor of the beast. I am not sure to what limit his knowledge may extend. Should I avoid claiming a property of so great value, which it is known that I possess, I will render the animal at least, liable to suspicion. It is not my policy to attract attention either to myself or to the beast. I will answer the advertisement, get the Ourang-Outang, and keep it close until this matter has blown over.'"

At this moment we heard a step upon the stairs.

"Be ready," said Dupin, "with your pistols, but neither use them nor show them until at a signal from myself."

The front door of the house had been left open, and the visitor had entered, without ringing, and advanced several steps upon the staircase. Now, however, he seemed to hesitate. Presently we heard him descending. Dupin was moving quickly to the door, when we again heard him coming up. He did not turn back a second time, but stepped up with decision, and rapped at the door of our chamber.

"Come in," said Dupin, in a cheerful and hearty tone.

A man entered. He was a sailor, evidently, – a tall, stout, and muscular-looking person, with a certain dare-devil expression of countenance, not altogether unprepossessing. His face, greatly sunburnt, was more than half hidden by whisker and *mustachio*. He had with him a huge oaken cudgel, but appeared to be otherwise unarmed. He bowed awkwardly, and bade us "good evening," in French accents, which, although somewhat Neufchatelish, were still sufficiently indicative of a Parisian origin.

"Sit down, my friend," said Dupin. "I suppose you have called about the Ourang-Outang. Upon my word, I almost envy you the possession of him; a remarkably fine, and no doubt a very valuable animal. How old do you suppose him to be?"

The sailor drew a long breath, with the air of a man relieved of some intolerable burden, and then replied, in an assured tone:

"I have no way of telling – but he can't be more than four or five years old. Have you got him here?"

"Oh no, we had no conveniences for keeping him here. He is at a livery stable in the Rue Dubourg, just by. You can get him in the morning. Of course you are prepared to identify the property?"

"To be sure I am, sir."

"I shall be sorry to part with him," said Dupin.

"I don't mean that you should be at all this trouble for nothing, sir," said the man. "Couldn't expect it. Am very willing to pay a reward for the finding of the animal – that is to say, any thing in reason."

"Well," replied my friend, "that is all very fair, to be sure. Let me think! – what should I have? Oh! I will tell you. My reward shall be this. You shall give me all the information in your power about these murders in the Rue Morgue."

Dupin said the last words in a very low tone, and very quietly. Just as quietly, too, he walked toward the door, locked it and put the key in his pocket. He then drew a pistol from his bosom and placed it, without the least flurry, upon the table.

The sailor's face flushed up as if he were struggling with suffocation. He started to his feet and grasped his cudgel, but the next moment he fell back into his seat, trembling violently, and with the countenance of death itself. He spoke not a word. I pitied him from the bottom of my heart.

"My friend," said Dupin, in a kind tone, "you are alarming yourself unnecessarily – you are indeed. We mean you no harm whatever. I pledge you the honor of a gentleman, and of a Frenchman, that we intend you no injury. I perfectly well know that you are innocent of the atrocities in the Rue Morgue. It will not do, however, to deny that you are in some measure implicated in them. From what I have already said, you must know that I have had means of information about this matter – means of which you could never have dreamed. Now the thing stands thus. You have done nothing which you could have avoided – nothing, certainly, which renders you culpable. You were not even guilty of robbery, when you might have robbed with impunity. You have nothing to conceal. You have no reason for concealment. On the other hand, you are bound by every principle of honor to confess all you know. An innocent man is now imprisoned, charged with that crime of which you can point out the perpetrator."

The sailor had recovered his presence of mind, in a great measure, while Dupin uttered these words; but his original boldness of bearing was all gone.

"So help me God," said he, after a brief pause, "I will tell you all I know about this affair; – but I do not expect you to believe one half I say – I would be a fool indeed if I did. Still, I am innocent, and I will make a clean breast if I die for it."

What he stated was, in substance, this. He had lately made a voyage to the Indian Archipelago. A party, of which he formed one, landed at Borneo, and passed into the interior on an excursion of pleasure. Himself and a companion had captured the Ourang-Outang. This companion dying, the animal fell into his own exclusive possession. After great trouble, occasioned by the intractable ferocity of his captive during the home voyage, he at length succeeded in lodging it safely at his own residence in Paris, where, not to attract toward himself the unpleasant curiosity of his neighbors, he kept it carefully secluded, until such time as it should recover from a wound in the foot, received from a splinter on board ship. His ultimate design was to sell it.

Returning home from some sailors' frolic the night, or rather in the morning of the murder, he found the beast occupying his own bed-room, into which it had broken from a closet adjoining, where it had been, as was thought, securely confined. Razor in hand, and fully lathered, it was sitting before a looking-glass, attempting the operation of shaving, in which it had no doubt previously watched its master through the key-hole of the closet. Terrified at the sight of so dangerous a weapon in the possession of an animal so ferocious, and so well able to use it, the man, for some moments, was at a loss what to do. He had been accustomed, however, to quiet the creature, even in its fiercest moods, by the use of a whip, and to this he now resorted. Upon sight of it, the Ourang-Outang sprang at once through the door of the chamber, down the stairs, and thence, through a window, unfortunately open, into the street.

The Frenchman followed in despair; the ape, razor still in hand, occasionally stopping to look back and gesticulate at its pursuer, until the latter had nearly come up with it. It then again made off. In this manner the chase continued for a long time. The streets were profoundly quiet, as it was nearly three o'clock in the morning. In passing down an alley in the rear of the Rue Morgue, the fugitive's attention was arrested by a light gleaming from the open window of Madame L'Espanaye's chamber, in the fourth story of her house. Rushing to the building, it perceived the lightning rod, clambered up with inconceivable agility, grasped the shutter, which was thrown fully back against the wall, and, by its means, swung itself directly upon the headboard of the bed. The whole feat did not occupy a minute. The shutter was kicked open again by the Ourang-Outang as it entered the room.

The sailor, in the meantime, was both rejoiced and perplexed. He had strong hopes of now recapturing the brute, as it could scarcely escape from the trap into which it had ventured, except by the rod, where it might be intercepted as it came down. On the other hand, there was much cause for anxiety as to what it might do in the house. This latter reflection urged the man still to follow the fugitive. A lightning rod is ascended without difficulty, especially by a sailor; but, when he had arrived as high as the window, which lay far to his left, his career was stopped; the most that he could accomplish was to reach over so as to obtain a glimpse of the interior of the room. At this glimpse he nearly fell from his hold through excess of horror. Now it was that those hideous shrieks arose upon the night, which had startled from slumber the inmates of the Rue Morgue. Madame L'Espanaye and her daughter, habited in their night clothes, had apparently been occupied in arranging some papers in the iron chest already mentioned, which had been wheeled into the middle of the room. It was open, and its contents lay beside it on the floor. The victims must have been sitting with their backs toward the window; and, from the time elapsing between the ingress of the beast and the screams, it seems probable that it was not immediately perceived. The flapping-to of the shutter would naturally have been attributed to the wind.

As the sailor looked in, the gigantic animal had seized Madame L'Espanaye by the hair, (which was loose, as she had been combing it,) and was flourishing the razor about her face, in imitation of the motions of a barber. The daughter lay prostrate and motionless; she had swooned. The screams and struggles of the old lady (during which the hair was torn from her head) had the effect of changing the probably pacific purposes of the Ourang-Outang into those of wrath. With one determined sweep of its muscular arm it nearly severed her head from her body. The sight of blood inflamed its anger into phrenzy. Gnashing its teeth, and flashing fire from its eyes, it flew upon the body of the girl, and imbedded its fearful talons in her throat, retaining its grasp until she expired. Its wandering and wild glances fell at this moment upon the head of the bed, over which the face of its master, rigid with horror, was just discernible. The fury of the beast, who no doubt bore still in mind the dreaded whip, was instantly converted into fear. Conscious of having deserved punishment, it seemed desirous of concealing its bloody deeds, and skipped about the chamber in an agony of nervous agitation; throwing down and breaking the furniture as it moved, and dragging the bed from the bedstead. In conclusion, it seized first the corpse of the daughter, and thrust it up the chimney, as it was found; then that of the old lady, which it immediately hurled through the window headlong.

As the ape approached the casement with its mutilated burden, the sailor shrank aghast to the rod, and, rather gliding than clambering down it, hurried at once home – dreading the consequences of the butchery, and gladly abandoning, in his terror, all solicitude about the fate of the Ourang-Outang. The words heard by the party upon the staircase were the Frenchman's exclamations of horror and affright, commingled with the fiendish jabberings of the brute.

I have scarcely anything to add. The Ourang-Outang must have escaped from the chamber, by the rod, just before the break of the door. It must have closed the window as it passed through it. It was subsequently caught by the owner himself, who obtained for it a very large sum at the *Jardin des Plantes*. Le Don was instantly released, upon our narration of the circumstances (with some comments from Dupin) at the bureau of the Prefect of Police. This functionary, however well disposed to my friend, could not altogether conceal his chagrin at the turn which affairs had taken, and was fain to indulge in a sarcasm or two, about the propriety of every person minding his own business.

"Let him talk," said Dupin, who had not thought it necessary to reply. "Let him discourse; it will ease his conscience, I am satisfied with having defeated him in his own castle. Nevertheless, that he failed in the solution of this mystery, is by no means that matter for wonder which he supposes it; for, in truth, our friend the Prefect is somewhat too cunning to be profound. In his wisdom is no *stamen*. It is all head and no body, like the pictures of the Goddess Laverna, – or, at best, all head and shoulders, like a codfish. But he is a good creature after all. I like him especially for one master stroke of cant, by which he has attained his reputation for ingenuity. I mean the way he has '*de nier ce qui est, et d'expliquer ce qui n'est pas.*'"[1]

Footnotes for 'The Murders in the Rue Morgue'
1. Rousseau – Nouvelle Heloise.

Spontaneous Combustion

Arthur B. Reeve

KENNEDY AND I had risen early, for we were hustling to get off for a week-end at Atlantic City. Kennedy was tugging at the straps of his grip and remonstrating with it under his breath, when the door opened and a messenger-boy stuck his head in.

"Does Mr. Kennedy live here?" he asked.

Craig impatiently seized the pencil, signed his name in the book, and tore open a night letter. From the prolonged silence that followed I felt a sense of misgiving. I, at least, had set my heart on the Atlantic City outing, but with the appearance of the messenger-boy I intuitively felt that the board walk would not see us that week.

"I'm afraid the Atlantic City trip is off, Walter," remarked Craig seriously. "You remember Tom Langley in our class at the university? Well, read that."

I laid down my safety razor and took the message. Tom had not spared words, and I could see at a glance at the mere length of the thing that it must be important. It was from Camp Hang-out in the Adirondacks.

"Dear old K.," it began, regardless of expense, "can you arrange to come up here by next train after you receive this? Uncle Lewis is dead. Most mysterious. Last night after we retired noticed peculiar odour about house. Didn't pay much attention. This morning found him lying on floor of living-room, head and chest literally burned to ashes, but lower part of body and arms untouched. Room shows no evidence of fire, but full of sort of oily soot. Otherwise nothing unusual. On table near body siphon of seltzer, bottle of imported limes, and glass for rickeys. Have removed body, but am keeping room exactly as found until you arrive. Bring Jameson. Wire if you cannot come, but make every effort and spare no expense. Anxiously, Tom Langley."

Craig was impatiently looking at his watch as I hastily ran through the letter.

"Hurry, Walter," he exclaimed. "We can just catch the Empire State. Never mind shaving – we'll have a stopover at Utica to wait for the Montreal express. Here, put the rest of your things in your grip and jam it shut. We'll get something to eat on the train – I hope. I'll wire we're coming. Don't forget to latch the door."

Kennedy was already half-way to the elevator, and I followed ruefully, still thinking of the ocean and the piers, the bands and the roller chairs.

It was a good ten-hour journey up to the little station nearest Camp Hang-out and at least a two hour ride after that. We had plenty of time to reflect over what this death might mean to Tom and his sister and to speculate on the manner of it. Tom and Grace Langley were relatives by marriage of Lewis Langley, who, after the death of his wife, had made them his proteges. Lewis Langley was principally noted, as far as I could recall, for being a member of some of the fastest clubs of both New York and London. Neither Kennedy nor myself had shared in the world's opinion of him, for we knew how good he had been to Tom in college and, from Tom, how good he had been to Grace. In fact, he had made Tom assume the Langley name, and in every way had treated the brother and sister as if they had been his own children.

Tom met us with a smart trap at the station, a sufficient indication, if we had not already known, of the "roughing it" at such a luxurious Adirondack "camp" as Camp Hang-out. He was unaffectedly glad to see us, and it was not difficult to read in his face the worry which the affair had already given him.

"Tom; I'm awfully sorry to—" began Craig when, warned by Langley's look at the curious crowd that always gathers at the railroad station at train time, he cut it short. We stood silently a moment while Tom was arranging the trap for us.

As we swung around the bend in the road that cut off the little station and its crowd of lookers-on, Kennedy was the first to speak. "Tom," he said, "first of all, let me ask that when we get to the camp we are to be simply two old classmates whom you had asked to spend a few days before the tragedy occurred. Anything will do. There may be nothing at all to your evident suspicions, and then again there may. At any rate, play the game safely – don't arouse any feeling which might cause unpleasantness later in case you are mistaken."

"I quite agree with you," answered Tom. "You wired, from Albany, I think, to keep the facts out of the papers as much as possible. I'm afraid it is too late for that. Of course the thing became vaguely known in Saranac, although the county officers have been very considerate of us, and this morning a New York Record correspondent was over and talked with us. I couldn't refuse, that would have put a very bad face on it."

"Too bad," I exclaimed. "I had hoped, at least, to be able to keep the report down to a few lines in the Star. But the Record will have such a yellow story about it that I'll simply have to do something to counteract the effect."

"Yes," assented Craig. "But – wait. Let's see the Record story first. The office doesn't know you're up here. You can hold up the Star and give us time to look things over, perhaps get in a beat on the real story and set things right. Anyhow, the news is out. That's certain. We must work quickly. Tell me, Tom, who are at the camp – anyone except relatives?"

"No," he replied, guardedly measuring his words. "Uncle Lewis had invited his brother James and his niece and nephew, Isabelle and James, junior – we call him Junior. Then there are Grace and myself and a distant relative, Harrington Brown, and – oh, of course, uncle's physician, Doctor Putnam."

"Who is Harrington Brown" asked Craig.

"He's on the other side of the Langley family, on Uncle Lewis's mother's side. I think, or at least Grace thinks, that he is quite in love with Isabelle. Harrington Brown would be quite a catch. Of course he isn't wealthy, but his family is mighty well connected. Oh, Craig," sighed Langley, "I wish he hadn't done it – Uncle Lewis, I mean. Why did he invite his brother up here now when he needed to recover from the swift pace of last winter in New York? You know – or you don't know, I suppose, but you'll know it now – when he and Uncle Jim got together there was nothing to it but one drink after another. Doctor Putnam was quite disgusted, at least he professed to be, but, Craig," he lowered his voice to a whisper, as if the very forest had ears, "they're all alike – they've been just waiting for Uncle Lewis to drink himself to death. Oh," he added bitterly, "there's no love lost between me and the relatives on that score, I can assure you."

"How did you find him that morning?" asked Kennedy, as if to turn off this unlocking of family secrets to strangers.

"That's the worst part of the whole affair," replied Tom, and even in the dusk I could see the lines of his face tighten. "You know Uncle Lewis was a hard drinker, but he never seemed to show it much. We had been out on the lake in the motor-boat fishing all the afternoon and – well, I must admit both my uncles had had frequent recourse to 'pocket pistols,' and I remember they referred to it each time as 'bait.' Then after supper nothing would do but fizzes and rickeys. I was disgusted, and after reading a bit went to bed. Harrington and my uncles sat up with Doctor Putnam – according to Uncle Jim – for a couple of hours longer. Then Harrington, Doctor Putnam, and Uncle Jim went to bed, leaving Uncle

Lewis still drinking. I remember waking in the night, and the house seemed saturated with a peculiar odour. I never smelt anything like it in my life. So I got up and slipped into my bathrobe. I met Grace in the hall. She was sniffing.

"'Don't you smell something burning?' she asked.

"I said I did and started down-stairs to investigate. Everything was dark, but that smell was all over the house. I looked in each room down-stairs as I went, but could see nothing. The kitchen and dining-room were all right. I glanced into the living-room, but, while the smell was more noticeable there, I could see no evidence of a fire except the dying embers on the hearth. It had been coolish that night, and we had had a few logs blazing. I didn't examine the room – there seemed no reason for it. We went back to our rooms, and in the morning they found the gruesome object I had missed in the darkness and shadows of the living-room."

Kennedy was intently listening. "Who found him?" he asked.

"Harrington," replied Tom. "He roused us. Harrington's theory is that uncle set himself on fire with a spark from his cigar – a charred cigar butt was found on the floor."

We found Tom's relatives a saddened, silent party in the face of the tragedy. Kennedy and I apologised very profusely for our intrusion, but Tom quickly interrupted, as we had agreed, by explaining that he had insisted on our coming, as old friends on whom he felt he could rely, especially to set the matter right in the newspapers.

I think Craig noticed keenly the reticence of the family group in the mystery – I might almost have called it suspicion. They did not seem to know just whether to take it as an accident or as something worse, and each seemed to entertain a reserve toward the rest which was very uncomfortable.

Mr. Langley's attorney in New York had been notified, but apparently was out of town, for he had not been heard from. They seemed rather anxious to get word from him.

Dinner over, the family group separated, leaving Tom an opportunity to take us into the gruesome living-room. Of course the remains had been removed, but otherwise the room was exactly as it had been when Harrington discovered the tragedy. I did not see the body, which was lying in an anteroom, but Kennedy did, and spent some time in there.

After he rejoined us, Kennedy next examined the fireplace. It was full of ashes from the logs which had been lighted on the fatal night. He noted attentively the distance of Lewis Langley's chair from the fireplace, and remarked that the varnish on the chair was not even blistered.

Before the chair, on the floor where the body had been found, he pointed out to us the peculiar ash-marks for some space around, but it really seemed to me as if something else interested him more than these ash-marks.

We had been engaged perhaps half an hour in viewing the room. At last Craig suddenly stopped.

"Tom," he said, "I think I'll wait till daylight before I go any further. I can't tell with certainty under these lights, though perhaps they show me some things the sunlight wouldn't show. We'd better leave everything just as it is until morning."

So we locked the room again and went into a sort of library across the hall.

We were sitting in silence, each occupied with his own thoughts on the mystery, when the telephone rang. It proved to be a long-distance call from New York for Tom himself. His uncle's attorney had received the news at his home out on Long Island and had hurried to the city to take charge of the estate. But that was not the news that caused the grave look on Tom's face as he nervously rejoined us.

"That was uncle's lawyer, Mr. Clark, of Clark & Burdick," he said. "He has opened uncle's personal safe in the offices of the Langley estate – you remember them, Craig – where all the property of the Langley heirs is administered by the trustees. He says he can't find the will, though he knows there was a will and that it was placed in that safe some time ago. There is no duplicate."

The full purport of this information at once flashed on me, and I was on the point of blurting out my sympathy, when I saw by the look which Craig and Tom exchanged that they had already realised it and understood each other. Without the will the blood-relatives would inherit all of Lewis Langley's interest in the old Langley estate. Tom and his sister would be penniless.

It was late, yet we sat for nearly an hour longer, and I don't think we exchanged a half-dozen sentences in all that time. Craig seemed absorbed in thought. At length, as the great hall-clock sounded midnight, we rose as if by common consent.

"Tom," said Craig, and I could feel the sympathy that welled up in his voice, "Tom, old man, I'll get at the bottom of this mystery if human intelligence can do it."

"I know you will, Craig," responded Tom, grasping each of us by the hand. "That's why I so much wanted you fellows to come up here."

Early in the morning Kennedy aroused me. "Now, Walter, I'm going to ask you to come down into the living-room with me, and we'll take a look at it in the daytime."

I hurried into my clothes, and together we quietly went down. Starting with the exact spot where the unfortunate man had been discovered, Kennedy began a minute examination of the floor, using his pocket lens. Every few moments he would stop to examine a spot on the rug or on the hardwood floor more intently. Several times I saw him scrape up something with the blade of his knife and carefully preserve the scrapings, each in a separate piece of paper.

Sitting idly by, I could not for the life of me see just what good it did for me to be there, and I said as much. Kennedy laughed quietly.

"You're a material witness, Walter," he replied. "Perhaps I shall need you some day to testify that I actually found these spots in this room."

Just then Tom stuck his head in. "Can I help?" he asked. "Why didn't you tell me you were going at it so early?"

"No, thanks," answered Craig, rising from the floor. "I was just making a careful examination of the room before anyone was up so that nobody would think I was too interested. I've finished. But you can help me, after all. Do you think you could describe exactly how everyone was dressed that night?"

"Why, I can try. Let me see. To begin with, uncle had on a shooting-jacket – that was pretty well burnt, as you know. Why, in fact, we all had our shooting-jackets on. The ladies were in white."

Craig pondered a little, but did not seem disposed to pursue the subject further, until Tom volunteered the information that since the tragedy none of them had been wearing their shooting jackets.

"We've all been wearing city clothes," he remarked.

"Could you get your Uncle James and your Cousin Junior to go with you for an hour or two this morning on the lake, or on a tramp in the woods?" asked Craig after a moment's thought.

"Really, Craig," responded Tom doubtfully, "I ought to go to Saranac to complete the arrangements for taking Uncle Lewis's body to New York."

"Very well, persuade them to go with you. Anything, so long as you keep me from interruption for an hour or two."

They agreed on doing that, and as by that time most of the family were up, we went in to breakfast, another silent and suspicious meal.

After breakfast Kennedy tactfully withdrew from the family, and I did the same. We wandered off in the direction of the stables and there fell to admiring some of the horses. The groom, who seemed to be a sensible and pleasant sort of fellow, was quite ready to talk, and soon he and Craig were deep in discussing the game of the north country.

"Many rabbits about here?" asked Kennedy at length, when they had exhausted the larger game.

"Oh, yes. I saw one this morning, sir," replied the groom.

"Indeed?" said Kennedy. "Do you suppose you could catch a couple for me?"

"Guess I could, sir – alive, you mean?"

"Oh, yes, alive – I don't want you to violate the game laws. This is the closed season, isn't it?"

"Yes, sir, but then it's all right, sir, here on the estate."

"Bring them to me this afternoon, or – no, keep them here in the stable in a cage and let me know when you have them. If anybody asks you about them, say they belong to Mr. Tom."

Craig handed a small treasury note to the groom, who took it with a grin and touched his hat.

"Thanks," he said. "I'll let you know when I have the bunnies."

As we walked slowly back from the stables we caught sight of Tom down at the boat-house just putting off in the motor-boat with his uncle and cousin. Craig waved to him, and he walked up to meet us.

"While you're in Saranac," said Craig, "buy me a dozen or so test-tubes. Only, don't let anyone here at the house know you are buying them. They might ask questions."

While they were gone Kennedy stole into James Langley's room and after a few minutes returned to our room with the hunting-jacket. He carefully examined it with his pocket lens. Then he filled a drinking-glass with warm boiled water and added a few pinches of table salt. With a piece of sterilised gauze from Doctor Putnam's medicine-chest, he carefully washed off a few portions of the coat and set the glass and the gauze soaking in it aside. Then he returned the coat to the closet where he had found it. Next, as silently, he stole into Junior's room and repeated the process with his hunting-jacket, using another glass and piece of gauze.

"While I am out of the room, Walter," he said, "I want you to take these two glasses, cover them, and number them and on a slip of paper which you must retain, place the names of the owners of the respective coats. I don't like this part of it – I hate to play spy and would much rather come out in the open, but there is nothing else to do, and it is much better for all concerned that I should play the game secretly just now. There may be no cause for suspicion at all. In that case I'd never forgive myself for starting a family row. And then again but we shall see."

After I had numbered and recorded the glasses Kennedy returned, and we went down-stairs again.

"Curious about the will, isn't it?" I remarked as we stood on the wide verandah a moment.

"Yes," he replied. "It may be necessary to go back to New York to delve into that part of it before we get through, but I hope not. We'll wait."

At this point the groom interrupted us to say that he had caught the rabbits. Kennedy at once hurried to the stable. There he rolled up his sleeves, pricked a vein in his arm, and injected a small quantity of his own blood into one of the rabbits. The other he did not touch.

It was late in the afternoon when Tom returned from town with his uncle and cousin. He seemed even more agitated than usual. Without a word he hurried up from the landing and sought us out.

"What do you think of that?" he cried, opening a copy of the Record, and laying it flat on the library table.

There on the front page was Lewis Langley's picture with a huge scare-head:

MYSTERIOUS CASE OF SPONTANEOUS COMBUSTION

"It's all out," groaned Tom, as we bent over to read the account. "And such a story!"

Under the date of the day previous, a Saranac despatch ran:

Lewis Langley, well known as sporting man and club member in New York, and eldest son of the late Lewis Langley, the banker, was discovered dead under the most mysterious circumstances this morning at Camp Hangout, twelve miles from this town.

The Death of "Old Krook" in Dickens's "Bleak House" or of the victim in one of Marryat's most thrilling tales was not more gruesome than this actual fact. It is without doubt a case of spontaneous human combustion, such as is recorded beyond dispute in medical and medico-legal text-books of the past two centuries. Scientists in this city consulted for the Record agree that, while rare, spontaneous human combustion is an established fact and that everything in this curious case goes to show that another has been added to the already well-authenticated list of cases recorded in America and Europe. The family refuse to be interviewed, which seems to indicate that the rumours in medical circles in Saranac have a solid basis of fact.

Then followed a circumstantial account of the life of Langley and the events leading up to the discovery of the body – fairly accurate in itself, but highly coloured.

"The Record man must have made good use of his time here," I commented, as I finished reading the despatch. "And – well, they must have done some hard work in New York to get this story up so completely – see, after the despatch follow a lot of interviews, and here is a short article on spontaneous combustion itself."

Harrington and the rest of the family had just come in.

"What's this we hear about the Record having an article?" Harrington asked. "Read it aloud, Professor, so we can all hear it."

"'Spontaneous human combustion, or catacausis ebriosus,'" began Craig, "'is one of the baffling human scientific mysteries. Indeed, there can be no doubt but that individuals have in some strange and inexplicable manner caught fire and been partially or almost wholly consumed.

"'Some have attributed it to gases in the body, such as carbureted hydrogen. Once it was noted at the Hotel Dieu in Paris that a body on being dissected gave forth a gas which was inflammable and burned with a bluish flame. Others have attributed the combustion to alcohol. A toper several years ago in Brooklyn and New York used to make money by blowing his breath through a wire gauze and lighting it. Whatever the cause, medical literature records seventy-six cases of catacausis in two hundred years.

"'The combustion seems to be sudden and is apparently confined to the cavities, the abdomen, chest, and head. Victims of ordinary fire accidents rush hither and thither frantically, succumb from exhaustion, their limbs are burned, and their clothing is all destroyed. But in catacausis they are stricken down without warning, the limbs are rarely burned, and only the clothing in contact with the head and chest is consumed. The residue is like a distillation of animal tissue, grey and dark, with an overpoweringly fetid odour. They are said to burn with a flickering stifled blue flame, and water, far from arresting the combustion, seems to add to it. Gin is particularly rich in inflammable, empyreumatic oils, as they are called, and in most cases it is recorded that the catacausis took place among gin-drinkers, old and obese.

"'Within the past few years cases are on record which seem to establish catacausis beyond doubt. In one case the heat was so great as to explode a pistol in the pocket of the victim. In another, a woman, the victim's husband was asphyxiated by the smoke. The woman weighed, one hundred and eighty pounds in life, but the ashes weighed only twelve pounds: In all these cases the proof of spontaneous combustion seems conclusive.'"

As Craig finished reading, we looked blankly, horrified, at one another. It was too dreadful to realise.

"What do you think of it, Professor" asked James Langley, at length. "I've read somewhere of such cases, but to think of its actually happening – and to my own brother. Do you really think Lewis could have met his death in this terrible manner?"

Kennedy made no reply. Harrington seemed absorbed in thought. A shudder passed over us as we thought about it. But, gruesome as it was, it was evident that the publication of the story in the Record had relieved the feelings of the family group in one respect – it at least seemed to offer an explanation. It was noticeable that the suspicious air with which everyone had regarded everyone else was considerably dispelled.

Tom said nothing until the others had withdrawn. "Kennedy," he burst out, then, "do you believe that such combustion is absolutely spontaneous? Don't you believe that something else is necessary to start it?"

"I'd rather not express an opinion just yet, Tom," answered Craig carefully. "Now, if you can get Harrington and Doctor Putnam away from the house for a short time, as you did with your uncle and cousin this morning, I may be able to tell you something about this case soon."

Again Kennedy stole into another bedroom, and returned to our room with a hunting-jacket. Just as he had done before, he carefully washed it off with the gauze soaked in the salt solution and quickly returned the coat, repeating the process with Doctor Putnam's coat and, last, that of Tom himself. Finally he turned his back while I sealed the glasses and marked and recorded them on my slip.

The next day was spent mainly in preparations for the journey to New York with the body of Lewis Langley. Kennedy was very busy on what seemed to me to be preparations for some mysterious chemical experiments. I found myself fully occupied in keeping special correspondents from all over the country at bay.

That evening after dinner we were all sitting in the open summer house over the boat-house. Smudges of green pine were burning and smoking on little artificial islands of stone near the lake shore, lighting up the trees on every side with a red glare. Tom and his sister were seated with Kennedy and myself on one side, while some distance from us Harrington was engaged in earnest conversation with Isabelle. The other members of the family were further removed. That seemed typical to me of the way the family group split up.

"Mr. Kennedy," remarked Grace in a thoughtful, low tone, "what do you make of that Record article?"

"Very clever, no doubt," replied Craig.

"But don't you think it strange about the will?"

"Hush," whispered Tom, for Isabelle and Harrington had ceased talking and might perhaps be listening.

Just then one of the servants came up with a telegram.

Tom hastily opened it and read the message eagerly in the corner of the summer house nearest one of the glowing smudges. I felt instinctively that it was from his lawyer. He turned and beckoned to Kennedy and myself.

"What do you think of that?" he whispered hoarsely.

We bent over and in the flickering light read the message:

New York papers full of spontaneous combustion story. Record had exclusive story yesterday, but all papers today feature even more. Is it true? Please wire additional details at once. Also immediate instructions regarding loss of will. Has been abstracted from safe. Could Lewis Langley have taken it himself? Unless new facts soon must make loss public or issue statement Lewis Langley intestate.

DANIEL CLARK

Tom looked blankly at Kennedy, and then at his sister, who was sitting alone. I thought I could read what was passing in his mind. With all his faults Lewis Langley had been a good foster-parent to his adopted children. But it was all over now if the will was lost.

"What can I do?" asked Tom hopelessly. "I have nothing to reply to him."

"But I have," quietly returned Kennedy, deliberately folding up the message and handing it back. "Tell them all to be in the library in fifteen minutes. This message hurries me a bit, but I am prepared. You will have something to wire Mr. Clark after that." Then he strode off toward the house, leaving us to gather the group together in considerable bewilderment.

A quarter of an hour later we had all assembled in the library, across the hall from the room in which Lewis Langley had been found. As usual Kennedy began by leaping straight into the middle of his subject.

"Early in the eighteenth century," he commenced slowly, "a woman was found burned to death. There were no clues, and the scientists of that time suggested spontaneous combustion. This explanation was accepted. The theory always has been that the process of respiration by which the tissues of the body are used up and got rid of gives the body a temperature, and it has seemed that it may be possible, by preventing the escape of this heat, to set fire to the body."

We were leaning forward expectantly, horrified by the thought that perhaps, after all, the Record was correct.

"Now," resumed Kennedy, his tone changing, "suppose we try a little experiment – one that was tried very convincingly by the immortal Liebig. Here is a sponge. I am going to soak it in gin from this bottle, the same that Mr. Langley was drinking from on the night of the – er – the tragedy."

Kennedy took the saturated sponge and placed it in an agate-iron pan from the kitchen. Then he lighted it. The bluish flame shot upward, and in tense silence we watched it burn lower and lower, till all the alcohol was consumed. Then he picked up the sponge and passed it around. It was dry, but the sponge itself had not been singed.

"We now know," he continued, "that from the nature of combustion it is impossible for the human body to undergo spontaneous ignition or combustion in the way the scientific experts of the past century believed. Swathe the body in the thickest of non-conductors of heat, and what happens? A profuse perspiration exudes, and before such an ignition could possibly take place all the moisture of the body would have to be evaporated. As seventy-five per cent or more of the body is water, it is evident that enormous heat would be necessary – moisture is the great safeguard. The experiment which I have shown you could be duplicated with specimens of human organs preserved for years in alcohol in museums. They would burn just as this sponge – the specimen itself would be very nearly uninjured by the burning of the alcohol."

"Then, Professor Kennedy, you maintain that my brother did not meet his death by such an accident" asked James Langley.

"Exactly that, sir," replied Craig. "One of the most important aspects of the historic faith in this phenomenon is that of its skilful employment in explaining away what would otherwise appear to be convincing circumstantial evidence in cases of accusations of murder."

"Then how do you explain Mr. Langley's death?" demanded Harrington. "My theory of a spark from a cigar may be true, after all."

"I am coming to that in a moment," answered Kennedy quietly. "My first suspicion was aroused by what not even Doctor Putnam seems to have noticed. The skull of Mr. Langley, charred and consumed as it was, seemed to show marks of violence. It might have been from a fracture of the skull or it might have been an accident to his remains as they were being removed to the anteroom. Again, his tongue seemed as though it was protruding. That might have been natural suffocation, or it might have been from forcible strangulation. So far I had nothing but conjecture to work on. But in looking over the living-room I found near the table, on the hardwood floor, a spot – just one little round spot. Now, deductions from spots, even if we know them to be blood, must be made very carefully. I did not know this to be a blood-spot, and so was very careful at first.

"Let us assume it was a blood-spot, however. What did it show? It was just a little regular round spot, quite thick. Now, drops of blood falling only a few inches usually make a round spot with a smooth border. Still the surface on which the drop falls is quite as much a factor as the height from which it falls. If the surface is rough the border may be irregular. But this was a smooth surface and not absorbent. The thickness of a dried blood-spot on a non-absorbent surface is less the greater the height from which it has fallen. This was a thick spot. Now if it had fallen, say, six feet, the height of Mr. Langley, the spot would have been thin – some secondary spatters might have been seen, or at least an irregular edge around the spot. Therefore, if it was a blood-spot, it had fallen only one or two feet. I ascertained next that the lower part of the body showed no wounds or bruises whatever.

"Tracks of blood such as are left by dragging a bleeding body differ very greatly from tracks of arterial blood which are left when the victim has strength to move himself. Continuing my speculations, supposing it to be a blood-spot, what did it indicate? Clearly that Mr. Langley was struck by somebody on the head with a heavy instrument, perhaps in another part of the room, that he was choked, that as the drops of blood oozed from the wound on his head, he was dragged across the floor, in the direction of the fireplace—"

"But, Professor Kennedy," interrupted Doctor Putnam, "have you proved that the spot was a blood-spot? Might it not have been a paint-spot or something of that sort?"

Kennedy had apparently been waiting for just such a question.

"Ordinarily, water has no effect on paint," he answered. "I found that the spot could be washed off with water. That is not all. I have a test for blood that is so delicately sensitive that the blood of an Egyptian mummy thousands of years old will respond to it. It was discovered by a German scientist, Doctor Uhlenhuth, and was no longer ago than last winter applied in England in connection with the Clapham murder. The suspected murderer declared that stains on his clothes were only spatters of paint, but the test proved them to be spatters of blood. Walter, bring in the cage with the rabbits."

I opened the door and took the cage from the groom, who had brought it up from the stable and stood waiting with it some distance away.

"This test is very simple, Doctor Putnam," continued Craig, as I placed the cage on the table and Kennedy unwrapped the sterilised test-tubes. "A rabbit is inoculated with human blood, and after a time the serum that is taken from the rabbit supplies the material for the test.

"I will insert this needle in one of these rabbits which has been so inoculated and will draw off some of the serum, which I place in this test-tube to the right. The other rabbit has not been inoculated. I draw off some of its serum and place that tube here on the left – we will call that our 'control tube.' It will check the results of our tests.

"Wrapped up in this paper I have the scrapings of the spot which I found on the floor – just a few grains of dark, dried powder. To show how sensitive the test is, I will take only one of the smallest of these minute scrapings. I dissolve it in this third tube with distilled water. I will even divide it in half, and place the other half in this fourth tube.

"Next I add some of the serum of the uninoculated rabbit to the half in this tube. You observe, nothing happens. I add a little of the serum of the inoculated rabbit to the other half in this other tube. Observe how delicate the test is—"

Kennedy was leaning forward, almost oblivious of the rest of us in the room, talking almost as if to himself. We, too, had riveted our eyes on the tubes.

As he added the serum from the inoculated rabbit, a cloudy milky ring formed almost immediately in the hitherto colourless, very dilute blood-solution.

"That," concluded Craig, triumphantly holding the tube aloft, "that conclusively proves that the little round spot on the hardwood floor was not paint, was not anything in this wide world but blood."

No one in the room said a word, but I knew there must have been someone there who thought volumes in the few minutes that elapsed.

"Having found one blood-spot, I began to look about for more, but was able to find only two or three traces where spots seemed to have been. The fact is that the blood spots had been apparently carefully wiped up. That is an easy matter. Hot water and salt, or hot water alone, or even cold water, will make quite short work of fresh blood-spots – at least to all outward appearances. But nothing but a most thorough cleaning can conceal them from the Uhlenhuth test, even when they are apparently wiped out. It is a case of Lady Macbeth over again, crying in the face of modern science, 'Out, out, damned spot.'

"I was able with sufficient definiteness to trace roughly a course of blood-spots from the fireplace to a point near the door of the living-room. But beyond the door, in the hall, nothing."

"Still," interrupted Harrington, "to get back to the facts in the case. They are perfectly in accord either with my theory of the cigar or the Record's of spontaneous combustion. How do you account for the facts?"

"I suppose you refer to the charred head, the burned neck, the upper chest cavity, while the arms and legs were untouched?"

"Yes, and then the body was found in the midst of combustible furniture that was not touched. It seems to me that even the spontaneous-combustion theory has considerable support in spite of this very interesting circumstantial evidence about blood-spots. Next to my own theory, the combustion theory seems most in harmony with the facts."

"If you will go over in your mind all the points proved to have been discovered – not the added points in the Record story – I think you will agree with me that mine is a more logical interpretation than spontaneous combustion," reasoned Craig. "Hear me out and you will see that the facts are more in harmony with my less fanciful explanation. No, someone struck Lewis Langley down either in passion or in cold blood, and then, seeing what he had done, made a desperate effort to destroy the evidence of violence. Consider my next discovery."

Kennedy placed the five glasses which I had carefully sealed and labelled on the table before us.

"The next step," he said, "was to find out whether any articles of clothing in the house showed marks that might be suspected of being blood-spots. And here I must beg the pardon of all in the room for intruding in their private wardrobes. But in this crisis it was absolutely necessary, and under such circumstances I never let ceremony stand before justice.

"In these five glasses on the table I have the washings of spots from the clothing worn by Tom, Mr. James Langley, Junior, Harrington Brown, and Doctor Putnam. I am not going to tell you which is which – indeed I merely have them marked, and I do not know them myself. But Mr. Jameson has the marks with the names opposite on a piece of paper in his pocket. I am simply going to proceed with the tests to see if any of the stains on the coats were of blood."

Just then Doctor Putnam interposed. "One question, Professor Kennedy. It is a comparatively easy thing to recognise a blood-stain, but it is difficult, usually impossible, to tell whether the blood is that of a man or of an animal. I recall that we were all in our hunting-jackets that day, had been all day. Now, in the morning there had been an operation on one of the horses at the stable, and I assisted the veterinary from town. I may have got a spot or two of blood on my coat from that operation. Do I understand that this test would show that?"

"No," replied Craig, "this test would not show that. Other tests would, but not this. But if the spot of human blood were less than the size of a pin-head, it would show – it would show if the spot contained even so little as one twenty-thousandth of a gram of albumin. Blood from a horse, a deer, a sheep, a pig, a dog, could be obtained, but when the test was applied the liquid in which they were diluted would remain clear. No white precipitin, as it is called, would form. But let human blood, ever so diluted, be added to the serum of the inoculated rabbit, and the test is absolute."

A death-like silence seemed to pervade the room. Kennedy slowly and deliberately began to test the contents of the glasses. Dropping into each, as he broke the seal, some of the serum of the rabbit, he waited a moment to see if any change occurred.

It was thrilling. I think no one could have gone through that fifteen minutes without having it indelibly impressed on his memory. I recall thinking as Kennedy took each glass, "Which is it to be, guilt or innocence, life or death?" Could it be possible that a man's life might hang on such a slender thread? I knew Kennedy was too accurate and serious to deceive us. It was not only possible, it was actually a fact.

The first glass showed no reaction. Someone had been vindicated.

The second was neutral likewise – another person in the room had been proved innocent.

The third – no change. Science had released a third.

The fourth—

Almost it seemed as if the record in my pocket burned – spontaneously – so intense was my feeling. There in the glass was that fatal, telltale white precipitate.

"My God, it's the milk ring!" whispered Tom close to my ear.

Hastily Kennedy dropped the serum into the fifth. It remained as clear as crystal.

My hand trembled as it touched the envelope containing my record of the names.

"The person who wore the coat with that blood-stain on it," declared Kennedy solemnly, "was the person who struck Lewis Langley down, who choked him and then dragged his scarcely dead body across the floor and obliterated the marks of violence in the blazing log fire. Jameson, whose name is opposite the sign on this glass?"

I could scarcely tear the seal to look at the paper in the envelope. At last I unfolded it, and my eye fell on the name opposite the fatal sign. But my mouth was dry, and my tongue refused to move. It was too much like reading a death-sentence. With my finger on the name I faltered an instant.

Tom leaned over my shoulder and read it to himself. "For Heaven's sake, Jameson," he cried, "let the ladies retire before you read the name."

"It's not necessary," said a thick voice. "We quarrelled over the estate. My share's mortgaged up to the limit, and Lewis refused to lend me more even until I could get Isabelle happily married. Now Lewis's goes to an outsider – Harrington, boy, take care of Isabelle, fortune or no fortune. Good—"

Someone seized James Langley's arm as he pressed an automatic revolver to his temple. He reeled like a drunken man and dropped the gun on the floor with an oath.

"Beaten again," he muttered. "Forgot to move the ratchet from 'safety' to 'fire.'"

Like a madman he wrenched himself loose from us, sprang through the door, and darted upstairs. "I'll show you some combustion!" he shouted back fiercely.

Kennedy was after him like a flash. "The will!" he cried.

We literally tore the door off its hinges and burst into James Langley's room. He was bending eagerly over the fireplace. Kennedy made a flying leap at him. Just enough of the will was left unburned to be admitted to probate.

The Dead Man's Dog

Zandra Renwick

BENCHLEY WAS surprised to find that the dead man's dog had followed her home.

She'd finished the job, taking great satisfaction in making everything sparkle and shine, and walked back to her motel. Tomorrow she'd catch the 8:42 bus home, and after three jiggling, jolting, jouncing hours across desert highway staring out the grimy window at sand and rocks she'd be watering her scraggly herb garden and making mushroom soup stock for next week. Her schedule was quite tight.

"Sorry," she told it as it slobbered and slurped water from the motel room's scratched plastic ice bucket, "but there really isn't room in my life for a dog."

The look on the dog's long face implied it understood her position completely, but that didn't prevent it from joining her on the sagging left seat of the two-person sofa to watch cable television reruns of a lesser-known crime show that had gone off the air long before Benchley had been born. The television police sauntered into a too-red spattered crime scene and began pointing to various supposed clues: a fingernail ripped from the assassin during the struggle; a torn scrap of clothing left behind; a melodramatic and wholly unlikely scrawl in blood from the victim's dying fingers, indicating on the dated linoleum the drug kingpin who'd orchestrated his murder.

"What a mess," Benchley said, idly stroking the dog's wide velvety head where it weighed down her knees. "They should've hired me to clean."

The dog's brows twitched as it gazed up into her face in what she read to be its wholehearted agreement.

The knock at the door felt intrusive in a way it didn't, usually. Benchley apologized to the dog for dislodging its head from her lap and went to answer. Frick stood there, on schedule, blunt meaty face coated with its usual light sheen of sweat. He pushed past her into the dingy room, froze when he saw the dog on the couch. The dog, Benchley was satisfied to note, ignored him.

"What's that?" he said, full chin jutting in the animal's direction.

Taking her cue from the dog and ignoring his question, Benchley held out her hand, palm up. She was only a cleaner, not a Cleaner, like Frick. The guy for whom she and Frick worked ran a tight but extremely small operation; her fee, in smooth flat fifties, fit snugly into a single letter-sized envelope. Easy to hand over.

"And I need a ride home tomorrow," she said. "Bus isn't going to work."

Frick snorted. "That's three hours each way, nothing but desert in between! You drive it if you want to. I got better things to do."

She shoved the envelope he handed her deep into the pocket of her cargo pants, zipped the pocket shut. "You know I don't drive. I need a ride home."

"No way is a dog going to slobber up my back seat."

"I need a ride home."

"I got allergies…" She stared at him until he shrugged. "All right, you little freak. But you owe me."

When Frick left the dog seemed relieved. Benchley joined the animal on the couch, intrigued by the way it shifted its weight to allow her to slide in beside it, how its head and paws flowed back over her lap like a liquid fur blanket, warm and forgiving. A high-pitched flatulent wheeze sounded and it shot her an apologetic look as a supremely unpleasant doggy aroma saturated the air.

"It's okay," she reassured it, flipping the channel with her thumb. "I've smelled worse."

* * *

The motel room phone ringing in the middle of the night was an unwelcome surprise. Benchley didn't do well with surprises. Between the dead man's dog following her home and the unexpected phone call, this job was turning particularly stressful.

Benchley picked up the phone and cradled the receiver to her ear. She could tell it was Frick on the other end of the line from his breathing, heavy, thick, echoing from his barrel-shaped chest even over the tinny hollowness of the line.

"There's been an Incident," he said. "Needs emergency cleaning."

She glanced at the red numbers of the cheap motel clock. Two forty-one A.M. "Emergency cleans get double rate," she said.

"This isn't the usual." His voice was tight. Excited. Tired. "This is more of what you might call a personal affair. Nothing to do with our employer."

"I don't do personal. Goodbye."

"Listen, you runty weirdo, you're going to owe me for that ride tomorrow. Do this first and we're even. Boss never needs to know anything outside the usual happened this trip. You think I didn't recognize that fucking dog? You think he'd let you keep something like that, something so obvious to tie any of us to a scene? That's not a *dog*, you little shit! It's *evidence*."

His ragged breathing filled the line, roaring in Benchley's ear as she imagined what her employer would have his Cleaner do to the dog if he knew where it came from. What he might do to her swam only peripherally near the thought. But the dog . . .

Benchley moved her feet under the cheap polyester satin of the coverlet. The dog shifted to accommodate her new position. A sudden unpleasantly sulphuric canine emission hit her olfactories like a brick to the nose.

"Okay," she said into the phone.

"Ten minutes," said Frick. The line went dead.

Black tennis shoes, black cap, black T-shirt and cardigan, cargo pants minus envelope, cleaning kit in the duffle. No socks; Benchley never could stand how they squeezed her ankles. She refilled the plastic ice bucket with water for the dog and slid the envelope under its warm ribs. The animal thumped its heavy tail twice but didn't otherwise move, only watched her from under velvet brows as she let herself out the motel room door.

A smooth black car eased into the parking lot with only its running lights on. Benchley slid into the back, hefting her cleaning duffel onto the seat beside her. Frick let the car roll out of the lot onto the street before firing up the headlights. His jacket was missing. A smear of blood stained his collar near his left ear. In the grey wash of headlights reflecting off asphalt the blood looked black rather than brown or rust or red.

They pulled into the driveway of a modest unkempt bungalow. Common midcentury cookie-cutter design, aluminum porch awning, scraggly row of parched roses behind a brick border. Benchley could tell someone had tried gardening but hadn't had the feel for it, or maybe lacked the patience. Gardening in arid climates required patience.

Frick cut the lights and rolled deep into the driveway, nosing up to the sagging front of a detached garage. He led the way in darkness to the back door, a typical nineteen fifties or early sixties kitchen entry. Someone had unscrewed the bulb in the cheap porchlight. When Frick used a key on his personal keyring to open the back door, Benchley pretended it wasn't strange.

The smell of the night-black kitchen hit her, familiar and ripe. "Is the mess contained to this room?" she asked. He grunted in a manner she took to be affirmative. She'd do a visual once-over of the other rooms afterward, as always. But it was good to get a sense of a job's parameters.

She dug her penlight from the front duffel pocket, clamped it in her teeth to painter-tape blackout plastic over the two small windows. She flipped the overhead light on to see Frick still hulking in the doorway, big and sweaty, hands shoved deep into pockets.

Two sticky blackish pools covered much of the cheap tile. Scraps of duct tape still clung to the chrome dinette chairs at the level where human wrists would fall, had a person or persons been confined involuntarily. There were no bodies, living or dead; the Cleaner always took care of those before he called her, the cleaner.

"This is a pretty big mess for a single Incident," she said, studying the pools.

"There were two of them," he said. "Two Incidents."

The hitch in his voice made her glance at his face. He too was studying the clotting red mess.

He said, "She was cheating on me."

Benchley nodded, as though an explanation had been given and not simply a reason or, as the police in the silly crime show she and the dog had been watching earlier would've called it, a motive. She'd never considered *why* or *what* or even *who* to be part of her job. No reason to alter her position on such matters now. She had a lot of work to do before dawn.

Benchley scrubbed and scoured and bleached. She shoveled soiled material into industrial-strength black bags. She paid attention to detail, a skill at which she excelled in a focused situation like this, like an Incident, where she could narrow the entire world down to a single bungalow, a single kitchen, a single tile or line of grout if need be to clean a mess. Outside, the world spun as it always did, millions of people doing millions of things, feeling millions and billions of feelings and sensations and elations and pains. An Incident was much simpler, less stressful with the unpredictable element of living removed. Easier to contain, easier to walk away from. She used to take comfort in the notion that making things clean meant no one else needed to be distressed by the awkwardness of finding the mess. In the beginning she'd clung to the thought she was sparing some sister or close neighbor or dear childhood friend from the task of scrubbing away the gore and the shit, the brain matter and skull fragments and shredded cartilage and tooth shards which might be all that remained of their departed loved one. She didn't think like that anymore. These days she simply took satisfaction in the gleam of scoured things, in a job complete, a job conscientiously done. She made everything sparkle and shine, and then she packed her bags, and went home until the next call came from Frick.

Her arms ached and her fingers were numb by the time she crumpled the last sheet of plastic into the last black sack and taped it shut. Her cursory inspection of the house came up clean, so far as she could tell, like Frick said it would. Her final task was to pluck his cigarette butts from the flower pot on the back porch and dump them into their own little sack. She raked them out from around the sharp woody stem of whatever flower had died there, leaving it to itself.

The sky was already lightening as they pulled into the motel lot. Frick left the motor running while Benchley let herself into the room. The dog waddled loose-hipped past her to urinate on the few blades of scraggled grass pushing up through the asphalt outside her room's door. She took the envelope from the bed and zipped it safe into her cargo pocket. It was still warm from a night spent under the dog.

When Benchley tossed her duffel into the back seat the dog clambered in after it without prompting. She expected a sharp protest from Frick when the animal's nails scrabbled for purchase on the vinyl interior but he simply stared out the front windshield, neither patient nor impatient. A cigarette dangled from his sausage fingers, ash long from inattention. After brief hesitation she closed the rear door and let herself into the front, into the passenger seat beside the Cleaner.

He turned to look at her with a faintly surprised air, as though being reminded of her existence. She watched him glance at the dog in his rearview mirror, but other than a tightening of his wide mouth and a disgusted shake of his head he made no objection.

In no time at all they'd reached the highway proper. The city fell away behind them, the road unfurling in front, an endless grey grosgrain ribbon dotted with yellow thread.

Fifty miles passed in silence before he said, "You know, if our employer ever finds out about that stupid dog, he'll kill us both."

Hot desert sun tilted hard and bright into Benchley's eyes as she studied him, slanting into the car even past the tinted glass of the windshield. "Not if we see him first," she said.

He grunted, almost an involuntary laugh but without the smile, without the mirth. The dog gave an exaggerated sigh from the back, followed by a flatulent whuffle loud enough to be heard above the rumble of tires on road.

Another fifty miles of desert scrolled by in a silence punctuated only occasionally by the dog's sleepy whimpers, by the click of the car's cigarette lighter popping up red and ready, by the brief crackle of paper and tobacco igniting as Frick held the glowing metal ember to the end of his next smoke. At a nondescript turnoff neither here nor there, a juncture Benchley hadn't noticed on the way to the job – would not have noticed had she travelled by bus and stared out the window at every crossing between one city and the next every day for a month – he exited the highway. The small side highway became a smaller road, which gradually grew even smaller. No houses, no shops. Some barbed wire fencing embedded in split wooden posts, but haphazardly erected, not seeming to enclose any particular thing or place, no observable people or animals to keep out or in on one side of a fence or the other.

"This is not where I live," Benchley said, looking out the window at a distant rock formation. Majestic, distinctive, not visible from the main highway they'd left. Nothing but rock jumbles and scrub-humped sand in every direction, no plants taller than dog-height, low and scruffy, dusty and prickled.

Frick veered onto another side road, this one unpaved. "Unusual circumstances," he said. "Need to make a detour."

Gravel crunched underneath, louder than asphalt. Sunshine reflecting off the ochre rock and grit cast everything in a peachy glow. When Frick at last drew the car to a stop the cessation of motion made Benchley's ears ring. Leaving keys in the ignition he got out, slammed the door shut behind him. The dog barked for the first time, once, short. She twisted in the seat to see it standing in the back, one thick paw on the window.

"Okay," she told it. She let herself out, opened the rear door for the dead man's dog to jump down. Wind whipped her short hair from under the edges of her cap. The trail they'd followed at a subtle but definite incline had brought them much higher in altitude than it had felt, gradually arriving. The path the car had come curved away and down, fresh tire marks in fine grit already being scrubbed away by wind. Far, far away she made out the glint of a vehicle passing on the highway, sun glancing off the hard shell of a camper or a rig. Hard to tell from this distance.

She slitted her eyes tighter against blowing grit. The dog squatted to urinate nearby on a clump of low scrub almost completely buried in the sand. Benchley had thought boy dogs lifted their legs, but this one only squatted, an arthritic-looking and shaky motion. Perhaps the dog was old. Benchley wouldn't know.

The trunk yawned wide. Crammed into the deep black-carpeted cavity were familiar black industrial sacks, humped and rounded by their contents, taped shut. She watched, squinting into the slicing wind, as Frick unloaded the top sacks, the ones Benchley had spent the night filling with soiled absorbent wipes, darker red at the bottom, lighter red in the middle layers, then almost clear on top where the material was saturated more with heavy-duty cleanser than anything else. A caustic chemical odor prickled the nostrils even in the desert, even in the wind, even past layers of plastic and tape.

The four black industrial sacks on the bottom layer of the trunk, nestled deepest in the crevices between wheel wells, were visibly heavier than the rest. Someone, not Benchley, had triple- and quadruple-taped the bags. Taping pattern was distinctive, like an artist's signature. Instead of Benchley's meticulous crisscrossed creases, these deepest bags, the first loaded, bore a brutal but efficient hash-marking pattern of tape. It was a good job, she could tell. Those bags had been taped by somebody who knew his business, somebody practiced in the art of cleaning.

With his meaty fists Frick heaved the last bag onto the ground and slammed the trunk shut. Benchley wanted to get back into the car. Instead she wrapped her hands over her upper arms, hugging herself tight against the sun and wind. She watched Frick grab the lightest bags two at a time and hurl them over the edge of the steep incline at the side of the path, practically a shallow canyon running parallel to the bowed segment of rutted gravel. He hitched up his pants and returned for two more bags, flung them over the edge so they tumbled down, rolling and bumping like black plastic boulders to join the others in a shower of pebbles and sand. The heaviest bags he carried one at a time, using both hands. No plastic split, nothing leaked or spattered or poked from any of the bags. He'd done a good job, wrapping and triple-bagging, taping.

The dog wandered over with its stiff awkward gait, nosed the final remaining bag.

"Get away from that, mutt!" snapped Frick, reaching for it. "But not too far, you hear? This is a good place."

He paused, his gaze sliding past the last thickly taped bag, past the dead man's dog, to Benchley. She snapped to attention, like lightning had zapped up her spine. She stepped lightly across the brush and gravel, put one hand on the dog's shaggy back. It glanced up at her, grotesque pink tongue lolling ridiculously far out of its mouth, before returning to nose at the black plastic.

"Come back to the car," she told the dog, tugging on its coat, watching Frick watch her. "Come get in so we can go home. Come."

Frick shook his head. "You know better than that. You know you got to get rid of evidence. All of it, no mess. Leave everything clean, right?"

"No." Benchley dropped to her knees and wrapped her arms around the dog. It wagged its tail but didn't turn its attention from a particularly skullshaped protuberance in the black plastic sack it nosed.

"Hey!" said Frick, tugging the sack from the dog's reach. This last sack must've been the heaviest; even the Cleaner's muscles visibly bulged in his thick forearms as he hefted it clear of the dog's nose.

Benchley was caught off guard when the dog lunged after the sack. She sprawled on the powdery grit, her arms suddenly empty. The sharp desert wind gusted a flurry of grit into her eyes as Frick and the dead man's dog scuffled in the sand, an oddly graceful tug-of-war over the shiny black plastic sack, one of them clamped to each side.

She scrubbed her face with balled fists trying to clear her vision, the sand painful even as her eyes watered. She pushed to her feet and staggered after the dog, scraping grit from her eyes as it puffed up in plumes to be huffed off in random gusts as the wind whistled up off the edge of the shallow canyon, scented slightly of chemical cleanser and drying blood.

The dog threw all its weight against the large man, its haunches sweeping a wide furrow in the sand as the Cleaner dragged it and the sack clenched in its jaws close to the cliff's rim. Benchley stumbled after them, thinking to add her weight to the animal's, to prevent the man from flinging dog and sack together into the canyon where they'd both tumble down the steep incline to smash onto the rocks at the bottom alongside the other discarded evidence.

Frick's city shoes sent rocks skittering over the sharp rim of the incline. His muscles bunched under his shirt as he prepared to heave and twist in one mighty motion, to sling the dead man's dog over the edge.

The dog let go.

Frick made no sound. Benchley, blinking through grit-seared eyes as she threw her arms around the dog's neck, thought she saw a triumphant smile suffuse the Cleaner's face as he staggered backward over the lip of the cliff, a look close to elation. He was there one moment, a hulking blot against the bright morning sky, and then he wasn't. She didn't hear him fall, only wind whistling through rocks, blowing over sand.

The dog slipped from her embrace to amble with its arthritic gait back to the parked car. When Benchley peered over the rim of the steep incline she saw a larger cloth-and-meat boulder lying near the plastic and tape ones, tucked in among the ochre stones and the sand-clogged tumbleweeds.

She left the car and everything inside. She walked the opposite direction from the highway, away from the distant glitter of cars going from here to there. The dog followed, slowly. When they came to the first small homestead – one cinderblock house, one windmilled water pump, one weedy garden staked over with clear tarp, one teardrop trailer out back with a rusted-off hitch and a lone corroded automobile propped on bricks – she knocked on the screen door and asked if her dog could have some water. The elderly lady, shriveled apple-doll small as though dehydrated by desert heat and wind, didn't behave as though it was odd for strangers to stagger up to her tiny front porch. She said her son had left his trailer, and Benchley and her dog could sleep there if they wanted, though it'd been sitting empty for many years now and was certainly a bit of a mess.

Benchley could tell the dog was tired, but it seemed to like the lady very much. So she accepted the offer with gratitude, and with the utmost assurance that she wasn't afraid of a bit of a mess, that she was in fact quite well practiced in the art of cleaning.

The Tale of the Three Apples

Scheherazade

Translated by Richard Francis Burton

THEY RELATE, O King of the age and lord of the time and of these days, that the Caliph Harun al-Rashid summoned his Wazir Ja'afar one night and said to him, "I desire to go down into the city and question the common folk concerning the conduct of those charged with its governance; and those of whom they complain we will depose from office and those whom they commend we will promote." Quoth Ja'afar, "Hearkening and obedience!" So the Caliph went down with Ja'afar and Eunuch Masrur to the town and walked about the streets and markets and, as they were threading a narrow alley, they came upon a very old man with a fishing-net and crate to carry small fish on his head, and in his hand a staff; and, as he walked at a leisurely pace, he repeated these lines:

> They say me: Thou shinest a light to mankind With thy lore as the night which the Moon doth uplight!
> I answer, "A truce to your jests and your gibes;
> Without luck what is learning? – a poor-devil wight!
> If they take me to pawn with my lore in my pouch,
> With my volumes to read and my ink-case to write,
> For one day's provision they never could pledge me;
> As likely on Doomsday to draw bill at sight."
> How poorly, indeed, doth it fare wi' the poor,
> With his pauper existence and beggarly plight:
> In summer he faileth provision to find;
> In winter the fire-pot's his only delight:
> The street-dogs with bite and with bark to him rise,
> And each losel receives him with bark and with bite:
> If he lift up his voice and complain of his wrong,
> None pities or heeds him, however he's right;
> And when sorrows and evils like these he must brave
> His happiest homestead were down in the grave.

When the Caliph heard his verses he said to Ja'afar, "See this poor man and note his verses, for surely they point to his necessities." Then he accosted him and asked, "O Shaykh, what be thine occupation?" and the poor man answered, "O my lord, I am a fisherman with a family to keep and I have been out between mid-day and this time; and not a thing hath Allah made my portion wherewithal to feed my family. I cannot even pawn myself to buy them a supper and I hate and disgust my life and I hanker after death." Quoth the Caliph, "Say me, wilt thou return with us to Tigris' bank and cast thy net on my luck, and whatsoever turneth up I will buy of thee for an hundred gold pieces?" The man rejoiced when he heard these words and said, "On my head be it! I will go back with you;" and, returning with them river-wards, made a cast and waited a while; then he hauled in the rope and dragged the net ashore and there appeared in it a chest padlocked and heavy. The Caliph examined it and lifted it finding it weighty; so he gave the fisherman two hundred dinars and sent him about his business; whilst Masrur, aided by the Caliph, carried the chest to the palace and set it down and lighted the candles. Ja'afar and Masrur then broke it open and found therein a basket of palm-leaves corded with red worsted. This they cut open and saw within it a piece of carpet which they lifted out, and under it was a woman's mantilla folded in four, which they pulled out; and at the bottom of the chest they came upon a young lady, fair as a silver ingot, slain and cut into nineteen pieces. When the Caliph looked upon her he cried, "Alas!" and tears ran down his cheeks and turning to Ja'afar he said, "O dog of Wazirs,[1] shall folk be murdered in our reign and be cast into the river to be a burden and a responsibility for us on the Day of Doom? By Allah, we must avenge this woman on her murderer and he shall be made die the worst of deaths!" And presently he added, "Now, as surely as we are descended from the Sons of Abbas,[2] if thou bring us not him who slew her, that we do her justice on him, I will hang thee at the gate of my palace, thee and forty of thy kith and kin by thy side." And the Caliph was wroth with exceeding rage. Quoth Ja'afar, "Grant me three days delay;" and quoth the Caliph, "We grant thee this." So Ja'afar went out from before him and returned to his own house, full of sorrow and saying to himself, "How shall I find him who murdered this damsel, that I may bring him before the Caliph? If I bring other than the murderer, it will be laid to my charge by the Lord: in very sooth I wot not what to do." He kept his house three days and on the fourth day the Caliph sent one of the Chamberlains for him and, as he came into the presence, asked him, "Where is the murderer of the damsel?" to which answered Ja'afar, "O Commander of the Faithful, am I inspector of murdered folk that I should ken who killed her?" The Caliph was furious at his answer and bade hang him before the palace-gate and commanded that a crier cry through the streets of Baghdad, "Whoso would see the hanging of Ja'afar, the Barmaki, Wazir of the Caliph, with forty of the Barmecides,[3] his cousins and kinsmen, before the palace-gate, let him come and let him look!" The people flocked out from all the quarters of the city to witness the execution of Ja'afar and his kinsmen, not knowing the cause. Then they set up the gallows and made Ja'afar and the others stand underneath in readiness for execution, but whilst every eye was looking for the Caliph's signal, and the crowd wept for Ja'afar and his cousins of the Barmecides, lo and behold! a young man fair of face and neat of dress and of favour like the moon raining light, with eyes black and bright, and brow flower-white, and cheeks red as rose and young down where the beard grows, and a mole like a grain of ambergris, pushed his way through the people till he stood immediately before the Wazir and said to him, "Safety to thee from this strait, O Prince of the Emirs and Asylum of the poor! I am the man who slew the woman ye found in the chest, so hang me for her and do her justice on me!" When Ja'afar heard the youth's confession he rejoiced at his own deliverance, but grieved and sorrowed for the fair youth; and whilst they were yet talking behold, another man well stricken in years pressed forwards through the people and thrust his way amid the populace till he came to Ja'afar and the youth, whom he saluted saying, "Ho thou the Wazir and Prince sans-peer! believe not the words of this youth. Of a surety none murdered the damsel but I; take her wreak on me this moment; for, an thou do not thus, I will require it of thee before Almighty Allah." Then quoth the young man, "O Wazir, this is an old man in his dotage who wotteth not whatso he saith ever, and I am he who murdered her, so do thou avenge her on me!" Quoth the old man, "O my son, thou art young and desirest the joys of the world and I am old and weary and surfeited with the world: I will offer my life as a ransom for thee and for the Wazir and his cousins. No one murdered the damsel but I, so Allah upon thee, make haste to hang me, for no life is left in me now that hers is gone." The Wazir marvelled much at all this strangeness and, taking the young man and the old man, carried them before the Caliph, where, after kissing the ground seven times between his hands, he said, "O Commander of the Faithful, I bring thee the murderer of the damsel!" "Where is he?"; asked the Caliph and Ja'afar answered, "This young man saith, I am the murderer, and this old man giving him the lie saith, I am the murderer, and behold, here are the twain standing before thee." The Caliph looked at the old man and the young man and asked, "Which of you killed the girl?" The young man replied, "No one slew her save I;" and the old man answered, "Indeed none killed her but myself." Then said the Caliph to Ja'afar, "Take the twain and hang them both;" but Ja'afar rejoined, "Since one of them was the murderer, to hang the other were mere injustice." [4] "By Him who raised the firmament and dispread the earth like a carpet," cried the youth, "I am he who slew the damsel;" and he went on to describe the manner of her murder and the basket, the mantilla and the bit of carpet, in fact all that the Caliph had found upon her. So the Caliph was certified that the young man was the murderer; whereat he wondered and asked him, "What was the cause of thy wrongfully doing this damsel to die and what made thee confess the murder without the bastinado, and what brought thee here to yield up thy life, and what made thee say Do her wreak upon me?" The youth answered, "Know, O Commander of the Faithful, that this woman was my wife and the mother of my children; also my first cousin and the daughter of my paternal uncle, this old man who is my father's own brother. When I married her she was a maid[5] and Allah blessed me with three male children by her; she loved me and served me and I saw no evil in her, for I also loved her with fondest love. Now on the first day of this month she fell ill with grievous sickness and I fetched in physicians to her; but recovery came to her little by little. and, when I wished her to go to the Hammam-bath, she said: – There is a something I long for before I go to the bath and I long for it with an exceeding longing. To hear is to comply, said I. And what is it? Quoth she, I have a queasy craving for an apple, to smell it and bite a bit of it. I replied: – Hadst thou a thousand longings I would try to satisfy them! So I went on the instant into the city and sought for apples but could find none; yet, had they cost a gold piece each, would I have bought them. I was vexed at this and went home and said: – O daughter of my uncle, by Allah I can find none! She was distressed, being yet very weakly, and her weakness increased greatly on her that night and I felt anxious and alarmed on her account. As soon as morning dawned I went out again and made the round of the gardens, one by one, but found no apples anywhere. At last there met me an old gardener, of whom I asked about them and he answered: – O my son, this fruit is a rarity with us and is not now to be found save in the garden of the Commander of the Faithful at Bassorah, where the gardener keepeth it for the Caliph's eating. I returned to my house troubled by my ill-success; and my love for my wife and my affection moved me to undertake the journey. So I gat me ready and set out and travelled fifteen days and nights, going and coming, and brought her three apples which I bought from the gardener for three dinars. But when I went in to my wife and set them before her, she took no pleasure in them and let them lie by her side; for her weakness and fever had increased on her and her malady lasted without abating ten days, after which time she began to recover health. So I left my house and betaking me to my shop sat there buying and selling; and about midday behold, a great ugly black slave, long as a lance and broad as a bench, passed by my shop holding in hand one of the three apples wherewith he was playing. Quoth I: – O my good slave, tell me whence thou tookest that apple, that I may get the like of it? He laughed and answered: – I got it from my mistress, for I had been absent and on my return I found her lying ill with three apples by her side, and she said to me: – My horned wittol of a husband made a journey for them to Bassorah and bought them for three dinars. So I ate and drank with her and took this one from her.6 When I heard such words from the slave, O Commander of the Faithful, the world grew black before my face, and I arose and locked up my shop and went home beside myself for excess of rage. I looked for the apples and finding only two of the three asked my wife: – O my cousin, where is the third apple?; and raising her head languidly she answered: – I wot not, O son of my uncle, where 'tis gone! This convinced me that the slave had spoken the truth, so I took a knife and coming behind her got upon her breast without a word said and cut her throat. Then I hewed off her head and her limbs in pieces and, wrapping her in her mantilla and a rag of carpet, hurriedly sewed up the whole which I set in a chest and, locking it tight, loaded it on my he-mule and threw it into the Tigris with my own hands. So Allah upon thee, O

Commander of the Faithful, make haste to hang me, as I fear lest she appeal for vengeance on Resurrection Day. For, when I had thrown her into the river and none knew aught of it, as I went back home I found my eldest son crying and yet he knew naught of what I had done with his mother. I asked him: – What hath made thee weep, my boy?; and he answered: – I took one of the three apples which were by my mammy and went down into the lane to play with my brethren when behold, a big long black slave snatched it from my hand and said, Whence hadst thou this? Quoth I, My father travelled far for it, and brought it from Bassorah for my mother who was ill and two other apples for which he paid three ducats. He took no heed of my words and I asked for the apple a second and a third time, but he cuffed me and kicked me and went off with it. I was afraid lest my mother should swinge me on account of the apple, so for fear of her I went with my brother outside the city and stayed there till evening closed in upon us; and indeed I am in fear of her; and now by Allah, O my father, say nothing to her of this or it may add to her ailment! When I heard what my child said I knew that the slave was he who had foully slandered my wife, the daughter of my uncle, and was certified that I had slain her wrongfully. So I wept with exceeding weeping and presently this old man, my paternal uncle and her father, came in; and I told him what had happened and he sat down by my side and wept and we ceased not weeping till midnight. We have kept up mourning for her these last five days and we lamented her in the deepest sorrow for that she was unjustly done to die. This came from the gratuitous lying of the slave, the blackamoor, and this was the manner of my killing her; so I conjure thee, by the honour of thine ancestors, make haste to kill me and do her justice upon me, as there is no living for me after her!" The Caliph marvelled at his words and said, "By Allah, the young man is excusable: I will hang none but the accursed slave and I will do a deed which shall comfort the ill-at-ease and suffering, and which shall please the All-glorious King."

And Shahrazad perceived the dawn of day and ceased saying her permitted say.

Now when it was the Twentieth Night, she said:

It hath reached me, O auspicious King, that the Caliph swore he would hang none but the slave, for the youth was excusable. Then he turned to Ja'afar and said to him, "Bring before me this accursed slave who was the sole cause of this calamity; and, if thou bring him not before me within three days, thou shalt be slain in his stead." So Ja'afar fared forth weeping and saying. "Two deaths have already beset me, nor shall the crock come of safe from every shock.[7] In this matter craft and cunning are of no avail; but He who preserved my life the first time can preserve it a second time. By Allah, I will not leave my house during the three days of life which remain to me and let the Truth (whose perfection be praised!) do e'en as He will." So he kept his house three days, and on the fourth day he summoned the Kazis and legal witnesses and made his last will and testament, and took leave of his children weeping. Presently in came a messenger from the Caliph and said to him, "The Commander of the Faithful is in the most violent rage that can be, and he sendeth to seek thee and he sweareth that the day shall certainly not pass without thy being hanged unless the slave be forthcoming." When Ja'afar heard this he wept, and his children and slaves and all who were in the house wept with him. After he had bidden adieu to everybody except his youngest daughter, he proceeded to farewell her; for he loved this wee one, who was a beautiful child, more than all his other children; and he pressed her to his breast and kissed her and wept bitterly at parting from her; when he felt something round inside the bosom of her dress and asked her, "O my little maid, what is in thy bosom pocket?"; "O my father," she replied, "it is an apple with the name of our Lord the Caliph written upon it. Rayhán our slave brought it to me four days ago and would not let me have it till I gave him two dinars for it." When Ja'afar heard speak of the slave and the apple, he was glad and put his hand into his child's pocket[8] and drew out the apple and knew it and rejoiced saying, "O ready Dispeller of trouble!"[9] Then he bade them bring the slave and said to him, "Fie upon thee, Rayhan! whence haddest thou this apple?" "By Allah, O my master," he replied, "though a lie may get a man once off, yet may truth get him off, and well off, again and again. I did not steal this apple from thy palace nor from the gardens of the Commander of the Faithful. The fact is that five days ago, as I was walking along one of the alleys of this city, I saw some little ones at play and this apple in hand of one of them. So I snatched it from him and beat him and he cried and said, O youth this apple is my mother's and she is ill. She told my father how she longed for an apple, so he travelled to Bassorah and bought her three apples for three gold pieces, and I took one of them to play withal. He wept again, but I paid no heed to what he said and carried it off and brought it here, and my little lady bought it of me for two dinars of gold. And this is the whole story." When Ja'afar heard his words he marvelled that the murder of the damsel and all this misery should have been caused by his slave; he grieved for the relation of the slave to himself, while rejoicing over his own deliverance, and he repeated these lines: –

> If ill betide thee through thy slave,
> Make him forthright thy sacrifice:
> A many serviles thou shalt find,
> But life comes once and never twice.

Then he took the slave's hand and, leading him to the Caliph, related the story from first to last and the Caliph marvelled with extreme astonishment, and laughed till he fell on his back and ordered that the story be recorded and be made public amongst the people. But Ja'afar said, "Marvel not, O Commander of the Faithful, at this adventure, for it is not more wondrous than the History of the Wazir Núr al-Dín Ali of Egypt and his brother Shams al-Dín Mohammed." Quoth the Caliph, "Out with it; but what can be stranger than this story?" And Ja'afar answered, "O Commander of the Faithful, I will not tell it thee, save on condition that thou pardon my slave;" and the Caliph rejoined, "If it be indeed more wondrous than that of the three apples, I grant thee his blood, and if not I will surely slay thy slave." So Ja'afar began in these words the Tale of Núr al-Dín Alí and His Son Badr al-Dín Hasan

When the Caliph Harun al-Rashid heard this story from the mouth of his Wazir, Ja'afar the Barmecide, he marvelled much and said, "It behoves that these stories be written in letters of liquid gold." Then he set the slave at liberty and assigned to the youth who had slain his wife such a monthly stipend as sufficed to make his life easy; he also gave him a concubine from amongst his own slave-girls and the young man became one of his cup-companions. "Yet this story," (continued Shahrazad) "is in no wise stranger than the tale of the Tailor and the Hunchback and the Jew and the Reeve and the Nazarene, and what betided them." Quoth the King, "And what may that be?" So Shahrazad began, in these words,[10] The Hunchback's Tale.

Footnotes for 'The Three Apples'
1. "Dog" and "hog" are still highly popular terms of abuse. The Rabbis will not defile their lips with "pig;" but say "Dabhar akhir" = "another thing."
2. The "hero eponymus" of the Abbaside dynasty, Abbas having been the brother of Abdullah the father of Mohammed. He is a famous personage in Al-Islam (D'Herbelot).
3. Europe translates the word "Barmecides." It is Persian from *bar* (up) and *makídan* (to suck). The vulgar legend is that Ja'afar, the first of the name, appeared before the Caliph Abd al-Malik with a ring poisoned for his own need; and that the Caliph, warned of it by the clapping of two stones which he wore *ad hoc*, charged the visitor with intention to murder him. He excused himself and in his speech occurred the Persian word "Barmakam," which may mean "I shall sup it up," or "I am a Barmak," that is, a high priest among the Guebres. See D'Herbelot s.v.
4. Arab. "Zulm," the deadliest of monarch's sins. One of the sayings of Mohammed,

popularly quoted, is, "Kingdom endureth with Kufr or infidelity (*i.e.* without accepting Al-Islam) but endureth not with Zulm or injustice." Hence the good Moslem will not complain of the rule of Kafirs or Unbelievers, like the English, so long as they rule him righteously and according to his own law.

5. All this aggravates his crime: had she been a widow she would not have had upon him "the claims of maidenhead," the premio della verginità of Boccaccio, x. 10.

6. It is supposed that slaves cannot help telling these fatal lies. Arab story-books are full of ancient and modern instances and some have become "Joe Millers." Moreover it is held unworthy of a free-born man to take over-notice of these servile villanies; hence the scoundrel in the story escapes unpunished. I have already noticed the predilection of debauched women for these "skunks of the human race;" and the young man in the text evidently suspected that his wife had passed herself this "little caprice." The excuse which the Caliph would find for him is the *pundonor* shown in killing one he loved so fondly.

7. The Arab equivalent of our pitcher and well.

8. *i.e.* Where the dress sits loosely about the bust.

9. He had trusted in Allah and his trust was justified.

10. This is one of the best tales for humour and movement, and Douce and Madden show what a rich crop of fabliaux, whose leading incident was the disposal of a dead body, it produced.

Oedipus King of Thebes
An Extract
Sophocles

[Publisher's Note: In this extract from Oedipus Rex, Oedipus begins to understand what happened during an incident earlier in the play, in which he visited the Oracle at Delphi and a fight broke out.]

JOCASTA.
Husband, in God's name, say what hath ensued
Of ill, that thou shouldst seek so dire a feud.

OEDIPUS.
I will, wife. I have more regard for thee
Than these. Thy brother plots to murder me.

JOCASTA.
Speak on. Make all thy charge. Only be clear.

OEDIPUS.
He says that I am Laïus' murderer.

JOCASTA.
Says it himself? Says he hath witnesses?

OEDIPUS.
Nay, of himself he ventures nothing. 'Tis
This priest, this hellish seer, makes all the tale.

JOCASTA.
The seer? – Then tear thy terrors like a veil
And take free breath. A seer? No human thing
Born on the earth hath power for conjuring
Truth from the dark of God.
Come, I will tell
An old tale. There came once an oracle
To Laïus: I say not from the God
Himself, but from the priests and seers who trod

His sanctuary: if ever son were bred
From him and me, by that son's hand, it said,
Laïus must die. And he, the tale yet stays
Among us, at the crossing of three ways
Was slain by robbers, strangers. And my son –
God's mercy! – scarcely the third day was gone
When Laïus took, and by another's hand
Out on the desert mountain, where the land
Is rock, cast him to die. Through both his feet
A blade of iron they drove. Thus did we cheat
Apollo of his will. My child could slay
No father, and the King could cast away
The fear that dogged him, by his child to die
Murdered. Behold the fruits of prophecy!
Which heed not thou! God needs not that a seer
Help him, when he would make his dark things clear.

OEDIPUS.
Woman, what turmoil hath thy story wrought
Within me! What up-stirring of old thought!

JOCASTA.
What thought? It turns thee like a frightened thing.

OEDIPUS.
'Twas at the crossing of three ways this King
Was murdered? So I heard or so I thought.

JOCASTA.
That was the tale. It is not yet forgot.

OEDIPUS.
The crossing of three ways! And in what land?

JOCASTA.
Phokis 'tis called. A road on either hand
From Delphi comes and Daulia, in a glen.

OEDIPUS.
How many years and months have passed since then?

JOCASTA.
'Twas but a little time before proclaim
Was made of thee for king, the tidings came.

OEDIPUS.
My God, what hast thou willed to do with me?

JOCASTA.
Oedipus, speak! What is it troubles thee?

OEDIPUS.
Ask me not yet. But say, what build, what height
Had Laïus? Rode he full of youth and might?

JOCASTA.
Tall, with the white new gleaming on his brow
He walked. In shape just such a man as thou.

OEDIPUS.
God help me! I much fear that I have wrought
A curse on mine own head, and knew it not.

JOCASTA.
How sayst thou? O my King, I look on thee
And tremble.

OEDIPUS (to himself).
Horror, if the blind can see!
Answer but one thing and 'twill all be clear.

JOCASTA.
Speak. I will answer though I shake with fear.

OEDIPUS.
Went he with scant array, or a great band
Of armèd followers, like a lord of land?

JOCASTA.
Four men were with him, one a herald; one
Chariot there was, where Laïus rode alone.

OEDIPUS.
Aye me! Tis clear now.
Woman, who could bring
To Thebes the story of that manslaying?

JOCASTA.
A house-thrall, the one man they failed to slay.

OEDIPUS.
The one man...? Is he in the house today?

JOCASTA.

Indeed no. When he came that day, and found
Thee on the throne where once sat Laïus crowned,
He took my hand and prayed me earnestly
To send him to the mountain heights, to be
A herdsman, far from any sight or call
Of Thebes. And there I sent him. 'Twas a thrall
Good-hearted, worthy a far greater boon.

OEDIPUS.

Canst find him? I would see this herd, and soon.

JOCASTA.

'Tis easy. But what wouldst thou with the herd?

OEDIPUS.

I fear mine own voice, lest it spoke a word
Too much; whereof this man must tell me true.

JOCASTA.

The man shall come. – My lord, methinks I too
Should know what fear doth work thee this despite.

OEDIPUS.

Thou shalt. When I am tossed to such an height
Of dark foreboding, woman, when my mind
Faceth such straits as these, where should I find
A mightier love than thine?

My father – thus
I tell thee the whole tale – was Polybus,
In Corinth King; my mother Meropê
Of Dorian line. And I was held to be
The proudest in Corinthia, till one day
A thing befell: strange was it, but no way
Meet for such wonder and such rage as mine.
A feast it was, and some one flushed with wine
Cried out at me that I was no true son
Of Polybus. Oh, I was wroth! That one
Day I kept silence, but the morrow morn
I sought my parents, told that tale of scorn
And claimed the truth; and they rose in their pride
And smote the mocker.... Aye, they satisfied
All my desire; yet still the cavil gnawed
My heart, and still the story crept abroad.
At last I rose – my father knew not, nor
My mother – and went forth to Pytho's floor

To ask. And God in that for which I came
Rejected me, but round me, like a flame,
His voice flashed other answers, things of woe,
Terror, and desolation. I must know
My mother's body and beget thereon
A race no mortal eye durst look upon,
And spill in murder mine own father's blood.
I heard, and, hearing, straight from where I stood,
No landmark but the stars to light my way,
Fled, fled from the dark south where Corinth lay,
To lands far off, where never I might see
My doom of scorn fulfilled. On bitterly
I strode, and reached the region where, so saith
Thy tale, that King of Thebes was struck to death....
Wife, I will tell thee true. As one in daze
I walked, till, at the crossing of three ways,
A herald, like thy tale, and o'er his head
A man behind strong horses charioted
Met me. And both would turn me from the path,
He and a thrall in front. And I in wrath
Smote him that pushed me – 'twas a groom who led
The horses. Not a word the master said,
But watched, and as I passed him on the road
Down on my head his iron-branchèd goad
Stabbed. But, by heaven, he rued it! In a flash
I swung my staff and saw the old man crash
Back from his car in blood.... Then all of them
I slew.

Oh, if that man's unspoken name
Had aught of Laïus in him, in God's eye
What man doth move more miserable than I,
More dogged by the hate of heaven! No man, kin
Nor stranger, any more may take me in;
No man may greet me with a word, but all
Cast me from out their houses. And withal
'Twas mine own self that laid upon my life
These curses. – And I hold the dead man's wife
In these polluting arms that spilt his soul....
Am I a thing born evil? Am I foul
In every vein? Thebes now doth banish me,
And never in this exile must I see
Mine ancient folk of Corinth, never tread
The land that bore me; else my mother's bed
Shall be defiled, and Polybus, my good
Father, who loved me well, be rolled in blood.
If one should dream that such a world began

In some slow devil's heart, that hated man,
Who should deny him? – God, as thou art clean,
Suffer not this, oh, suffer not this sin
To be, that e'er I look on such a day!
Out of all vision of mankind away
To darkness let me fall ere such a fate
Touch me, so unclean and so desolate!

The Bulldog Ant Is Not a Team Player

Dan Stout

SCIENTISTS BOTH cruel and curious have demonstrated that a Bulldog Ant cut in two will lash out at anything nearby, including itself. The heads and bodies bite and sting their missing halves until either death or their nest mates claim them. The crew that hit Wayne Jewellers was like that – solid planning, flawless execution, but three days in a cabin and they were at each other's throats.

Take, for example, the way Kit Rosland drowned Teddy Wilson in the toilet. Teddy had saved their lives, darting the getaway car down side streets and arranging for the second vehicle they swapped into. Now he lay slumped into the toilet, his forehead resting in the curve of the bowl while Kit stood over him, trying to listen over the sound of her own panting breath. The other two in the crew – Henry and Matt – should be asleep, but she couldn't be sure if they'd been drunk enough to slumber through her fight with Teddy.

She leaned on the vanity, waiting for her heart to calm and her limbs to stop shaking. When she was steadier, she washed her hands. It made her feel cleaner, even if it didn't do anything to combat the rank smell of sweat and urine. She wondered if she should bother doing anything with the body, or if that was only postponing the inevitable. Matt and Henry would surely notice that their happy little family had been reduced by a full fourth. She decided her best bet was to get dressed fast and prepare to bolt. She exited the bathroom cautiously. There was no noise from the bedroom, the one Matt and Henry shared. Kit had let Teddy take the other bedroom. She preferred the living room couch; it was easier to monitor the comings and goings of the others, and she didn't feel cornered the way she might in one of the bedrooms.

She didn't like being in this situation. She might have been content to stick with the plan, to wait it out in the woods drinking beer and shooting the cans full of holes with a BB gun, but Teddy had started giving her looks. Hard looks. When the conversation in the cabin lapsed, Kit swore she could feel him – hell, she could damn near hear him looking at her. The crow's feet around his eyes crackled like old leaves on pavement when he gave her that look, the one whose message was clear: "I want what you have."

She'd felt that look from belligerent drunks in bars, from her classmates in university, from the bums and whores who watched her walk out of a restaurant with a stomach full of food and a wallet full of cash. It was Envy, a desire to take her and the things that belonged to her. It made her tired to see it.

When Teddy had reached the point where he was clearly ready to move on her, Kit moved first. Pretending to sleep on her couch, she waited for him to take a leak. A five-count later she was up and to the door. She hadn't even needed to pop the lock, he'd left it not only unlocked but un-latched. Sloppy.

She could hear the tinkle of piss on porcelain, and as she slid past the door she found comfort in the heft of her makeshift blackjack: a sock full of BBs. The toilet faced outward, so Teddy's back was to her as he relieved himself. When she hit him, Teddy's head pitched forward and cracked into the wall. Reflexively, he covered his pecker with his hands, but that wasn't where she was aiming. She kicked the side of his knee. Kicked hard, and he dropped. On the way down she hit him again with the blackjack. Teddy landed across the toilet, head down, not looking at her, not looking at anything.

It was a small amount of wrestling to reposition him, but Teddy wasn't a big guy, and she got his head into the toilet without too much trouble. He'd started to kick, right at the end, but by then her back was wedged against the wall and the leverage was in her favor.

* * *

Back in the living room, she reached for her clothes, which lay across a gym bag tucked beneath the couch. There was a soft click as the other bedroom door opened. Silently she rolled onto the couch, lying still. Someone walked to the bathroom. She couldn't see if it was Henry or Matt's oversized frame. The light clicked on, streaming out from underneath the door. Kit tensed, ready for the yelling to start, but there was nothing. After a moment, the sink began to run.

She jumped up, considered making a break for it. Instead she stepped on the coffee table, and reached into the overhead light, loosening the bulbs. She just had time to regain her seat on the couch when the bathroom door opened, and Henry walked out. The bathroom light was still on, and he was back-lit, reducing him to just a silhouette.

"Hiya Kit." He walked towards her, very slowly, drying his hands on a towel. "You mind if I have a sit-down?"

She said nothing. She knew there was no stopping Henry, only making things enough of a pain in the rear that he'd give up and walk away of his own accord.

Henry stepped out of the shaft of the bathroom light, sliding into the darkness with her. "I notice that Teddy had a little accident. You know anything about that?" He moved slow in the dark, his eyes not yet adjusted from the bathroom light.

She wished to hell that she'd had time to put on clothes. Yoga pants and a t-shirt seemed an awful outfit to wear for this confrontation. And if things went poorly, it would be an awful outfit to die in.

Holding the towel in his left hand, Henry reached with his right to turn on the light. The loosened bulbs didn't respond, and he didn't bother trying it twice. He was moving towards the recliner now, next to the couch. "I think we need to talk about how that affects the take from this job."

He sat down in the La-z-boy, his slippered feet looking ridiculous on a dangerous man. He raised his hand, and Kit pulled away, ready to fight. But instead he reached for the lamp. *Aw Hell,* she thought, *I forgot to take the bulb out of—*

With a click the end table lamp came on. Henry looked at her, wearing that little smile that annoyed her so much. The one that looked like he practiced it in the mirror. He didn't move, one hand on the lamp, the other holding the towel on his lap, light blue with dark crimson stains on it. He didn't look away from her eyes. "It's a pretty healthy take, when split two ways, don't you think?"

"And Matt?" she asked. Her southern Ohio accent stretched the syllables like honey on a hot day.

"Yeah... Matt's not going to be playing with us anymore." He withdrew his hand from the lamp, slowly. He was trying not to spook her. "And I think the same's true of Teddy, right?"

"Pretty much."

"I s'pose he kinda had it coming. And Matt... well, Matt was always sort of the weakest link, don't you think?"

Henry always did that – end sentences with a question. It was something he'd picked up from some sales infomercial. But in this case he was right. Kit shrugged an assent. "He probably would've talked sooner or later."

"Well, then I'm glad that we could establish a base line for our negotiations."

She looked at Henry, studied his face, the line of his lips, tried to see past his friendly poker face to the shark beneath.

"Yeah, negotiations," he said. "We already agree that we're the two who should get the profits from this job. Now we just have to decide how we'll split them up."

"Isn't that a little cold?"

"You just drowned a man in his own piss."

"Fine. 50/50. We go our own ways."

"80/20 and I take the car."

"You can't leave me without a car. What am I supposed to do, hitch a ride with that old couple in their RV?" She pointed to the west, towards the only nearby cabin.

"It's a favor to you. Cops'll be looking for it."

"No, they won't."

"Yes, they will." His voice grew sharper at being contradicted. "Any car lifted in the last week is going to be flagged once they find our ditched getaway." He shrugged in a what-can-you-do fashion. "That thing's a liability."

"The car we're in was picked up months ago and has clean plates. Teddy was smarter than that."

"If he was all that smart he'd still be alive, right?"

"He was smart about cars. Not about staying alive."

"You're smart about security." He didn't ask if she was smart enough to stay alive.

Kit was tensing, ready to run or pounce. She felt naked and wished again that she'd had time to get dressed. She wondered how much of Henry was fat and how much was muscle, wondered if she could wrap the cord of the table lamp around his thick throat.

Her nerves must have shown, because Henry softened his voice, took the edge out of it. Kit thought it made him seem even more like a snake about to strike. "I ran the show," he said, "and you took out the alarm system. You deserve a cut. The other two? Muscle and drivers we could have picked up anywhere."

She turned her head away, but kept him in the edge of her vision. "You going to do anything to clean up this place?"

"Nah, no point."

"We could take the bodies to the woods, give us a couple days, maybe."

"Why bother? We leave here two days before the rental is up, it's the same effect. You need to think further into the game, Kit." He was still covering the towel with his left hand, fingering the fringe at its end.

She nodded, trying to appear reasonable. "Sixty/forty. It was your plan, you deserve a majority cut."

"Yes, I do," he said. "Seventy-five/twenty-five. You keep your full original share and walk out of here alive."

"Sure you could take me?" She cocked her jaw, just slightly, but it was a challenge.

"Sure enough that I didn't bother to stick you yet." Henry shifted his left hand, revealing the long and ugly knife wrapped in the towel.

Kit stared at it, at the coagulating blood which hadn't quite rinsed off the blade. When she spoke her voice was cold. "You planned this the whole time."

"You didn't?"

"Teddy was self-defense." Her voice rose.

"Looked to me like you hit him from behind while he was taking a whiz."

"He was getting squirrelly on me."

Now that the knife was out in the open, Henry played with it while they talked. He watched her eyes track it for a while, then set it down on the arm of the chair. She got the message: he was so confident, he didn't need the knife. He just didn't want her to forget he had it, either.

"Twenty-five percent of this take's a good cut."

"Make it thirty."

He started to respond, but she cut him off. "The extra 5 is for taking care of Teddy."

Henry stared at her, round cheeks obscuring his dark eyes. She knew he was doing math, figuring just how much trouble she was worth. Going in her favor was the fact that Henry wasn't really a fighter. She'd been surprised that it had been him to come out of that bedroom. He must have gotten Matt drunker than she thought. Finally, just as she began to think that he was going to come after her anyway, he gave in.

"Fine," he said, "70/30. I'll take the car." He stood up, finished with her.

"It's a liability."

"You convinced me otherwise." He kept facing her as he walked to the closet where the stash was secured. He may have won, but he clearly wasn't going to turn his back to her. "And even if it is," he said, opening the closet, "don't you think—"

He cut off, must have seen movement or heard the 'click' as the closet door opened, but still the shotgun blast caught him under the jaw and there wasn't much left of Henry after that. Kit had spent some time positioning the shotgun at just the right angle, its stock wedged into the corner with the luggage stand and a simple pulley switch connecting the trigger to the closet doorknob.

She reached under the couch and pulled out her travel bag. All evidence of a fourth person, and certainly any sign of a female, had already been picked clean from the cabin. The security tapes at the jewelry store showed two men, and the cops knew there was a driver, but no one had seen her. At the cabin she'd been especially careful not to be seen by their only neighbors, the elderly couple with the RV. She stepped lightly over Henry's body as she retrieved the satchel with its glittery, precious contents. The police would find two murdered crooks, and another caught in one of his dead partners' traps, their car sitting in the driveway. The cops would assume that no diamonds meant that they'd been stashed somewhere else before hiding out. Just another heist that would never be solved.

She was out the door, and across the field towards the older couple's cabin. She knew that there was a spot behind the AC roof unit on the RV where the couple had a tarped-over equipment bag, for bikes or backpacks or whatever. She could fit under there, long enough at least for them to get to another truck stop, another campground. From there she'd hitchhike, or carjack someone. Whatever it took to make it clear, Kit knew she could do it.

Because she was alive. And because nobody thought further into the game than she did.

Chit Chit

Steve Toase

DIESEL FUMES leaked through the rusted floor into the back of the transit van and tainted every mouthful of air. I covered my face with my sleeve and tried to breathe as shallow as possible, not that it made much difference.

"Why couldn't you steal something decent?" I said, hardly able to hear my own voice over the engine noise. Vibrations from the worn suspension rattled me against the bodywork.

Karl half looked over his shoulder while trying to keep his attention on the road.

"I told you. There was nothing else available at such short notice, and a flash car was going to attract too much attention up here."

"You couldn't get a Landrover? A Range Rover? Those wouldn't attract attention."

Chloe tapped me on the leg and shook her head. She sat opposite on the thin wooden seat, combat jacket collar folded up over her face.

She didn't need to remind me Karl was quick to temper. I'd seen the aftermath more than once. I looked back toward the driver's seat, and saw him gripping the steering wheel, knuckles almost popping out of the skin. Beside him Mick turned the radio on, his gold sovereign rings reflecting the moonlight, music struggling to be heard over the van trying to shake itself apart.

I still didn't understand why the job needed four of us for a simple recovery, but it wasn't really my place to understand the logistics. Apparently the client had insisted on it, and the client was always right.

We were far from any town, roads little more than grooves worn into the landscape. Each corner was a game of chicken with an unknown opponent.

I'd worked with Karl a few times over the years. I'd trust him to drive at speed down country roads far more than I would order me a beer in a pub. As long as he didn't have to talk to the public there was a chance someone wouldn't end up in hospital.

It was Chloe who'd brought us together. Had the link with the client. I saw her open Signal on her phone once more and update them on our progress. I'd worked with all three separately in the past, but never on a single job. At first I didn't know why they brought me in, but it sort of made sense.

After what happened to Pasha I'd retired to a small Romanian port on the Black Sea, far from my previous employer's influence, but money only lasts so long, and I had experiences a bank robber, a debt collector and a con-woman didn't. Reaching into my pocket I brought out the creased map to check the route one more time.

The target was hidden in the corner of a small piece of moorland called Black Horse Acre. Over the years I'd searched for many different things in night-time fields. Unexcavated roman artefacts on archaeology sites. Sawn-off shotguns stuffed in mouldy holdalls. Caches of military grade explosives. Each one needed a specific search method. Horse skulls? They were harder to find. They needed intelligence, and intelligence needed an informer.

* * *

I recognised the mark from several videos on YouTube, though he looked different wearing farm stained tweeds instead of his ribbon fluttered mummer's costume. Grabbing myself a bourbon I sat down on the next table, and watched him for a few minutes as I sipped the harsh, cheap, spirit. Several ash smeared horse skulls stared down at me from the wall, bottle glass ground into the eye sockets.

I knew from Chloe's research that he never met anyone, every night just sitting by himself and drinking a single pint. A picture of rural isolation and misery. That research also told me he used to drink more, a lot more, and that whiskey loosened his tongue in a way that polite conversation couldn't.

Usually Chloe did the information gathering. Might be cliché, but people open up to a well spoken young woman in expensive clothes, and when I say people I mean men. Not so much on the edge of the moors. In farming villages smart suits and posh accents mean authority, and authority meant someone poking around where they didn't belong.

Horse brasses glittered the light from the open fire. The taproom was too hot and I took off my jacket, tucking it on the windowsill.

"Can I join you?" I said, turning my chair around before the mark had chance to object. His beer was untouched. He shrugged and lifted the glass, coating his cracked lips in foam but barely drinking anything.

"What do you have there?" he said, as if noticing my glass for the first time.

"Bourbon, but it's pretty poor stuff. Got to make do I suppose."

"Scotch is better," he said, with the certainty of a man making a self obvious proclamation.

"I'm sure you're right," I said, finishing the shot in one. He flinched at that. "But I know next to nothing about single malt. What would you recommend?"

He turned and looked at the bar.

"Start with a Highland Park," he said.

I came back and placed the second glass in front of him.

"As a thank-you," I said.

There was a flicker of doubt in his eyes as he stood at the top of a personal hill reaching for a treat he could no longer afford for himself. His scarred hand hesitated on the table. I lifted my glass and waited while his doubts left and he returned my cheers.

By the sixth drink we were best friends. By the seventh he was talking freely about the mummers, and by the tenth he'd marked on the Ordnance Survey map exactly where the horse skulls were buried in the field.

* * *

"We can't leave that there," Mick said, turning to stare at the van parked white and beacon-like beside the dry stone wall. The overheating engine crackled like burning leaves. "Someone will see it."

Karl looked around as if trying to find something lost.

"No garages. We'll just have to chance it. Unless you fancy driving it down to that village we passed and hiking back up while we shelter from the weather under a non-existent tree."

Mick said nothing, and walked to the back doors. He was a big guy, heavily tattooed with a taste for post pub fighting in car-parks. He was also very effective in problem solving, and the problem for now was keeping a lid on Karl's temper until we'd finished this part of the job. He passed me a shovel and closed the doors.

"Let's get going then."

* * *

The plan was always for Karl to stop with the Transit. Just in case we needed to get started fast. While he waited he doubled as look out, and interference if the police turned up. Though he would tear a nightclub to shreds over some imagined slight, in the presence of the Police he was always polite, forthcoming and helpful. Hidden talents. We all had them.

Mick, Chloe and I walked across the first field, threading our way through nettles and patches of stagnant water. The damp had got into my leg and stiffened my old knee injury, finding the metal and cooling it against the bone. Reminding me why I always got nervous going around country roads in the dark.

"He's the weak link, you know," Mick said, when he thought we were out of Karl's earshot. I said nothing, still unconvinced and unwilling to speak just in case.

"Someone always is," Chloe said. She turned her phone off, the stars and moon bright enough to navigate by. The heavy scent of peat washed down from the higher slopes on the breeze.

I led the way over the wall into the next field. I was the one with experience of stomping around the countryside at night finding lost artefacts. My workplace.

Chloe followed me, took the sketch map and looked around Black Horse Acre.

I didn't know if the client wanted the skulls for trophies or disruption, I didn't need to, but my money was on the latter. If it was a trophy we'd be revisiting the village pub after closing time. A full ritual skull was a far more impressive dinner party talking point than one freshly maggot skinned in the ground, still rot yellowed and dirt streaked.

"Over there," Chloe said, pointing to a far corner where the dry stone walls tapered to meet at a narrow point.

She tried to pretend she didn't belong, but I'd known her for many years and knew that she'd earned the right to be there as much as any of us. If Karl did lose his rag I'd let her deal with him. His fragile ego would be far more damaged by a beating from a hundred and twenty five pound woman. Baggy jumpers and designer jeans could hide a lot of battle scars and Chloe had been in a lot of battles.

* * *

This was where I came in. I knew dirt. I knew topsoil and subsoil. I knew clay, silt, and bedrock. I knew when soil had been spade turned, and I was very, very good at finding things. I used to find changes in soil as a professional. Dig up old stuff hidden from sight for thousands of years. Qualifications and everything. Later in life? Let's say I was more work for hire than public service.

The ground was covered in thistles and patches of heather. Clumps of grass that even moorland sheep would pass on. I ran my hand over the ground. Felt the earth for any slight disturbance. The presence of something that should not be there.

Soil never goes back the same. Put a shovel in the earth and the land changes forever. Do it recently enough and someone like me will find it.

"Start there," I said, pointing to a clump of forget-me-nots growing amongst the choke of plants.

No-one questioned me. We all knew our jobs, and mine was to say where to look. The only thing I couldn't tell was how deep. How long we would be stood around in the corner of that field.

Mick started digging, hefting each shovelful of dirt to one side. Chloe just stood and watched. I noticed that her mobile had re-appeared, filming the job in progress so the client knew everything was going smoothly. Live-streaming. No escaping the signal, even on the moors.

I glanced toward the road. The van was still in place, and I thought I saw Karl moving around trying to keep himself warm. He never could keep still. Too much nervous energy.

"It's empty." Mick stood up and leant on the spade's handle, leaving room for myself and Chloe to kneel down. She turned her phone and switched on the torch.

There were no skulls but the hole was far from empty. Strands of horse hair stuck to the sides, tangled in the forget-me-knot roots. The rough trench reeked of abattoirs and tanning pits. I reached my hand back and Mick passed me the spade. Using the blade I scraped the bottom layer of soil away at the base. Hundreds of maggots came to life, until then hidden under a thin spread of silt. Shuffled and twitched like severed muscle. I flinched and stood up, pointed to Chloe's hand and she disconnected the video feed.

"Someone's beaten us to it," I said, stretching out my back. "They've already got the skulls. We can't do any more."

"Are you sure? These clients," she paused. "I don't want to go back to them empty-handed."

"Then I suggest you go to a stables and decapitate a couple of mares because there's fuck all under the ground here," Mick said. I watched him reach into his pocket for a packet of tobacco, slow and deliberate, resting the cigarette paper on his thumb and forefinger while he crumbled in his addiction.

"We need to check," Chloe said. "At least to say we've tried."

I nodded, took off my coat and hooked it on the limestone wall. Working fast I dug three more holes, cutting through the roots and stacking the dirt behind me. The quicker I finished the quicker I could get back out of the country. As soon as the metal blade hit bedrock I moved onto the next. Mick smoked and Chloe typed messages I couldn't see. I left them to what they needed to do. Dealing in their own ways with how things were panning out.

* * *

After the crash all those years ago all the memories faded, apart from the sound. The noise of bone on metal is very particular. One hardened substance giving way to another. Neither coming off unscathed. If Chloe and Mick hadn't turned toward the van I would have thought it was another flashback. I'd not had one for a while. When I saw them looking in the same direction, well, it seemed a lot less likely.

Mick dropped his roll-up into the grass and stamped it cold.

"I'll go and have a look," he said, reaching to his belt for his knife.

"We'll all go," Chloe said. Something glinted across her knuckles, but in the darkness I couldn't tell if it was jewellery or a weapon. Maybe both.

I nodded, and followed them back across the field. We all walked in silence, making our own plans to deal with whatever was waiting for us. We were all capable and did not need to compare notes in situations like this.

Karl was no longer there, apart from a gouge of skin still attached to the ripped open metal of the driver's door. We moved around the vehicle falling into roles. I took the front, while Mick examined the wheels and Chloe checked out the rear compartment.

The bonnet had been torn open, inside the engine block shattered. Oil and water pooled underneath, collecting in the potholes of the lay-by, like the van had voided itself with fear.

Mick sat by the front wheel, running his finger over the buckled rim.

"Something's not right about this."

"You mean the van getting vandalised and Karl disappearing?" I knelt beside him, wincing as the surgical steel in my leg continued to remind me it was still there.

"The damage. Why not just slash the tires? This looks like something has gripped the rim and gnawed through the sidewall."

He was right. Wire sprung from underneath the rubber like splintered bone, the metal of the wheel buckled and torn.

"The back too," Chloe said. "Looks like it's been chewed free."

"And Karl?"

She shrugged, in a way that reminded me how hard it was for her to make a living in this business. How hard she had to be in return.

"We have to put him down to collateral. Get ourselves somewhere secure and regroup."

I nodded and stood, looked back to where we'd just been.

The figure was two fields away, dressed in white, its yellowed head streaked and stained to shadow. I watched for any movement but there was none. It did not approach or retreat, just stayed there watching us, limbless and empty eyed.

"I think we've got problems," I said. Chloe glanced up, and reached into her pocket for her phone. I watched her scroll a map to a destination, fingers zooming and scanning.

"There's a disused cottage about half a mile away. We get there and we wait."

I glanced toward the field once more. The figure had climbed the wall while our attention was elsewhere and was moving through the stagnant water and thistles toward us, each step marked by the chit chit of skinless jaws.

* * *

You can ignore chronic pain you need to. You focus on the next thing because if you let the discomfort overwhelm you, that's your life worn away. I ignored my knee and ran, following Chloe and the glimmer of the mobile screen as she tried to keep track of the route. Behind us the figure was at the dry stone wall. Over the wall. Beside the van.

Mick was behind me, the tar in his lungs making each breath an effort.

There's an old joke with the punchline, 'I don't need to be faster than the bear. I just need to be faster than you.' I looked behind me at Mick, ignored the nerves in my leg that were trying to get me to slow down, and sped up after Chloe.

I don't know when Mick fell. I was too busy concentrating on following Chloe to the shelter of the cottage. She held the door open as I ran inside and collapsed on the floor, my knee finally giving way. While I recovered she locked us in and barricaded the way with mould infested chairs, and rotten sideboards.

"Are you OK?" she said, crouching beside me, and checking my pulse.

"As long as we don't have to run for a while, I'll be fine," I said. I tried to stand but all the pain I'd switched off came back in one single wave and I collapsed back to the floor.

"Did you see it?" I said, reaching into my pocket for a blister-pack of painkillers. They wouldn't work straight away but soon enough.

"I was too busy finding somewhere to run to," she said. She took off her coat and dropped it over the back of a dining chair. "Did you?"

I nodded.

"It had a horse's skull for a head."

She smiled as if trying to reassure a toddler.

"You're just seeing things. That knee injury distracting you, and the target playing on your mind."

"I know what I saw. Even at that distance."

"It's your first job in a while isn't it?" I nodded, because there was nothing to disagree with. "Adrenaline can do funny things."

The argument wasn't worth having, and we had more real world concerns than something I might or might not have seen.

"Get a fire lit," I said. "Then we can start planning how to get out of here."

She nodded and started to break up an old bed in the corner of the room, stamping the slats until they fitted on the hearth. Using handfuls of wallpaper as kindling. Soon flames blazed in the grate, smoke billowing into the room as if the chimney did not want to accept the offering.

I pulled myself up onto a chair and stretched out my knee, waiting for the drugs to kick in.

"What now?" I said, trying to get comfy.

"Now we wait until dawn," she said, placing her phone on the mantelpiece. "There's no cover, and I can't arrange an extraction until first thing. Someone is bound to report the van, so we don't want to be just wandering the moors waiting to be picked up."

The rattling interrupted her, coming from both sides of the building at once.

"Stay here," she said. I watched her climb the stairs to the first floor and listened as she moved from front to back of the building.

"And?"

"It's caught up with us. Trying to find a way in, but the building's secure for now."

"It? Can it be in two places at once? That noise came from the front and back at the same time."

"There's only one," she said. "You only saw one."

A white shape crossed in front of the window, then crossed back. I listened to the footsteps, first through the dirt of abandoned flower beds, then onto the stone path. I did not need to see it to know where it had gone.

The sound of banging on the door was incessant, splintering the old planks until cold air chased away any heat from the feeble fire. I looked around for Chloe. She was still upstairs.

"Chloe," I shouted, because we were far past concealing our names. "This barrier isn't going to hold forever."

Still no sound came down from the top floor.

It took me a moment to realise that the back door was also under attack, a moment longer to remember that it hadn't been reinforced.

Using the chair as a walking frame I limped across to the mantelpiece. To Chloe's phone. The screen glowed intermittently as message after message came in unanswered. I picked it up and pressed the display, left unlocked for speed. Read the message thread.

"Two targets secured. Third ready and unable to retreat to a safer location."

"Understood. Secure yourself out of the way and let them do what they need to. The transfer will be done when all three are created."

"When can you extract me?"

"As soon as all three targets have been transformed."

I slid her phone into my pocket and looked toward the back door. The creature ducked under the lintel and came into the cottage, horse's skull blackened with soot and ash, the white shroud almost glowing in the darkness. Where fabric and bone met I saw vertebrae exposed and strung with torn muscle. The cottage filled with the scent of charred fur, sweat, and urine soaked stables.

The creature stood staring for a moment, then walked forward, almost toppling with each step. The shroud lifted as it went to steady itself and an arm reached out. Gold sovereign rings glittered against tattooed hands. I ran toward the stairs as the front door finally gave way, hoping that the low arch would keep the creatures on the ground floor.

"I can't let you up," Chloe said, blocking the way. "I don't get paid unless all three of you are given and I really need to get paid." She held the knife low and, because of the difference in height, very close to my throat.

"Mick and Karl down there?"

She nodded. "And soon you. Three skulls. Three sacrifices. Three horses for the villages."

"How much are they paying you?" I asked, all the time watching where her gaze was.

"Paying me in kind. Money is not a problem. Sometimes you need a job doing in return. I'm sure you understand."

My intention was only ever to get beyond Chloe, into the safety of the second floor. As I launched myself forward she lunged with the knife. I grabbed her wrist and pulled, stepping past as I did. She lost her footing and fell down the flight of stairs. I couldn't keep my balance and slipped myself, catching the banister and wedging myself in the stairwell, just able to see the hobby horses moving onto the fallen Chloe.

They did not decapitate her. Instead the things that were once Mick and Karl gripped her head and slowly massaged her skull. The plates, solid since childhood, loosened along their seams and moved over each other, collapsing and shifting. They carried on manipulating, readying her for the next stage. Bone ground against bone. Her scalp snagged in the joins, tearing and cooking with friction. The cottage filled with the stench of burnt hair.

From under its shroud the creature with tattooed arms produced the third horse's skull, jaw already wired to chitter, and slid it over Chloe's now softened head.

Noises that might have been protests escaped from Chloe's shattered throat and just as the new adornment fitted into place the other two creatures reached out together and tore free her jaw, pulling away the skin and muscle from around her neck.

They were three now, united in their transformation. Creatures of the moor and the ritual. The Obby 'Oss and the Grey Mary. Mari Lwyd. The clatter against the door in the night that brings fear and nightmares to those inside.

With their triumvirate complete they turned away from me and walked out of the cottage into the darkness. In my pocket Chloe's phone rang. I pressed the green answer button and the speaker button.

"It was meant to be you, you know," the voice said.

I recognised it, though I'd only had one conversation with the owner, in a deserted taproom, overlooked by horse brasses and ash streaked skulls. He sounded different. In control. As if he was someone who never lost grip of a situation, even when he was on the outside of half a bottle of expensive single malt. "But that doesn't matter. We have our three horses now, ready for the winter plays. You can leave and make safe passage off the moors."

"And payment?" I said. I was used to keeping my voice steady in dangerous situations. At that moment I struggled.

"Your return flight is paid for. Consider yourself lucky you're leaving at all."

* * *

The knee injury happened a long time before the job with Chloe, Mick and Karl on that deserted moor, but it's not the car crash I remember when cold gets into the surgical steel. It's the sight of a scalp being massaged and softened as a face collapses in on itself. Then I sit up all night with the lights on waiting for the memory of scorched hair and torn scalp to fade, but it never does.

The Ringer

Chapters I–XV

Edgar Wallace

Chapter I

THE ASSISTANT COMMISSIONER OF POLICE pressed a bell on his table, and, to the messenger who entered the room a few seconds after: "Ask Inspector Wembury if he will be good enough to see me," he said.

The Commissioner put away into a folder the document he had been reading. Alan Wembury's record both as a police officer and as a soldier was magnificent. He had won a commission in the war, risen to the rank of Major and had earned the Distinguished Service Order for his fine work in the field. And now a new distinction had come to him.

The door opened and a man strode in. He was above the average height. The Commissioner looked up and saw a pair of good-humoured grey eyes looking down at him from a lean, tanned face.

"Good morning, Wembury."

"Good morning, sir."

Alan Wembury was on the sunny side of thirty, an athlete, a cricketer, a man who belonged to the out-of-doors. He had the easy poise and the refinement of speech which comes from long association with gentlemen.

"I have asked you to come and see me because I have some good news for you," said the Commissioner.

He had a real affection for this straight-backed subordinate of his. In all his years of police service he had never felt quite as confident of any man as he had of this soldierly detective.

"All news is good news to me, sir," laughed Alan.

He was standing stiffly to attention now and the Commissioner motioned him to a chair.

"You are promoted divisional inspector and you take over 'R' Division as from Monday week," said the chief, and in spite of his self-control, Alan was taken aback. A divisional inspectorship was one of the prizes of the C.I.D. Inevitably it must lead in a man of his years to a central inspectorship; eventually inclusion in the Big Four, and one knows not what beyond that.

"This is very surprising, sir,'" he said at last. "I am terribly grateful. I think there must be a lot of men entitled to this step before me—"

Colonel Walford shook his head.

"I'm glad for your sake, but I don't agree," he said. And then, briskly: "We're making considerable changes at the Yard. Bliss is coming back from America; he has been attached to the Embassy at Washington – do you know him?"

Alan Wembury shook his head. He had heard of the redoubtable Bliss, but knew little more about him than that he was a capable police officer and was cordially disliked by almost every man at the Yard.

"'R' Division will not be quite as exciting as it was a few years ago," said the Commissioner with a twinkle in his eye; "and you at any rate should be grateful."

"Was it an exciting division, sir?" asked Alan, to whom Deptford was a new territory.

Colonel Walford nodded. The laughter had gone out of his eyes; he was very grave indeed when he spoke again.

"I was thinking about The Ringer – I wonder what truth there is in the report of his death? The Australian police are almost certain that the man taken out of Sydney Harbour was this extraordinary scoundrel."

Alan Wembury nodded slowly.

The Ringer!

The very name produced a little thrill that was unpleasantly like a shiver. Yet Alan Wembury was without fear; his courage, both as a soldier and a detective, was inscribed in golden letters. But there was something very sinister and deadly in the very name of The Ringer, something that conjured up a repellent spectacle...the cold, passionless eyes of a cobra.

Who had not heard of The Ringer? His exploits had terrified London. He had killed ruthlessly, purposelessly, if his motive were one of personal vengeance. Men who had good reason to hate and fear him, had gone to bed, hale and hearty, snapping their fingers at the menace, safe in the consciousness that their houses were surrounded by watchful policemen. In the morning they had been found stark and dead. The Ringer, like the dark angel of death, had passed and withered them in their prime.

"Though The Ringer no longer haunts your division, there is one man in Deptford I would like to warn you against," said Colonel Walford, "and he—"

"Is Maurice Meister," said Alan, and the Commissioner raised his eyebrows in surprise.

"Do you know him?" he asked, astonished. "I didn't know Meister's reputation as a lawyer was so widespread."

Alan Wembury hesitated, fingering his little moustache.

"I only know him because he happens to be the Lenley's family lawyer," he said.

The Commissioner shook his head with a laugh. "Now you've got me out of my depth: I don't even know the Lenleys. And yet you speak their name with a certain amount of awe. Unless," he said suddenly, "you are referring to old George Lenley of Hertford, the man who died a few months ago?"

Alan nodded.

"I used to hunt with him," mused the Commissioner. "A hard-riding, hard-drinking type of old English squire. He died broke, somebody told me. Had he any children?"

"Two, sir," said Alan quietly.

"And Meister is their lawyer, eh?" The Commissioner laughed shortly. "They weren't well advised to put their fortune in the hands of Maurice Meister."

He stared through the window on to the Thames Embankment. The clang of tram bells came faintly through the double windows. There was a touch of spring in the air; the bare branches along the Embankment were budding greenly, and soon would be displayed all their delicate leafy splendour. A curious and ominous place, this Scotland Yard, and yet human and kindly hearts beat behind its grim exterior.

Walford was thinking, not of Meister, but of the children who were left in Meister's care.

"Meister knew The Ringer," he said unexpectedly, and Wembury's eyes opened.

"Knew The Ringer, sir?" he repeated.

Walford nodded.

"I don't know how well; I suspect too well – too well for the comfort of The Ringer if he's alive. He left his sister in Meister's charge – Gwenda Milton. Six months ago, the body of Gwenda Milton was taken from the Thames." Alan nodded as he recalled the tragedy. "She was Meister's secretary. One of these days when you've nothing better to do, go up to the Record Office – there was a great deal that didn't come out at the inquest."

"About Meister?"

Colonel Walford nodded.

"If The Ringer is dead, nothing matters, but if he is alive" – he shrugged his broad shoulders and looked oddly under the shaggy eyebrows at the young detective – "if he is alive, I know something that would bring him back to Deptford – and to Meister."

"What is that, sir?" asked Wembury.

Again Walford gave his cryptic smile.

"Examine the record and you will read the oldest drama in the world – the story of a trusting woman and a vile man."

And then, dismissing The Ringer with a wave of his hand as though he were a tangible vision awaiting such a dismissal, he became suddenly the practical administrator.

"You are taking up your duties on Monday week. You might like to go down and have a look round, and get acquainted with your new division?"

Alan hesitated.

"If it is possible, sir, I should like a week's holiday," he said, and in spite of himself, his tanned face assumed a deeper red.

"A holiday? Certainly. Do you want to break the good news to the girl?" There was a good-humoured twinkle in Walford's eyes.

"No, sir." His very embarrassment seemed to deny his statement. "There is a lady I should like to tell of my promotion," he went on awkwardly. "She is, in fact – Miss Mary Lenley."

The Commissioner laughed softly.

"Oh, you know the Lenleys that much, do you?" he said, and Alan's embarrassment was not decreased.

"No, sir; she has always been a very good friend of mine," he said, almost gently, as though the subject of the discussion were one of whom he could not speak in more strident tones. "You see, I started life in a cottage on the Lenley estate. My father was head gardener to Squire Lenley, and I've known the family ever since I can remember. There is nobody else in Lenley village" – he shook his head sadly – "who would expect me – I—" He hesitated, and Walford jumped in.

"Take your holiday, my boy. Go where you jolly well please! And if Miss Mary Lenley is as wise as she is beautiful – I remember her as a child – she will forget that she is a Lenley of Lenley Court and you are a Wembury of the gardener's cottage! For in these democratic days, Wembury," – there was a quiet earnestness in his voice – "a man is what he is, not what his father was. I hope you will never be obsessed by a sense of your own unworthiness. Because, if you are" – he paused, and again his eyes twinkled – "you will be a darned fool!"

Alan Wembury left the room with the uneasy conviction that the Assistant Commissioner knew a great deal more about the Lenleys than he had admitted.

Chapter II

IT SEEMED THAT the spring had come earlier to Lenley village than to grim old London, which seems to regret and resist the tenderness of the season, until, overwhelmed by the rush of crocuses and daffodils and yellow-hearted narcissi, it capitulates blandly in a blaze of yellow sunshine.

As he walked into the village from the railway station, Alan saw over the hedge the famous Lenley Path of Daffodils, blazing with a golden glory. Beyond the tall poplars was the roof of grey old Lenley Court.

News of his good fortune had come ahead of him. The bald-headed landlord of the Red Lion Inn came running out to intercept him, a grin of delight on his rubicund face.

"Glad to see you back, Alan," he said. "We've heard of your promotion and we're all very proud of you. You'll be Chief of the Police one of these days."

Alan smiled at the spontaneous enthusiasm. He liked this old village; it was a home of dreams. Would the great, the supreme dream, which he had never dared bring to its logical conclusion, be fulfilled?

"Are you going up to the Court to see Miss Mary?" and when he answered yes, the landlord shook his head and pursed his lips. He was regret personified. "Things are very bad up there, Alan. They say there's nothing left out of the estate either for Mr. John or Miss Mary. I don't mind about Mr. John: he's a man who can make his way in the world – I wish he'd get a better way than he's found."

"What do you mean?" asked Alan quickly. The landlord seemed suddenly to remember that if he was speaking to an old friend he was also speaking to a police officer, and he became instantly discreet.

"They say he's gone to the devil. You know how people talk, but there's something in it. Johnny never was a happy sort of fellow; he's forgotten to do anything but scowl in these days. Poverty doesn't come easy to that young man."

"Why are they at the Court if they're in such a bad way? It must be an expensive place to keep up. I wonder John Lenley doesn't sell it?"

"Sell it!" scoffed the landlord. "It's mortgaged up to the last leaf on the last twig! They're staying there whilst this London lawyer settles the estate, and they're going to London next week, from what I hear."

This London lawyer! Alan frowned. That must be Maurice Meister, and he was curious to meet the man about whom so many strange rumours ran. They whispered things of Maurice Meister at Scotland Yard which it would have been libel to write, slander to say. They pointed to certain associations of his which were unjustifiable even in a criminal lawyer, whose work brought him into touch with the denizens of the underworld.

"I wish you'd book me a room, Mr. Griggs. The carrier is bringing my bag from the station. I'll go to up the Court and see if I can see John Lenley."

He said "John," but his heart said "Mary." He might deceive the world, but he could not deceive his own heart.

As he walked up the broad oak-shaded drive, the evidence of poverty came out to meet him. Grass grew in the gravelled surface of the road; those fine yew hedges of the Tudor garden before which as a child he had stood in awe had been clipped by an amateur hand; the lawn before the house was ragged and unkempt. When he came in sight of the Court his heart sank as he saw the signs of general neglect. The windows of the east wing were grimy – not even the closed shutters could disguise their state; two windows had been broken and the panes not replaced.

As he came nearer to the house, a figure emerged from the shadowy portico, walked quickly towards him, and then, recognising, broke into a run.

"Oh, Alan!"

In another second he had both her hands in his and was looking down into the upturned face. He had not seen her for twelve months. He looked at her now, holding his breath. The sweet, pale beauty of her caught at his heart. He had known a child, a lovely child; he was looking into the crystal-clear eyes of radiant womanhood. The slim, shapeless figure he had known had undergone some subtle change; the lovely face had been moulded to a new loveliness.

He had a sense of dismay. The very fringe of despair obscured for the moment the joy which had filled his heart at the sight of her. If she had been beyond his reach before, the gulf, in some incomprehensible manner, had widened now.

With a sinking heart he realised the gulf between this daughter of the Lenleys and Inspector Wembury.

"Why, Alan, what a pleasant sight!" Her sad eyes were brightened with laughter. "And you're bursting with news! Poor Alan! We read it in the morning newspaper."

He laughed ruefully.

"I didn't know that my promotion was a matter of world interest," he said.

"But you're going to tell me all about it." She slipped her arm in his naturally, as she had in the days of her childhood, when the gardener's son was Mary Lenley's playmate, the shy boy who flew her kite and bowled and fielded for her when she wielded a cricket bat almost as tall as herself.

"There is little to tell but the bare news," said Alan. "I'm promoted over the heads of better men, and I don't know whether to be glad or sorry!"

He felt curiously self-conscious and gauche as they paced the untidy lawn together.

"I've had a little luck in one or two cases I've handled, but I can't help feeling that I'm a favourite with the Commissioner and that I owe my promotion more to that cause than to any other."

"Rubbish!" she scoffed. "Of course you've had your promotion on merit!"

She caught his eyes looking at the house, and instantly her expression changed.

"Poor old Lenley Court!" she said softly. "You've heard our news, Alan? We're leaving next week." She breathed a long sigh. "It doesn't bear thinking about, does it? Johnny is taking a flat in town, and Maurice has promised me some work."

Alan stared at her.

"Work?" he gasped. "You don't mean you've got to work for your living?"

She laughed at this.

"Why, of course, my dear – my dear Alan. I'm initiating myself into the mysteries of shorthand and typewriting. I'm going to be Maurice's secretary."

Meister's secretary!

The words had a familiar sound. And then in a flash he remembered another secretary, whose body had been taken from the river one foggy morning, and he recalled Colonel Walford's ominous words.

"Why, you're quite glum, Alan. Doesn't the prospect of my earning a living appeal to you?" she asked, her lips twitching.

"No," he said slowly, and it was like Alan that he could not disguise his repugnance to the scheme. "Surely there is something saved from the wreck?"

She shook her head.

"Nothing – absolutely nothing! I have a very tiny income from my mother's estate, and that will keep me from starvation. And Johnny's really clever, Alan. He has made quite a lot of money lately – that's queer, isn't it? One never suspected Johnny of being a good business man, and yet he is. In a few years we shall be buying back Lenley Court."

Brave words, but they did not deceive Alan!

Chapter III

HE SAW HER LOOK over his shoulder, and turned. Two men were walking towards them, Though it was a warm day in early summer, and the Royal Courts of Justice forty miles away, Mr. Meister wore the conventional garb of a successful lawyer. The long-tailed morning coat fitted his slim figure faultlessly, his black cravat with its opal pin was perfectly arranged. On his head was the glossiest of silk hats, and the yellow gloves which covered his hands were spotless. A sallow, thin-faced man with dark, fathomless eyes, there was something of the aristocrat in his manner and speech. "He looks like a duke, talks like a don and thinks like a devil," was not the most unflattering thing that had been said about Maurice Meister.

His companion was a tall youth, hardly out of his teens, whose black brows met at the sight of the visitor. He came slowly across the lawn, his hands thrust into his trousers pockets, his dark eyes regarding Alan with an unfriendly scowl.

"Hallo!" he said grudgingly, and then, to his companion: "You know Wembury, don't you, Maurice – he's a sergeant or something in the police."

Maurice Meister smiled slowly.

"Divisional Detective Inspector, I think," and offered his long, thin hand. "I understand you are coming into my neighbourhood to add a new terror to the lives of my unfortunate clients!"

"I hope we shall be able to reform them," said Alan good-humouredly. "That is really what we are for!"

Johnny Lenley was glowering at him. He had never liked Alan, even as a boy and now for some reason, his resentment at the presence of the detective was suddenly inflamed.

"What brings you to Lenley?" he asked gruffly. "I didn't know you had any relations here?"

"I have a few friends," said Alan steadily.

"Of course he has!" It was Mary who spoke. "He came to see me, for one, didn't you, Alan? I'm sorry we can't ask you to stay with us, but there's practically no furniture left in the house."

John Lenley's eyes snapped at this.

"It isn't necessary to advertise our poverty all over the kingdom, my dear," he said sharply. "I don't suppose Wembury is particularly interested in our misfortunes, and he'd be damned impertinent if he was!"

He saw the hurt look on his sister's face, and his unreasonable annoyance with the visitor was increased. It was Maurice Meister who poured oil upon the troubled water.

"The misfortunes of Lenley Court are public property, my dear Johnny," he said blandly. "Don't be so stupidly touchy! I, for one, am very glad to have the opportunity of meeting a police officer of such fame as Inspector Alan Wembury. You will find your division rather a dull spot just now, Mr. Wembury. We have none of the excitement which prevailed when I first moved to Deptford from Lincoln's Inn Fields."

Alan nodded.

"You mean, you're not bothered with The Ringer?" he said.

It was a perfectly innocent remark, and he was quite unprepared for the change which came to Meister's face. He blinked quickly as though he had been confronted with a brilliant light. The loose mouth became in an instant a straight, hard line. If there was not fear in those inscrutable eyes of his, Alan Wembury was very wide of the mark.

"The Ringer!" His voice was husky. "Ancient history, eh? Poor beggar, he's dead!"

He said this with almost startling emphasis. It seemed to Alan that the man was trying to persuade himself that this notorious criminal had passed beyond the sphere of human activity.

"Dead...drowned in Australia."

The girl was looking at him wonderingly.

"Who is The Ringer?" she asked.

"Nobody you would know anything about, or ought to know," he said, almost brusquely. And then, with a little laugh: "We're all talking 'shop,' and criminal justice is the worst kind of 'shop' for a young lady's ears."

"I wish to heaven you'd find something else to talk about," growled John Lenley fretfully, and was turning away when Maurice Meister asked: "You are at present in a West End division, aren't you, Wembury? What was your last case? I don't seem to remember seeing your name in the newspapers."

Alan made a little grimace.

"We never advertise our failures," he said. "My last job was to inquire into some pearls that were stolen from Lady Darnleigh's house in Park Lane on the night of her big Ambassadors' party."

He was looking at Mary as he spoke. Her face was a magnet which lured and held his gaze. He did not see John Lenley's hand go to his mouth to check the involuntary exclamation, or the quick warning glance which Meister shot at the young man. There was a little pause.

"Lady Darnleigh?" drawled Maurice. "Oh, yes, I seem to remember...as a matter of fact, weren't you at her dance that night, Johnny?"

He looked at the other and Johnny shook his shoulder impatiently.

"Of course I was...I didn't know anything about the robbery till afterwards. Haven't you anything else to discuss, you people, than crimes and robberies and murders?"

And, turning on his heel, he slouched across the lawn.

Mary looked after him with trouble in her face.

"I wonder what makes Johnny so cross in these days – do you know, Maurice?"

Maurice Meister examined the cigarette that burnt in the amber tube between his fingers. "Johnny is young; and, my dear, you mustn't forget that he has had a very trying time."

"So have I," she said quietly. "You don't imagine that it is nothing to me that I am leaving Lenley Court?" Her voice quivered for a moment, but with a resolution that Alan could both understand and appreciate, she was instantly smiling. "I'm being very pathetic; I shall be weeping on Alan's shoulder if I am not careful. Come along, Alan, and see what is left of the rosery – perhaps when you have seen its present condition, we will weep together!"

Chapter IV

JOHNNY LENLEY looked after them until they had disappeared from view. His face was pale with anger, his lips trembled.

"What brings that swine here?" he demanded.

Maurice Meister, who had followed across the lawn, looked at him oddly.

"My dear Johnny, you're very young and very crude. You have the education of a gentleman and yet you behave like a boor!"

Johnny turned on him in a fury.

"What do you expect me to do – shake him cordially by the hand and bid him welcome to Lenley Court? The fellow's risen from the gutter. His father was our gardener—"

Maurice Meister interrupted him with a chuckle of malicious enjoyment.

"What a snob you are, Johnny! The snobbery wouldn't matter," he went on in a more serious tone, "if you would learn to conceal your feelings."

"I say what I think," said Johnny shortly.

"So does a dog when you tread on his tail," replied Maurice. "You fool!" he snarled with unexpected malignity. "You half-wit! At the mention of the Darnleigh pearls you almost betrayed yourself. Did you realise to whom you were talking, who was probably watching you? The shrewdest detective in the C.I.D.! The man who caught Hersey, who hanged Gostein, who broke up the Flack Gang."

"He didn't notice anything," said the other sulkily, and then, to turn the conversation to his advantage: "You had a letter this morning, was there anything about the pearls in it – are they sold?"

The anger faded from the lawyer's face; again he was his suave self.

"Do you imagine, my dear lad, that one can sell fifteen thousand pounds' worth of pearls in a week? What do you suppose is the procedure – that one puts them up at Christie's?"

Johnny Lenley's lips tightened. For a while he was silent. When he spoke his voice had lost some of its querulous quality.

"It was queer that Wembury was on the case – apparently they've given up hope. Of course, old Lady Darnleigh has no suspicion—"

"Don't be too sure of that," warned Meister. "Every guest at No. 304, Park Lane, on that night is suspect. You, more than any, because everybody knows you're broke. Moreover, one of the footmen saw you going up the main stairs just before you left."

"I told him I was going to get my coat," said Johnny Lenley quickly, and a troubled look came to his face. "Why did you mention that I was there to Wembury?"

Maurice laughed.

"Because he knew; I was watching him as I spoke. There was the faintest glint in his eyes that told me. I'll set your mind at ease; the person at present under suspicion is her unfortunate butler. Don't imagine that the case has blown over – it hasn't. Anyway, the police are too active for the moment for us to dream of disposing of the pearls, and we shall have to wait a favourable opportunity when they can be placed in Antwerp."

He threw away the end of the thin cigarette, took a gold cigarette-case from his waistcoat pocket, selected another with infinite care and lit it, Johnny watching him enviously.

"You're a cool devil. Do you realise that if the truth came out about those pearls it would mean penal servitude for you, Maurice?"

Maurice sent a ring of smoke into the air.

"I certainly realise it would mean penal servitude for you, my young friend. I fancy that it would be rather difficult to implicate me. If you choose for your amusement to be a robber baron, or was it a Duke of Padua? – I forget the historical precedent – and engage yourself in these Rafflesish adventures, that is your funeral entirely. Because I knew your father and I've known you since you were a child, I take a little risk. Perhaps the adventure of it appeals to me—"

"Rot!" said Johnny Lenley brutally. "You've been a crook ever since you were able to walk. You know every thief in London and you've 'fenced'—"

"Don't use that word!" Maurice Meister's deep voice grew suddenly sharp. "As I told you just now, you are crude. Did I instigate this robbery of Lady Darnleigh's pearls? Did I put it into your head that thieving was more profitable than working, and that with your education and entry to the best houses you had opportunities which were denied to a meaner – thief?"

This word was as irritating to Johnny Lenley as "fence" had been to the lawyer.

"Anyway, we are in, the same boat," he said. "You couldn't give me away without ruining yourself. I don't say you instigated anything, but you've been jolly helpful, Maurice. Some day I'll make you a rich man."

The dark, sloe-like eyes turned slowly in his direction. At any other time this patronage of the younger man would have infuriated Meister; now he was only piqued.

"My young friend," he said precisely, "you are a little over-confident. Robbery with or without violence is not so simple a matter as you imagine. You think you're clever—"

"I'm a little bit smarter than Wembury," said Johnny complacently.

Maurice Meister concealed a smile.

It was not to the rosery that Mary led her visitor but to the sunken garden, with its crazy paving and battered statuary. There was a cracked marble bench overlooking a still pool where water-lilies grew, and she allowed him to dust a place for her before she sat down.

"Alan, I'm going to tell you something. I'm talking to Alan Wembury, not to Inspector Wembury," she warned him, and he showed his astonishment.

"Why, of course..." He stopped; he had been on the point of calling her by name. "I've never had the courage to call you Mary, but I feel – old enough!"

This claim of age was a cowardly expedient, he told himself, but at least it was successful. There was real pleasure in her voice when she replied: "I'm glad you do. 'Miss Mary' would sound horribly unreal. In you it would sound almost unfriendly."

"What is the trouble?" he asked, as he sat down by her side.

She hesitated only a second.

"Johnny," she said. "He talks so oddly about things. It's a terrible thing to say, Alan, but it almost seems as though he's forgotten the distinction between right and wrong. Sometimes I think he only says these things in a spirit of perversity. At other times I feel that he means them. He talks harshly about poor, dear father, too. I find that difficult to forgive. Poor daddy was very careless and extravagant, but he was a good father to Johnny – and to me," she said, her voice breaking.

"What do you mean when you say Johnny talks oddly?"

She shook her head.

"It isn't only that: he has such strange friends. We had a man here last week – I only saw him, I did not speak to him – named Hackitt. Do you know him?"

"Hackitt? Sam Hackitt?" said Wembury in surprise. "Good Lord, yes! Sam and I are old acquaintances!"

"What is he?" she asked.

"He's a burglar," was the calm reply. "Probably Johnny was interested in the man and had him down—"

She shook her head.

"No, it wasn't for that." She bit her lip. "Johnny told me a lie; he said that this man was an artisan who was going to Australia. You're sure this is your Sam Hackitt?"

Alan gave a very vivid, if brief, description of the little thief.

"That is he," she nodded. "And, of course, I know he was an unpleasant sort of man. Alan, you don't think that Johnny is bad, do you?"

He had never thought of Johnny as a possible subject for police observation. "Of course not!"

"But these peculiar friends of his—?"

It was an opportunity not to be passed.

"I'm afraid, Mary, you're going to meet a lot of people like Hackitt, and worse than Hackitt, who isn't a bad soul if he could keep his fingers to himself."

"Why?" she asked in amazement.

"You think of becoming Meister's secretary – Mary, I wish you wouldn't."

She drew away a little, the better to observe him.

"Why on earth, Alan...? Of course, I understand what you mean. Maurice has a large number of clients, and I'm pretty sure to see them, but they won't corrupt my young mind!"

"I'm not afraid of his clients," said Alan quietly. "I'm afraid of Maurice Meister."

She stared at him as though he were suddenly bereft of his senses.

"Afraid of Maurice?" She could hardly believe her ears. "Why, Maurice is the dearest thing! He has been kindness itself to Johnny and me, and we've known him all our lives."

"I've known you all your life, too, Mary," said Alan gently, but she interrupted him.

"But, tell me why?" she persisted. "What do you know against Maurice?"

Here, confronted with the concrete question, he lost ground.

"I know nothing about turn," he admitted frankly. "I only know that Scotland Yard doesn't like him." She laughed a low, amused laugh.

"Because he manages to keep these poor, wretched criminals out of prison! It's professional jealousy! Oh, Alan," she bantered him, "I didn't believe it of you!"

No good purpose could be served by repeating his warning. There was one gleam of comfort in the situation; if she was to work for Meister she would be living in his division. He told her this.

"It will be rather dreadful, won't it, after Lenley Court?" She made a little face at the thought. "It will mean that for a year or two I shall have no parties, no dances – Alan, I shall die an old maid!"

"I doubt that," he smiled, "but the chances of meeting eligible young men in Deptford are slightly remote," and they laughed together.

Chapter V

MAURICE MEISTER stood at the ragged end of a yew hedge and watched them. Strange, he mused, that never before had he realised the beauty of Mary Lenley. It needed, he told himself, the visible worship of this policeman to stimulate his interest in the girl, whom in a moment of impulse, which later he regretted, he had promised to employ. A bud, opening into glorious flower. Unobserved, he watched her; the contour of her cheek, the poise of her dark head, the supple line of her figure as she turned to rally Alan Wembury. Mr. Meister licked his dry lips. Queer that he had never thought that way about Mary Lenley. And yet...

He liked fair women. Gwenda Milton was fair, with a shingled, golden head. A stupid girl, who had become rather a bore. And from a bore she had developed into a sordid tragedy. Maurice shuddered as he remembered that grey day in the coroner's court when he had stood on the witness stand and had lied and lied and lied.

Turning her head, Mary saw him and beckoned him, and he went slowly towards them.

"Where is Johnny?" she asked.

"Johnny at this moment is sulking. Don't ask me why, because I don't know."

What a wonderful skin she had – flawless, unblemished! And the dark grey eyes, with their long lashes, how adorable! And he had known her all her life and been living under the same roof for a week, and had not observed her values before!

"Am I interrupting a confidential talk?" he asked.

She shook her head, but she did not wholly convince him. He wondered what these two had been speaking about, head to head. Had she told Alan Wembury that she was coming to Deptford? She would sooner or later, and it might be profitable to get in first with the information.

"You know, Miss Lenley is honouring me by becoming my secretary?"

"So I've heard," said Alan, and met the lawyer's eyes. "I have told Miss Lenley" – he spoke deliberately; every word had its significance – "that she will be living in my division...under my paternal eye, as it were."

There was a warning and a threat there. Meister was too shrewd a man to overlook either. Alan Wembury had constituted himself the girl's guardian. That would have been rather amusing in other circumstances. Even as recently as an hour ago he would have regarded Alan Wembury's chaperonage as a great joke. But now...

He looked at Mary and his pulse was racing.

"How interesting!" his voice was a little harsh and he cleared his throat. "How terribly interesting! And is that duty part of the police code?"

There was the faintest sneer in his voice which Alan did not miss.

"The duty of a policeman," he said quietly, "is pretty well covered by the inscription over the door of the Old Bailey."

"And what is that?" asked Meister. "I have not troubled to read it."

"'Protect the children of the poor and punish the wrongdoer,'" said Alan Wembury sternly.

"A noble sentiment!" said Maurice. And then: "I think that is for me."

He walked quickly towards a telegraph messenger who had appeared at the end of the garden.

"Is Maurice annoyed with you?" asked Mary.

Alan laughed.

"Everybody gets annoyed with me sooner or later. I'm afraid my society manners are deplorable."

She patted the hand that lay beside hers on the stone bench.

"Alan," she said, half whimsically, half seriously, "I don't think I shall ever be annoyed with you. You are the nicest man I know."

For a second their hands met in a long, warm clasp, and then she saw Maurice walking back with the unopened telegram in his hand.

"For you," he said jovially. "What a thing it is to be so important that you can't leave the office for five minutes before they wire for you – what terrible deed has been committed in London in your absence?"

Alan took the wire with a frown. "For me?" He was expecting no telegram. He had very few personal friends, and it was unlikely that his holiday would be curtailed from headquarters.

He tore open the envelope and took out the telegram. It was closely written on two pages. He read:

VERY URGENT STOP RETURN AT ONCE AND REPORT TO SCOTLAND YARD STOP BE PREPARED TO TAKE OVER YOUR DIVISION TOMORROW MORNING STOP AUSTRALIAN POLICE REPORT RINGER LEFT SYDNEY FOUR MONTHS AGO AND IS BELIEVED TO BE IN LONDON AT THIS MOMENT MESSAGE ENDS.

The wire was signed "Walford."

Alan looked from the telegram to the smiling old garden, from the garden to the girl, her anxious face upturned to his.

"Is anything wrong?" she asked.

He shook his head slowly.

The Ringer was in England!

His nerves grew taut at the realisation. Henry Arthur Milton, ruthless slayer of his enemies – cunning, desperate, fearless.

Alan Wembury's mind went back to Scotland Yard and the Commissioner's office. Gwenda Milton – dead, drowned, a suicide!

Had Maurice Meister played a part in the creation of that despair which had sent her young soul unbidden to the judgment of God? Woe to Maurice Meister if this were true!

Chapter VI

THE RINGER was in London!

Alan Wembury felt a cold thrill each time the thought recurred on his journey to London.

It was the thrill that comes to the hunter, at the first hint of the man-slaying tiger he will presently glimpse.

Well named was The Ringer, who rang the changes on himself so frequently that police headquarters had never been able to circulate a description of the man. A master of disguise, a ruthless enemy who had slain without mercy the men who had earned his hatred.

For himself, Wembury had neither fear nor hatred of the man he was to bring down; only a cold emotionless understanding of the danger of his task. One thing was certain – the Ringer would go to the place where a hundred bolts and hiding places were ready to receive him.

To Deptford...?

Alan Wembury gave a little gasp of dismay. Mary Lenley was also going to Deptford – to Meister's house, and The Ringer could only have returned to England with one object, the destruction of Maurice Meister. Danger to Meister would inevitably mean danger to Mary Lenley. This knowledge took some of the sunlight of the spring sky and made the grim facade of Scotland Yard just a little more sinister.

Though all the murderers in the world were at large, Scotland Yard preserved its equanimity. He came to Colonel Walford's room to find the Assistant Commissioner immersed in the particulars of a minor robbery.

"You got my wire?" said Walford, looking up as Alan came in. "I'm awfully sorry to interrupt your holiday. I want you to go down to Deptford to take charge immediately und get acquainted with your new division."

"The Ringer is back, sir?"

Watford nodded. "Why he came back, where he is, I don't know – in fact, there is no direct information about him and we are merely surmising that he has returned."

"But I thought—"

Walford took a long cablegram from the basket on his table. "The Ringer has a wife. Few people know that," he said. "He married her a year or two ago in Canada. After his disappearance, she left this country and was traced to Australia. That could only mean one thing. The Ringer was in Australia. She has now left Australia just as quickly as she left this country; she arrives in England tomorrow morning."

Alan nodded slowly.

"I see. That means that The Ringer is either in England or is making for this country."

"You have not told anybody?" the Commissioner asked. "I'd forgotten to warn you about that. Meister was at Lenley Court, you say? You didn't tell him?"

"No, sir," said Alan, his lips twitching. "I thought, coming up in the train, that it was rather a pity I couldn't – I would like to have seen the effect upon him!"

Alan could understand how the news of The Ringer's return would flutter the Whitehall dovecotes, but he was unprepared for the extraordinarily serious view which Colonel Walford took of the position.

"I'll tell you frankly, Wembury, that I would much rather be occupying a place on the pension list than this chair at Scotland Yard when that news is published."

Alan looked at him in astonishment; the Commissioner was in deadly earnest.

"The Ringer is London's favourite bogy," Colonel Walford said, "and the very suggestion that he has returned to England will be quite sufficient to send all the newspaper hounds of Fleet Street on my track. Never forget, Wembury, he is a killer, and he has neither fear nor appreciation of danger. He has caused more bolts to be shot than any other criminal on our list! The news that this man is at large and in London will arouse such a breeze that even I would not weather it!"

"You think he'll be beyond me?" smiled Alan.

"No," said Walford surprisingly, "I have great hopes of you – and great hopes of Dr. Lomond. By the way, have you met Dr. Lomond?"

Alan looked at him in surprise. "No, sir, who is he?"

Colonel Walford reached for a book that lay on his table, "He is one of the few amateur detectives who have impressed me," he said. "Fourteen years ago he wrote the only book on the subject of the criminal that is worth studying. He has been in India and Tibet for years and I think the Under-Secretary was fortunate to persuade him to fill the appointment."

"What appointment, sir?"

"Police surgeon of 'R' Division – in fact, your new division," said Walford. "You are both making acquaintance with Deptford at the same time."

Alan Wembury turned the closely-set pages of the book. "He is a pretty big man to take a fiddling job like this," he said and Walford laughed.

"He has spent his life doing fiddling jobs – would you like to meet him? He is with the Chief Constable at the moment."

He pressed a bell and gave instructions to the messenger who came. "Lomond is rather a character – terribly Scottish, a little cynical and more than a little pawky."

"Will he help us to catch The Ringer?" smiled Alan and he was astonished to see the Commissioner nod.

"I have that feeling," he said.

The door opened at that moment and a tall bent figure shuffled in. Alan put his age at something over fifty. His hair was grey, a little moustache drooped over his mouth and the pair of twinkling blue eyes that met Alan's were dancing with good-humour. His homespun suit was badly cut, his high-crowned felt hat belonged to the seventies.

"I want you to meet Inspector Wembury who will be in charge of your division," said Walford and Wembury's hand was crushed in a powerful grip.

"Have ye any interesting specimens in Deptford, inspector? I'd like fine to measure a few heids."

Alan's smile broadened.

"I'm as ignorant of Deptford as you – I haven't been there since before the war," he said.

The doctor scratched his chin, his keen eyes fixed on the younger man, "I'm thinkin' they'll no' be as interesting as the Lolos. Man, there's a wonderful race, wi' braci-cephalic heads, an' a queer development of the right parietal..."

He spoke quickly, enthusiastically when he was on his favourite subject.

Alan seized an opportunity when the doctor was expounding a view on the origin of some mysterious Tibetan tribe to steal quietly from the room. He was not in the mood for anthropology.

An hour later as he was leaving Scotland Yard he met Walford as he was coming out of his room and walked with him to the Embankment, "Yes – I got rid of the doctor," chuckled the colonel, "he's too clever to be a bore, but he made my head ache!" Then suddenly: "You're handing over that pearl case to Burton – the Darnleigh pearls I mean. You have no further clue?"

"No, sir," said Alan. He had almost forgotten that there was such a case in his hands.

The Commissioner was frowning. "I was thinking, after you left, what a queer coincidence it was that you were going to Lenley Court. Young Lenley was apparently at Lady Darnleigh's house on the night of the robbery," and then, seeing the look that came to his subordinate's face, he went on quickly: "I'm not suggesting that he knew anything about it, of course, but it was a coincidence. I wish we could clear up that little mystery. Lady Darnleigh has too many friends in Whitehall for my liking and I get a letter from the Home Secretary every other day asking for the latest news."

Alan Wembury went on his way with an uneasy mind. He had known that Johnny was at the house on the night of the robbery but he had never associated "the Squire's son" with the mysterious disappearance of Lady Darnleigh's pearls. There was no reason why he should, he told himself stoutly. As he walked across Westminster Bridge he went over again and again that all too brief interview he had had with Mary.

How beautiful she was! And how unapproachable! He tried to think of her only, but against his will a dark shadow crept across the rosy splendour of dreams: Johnny Lenley.

Why on earth should he, and yet – the Lenleys were ruined... Mary was worried about the kind of company that Johnny was keeping. There was something else she had said which belonged to the category of unpleasant things. Oh, yes, Johnny had been "making money" Mary told him a little proudly. How?

"Rot!" said Alan to himself as an ugly thought obtruded upon his mind. "Rubbish!"

The idea was too absurd for a sane man to entertain. The next morning he handed over all the documents in the case to Inspector Burton and walked out of Scotland Yard with almost a feeling of relief. It was as though he had shaken himself clear of the grisly shadow which was obscuring the brightness of the day.

The week which followed was a very busy one for Alan Wembury. He had only a slight acquaintance with Deptford and its notables. The grey-haired Scots surgeon he saw for a minute or two, a shrewd old man with laughing eyes and a fund of dry Scottish humour, but both men were too busy in their new jobs to discuss The Ringer.

Mary did not write, as he had expected she would, and he was not aware that she was in his district until one day, walking down the Lewisham High Road, somebody waved to him from an open taxicab and turning, he saw it was the girl. He asked one of his subordinates to find out where she and Johnny were staying and with no difficulty located them at a modern block of flats near Malpas Road, a building occupied by the superior artisan class. What a tragic contrast to the spacious glories of Lenley Court! Only his innate sense of delicacy prevented his calling upon her, and for this abstention at least one person was glad.

Chapter VII

"I SAW YOUR copper this morning," said Johnny flippantly. He had gone back to lunch and was in a more amiable mood than Mary remembered having seen him recently.

She looked at him open-eyed.

"My 'copper'?" she repeated.

"Wembury," translated Johnny. "We call these fellows 'busies' and I've never seen a busier man," he chuckled. "I see you're going to ask what' busy' means. It is a thieves' word for detective."

He saw a change come to her face.

"'We' call them?" she repeated. "You mean 'they' call them, Johnny."

He was amused as he sat down at the table.

"What a little purist you're becoming, Mary," he said. "We, or they, does it matter? We're all thieves at heart, the merchant in his Rolls and the workman on the tram, thieves every one of them!"

Very wisely she did not contest the extravagant generalisation.

"Where did you see Alan?"

"Why the devil do you call him by his Christian name?" snapped Johnny. "The man is a policeman, you go on as though he were a social equal."

Mary smiled at this as she cut a round of bread into four parts and put them on the bread plate.

"The man who lives on the other side of the landing is a plumber, and the people above us live on the earnings of a railway guard. Six of them, Johnny – four of them girls."

He twisted irritably in his chair. "That's begging the question. We're only here as a temporary expedient. You don't suppose I'm going to be content to live in this poky hole all my life? One of these days I'll buy back Lenley Court."

"On what, Johnny?" she asked quietly.

"On the money I make," he said and went back to his bete noire. "Anyway, Wembury isn't the sort of fellow I want you to know," he said. "I was talking to Maurice about him this morning, and Maurice agrees that it is an acquaintance we ought to drop."

"Really?" Mary's voice was cold. "And Maurice thinks so too – how funny!"

He glanced at her suspiciously.

"I don't see anything amusing about it," he grumbled. "Obviously, we can't know—"

She was standing facing him on the other side of the table, her hands resting on its polished surface.

"I have decided to go on knowing Alan Wembury," she said steadily. "I'm sorry if Maurice doesn't approve, or if you think I'm being very common. But I like Alan—"

"I used to like my valet, but I got rid of him," broke in Johnny irritably.

She shook her head.

"Alan Wembury isn't your valet. You may think my taste is degraded, but Alan is my idea of a gentleman," she said quietly, "and one cannot know too many gentlemen."

He was about to say something sharp, but checked himself, and the matter had dropped for the moment.

The next day Mary Lenley was to start her new life. The thought left her a little breathless. When Maurice had first made the suggestion that she should act as his secretary the idea had thrilled her, but as the time approached she had grown more and more apprehensive. The project was one filled with vague unpleasant possibilities and she could not understand why this once pleasing prospect should now have such an effect upon her.

Johnny was not up when she was ready to depart in the morning, and only came yawning out of his bedroom when she called him.

"So you're going to be one of the working classes," he said almost jovially. "It will be rather amusing. I wouldn't let you go at all, only—"

"Only?" she waited.

Johnny's willingness that she should accept employment in Maurice's office had been a source of wonder to her, knowing his curious nature.

"I shall be about, keeping an eye on you," he said good-humouredly.

A few minutes later she was hurrying down crooked Tanners Hill toward a neighbourhood the squalor of which appalled her. Flanders Lane has few exact parallels in point of grime and ugliness, but Mr. Meister's house was most unexpectedly different from all the rest.

It stood back from the street, surrounded by a high wall which was pierced with one black door which gave access to a small courtyard, behind which was the miniature Georgian mansion where the lawyer not only lived but had his office.

An old woman led her up the worn stairs, opened a heavy ornamental door and ushered her into an apartment which she was to know very well indeed. A big panelled room with Adam decorations, it had been once the drawing-room of a prosperous City merchant in those days when great gentlemen lived in the houses where now the poor and the criminal herded like rats.

There was an air of shabbiness about the place and yet it was cheerful enough. The walls were hung about with pictures which she had no difficulty in recognising as the work of great masters. But the article of furniture which interested her most was a big grand piano which stood in an alcove. She looked in wonder at this and then turned to the old woman.

"Does Mr. Meister play this?"

"Him?" said the old lady with a cackle of laughter. "I should say he does!"

From this chamber led a little doorless ante-room which evidently was used as an office, for there were deed boxes piled up against one wall and a small desk on which stood a covered typewriter.

She had hardly taken her survey when the door opened and Maurice Meister came quickly in, alert and smiling. He strode toward her and took both her hands in his.

"My dear Mary," he said, "this is delightful!"

His enthusiasm amused her.

"This isn't a social call, Maurice," she said. "I have come to work!"

She drew her hands free of his. Had they always been on these affectionate terms, she wondered. She was puzzled and uneasy. She tried to reconstruct from her memory the exact relationship that Maurice Meister had stood to the family. He had known her since she was a child. It was stupid of her to resent this subtle tenderness of his.

"My dear Mary, there's work enough to do – title deeds, evidence," he looked vaguely round as though seeking some stimulant to his imagination.

And all the time he looked he was wondering what on earth he could find to keep her occupied.

"Can you type?" he asked.

He expected a negative and was amazed when she nodded.

"I had a typewriter when I was twelve," she smiled. "Daddy gave it to me to amuse myself with."

Here was relief from a momentary embarrassment. Maurice had never wished or expected that his offer to employ the girl should be taken seriously – never until he had seen her at Lenley Court and realised that the gawky child he had known had developed so wonderfully.

"I will give you an affidavit to copy," he said, searching feverishly amongst the papers on his desk. It was a long time before he came upon a document sufficiently innocuous for her to read. For Maurice Meister's clientele was a peculiar one, and he, who through his life had made it a practice not to let his right hand know what his left hand did, found a difficulty in bringing himself to the task of handing over so much of his dubious correspondence for her inspection. Not until he had read the paper through word by word did he give it to her.

"Well, Mary, what do you think of it all?" he demanded, "and do, please, sit down, my dear!"

"Think of it all? This place?" she asked, and then, "You live in a dreadful neighbourhood, Maurice."

"I didn't make the neighbourhood. I found it as it is," he answered with a laugh. "Are you going to be very happy here, Mary?"

She nodded. "I think so. It is so nice working for somebody one has known for so long – and Johnny will be about. He told me I should see a lot of him."

Only for a second did the heavy eyelids droop. "Oh," said Maurice Meister, looking past her. "He said you'd see a lot of him, eh? In business hours, by any chance?"

She did not detect the sarcasm in his tone.

"I don't know what are your business hours, but it is rather nice, isn't it, having Johnny?" she asked. "It really doesn't matter working for you because you're so kind, and you've known me such a long time, but it would be rather horrid if a girl was working for somebody she didn't know, and had no brother waiting on the doorstep to see her home."

He had not taken his eyes from her. She was more beautiful even than he had thought. Hers was the type of dainty loveliness which so completely appealed to him. Darker than Gwenda Milton, but finer. There was a soul and a mind behind those eyes others; a latent passion as yet unmoved; a dormant fire yet to be kindled. He felt her grow uncomfortable under the intensity of his gaze, and quick to sense this, he was quicker to dispel the mist of suspicion which might soon gather into a cloud.

"I had better show you the house," he said briskly, and led her through the ancient building.

Before one door on the upper floor he hesitated and finally, with an effort, slipped the key in the lock and threw open the door.

Looking past him, Mary saw a room such as she had not imagined would be found in this rather shabby old house. In spite of the dust which covered everything it was a beautiful apartment, furnished with a luxury that amazed her. It seemed to be a bed and sitting-room, divided by heavy velvet curtains which were now drawn. A thick carpet covered the floor, the few pictures that the room contained had evidently been carefully chosen. Old French furniture, silver light brackets on the walls, every fuse and every fitting spoke of lavish expenditure.

"What a lovely room!" she exclaimed when she had I recovered her breath.

"Yes...lovely." He stared gloomily into the nest which had once known Gwenda Milton, in the days before tragedy had come to her. "Better than Malpas Mansions, Mary, eh?" The frown had vanished from his face; he was his old smiling self. "A little cleaning, a little dusting, and there is a room for a princess – in fact, my dear, I shall put it entirely at your disposal."

"My disposal!" she stared at him. "How absurd, Maurice! I am living with Johnny and I couldn't possibly stay here, ever."

He shrugged.

"Johnny? Yes. But you may be detained one night – or Johnny may be away. I shouldn't like to think you were alone in that wretched flat."

He closed and locked the door and followed her down the stairs.

"However, that is a matter for you entirely," he said lightly. "There is the room if you ever need it."

She made no answer to this, for her mind was busy with speculation. The room had been lived in, she was sure of that. A woman had lived there – it was no man's room. Mary felt a little uneasy. Of Maurice Meister and his private life she knew nothing. She remembered vaguely that Johnny had hinted of some affair that Meister had had, but she was not curious.

Gwenda Milton!

She remembered the name with a start. Gwenda Milton, the sister of a criminal. She shivered as her mind strayed back to that gorgeous little suite, peopled with the ghost of a dead love, and she had the illusion that a white face, tense with agony, was peering at her as she sat at the typewriter. She looked round with a shudder, but the room was empty and from somewhere near at hand she heard the sound of a man humming a popular tune.

Maurice Meister did not believe in ghosts.

Chapter VIII

ON THE AFTERNOON of the day that Mary Lenley went to Meister's house the Olympic was warped into dock at Southampton. The two Scotland Yard men who had accompanied the ship from Cherbourg, and who had made a very careful scrutiny of the passengers, were the first to land and took up their station at the foot of the gangway. They had a long time to wait whilst the passport examinations were taking place, but soon the passengers began to straggle down to the quay.

Presently one of the detectives saw a face which he had not seen on the ship. A man of middle height, rather slight, with a tiny pointed beard and a black moustache appeared at the ship's side and came slowly down.

The two detectives exchanged glances and as the passenger reached the quay one of them stepped to his side and said: "Excuse me, sir, I did not see you on the ship."

For a second the bearded man surveyed the other coldly. "Are you making me responsible for your blindness?" he asked.

They were looking for a bank robber who had crossed from New York, and they were taking no chances. "May I see your passport?"

The bearded passenger hesitated, then slipping his hand into his inside pocket pulled out, not a passport but a leather note-case. From this he extracted a card. The detective took it and read:

> CENTRAL INSPECTOR BLISS.
> C.I.D. Scotland Yard. Attached Washington Embassy.

"I beg your pardon, sir."

The detective pushed the card back into the other's hand and his attitude changed.

"I didn't recognise you, Mr. Bliss. You hadn't grown a beard when you left the Yard."

"Who are you looking for?" he asked harshly.

The second detective gave a brief explanation.

"He's not on the ship, I can tell you that," said Bliss, and with a nod turned away.

He did not carry his bag into the Customs, but depositing it at his feet, he stood with his back to the wall of the Custom House and watched the passengers disembark. Presently he saw the girl for whom he had been looking.

Slim, svelte, immensely capable, entirely and utterly fearless – this was the first impression Inspector Bliss had received. He never had reason to revise his verdict. Her olive skin was faultless, the dark eyes under delicately pencilled eyebrows were insolent, knowledgeable. Here was a girl not to be tampered with, not to be fooled; an exquisite product of modernity. Expensively and a little over-dressed, perhaps. One white hand glittered with diamonds. Two large stones flashed on the lobes of her pink ears. As she brushed past him there came to the sensitive nostrils of Mr. Bliss the elusive fragrance of a perfume that was strange to him.

She had come on board at Cherbourg, and it was, he thought, a remarkable coincidence that they should have travelled to England on the same boat, and that she had not recognised him. Following her into the Custom House, he watched her thread her way through piles of luggage under the indicator M. His own customs examination was quickly finished. He handed his bag to a porter and told him to find a seat in the waiting train, and then he strolled toward where the girl, now hidden in the little crowd of passengers, was pointing out her baggage to the customs officer.

As though she were aware of his scrutiny she looked over her shoulder twice, and on the second occasion their eyes met, and he saw a look of wonder – or was it apprehension? – come into her face.

When her head was turned again, he approached nearer, so near that looking round, she almost stared into his face, and gasped.

"Mrs. Milton, I believe?" said Bliss.

Again that look. It was fear, beyond doubt.

"Sure! That's my name," she drawled. She had the soft cultured accent of one who had been raised in the Southern States. "But you certainly have the advantage of me."

"My name is Bliss. Central Inspector Bliss of Scotland Yard," he said.

Apparently the name had no significance, but as he revealed his calling, he saw the colour leave her cheeks, to flow back again instantly.

"Isn't that interesting?" she said, "and what can I do for – Central Inspector Bliss of Scotland Yard?"

Every word was like a pistol shot. There was no doubt about her antagonism.

"I should like to see your passport."

Without a word she took it from a little hand-bag and handed it to him. He turned the leaves deftly and examined the embarkation stamps.

"You've been in England quite recently?"

"Sure! I have," she said with a smile. "I was here last week. I had to go to Paris for something. From there I made the trip from Cherbourg – I was just homesick to hear Americans talking."

She was looking hard at him, puzzled rather than frightened.

"Bliss?" she said thoughtfully, "I can't place you. Yet, I've got an idea I've met you somewhere."

He was still examining the embarkation marks.

"Sydney, Genoa, Domodossola – you're a bit of a traveller, Mrs. Milton, but you don't move quite so fast as your husband."

A slow smile dawned on the beautiful face.

"I'm too busy to tell you the story of my life, or give you a travelogue," she said, "but maybe you want to see me about something more important?"

Bliss shook his head. In his sour way he was rather amused.

"No," he said, "I have no business with you, but I hope one day to meet your husband."

Her eyes narrowed.

"Do you reckon on getting to heaven too?" she asked sardonically. "I thought you knew Arthur was dead?"

His white teeth appeared under his bearded lips for a second.

"Heaven is not the place I should go to meet him," he said.

He handed back her passport and turning on his heel walked away.

She followed him with her eyes until he was out of sight, and then with a quick little sigh turned to speak to the customs officer. Bliss! The ports were being watched.

As she walked along the platform she examined each carriage with a careless eye. After a while she found the man she sought. Bliss sat in the corner of the carriage, apparently immersed in a morning newspaper.

"Bliss!" she said to herself. "Bliss!"

Where had she seen his face before? Why did the sight of this dour- looking man fill her soul with terror? Cora Ann Milton's journey to London was a troubled one.

Chapter IX

WHEN JOHNNY LENLEY called at Meister's house that afternoon, the sight of his sister hard at work with her typewriter was something of a shock to him. It was as if he recognised for the first time the state of poverty into which the Lenleys had fallen.

She was alone in the room when he came and smiled up at him from a mass of correspondence.

"Where's Maurice?" he asked, and she indicated the little room where Meister had his more important and confidential interviews which the peculiar nature of his clientele demanded.

"That's a rotten job, isn't it?"

He hoped she would say "no" and was relieved when she laughed at the question.

"It is really very interesting," she said, "and please don't scowl, Johnny, this is less boring than anything I have done for years!"

He looked at her for a moment in silence; he hated to see her thus – a servant. Setting his teeth he crossed the room and knocked at the door of Meister's private bureau.

"Who is there?" asked a voice.

Johnny tried to turn the handle but the door was locked. Then he heard the sound of a safe closing, the bolt slipped back and the lawyer appeared.

"What is the secret?" grumbled Johnny as he entered the private apartment.

Meister closed the door behind him and motioned him to a chair.

"I have been examining some rather interesting pearls," he said meaningly, "and naturally one does not invite the attention of all the world to stolen property."

"Have you had an offer for them?" asked Johnny eagerly.

Maurice said he had. "I want to get them off to Antwerp tonight," he said.

He unlocked the little safe in the corner of the room, took out a flat cardboard box, and removing the lid he displayed a magnificent row of pearls embedded in cotton wool.

"There are at least twenty thousand pounds worth," said Johnny, his eyes brightening.

"There is at least five years' penal servitude," said Maurice brutally, "and I tell you frankly, Johnny, I'm rather scared."

"Of what?" sneered the other. "Nobody is going to imagine that Mr. Meister, the eminent lawyer, is 'fencing' Lady Darnleigh's pearls." Johnny chuckled as the thought occurred to him. "By gad! You'd cut a queer figure in the dock at the Old Bailey, Maurice, Can't you imagine the evening newspapers running riot over the sensational arrest and conviction of Mr. Maurice Meister, late of Lincoln's Inn Fields, and now of Flanders Lane, Deptford."

Not a muscle of Maurice's face moved, only the dark eyes glowed with a sudden baleful power.

"Very amusing," he said evenly. "I never credited you before with an imagination." He carried the pearls to the light and examined them, before he replaced the cardboard lid.

"You have seen Mary?" he asked in a conversational tone.

Johnny nodded.

"It is beastly to see her working, but I suppose it is all right. Maurice—"

The lawyer turned his head.

"Well?"

"I've been thinking things over. You had a girl in your service named Gwenda Milton?"

"Well?" said Maurice again.

"She drowned herself, didn't she? Have you any idea why?"

Maurice Meister was facing him squarely now. Not so much as a flicker of an eyelid betrayed the rising fury within him.

"The jury said—" he began.

"I know what the jury said," interrupted Johnny roughly, "but I have my own theory."

He walked slowly to the lawyer and touched him lightly on the shoulder as he emphasised every word.

"Mary Lenley is not Gwenda Milton," he said. "She is not the sister of a fugitive murderer, and I am expecting a little better treatment for her than Gwenda Milton received at your hands."

"I don't understand you," said Meister. His voice was very low and distinct.

"I think you do." Johnny nodded slowly. "I want you to understand that there will be very serious trouble if Mary is hurt! They say that you live in everlasting fear of The Ringer – you would have greater cause to fear me if any harm came to Mary!"

Only for a second did Maurice drop his eyes.

"You're a little hysterical, Johnny," he said, "and you're certainly not in your politest mood this morning. I think I called you crude a week ago, and I have no reason to revise that description. Who is going to harm Mary? As for The Ringer and his sister, they are dead!"

He picked up the pearls from the table, again removed the lid and apparently his eyes were absorbed in the contemplation of the pearls again.

"As a jewel thief—"

He got so far when there came a gentle tap at the door.

"Who's there?" he asked quickly.

"Divisional Inspector Wembury!"

Chapter X

MAURICE MEISTER had time hastily to cover the pearls, toss them back into the safe and lock it before he opened the door. In spite of his iron nerve, the sallow face of the lawyer was drawn and white, and even his companion showed signs of mental strain as Alan appeared. It was Johnny who made the quicker recovery.

"Hallo, Wembury!" he said with a forced laugh. "I don't seem to be able to get away from you!"

There was evidence of panic, of deadly fear, something of breathless terror in the attitude of these men. What secret did they hold in common? Alan was staggered by an attitude which shouted "guilt" with a tongue of brass.

"I heard Lenley was here," he said, "and as I wanted to see him—"

"You wanted to see me?" said Johnny, his face twitching. "Why on earth should you want to see me?"

Wembury was well aware that Meister was watching him intently. No movement, no gesture, no expression was lost on the shrewd lawyer. What were they afraid of? Alan wondered, and his heart sank when, looking past them, he saw Mary at her typewriter, all unconscious of evil. "You know Lady Darnleigh, don't you?" he asked.

John Lenley nodded dumbly.

"A few weeks ago she lost a valuable string of pearls," Alan went on, "and I was put in charge of the case."

"You?" Maurice Meister's exclamation was involuntary.

Alan nodded. "I thought you knew that. My name appeared in the newspapers in connection with the investigations. I have handed the case over to Inspector Burton, and he wrote me this morning asking me if I would clear up one little matter that puzzled him."

Mary had left her typewriter and had joined the little group. "One little matter that was puzzling him?" repeated John Lenley mechanically. "And what was that?"

Wembury hesitated to put the question in the presence of the girl. "He wanted to know what induced you to go up to Lady Darnleigh's room."

"And I have already given what I think is the natural explanation," snapped Johnny.

"That you were under the impression you had left your hat and coat on the first floor? His information is that one of the footmen told you, as you were going upstairs, that the coats and hats were on the ground floor."

John Lenley avoided his eyes. "I don't remember," he said. "I was rather rattled that night. I came downstairs immediately I recognised my mistake. Is it suggested that I know anything about the robbery?" His voice shook a little.

"Of course no such suggestion is put forward," said Wembury with a smile, "but we have to get information wherever we can."

"I knew nothing of the robbery until I read about it in the newspapers and—"

"Oh, Johnny," Mary gasped the words, "you told me when you came home there had been a—"

Her brother stared her into silence. "It was two days after, you remember, my dear," he said slowly and deliberately. "I brought the newspaper in to you and told you there had been a robbery. I could not have spoken to you that night because I did not see you."

For a moment Alan wondered what the girl was going to say, but with a tremendous effort of will she controlled herself. Her face was colourless, and there was such pain in her eyes that he dared not look at her.

"Of course, Johnny, I remember...I remember," she said dully. "How stupid of me!"

A painful silence followed.

Alan was looking down at the worn carpet; his hand was thrust into his jacket pocket. "All right," he said at last. "That, I think, will satisfy Burton. I am sorry to have bothered you." He did not look at the girl: his stern eyes were fixed upon Johnny Lenley. "Why don't you take a trip abroad, Lenley?" He spoke with difficulty. "You are not looking quite as well as you might."

Johnny shifted uneasily under his gaze. "England is good enough for me," he said sulkily. "What are you, Wembury, the family doctor?"

Alan paused. "Yes," he said at last, "I think that describes me," and with a curt nod he was gone.

Mary had gone back to her typewriter but not to work. With a gesture Maurice led the young man back to his room and closed the door quietly.

"I suppose you understand what Wembury meant?" he said.

"Not being a thought reader, I didn't," replied Johnny. He was hovering between rage and amusement. "He has got a cheek, that fellow! When you think that he was a gardener's boy..."

"I should forget all that," said Mr. Meister savagely. "Remember only that you have given yourself away, and that the chances are from today onward you will be under police observation – which doesn't very much matter, Johnny, but I shall be under observation, too, and that is very unpleasant. The only doubt I have is as to whether Wembury is going to do his duty and communicate with Scotland Yard. If he does you will be in serious trouble."

"So will you," replied Johnny gruffly. "We stand or fall together over this matter, Maurice. If they find the pearls where will they be? In your safe! Has that occurred to you?"

Maurice Meister was unruffled, could even smile.

"I think we are exaggerating the danger to you," he said lightly. "Perhaps you are right and the real danger is to me. They certainly have a down on me, and they'd go far to bring me to my knees." He looked across at the safe. "I wish those beastly things were a thousand miles away. I shouldn't be surprised if Mr. Wembury returned armed with a search warrant, and if that happened the fat would be in the fire!"

"Why not post them to Antwerp?" asked the other.

Meister smiled contemptuously.

"If I am being watched, as is very likely," he said, "you don't suppose for one moment that they would fail to keep an eye on the post office? No, the only thing to do with those wretched pearls is to plant them somewhere for a day or two."

Johnny was biting his nails, a worried look on his face.

"I'll take them back to the flat," he said suddenly. "There are a dozen places I could hide them." If he had been looking at Maurice he would have seen a satisfied gleam in his eyes.

"That is not a bad idea," said the lawyer slowly. "Wembury would never dream of searching your flat – he likes Mary too much."

He did not wait for his companion to make up his mind, but, unlocking the safe, took out a box and handed it to the other. The young man looked at the package dubiously and then slipped it into his inside pocket.

"I'll put it into the box under my bed," he said, "and let you have it back at the end of the week."

He did not stop to speak to Mary as he made his way quickly through the outer room. There was a sense of satisfaction in the very proximity of those pearls, for which he had risked so much, that gave him a sense of possession, removed some of the irritable suspicion which had grown up in his mind since Meister had the handling of them.

As he passed through crowded Flanders Lane a man turned out of a narrow alley and followed him. As Johnny Lenley walked up Tanners Hill, the man was strolling behind him, and the policeman on point duty hardly noticed him as he passed, never dreaming that within reach of his gloved hand was the man for whom the police of three continents were searching – Henry Arthur Milton, otherwise known as The Ringer.

Chapter 11

LONG AFTER LENLEY had taken his departure Maurice Meister strode up and down his tiny sanctum, his hands clasped behind him.

A thought was taking shape in his mind – two thoughts indeed, which converged, intermingled, separated and came together again – Johnny Lenley and his sister.

There had been no mistaking the manner in Lenley's voice. Meister had been threatened before and now, so far from moving him from his half-formed purpose, it needed only the youthful and unbalanced violence of Johnny Lenley to stimulate him in the other direction. He had seen too much of Johnny lately. Once there was a time when the young man was amusing – then he had been useful. Now he was becoming not only a bore but a meddlesome bore. He opened the door gently and peeped through the crack. Mary was sitting at her typewriter intent upon her work.

The morning sun flooded the little room, and made a nimbus about her hair. Once she turned her face in his direction without realising that she was being watched. It was difficult to find a fault in the perfect contour of her face and the transparent loveliness of her skin. Maurice fondled his chin thoughtfully. A new interest had come into his life, a new chase had begun. And then his mind came uneasily back to Johnny.

There was a safe and effective way of getting rid of Johnny, with his pomposity, his threats and his stupid confidence.

That last quality was the gravest danger to Maurice. And when Johnny was out of the way many difficulties would be smoothed over. Mary could not be any more adamantine than Gwenda had been in the earliest stages of their friendship.

Inspector Wembury!

Maurice frowned at the thought. Here was a troublemaker on a different plane from Lenley. A man of the world, shrewd, knowledgeable, not lightly to be antagonised. Maurice shrugged his shoulders.

It was absurd to consider the policeman, he thought. After all, Mary was not so much his friend as his patroness. She was wholly absorbed in her work when he crossed the room and went softly up the stairs to the little suite above.

As he opened the door he shivered. The memory of Gwenda Milton and that foggy coroner's court was an ugly one. A little decoration was needed to make this room again as beautiful as it had been. The place must be cleaned out, decorated and made not only habitable but attractive. Would it attract Mary – supposing Johnny were out of the way? That was to be discovered. His first task was to settle with John Lenley and send him to a place where his power for mischief was curtailed. Maurice was a wise man. He did not approach or speak to the girl after the interview with her brother, but allowed some time to elapse before he came to where she was working.

The little lunch which had been served to her was uneaten.

She stood by the window, staring down into Flanders Lane, and at the sound of his voice she started.

"What is the matter, my dear?" Maurice could be very fatherly and tender. It was his favourite approach.

She shook her head wearily. "I don't know, Maurice. I'm worried – about Johnny and the pearls."

"The pearls?" he repeated, in affected surprise. "Do you mean Lady Darnleigh's pearls?"

She nodded. "Why did Johnny lie?" she asked. "It was the first thing he told me when he came home, that there had been a robbery in Park Lane and that Lady Darnleigh had lost her jewels."

"Johnny was not quite normal," he said soothingly. "I shouldn't take too much notice of what he said. His memory seems to have gone to pieces lately."

"It isn't that." She was not convinced. "He knew that he had told me, Maurice: there was no question of his having forgotten." She looked up anxiously into his face. "You don't think—" She did not complete the sentence.

"That Johnny knew anything about the robbery? Rubbish, my dear! The boy is a little worried – and naturally! It isn't a pleasant sensation to find yourself thrown on to the world penniless as Johnny has. He has neither your character nor your courage, my dear."

She sighed heavily and went back to her desk, where there was a neat little pile of correspondence which she had put aside. She turned the pages listlessly and suddenly withdrew a sheet.

"Maurice, who is The Ringer?" she asked.

He glared back at the word.

"The Ringer?"

"It's a cablegram. You hadn't opened it. I found it amongst a lot of your old correspondence."

He snatched the paper from her. The message was dated three months before, and was from Sydney. By the signature he saw it was from a lawyer who acted as his agent in Australia, and the message was brief: "Man taken from Sydney Harbour identified, not Ringer, who is believed to have left Australia."

Mary was staring at the lawyer. His face had gone suddenly haggard and drawn; what vestige of colour there had been in his cheeks had disappeared.

"The Ringer!" he muttered..."Alive!"

The hand that held the paper was shaking, and, as though he realised that some reason for his agitation must be found, he went on with a laugh: "An old client of mine, a fellow I was rather keen on – but a scoundrel, and more than a scoundrel."

As he spoke he tore the form into little pieces and dropped the litter into the wastepaper basket. Then unexpectedly he put his arm about her shoulder.

"Mary, I would not worry too much about Johnny if I were you. He is at a difficult age and in a difficult mood. I am not pleased with him just now."

She stared at him wonderingly.

"Not pleased with him, Maurice? Why not?"

Maurice shrugged his shoulders.

"He has got himself mixed up with a lot of unpleasant people – men I would not have in this office, and certainly would not allow to associate with you."

His arm was still about her shoulder, and she moved slightly to release herself from this parental embrace. She was not frightened, only a little uncomfortable and uneasy, but he allowed his arm to drop as though his gesture had been born in a momentary mood of protection, and apparently did not notice the movement by which she had freed herself.

"Can't you do something for him? He would listen to you," she pleaded.

But he was not thinking of Johnny. All his thoughts and eyes were for the girl. She was holding his arms now, looking up into his face, and he felt his pulses beating a little faster. Suppose Johnny took the detective's advice and went off to the Continent with the pearls – and Mary! He would find no difficulty in disposing of the necklace and would secure a sum sufficient to keep him for years. This was the thought that ran through Meister's mind as he patted the girl's cheek softly.

"I will see what can be done about Johnny," he said. "Don't worry your pretty head any more."

In his private office Meister had a small portable typewriter. Throughout the afternoon she heard the click-click of it as he laboriously wrote his message of betrayal.

That evening, when Inspector Wembury came back to Flanders Lane Police Station, he found a letter awaiting him. It was typewritten and unsigned and had been delivered by a district messenger from a West Central office. The message ran:

The Countess of Darnleigh's pearl necklace was stolen by John Lenley of 37, Malpas Mansions. It is at present in a cardboard carton in a box under his bed.

Alan Wembury read the message and his heart sank within, him, for only one course was open to him, the course of duty.

Chapter XII

WEMBURY knew that he would be well within his rights if he ignored this typewritten message, for anonymous letters are a daily feature of police life. Yet he realised that it was the practice that, if the information which came thus surreptitiously to a police station coincided with news already in the possession of the police, or if it supported a definite suspicion, inquiries must be set afoot.

He went to his little room to work out the problem alone. It would be a simple matter to hand over the inquiry to another police officer, or even to refer it to...But that would be an act of moral cowardice.

There was a small sliding window in the door of his office which gave him a view of the charge room, and as he pondered his problem a bent figure came into his line of vision and, acting on an impulse, he jumped up from the table, and, opening the door beckoned Dr. Lomond. Why he should make a confidant of this old man who was ignorant of police routine he could not for the life of him explain. But between the two men in the very short period of their acquaintance there had grown a queer understanding.

Lomond looked round the little room from under his shaggy brows.

"I have a feeling that you're in trouble, Mr. Wembury," he said, his eyes twinkling.

"If that's a guess, it's a good one," said Alan.

He closed the door behind the police surgeon and pushed forward a chair for him. In a few words he revealed the problem which was exercising his mind, and Lomond listened attentively.

"It's verra awkward." He shook his head. "Man, that's almost like a drama! It seems to me there's only one thing for you to do, Mr. Wembury – you'll have to treat John Lenley as though he were John Smith or Thomas Brown. Forget he's the brother of Miss Lenley, and I think," he said shrewdly, "that is what is worrying you most – and deal with this case as though it were somebody you had never heard of."

Alan nodded slowly.

"That, I'm afraid, is the counsel I should give myself, if I were entirely unprejudiced in the matter."

The old man took a silver tobacco box from his pocket and began slowly to roll a cigarette.

"John Lenley, eh?" he mused. "A friend of Meister's!"

Alan stared at him. The doctor laid significant emphasis on the lawyer's name.

"Do you know him?"

Lomond shook his head.

"Through my career," he said, "I have followed one practice when I come to a strange land – I acquire the local legends. Meister is a legend. To me he is the most interesting man in Deptford, and I'm looking forward to meeting him."

"But why should Johnny Lenley's friendship with Meister—" began Alan, and stopped. He knew full well the sinister importance of that friendship.

Maurice Meister was something more than a legend: he was a sinister fact. His acquaintance with the criminal law was complete. The loopholes which exist in the best drawn statutes were so familiar to him that not once, but half a dozen times, he had cleared his clients of serious charges. There were suspicious people who wondered how the poor thieves who employed him raised the money to pay his fees. There were ill-natured persons who suggested that Meister paid himself out of the proceeds of the robbery and utilised the opportunities he had as a lawyer to obtain from his clients the exact location of the property they had stolen. Many a jewel thief on the run had paused in his flight to visit the house in Flanders Lane, and had gone on his way, leaving in the lawyer's hands the evidence which would have incriminated him. He acted as a sort of banker to the larger fry, and exacted his tribute from the smaller.

"Let me see your anonymous letter," said the doctor.

He carried the paper to the light and examined the typewritten characters carefully.

"Written by an amateur," he said. "You can always tell amateur typists, they forget to put the spaces between the words; but, more important, they vary the spaces between the lines."

He pursed his lips as though he were about to whistle.

"Hum!" he said at last. "Do you rule out the possibility that this letter was written by Meister himself?"

"By Meister?" That idea had not occurred to Alan Wembury. "But why? He's a good friend of Johnny's. Suppose he were in this robbery, do you imagine he would trust John Lenley with the pearls and draw attention to the fact that a friend of his was a thief?"

The doctor was still frowning down at the paper.

"Is there any reason why Meister should want John Lenley out of the way?" he asked.

Alan shook his head.

"I can't imagine any," he said, and then, with a laugh: "You're taking rather a melodramatic view, doctor. Probably this note was written by some enemy of Lenley's – he makes enemies quicker than any man I know."

"Meister," murmured the doctor, and held the paper up to the light to examine the watermark. "Maybe one day you'll have an opportunity, inspector, of getting a little of Mr. Meister's typewriting paper and a specimen of lettering."

"But why on earth should he want Johnny Lenley out of the way?" insisted Alan. "There's no reason why he should. He's an old friend of the family, and although it's possible that Johnny has insulted him, that's one of Johnny's unpleasant little habits. That's no excuse for a civilised man wanting to send another to penal servitude—"

"He wishes Mr. John Lenley out of the way" – Lomond nodded emphatically. "That is my eccentric view. Inspector Wembury, and if I am an eccentric, I am also a fairly accurate man!"

After the doctor left, Alan puzzled the matter over without getting nearer to the solution. Yet he had already discovered that Dr. Lomond's conclusions were not lightly to be dismissed. The old man was as shrewd as he was brilliant. Alan had read a portion of his book, and although twenty years old, this treatise on the criminal might have been written a few weeks before.

He was in a state of indecision when the telephone bell in his room shrilled. He took up the instrument and heard the voice of Colonel Walford.

"Is that you, Wembury? Do you think you can come up to the Yard? I have further information about the gentleman we discussed last week."

For the moment Alan had forgotten the existence of The Ringer. He saw now only an opportunity of taking counsel with a man who had not only proved a sympathetic superior, but a very real friend.

Half an hour later he knocked at the door of Colonel Walford's room, and that moment was one of tragic significance for Mary Lenley.

Chapter XIII

JOHN LENLEY, after a brief visit to his house, where, behind a locked door, he packed away carefully a small cardboard box, had gone to town to see a friend of the family.

Mary came home to an empty flat. Her head was aching, but that was as nothing to the little nagging pain at her heart. The little supper was a weariness to prepare – almost impossible to dispose of.

She had eaten nothing since breakfast, she remembered, and if she had failed to recall the fact, the queer and sickly sensation of faintness which had come over her as she was mounting the stone steps of Malpas Mansions was an unpleasant reminder of her abstinence.

She forced herself to eat, and was brewing her second cup of tea when she heard a key turn in the lock and John Lenley came in. His face was as black as thunder, but she had ceased to wonder what drove Johnny into those all too frequent tempers of his. Nor was there need to ask, for he volunteered the cause of his anger.

"I went out to the Hamptons' to tea," he said, as he sat down at the table with a disparaging glance at its meagre contents. "They treated me as though I were a leper – and those swine have been entertained at Lenley Court times without number!"

She was shocked at the news, for she had always regarded the Hamptons as the greatest friends of her father.

"But surely, Johnny, they didn't – they weren't horrible because of our – I mean because we have no money?"

He growled something at this.

"That was at the back of it," he said at last. "But I suspect another cause."

And then the reason flashed on her, and her heart thumped painfully.

"It was not because of the Darnleigh pearls, Johnny?" she faltered.

He looked round at her quickly.

"Why do you ask that? – Yes, it was something about that old fool's jewellery. They didn't say so directly, but they hinted as much."

She felt her lower lip trembling and bit on it to gain control.

"There is nothing in that suggestion, is there, Johnny?" It did not sound like her voice – it was a sound that was coming from far away – a strange voice suggesting stranger things.

"I don't know what you mean!" he answered gruffly, but he did not look at her.

The room spun round before her eyes, and she had to grasp the table for support.

"My God! You don't think I am a thief, do you?" she heard him say.

Mary Lenley steadied herself.

"Look at me, Johnny!" Their eyes met. "You know nothing about those pearls?"

Again his eyes wandered. "I only know they're lost! What in hell do you expect me to say?" He almost shouted in a sudden excess of weak anger. "How dare you, Mary...cross-examine me as though I were a thief! This comes from knowing cads like Wembury...!"

"Did you steal Lady Darnleigh's pearls?"

The tablecloth was no whiter than her face. Her lips were bloodless. He made one effort to meet her eyes again, and failed.

"I—" he began.

Then came a knock at the door. Brother and sister looked at one another.

"Who is that?" asked Johnny huskily.

She shook her head.

"I don't know; I will see."

Her limbs were like lead as she dragged them to the door; she thought she was going to faint. Alan Wembury stood in the doorway, and there was on his face a look which she had never seen before.

"Do you want me, Alan?" she asked breathlessly.

"I want to see Johnny."

His voice was as low as hers and scarcely intelligible. She opened the door wider and he walked past her into the dining-room. Johnny was standing where she had left him, by the little round table covered with the remains of the supper, and the clang of the door as Mary closed it came to his ears like the knell of doom.

"What do you want, Wembury?" John Lenley spoke with difficulty. His heart was beating so thunderously that he felt this man must hear the roar and thud of it.

"I've just come from Scotland Yard." Alan's voice was changed and unnatural. "I've seen Colonel Walford, and told him of a communication I received this afternoon. I have explained the" – he sought for words – "the relationship I have with your family and the regard in which I hold it, and just why I should hesitate to do my job."

"What is your job?" asked Lenley after a moment of silence.

"Immediately, I have no business." – Wembury chose his words deliberately and carefully. "Tomorrow I shall come with a warrant to search this house for the Darnleigh pearls."

He heard the smothered sob of the girl, but did not turn his head.

John Lenley stood rigid, his face as white as death. He was ignorant of police procedure, or he would have realised how significant was Alan's statement that he did not possess a search warrant. Wembury sensed this ignorance, and made one last desperate effort to save the girl he loved from the tragic consequences of her brother's folly.

"I have no search warrant and no right to examine your flat," he said. "The warrant will be procured by tomorrow morning."

If John Lenley had a glimmering of intelligence, and the pearls were hidden in the flat, here was a chance to dispose of them, but the opportunity which Alan offered was not taken.

It was sheer mad arrogance on Lenley's part to reject the chance that was given to him. He would not be under any obligation to the gardener's son!

"They are in a box under the bed," he said. "You knew that or you wouldn't have come. I am not taking any favours from you, Wembury, and I don't suppose I should get any if I did. If you feel any satisfaction in arresting a man whose father provided the cottage in which you were born, I suppose you are entitled to feel it."

He turned on his heel, walked into his room, and a few seconds later came back with a small cardboard box which he laid on the table. Alan Wembury was momentarily numbed by the tragedy which had overwhelmed this little household. He dared not look at Mary, who stood stiffly by the side of the table. Her pallid face was turned with an agonised expression of entreaty to her brother, and it was only now that she could find speech.

"Johnny! How could you!"

He wriggled his shoulders impatiently.

"It is no use making a fuss, Mary," he said bluntly. "I was mad!"

Turning suddenly, he caught her in his arms, and his whole frame shook as he kissed her pale lips.

"Well, I'll go," he said brokenly, and in another instant had wrenched himself free of her kiss and her clinging hands, and had walked out of the room a prisoner.

Chapter XIV

NEITHER ALAN WEMBURY nor his prisoner spoke until they were approaching Flanders Lane Police Station, and then Johnny asked, without turning his head.

"Who gave me away?"

It was only the rigid discipline of twelve years' police work that prevented Alan from betraying the betrayer.

"Information received," he answered conventionally, and the young man laughed.

"I suppose you've been watching me since the robbery," he said. "Well, you'll get promotion out of this, Wembury, and I wish you joy of it."

When he faced the desk sergeant his mood became a little more amiable, and he asked if Maurice Meister could be intimated. Just before he went to the cell he asked, "What do I get for this, Wembury?"

Alan shook his head. He was certain in his mind that, though it was a first offence, nothing could save Johnny Lenley from penal servitude.

It was eleven o'clock at night, and rain was falling heavily, when Alan came walking quickly down the deserted stretch of Flanders Lane, towards Meister's house. From the opposite side of the road he could see above the wall the upper windows; one window showed a light. The lawyer was still up, possibly was interviewing one of his queer clients, who had come by a secret way into the house to display his ill-gotten wares or to pour a tale of woe into Meister's unsympathetic ear. These old houses near the river were honeycombed with cellar passages, and only a few weeks before, there had been discovered in the course of demolition a secret room which the owner, who had lived in the place for twenty years, had never suspected.

As he crossed the road, Alan saw a figure emerge from the dark shadow of the wall which surrounded the lawyer's house. There was something very stealthy in the movements of the man, and all that was police officer in Wembury's composition, was aroused by this furtiveness. He challenged him sharply, and to his surprise, instead of turning and running, as the Flanders Laner might be expected to do in the circumstances, the man turned and came slowly towards him and stood revealed in the beam of Inspector Wembury's pocket lamp, a slight man with a dark, bearded face. He was a stranger to the detective, but that was not remarkable. Most of the undesirables of Deptford were as yet unknown to Alan.

"Hallo! Who are you, and what are you doing here?" he asked, and immediately came the cool answer:

"I might ask you the same question!"

"I am a police officer," said Alan Wembury sternly, and he heard a low chuckle.

"Then we are brothers in misfortune," replied the stranger, "for I am a police officer, too. Inspector Wembury, I presume?"

"That is my name," said Alan, and waited.

"I cannot bother to give you my card, but my name is Bliss – Central Detective Inspector Bliss – of Scotland Yard."

Bliss? Alan remembered now that this unpopular police officer had been due to arrive in England on that or on the previous day. One fact was certain: if this were Bliss, he was Alan's superior officer.

"Are you looking for something?" he asked.

For a while Bliss made no reply.

"I don't know what I'm looking for exactly. Deptford is an old division of mine, and I was just renewing acquaintance with the place. Are you going to see Meister?"

How did he know it was Meister's house, Alan wondered. The lawyer had only gone to live there since Bliss had left for America. And what was his especial interest in the crook solicitor? As though he were reading the other's thoughts, Bliss went on quickly: "Somebody told me that Meister was living in Deptford. Rather a 'come down' for him. When I knew him first, he had a wonderful practice in Lincoln's Inn."

And then with an abrupt nod he passed on the way he had been going when Wembury had called him back. Alan stood by the door of Meister's house and watched the stranger till he was out of sight, and only then did he ring the bell. He had some time to wait, time for thought, though his thoughts were not pleasant. He dared not think of Mary, alone in that desolate little flat, with her breaking heart and her despair. Nor of the boy he had known, sitting on his plank bed, his head between his hands, ruin before him.

Presently he heard a patter of slippered feet coming across the courtyard, and Meister's voice asked: "Who is that?"

"Wembury."

A rattle of chains and a shooting of bolts, and the door opened. Though he wore his dressing-gown, Wembury saw, when they reached the dimly lit passage, that Meister was fully dressed; even his spats had not been removed.

"What is the trouble, Mr. Wembury?"

Alan did not know how many people slept in the house or what could be overheard. Without invitation he walked up the stairs ahead of the lawyer into the big room. The piano was open, sheets of music lay on the floor. Evidently Meister had been spending a musical evening. The lawyer closed the door behind him.

"Is it Johnny?" he asked.

Was it imagination on Alan's part, or was the lawyer's voice strained and husky.

"Why should it be Johnny?" he demanded. "It is, as a matter of fact. I arrested him an hour ago for the Darnleigh pearl robbery. He has asked me to get into communication with you."

Maurice did not reply: he was looking down at the floor, apparently deep in thought.

"How did you come to get the information on which he was arrested, or did you know all the time that Johnny was in this?" he asked at last.

Alan was looking at him keenly, and under his scrutiny the lawyer shuffled uneasily.

"I am not prepared to tell you that – if you do not know!" he said. "But I have promised Lenley that I will carry his message to you, and that ends my duty so far as he is concerned."

The lawyer's eyes were roving from one object in the room to another. Not once did he look at Wembury.

"It is curious," he said, shaking his head sorrowfully, "but I had a premonition that Johnny had been mixed up in this Darnleigh affair. What a fool! Thank God his father is dead—"

"I don't think we need bother our heads with pious wishes," said Alan bluntly. "The damnable fact is that Lenley is under arrest for a jewel robbery."

"You have the pearls?"

Alan nodded.

"They were in a cardboard box – there was also a bracelet stolen, but that is not in the box," he said slowly. "Also I have seen a sign of an old label, and I think I shall be able to trace the original owner of the box."

And then, to his astonishment, Meister said: "Perhaps I can help you. I have an idea the box was mine. Johnny asked me for one a week ago. Of course, I had no notion of why he wanted it, but I gave it to him. It may be another box altogether, but I should imagine the carton is mine."

Momentarily Alan Wembury was staggered. He had had a faint hope that he might be able to connect Meister with the robbery, the more so since he had discovered more than he had told. The half-obliterated label had obviously been addressed to Meister himself, yet the lawyer could not have been aware of this fact. It was one of the slips that the cleverest criminals make. But so quick and glib was he that he had virtually destroyed all hope of proving his complicity in the robbery – unless Johnny told. And Johnny was not the man who would betray a confederate.

"What do you think he will get?" asked Maurice.

"The sentence? You seem pretty certain that he is guilty."

Maurice shrugged. "What else can I think – obviously you would not have arrested him without the strongest possible evidence. It is a tragedy! Poor lad!"

And then all the dark places in this inexplicable betrayal were lit in one blinding flash of understanding. Mary! Wembury had scoffed at the idea that Meister wished to get her brother out of the way. He could see no motive for such an act of treachery. But now all the hideous possibilities presented themselves to him, and he glared down at the lawyer. He knew Meister's reputation; knew the story of Gwenda Milton; knew other even less savoury details of Meister's past life. Was Mary the innocent cause of this wicked deed? Was it to gain domination over her that Johnny was being sent into a living grave? This time Meister met his eyes and did not flinch.

Chapter XV

"I DON'T think you need trouble about Miss Lenley." Alan's voice was deadly cold. "Fortunately she lives in my division, and she trusts me well enough to come to me if she's in any trouble."

He saw the slow smile dawn upon the lawyer's face.

"Do you think that is likely. Inspector Wembury?" Meister asked. His voice had a quality of softness which was almost feline. "As I understand, you had the unhappy task of arresting her brother: is she likely to bring her troubles to you?"

Alan's heart sank. The thought of Mary's attitude towards him had tortured him since the arrest. How could she continue to be friendly with the man who was immediately responsible for the ruin and disgrace of her brother?

"The Lenleys are an old family," Meister went on. "They have their modicum of pride. I doubt if poor Mary will ever forgive you for arresting her brother. It will be terribly unjust, of course, but women are illogical. I will do what I can for Miss Lenley, just as I shall do what I can for Johnny. And I think my opportunities are more obvious than yours. Can I see Johnny to-night?"

Alan nodded.

"Yes, he asked me if you would see him at once, though I'm afraid you can do very little for him. No bail will be granted, of course. This is a felony charge."

Maurice Meister hurried to the door that led to his room, slipping off his dressing-gown as he went.

"I will not keep you waiting very long," he said. Left alone in the big room, Alan paced up and down the worn carpet, his hands behind him, his chin on his breast. There was something subtly repulsive in this atmosphere. The great piano, the faded panelling, the shabby richness of the furnishing and decoration. The room seemed to be over-supplied with doors: he counted four, in addition to the curtain which hid the alcove. Where did all these lead to? And what stories could they tell, he wondered.

Particularly interested was he in one door which was heavily bolted and barred, and he was staring at this when, to his amazement, above the frame glowed suddenly a long red light. A signal of some kind – from whom? Even as he looked, the light died away and Meister came in, struggling into his overcoat.

"What does that light mean, Mr. Meister?"

The lawyer spun round. "Light? Which light?" he asked quickly, and following the direction of the detective's finger, he gasped. "A light?" incredulously. "You mean that red lamp? How did you come to notice it?"

"It lit up a few minutes ago and went out again." It was not imagination on his part: the lawyer's face had gone a sickly yellow.

"Are you sure?" And then, quickly: "It is a substitute for a bell – I mean, if you press the bell on the outer door the lamp lights up; bells annoy me."

He was lying, and he was frightened too. The red lamp had another significance. What was it?

In those few seconds Meister had become ill at ease, nervous; the hand that strayed constantly to his mouth trembled. Glancing at him out of the corner of his eye, when he thought he was free from observation, Alan saw him take a small golden box from his pocket, pinch something from its contents and sniff at his thumb and finger. "Cocaine," guessed Wembury, and knew that his theory was right when almost immediately the lawyer became his old buoyant self.

"You must have imagined it – probably a reflection from the lamp on the table," he said.

"But why shouldn't there be somebody at the front door?" asked Alan coolly, and Meister made an effort to correct his error.

"Very probably there is," He hesitated. "I wonder if you would mind, inspector – would it be asking you too much to go down to the front gate and see? Here is the key!"

Alan took the key from the lawyer's hand, went downstairs across the courtyard and opened the outer gate. There was nobody there. He suspected, indeed he was sure, that the lawyer had asked him to perform this service because he wished to be alone in the room for a few minutes, possibly to investigate the cause of and reason for that signal.

As he went up the stairs he heard a sharp click as though a drawer had closed, and when he came into the room he found Meister pulling on his gloves with an air of nonchalance.

"Nobody?" he asked. "It must have been your imagination, inspector, or one of these dreadful people of Flanders Lane playing a trick."

"The lamp hasn't lit since I left the room?" asked Alan, and when Meister shook his head, "You are sure?"

"Absolutely," said the lawyer, and too late saw he was trapped.

"That is very curious." Wembury looked hard at him. "Because I pressed the front door bell, and if the lamp was what you said it was, it should have lit up again, shouldn't it?"

Meister murmured something about the connections being out of order, and almost hustled him from the room.

Alan was not present at the interview at the police station. He left Meister in the charge of the station sergeant, and went home to his lodgings in Blackheath Road with a heavy heart. He could do nothing for the girl; not so much as suggest a woman who would keep her company. He could not guess that at that moment, when his heart ached for her, Mary had a companion, and that companion a woman.

The complete and unabridged text is available online, from *flametreepublishing.com/extras*

The Mystery of the Boat Express

Victor L. Whitechurch

IT WAS A GUSTY, stormy morning in January, with the wind blowing a cold rain from the north-west. There were very few passengers by the Great Southern Boat train to Porthampton that morning, for it was not the day one would choose, if one could help it, for a cross-Channel journey, especially as the telegram from the coast on the station notice-board proclaimed that the Channel was "rough and stormy."

It wanted but three minutes to the starting of the train. A passenger came running from the booking office, a man of about forty years of age, with fair beard and moustache, carrying a small Gladstone bag, a soft hat pulled well down over his eyes, and the collar of his great coat turned up.

"What class, sir?" asked the guard as he drew near.

"Second – please," replied the man.

The guard noticed that he spoke with a slight foreign accent, and opened the door of an empty compartment. The passenger glanced hurriedly along the train, and then got in.

"Will you please lock the door? I do not wish to be disturbed."

The guard took the proffered half-crown, drew a key from his pocket, and turned the lock. The man pulled up the window.

One or two more belated passengers came hurrying to the train – one just as it was about to start. The latter looked hastily into each carriage as he moved along the train.

"Now then, sir – in here, please!" And the guard opened the door of a compartment, blew his whistle, and the train started.

At Porthampton the guard remembered the locked door, and ran down the platform to release the passenger. He opened the door, and gave a start of surprise.

The occupant of the compartment was huddled up in a heap upon the floor on the further side, his head, with its back to the guard, leaning against the edge of the seat. And staining the cushion of the seat, and the man's shoulder, were splashes of blood.

The guard gave a cry of alarm; a few station officials and passengers pressed forward. One of the latter, an elderly gentleman, exclaimed:

"Then it was a shot I heard!"

"I'll trouble you for your name and address, then, please sir," said a quiet voice. "I am one of the company's detectives."

The other produced his card.

"I am the manager of the City and Southern Bank," he said.

"All right, sir – now let's have a look at the poor chap, and you shall tell us your story later. Someone fetch a doctor."

He went into the compartment, and gently raised the head of the unfortunate man.

"He's dead, I'm afraid – looks as if he shot himself."

"There's a revolver on the seat," exclaimed the guard.

The detective took it up, glanced at it sharply, and put it into his pocket.

"Was he travelling alone?"

"Yes," replied the guard.

"Anyone in the next compartments?"

"This is at the end of the coach. No one was in the next. I'm certain of that."

A doctor came bustling up. They lifted the body on to the seat, and the medical man made an examination.

"A bullet through the brain," he said. "Life must have been extinct for nearly an hour."

"You say you heard a shot, sir?" asked the detective of the bank manager.

"Yes – some time ago. I thought it was a fog signal. I little imagined it meant suicide. Do you want me? I am on my way to Paris, but I shall be back tomorrow."

"You could attend the inquest here if we held it tomorrow evening?"

"Certainly."

The whistle of the steamer sounded, and the little group of passengers hurried away. The detective looked at the doctor, raising his eyebrows.

"Queer, I think, sir?" he asked.

The doctor nodded.

"Half-a-minute," said the other.

He darted out of the carriage.

"Jenkins," he said to a subordinate on the platform, "it's lucky you're here. I want you to board the boat and cross on her. Bring back an account of all the passengers, if you can – there's not a score of them."

"Very good, sir."

The detective went back to the carriage.

"I understand a revolver was found," said the doctor. "Where?" The other showed the exact spot on the seat where the weapon had been lying. Then he took it from his pocket and showed it to the doctor. The latter examined it.

"As you say – it's queer," he said. "D'you see what he's got in his right hand?"

The detective looked.

"A handkerchief!" he exclaimed. "Will you see about getting the body to the waiting-room, sir? It may as well lie there. I'll examine the clothes afterwards. I've some work to do here first."

He was a long time in the compartment, and before he left he summoned the guard once more. That night the evening papers had a paragraph stating that an unknown man had apparently committed suicide by shooting himself in the Porthampton boat express. The detective smiled when he read it. His smile changed into a frown, however, when Jenkins returned by the night boat and handed in his report.

"Nothing suspicious about any of them," he said.

"Then he must have slipped off on this side – out of the station," replied his chief enigmatically, "I've bungled it a little."

At the inquest the guard was the first to give evidence. He mentioned that the deceased had spoken to him with a German accent.

"How do you know that?" asked the coroner.

"You can't be guard of the boat train for five years running, sir, without picking up hints. I can generally spot a Frenchman or a German."

He concluded by giving a brief account of his discovery of the body. The coroner asked a few questions, adding:

"No one else could have got in with him?"

"Impossible, sir. The further door was locked already, and, as I said, he asked for the other to be locked."

"He seemed to want to be alone?" asked a juryman.

"Yes."

The juryman nodded sagaciously.

"Suicide – premeditated," he murmured.

Mr. Clinton, the bank manager, was allowed to give evidence next, as he was anxious to catch the last train back to town.

"I was travelling in the compartment next but two to the deceased's," he said, "and was half dozing over a book when I heard a slight report. The wind was very high and both windows were shut."

"A report of a pistol?"

"I didn't think so at the time. There were three other passengers with me, and we all imagined it was probably a detonator on the line, such as is used in fogs or in warning the driver that a gang of men are at work. I am interested in railway matters, and I jumped up at once and looked out of both windows. There was nothing to be seen, and the train did not slacken speed, so we all thought no more about it till I was told at Porthampton what had happened."

"When did you hear the shot?"

"About half an hour after leaving London."

Next came the doctor. He stated, concisely, that death had been caused by a bullet which had entered the deceased's head at the right temple, passed through the skull, and carried away a piece of the bone on the further side. He agreed that the time which had elapsed might reasonably coincide with the shot that Mr. Clinton had heard, and described how he found the body lying on the floor close to the further door.

"As a man might naturally have fallen after he had shot himself?" asked the juryman who had spoken before.

"I don't think so," replied the doctor shortly.

A sensation ran round the court.

"Why not?" asked the coroner.

"There are circumstances in the case which are baffling. The wound was just in the position likely for a man who had shot himself with a pistol, holding it in his right hand with the muzzle against his temple. Death must have been instantaneous. But the strange thing is that the deceased was clutching a handkerchief with his right hand, and that there were no powder marks round the wound. The shot must have been fired at a further distance."

"But," said the coroner, "I understand that a revolver was found in the compartment?"

"It was found before I was on the spot," replied the doctor, "and the next witness will tell you more about it. It is not my professional business," he went on, "to hazard speculation; but I do say emphatically that, in my opinion, it is certainly not a case of suicide."

The detective corroborated what the doctor had said.

"Tell us about the revolver, please," said the coroner. "It was lying on the seat – away from the deceased. It was loaded in every chamber, and had not been discharged recently. The barrel was quite clean inside.

"I examined the compartment carefully," he went on, "and although, as the doctor has told you, the bullet went through the skull, carrying away a piece of the bone, I could find neither bone nor bullet – nor any mark of either – in the carriage."

"Was the window open?" asked a juryman.

"Yes – at the end where the body had fallen. The other was shut. I know what your question implies; but, if the man had been shot by someone outside the open window, the bullet mark would have been found at the opposite end of the compartment. If, on the other hand, the bullet, after penetrating the skull, had gone out of the open window, the shot must have been fired inside, which appears impossible, especially as both doors were found locked; and the murderer could not have opened the other window from outside and then fired through it."

"What is your opinion, then?" asked the Coroner.

"Murder," he replied, "but how I cannot say."

"You have taken steps?"

"As far as is possible."

He stated further that there was no clue to identify the dead man. "He carried no papers, his bag only contained clothing, and his linen was not marked."

"Nothing else?"

The witness hesitated.

"There was something which might be a possible clue, sir; but I will ask you not to make me mention it – at present."

An adjournment was made for a fortnight at the request of the police. But at the adjournment the detective said bluntly that he had no more evidence, and the inspector of police who was in charge of the case was equally reticent.

Finally, the jury returned the rather strange verdict of "Found shot – apparently by some person unknown," and the newspapers curtly referred to the case as "another unsolved railway mystery."

So much for the story. I had the sequel from the very man who unravelled the mystery, now retired from business on a comfortable pension. He was telling me some of his exploits one day, when I happened to mention the Porthampton Murder.

"That was a curious affair," I said. "You never solved it, did you?"

He filled and lit his pipe thoughtfully.

"I can't say I didn't do that," he replied; "but" – and he laughed – "I wasn't allowed to get the credit of it. The official police stopped me. Look here," he went on, "it happened five years ago, and is forgotten; I don't mind telling you the tale, if you like."

"I'd better begin at the start," he continued. "I was pretty convinced from the first that the murderer – if there were one – had been on the train, and probably given us the slip at Porthampton Station. But I had very little to go upon. As a sort of forlorn hope, however, it dawned upon me that something might be discovered if I found the exact spot on the line where the bank manager – Mr. Clinton – had heard the shot. He had said it was about half an hour after leaving London. I ran up to town the morning after the inquest, and called on him.

"'Can't you recollect exactly where it was on the line?' I asked.

"He thought for a minute.

"'Let me see – yes, I can. We ran through Hazleton Station a minute or so afterwards.'

"'Hazleton;' I exclaimed. 'A big village, I think? Now, Mr. Clinton, when you looked out, you're sure you saw no one – on the footboard, for example?'

"'Positive. I couldn't have helped seeing anyone if he had been there. I glanced both up and down the track on both sides.'

"I took the next train to Hazleton, determined to patrol the line for a mile or so up from the station. It was just a remote possibility that I might find something – perhaps, even, a pistol!

"It was a fruitless search, however. So, giving it up, I made up my mind to seek a place of refreshment. A road ran parallel with the up side of the line, quite close. I climbed over the palings for easier walking, and got into the road. There were a few small houses, almost new, of the suburban villa type, for Hazleton was getting a name as a picturesque neighbourhood, being only half-an-hour's run from town.

"As I walked along, thinking that the train must have been passing close by the spot when the mysterious tragedy happened, my glance fell on the gatepost of one of the villas. On it was the name of the house, 'The Maples.'

"I gave a start, and I'll tell you why. You may remember that at the inquest I stated there was a small, possible clue, which I wished to keep to myself. In the pocket of the murdered man I had found a current number of a newspaper, on the outside cover of which was scrawled in pencil those very words – 'The Maples.'

"At once I made up my mind. I found my way to the only newspaper shop in the village, and made some inquiries. At what hour could I have a morning paper delivered? I was told the newspaper train arrived pretty early, and that the boy started on his rounds at seven. I chatted away, leading the conversation up to 'The Maples.' Yes, they sent papers to that house.

"'Who lives there?' I asked casually.

"'Foreigners, I think, sir. They haven't been long at Hazleton. I've quite forgotten their name for the moment.'

"I was evidently on a track. Sometimes boldness is the best action for discovering things, so I determined to call at 'The Maples.' The point was this: The paper found on the man had evidently been left at this house the very morning he was murdered. The obvious deduction was that the poor wretch himself had been in the house.

"The door was opened by a fair-haired young woman, with a pale, anxious face. I saw, at a glance, she had been crying.

"'What is it, please, you want?' she asked nervously, with a strong foreign accent.

"I came to the point at once.

"'Information about a fellow-countryman of yours who left this house early on Tuesday morning and was found dead in the Porthampton boat express,' I said.

"She clasped her hands together, and gave a little cry.

"'*Ach!*' she exclaimed, 'are you of the *English* police?'

"'Not exactly,' I replied, 'I am in the service of the railway company.'

"She hesitated. I thought she was about to faint. Then, pulling herself together with an effort, she said:

"'Will you come in? You need not fear – there is no one else in the house.'

"She led me into a sitting-room, sat down, wringing her hands, and said, in a low voice:

"'He was my brother!'

"'Your brother? But if you knew – why have you not identified him?'

"She shook her head.

"'I was afraid – they might kill me, too – *Himmel* – but you do not know how I am suffering.'

"'Then you know he was murdered?' I asked in surprise.

"She nodded.

"'I saw it,' she gasped, 'it has haunted me ever since – it was terrible – and I could do nothing. Poor André!'

"'Come,' I said, 'you must tell me everything. I want to be your friend.'

"'But – but,' she faltered, 'it is the police whom I fear – and the others. You do not know.'

"'My dear young lady,' I said, 'I assure you you have nothing to fear from the police. They are only too anxious to find the murderer. And, if you know, you can help them.'

"She shook her head again.

"'You do not understand,' she said. There was a long pause. Then she spoke again, more calmly:

"'I will tell you,' she said. 'Since you have discovered so much. I was afraid of this. My name is Cambon. André and I are natives of Alsace, of French extraction, but of German nationality. And, you see, we were both in the Secret Service of the German Government. I cannot tell you how it all happened, but Herr

Otto Schuster had us in his hands – he is a bad man. It began by accident; a little sketch that I made of one of your English forts, and André mentioned it. Schuster paid us for it; we were poor, and ever since he has held us in his hand.'

"'There is a retired officer of your artillery living here in Hazleton, Major Dent. He had invented a new gun, and your War Office was going to make experiments with it. Schuster told us we must come down here and try and get the drawings, so he took this house for us. We got to know the Major – I taught his little girl German, and – well I got hold of the plans and made a rough copy.'

"'And sold it to Schuster?'

"'No. That is why it all happened. It was Pierre Duprez who interfered. You do not know him? Oh, he is one of the cleverest spies of the French Government, and he found out what we were doing. He came here and saw my brother, just as we were about to send the plans to Schuster. He appealed to Andre's French parentage – he entreated – reviled him for being a false Alsatian – for many of us still hate the Germans, though we obey them. And André gave way. He gave the plans to Pierre Duprez, and Duprez was to pay him twenty thousand francs – to his order at a bank in Paris. We meant to retire then – to get away from the power of Otto Schuster. That was last Monday, and Duprez took the plans back with him to London.

"'It was early on Tuesday morning that the warning came, by the first post. Pierre Duprez sent it. He said that Schuster had found out, and advised my brother to go to Paris at once. There was scarcely time to arrange anything, for André saw that he must take the next train to town to catch the boat express. I packed up a few things in his bag, and he put in his revolver. He was very nervous and afraid of Schuster, and said he should keep the weapon ready during the whole journey. I was to follow him in a few days' time. Then we arranged a signal, so that I should know he had caught the express. He was to wave his handkerchief from the window as the train passed this house.

"'Can you guess now? Schuster must have tracked him to the train, but was too late to get in with him. I stood just outside the front door, waiting. Then the train came in sight, and I saw André leaning out of the window, waving his handkerchief. I waved mine in return. Schuster must have seen me doing so, and that evidently gave him the idea that André was leaning out of the carriage, and that an unexpected chance of killing him had offered itself.

"'For, suddenly, just as the train was opposite the house, I saw a man's head and arm come out of a window two compartments behind my brother. Something shone in his hand; he leant forward, took aim at André, there was a flash, and I saw my brother fall back into the carriage, while Schuster, for it was near enough to recognise him, immediately retired into his.'

"Now I understood why no traces of bone or bullet were found. The latter went through Cambon's head while it was outside the carriage.

"Well, by strong arguments, I prevailed upon his sister to go to town with me at once. Now she had told her story a new idea seemed to have got possession of her. The phase of fright was passing. Vengeance was taking its place.

"'Yes, I will go with you,' she said, 'I don't care what your police do with me – if they find Otto Schuster.'

"But I had my doubts and said nothing. It was as I had expected. The Chief Inspector at Scotland Yard took down the information without comment, thought for a few minutes, and then said:

"'I will ask you to stay here a short time, I am going to the Foreign Office. This is a very peculiar matter, and I cannot handle it without advice.'

"In an hour's time he was back. A grim smile was on his face. He turned to Fräulein Cambon.

"'It may be some satisfaction to you to know that any charge against you for purloining valuable secrets has fallen through. Major Dent is not so artless as you supposed. His drawings were under lock and key at the War Office.'

"But—!' she began, in astonishment.

"'What you copied were old designs, of no value,' he interrupted drily, 'as M. Duprez will doubtless discover before long.'

"She sprang from her seat.

"'So!' she cried, 'André has been murdered for nothing! But you will find this Schuster – ah, you English police are so clever! You will hang him, yes—'

"The Chief waved his hand.

"'Madam,' he said, 'my instructions are simply to see that you leave the country at once. With the rest we have nothing to do. When one enters the Secret Service of a Government one takes all risks, and you and your brother ought to have known this. You will understand,' he went on, turning to me, 'that nothing is to be done by us, and that you are to proceed no further.'

"'You will not find Schuster. You will not avenge my poor brother?' she shrieked.

"He shook his head.

"'Then,' she said, in a low voice, 'I will avenge André myself. I will never rest until—'

"The Chief cut her short. He evidently had little sympathy with spies.

"'You may do what you please, madam, but I warn you that it must not be in this country.'

"Whether she carried out her threat or not I often wonder. At all events Otto Schuster, the German Secret Service agent, was found stabbed in the back in one of the narrow streets of Genoa not a year afterwards, and I have sometimes thought it may have been the sequel to the Porthampton boat express mystery."

Biographies & Sources

Jeremy Bates

Dinner Date

USA Today and #1 Amazon overall bestselling author Jeremy Bates has published more than twenty novels and novellas, which have been translated into several languages, optioned for film and TV, and downloaded more than one million times. *Midwest Book Review* compares his work to 'Stephen King, Joe Lansdale, and other masters of the art'. He has won both an Australian Shadows Award and a Canadian Arthur Ellis Award. He was also a finalist in the Goodreads Choice Awards, the only major book awards decided by readers. His two main series are *World's Scariest Places* (based on real places) and *World's Scariest Legends* (based on real legends).

Jesse Bethea

The Peculiar Affliction of Allison White

(First Publication)

Jesse Bethea is an award-winning author, journalist and videographer from Fairfax, Virginia. His articles for ColumbusUnderground.com have been recognized several times by the Ohio Society of Professional Journalists. His first novel, *Fellow Travellers*, won the Ohio Writers' Association's Great Novel Contest in 2019, was published in January 2021, and is currently available worldwide. He lives in Columbus, Ohio with his wife Melissa and their three cats.

Allan Burd

The Grim

(Originally Published in the Bram Stoker nominated anthology *A New York State of Fright: Horror Stories from the Empire State*, 2019)

Allan Burd is a science fiction and action horror author hailing from Long Island, New York that loves penning exciting stories about the supernatural and aliens. He also occasionally dabbles in children's books and short stories. His first novel published in 2009, *The Roswell Protocols*, about a second crashed UFO, got the ball rolling and he's been writing ever since. He is a member of the Horror Writers Association (HWA). For more information visit allanburd.com.

Laura J. Campbell

She Walks

(First Publication)

Laura J. Campbell lives and writes in Houston, Texas. Her background includes molecular biology, criminal defense law, and running long distance races. She is encouraged in her writing by her husband, Patrick, and children, Alexander and Samantha. In 2007, Laura was awarded the James B. Baker Award for short story for her science fiction tale, '416175'. Her short stories have appeared in *Pressure Suite: Digital Science Fiction Anthology 3*, *Under the Full Moon's Light*, *Suspense Unimagined*, *Gods & Services*, *Luna Station Quarterly*, *A Celebration of Storytelling*, and other publications. Her two novels, *Blue Team One* and *Five Houses*, and a collection of her first short stories entitled *No Lesser Angels, No Greater Devils*, are currently available online.

Ramsey Campbell

A Name for Every Home

(Originally Published in *Nowhereville: Weird is Other People*, ed. Scott Gable and C. Dombrowski, 2019. © Ramsey Campbell 2019.)

The Oxford Companion to English Literature describes Ramsey Campbell as 'Britain's most respected living horror writer'. He has been given more awards than any other writer in the field, including the Grand Master Award of the World Horror Convention, the Lifetime Achievement Award of the Horror Writers Association, the Living Legend Award of the International Horror Guild and the World Fantasy Lifetime Achievement Award. Among his novels available from Flame Tree Press are *Thirteen Days by Sunset Beach*, *The Wise Friend*, *Somebody's Voice*, and *The Searching Dead*, the first volume of his trilogy *The Three Births of Daoloth*.

D.R. Cartwright

Screams Don't Echo

(First Publication)

D.R. Cartwright started writing at a very young age, sampling different genres, but found herself more at home writing Horror and Fantasy. While she continues to work on bringing life to her Dark Fantasy series, *The Egaean Archives*, she has self-published a few short novels on Amazon, *Son of Jack* and *Tunnel*, as well as numerous short stories. She lives with her husband and two Persian cats, and finds inspiration in anything dark and macabre. It's no wonder her husband sleeps with one eye open.

Irvin S. Cobb

The Belled Buzzard

(Originally published in *The Escape of Mr. Trimm*, 1909)

Irvin Shrewsbury Cobb (1876–1944) was an American author, editor and columnist who was originally from Kentucky but then in 1904 relocated to New York, where he lived for the rest of his life. He wrote for the *New York World* newspaper as one of their highest paid employees, having worked his way up from his first job with the *Paducah Daily News* when he was seventeen. He is best known for his short story collection *Old Judge Priest* (1915) and his humorous *Speaking of Operations* (1916).

Wilkie Collins

The Dream Woman

(Originally published as 'The Ostler' in *The Holly-Tree Inn*, 1855.)

William Wilkie Collins (1824–1889) was born in London's Marylebone and he lived there almost consistently for 65 years. Writing over 30 major books, 100 articles, short stories and essays and a dozen or more plays, he is best known for *The Moonstone* and *The Woman in White*. He was good friends with novelist Charles Dickens with whom he collaborated as well as took inspiration from to help write novels like *The Lighthouse* and *The Frozen Deep*. Finally becoming internationally reputable in the 1860s, Collins truly showed himself as the master of his craft as he wrote many profitable novels in less than a decade and earned himself the title of a successful English novelist and playwright.

Richard Harding Davis

Gallegher

(Originally Published in *Gallegher and Other Stories*, 1891)

Born in Philadelphia, Pennsylvania, Richard Harding Davis (1864–1916) was an American journalist, playwright and author. His mother was the successful novelist Rebecca

Harding Davis and his father was a newspaper editor. Davis published his first collection of short stories while at university, going on to become a prominent journalist. He acted as a war correspondent during the Spanish-American War of 1898, the Second Boer War, and World War I, and wrote unflinchingly on delicate issues like execution. Davis travelled widely and gained a reputation as an intrepid adventurer, producing a number of thriller spy novels.

Charles Dickens

The Convict's Return
(Originally published in *The Pickwick Papers*, 1836)
The Old Man's Tale About The Queer Client
(Originally published in *The Pickwick Papers*, 1836)
The iconic and much-loved Charles Dickens (1812–1870) was born in Portsmouth, England, though he spent much of his life in Kent and London. At the age of 12 Charles was forced into working in a factory for a couple of months to support his family. He never forgot his harrowing experience there, and his novels always reflected the plight of the working class. A prolific writer, Dickens kept up a career in journalism as well as writing short stories and novels, with much of his work being serialized before being published as books. He gave a view of contemporary England with a strong sense of realism, yet incorporated the occasional ghost and horror elements. He continued to work hard until his death in 1870, leaving *The Mystery of Edwin Drood* unfinished.

Robert Eustace

To Prove An Allibi
(Originally Published in *A Master of Mysteries*, by L. T. Meade and Robert Eustace, 1898)
Working under the pseudonyms Robert Eustace and Eustace Robert Rawlings, English doctor Eustace Robert Barton (1854–1943) authored several works of mystery and crime fiction. His scientific and medical expertise often informed his work, both thematically (his stories are known for their preoccupation with scientific innovation) and in terms of key plot components. He frequently collaborated with other authors, including L.T. Meade, Edgar Jepson, and Dorothy L. Sayers, supplying them with necessary supporting medical and scientific information.

F. Scott Fitzgerald

The Great Gatsby
(Originally Published in 1925)
Francis Scott Key Fitzgerald (1896–1940) was an American novelist and short story writer, primarily known for portraying the decadence and excess of the Jazz Age, a term for the 1920s and 30s during which jazz music flourished. Most of Fitzgerald's published work was in the form of short stories; however, he is most well-known for his third novel, *The Great Gatsby* as well as *The Beautiful and the Damned* (1922) and *Tender is the Night* (1934).

Robert Ford

T.H.O.R.N.: The Human Organ Repossession Network
(First Publication)
Robert Ford has written the novels *Burner*, *The Compound*, and *Blood Roses*, a supernatural western. He has also published a collection of his short fiction titled *The God Beneath My Garden*, and a novella collection, *Inner Demons*. He collaborated with

John Boden on the novellas *Rattlesnake Kisses*, *Cattywampus*, and *Black Salve*, in the *Knucklebucket Thang* series. He has also collaborated with Matt Hayward on the novel *A Penny for Your Thoughts*. Robert lives in Central Pennsylvania, and is usually hard at work on at least two projects at a time. You can find out more about his upcoming releases at robertfordauthor.com.

Anna Katharine Green
The Second Bullet
(Originally published in *The Golden Slipper and Other Problems for Violet Strange*, 1915)
Mother of detective fiction Anna Katharine Green (1846–1935) was born in Brooklyn, New York. A poet even at a young age, she later turned her hand to detective novels, perhaps partly inspired by stories from her lawyer father. She enjoyed immediate success with *The Leavenworth Case*, the first outing for the amiable but eccentric Inspector Ebenezer Gryce. Having found a successful formula, but always coming up with original and intriguing plots, Green went on to write around 30 novels as well as several short stories. She created interesting detective heroes and established several conventions of the genre, her name becoming synonymous with popular, original and well-written detective fiction.

Henry James
A Tragedy of Error
(Originally Published in *The Continental Monthly 5*, February 1864)
Henry James (1843–1916) was born in New York City, though spent a lot of time in England, with the dynamic between Europe and America playing a key role in his novels. Writing a massive amount of literary works throughout his lifetime, he published over 112 tales, 20 novels, 16 plays and various other autobiographies and literary criticisms. Each work is filled with characters of great social complexity as most of his works reflect his own complicated perspectives and satirical personality. James's works include *Daisy Miller*, *The Turn of the Screw*, *The Ambassadors*, *The Golden Bowl* and *The Portrait of a Lady*. James strongly believed novels had to be a recognizable representation of the realistic truth as well as filled with imaginative action.

Tyler Jones
"Trigger"
(First Publication)
Tyler Jones is the author of *Criterium*, *The Dark Side of the Room*, *Almost Ruth*, and the story collection *Burn the Plans*. His work has appeared in the anthologies *Burnt Tongues* (edited by Chuck Palahniuk), *One Thing Was Certain*, *101 Proof Horror*, *Campfire Macabre*, *Paranormal Contact*, and in *Dark Moon Digest*, *Aphotic Realm*, *Coffin Bell*, *Cemetery Dance*, *LitReactor*, and *The NoSleep Podcast*. His stories have been optioned for film. He lives in Portland, Oregon, and you can find out more at tylerjones.net.

Theresa Konwinski
Justice
(First Publication)
Theresa Konwinski is a retired registered nurse, wife and mother of two grown children. She became interested in writing as a kid, beginning with poetry, but life's path deviated

from creative writing. It wasn't until after she retired that she began to devote time and energy to telling stories. Theresa's writing influences are Ray Bradbury, John Irving, James Michener, and Alice Sebold, but she admits to a strong attraction to Stephen King and Thomas Harris as well. She has written four books: *An Extraordinary Year*; *Ragged Road*; *Seven Secrets*; and *Love¹⁰*, her most 'non-fiction' piece of fiction.

Alexes Lester

Shadows

(First Publication)

Alexes Lester lives and works in Toronto, Canada. She enjoys writing horror, dark fantasy and science fiction short stories but has also published creative nonfiction. Many's the time she can be found reading gothic horror aloud to her cat, who is never impressed enough to show affection. Her most recent work can be found in *Kzine*, issue 29, *Chicken Soup for the Soul: Life Lessons from the Cat*, and *Be Their Voice: An Anthology for Rescue*.

Robert Lopresti

The Present

(Originally Published in *The Strand Magazine*, 2013, and won the Derringer Award for Best Short Mystery Story)

Robert Lopresti is a retired librarian and the author of more than seventy short stories. He has won the Derringer and Black Orchid Novella Awards, and been nominated for the Anthony. He has been reprinted in *Best American Mystery Stories* and *Year's Best Dark Fantasy and Horror*. His most recent novel is *Greenfellas*, a comic caper about the Mafia trying to save the environment. He is the current president of the Short Mystery Fiction Society. Read more about Robert at roblopresti.com.

Guy de Maupassant

The Horrible

(Originally Published in *The Entire Original Maupassant Short Stories*, 1903)

Henri René Albert Guy de Maupassant (1850–93) was born at the Château de Miromesnil in France, and is considered the father of the modern short story. He is perhaps known best for *The Necklace*, though his most stunning success is possibly his first published novel *Boule de Suif*, which was inspired by his time serving during the Franco-Prussian War. Maupassant developed syphilis early on in his life, causing him to develop a mental disorder coupled with nightmarish visions. These visions enabled Maupassant to write his most convincing works of horror fiction.

Tom Mead

Invisible Death

(Originally Published in *Mystery Weekly*, 2018)

Tom Mead is a UK-based author and active member of the Crime Writers' Association. His work has appeared in *Ellery Queen Mystery Magazine*, *Alfred Hitchcock Mystery Magazine*, *Lighthouse*, *Litro Online* and numerous others. His particular interest is classic locked-room mysteries, and he has written many stories in tribute to the masters of the genre, such as John Dickson Carr and Paul Halter. Most recently his story 'Heatwave', originally published in Flame Tree's *Detective Thrillers* collection, was selected by Lee Child and Otto Penzler for inclusion in their forthcoming *Best Mystery Stories of the Year* anthology.

L.T. Meade

To Prove An Allibi

(Originally Published in *A Master of Mysteries*, by L. T. Meade and Robert Eustace, 1898)

Elizabeth Thomasina Meade Smith (1844–1914), writing under the pen name L.T. Meade, was an enormously prolific English author – so much so that eleven out of her approximate three hundred works were published posthumously. Recognized today as an early feminist, she belonged to the progressive Pioneer Club and the founder and editor of Atalanta, a monthly periodical for girls. Smith wrote across numerous genres, occasionally collaborating with other authors, such as Robert Eustace. Her and Eustace's partnership also yielded some notable female villains, including Madame Koluchy, criminal mastermind and leader of the 'Brotherhood of the Seven Kings'.

Marshall J. Moore

Monsters

(First Publication)

Marshall J. Moore is a writer, filmmaker, and martial artist who was born and raised on Kwajalein, a tiny Pacific island. He has travelled to nearly thirty countries, once sold a thousand dollars' worth of teapots to Jackie Chan, and on one occasion was tracked down by a bounty hunter for owing $300 in overdue fees to the Los Angeles Public Library. He lives in Atlanta, Georgia with his wife Megan and their two cats. You can find him on Facebook at Marshall J. Moore – Author, Twitter at @Kwaj14, and Instagram at @kwajmarshall.

Thomas More

Princes in the Tower (extract)

(Originally Published in *The History of King Richard III, c.* 1535)

Sir Thomas More (1478–1535) was a lawyer and judge as well as an author and philosopher. He also served Henry VIII as Lord High Chancellor of England from October 1529 to May 1532. The extract included here is from a *History of King Richard III*, which he never finished. It is unlikely to be historically accurate, but is a great work of literary value and it's known to have influenced William Shakespeare's play, *Richard III*. As well as *Richard III* More's best-known and most controversial work was *Utopia*, his exploration of a perfect society, which gave rise to the genre of utopian and dystopian literature.

Margaret Murphy

Foreword

Margaret Murphy has written 11 internationally acclaimed and bestselling psychological thrillers under her own name, and five forensic thrillers as Ashley Dyer and AD Garrett. She is a past Chair of the Crime Writers Association (CWA), founder of Murder Squad, and a former RLF Writing Fellow and Reading Round Lector. A Short Story Dagger, HRF Keating, and CWA Red Herring award winner, she has also been shortlisted for the 'First Blood' critics award and CWA Dagger in the Library. Margaret is patron of Smithdown Litfest in Liverpool and co-founder of Perfect Crime UK, Liverpool's first ever crime festival.

Jane Nightshade

Rockin' Around the Murder Tree

(Originally Dramatized on *NoSleep Podcast*, Christmas 2019 Bonus Episode, and Released as a Kindle Single, 2019)

A native Californian, Jane Nightshade is a former corporate writer turned horror, sci-fi, and crime writer. Her non-fiction writing about horror and crime film/television has appeared online at Horrornews.net, *Horrified Magazine* (horrifiedmagazine.co.uk), *Ghouls Magazine* (ghoulsmagazine.com), and *Mandatory Midnight* (davidpaulharris.com). Her fiction has appeared in several anthologies and has been dramatized by *NoSleep Podcast* and *Octoberpod*. She is the author of *The Drowning Game: A Novella of the Supernatural*, available in digital form on Amazon. Online, Jane mostly hangs out on Twitter @JaneNightshade. She also blogs at hive.blog/@janenightshade.

Christi Nogle
Move-in Weekend
(Originally Produced as an Audio Podcast Narration on *Tales to Terrify*, February 2021)
Christi Nogle's debut novel, *Beulah*, is coming in early 2022 from Cemetery Gates Media. Her short stories have appeared in over forty publications including *Tales to Terrify* (where 'Move-in Weekend' debuted), *PseudoPod*, and *Dark Matter Magazine* along with anthologies such as C.M Muller's *Nightscript* series and Flame Tree's *American Gothic Short Stories*. Christi is a member of HWA, SFWA, and Codex Writers' Group. She teaches college composition and lives in Boise, Idaho with her partner Jim and their gorgeous dogs. Follow her at christinogle.com or on Twitter @christinogle.

Baroness Emma Orczy
The Ninescore Mystery
(Originally Published in *Lady Molly of Scotland Yard*, 1910)
Baroness Emma Orczy (1865–1947) was born in Tarnaörs, Heves County, Hungary. She spent her childhood in Budapest, Brussels and Paris before moving to London when she was 14. After her marriage to a young illustrator, she worked as a translator and illustrator to supplement their low income. Baroness Orczy's first novel, The Emperor's Candlesticks, was a failure but her later novels faired better. She is most famous for the play 'The Scarlet Pimpernel', which she wrote with her husband. She went on to write a novelization of it, as well as many sequels and other works of mystery fiction and adventure romances.

Michael Penncavage
The Walker
(First Publication)
Michael Penncavage's fiction can be found in over 100 magazines and anthologies from 7 different countries, such as *Alfred Hitchcock Mystery Magazine* (USA), *Here and Now* (England), *Tenebres* (France), *Crime Factory* (Australia), *Reaktor* (Estonia), *Speculative Mystery* (South Africa), and *Visionarium* (Austria). His other stories include 'The Cost of Doing Business', which won the Derringer Award for best mystery; 'The Converts', which was filmed as a short movie; and 'The Landlord', which was adapted into a play. He has also been published by *IDW* and *Ahoy Comics*. Michael has been an Associate Editor for *Space and Time Magazine* as well as the Editor of the horror/suspense anthology *Tales from a Darker State*.

Edgar Allan Poe
Murders in the Rue Morgue
(Originally Published in *Graham's Magazine*, 1841)
Versatile writer, Edgar Allan Poe (1809–49) was born in Boston, Massachusetts. Poe is well

known for being an author, poet, editor and literary critic during the American Romantic Movement. Poe is generally considered the inventor of the detective fiction genre, and his works are famously filled with terror, mystery, death and haunting. His better known works include The Tell Tale Heart, The Raven and The Fall of the House of Usher. The dark, mystifying characters from his tales have captured the public's imagination and reflect the struggling, poverty-stricken lifestyle he lived his whole life.

Arthur B. Reeve

Spontaneous Combustion

(Originally Published in *The Silent Bullet*, 1910)

Arthur B. Reeve (1880–1936) was born in New York, graduating from Princeton and going on to study law. However he ended up working as an editor and journalist, writing about several famous crime cases, before gaining wide popularity for his stories about fictional detective Professor Craig Kennedy, the first of which were published in Cosmopolitan magazine. Kennedy shares many similarities with both Conan Doyle's Holmes and Freeman's Dr. Thorndyke, as he solves crimes with science, logic and a knowledge of technology, as well as having a companion in several stories who chronicles his work, very similarly to Watson.

Zandra Renwick

The Dead Man's Dog

(Originally Published in *Alfred Hitchcock's Mystery Magazine*, 2019)

Zandra Renwick lives in a crumbling stone heritage home in the heart of Canada's capital city. Her fiction has been translated, podcast, performed on stage, and is currently in development for television. Her stories 'The Dead Man's Dog' and 'Killer Biznez' were shortlisted back to back in sequential years for the Crime Writers of Canada's annual awards for outstanding Canadian crime and mystery writing. More information at zandrarenwick. com, or on various virtual haunts at @zandrarenwick.

Scheherazade

The Three Apples

(Originally Published in *The Book of the Thousand Nights and a Night, Volume I,* c. 1706–1721)

Scheherazade is the storyteller in the Middle Eastern collection of tales, *One Thousand and One Nights*. She is described in the collection as being well-read, with an impressive knowledge of rulers and history, poetry and philosophy, as well as the sciences and arts. She was a kind person, polite and pleasant. *One Thousand and One Nights* was collected over many centuries by various authors, translators and scholars. Many of the tales trace their roots back to ancient and medieval Arabic, Indian, Persian and Mesopotamian mythology.

Sophocles

Oedipus King of Thebes (extract)

(Originally Published in *Oedipus Rex, c.* 429 BC)

Sophocles (c. 497/6–406/5 BC) is an ancient Greek playwright. He wrote over one hundred plays, but only very few have them survived: *Ajax, Antigone, Women of Trachis, Oedipus Rex, Electra, Philoctetes* and *Oedipus at Colonus*. We know that Sophocles was celebrated as a great success in Athens and his plays continue to be studied and loved all over the world.

Dan Stout
The Bulldog Ant Is Not a Team Player
(Originally Published in *Plan B Magazine*, 2014)
Dan Stout lives in Columbus, Ohio, where he writes noir with a twist of magic and a disco chaser. His prize-winning fiction draws on travels throughout Europe, Asia, and the Pacific Rim as well as an employment history spanning everything from subpoena server to assistant well driller. Dan's stories have appeared in publications such as *The Saturday Evening Post*, *Nature*, and *NXS*. He is the author of *The Carter Archives*, a series of noir fantasy novels from DAW Books. To say hello, visit him at www.DanStout.com.

Steve Toase
Chit Chit
(First Publication)
Steve Toase was born in North Yorkshire, England, and now lives in Munich, Germany. He writes regularly for *Fortean Times* and *Folklore Thursday*. His fiction has appeared in *Nightmare Magazine*, *Shadows & Tall Trees 8*, *Analog – Science Fiction and Fact*, *Three Lobed Burning Eye*, *Shimmer*, and *Lackington's* amongst others. Three of his stories have been reprinted in Ellen Datlow's *Best Horror of the Year* series. His debut short story collection 'To Drown in Dark Water' is now out from Undertow Publications (undertowpublications.com/shop/to-drown-in-dark-water). He also likes old motorbikes and vintage cocktails. See more at stevetoase.co.uk.

Edgar Wallace
The Ringer (Chapters I–XV)
(Originally Published in 1929)
Edgar Wallace (1875–1932) was born illegitimately to an actress, and adopted by a London fishmonger and his wife. On leaving school at the age of 12, he took up many jobs, including selling newspapers. This foreshadowed his later career as a war correspondent for such periodicals as the *Daily Mail* after he had enrolled in the army. He later turned to writing stories inspired by his time in Africa, and was incredibly prolific over a large number of genres and formats. Wallace is credited as being one of the first writers of detective fiction whose protagonists were policemen as opposed to amateur sleuths.

Victor L. Whitechurch
The Mystery of the Boat Express
(Originally Published in *Stories of the Railway*, 1912)
Victor Lorenzo Whitechurch (1868–1933) was a clergyman, educated at Chichester Theological College in England. He was also a fiction writer, best known for characters such as the vegetarian, fitness fanatic and detective Thorpe Hazell; and spy Ivan Koravitch. Whitechurch wrote several stories inspired by his clerical vocation, however he was also a railway enthusiast, as evidenced by his many railway mysteries featuring the detective Godfrey Page and later better developed with his Thorpe Hazell stories. The eccentric nature of Hazell was intended as a contrast to Sherlock Holmes.

FLAME TREE PUBLISHING
Epic, Dark, Thrilling & Gothic

New & Classic Writing

Flame Tree's Gothic Fantasy books offer a carefully curated series of new titles, each with combinations of original and classic writing:

*Chilling Horror • Chilling Ghost • Science Fiction
Murder Mayhem • Crime & Mystery • Swords & Steam
Dystopia Utopia • Supernatural Horror • Lost Worlds
Time Travel • Heroic Fantasy • Pirates & Ghosts • Agents & Spies
Endless Apocalypse • Alien Invasion • Robots & AI • Lost Souls
Haunted House • Cosy Crime • American Gothic • Urban Crime
Epic Fantasy • Detective Mysteries • Detective Thrillers • A Dying Planet
Footsteps in the Dark • Bodies in the Library • Strange Lands
Lovecraft Mythos • Terrifying Ghosts • Black Sci-Fi • Chilling Crime*

**Also, new companion titles offer rich collections of
classic fiction, myths and tales in the gothic fantasy tradition:**

*Charles Dickens Supernatural • George Orwell Visions of Dystopia
H.G. Wells • Lovecraft • Sherlock Holmes • Edgar Allan Poe • Bram Stoker Horror
Mary Shelley Horror • M.R. James Ghost Stories • The Divine Comedy
Hans Christian Andersen Fairy Tales • Brothers Grimm Fairy Tales
Alice's Adventures in Wonderland • King Arthur & The Knights of the Round Table
The Wonderful Wizard of Oz • The Age of Queen Victoria • Ramayana
One Thousand and One Arabian Nights • Persian Myths & Tales • African Myths & Tales
Celtic Myths & Tales • Greek Myths & Tales • Norse Myths & Tales • Chinese Myths & Tales
Japanese Myths & Tales • Native American Myths & Tales • Irish Fairy Tales
Heroes & Heroines Myths & Tales • Gods & Monsters Myths & Tales
Witches, Wizards, Seers & Healers Myths & Tales*

Available from all good bookstores, worldwide, and online at
flametreepublishing.com

See our new fiction imprint
FLAME TREE PRESS | FICTION WITHOUT FRONTIERS
New and original writing in Horror, Crime, SF and Fantasy

And join our monthly newsletter with offers and more stories:
FLAME TREE FICTION NEWSLETTER
flametreepress.comflametreepress.com

GOTHIC FANTASY

For our books, calendars, blog
and latest special offers please see:
flametreepublishing.com